THE Peacock THRONE

SUJIT SARAF

SCEPTRE

Copyright © 2007 by Sujit Saraf

First published in Great Britain in 2007 by Hodder & Stoughton
A division of Hodder Headline

The right of Sujit Saraf to be identified as the Author of the Work
has been asserted by him in accordance with the Copyright,
Designs and Patents Act 1988.

A Sceptre Book

2

A CIP catalogue record for this title is available from the British Library

Hardback ISBN 978 0 340 89969 4
Trade Paperback ISBN 978 0 340 89970 0

Typeset in Sabon by Hewer Text UK Ltd, Edinburgh
Printed and bound by Clays Ltd, St Ives plc

Hodder Headline's policy is to use papers that are natural,
renewable and recyclable products and made from wood grown in
sustainable forests. The logging and manufacturing processes are expected
to conform to the environmental regulations of the country of origin.

Hodder & Stoughton Ltd
A division of Hodder Headline
338 Euston Road
London NW1 3BH

To Bajrang Lal and Triveni Devi

AUTHOR'S NOTE

In this novel I have aimed to draw an authentic portrait of modern India, so it necessarily features some notorious public events as well as certain well-known public figures such as presidents and prime ministers. But as will be readily understood, it is from start to finish a work of the imagination, and the characters and their actions in the story are entirely fictional.

CONTENTS

Old Delhi Railway Station

Mahatma Gandhi Park

Kucha Bansilal

Town Hall

C H A N D N I

Khari Baoli

Katra Badami

Fatehpuri Masjid

Mangat Ram Nawal Kishor

Paratha Gali

Kinari Bajar

Bhagwan Das and Sons

Shraddhanand Marg (GB Road)

Ballimaran

Ghalib Shoe House

Sparrows

Chawri Bajar

842

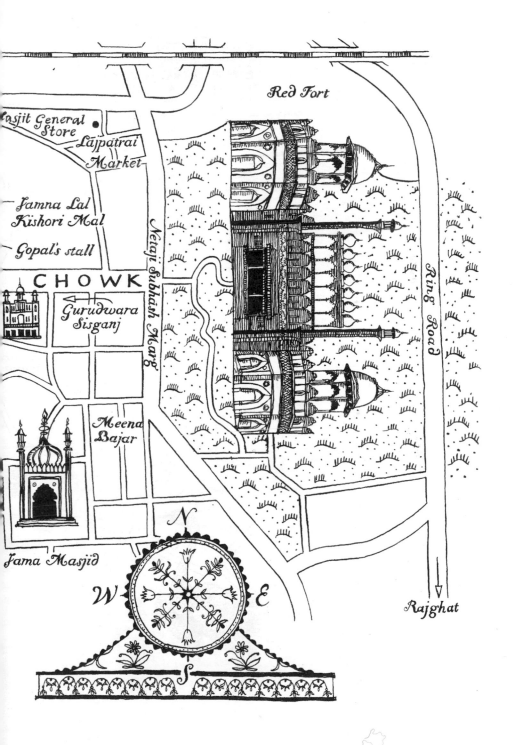

Red Fort

Masjit General Store

Lajpatrai Market

Jamna Lal Kishori Mal

Gopal's stall

CHOWK

Gurudwara Sisganj

Netaji Subhaish Marg

Meena Bajar

Ring Road

Jama Masjid

N
W   E
S

Rajghat

1984

Gopal Pandey wakes up with a twitch in his left eye and a curse on his tongue, and knows it is a bad day. It is past eight on the luminous face of his old wristwatch. He sits up slowly, propping himself against turmeric sacks, then lies down again with a sigh. It is still dark behind the sacks, but he knows the sun has risen high in the sky.

'Wake up and catch the thief, Gopal Bhai!' screams Hameed.

Gopal shuts both eyes and dreams. He sits cross-legged in his stall and a long line of customers stretches from one end of Chandni Chowk to the other, diffidently awaiting their turn, teacups in hand, coins jangling in their kurta pockets. 'There are many stalls in Chandni Chowk,' they say, 'but we want Gopal Pandey's chai.'

'Catch the thief, Gopal Bhai! He just made off with a sack.'

Gopal opens his twitching eye.

'Another sack! Sethji will throw you out today.'

Gopal sits up in horror, so quickly that blood rushes from his head. Squatting next to the sacks is Hameed, eyes glinting even in darkness.

'This is an unfortunate day,' sighs Gopal.

'Every day is unfortunate,' says Hameed, knowledgeably.

'Where is the thief?'

Without answering, Hameed chuckles and disappears down the ladder. Gopal rolls off the sack and crawls to the edge of the room, staying close to the wall where ventilators light his path. Three months ago, Seth Sushil Jain installed lengths of fabric on them. Curtains, said everyone, would make the kholi look more comfortable. At the same time, the seth began to move steel trunks into the kholi, which had been reserved previously for sacks of turmeric. Gopal hates those trunks. They have sharp corners he bumps into, and they are stacked against the curtained ventilators, shutting out half of his light. But what is this? A tin, from which emerges the unmistakable odour of asafoetida. Is the seth intent on ruining his own stock? How can you place turmeric and asafoetida in the same room when each will destroy the other? Gopal crawls to the end of the kholi, where a rectangular opening in the floor supports the top of a ladder. He climbs down, blinded by sudden light streaming through steel grilles on the third floor. At the base of the ladder he slips his feet into chappals, collects his dhoti round his waist, caresses his teeth with his tongue, clears his throat, slips on his spectacles and goes downstairs. At the base of the stairwell, he brushes into Hameed again. 'There is no thief,' grumbles Gopal.

Hameed laughs and heaves a sack up the staircase, brushing against Gopal and giving him a slight coat of turmeric. Gopal emerges from the stairwell and feels the eyes of Seth Sushil Jain on him. He is already late. He does not want to be drawn into a discussion on thieves and robberies and the number of hours he has slept when he should have kept watch. He rearranges his dhoti nervously and shuffles past the seth, making a great show of being in a hurry.

Seth Sushil Jain owns all three floors of Katra Badami. It is an old mansion whose third floor has been converted into godowns and storehouses for sacks of spices. The second floor houses wholesale-business offices, and the ground floor has been divided into more than thirty shops, which have further divided themselves into cubicles atop each other. Sushil Jain sits in one cubicle, his own shop merely a front for the much larger bounty he collect from his tenants in other cubicles. The main passage that runs the length of the katra – before it opens out into the crowded market of Khari Baoli – is lined with sacks of sugar and jaggery, sakoti, biznor, bulandshahar, modi, douralla, simbhauli and agota. Gopal threads his way along the passage – avoiding carts of cinnamon sacks and sneezing men – emerges into Khari Baoli and unlocks his bicycle from the police post outside the katra.

He cycles away and turns into a lane behind the old post office where, a few years ago, the Corporation had laid out a line of toilets. Now they are used to store rotting grain and rat-infested oilseeds, but the hand-pump still works. Gopal withdraws a can from the hooks on his bicycle, fills it at the pump, pulls up his dhoti and walks carefully round the toilet walls to the grass behind them, where he squats and shits. Then he cycles back to Katra Badami, retrieves his clothes and bathes under a tap on the ground floor.

It is a warm Wednesday morning. Khari Baoli sits noisily under the October sun, a wide river transformed into a narrow stream by mounds of almonds and figs from Afghanistan, walnuts and cashews from America, munacca and chirgozey from Kashmir. Gopal notes, with some surprise, that most shops, behind mountains of urad, moong, gram, masoor, rajmash, chitra and lobia, appear to be shuttered. Men sit around on trailers and rickshas when they should be carting sacks of peppercorns. Further down the road, where Khari

Baoli veers right to meet Chandni Chowk, Gopal discovers the source
of this listlessness. Three police jeeps screech to a stop outside a shop
whose shutters are half open. In its semi-darkness, behind a swarm of
flies and drums of groundnut oil, he sees a man get up hastily, bound
out of the shop, slip through the clumsy cordon thrown by the police
and run into a lane, followed by two constables. The rest stand guard
in the street, where other shutters are hurriedly pulled down. A frantic
sound wafts through the air.

'SDM! SDM! SDM . . .'

The sub-divisional magistrate stands in the centre of Khari Baoli,
tapping a baton on the palm of his right hand and surveying a
shuttered market. He has come to take oil samples and test them
for contamination. This is his third visit to Khari Baoli. The first two
were foiled by the shopkeepers, who got wind of his arrival, shut their
shops and went home. This time he has relied on stealth, yet his
constables are not quick enough to corner anyone.

Gopal gets off his bicycle and watches the policemen. At the far end
of the street, a small crowd of shopkeepers has slowly grown to a
procession. Their spirits rise as their numbers increase. At first they
cower, then stand defiantly and move a few steps toward the SDM.
Someone complains gingerly that the SDM is harassing shopkeepers.
Who can trust police laboratories? Who can vouch for the fairness of
those tests? And even if they are fair, it is not the shopkeepers' fault
that oil drums are contaminated. They do not produce the oil, just buy
and sell it. The right place to stop adulteration is the Delhi–Haryana
border, where trucks should be inspected. This is merely a ploy by the
SDM to increase his monthly allowance. Why should they suffer
silently?

The crowd grows in size and courage. Someone shouts an insult.
Someone repeats it. They begin to advance on the SDM, who is now
ringed by confused constables.

'SDM, *haay haay*! SDM, *haay haay*!'

Gopal straddles his bicycle wearily and passes through the crowd,
ringing the bell to avoid brushing against anyone, grateful he does not
own a shop. Yet some day he hopes to sit behind mounds of chillies,
almonds, walnuts and figs, and sacks of wheat, atta, maida, suji . . .
He turns into Chandni Chowk near Fatehpuri Masjid, then takes a
detour into Dudhiya Gali to buy milk. The lane is so narrow that he
must get off the bicycle and push it. He does not trust his steering skills
in the obstacle course created by the metal vats of curd and paneer that

lie in his way. Every time his bicycle scrapes against one, the curd trembles. Like the tyres on a fat woman, he thinks wickedly, then brushes away the thought. At the milk stall, he stands his bicycle against a drum and unhooks his pails, regarded with some impatience by Banwari Lal, who owns the stall, and Ram Bibek, who owns the barber's chair outside it.

'You are late,' says Banwari Lal.

Gopal mechanically replies, 'This is an unfortunate day.'

'Every day is unfortunate . . .'

Banwari is busy washing cauldrons at the hand-pump outside his stall, readying them for a fresh setting of curd. Bits of curd stick to their sides, inviting a cloud of flies that dissolves whenever a spray of water hits it. Banwari motions to Gopal, who fills his pails from two large drums placed in front of the stall and hangs them back on his bicycle. Then he sits down on the chair and Ram Bibek shaves him.

'Your stubble is going grey,' grumbles Ram Bibek.

'I am not yet forty,' Gopal retorts.

'Age does not defeat a man, but the cares of the world. How many children do you have, Gopal Bhai?'

Gopal's face wears a mournful expression. 'One. And you?'

Ram Bibek produces a scornful sound that lies between a shriek and a hiss. 'Seven, and all well settled!'

Gopal says nothing. Banwari has finished washing the cauldrons, and his place at the hand-pump is now occupied by three children who are taking a raucous bath. Gopal watches them, his face turned up to the sky in Ram Bibek's hands, his eyes lowered to seek out the children – two girls and a boy. The girls are naked, the boy wears pants that ride bony buttocks. The girls are five or six, and the boy looks around ten, which makes him master of the team. He directs who should have hand-pump privileges, who plies its handle and who gets blissful moments under the stream of water. The boy is thin – the skin on his chest, almost black, is stretched tightly over his ribs. His hair is a dull golden mass of neglect. There is something odd in the way he handles the pump. He pushes the handle down with his left hand – using the weight of his body to overcome the stubborn valve – then uses the same hand to guide the girls under the spout. Gopal's eyes seek out the right hand, to find it is cut off at the wrist, leaving a stump that healed long ago.

Ram Bibek is amused by Gopal's interest in the boy. 'Bangladeshi!' He snorts.

Gopal nods. The boy is certainly a Musalman, not a Hindu, from Bihar, Uttar Pradesh or Bangladesh, yet he is so much like his own son, Mukesh, even though Mukesh is sixteen with lighter skin and two hands. Yet Mukesh lives with the same abandon, the same steady authority over other children. These are bad omens – the SDM raid, the crowds in Khari Baoli, and now this appearance of a Musalman boy with only one hand who reminds him of Mukesh . . . And his left eye still twitches. 'This is an unfortunate day,' he repeats.

Ram Bibek does not reply. He has finished shaving Gopal's face and flicks shaving cream from his forearm with his razor. It lands in snowy hillocks outside Banwari's stall, and a few drops bounce into the cauldrons of milk.

'You should be careful,' Gopal scolds him. 'Banwari will not let you use the hand-pump if you dirty his milk.'

'Better to have cream than water in it,' Ram Bibek replies.

Gopal laughs.

'No fitkari today,' says Ram Bibek.

Gopal shrugs. He does not like the burning sensation alum produces anyway. The one-handed boy has run dripping from the pump, chasing the girls out of Dudhiya Gali, laughing and swearing in an unfamiliar language. Bengali, thinks Gopal, yet not the Bengali he heard as a child in Sasaria, which is not far from Bengal. Ram Bibek offers to clean his ears but Gopal refuses: he prefers ear-cleaner boys who have small, dainty hands. He hooks the milk pails into metal rings behind his bicycle saddle and rides back into Chandni Chowk.

It is now nine. The SDM raid in Khari Baoli is of no concern to Chandni Chowk. Shops are opening: shutters clank up to reveal showrooms; windows are noisily thrust open on upper floors.

Deep inside Chandni Chowk, mid-way between Fatehpuri Masjid and Red Fort, a large peepul tree is weighed down with signboards and banners: 'We accept torn money; Try not to follow the crowd; Full body massage'. The largest board hangs from the thickest branch, which extends into Chandni Chowk: 'Jamna Lal Kishori Mal – Sarees and Blouses'. The tree shelters a red Hanuman temple, whose collapsible gates are pulled open squeakily by the pujari as Gopal passes. Someone calls, 'You must oil the gates, panditji.'

The pujari ignores the advice and continues his assault on the gates, which screech in their tracks, then yield. Gopal turns into Kucha Bansilal, the lane next to the temple, and stops near an electrical junction box attached to the wall, protruding into the lane at a height of six feet. The showroom facing it is emblazoned with the same board as the peepul tree's: 'Jamna Lal Kishori Mal – Sarees and Blouses'. A drain flows under the box, and is bridged by three planks that create a platform for a wooden chest, four feet high and seven feet long, the bottom screwed to the platform and the top two feet below the junction box.

Gopal unlocks the chest, lifts the lid and ties it to the box. The front wall of the chest falls away, creating the compartment that is his stall. He brings out a ladder, rests it against the wall, hoists up his bicycle and secures its hooks to louvres in the box. The junction box has been long forgotten by the Corporation. It provides the stall with a ceiling: on hot days, such as this, it blocks out the sun; on rainy days it can be extended with sticks and a tarpaulin to form an awning. At night, an electric light bulb hangs from it, drawing power from the wires above. At times it swings open to reveal an array of wires and switches.

Gopal unhooks his milk pails and places them inside the stall next to cans of sugar, tea and cardamom, slips off his chappals, crawls into the stall and begins to pump an oil stove for the first batch of tea.

Across the narrow lane, the signboard of Jamna Lal Kishori Mal is receiving a listless dusting from Chotu, the boy who opens the shop every morning. The showroom spills into the lane in the form of a concrete slab where customers can remove their shoes, leaving a passage no more than four feet wide between it and Gopal's stall. Not many people pass through, because Kucha Bansilal withers away beyond this point, lined with wholesale dealers whose customers rarely come into their shops. There are no outlets of any consequence beyond Jamna Lal Kishori Mal, although the narrow lane continues and eventually opens out into a municipal park that borders the Old Delhi railway station.

Chotu finishes dusting the board and begins to sweep the mattress that lies inside the showroom. At the far end of it, next to an alcove set into the wooden cabinets lining the wall, sits Seth Sohan Lal, owner of the showroom, his hands folded, eyes half shut and lips moving rapidly as he forms the words of his morning puja. Chotu circles him, thrashing about with a bamboo broom whose reeds occasionally prick Sohan Lal through his dhoti.

'Watch what you're doing, Chotu,' scolds Sohan Lal mildly.

He does not want to be rude early in the morning, especially in his present frame of mind. He has just measured out three drops of aniseed into a bottle of lemongrass oil, and rubbed the concoction over his hands and neck, and behind his ears. The mixture gives off a sweet smell, which will stay with him all day. He resumes his puja, looking at the figurines in the alcove. Lakshmi, made of polished silver, wears a blouse embroidered with gold threads. Her skirt overflows the alcove and displays its golden brocade. Vishnu, next to her, wears a simple yellow dhoti, his upper body bare, with a brilliant brass chest. Both Vishnu and Lakshmi are adorned with a nimbus of filigreed silk behind their heads. Sohan Lal would have preferred gold-plated figurines, but he cannot trust Chotu. Even gods need protection. He carefully rearranges the folds of Lakshmi's skirt and peels away stale flowers from the previous day. He has brought fresh garlands in a paper cone, which he now lays round the figurines, then dips his ring finger into a brass tumbler and sprinkles gangaajal on Lakshmi, followed by a new coat of vermilion for the parting in her hair and a scattering of flower petals. He rings a silver bell and sings the final aarti in a toneless voice.

Gopal hears Sohan Lal's aarti and bows his head respectfully. The seth is a formidable man, a man of substance, who has pulled himself up to his present position over the last thirty years. He has propitiated Lakshmi, no doubt, going by the stones on his fat fingers, the lustre of his silk kurta and the flood of customers to his spotless shop. He is a good man, a staid man, a man with a family . . . A hissing sound breaks Gopal's reverie. The tea has boiled over. He quickly removes the pan from the stove and salvages what he can, then wipes the spill off the polythene sheet that lines the floor of his stall. This is an unfortunate day . . . Hopefully the seth has not witnessed the accident, or he will send a rebuke across the lane. He does not like clumsiness.

Sohan Lal finishes his aarti, sprinkles a few more drops of gangaajal on the figurines, shakes his hand dry and wipes the vermilion from his fingers on a silk handkerchief. From a Sunmica-topped drawer he withdraws a tiny bottle and pulls out its wooden cork. With his index finger pressed to the mouth, he turns it upside-down, holds it for a second, straightens it, removes his finger and squeezes his earlobes – right, then left – between thumb and finger. Then he rubs attar molshri under his chin, on his wrists and throat, puts the cork back into the bottle and restores it to its drawer. The sweet smell of molshri wafts into his nostrils, mixing with aniseed and lemongrass. He shuts his eyes, enjoying a fragrance that has never existed before in these exact proportions. As the first rush of attar dissipates, he opens his eyes, touches his ears, sighs and prepares for his customers.

Gopal sniffs in disapproval. The seth is a fop, a show-off. The attar smell mixes with sewage before it reaches him in a gale of pungency. It will stay all day, assaulting him, forming an unpleasant amalgam with the cardamom and cloves in his tea. He is a poor man, unable to afford attar, yet when Lakshmi lets fall her benign gaze on him . . .

There is a disturbance at the entrance to the lane. A man has charged in and is coming his way in great agitation. It is Ibrahim Mian, shouting his name, arms flailing, beard trembling, yellow teeth splayed out in a mouth that is perpetually open.

'Gopal Bhai!'

Gopal regards him with consternation. He knows he must offer him tea. It is not a good omen when the first cup of the day is supplied free.

'It is all finished!' says Ibrahim, breathlessly. 'Shut your stall! They have killed her.'

Gopal is annoyed: he knows the seth frowns on commotion in the kucha.

'There will be trouble! They have killed the bitch. Even a prime minister has to pay for her sins.'

Across the lane, Sohan Lal's jaw drops, hand arrested in mid-motion as it travelled upward to give his nose another whiff of attar. 'Who told you?' he gasps.

Ibrahim eyes the seth suspiciously, then looks away. He continues to talk to Gopal, ignoring the seth but aware that he is listening. 'Everyone knows. It is all over the market.'

'Are you sure?' Sohan Lal asks coldly.

'It is on television. There is a great crowd outside the All India Institute. That is where they took her. The bitch . . . Shut your stall, Gopal Bhai. Let us go!'

Gopal sits obstinately. 'Why?'

Ibrahim makes an impatient sound. 'Did I not tell you? There will be trouble, there will be killing—'

'Why would they kill me?' demands Gopal.

From across the kucha, Sohan Lal persists, choosing his words carefully. 'How did she die?'

'Shooting in the prime minister's residence. Sixteen bullets. Her own security guards. Two Sikhs. One sardar alone cannot be trusted, what can you expect when two get together?'

Sohan Lal brings his hands together and shuts his eyes for a moment, then reaches for the telephone and begins to dial furiously.

'They have already shut down everything,' says Ibrahim conspiratorially to Gopal. 'Every shop in Ballimaran, Chawri Bajar, Khari Baoli, Nai Sarak . . .'

'What about your shoe shop?'

Ibrahim snorts in contempt. 'Sharief Mirza is still sitting there! I told him, "Even dogs have deserted the lanes of Ballimaran. Who will come to buy your shoes?" He said, "I am the owner, not a clerk. My grandfather sat in this shop through Partition. Who is Indira Gandhi to shut it down?"'

'Poor man.'

'So I told him! I said, "Considering I am not the owner, I must save my own life before the shop!" And I left Ballimaran.'

'But the rest of Chandni Chowk—'

'Everyone is going home! Take your bicycle and leave!'

Trembling, Gopal begins to put away his stove and cans. Ibrahim notices the pan on the stove, which has some tea left inside it even after the spill. 'A cup of chai first?' he suggests hopefully.

Gopal reaches into the junction box and brings out a glass tumbler. Ibrahim frowns, and the yellow teeth are bared. When he speaks his voice threatens as much as it implores: 'Maybe I can drink from your regular cup today. There is no difference between Hindu and Musalman now. Both have turned against the sardar.'

Gopal shakes his head, fills Ibrahim's glass and extends it toward him. He cannot give a regular cup to a Musalman and risk losing his business because Sohan Lal's eyes are on him. Ibrahim accepts the glass sulkily and sips. 'Why will anyone do anything to me?' asks Gopal. 'I am not a political man.'

Ibrahim considers this. 'Your son is a political man,' he says tartly.

Gopal does not reply. The accusation stings. Ibrahim drains the tumbler, puts it back in the junction box, and turns to go. 'I will not pay today,' he says.

It is an unnecessary announcement, because Ibrahim never pays. Gopal asks anyway, as he always does, 'Why?'

Ibrahim shrugs. His manner implies that the answer is obvious. Gopal stands up, slips on his chappals, loosens the lid and shuts his box. Ibrahim sidles up close to him, overpowering attar molshri with his own leathery smell.

'I am glad they have killed her,' he says viciously. 'She was a whore who castrated our men and had our women raped. Someone *had* to kill her . . .'

Gopal shrugs uncomfortably. 'I am not a political man, Ibrahim Mian. I hope it did not hurt too much . . .'

'You do not understand, Gopal Bhai, because you are not a Musalman.'

'But it was sardars who killed her!' protests Gopal.

'There is no difference. Musalmans, sardars, Hindus, everyone hated her. But there will be trouble for sardars.'

'It is an unfortunate day,' sighs Gopal.

'It is not safe to walk in Chandni Chowk,' says Ibrahim.

Gopal trembles, thinking of his son Mukesh.

2

The two girls melt away into Dudhiya Gali, giggling and fighting, leaving watery imprints of their feet on dry asphalt. Gauhar calls after them, then leaves the hand-pump and wanders back into Chandni Chowk. He does not care about the girls. He must find Ma and Baba, whom he has not seen for three days. He rearranges his soaking, matted hair, combing it roughly with the fingers of his left hand. Dripping shorts cling to his legs. Drops of water glisten on his thin shoulders and chest, but the sun quickly dries them. He thrusts his hand into a wet pocket, the stump into another, and surveys the scene in Chandni Chowk. Buildings on either side seem to lean into the street as they move upward. It is quieter than it has been in the last three days. There should have been carts, rickshas, thelas and more people. There should be bells, whistles, horns and the constant roar of traffic. Yet half the shops are shuttered. Straight ahead, seen through a maze of electrical wires that criss-cross the street, the indistinct form of Red Fort looms against the horizon. He last saw Ma and Baba behind this fort three days ago.

He walks toward the fort without much hope. He knows already that they are not in the settlements behind it. He does not like this city, where his stomach has never been full and his baba never at his side.

They should never have left Binodpur. Perhaps his friends there still look for him to play kabaddi. Or maybe they have found a replacement, and Shahid has a new team-mate. That puny bastard with two hands! He must go back and beat him to a pulp . . . They had left Binodpur one dark night, and walked for hours in the forest. Baba held his hand, pulling him along through thickets and groves – Baba, Ma and himself, with Bhola Dada, who walked in front and showed the way. Bhola Dada had arrived in Binodpur a few days before, talking, cajoling, laughing, sitting around. He seemed to know everyone yet had nothing to do. With his well-oiled hair, smooth moustache and fleshy jowls, he alone in the village had an air of contentment. And now they were walking through the forest with him, rapidly, as if someone was in pursuit. Baba slowed down as they approached a police check-post on the bank of a river. Bhola Dada laughed at his timidity. 'Bangladesh Rifles!' he said contemptuously.

They walked through the check-post unmolested, and descended a steep embankment to the river, where a boat appeared from the darkness, summoned miraculously. They clambered into it, Bhola Dada hurrying them into the hull and pushing them down on wooden planks. The boat slid soundlessly into the river, gliding on a calm, black surface. For a while he could see the indistinct outline of the shore, and then they were surrounded by water. Only the boatman and Bhola Dada knew their whereabouts. In pitch darkness, he could still see Bhola Dada's glinting eyes, and then his white teeth, because he had turned to address Gauhar. 'This is the river Ichchamati,' said Bhola Dada. 'It grants every wish.'

Gauhar is at the eastern end of Chandni Chowk now, watched over by the great fort. Rickshas and cycles wait at the red signal where Chandni Chowk opens into a wide, grassy expanse, whose eastern border is delineated by the walls of Red Fort. A police jeep tears through the signal, siren wailing, constables in khaki uniform sitting in the back with guns at the ready. The signal turns green and rickshas rush toward it, horns blowing continually. Gauhar joins the flood and is carried along to the fort wall. He feels a tightness in his stomach, but this is not Binodpur, where you can find an open field and squat wherever you want. This is not even the settlement behind the fort wall – the wall is very long, he cannot possibly walk round it – where he can sneak away to an open drain. This is a wide open city, with a thousand eyes watching him from cars, scooters and buses, and police check-posts at every corner. Yet the tightness in his stomach will not go away. He comes to the brink of a dry moat, beyond which lies the red sandstone wall of the fort. He scuttles down the slope until he is hidden from view, and discovers a row of sputtering sprinklers. Here he squats and shits. Just as he begins to wash himself in a sprinkler, a shout goes up above him beyond the walls of the moat. He looks up. Three policemen, batons in hand, are charging down at him, crying, '*Pakaro! Pakaro!*' He pulls up his shorts – still wet from the hand-pump – scampers up the moat wall and runs.

The boat had pulled into a dark bay on the opposite shore of the Ichchamati. Bhola Dada jumped off with surprising energy, leaving the boat shaking violently and almost throwing Ma into the water. They stepped off into the knee-deep water, steadying themselves by holding on to each other, and waded toward land, admonished to remain silent by Bhola Dada, whose composure on the previous shore had been replaced with extreme nervousness. The boatman was now the leader of the party, choosing his steps carefully in the treacherous water, heading for a grove of trees that arched over the river. A sudden shot was fired into the air, somewhere on the riverbank above them.

'BSF! BSF!' screamed the boatman. He rushed toward the trees and disappeared into darkness, as Bhola Dada watched in consternation. At the same time a flashlight appeared inside the grove, combing the water until it found them and stayed on them.

Baba turned to Bhola Dada. 'BSF?'

'Border Security Force,' said Bhola Dada, impatiently. 'Indian.'

Baba gave a cry of despair, and Ma began to cry. Bhola Dada scolded them, then stomped through the water toward the flashlight, creating swirls of current that rode up their waists. They stood shivering, although it was a warm night. Bhola Dada was saying something to the men behind the flashlight, who were now plainly visible as Indian policemen in khaki uniforms. The conversation was unfriendly, and seemed to become heated. Then the flashlight went out and Bhola Dada called to Baba roughly. Baba waded ashore, pulling Ma with one hand and Gauhar with the other, sacks of clothes and food slung on his shoulders. Gauhar was the last one ashore, dragged up the muddy bank by an impatient Bhola Dada.

The next morning they ventured into town to buy rice. It was the busiest market Gauhar had ever seen. There were shops selling bangles, pearls, necklaces, pots, pans, blankets, rice, onions . . . There were such large heaps of potatoes, such mounds of rice and meat. He walked in wonder behind Baba, watching his green lungi flap against his legs, and pulling at the saree that clung to his mother's frame, still damp from last night.

'Is this Dhaka?' he asked Ma.

She turned on him. 'Never say Dhaka again!'

Gauhar was confused by her violence. He had always imagined they would go to Dhaka some day. Shahid had been there, and had spoken favourably of the city when compared with Binodpur, or even the entire Jessore district. 'Which other city could be so large?' he wondered aloud.

'This is Bongaon,' said Baba, proudly. 'You now live in Bongaon.'

The policemen are still after him – he can hear their '*Pakaro! Pakaro!*' He bounds across the grass, crosses the street – ignoring the stream of traffic, which parts to avoid him – and enters a lane near the bird hospital, hoping it will open out into a field where he can squat again. But it turns into another lane, and then another, until he is lost somewhere in Chandni Chowk, running from one lane to the next. He has shaken off the policemen but he does not want to stop. He slows down only when he is breathless and gasping and cannot run any more. He cannot read the writing on boards strung above the shops. The letters look different from the Arabic *alif*, *be*, *te*, *se* he has learned in Binodpur. He sits down on a concrete platform outside a shop. This Delhi is a large city, much larger than Binodpur, larger than Bongaon, even. He does not understand these lanes, the people are unfamiliar, and he wishes he was back in Binodpur, sleeping in his cot next to Ma and Baba . . . He shifts uncomfortably on the concrete platform, aware that it belongs to a shop. Inside, a man in a large turban sits cross-legged, fanning himself with a handkerchief. Should he ask the man for food? Or will he be asked to get off the platform if he draws attention to himself?

He lies down on the platform, curls into a ball and drifts into sleep, thinking of Ma, Baba, rice, fish, Bhola Dada, jalebis and the bus journey from Bongaon to Calcutta. He is woken by a stone that bounces off the platform. He sits up, frightened, and folds his hands in supplication. It is a gesture he has learned recently, having seen his father employ it seven days ago in the bus to Calcutta. There was his father in a green lungi, standing with hands folded while a policeman stood over him, growling, 'Bangladeshi, Bangladeshi . . .' So he brings his hands together and shuts his eyes. '*Maaro! Maaro!*' someone shouts. Gauhar opens his eyes, wondering who wants to kill him. A hail of stones hits the metal signboard and lands at his feet, while a few bounce into the shop. Gauhar jumps off the platform as the man in the turban comes forward to challenge the stone-throwers. Someone shouts, 'Indira Gandhi *amar rahe*!'

The turbaned man holds up his hands to calm them, then flings abuse, but is cowed by the rage of the crowd and begins to pull down his metal shutter, inviting another shower of stones. There are renewed shouts of '*Maaro*! Sardar! Sardar!'

Ah, thinks Gauhar with relief, they want to kill the fat one in the turban, not me.

'Pakistan *murdabad*! Khalistan *murdabad*!' someone shouts.

Gauhar looks around excitedly. A man brandishes a stick, another holds a trident, a weapon Gauhar had seen for the first time in Calcutta. There is going to be a fight! He picks up a stone from the platform and recedes into the crowd.

The sardar has almost finished with his shutter, but to lock it he must step outside the shop. He considers the crowd – which has been partially mollified by his retreat – holds up a conciliatory hand and steps out gingerly to the concrete platform. Gauhar raises his arm, takes aim, and hurls the stone with full force. It hits the sardar just below the turban, drawing blood from his temple. A sudden silence falls upon the crowd. The sardar looks up in shock and fear, and the mob seems to draw back. Three men in white kurtas climb the platform and form a shield round him, urging the crowd to disperse.

'*Maaro*!' someone shouts again.

The men in kurtas scold the slogan-shouter and challenge the stone-thrower to come forward, as the sardar hurriedly locks his shutter. The crowd now exhales consciously, everyone looking at everyone else to spot the stone-thrower. The men escort the sardar away from the scene, hurrying him along until he has safely turned the corner. The crowd begins to disperse. Gauhar backs away quietly, hands in pockets, and turns into Paratha Gali, his heart beating uncontrollably.

They had stayed in Bongaon for a few days, then taken a bus to Calcutta, eighty kilometres away. He had not wanted to go. What was wrong with Bongaon? he asked Baba. 'We must go to Calcutta and then we must go west,' Baba had said, as if the west was a town where everyone obviously went. Before they reached Calcutta they were taken off the bus by policemen. He had never known such fear. His father stood surrounded by policemen, green lungi flapping in the wind, hands folded. But Bhola Dada seemed to know everyone, and soon they were on a train to Delhi. No one on it spoke Bengali, and

Baba brought a finger to his lips every time Gauhar opened his mouth. 'You are from Murshidabad,' Baba whispered to him. 'Never forget you are from Murshidabad.' By the time the train had crossed large bridges and arrived in Delhi, Bhola Dada had disappeared.

They pushed through the crowds at Delhi railway station, staying close together with Baba holding Ma with one hand and Gauhar with the other, and walked through streets with such tall buildings that Gauhar's neck ached from looking up. Then they circled a great red wall and arrived at a village where Baba knew someone. It was an odd-looking village, with tents much smaller than the houses in Binodpur, made of tins, tarpaulins and cans. Inside one such tent they spent their first night, sleeping fitfully while Baba spoke for a long time with the man who lived in it. The next morning Gauhar asked the name of their new town. 'Naresh Colony,' said Baba.

Paratha Gali is awash with the fragrance of ghee. Gauhar passes countless stalls stacked with parathas, potatoes and chillies next to cauldrons of boiling oil. Large griddles hold a dozen parathas that are flipped over every few seconds, until each is crisp and golden. He has seen parathas in Binodpur and Bongaon, small, thin ones, not big stuffed ones like these. And he has never seen such pickles, such arrangements of banana, tamarind, watermelon, pumpkin, mint . . . Is there anything that cannot be pickled here? He has not eaten since last evening, when Baba bought him aloo puri in Chandni Chowk just before Gauhar lost him in the crowd. How much do these parathas cost? Can he ask them to give him one in return for some work? Perhaps he can man that griddle, wash it when it cools, lay it on the stove. Wooden signboards hang before every shop, in languages he does not understand, until he comes upon one in Urdu – 'Arya Restaurant. Prove our parathas are not made with pure desi ghee and get a reward of one thousand rupees!'

He reads haltingly, but the claim lights a fire in his belly. Weakened by hunger, he is unable to tear his eyes from the chutneys and pickles that lie beneath the board. The man behind the griddle frowns. Gauhar points to a stack of parathas lying shamelessly on the side. 'Twelve rupees,' says the man, suspiciously. Gauhar stands mute. 'Or twenty-five,' says the man, with a scornful glint in his eyes, pointing to a solitary fat paratha that bulges with stuffing. He chuckles at Gauhar's confusion, then gets serious. 'This is seven rupees,' he says, pointing to a thin roti. 'This is a methi paratha, with a stuffing of grams and fenugreek seeds. Just seven rupees!'

The description and the prices mean nothing to Gauhar. He digs deep into his left pocket and brings out three coins. His mother gave them to him when they arrived in Delhi three days ago, as they stepped off the train. He considers them. They are the last of his money. Slowly, he extends his left palm to the man behind the griddle.

'What is this?' exclaims the man, impatiently. 'What coins are these?'

Gauhar stands stubbornly, palm open. The man takes his coins, considers them, then hurls them back at him. 'Bangladeshi!' he mutters.

Gauhar stays rooted to the spot. The parathas are spread over the hot griddle, stuffed with aloo, daal, sugar, mattar paneer . . . He puts out his hand to touch them, feel them, smell them a little better, clasp them, squeeze them, roll them up. They are soft and warm, and release the scent of ghee when squeezed. Then he is running blindly through Paratha Gali clutching a hot methi paratha, away from the stalls, away from the frenzied calls, the boy who lunged at him, the people who turn to look at him in amusement, and the shouts of '*Pakaro*! *Pakaro*!' and 'Bangladeshi', followed by '*Chor*! *Chor*!'

In the last three days Gauhar has met everyone who lives in Naresh Colony, which lies along the walls of a great Musalman fort where once an emperor had ruled all of Hindustan, said Baba. The best tents in it are the ones adjacent to the fort wall, because they have at least one flank that is protected from rain and wind. But those spaces are all taken, and the wall-tents were pitched years ago. The many boys in the colony are from towns and districts Gauhar has heard of – Satkhira, Jessore, Khendiah, Meherpur, Rajshahi, Nababganj and Joypurghat, South Dinajpur – but they whisper the names softly, and only when coaxed. Aloud, they say they are from Nadia, Murshidabad, Malda or Cooch Behar. Gauhar likes the boys. He has been around with them, circling the great fort and picking rags, which he exchanged for money that he gave to Baba. 'We will soon have our own tent,' Baba said yesterday, 'and we will soon have a ration card, and there is talk that Naresh Babu will visit us.'

'Who is Naresh Babu?' Gauhar had asked.

'The king of Naresh Colony,' Baba had said.

This morning, he woke up early and noticed that Baba and Ma were not there. The sun, visible in the sky from where he lay, cast a red glow on the eastern wall of the fort. The tent, with many holes in it, was lit brilliantly, and the mat where Baba and Ma had lain was bare. He waited for them to return until the sun had climbed higher and cast the wall of the fort into shadow, turning it a dull brown. He walked about the colony, peered under tarpaulins, cast about among pots and pans, asked his new friends. Some laughed, some shook their heads, some pointed vaguely here and there, but no one seemed to care much. He wandered outside the colony and walked down Chandni Chowk, heading straight for Fatehpuri Masjid, then turned into a lane where vats of curd stood in the roadway. The curd shook delightfully as he brushed against the vats. It was there that he had met the two girls with whom he had washed at a pump . . . But now he must run because he can still hear '*Pakaro! Pakaro!*'

He crumbles half of the paratha and stuffs it into his mouth, chewing greedily, then ducks under poles and benches, emerges into Chandni Chowk and loses himself in the crowd, relishing the flavours of the paratha. A haze has descended over Chandni Chowk, caused by a thousand cars and scooters, which seem to be driving away from something. The street is emptying. There are many more police jeeps now, sirens blaring. He wonders fearfully if the policemen have assembled to catch him and confiscate his paratha. He runs back toward Red Fort, staying close to the edge of the street, wishing they had stayed in Binodpur or at least in Bongaon. This Delhi, this Chandni Chowk: it has swallowed Baba and Ma, who always held his hand tightly in Bongaon so he would not get lost. He grips the last piece of paratha in his left hand. The ball of flour in his mouth slides down his throat, and he coughs, bringing tears to his eyes.

Why did she have to die today? Chitra asks herself in exasperation.

All right, many people hated her and wanted her dead. Oh, yes, she had hurt the 'Sikh psyche' – as newspapers pointed out with maddening repetitiveness – she had sent her army into Golden Temple, she had outraged the entire Sikh population . . . but why must she die on the very day that Chitra stands on the cusp of a new dawn? Today represents a beginning, the birth of hope, the morning of many happy lives, not the end of a troubled, pointless one. Yet she is dead, lying bullet-riddled in the All India Institute of Medical Sciences. At this very moment, perhaps, they are taking her body to lie in state, for mourners to file past and television cameras to pan over, while she, Chitra, stands in a bare corridor and prepares to deliver the few lines that will inaugurate Sparrows, her school for destitute children. It is the culmination of three years' knocking and imploring, during which she has alienated friends and angered the Municipal Corporation of Delhi. 'We will not sanction a charity house for Bangladeshis,' say Corporation officials. 'We will not give you land and money to turn them into vote-banks. And who are you anyway? Do you have a government position? Have you been asked to look into the matter by a councillor, a Member of Parliament or a minister?'

Chitra smiles without humour. Here is Sparrows, home to thirteen impoverished children. There has been no councillor, no Member of Parliament and no minister. There has only been Suleman Mian, the lean, energetic young man who now awaits her in the next room. She knows little about him except that he is 'local', as he never tires of reminding her, raised in the lanes where Sparrows now stands, and loved by 'his people', a term he applies to anyone who lives or works in the web of lanes behind Jama Masjid. Whatever the substance of his claims, he has secured for her a building and enough money for her experiment. And here she is – reflected in the glass panes of a wooden cupboard – ready to begin.

She assesses her reflection. She is twenty-seven, but she has always considered herself mature for her age. It was in her nature to oppose beauty contests and fight elections in college, as she now lets the streak of premature grey shine in her hair. She is tall, large-boned but never plump. In the last three years she has, almost unconsciously, created herself in an image well understood among the culturally aware in Delhi – flowing black hair, large red bindi, handloom saree with tribal patterns and plain kolhapuri chappals, combining taste with modesty, fashionable college graduate with no-frills social worker.

She is not displeased with her appearance in the glass pane. A mature woman, a woman of substance. She raises an arm to silence the children – as she plans to do after she enters the room – and mouths her opening words. *It is a new beginning for you, my children, but the end of an era for our country. A great tragedy has befallen us . . .* How does one say 'tragedy' in Hindi? Should she have written the speech down? Her Hindi is not fluent. She had no occasion to use it in college, except in jokes, half-sentences, insults and the limited exchange required at tea stalls. She has brushed up her command of it in dealings with government servants, but the Hindi of officialdom is a pidgin language, confined to a few phrases about giving and receiving money. How can it compare with this, her maiden speech, her first formal contact with the children who will shape her life?

She corrects herself hastily: it is she who will shape the lives of the children. There will be no time to think about herself as she dedicates her life to thirteen little boys and girls discarded by society, with many more to follow. She walks resolutely into the room.

Suleman does not rise from his chair when she enters. The children clap. She holds up an arm and they fall silent with surprising docility. She stands still for a moment, looking around in confusion: she has never seen the room filled with children. They have been brought into the building over the last few days and have slept in its courtyard, played in the lanes around it and run up the steps of Jama Masjid to act as guides for American tourists, but this is the first time she has seen them all seated together – cross-legged on coir mats, with notebooks and pencils in their hands. The room – the same drab room she has swept and recently decorated with pictures of Gandhi and Nehru, inspirational slogans and the letters of the Hindi alphabet – presents itself anew as an object of wonder, a place of learning.

She faces the children and folds her hands. The children respond with shouts of 'Hello' and 'Good morning'. She smiles. 'I am going to give you some bad news,' she says. The children laugh and clap. They have just been fed roti and pickle bought at a stall behind Jama Masjid, and appear to feel secure and comfortable. They seem to have already organised themselves into teams. Three sit round Mussabir, who at twelve is the oldest boy. Chitra found him picking rags in Daryaganj, and enticed him to Sparrows with promises of food. He is a thin, gangly boy, who does not know where his parents are and she suspects – almost knows – that he is Bangladeshi. More than half of them have the same story: brought from Bangladesh by desperate parents and abandoned as soon as convenient. Mussabir has no memory of his family. He has foraged in the drains of Chandni Chowk for four years, stolen food, fought for pavement space, and is quite comfortable in his empire. She has held on to him for the last six days with difficulty. Her usual bait is food, and the promise of more. He has spent the last few nights in the building – he will not tell her where he goes during the day – and has built up a following of younger boys, who now watch his face carefully, to get cues on how to respond to the world. Mussabir himself sits in regal indifference, glancing at the nine children who have not yet discovered his eminence and still sit cross-legged on the mat. He sprawls, of course. His legs are thrown out, and his notebook lies forgotten by his side.

Near the front edge of the mat are two girls whom Chitra found begging outside a stall three years ago. Jolly and Sheila – the names are certainly fake, taken by them from a film – were the inspiration for Sparrows. Chitra had taken them to a night shelter, which would not accept them because it was for males. She bought them a frock each. She saw them every few weeks in Chandni Chowk on her frequent visits to Town Hall. They would stand at the gate in the frocks and she would give them money, then enter the compound for her next meeting with obscure officials, prepared to haggle again for a building where she could create a shelter and school. Now the girls, eight years old, sit at the front, oblivious of Mussabir, wearing the same frocks, looking up at her wide-eyed.

The children sense her indecision and begin to chatter again. Mussabir looks at her with contempt, and his acolytes giggle.

'Something unfortunate has happened to our country,' she says. She hopes they will calm down and give the moment the dignity it deserves. But they laugh again. 'Our prime minister has been killed,' she tells them. The words come out bluntly in Hindi, not with the measured emotion she had practised. She sighs. Hindi is a crude language – a language of the street – without sensitivity or refinement.

The children's laughter metamorphoses into a confused murmur. Mussabir's acolytes look at him. Sheila and Jolly titter. Chitra considers the possibility that they do not know who, or what, the prime minister is. She feels sorry for herself. What is she, a graduate of Delhi's most prestigious college, doing here? Why is she standing amid half-naked orphans, beggars and Bangladeshis? Which self-destructive gene has driven her to this kind of life? But this is not the time to doubt herself. She ploughs on stubbornly. 'I had hoped to teach you a lesson today, because it is our first day. Instead we will sing a prayer – a prayer for our prime minister.'

The children break into applause. Embarrassed, she casts a glance to the right, where Suleman sits inscrutably on a steel chair. He looks straight ahead and seems not to notice the applause. She brings a horrified finger to her lips. So boisterous on such a day! But she must

get them to sing. She begins softly: 'Allah *tero naam,* Ishwar *tero naam*
. . .' Your name is Allah, your name is Ishwar . . . She is not a
practised singer, and her voice trembles. She notices Suleman is
frowning. She has never known what to make of him. Should she
treat him as a friend who used his boundless drive to arrange for the
money, the building, the budget for Sparrows? He bestows his
kindness imperiously. His favours are disbursed not because the task
is important but because he is in a position to offer them. His eyes
have sharp, pinpoint pupils that make her uncomfortable. He always
looks impatient, as if the present task is holding up the ones that will
come after it. She stops singing: the children have not joined in.

'Let it be,' says Suleman. He has turned to her with a humourless
smile that makes her cringe. 'They are children,' he says. 'They have
not heard of Indira Gandhi.'

But a ripple runs through the children. The name brings instant
recognition among them. Some laugh, some clap, and a slogan rises
from the back. 'Indira Gandhi *randii hai!*'

The children roar with laughter. Chitra is horrified. What would
Corporation officials say? We give you money and you teach children
to call the prime minister a whore! She walks through them to the
source of the blasphemy. Mussabir Hussein sits comfortably, legs
splayed, turning a friendly face up to her. Chitra stands helpless before
him, a little like a child herself. What should she do? She could slap
him, rap his palm with a wooden ruler, drag him up by the ear and
have him stand in the corner . . . But she cannot do any of these on the
first day. She had counted on having well-behaved children who
understood the importance of this moment. How was she to know
she would have to discipline them? And how was she to know Indira
would choose to be shot that morning?

She turns, almost against her will, to Suleman. His white kurta is
arranged neatly round him. His pyjamas are white too, pressed
flawlessly, and wrapped tightly round his legs, one of which is
comfortably thrown over the other. He speaks, and his pencil moustache wiggles: 'Children say such things, madam. She was an old
woman, after all.'

Chitra shakes her head, then walks back to him. She will forgive
Mussabir, and she will also forgive Suleman. She had first approached
Naresh Agrawal, Member of Parliament for Chandni Chowk. He had
been courteous, but offered no more than vague promises of help.
Suleman, in his dry, distant manner, had rescued her. It is because of

his kindness, or ambition, or whatever it is, that she stands among these children and dreams of a future for them.

She sits on her chair, next to Suleman, and asks him if he wants to make a speech. He demurs. It is not his style to thrust himself forward, she thinks. He is only twenty-eight, but his self-assurance is that of an older man. What should she do now? She cannot teach them a lesson. She cannot get them to sing a song. And she cannot say anything that will do justice to the moment, because she must say it in Hindi. It would have been convenient to deliver a short speech in English. What moving imagery she would use! What rousing words! What had Nehru said on Gandhi's death? "The light has gone out of our lives . . ." English is so much kinder on the tongue!

She checks herself. This is vanity, romance, literary folly! Here is her family of thirteen – Mussabir, Jolly, Sheila, Raju, Anju, Manpreet, Robert, Babloo, Suraj, Sonu, Afroz, Anil and Muhammad Akram. Here are her children – half naked, illiterate, awaiting deliverance. Words cannot deliver them from misfortune.

'We will stay silent for a moment,' she says.

She looks at Suleman for his agreement. He lowers his eyelids. Mussabir is quiet, perhaps bored with rebellion, and shuts his eyes. His followers copy him. Sheila and Jolly sit demurely at the front. The other children fall silent when they sense that the room is quiet. The moment stretches. She steals another glance at Suleman and wonders if he is asleep.

Mussabir's sudden expletive shreds the silence: '*Saalaa*!' A scuffle has broken out on the far right where he sits. Behind him, the open door leads out to the lane and a boy, smaller than Mussabir, thin, dark, with dirty matted hair, stands there. He holds something in his left hand – perhaps a roti – that Mussabir is trying to wrest from him. The children shout encouragement. Mussabir laughs, but he is panting with the exertion. The other boy lifts his right hand – it ends in a stump – and brings it down hard on Mussabir's shoulders. Mussabir leaps back in pain, holding a piece of the prize. He stuffs it into his mouth to great applause. The smaller boy hastily devours the last of what is in his hand, then lowers his head and slams it into Mussabir's belly.

With difficulty Chitra separates them. Mussabir is furious, and the smaller boy fearful. He stands behind her, protected from Mussabir, crying, rubbing his face ineffectually with his stump. Mussabir slinks away sullenly. Children surround the new boy. Chitra looks carefully at him. His shorts appear to be damp, and he seems curiously clean. The stump is evidently from an old injury that has long healed. 'You can go now,' she says to him. 'No one will harm you.'

The boy does not move. He looks up at her with wide eyes. It occurs to her that he is another Mussabir – a younger, greener one.

'The budget is for thirteen,' calls Suleman.

She does not like his presumption. She runs a hand over the boy's rough hair. 'What is your name?'

The boy looks blank, as if he does not understand Hindi. Then he folds his hands and answers, in a studied manner he must have been taught by his parents: 'Gauhar Muhammad.'

'Where is your father?'

The boy does not answer. At the other end of the room, Suleman rises in his chair. 'What did you say your name was?'

'Gauhar Muhammad.'

'Where are you from?' asks Suleman.

The boy hesitates before he answers. 'Murshidabad.'

Suleman smiles. 'Keep him here, madam,' he says. 'Fourteen mouths cost no more than thirteen.'

Chitra knows, without asking, that the boy is a Musalman just arrived in Delhi. His accent is odd. His Hindi sounds like the Bengali of Bangladeshi children.

'You can stay here,' says Suleman, to the boy, then bends to look at him intently. Chitra wonders if his eyes are full of kindness or mere curiosity. 'Allah gives, always!' Suleman whispers loudly.

She wonders at his sudden piety. Mussabir, near the door, makes an impatient sound. He does not like the boy. Although small and weak – what sort of fight can a one-handed freak put up? – he is too large to be incorporated easily into his team. He is an aberration, an un-welcome recruit, a potential power centre. Mussabir stares angrily at Chitra, trying to will her into changing her mind. He is aware that Suleman, against whom he feels helpless, is the mover behind the decision. And it is somehow the fault of that whore who has died. He screams: 'Indira Gandhi *randii hai*!'

A crowd of whores watches from the third-floor balcony of Kotha 842, peering through metal grilles, squeezed between petticoats and skirts strung out to dry. Their rouged cheeks are wrinkled with mirth and their betel-red mouths fall open in laughter, releasing streams of betel juice that rain down to the street below. Outside the police check-post across the street, the station house officer stands with his baton poised. Beneath the balcony, the bai waits, arms akimbo, but gives no instructions to her pahalvan to break up the fight as Gita hits Ramvilas with all her strength. She is the goddess Durga personified, and does not care if every pahalvan, bai, cat and dog in GB Road wants her to stop, begs her to desist before she beats the life out of this bastard. Let them try to prise her off, let them threaten her with sticks and starvation, let them tie her up and throw her into a dungeon, she will not let this one go until he pays! Fifteen is what they agreed on. After she has given two to the babu, five to the bai, two to the pahalvan, one to the owner and one to the SHO, she will be left with four rupees. Four rupees for four hours! How can she let him cheat her? He is not a quick customer who takes what he wants, pays and leaves. He is the type who likes to spend an entire morning in the kotha, lying in bed and having tea served to him as if she were his wife. He insists that mornings – which come after such long nights – are hours of business. She will tear him apart, flay the hide off his skinny bones and hang it out to dry on the grilles with the blouses and sarees. She brings down a rubber chappal on his skull, again and again, with a torrent of abuse. He has turned away his face, and now he has raised both arms to cover his head. What a small, childlike skull! And what delicate arms! How can such a limp man intimidate her so? How has she been so weak as to let him violate her?

Ramvilas crouches, hands covering his face, his head and his shoulder, trying to anticipate where the next blow will descend. He knows he has made a tactical mistake by running out into the street when she advanced on him. A whore in a kotha turns into a harpy in the street. Inside, he could have grabbed her by the hair and hurled her on to the bed, or at least run round the corridors to protect himself. Here, with the whores of GB Road and the shopkeepers watching, he cannot even stand up. His face burns with tracks scoured

by her nails. What talons the bitch has! And painted with the varnish
he has bought her! 'A courtesan should be kept in her place,' says
Vatsyayan of the *Kama Sutra*, 'not unduly flattered with gifts . . .'
And how did she get her hands on his chappals? He must get away,
beyond her reach. Once he is on his feet she will not be able to keep up.
He has to go only as far as the end of GB Road. She will not dare to
follow him round the corner. He brings up one knee and plants a bare
foot on the ground. Using this leg as a lever he heaves himself up.
Thwack! A chappal lands on his left shoulder, which collapses under
the impact. He is back on the ground, sprawled on his stomach.

The whores on the third-floor balcony giggle and clap loudly. The
bai frowns and looks up impatiently. Too many of her girls are behind
the grilles. Too many cleavages, dull red teeth, pendulous lips. And a
crowd has begun to form in the street. Rickshas have stopped, cycles
stand by, shopkeepers scowl behind their counters. She can sense the
SHO weighing his options, calculating the exact moment at which he
should break up the fight. By night the denizens of GB Road are
whores and bais, but by day this is a market. The SHO has strict
instructions from the assistant commissioner of police not to let night
intrude on day. People come here to buy water-pumps, bathroom tiles,
Western-style commodes and wash-basins. They walk in the street, sit
on rickshas and scooters, haul away motors and pumps without
looking up at the grilles. Should they do so, they will see a petticoat
or a saree but rarely a woman. The bai allows her girls to lean over the
balcony, in groups of three, to watch the street, but only in accordance
with a strict dress code. They yearn for sunlight, and they appear
innocent enough when clothed. But to run out into the street and make
a scene at noon? The SHO will surely turn up this evening, when the
market has closed and GB Road has reverted to its primeval calling, to
demand money for this. She will have no choice but to pay. She does
not want a falling-out with the police.

The bai nods at the pahalvan, a stocky man of thirty whose father
was also a bouncer in the kotha. He pulls up his lungi and ties it round
his knees in preparation for the dirty business. Then he steps forward,
grabs Gita's arms and pulls her away. She flails and shrieks, but he
hauls her toward the kotha, a few steps at a time. He is amused by this
turn of events. It is his duty to defend Gulmohar – which is Gita's
trade name – against her predators, not to protect the predators from
her. Yet this man – who continues to sprawl on the ground even after
Gulmohar has been plucked away – seems an unlikely carnivore. He is

dressed in white cotton kurta-pyjamas like a politician and, instead of proper sandals, wears rubber chappals which presently adorn Gulmohar's hands. He is probably thirty but his hair is thinning and he will soon be bald. He has not an ounce of flesh on his bones – a slight man who looks like he has learned to ingratiate himself with the more powerful to get by in a brutal world. Instead of seizing her by the hair as a man should, he had crouched on all fours and let Gulmohar thrash him, protesting only mildly when the pain became too intense. At one point, he may even have smiled, as if amused to be beaten in public by a whore who is only seventeen. Instead of fighting back, he kept plying her with palliatives, murmured so softly that only the pahalvan, standing close by, could hear them – 'Go easy on me, my Fatehpuri Begum, my Jahanara, my Roshanara, my Mumtaz Mahal . . .'

'Let go of me!' yells Gita in broken Hindi.

The pahalvan laughs and pulls her into the stairwell next to Agrawal Pump House. He holds her until the bai grabs her arm and drags her upstairs.

'I will kill him!' says Gita.

The pahalvan laughs again at her accent. These Nepali girls! Narrow eyes, creamy skin, smooth arms, oval face, fiery spirit, but they never learn proper Hindi. It is a good thing no one comes to the kotha to hear her speak.

The bai comes running down the staircase, having deposited Gita safely into the arms of Parvati. She cannot let the man leave like this. She rushes past the waiting pahalvan into GB Road, where the crowd has begun to disperse. The grilles on either side of the street are emptying, as disappointed whores go back to their rooms.

Ramvilas rises, holding up both hands to cover his face against blows that no longer rain on him. He is clearly in love with Gulmohar, thinks the bai with satisfaction, or he would not have tolerated the violence. The slippers must have hurt because he is such a delicate man, perhaps weak-willed, besotted with the girl. She does not mind customers who fall in love with whores, but it is inconvenient when it interferes with business, when the lover wants to spend all morning in the kotha and expects his beloved to fuss over him. A girl needs rest after a night's work. She cannot continue the ritual of playing wife, lover, courtesan and slave for more than ten hours at a stretch. What is more, Gulmohar is barely seventeen. She has known less than a dozen men. But this one is foolish enough to think he took her virginity. You can hardly tell with such young women. They are fresh as virgins for at least a few nights. But they do not wear well, unlike the hard women of the bai's generation, who could pass for tender flesh in the twilight decade of their thirties. In those days women were like candles, burning steadily into middle age. These girls are like fire-crackers: they sparkle for a few moments – the first two years, if that many – and are then extinguished to serve the rest of their lives at break-even rates, which bring little profit to her or the owner. She has kept this girl on a light load for the last few weeks, giving her a few other men but largely reserving her for this one. She does not want Gulmohar to wear out too soon. With luck, she will have thirty years of supple skin, firm breasts, strong thighs and flat belly, as long as she does not get pregnant.

The bai sighs. Let it be. It does the girl good to slap her customers every few days. The drops of venom will prolong her freshness, and the wretch in the street will drink it gratefully in a masochist trance. But now she must attend to the wretch. She must be solicitous, she must offer help, she must ensure he will return to the kotha and Gulmohar. She offers him a plump arm, which he gratefully grabs to heave himself up. He stands, bewildered, then brings out a hand-kerchief and wipes his forehead.

'She is not broken in,' says the bai, helpfully.

Ramvilas nods. His chief concern, as he smoothes back his oily hair, is the SHO, who still stands at the edge of the street. The crowd has dispersed. Rickshas and cycles swerve round them. No one stops to look, but the SHO has his eye firmly on them.

'I will teach her a lesson tonight,' promises the bai.

Ramvilas holds up a limp hand – the one that had rested on her arm – in protest. 'There is no need for that,' he says. 'I will come back tonight and settle this myself.'

The bai bestows a beatific smile on him. Happy customer, generous customer, benevolent customer! A wonderful man, well-groomed, clean-shaven, unthreatening consumer of beauty, not an overbearing fat giant who will crush poor Gulmohar under his weight. Why, if she were younger she would have taken him herself. But the poor man is bleeding from the furrows Gulmohar dug into his cheeks. The bai signals to the pahalvan, who runs inside the kotha and comes back with cotton wool and a bottle of Dettol. 'Hold still! I will take care of you,' she says.

From the first-floor grille in the kotha balcony, Gita watches the scene below. Parvati stands with her, a restraining hand on her arm, and admonishes her: 'You must control yourself, Gulmohar.'

Gita snorts. She does not like Parvati, and she does not like being called Gulmohar. 'It is a flower,' the bai said to her. 'It will make people swoon over you to catch a whiff of your fragrance.' How often has Gita heard this flower talk! When she was ten, her uncle Jangbahadur had come to Sindhupalchowk district to meet her father. He had cast one glance at her and said to her father, 'What a beautiful flower you have in your garden.' Her father had laughed. Everyone laughed at Jangbahadur's jokes because he was from Kathmandu.

At sixteen she was sent there to live with Jangbahadur and his second wife. She did not want to go, but her father said it was best for her. There were no prospects for a young girl in a village. Who would marry her? In Kathmandu a girl could earn a living. She could find herself a young man to take care of her, which was why girls from Dhading, Nuwakot and Sindhupalchowk district were all flocking to the city. Those who had aunts and uncles in Kathmandu considered themselves fortunate, because they had a home and loving relatives to start them off. Affectionate Jangbahadur had certainly turned out to be. He had embraced her when she arrived, and never missed the opportunity to give her a peck on the cheek. A few days later, he had set her up as a waitress. 'This is the first step,' he told her, 'on your way to a future that will dazzle your father.'

The restaurant was hard work. She was up at five in the morning and worked until ten at night, lighting stoves, pumping water and slicing vegetables. During restaurant hours she waited on customers. That was the best part of her day, because she was allowed to dress in a new frock Jangbahadur bought her. She served with a warm smile, and allowed her brown hair to sway when she stood over customers to set down their plates and glasses. One day a young man left three rupees on the table for her. She thought he had made a mistake, but he was back the next day, saying he had been deliberately generous with his tip. 'You are a beautiful woman,' he said, as he looked directly at her, 'and I know your uncle Jangbahadur very well.' She was pleased.

She reported the incident to Jangbahadur. 'I know the boy,' said her uncle. 'He is a garment importer, very successful, very rich. He will make someone a wonderful husband.'

Bikram came to the restaurant almost every day, and his tips grew with time. He was not bad-looking – in his thirties, a bit fleshy, clean and sunny. His plumpness spoke of prosperity, not neglect. She began to preen herself in the kitchen, arranging her hair, using perfume, self-conscious when she approached his table, knowing that he came to the restaurant only to see her. On the days he did not come she was indifferent to her work. 'I have been to Delhi,' he would say, when he returned after a long absence, 'to buy salvaar-kameez and sarees.' She found out that he went regularly to Delhi to import garments, which he sold to shopkeepers in Kathmandu. 'Delhi is a great city,' he told her, 'a wonderful world of forts, gardens, monuments, roads, cars and skyscrapers.' When he asked her to come with him she did not hesitate. She asked Jangbahadur for his permission. She was not a bold girl, and would not have gone if her uncle had not given his blessing. 'You are seventeen and can make your own decisions,' said Jangbahadur, 'but I do not want to answer to your mother in Sindhupalchowk.' He brought her face so close to his that she could see the dark lines in his gums and feel his breath on her cheeks. 'You will break many hearts with your almond eyes,' he said. Then his lips fell open and he slobbered over her face. She pulled away and spent the night packing her clothes into a suitcase. She was not sure he had given her permission to go, but she was certain he was dangerous. She had to go with Bikram, who was younger, warmer and much more likeable. She would become a partner in his garment-import business. In a great city like Delhi, a woman could become anything she wanted – a beautician, a shop-girl or a waitress in a five-star hotel, serving white men from foreign countries.

She met Bikram early in the morning at a bus stop. 'Let us go and get married,' she said.

Bikram laughed. He ran his hand over the parting in her hair, index finger and thumb depositing a line of imaginary vermilion. 'Now we are married,' he said. She laughed and he pulled her close. She liked that. He was kind, solicitous and generous. They crossed the border into India in a bus, then took a train to Delhi. In Delhi they always travelled by bus – never by taxi – because Bikram wanted to save money for the sarees they would buy to take home. She did not mind. What wonderful sights he showed her! India Gate and Parliament House and Red Fort . . . They spent three days wandering around Kinari Bajar and Khari Baoli, walking up and down Chandni Chowk, eating jalebis and dahi bhallas and mouth-watering parathas . . . but never buying the sarees and salvaar-kameez they had come for. They walked for hours, scouring the market for good sarees, negotiating in a dozen shops but never buying anything. 'The rates are too high,' said Bikram.

'If you will not buy sarees for the business you can buy one for me,' she said.

He agreed, with a reluctance that hurt her. 'All right,' he said, 'I will buy you a georgette saree.'

The seth who owned the shop had smiled scornfully. 'We do not sell georgette sarees,' he said, 'because georgette is cheap and this is Jamna Lal Kishori Mal.' His entire stock, he said, was organdie, French chiffon and nylon.

They walked out of the shop in disgrace. Bikram was indifferent; she was furious. That night he raped her for the first time. Although he had taken to holding her hand when helping her out of buses, he had been careful not to brush against her on the first two nights they had spent in Delhi, in a fifth-floor room in Chandni Chowk. She was accustomed to the casual, unspoken intimacy that had developed between them from sharing the same room, toilet and travelling compartment. On the third night, after their argument about the georgette saree had fanned itself into a violent quarrel, he drew her to him calmly and deliberately. She had never known such intimacy. At first she was pleasantly surprised, then shocked. No one in the building, where at least a hundred people slept in cubicles like theirs, answered her cries for help, as if the room was a solitary box suspended in space. The next two nights he raped her again.

On their sixth morning, he woke her up before dawn and led her to a market for water-pumps and bathroom tiles. 'There are no saree shops here,' she said, 'and all the shops are closed.'

'We have not come to buy,' he replied cryptically. 'We have come to sell.' He held her hand and she walked with him willingly. She no longer regarded his intrusion on her as criminal. This was what a husband demanded, he had told her, and the pain would soon turn to pleasure. They walked through the deserted market, hand in hand, passing shuttered shops and sleeping beggars. Daylight was still an hour away. Next to Agrawal Pump House – closed, its electronic signboard flashing in Hindi – he turned into a building and led her up a dark staircase that opened into a landing and then a waiting room with stacks of bunk beds, curtains drawn over each one. Boys played marbles on the linoleum floor; girls played Ludo. The walls were covered with pictures of Gandhi, Nehru, Guru Nanak and Sai Baba. She asked Bikram where they were.

'Girls' hostel,' he said.

She could not understand why everyone was up so early, or what function was served by the bunk beds and curtains. A plump woman came into the room, followed by a troupe of six or seven younger girls. She was about forty, Gita decided, not unlike her mother but more confident and self-assured. She looked hard at Gita, clucked, and exchanged quick looks with the girls.

'This is Shanti Bai,' said Bikram.

Gita said namaste to her.

The bai whispered in Bikram's ear – Gita was shocked by the familiarity – and giggled. Tea was brought in on a steel tray. The bai had a glass, Bikram had a glass, and Gita sipped hers. Bikram asked the bai why the other girls would not drink tea. 'Roza,' said the bai.

When they had finished their tea, Bikram told Gita he was planning to go to Ludhiyana and Jalandhar to buy yarn. 'They make good yarn there,' he said. 'Stay here until I return. The bai will take care of you.'

She did not want Bikram to go. She clung to him, letting her tears flow freely.

'This is childish behaviour!' Bikram scolded her. 'I have complete faith in the bai, and I will be back in a few days.'

'I do not know the bai,' she protested. 'And what is roza?'

'Musalman fast,' said Bikram. 'Not for you. The bai will give you something to eat if you are hungry. Even the girls will eat early in the morning.'

'Are all these girls waiting for their husbands to come back?' she asked.

Bikram laughed. She stepped back in fear and confusion. The second time he had assaulted her he had called her his flower, his rose, his champa, his rajnigandha . . . He had hugged her and whispered those words into her ear. Surely she had acquired some rights over him? Should she cling to him and refuse to be parted from him? She put her slender arms round his plump body, then drew back, embarrassed. She did not want the bai and the girls to see her like that.

'A few days,' said Bikram, as he left. 'Then we will go back to Kathmandu.'

The last glimpse she had of him was when he stopped at the door, parted the curtain, glanced at her and walked down the staircase. It might have been a look of longing, but she was not sure.

The girls took her inside, fussing over her. There were four of them, all in their twenties, thought Gita. They were dressed in white salvaar-kameez with long dupattas that they kept tightly wrapped round their bodies. Their modesty caused Gita some anxiety. She wished she had not worn such a low-cut blouse. Children – at least a dozen – followed them from room to room, until they sat down on a carpet, surrounded by walls plastered with posters of Amitabh Bachchan and Dharmendra, and other film stars she did not recognise.

The girls saw her looking at the pictures and laughed. 'We don't have Gandhi and Sai Baba in this room.'

The girls introduced themselves. This is Manju, this is Nasreen, this is Lilly, this is Parvati . . . Gita asked about the children. Did they live in the girls' hostel too? Whose were they?

Parvati laughed. 'We are a family.'

'The three biggest ones are my sons,' said Manju.

'The two little girls belong to me,' said Nasreen.

'I thought the little girl was mine!' screamed Parvati.

'She's mine,' insisted Nasreen. 'She has my eyes.'

'All of them call me Mother,' shrieked Lilly.

And they exploded into laughter. Gita laughed too, as did the children. Then she thanked them all for their kindness. 'I will stay with you for a few days,' she said. 'Until my husband comes back from Ludhiyana.'

Nasreen giggled. 'This is your sasuraal, your husband's home.'

'All your sasuraals are in this house,' added Manju, 'because all your husbands live here!'

Gita laughed, not knowing what they meant. She pointed to the outer room, where the bai was. 'Who is she?'

'Mummy? She is your mother-in-law!' yelled Parvati.

At which they all laughed again. Suddenly Nasreen held up her hand and everyone fell silent. The distant call of a mulla, broadcast over loudspeakers strung across GB Road, floated into the room. 'I have heard the azan!'

Lilly brought out a steel plate of samosas and they sat in a circle to eat. The children ate ravenously.

'We are not all Musalmans,' explained Manju, 'but we like to eat when Nasreen does. In a few days the month of Ramzan will end and we will have to go hungry all night!'

'Don't be shy,' said Nasreen. 'You must eat if you want to work.'

Gita took a bite out of a samosa.

'You have such smooth, creamy skin,' said Nasreen.

When the meal was finished, the girls went to sleep and the bai took Gita upstairs.

'This is my room,' said the bai. 'You will sleep here for now.'

Gita spent two anxious weeks in the kotha, watching the girls sleep through mornings, wake up in the afternoons, play Ludo, wash their clothes, cook, giggle, quarrel and sing. She took care of the children while the girls cooked. At night the bai would lock her into her room. 'We want you to be safe,' she would say. Every morning Gita asked her about Bikram. Had she heard from him? The bai would pull her into her arms and caress her, braid her hair and say nothing, jaws moving inexorably as they masticated the remains of her paan.

'You must take better care of yourself,' said the bai, reprovingly. 'You will lose your looks, Gulmohar.'

'My name is Gita Tamang!'

'But Gulmohar is much prettier,' said the bai. Then she took Gita's face into her hands, as Jangbahadur had done in Kathmandu. 'You have beautiful almond eyes. Such light skin, such smooth arms, such black hair!'

A week later, Gita first saw Ramvilas in her room, standing over her bed. She did not know what to make of him. He was a slight man, and looked intimidated. She fought him all night, bit him, slapped him. When she yielded it was only because she was exhausted and wanted to sleep. He hugged her, called her his Mumtaz Mahal, then emptied a fragrant bottle over her naked body. 'This is attar chameli, my Gulmohar, mixed with a few drops of attar bela. I just poured two hundred rupees over you!'

'You must be very rich,' she said in wide-eyed wonder.

'I am the emperor of Delhi,' he declared. When he left he gave her five rupees. Soon after, the bai entered the room and took the note. She sniffed the air. 'What is that smell?'

'Something he brought in a bottle,' said Gita.

The bai laughed and held Gita's face in her hands again. 'He loves you very much. You will bring him a lot of joy.'

And she has brought him much joy, thinks Gita bitterly, as she has brought much joy to Bikram. Her cousin Gauri, who had returned to Sindhupalchowk district two months after her wedding, had told her that husbands were unpredictable: they sometimes beat you, sometimes hugged you tenderly, sometimes did not speak to you for days. 'You are my rose,' Bikram had said, 'my champa, my rajnigandha . . .' Ah, she would have forgiven him the pain of that night in Chandni Chowk! A husband had the right to do such things. She would have put up with everything – beatings, harsh words, sulks, fits of temper.

Did he not know that? Had she been too demanding? She should never have asked for a georgette saree. If only he would take her back . . .

Three days ago she had begged the bai to send her back to Sindhupalchowk district. The bai turned away without answering. She ran, crying, to Parvati, who hugged her and said, 'A whore makes the kotha her home.'

'Do not call me a whore!' Gita had sobbed.

But there is no other word for it, she thinks mournfully, as she watches the bai minister to Ramvilas in the street. A whore betrothed to a new Bikram – that jackal in the street. He has come to her every night for forty days. He brings a new bottle of attar every time he comes, a new gift, a new trinket, all of which the bai takes away. Lately he has begun to spend mornings with her too. Very well, she will let him feed off her but she will make him pay. Yet he will not go beyond twelve rupees even when he agrees to give her fifteen. Such chicanery from a man who wastes hundreds on attar! She does not want the attar or the baubles. She wants him to give her money, and he is inexplicably tight-fisted when she asks.

Her anger rises anew as she looks down into GB Road, where the bai has finished rubbing Dettol on Ramvilas's wounds. He whines like a child when the Dettol touches raw skin. She should have dug harder and excoriated the face. She should have drawn more blood!

'You have scratched the poor man badly,' laments Parvati.

Gita strains angrily against the steel grille. She cannot allow Ramvilas to present his pitiful face to the world and claim victimhood. 'Fifteen!' she screams.

The SHO, who had been losing interest in the matter, looks up disapprovingly, and Ramvilas takes a step back, afraid of the force of her words.

'We must not have any trouble,' says the SHO, sententiously.

'We agreed on fifteen!' cries Gita.

The bai signals urgently to Parvati that she must gag Gita. Parvati traps her in the crook of her arm and brings round a hand to cover the mouth. The bai shakes her head. 'To be screaming out rates in an open market!' She sighs. A girl with spirit is an asset, but one with too much can destroy the kotha. She has been kind to this girl: she left her alone for three whole weeks after Bikram delivered her to the kotha – haste, she knows, may lead to complications. Bikram had told her the girl was a virgin, but she had known better. She repeated the claim, of course, to Ramvilas, knowing he was too clumsy to know the difference.

Ramvilas lets out a long 'Aaaarrgh', perhaps to arouse the SHO's pity.

In spite of the situation the bai is amused. 'Did you really promise fifteen to Gulmohar?' she asks kindly.

Ramvilas nods. The bai cannot suppress a smile. She had smiled when Ramvilas first presented himself to her forty days ago. He had been recommended by someone she knew. She had listed the virtues of her kotha, hoping to push up her rates. 'This is a Class A establishment,' she had said with studied indifference. 'Rooms have toilets and beds, and all customers are students and shopkeepers. No truck drivers – they bring diseases. None of my girls works with more than five men in one night.'

Ramvilas had nodded knowledgeably. She knew immediately that he was ignorant of such nuances. 'In a Class B, a girl may have as many as ten in every shift,' she warned.

Ramvilas had raised his eyebrows and expressed relief that this was a Class A kotha. She allowed him to spend a night with Gulmohar after considering him carefully. He was a small, harmless man with thin shoulders, delicate features and deliberate speech. She knew he was married and employed. He would not be too harsh with a seventeen-year-old, if only because he was concerned about his reputation. He was, in some ways, the ideal first man for a girl like Gulmohar. She told him Gulmohar was twenty-three, which is what she tells anyone who asks. Yet for all her care the situation has spun out of control.

'No trouble,' repeats the SHO, unmoved by Ramvilas's cry of pain, but resolved that the situation must yield some income for him.

'He promised her fifteen,' says the bai pointedly to the SHO. 'How can people live on less than that?' She can see the SHO's mind working, in recognition of his own stake in the fifteen rupees.

Suddenly he looks officious. 'Give her fifteen,' he commands Ramvilas.

On the balcony, Gita struggles unsuccessfully in the crook of Parvati's arm. 'Keep still!' Parvati scolds.

'I do not want any trouble,' says the SHO, again. 'There is tension in Chandni Chowk. They have shot Indira in her house on Safdarjung Road.'

Ramvilas snaps to attention. 'Did you say they have shot Indira?'

The SHO does not deign to confirm this. He makes a motion with his thumb and forefinger, indicating that it is time to pay up. Ramvilas brings out a red velvet pouch from his kurta pocket and extricates two notes – ten and five – which he hands sheepishly to the bai. She snatches them and stuffs them into her blouse. The eyes of the SHO follow the notes greedily, all the way to their final resting place, where they linger lustfully.

'Who the fuck is Indira?' screams Gita from the balcony, having shaken off Parvati's cupped hand. She does not care for an answer. She has never heard of this woman and is not inclined to find out who she is. Her pride has been mollified by the fifteen rupees. 'Fuck you!' she continues. 'And fuck this Indira!' She throws Ramvilas one last look of contempt, slaps away Parvati's arm, turns and stalks regally into the kotha, leaving Parvati on the balcony.

'Teach the bitch some manners,' mutters the SHO, to the bai. 'Such a sharp tongue at twenty-three!'

The bai makes a gesture of helplessness. Ramvilas, his face bloody but his manner exuberant, dusts off his kurta, smoothes it down, removes creases from his pyjamas, slips his feet into his chappals, and turns to the SHO again. 'When did this happen?'

The SHO snorts. 'Where have you been all morning, babu? Four hours ago.'

'Did they kill her?'

'How should I know? She is in the All India Institute.'

Ramvilas brings out his bloodstained handkerchief again, and dabs his face where the Dettol stings. He runs a finger through his hair and rearranges his kurta collar. His right hand brings out the red velvet pouch, from which he withdraws a five-rupee note. 'Give this to Gulmohar,' he says, to the bai.

The bai brightens. That beating the girl gave him was for her own good, she tells herself. It has softened the man. He will never threaten her again, he will never go back on his word, and he will always pay well. She speaks to him in honeyed tones: 'You are very generous, Ramvilas Babu. You must love Gulmohar very much.'

Ramvilas pulls out another five-rupee note and holds it out. 'Keep this for yourself.'

The SHO licks his lips.

'And this is for you,' says Ramvilas to him. 'Buy yourself a box of gulabjamun.'

The SHO, wide-eyed, accepts the money with both hands and a salute. Ramvilas replaces the pouch in his kurta pocket and sets off with a flourish, walking triumphantly down GB Road, none the worse for his humiliation, leaving behind him a flattered bai and a disarmed SHO.

Sohan Lal sits in his shop near the Lakshmi alcove, worried. Every time a roar goes up in Chandni Chowk, he trembles and casts fearful glances at the closed doors. They are made of wood, latched from the inside, not strong enough to survive a sustained assault, especially if those outside carry rods and axes. He shut them soon after he heard the news from the Musalman. He does not trust the man, although he sees him often in Gopal's stall. Gopal himself is harmless – who feels threatened by a bald chaivala? But you cannot trust a yellow-toothed Musalman . . . He has asked Chotu to stand outside Kucha Bansilal, where it joins Chandni Chowk under the peepul tree, and look for signs of trouble. Hopefully, Chotu will let him know before they arrive. He is a smart, intelligent boy, quick at spotting customers in Chandni Chowk and luring them to Jamna Lal Kishori Mal. But that promptness is the result of the commissions he gets – almost four per cent on some sales. Will he show the same alacrity when he sees signs of trouble? The boy can be forgetful and careless. Perhaps he should have been offered something in return for keeping watch, because he will lose his commissions today. Who will come to buy sarees at a time like this?

For a few moments Sohan Lal entertains the idea of locking up and going home. He can sneak out through the other end of the lane, and Chotu can ask the driver to take the car to the railway station so he can avoid Chandni Chowk altogether . . . But his enthusiasm ebbs as he looks round the shop. Three days ago, he had had it cleaned and all the cotton and chiffon packed away. No one will buy chiffon in November and December. The walls are now gilded with silk sarees in preparation for Divali and the approaching winter months – Banarasi silk, Mysore silk, Kanjeevaram silk, synthetic silk, all with delicate filigree in gold and silver. There is stock worth five lakhs here. A man cannot leave five lakhs of stock and go home when rioters are lurking beyond the doors.

The smell of attar molshri assaults him again, cloying at such a high concentration. He frowns. He should not have wasted aniseed and lemongrass – good oils – if he had planned to dab molshri on his wrists. He should not be here at all, sitting alone on the mattress, while crooks and hoodlums roam the length of Chandni Chowk. He should be home, sipping tea and watching the news on television. But

how is a man to know? Such events should happen early in the
morning, before people have begun their day, so that they can adjust
their schedules. Yet there is some consolation in all this: for him, a day
of business has been ruined, but for the nation, an age of oppression
has ended. What is one day in the life of a man? He will recover
whatever he loses today ten-fold when people come in droves to
celebrate her death. She was a blight on the nation, a great burden on
her shoulders, a chain around her feet. Trouble is in store for the Sikhs
who killed her, Sikhs who collaborated and Sikhs who are bystanders.
For the rest, there is deliverance. And for the IPP, there may be sweet
victory at the end. Sometimes, a man must sacrifice a day of business
for his party.

Sohan Lal reaches for the telephone and dials home. Ramesh
answers. He is excited.

'Yes, of course I know!' says Sohan Lal, sourly.

News of the assassination has travelled fast. People knew even
before they heard it on television, but Ramesh cannot contain himself.
He describes in great detail what the announcers have said. 'They have
it all on tape!' he gushes. 'They have filmed the entire shooting! How
they aimed their guns at her, how they opened fire . . .'

Sohan Lal groans.

'What a shameful act,' says Ramesh. 'What horrible people!'

Sohan Lal says nothing. The boy is twenty, a political neophyte. He
regurgitates what they say on television. He imagines himself in a
never-ending drama, mouthing the right lines and following the right
directions.

'I am glad I woke up late today,' continues Ramesh, 'or I would
have been in the shop when it happened.'

It pains Sohan Lal to hear his son say this. Does he not realise that
his father is sitting in the shop at this very moment while he thanks
Providence for being far away? Should there not be an expression of
concern for his father's safety? Granted, the boy is insensitive. All men
are at twenty. But is he tactless too?

'You should come home, babuji.'

This consoles Sohan Lal. Youth retains a pinch of shame, he tells
himself. It is my fate to leave my bed and come to Chandni Chowk
every morning. It is I who must rise at six, take a bath, nibble a few
almonds, drink a cup of tea and set out into the world, as I first did
thirty years ago. 'I cannot just leave the shop and come home,' he tells
Ramesh.

Then he waits for the protestations. Ramesh should raise his voice in alarm, offer to dash to Chandni Chowk on his scooter and bring his father home.

'Yes,' says a chastened Ramesh. 'There is stock in the shop, I forgot.'

Twice wrong, thinks Sohan Lal. Imprudent haste in business combined with dereliction of duty to his father. But this is the new generation he must live with. This is the generation created by Nehru and Indira. This is the new India. A man of forty-nine must guard his stock, protected by a scoundrel of a tout, an unmanly chaivala and a Musalman with yellow teeth, while his son of twenty sips tea safely at home.

'Turn on your television, babuji!' implores Ramesh. 'They are showing the crowds outside the All India Institute. Live telecast!'

'Tell your mother I will be late,' says Sohan Lal drily.

'They are saying there may be trouble in Chandni Chowk,' warns Ramesh. 'Be careful.'

Sohan Lal ends the conversation with a heavy heart. His son speaks of trouble in Chandni Chowk as if he were discussing rates in the bullion market – as if his father were not sitting in Chandni Chowk at that very moment.

At the end of Sohan Lal's gaddi, where it meets the wooden cabinets, Ramesh has installed a small television, so that he can watch cricket matches. Sohan Lal switches it on. A great swarm of people is massed outside the All India Institute of Medical Sciences, held back by policemen. Vans filled with riot police pass through. White Ambassador cars bearing VIPs are frantically waved through the crowd with much squeezing, pushing and pulling. The announcer says, again and again, that she is in a critical condition but will survive, but Sohan Lal knows this is the end. When a great tree falls, it cannot be raised again. The crowd seems to know this too. 'Indira was our mother,' shouts someone, 'and we will avenge her.' Avenge her against whom? wonders Sohan Lal. Against the two Sikh bodyguards who killed her? But one is already dead and the other is dying, shot by security officers. Against the Sikhs who hated her? But you will not know whom to single out. Will you start with the president, who is a Sikh, and who was her shoeshine boy until she raised him to his present position? 'The president is in the Middle East somewhere – in Muscat, perhaps – and he is on his way back,' says the announcer.

'Indira Gandhi *amar rahe*!' shouts the crowd.

'Khalistan *murdabad*!' says someone close to the microphone.

Footage of her body being brought to the Institute is repeated. As she is wheeled in, a group of men comes into the foreground, screaming, '*Kachchhaa karaa aur kirpaan, bhej denge* Pakistan!'

Sohan Lal trembles. So that is what they are saying on television – send all sardars to Pakistan . . . He is glad he is not a sardar. Sardars are too noisy, too large, too physical, too aggressive. They laugh too much, cry often, rejoice violently and mourn piteously. For him, there is comfort in being invisible, unnoticeable and colourless. There is wisdom in the moderation of his forefathers. Life should be lived in the correct proportions of joy, sorrow, success and failure, all superlatives regarded with suspicion – dazzling success or bottomless failure. Wealth must be accumulated slowly and steadily, not conjured overnight through see-mingly brilliant schemes. The bird that flies in quickly is just as quick to fly away. He is proud of his moderation over thirty years, during which he has gradually raised himself higher. True, his kurta is silk and the attar he uses is the finest, but his slippers are still made of rubber and his dhoti of cotton. His house is modest, not one of those flashy new bungalows his son covets, and his shop is unassuming, even if the cash-box is overflowing with bundles of hundred-rupee notes.

The thought of those bundles sends a jolt through his heart. Why has he kept so much money lying around? To keep stock is one thing – a saree shop must have sarees – but to have seven lakhs in currency protected by a mere steel safe? He is a fool not to have sent Ramesh to the bank yesterday. Comfort at his own prudence is replaced with irritation at Ramesh's ineptitude. Why did the boy leave early yester-day? Should he not have remembered to complete his daily deposit? How will he ever take over the business if he displays such a casual attitude to money?

The smell of molshri nags at him. He must open the doors to let in some fresh air. Yet how can he, with those animals screaming in Chandni Chowk? And where is Chotu, that ingrate, sent to gather news of the disturbance?

He shuts his eyes and composes himself. He must not panic: he must display the cool self-assurance that has made Jamna Lal Kishori Mal what it is. Perhaps he can take the money home with him. But Chotu will notice, or the driver will. If they do not, the servants at home will. It is never a good idea to keep too much money at home, where he has much less privacy than he has at the shop. The bank must have closed because of Indira, so it will not accept the money.

The television rambles on. 'There is turmoil in the financial markets,' says the announcer.

Sohan Lal groans. How many blows can a man take in one day? The rupee will not hold up in such a storm. It has never been strong, and now it will plunge – it will crash to nothing. Briefly he is gripped by terror, his vow of composure forgotten. Slowly, a notion gathers in his mind, first in outline and then in detail. From time to time, he stows away a few lakhs with his nephew abroad. The scheme was first suggested to him by Sardar Kartar Singh, a friend, associate and fellow member of the IPP committee. Kartar Singh himself arranged the first transfer. 'The dollar is much more stable,' he had said. 'It will always rise against the rupee.' His declaration had been prescient because Indira had devalued the rupee soon after. Sohan Lal had leaned on the bolsters in his gaddi and chuckled to himself when the news rippled through the market. Over the last few years he has done more business with Kartar Singh, transferring many lakhs to his nephew in New York, and watching smugly as the rupee has slid against the dollar. And here he is now, sitting with almost seven lakhs in his safe, unable to deposit it in a bank, awaiting the imminent fall of the rupee. He casts a reverent look toward the Lakshmi alcove and folds his hands. Lakshmi knows best what she is doing for her devotees, and she is always at work!

From a string wrapped tightly round his waist, he pulls out the brass key to his steel safe, opens it as silently as he can – the door is not well oiled and needs a few thumps – then gazes at the pillars of banknotes stacked inside. He brings out the bundles, one by one, and arranges them in neat piles on the gaddi. He counts sixty-three bundles of hundred-rupee notes, each secured neatly with a rubber band, counted and double-counted with its hundred leaves aligned perfectly, their heads facing the same way. He is proud of his skill in handling money, in shaking a disorderly sheaf until each note falls into place, obeying the irresistible command of hands which have caressed much wealth. Sixty-three bundles: six lakhs and thirty thousand.

He raises a corner of the mattress and brings out five cloth belts fitted with metal buckles. They are long tubes sewn by his wife Rukmini many years ago, when it became clear that Chandni Chowk was unsafe for his staff when they took money to the bank. Even now, he knows there are people who stake out the street and await bank deliveries that happen at the same time every day. It is easy to walk up to a man, flash a discreet knife, grab his bag and run. It is much more difficult to accost him – even if you can guess he has money – when the cash is strapped round his body. For five years, this is how Sohan Lal has sent money to the bank every day. It is now Ramesh's daily chore, one of the few things Sohan Lal no longer entrusts to his staff.

The belts are narrow, designed so that the money cannot slip out. Sohan Lal holds up each one and laboriously stuffs it with bundles, ten to a belt. That leaves thirteen bundles on the mattress. He has no more belts so he puts these back into the safe. Then, still cross-legged, he pulls his silk kurta over his head and lays it on the gaddi, spread out so that it will not crease. He ties the five cloth belts round himself one by one, starting at his chest and working down to his waist. He secures the last belt with difficulty, pulling the buckle tight over his navel and using the last hole – the one meant for the fattest waist – with some disappointment. It cuts a ribbon into his flesh, reminding him of his growing spare tyre. He retrieves the kurta and thrusts his head into it. The bundles, which cover his trunk like armour, are bulky. As he struggles to pull the kurta down over his chest, a sound from the kucha strikes dread into his heart. He stops in mid-motion, hands clutching the kurta's ends nervously, body shaking stiffly inside its coat of money. Through the translucent fabric he can see that a side-door has opened. He forgot to lock it! In the rectangle of light created by the open door stands the figure of Chotu, watching him curiously.

'There is no trouble in Chandni Chowk,' says Chotu, 'just some stoning and slogan-shouting by Congress workers.'

'Get out of the shop, thief!' screams Sohan Lal.

Chotu draws back in confusion but does not leave. He stands on the concrete slab that serves as doormat to the shop, watching Sohan Lal in bewilderment, eyes riveted on the insubordinate kurta.

Sohan Lal wonders how much the boy has seen. 'It is hot,' he says weakly, hoping this will explain his state of undress.

Chotu leans forward dutifully and switches on the ceiling fan. With sudden clarity Sohan Lal notices the open safe, thirteen bundles lying in embarrassing nakedness on the exposed shelf, and the metal buckle of the last belt, which girdles his stomach like a serpent. 'I asked you to stand in the street,' he grumbles.

'It is not safe,' says Chotu.

'You just said there would be no trouble.'

'They have stoned the picture of Agrawalji.'

Even in his present discomfort Sohan Lal cannot suppress a smile. A picture of Naresh Agrawal, Member of Parliament, is not often stoned in Chandni Chowk. But he must not let the boy stand there. He must distract him, find him something to do. 'They will not harm you,' he says reassuringly. 'You are not a sardar. Go to Lala Surajmal and ask him if we can meet at six this evening. Inform Jugal Kishor too. Tell them to come to Kucha Bansilal at six. They should bring Ramvilas with them. And shut the door behind you.'

Chotu hesitates, then goes out, and the rectangle of light closes. Sohan Lal brutally forces the kurta down over his chest and belly, dragging it over tyres of money. Small rips in the silk seams do not engage his attention. There is no telling what that conniving thief has seen. The boy is a regular spy: perhaps he stood behind the door and watched everything through a crack.

With great difficulty, Sohan Lal raises his body into standing position. The belts have stiffened his trunk, making it impossible to bend over. The first one rides high above his chest, reaching his collarbone. The last sags and almost slides down over his dhoti to his legs. He realises that when he was sitting down, his belly had been pushed out, so now he can tighten the last two belts a notch each. He reaches for his cap and stick and prepares to leave the shop, then feels a stab of indecision. Should he be going to Kartar Singh on such a day? Kartar Singh may not be in his store. He is a sardar, after all, and everyone knows they are in trouble now that they have killed Indira. It is no use trying to telephone him. He is too careful to pick up the phone at such a time. What if the rupee holds up? Would he then feel like a fool who had panicked needlessly? But it has slid inexorably over the last few years and the money will be safer in New York, beyond the reach of income-tax inspectors. He will go to Kartar Singh.

There is a knock on the door.

This is Yamaraj himself, the Lord of Death come to take me away from this world, thinks a horrified Sohan Lal. This is Chotu, wielding a metal rod, followed by his hoodlum friends! This is how my last moments will be lived out! This is where Ramesh will find my body, and blame himself for not coming to my aid! 'Go away!' screams Sohan Lal. 'I am in the middle of my puja!'

'Sethji,' says the tentative voice of the chaivala. 'Would you like some chai?'

Sohan Lal is both relieved and irritated. Why is the chaivala peddling tea on a day like this? He should shut his stall and go home, as the rest of Chandni Chowk has done. And he should dispatch that yellow-toothed Musalman who hovers round the stall like a plague.

'How can you make tea at a time like this?' he demands.

Gopal hears the annoyance in Sohan Lal's voice and is intimidated. Will people stop drinking tea now that Indira Gandhi is dead?

'Go away!' says Sohan Lal. 'Shut your stall and go home. There is going to be trouble in Chandni Chowk.'

He waits for the chaivala's protest, but the man seems to have withdrawn. The fool, drain-squatter in checked shirt and cotton dhoti, bumpkin who has over-reached, fat bald idiot with foggy spectacles . . . Sohan Lal checks himself, reminded of the layer of softness round his own belly. He must take better care of his diet – the bundles are choking him. He must leave immediately. He walks to the alcove and rearranges, for the third time that morning, the gold-filigreed skirt of Lakshmi. With his ring finger he scoops up a drop of gangaajal from her feet and sprinkles it over his own head, causing it to disintegrate into a hundred tiny droplets. He presses his cap down on his head before the droplets can roll off. Thus he shall walk the dangerous streets of Chandni Chowk, protected by the waters of Ganga herself, sanctified at her feet. He steps off the gaddi and slips his feet into black rexine shoes.

The television shows pictures of young men with sticks, dancing round a shrine, a temple to Indira, hastily constructed outside the All India Institute. The men turn menacingly to the camera, hurl abuse, and deliver their warning to all sardars – 'Indira is our mother and we will avenge her.'

It is better to leave the television on, thinks Sohan Lal, so people will think someone is inside the shop. He removes the metal chain that latches the main door, steps out, locks it, replaces the key in his kurta pocket, and walks briskly through Kucha Bansilal to its junction with Chandni Chowk, ignoring the snigger of the yellow-toothed Musalman who crouches with the chaivala.

Ibrahim crinkles his nose and makes a face. Sohan Lal's emergence from the shop has delivered a sharp whiff of attar molshri into his nostrils. 'He carries the smell of sin,' he whispers.

Gopal replenishes Ibrahim's glass tumbler with the tea meant for Sohan Lal, remembering with a sigh that now this tea is free.

'The seth is fatter today,' remarks Ibrahim. 'Look how stiffly he walks, as if he's stuck in a tube.'

Gopal is forlorn. He has counted the cups downed by Ibrahim Mian. Four in the last hour, with no prospect of payment. The seth has gone for the day. No more customers, just hoodlums and crooks. And among them, perhaps, Mukesh. What is he doing? Shattering windows? Uprooting telephone poles? Setting houses on fire? Ah, a man should never be blessed with a son.

Ibrahim is in an expansive mood with his fourth cup. 'Indira was a kafir,' he says. 'No one will mourn her. But I have to go to the office.'

'You have no office, Ibrahim Mian.'

'Office,' repeats Ibrahim. 'They will tell me what to do.'

Gopal does not understand. His thoughts converge on the fourth cup. 'Will you pay now?'

Ibrahim casts a look of strained tolerance at him. 'Do you not understand what she did to the country, Gopal Bhai? Do you remember how her son locked up Musalmans and cut off their balls in the Emergency?'

'That was in 'seventy-five,' says Gopal.

'We have not forgotten!' hisses Ibrahim. He shakes his head and stares into space, overwhelmed by the task of recounting all of Indira's misdeeds.

Gopal puts an arm round him. 'I know you have suffered,' he says. For a moment he wonders how Ibrahim has suffered. Then his thoughts drift back to his son.

Ibrahim stands up and stretches. 'There is much suffering in the world, Gopal Bhai. You suffer too, but you do not know it. Did you see how the seth waddled, how the rolls of fat danced all over his body? Why do you think he is getting fat? He feasts on your body, Gopal Bhai. He is growing fat on your blood.'

Sohan Lal emerges from Kucha Bansilal, short of breath. He is not used to walking so quickly. He turns left in Chandni Chowk, away from the peepul tree and the Hanuman temple. A police van is parked under the tree, but there is no sign of trouble. Constables stand around listlessly, batons in hand. Chandni Chowk is deserted. Most shops have lowered their shutters. Kartar Singh's store is in Lajpatrai

Market at the eastern end of Chandni Chowk, near Red Fort. Sohan
Lal walks quickly, and first becomes aware of a crowd as he
approaches Gurudwara Sisganj. The crowd worries him. He crosses
to the other side of the street. Once he is past Gurudwara Sisganj, he
thinks, he can continue safely to Lajpatrai Market. 'The gurudwara is
sacred space,' say the sardars. 'It is the temple of our guru,' they claim,
'so the police cannot violate it.' He has heard that there is an army of
Sikhs, a Khalsa army, inside, armed with spears and kirpaans,
although Kartar Singh swears this is not true.

The crowd is small, no more than fifty people. It has gathered
round the white marble steps that lead into the gurudwara. At the top
of the steps, outside the main door, a few sardars stand guard with
ceremonial kirpaans in their hands. They seem to be arguing with the
crowd, but there is no sign of violence. A few sardars can still be seen
washing the marble steps, and a dozen are taking off their shoes in the
hall to the right of the building. The argument between the sardars
and the crowd heats up, and someone in the street shouts, 'Indira was
our mother and we will avenge her!'

Sohan Lal stops. He is a careful man, immune to impulses. To him,
boldness is another word for foolhardiness. So far, this appears to be
no more than an argument, but there is no telling where it will lead.
He turns and walks back toward Kucha Bansilal. He will take a longer
route through lanes that lead round the gurudwara and will deposit
him directly inside Lajpatrai Market. He passes Kucha Bansilal and
continues westward. The police van still stands under the peepul tree
but the constables are gone. 'Jamna Lal Kishori Mal – Sarees and
Blouses,' says the sign. He bows his head, and shuts his eyes
momentarily when he passes the Hanuman temple, noticing with
consternation that the pujari has drawn the gates. Why should God
fear the violence of men?

He turns into a lane and feels safer. He rarely comes here nowadays
but has fond memories of these lanes. 'Do not go to Delhi,' his uncles
had told him. 'It is a den of vice, a hive of thieves, prostitutes, robbers
and pimps. What will a simple boy like you do among such people?
We have a good business of our own – a steady business, three
generations old. You can sit on the gaddi all your life, chew paan,
serve your customers and watch your wealth grow. Life is not lived in
bursts of success and failure,' said the uncles. 'It is lived slowly,
gradually, in moderation, staying on the right side of both God and
man . . .'

Sohan Lal did not want to stay in Bikaner. His uncles thought it was a great city, having arrived from the much smaller town of Nawalgarh. But Sohan Lal had been to Delhi. He had seen Chandni Chowk, walked in its lanes, wandered around Lajpatrai Market and Khari Baoli. He had seen Punjabi refugees – who came in lakhs after Partition – prosper in small shops and cubicles. He knew it was important for his uncles that he stay in Bikaner. His father was dead, and they wanted his share of the capital to remain invested in the business.

Two months after the death of his father Sohan Lal found himself, at the age of eighteen, in Chandni Chowk, working for Seth Ghanshyam Das, a distant uncle, and cushioned by his capital, which he had withdrawn from the business in Bikaner. He had promises of a loan from Ghanshyam Das, to be given after five years, when he hoped to start his own business. He walked through Khari Baoli, Chawri Bajar, Nai Sarak and Lajpatrai Market, studied the shops and stalls, and turned in his mind an ever-changing vision of what his shop might look like. He was determined not to go into the cloth business, and he had decided he would not sell sweets. Chandni Chowk offered unlimited possibilities – toys, cosmetics, kitchenware, photo albums, gold, silver, cotton, jewellery, yarn, fruit, grains, spices, shoes, rexine, leather, hardware, water-pumps, wash-basins, paper, cardboard, pipes, bicycles, spectacles, kites, fireworks, fans, wedding rings, air-conditioners, printing presses . . . He had seen people make money from selling peacock feathers, hearing-aids and horoscopes. This, he told himself, was the market of India, where the country congregated to buy and sell. Surely there was space enough for him in the great scheme?

After he had worked for Ghanshyam Das for four years, his uncles found him a match in Bikaner. He went home hesitantly, aware that a man of twenty-two must be married off yet unhappy that his marriage had preceded the loan. Immediately after the wedding, he had returned to Delhi and sought an audience with Ghanshyam Das. The loan was given grudgingly at eighteen per cent – a back-breaking rate for a business and a criminal rate for a relative – and he wrote his first letter to Rukmini, addressed to his nephew who read it to her. 'I have my own business now,' he wrote, 'and I will soon bring you to Delhi.'

That promise had been difficult to fulfil. Rents had already begun to rise in Chandni Chowk. He spent much of his time in his shop, and at night slept there on a mattress. His meals were eaten in a communal kitchen where he found good Marwari food. He did not trust the so-called vegetarian restaurants in a big city like Delhi: although they did not serve chicken or mutton, they thought it was all right to make omelettes, and cut onions and garlic in plain view of customers.

From the day he opened its doors the shop prospered. There is something of the trader in every Marwari's blood, his father had assured him, and he was right. Sohan Lal never had a bad year, although in the beginning he struggled to make a profit because of the high interest on the loan. More than once he thought of defaulting. The loan was kachchha money, undocumented, invisible, impossible to litigate against. Ghanshyam Das had no hold over him except the pressure of public opinion and family ties. Had he defaulted, nothing more than his reputation would have been sullied.

During the first six years of his marriage, he rarely went to Bikaner. When he did, he spent little time with Rukmini because he was closeted with his uncles, who enquired anxiously about his prospects, perhaps in the hope that he would admit defeat and return to them. He was firm that Rukmini should continue to live with his mother – a man in debt should not have the cares of a household thrust on him.

As soon as he had paid the last rupee to Seth Ghanshyam Das, he brought Rukmini to Delhi. And in their rented flat, which she kept spotlessly clean – his mother had prepared her well – their first son was born, fully seven years after their wedding. The date is clear in his mind – 27 May 1964 – as is the time: it was three in the afternoon. The sun had scorched Chandni Chowk into submission; the fan overhead whirred fecklessly. He remembers standing outside the room, anxiously listening for the first cry of a newborn that would tell him everything was all right.

Suddenly, Pratap Munshi, his accountant at the time, rushed into the house trembling with excitement. 'Jawahar Lal Nehru has passed away,' he declared.

'I am waiting for a birth,' Sohan Lal had replied coldly. 'Why do you bring me news of a death?'

'Because the spirit of Nehruji will be reborn in the child,' said Pratap Munshi. As he finished speaking, Sohan Lal heard the heart-warming trill of a child inside the room.

He knocked impatiently, knowing it was improper to appear impulsive. The face of his mother, when she opened the door, told him all he needed to know. It was a boy. He looked at the men –

uncles, cousins – standing outside the room with him, and sensed envy in their eyes. He knew then that Lakshmi sends blessings to those who are debt-free and industrious, while she flings terrible wrath on the indebted and indolent.

Lakshmi was less predictable, however, than he had believed. In the next three years Rukmini gave birth to two girls. Despairing, he took her to a hospital and had the lady doctor make it so she would have no more children. Two girls were unfortunate, but three would have been too great a burden. This was also when he was beginning to attend Congress Party meetings at which talk of family planning was frequent. 'Two or three children and no more,' said the family-planning slogan. He was happy to acquiesce, so there it stopped: one boy and two girls. He would have preferred two boys and one girl. The two boys would take over the shop and the girl would be married off with great pomp, jewel of her father's heart, darling sister to two adoring brothers . . . But Lakshmi has been fair enough. He knows people who have three daughters, four daughters, five daughters, and not a single son to recoup the wealth that must flow out of the family when the girls are married off. His economy of children endeared him to the Congress Party committee, but he soon drifted away from it toward the Jan Sangh, which had always regarded family planning with suspicion. He wonders now if he was too enthusiastic about the whole family-planning business. It was all right for Indira Gandhi to push it: she already had two sons. Was it fair to impose it on the entire country? His fourth child might have been a son! This causes him a stab of pain, but he recovers and scolds himself. Here he walks in a suit of banknotes, debt-free, father of a grown-up boy, prepared to marry off two daughters when the time comes, on his way to securing five lakhs in stable dollars. What cause should such a man have to worry?

It is now thirty-one years since he left Bikaner, and he is reconciled to the idea of a cloth business, of selling sarees and blouses as his father had done in Bikaner, and his grandfather in Nawalgarh. Perhaps his uncles were right: a man needs no more than his own saree shop, in which he can recline on the gaddi, rest his elbows on bolsters, chew paan and serve his customers. True, he is much wealthier than his uncles' families. He stopped selling georgette sarees a long time ago, and will soon phase out cotton and chiffon. 'Jamna Lal Kishori Mal, Banarasi and Kanjeevaram silk only . . .' But a saree shop cannot rise to the level of a bullion business, as his uncles would have pointed out, had they still been alive. In one respect he has heeded their advice. He still clears the ground carefully before placing his foot on it.

The cloth belts have ridden up his trunk. The uppermost one is visible above the neckline of his kurta, and the one at his waist strains against his belly. Its metal buckle pinches him. I should not worry, he consoles himself. I am encased in tyres, but they can pass off as extra folds of a kurta. In any case the lanes are deserted. If a man can keep his wits about him, there is money to be made from the death of prime ministers. She is surely dead, although All India Radio has made no such announcement. Even the men outside Gurudwara Sisganj seem to think so. Indira was our mother and we will avenge her . . . Indira *was*, she no longer *is*. Indira, the whore of Emergency, fiend of Operation Bluestar, blight on the nation, curse on its democracy . . . We will avenge her. You need sons to avenge you, Sohan Lal thinks wistfully.

The lanes lead Sohan Lal to the bird hospital, where he joins Chandni Chowk again, crosses the street and enters Lajpatrai Market. Most shops are closed. Some have left their shutters half open, fear competing with greed. Some sit shamelessly with the shutters wide, starved of customers, television sets on their counters to attract people. Every screen shows scenes outside the All India Institute of Medical Sciences, where they have taken the body – although Door-darshan still does not say she is dead.

Kartar Singh has not bothered to roll down his shutter. 'Jasjit General Store,' says the electrical sign, with a subtext taken from a fan promotion proclaiming the greatness of India – 'Meraa Bharat Mahaan'. The shop sits at a corner under an old haveli – once the mansion of a courtier in Red Fort – that has been converted into commercial cubicles. The counter is adorned with a dozen table fans of different colours and sizes. Four young men stand near them, their backs to the lane, looking at the store wall where leather belts, photo albums, batteries, purses and electrical mixers are displayed on glass shelves. Sohan Lal frowns. Why should there be customers in Kartar Singh's shop when the market is deserted? There is no television in his shop, nothing to attract onlookers. No one could want to buy electric fans at a time like this. These might be Congress workers, come to stir trouble. Or police spies. He approaches the shop carefully, aware that the money is rustling under his kurta. He cannot brush against the men, whoever they are. He finds an opening between them, pushes his way to the counter, and waits for Bishan – Kartar Singh's clerk – to notice him. He is conscious of the belts digging into his flesh. The men on either side can probably feel the bundles pressing against them, but he does not care. He will soon be relieved of his load.

Bishan turns, leather belt in hand, breathless with activity, and sees Sohan Lal. 'Which fan would you like to see, sethji?' he asks.

Bishan is about twenty, almost the same age as Ramesh. He is a Jat – much taller than Ramesh – and has the calm assurance that Sohan Lal wishes for in his son. He has worked for Kartar Singh since childhood, and is adept with electrical appliances. He can open digital watches, stereos, electric fans, mixers and motors. He can replace resistors, change fuses and stabilise turntables. He salvages parts from obsolete electronic gadgets, which Kartar Singh passes off as new and inserts into gadgets in need of repair. Bishan is also in the know about Kartar Singh's other business, serving as gatekeeper and short-listing agent, familiar with regular customers, dismissive of new ones. He knows Sohan Lal well.

There is nothing exceptional about the boy, Sohan Lal tells himself. His self-assurance is merely a strain in his Jat blood, an evolutionary trait in a man whose forefathers worked the fields. Place a Jat behind a counter and he looks imposing. Place him behind the books and he is no match for a Bania like Ramesh, who was born to prosper by his wit and resourcefulness, not by his bearing. Thus consoled, Sohan Lal answers, 'The white one with six blades.'

'Bajaj has stopped making fans with six blades,' replies Bishan. 'But let me ask Kartar Singhji.'

Bishan telephones Kartar Singh and tells him Seth Sohan Lal is looking for a white fan with six blades.

'Kartar Singhji says you can come tomorrow,' says Bishan to Sohan Lal. 'He will have them brought out for you.'

The young men are growing impatient with Bishan. He has deserted them for Sohan Lal. Now he goes back to them and hands them the leather belt. It is passed round. Comments are made on its roughness. 'It is genuine leather,' says Bishan, 'unfinished leather, which is rough because it is expensive.' The men look doubtfully at each other. They are used to rexine imitations, which are smooth and shiny.

Sohan Lal leaves the counter and finds his way into a narrow lane next to the haveli. At the far end of the building he pushes open a door and enters an unlit corridor. He feels his way carefully along the passage and knocks on a white door. Kartar Singh immediately opens it and Sohan Lal steps inside. '*Sat sri akaal*, Kartar Singhji,' says Sohan Lal.

Kartar Singh ignores the '*Sat sri akaal*' – he is uncomfortable with religious greetings in public – and holds Sohan Lal's hands, covering them with his own. Then he gives the seth a knowing pat on the back, which resounds with the crispness of banknotes. He laughs, but although his beard shakes violently and his chest heaves with mirth, Sohan Lal can sense that he is nervous.

The room is windowless, located directly behind the store. The main door – through which Sohan Lal entered – opens on to the corridor that leads to the back of the building. A second door opens into the store, where it is hidden behind shelves of Bournvita. The floor is linoleum, but most of it is taken up by a mattress covered with a white sheet. A dozen telephones sit next to the wall, where the mattress runs along it. A maze of wires emerges from the telephones, groups itself into a bunch, then separates to disappear at various points in the wall.

Kartar Singh, a large man who looks older than his forty years, sits cross-legged on the mattress and waits for Sohan Lal, who raises his kurta and unbuckles the five belts, starting with the lowest. 'This is not a good time, sethji,' says Kartar Singh.

Sohan Lal does not reply. He breathes heavily, released from the belts, now in a heap at his feet. He slips off his chappals and lowers himself on to the mattress with a deep sigh. 'I have come this far,' he says. 'You cannot send me back now.'

Kartar Singh nods. He will never turn away a customer. 'Is there trouble in Chandni Chowk?' he asks anxiously.

Sohan Lal makes an impatient gesture. 'They are shouting slogans outside Sisganj. I don't think they will do anything more than that.'

'What are they shouting?' asks Kartar Singh.

Sohan Lal hesitates. He can see that Kartar Singh is on edge, and he does not want anything to interfere with his present business.

'"Indira was our mother and we will avenge her."'

Kartar Singh lowers his head.

'People say many things in passion,' adds Sohan Lal quickly. 'They are Congress workers, paid to say such things. We both know that no one will shed tears for the whore. I have called a committee meeting this evening at six. Lala Surajmal will be there and Jugal Kishor will come. Perhaps you too. We should talk this over. There may be elections.'

Kartar Singh nods, unconvinced. 'They were her own security guards, weren't they?' he asks suddenly.

'Yes, but it does not matter now,' says Sohan Lal, with some irritation. 'Two of them. One was shot instantly by the Tibetan police, I think. The other is still alive. They will torture him until he tells them everything. I have heard that the whole shooting is on tape, filmed by the BBC. She was about to give them an interview when the guards fired. The BBC was waiting with running cameras.'

'They will never show us that tape,' Kartar Singh sighs. 'We will never know what happened.'

Sohan Lal is annoyed. Why must they dwell on Indira while his money lies exposed? Can they not pretend she is alive until his business is concluded? When they announce it officially, he will shutter his shop and go into mourning. 'She is not dead yet,' he says soothingly. 'She is still at the All India Institute. They will do everything they can for her.'

'She is dead,' insists Kartar Singh. 'The BBC has announced it.'

'All India Radio has not.'

Kartar Singh throws up his hands with an air of bravado. 'People say there will be trouble. I say to them, "When has there not been trouble in Delhi?" When they kill Hindus in Punjab there is trouble in Delhi. When they explode a bomb in Bihar there is trouble in Delhi. Someone in Delhi is always trying to kill Sikhs! What is new about that? Sikhs know how to live with trouble.'

'Of course,' Sohan Lal agrees.

'What is the total amount?' Kartar Singh asks.

Ah, thinks Sohan Lal, we are finally talking business. 'Five lakhs.'

'Where to?'

'Ranjan, the same boy.'

'New York?'

Sohan Lal nods. 'You do not usually send such a large amount in one transaction,' says Kartar Singh.

'These are unusual times,' says Sohan Lal.

Kartar Singh picks up each belt and inspects it, then runs his hands inside the tubes but does not pull out the bundles. 'What is the rate?' asks Sohan Lal.

'Seven per thousand.'

'That is robbery!'

Kartar Singh raises his hands heavenward. 'Times are difficult for everyone, sethji. This business is not what it used to be. The government does not want you to transfer money through havala, because its banks lose the commission. All rates have gone up. Agents want two per thousand. SHOs have raised rates, and even constables now make more from the havala business than we do.'

'All right,' says Sohan Lal, evenly. He does not much mind the higher rates, and does not expect Kartar Singh to lower them for him. He has merely raised the customary objection that every buyer should. Kartar Singh tots up the numbers on a calculator.

'You should get one of those new machines,' says Sohan Lal. 'It is called a computer. It can add up numbers in a flash. Especially for you, who must convert from rupees to dollars every day.'

'I add less and less these days,' says Kartar Singh. 'People have begun to avoid havala. Too much interference by the police.' He finishes with the calculator. 'Thirty-five hundred for the rate, two hundred for the SHO and fifty for Bishan. That is thirty-seven hundred and fifty.'

'Bishan gets a cut?' asks Sohan Lal, horrified.

Kartar Singh shrugs. 'I need to keep everyone happy.'

Sohan Lal shakes his head in sympathy.

'Delivery by tomorrow,' says Kartar Singh. 'New York. Four lakhs, ninety-six thousand two hundred and fifty, at the dollar-buying rate. You will get tomorrow's rate.'

'The code?' asks Sohan Lal.

Kartar Singh considers. 'Operation Bluestar,' he says.

Sohan Lal chuckles nervously. 'All right, Operation Bluestar.'

'It is settled then,' says Kartar Singh. 'Delivery tomorrow in dollars in New York.'

Sohan Lal rises with difficulty, using his hands to push himself up. He steps off the mattress and stands barefoot on the linoleum. He feels the tug of his cloth belts. He does not want to walk away from the money: it suddenly seems unsafe. 'I should perhaps bring back the money tomorrow, when things will have settled down.'

Kartar Singh is surprised at the seth's loss of poise. 'I have never failed you, sethji.'

'There are four young men at the counter,' says Sohan Lal.

'What of it? This is a store.'

'The market is closed,' emphasises Sohan Lal. 'No one is buying anything.'

Kartar Singh smiles. 'Why should I chase away customers?'

But Sohan Lal cannot shake off his premonition. 'Bishan,' he says. 'The boy. Do you trust him?'

'Of course! I have raised him. He was ten when I first placed him at the counter. He is like a son to me. Go home and watch television, sethji.'

Kartar Singh begins to stow away the belts in a steel safe set against the wall.

'Will you not count it?' asks Sohan Lal.

'Your money needs no counting,' says Kartar Singh, obsequiously.

Sohan Lal slips his feet silently into his chappals and moves toward the white door, then stops and lingers. He cannot resist grumbling about the higher rate. 'It used to be five per thousand.'

'The rates I gave you are from last month, because we have known each other so long. They change every hour, but I cannot keep track. Maybe this computer you speak of can calculate the rates every hour, but I can add them up only once a day. My loss is your gain, sethji.'

'When you have a computer you will charge even more,' says Sohan Lal, wistfully.

Kartar Singh stands up with a laugh and opens the white door. Sohan Lal walks down the dim corridor, finds the outer door and goes out. He wishes he had not come to Kartar Singh. All smugness at his forethought is replaced with a presentiment of disaster. 'This is mere superstition,' he says, in an effort to cheer himself. He passes the store and sees that the young men are still busy, comparing leather belts. Is a belt really that difficult to select?

Lajpatrai Market has almost completely closed down. No television sets, no half-open shutters, no cycles, no rickshas. This is the silence of death, thinks Sohan Lal. If only it would last until tomorrow when his money is delivered safely to Ranjan in New York! Then they can burn down Delhi or hammer it to rubble in memory of Indira. She shed so much blood while she lived. It is fitting that more be shed now she is dead.

As soon as Sohan Lal leaves, Kartar Singh reopens the safe and brings out the money to count it. He studies the cloth belts with admiration.

They are sewn neatly, and they fit tightly round the bundles of banknotes without distorting them. The arrangement is too perfect to be disturbed, so he decides not to squeeze them out. This is how he will take them to Chawri Bajar tomorrow – where he puts his havala money to work in the form of high-interest loans – and have the clerks count the money.

He calls his man at the telephone exchange and asks to be connected to New York. He is told it will take an hour. He decides to wait and presses the intercom buzzer. Bishan picks up in the store.

'Bring me a cup of tea,' says Kartar Singh.

While he waits, the images he saw on television a few hours ago return to him, and he shudders. Men around the van that brought her to the Institute were screaming abuse whose meaning he well understood. Why were the police letting them get away with such slogans? And why had Doordarshan shown them again and again baying for the blood of Sikhs? The channel is, after all, controlled by the same Congress Party whose prime minister has been killed. This is an unfriendly country, he thinks wistfully. He wishes his relatives in Canada were closer to the family. They are distant cousins, not brothers or nephews as so many traders in Lajpatrai Market claim to have. If he was more intimate with them, he would have sold his flat in Trilokpuri and emigrated to Canada, taking Sukhbir and their son Jasjit with him. He would be rid of this bloodthirsty city, its foul-mouthed people and intolerable cruelty.

There is a loud knock on the white door. He starts, but it is only Bishan with the tea. 'It is hot, be careful!' he cautions.

'Knock softly in the future,' scolds Kartar Singh. 'You frightened me.'

Bishan giggles.

'How does the market look?' Kartar Singh asks.

'It is closed.'

'Shut the store and go home,' says Kartar Singh. 'No one will come today.'

'We have many customers.'

Kartar Singh frowns. He had shrugged off the question when Sohan Lal raised it, but it bothers him now. Why are there customers in his store when the market is closed?

'Send them away,' he says. 'Shut the store and go home.'

Bishan looks puzzled. 'What reason do you have to fear?'

Kartar Singh waves him away, secures the door and settles down to wait for the call to New York. Bishan's soothing words, turned repeatedly in his mind, become increasingly ominous. 'What reason do you have to fear?' he asked. There had been something in his manner, a glint in his eye . . .

Kartar Singh can hear two voices through the wall. In the store, someone is haggling over the price of a leather belt. The other voice is Bishan's, extolling its virtues. Kartar Singh grits his teeth. What a fool! Why will Bishan not let the man pay, then go home? He presses the buzzer again, insistently, until Bishan picks up. 'Take his money and give him the belt!' he barks.

'It is not time yet,' Bishan says, and hangs up.

Kartar Singh is dumbfounded. It is not time yet for *what*? There is a certain familiarity in the way the boy banters with the other voices. And there are at least four of them. He takes a deep draught of tea, drains the glass, and pats his face with his handkerchief, ashamed of his suspicions. Why, Bishan is almost like a son to him.

The voices grow louder. There is laughter. The men do not sound like customers! And why is Bishan laughing with them?

A loud crash thunders through the wall. Something has fallen to the floor. Kartar Singh cowers in horror. The crash is followed by another. His table fans are slipping off the counter one by one! But how can they slip by themselves? The counter is wide and the fans have stable bases. They are being thrown deliberately!

'Khalistan *murdabad*!' someone shouts.

For a moment Kartar Singh stops breathing. Crash follows crash. They are sweeping his bottles, mixers, blowers and shavers off the counters. Bishan has probably run away. The coward! Yet he is only a boy. They will kill him if he intercedes. Kartar Singh's eyes fill with tears. This is a test, *Sachche Padshah*! He will sit still. He will hand over his life to the care of the True King. Let the bastards spit on him! They will destroy what they see and continue, triumphant, to the next open shop. The store does not add much to his income anyway. The entire stock is worth one lakh. Let them have it all! He will begin anew, this time among human beings, not bloodthirsty hounds.

'Indira was our mother and we will avenge her!' someone shouts.

Kartar Singh shuts his eyes. He will live through this! Among the crashes and screaming, a sound arises – at first faint, then insistent, and eventually unmistakable. Someone is attacking the glass shelves that hide the red door to the back room. They crash on to the floor. The cans of Bournvita and Horlicks are swept away. Bishan! Only

Bishan could have told them about the door. Behind the shelves a false wall is secured by a hidden clasp. He hears a click as it is undone. The red door is now exposed to them, and they begin to pound on it from the other side.

The telephone rings. Perhaps it is Kartar Singh's man at the exchange, ready to connect him to New York. He curses. It is Sohan Lal's business or his life! The door is sagging under the blows. At any moment now it will fly off its hinges. On the other side stands Bishan with his hoodlums. The ungrateful bastard! Never trust a Jat!

'Indira Gandhi *amar rahe*!' shout the men. 'Khalistan *murdabad*!'

'Give us the sardar!' someone laughs.

A voice answers, and it is Bishan's: 'You take the sardar, I will take the money.'

Kartar Singh frantically locks the steel safe, stuffs Sohan Lal's cloth belts into a jhola and runs to the other door. He squeezes out as the red door is shredded into a dozen slivers by an axe and they charge into the room. 'Don't let him get away!' someone shouts.

Kartar Singh quickly locks the white door from the outside and recoils as the axe falls on its inner surface. He runs down the corridor. A lone electric bulb barely illuminates it, but he could walk along it blindfolded. When he emerges from the building, he hears them throwing his stools, counters and chairs into the street.

He is a large man, unused to exercise. It is not long before he is gasping for breath and slowing down. He is overwhelmed by self-pity. Will he get out of Chandni Chowk alive? But then he thinks of Jasjit and laughs at his fatalism. Of course he will. He will stick to the lanes around Chandni Chowk. They are safer than the street. He must get word to Sukhbir and Jasjit. Sukhbir is at home, perhaps sitting down with her gutkas at this moment, about to begin Japji Sahib. 'One breath of Japji Sahib protects you from danger,' she says, 'even if you don't know all the lines.' He must exhume those lines now from the recesses of his mind . . . And Jasjit is watching a matinée in Vishaal cinema, unless the film has finished and he is drinking chai somewhere in Chandni Chowk, unaware of the danger. He will not leave Jasjit defenceless. He will find an open store – one that looks friendly – and ask the man if he may use his telephone. He will tell Sukhbir to open the door to no one and shut herself inside the bedroom, and he himself will go looking for Jasjit in Vishaal cinema, if they are still showing films on such a day. Then they will go home to Trilokpuri together. They will find an autoricksha, perhaps one driven by a sardar. They will pack and lock up the flat. He will take Sukhbir away for a few days. Jasjit can stay with friends he trusts, or come too. They will go to Simla or Kanpur. They will manage.

Chandni Chowk is crowded. Everyone seems to be waiting for something to happen. Police jeeps with flashing beacons cruise the streets. Rooftops are filled with people looking down for signs of trouble. There have been stray incidents of violence. Someone threw stones at a sardar's shop in Ballimaran, but ran away before the matter could get out of hand. A ricksha ploughed through a group of people in Nai Sarak, but that appears to have been an accident. 'It is not a communal incident,' says the assistant commissioner of police, speaking into the camera. Four young men, all 'lumpen elements', according to the ACP, attacked a general store owned by a sardar and ran away with leather belts. An irate mob has formed outside Fatehpuri Masjid round a passionate speaker who invokes the fury of Mother India. The ACP says that 'The matter is being investigated and all rabble-rousers will be arrested.' He is not too concerned about Fatehpuri Masjid because, he says, it is not a 'communal disturbance'. The crowd outside the mosque sways and heaves, then moves through Chandni Chowk in a disorganised, confused manner.

The epicentre of this earthquake, should it come, is Gurudwara Sisganj, on which most eyes are focused. The rooftops next to it are choked with onlookers, while in the street the mass of people has formed a large clearing at the entrance, afraid to go too close but eager not to miss anything. Ramvilas stands at the edge of this gathering, inside a closed stall. The wooden planks that shutter it have gaps between them, through which he can comfortably scan the crowd. Scattered throughout it are some familiar faces – people he has cultivated over the years because they are useful: they can give you a riot in two hours, a fire in thirty minutes, or a knifing the next day. They are the tools of his trade as an organiser, an amorphous group belonging to no organisation, unknown to each other, interacting only with him. His instructions to them are vague, because he himself has received no specific direction from Lala Surajmal. He knows instinctively that trouble will help, but not if a full-blown pogrom against sardars will be advantageous to the IPP. The Indian People Party, in its astonishing transformation from a caucus of traders to the great hope of a middle class that has always viewed Congress with suspicion, has yet to gain the confidence of Sikhs. At best, this trouble could be used to smear Congress. It must be because of his tentative command that the men – the few he recognises – stand uncertainly. It is also possible that they are serving as 'Congress Party activists' today – they render services to both sides with equal frequency.

A stream of light falls across his face and he steps back. He does not want to be seen. A rush of wind sears his cheek. He pats it carefully, avoiding the scratches dug into it this morning.

A man – a sardar – emerges from a lane beyond Gurudwara Sisganj and walks toward it. Ramvilas cannot see him distinctly from this distance. A fat sardar, most likely, from the way he walks. He seems exhausted, and carries something that looks like a bag. He spots the crowd and draws back instinctively. Almost everyone in the crowd notices him at the same time, as if they possess one pair of eyes driven by one relentless mind. A thousand faces turn to him. There is a brief moment when the street falls silent – the crowd considers its prey, the sardar is struck dumb. Then he runs, but instead of retreating and losing himself in the lanes, he makes the mistake of running straight into the crowd, perhaps blinded by urgency.

The crowd is stunned. It draws back a little, like a herd of cows about to stampede at the charge of a bull. What gives the sardar such courage? Perhaps the load that weighs down the jhola in his hand. A bomb? A bottle of kerosene? Then the situation suddenly defines itself. It is only a sardar, a fat sardar – one man against a thousand with fear written on his brow. 'Kill the Khalistani bastard!' someone shouts. 'Khalistan *murdabad*! Indira Gandhi *amar rahe*!' The crowd advances toward him, eyes fixed on the hateful turban that bobs up and down as he runs.

Blood shall be spilled today, thinks Ramvilas. From his hideout he cannot see the sardar clearly, but can sense the nervousness in the air. He leaves the stall through a back door and walks away from the scene. He has no interest in bloodshed. In his mind, only the vulgar are voyeurs of violence.

The sardar reaches Gurudwara Sisganj, and the mob swoops on

him. Just before they can encircle him, a full battalion of Sikhs emerges from the gurudwara, dressed in blue and yellow salvaars, resplendent with silk sashes, armed with kirpaans held high above their heads. The advancing mob falters. The sardar is within reach – such tender meat! – but is now surrounded by a dazzling sea of blue and yellow. In spite of the men Ramvilas has seeded in the crowd, it consists largely of clerks, rickshavalas, accountants and traders. They have never fought street battles. They stand a few feet from the Sikh army and hurl abuse, obstinacy competing with fear. Their numbers are far larger than the Sikh army, but they carry no kirpaans, they have no dazzling uniforms and their anger is unfocused, undefined. 'Khalistan *murdabad*!' they scream. 'Indira was our mother and we will avenge her . . .'

The sardar stands between two armies, bewildered. The sensible course is to run into the array of Sikh skirts and be absorbed safely, but he is not in control of his reason, as if destiny has willed him to destruction. The Sikhs in full regalia look more threatening to him than harmless clerks in kurtas, shirts, trousers and pyjamas. After hesitating momentarily, he tears through the clerks and emerges on the other side unharmed, before the Sikh army can stop him or the clerks lay their hands on him. A roar erupts from the crowd when it realises the sardar has been separated from his army. Its courage redoubled, the mob reverses course and gives chase, as the sardar hops on to the footpath and disappears into Kucha Bansilal.

'Get the Khalistani bastard!' someone shouts. 'He slipped into the lane!'

'Kucha Bansilal!'

Kartar Singh slows down, overwhelmed by self-pity. God will bear witness that he tried to walk through bloodthirsty wolves but could not get to Vishaal cinema. God will protect Jasjit. He is only human, he cannot do much more. His legs are beginning to give way. This is the end – this is how it all ends! Jasjit will survive – if they spare him – but what will Sukhbir do? At this very moment she is perhaps reciting a gutka. Does this kucha lead somewhere? What if it is a dead-end? They will corner him like a rat! Perhaps someone in the kucha can give him shelter. People must live on the upper floors.

He looks up, scanning closed windows and drawn curtains. The kucha is dead. Its businessmen have gone home and its residents – if there are any – have no pity in their hearts. His eyes rest on a signboard, the largest in the lane, 'Jamna Lal Kishori Mal – Sarees and Blouses'. He cannot believe his luck. He has never before come to Sohan Lal's shop, but there can be no mistake: he has heard the name countless times in committee meetings. He shuts his eyes in gratitude. *Sachche Padshah*! Of the hundred lanes in Chandni Chowk, You bring me to one where I shall get succour!

He beats on the closed doors. He can hear the television inside, chanting the same ominous slogan that they are repeating outside the kucha. 'Khalistan *murdabad*! Khalistan *murdabad* . . .' They are coming for him! Why does Sohan Lal not open the door? Can he not hear his cries?

He looks about the lane desperately. There is an electrical junction box in the wall on the other side. Maybe he can climb up and hide above it. There is enough space for a person there, but the box is at least six feet off the ground. Who will help him up? His body does not have the strength to make such a leap. Below the junction box the lid of a large wooden chest is propped open and tied to the junction box. There are pans, tins, glass tumblers, cups, a stove, bottles of sugar and cardamom. A chai stall. Could he pass as a chaivala? Ah, futile thought! Who would mistake a fat sardar for a chaivala? And have not a thousand pairs of eyes seen him? He throws the jhola into the wooden chest, thinking he will hide it there. The sounds outside the kucha are louder now. He places one foot inside the chest, then the other, and lowers himself into a crouching position, the jhola by his side. He does not fit – the chest is too small. Thus he stays for a few seconds, suspended in a half-crouch, feet planted inside the chest, turban showing above its walls. The crowd is almost upon him. Perhaps they will take pity when they see him like this? But these are not human beings.

With a great effort, he squeezes himself lower in the chest, unties the lid from the junction box, and lets it drop over his head. It hits him hard, but his turban absorbs much of the impact. He is now curled in a foetal position, upright, suspended like a biological specimen within six walls that push on him from every side, face pressed to his knees, hips rubbing painfully against the chest, which might splinter apart at any moment.

The crowd washes by him, missing him by seconds. 'He is in the lane somewhere!' someone shouts. 'He must have run into a building! Look deeper inside the kucha! Scour the drains! He is hiding inside the slush like a rat!'

He listens to them talking to each other for twenty minutes. The chest seems to adjust itself to his bulk, or perhaps his body finds previously unexplored spaces and flows into them. He is able to take a few deep breaths and wrap his arms round his knees. As long as he remains silent and does not move, he is probably safe. The chest is screwed into the wooden planks beneath it, so it will not tip over. The jhola lies crushed on his side, its cloth belts curled like snakes.

The sounds gradually die away, but he is too frightened to push up the lid. He will stay like this for a while, perhaps another twenty minutes, then take a peek over the chest walls.

It is almost dark when Gopal returns from Kucha Mahajani in despair. He has spent two hours looking for Mukesh. He went first to Seth Jhunjhunwala's shop and found it closed. He stood before the shop for a long time, hoping the doors would open to reveal his son sitting inside, weighing silver. A vain hope, because the seth had thrown out Mukesh four months ago over that diamond theft, which Mukesh claims he is innocent of. He still goes to the shop to plead with the seth, and Gopal had hoped he would be there today. After an hour waiting outside, Gopal had plodded down the kucha to Seth Jhunjhunwala's foundry, thinking Mukesh might be loitering there among the furnaces, watching them melt silver, helping with electrolysis and casting. After two hours of fruitless scouring, he knew Mukesh was nowhere in the bullion market. He could be in a hundred other places in Chandni Chowk. There were so many katras and kuchas, so many lanes and buildings and havelis. Gopal decided to return to Kucha Bansilal.

Turning into the lane with a heavy heart, Gopal is surprised to find the lid of his box closed. He had left it open – no one steals from a chai stall. He lifts the lid, and the first object that greets his eye – in the semi-darkness of dusk – is a blue turban that pops upward, like a spring released from a clasp. Gopal cowers back in fear. 'Ganga *Maiya*!'

'Do not kill me!' begs the sardar.

Gopal uncovers his eyes. The sardar does not appear to be threatening him. Indeed, he is in an awkward position, wedged tightly into the box, arms wrapped round his legs, unable to move. His eyes are bloodshot, like those of a hunted animal. 'Who are you, sardarji?'

'Let me stay here until dark,' pleads Kartar Singh, 'or they will kill me!'

Gopal does not know what to do with the sardar. Perhaps the man will buy a cup of tea. A customer, finally, on this horrible day. 'Let me make you chai. You have some money?'

Kartar Singh does not reply.

'Why are you here?' asks Gopal. 'They are chasing down sardars all over Chandni Chowk. You should be at home, watching television.'

'I was trying to go to Vishaal cinema.'

Gopal is dumbfounded: how could a man watch a film on such a day?

Kartar Singh senses his confusion. 'I am looking for my son,' he adds softly. 'He is at Vishaal cinema.'

'Ah!' groans Gopal. 'I am looking for my son too . . .'

They fall silent, united in anxiety. Gopal notices that the sardar is uncomfortable inside the box. 'What is that against your knees?'

'A jhola,' says Kartar Singh, reluctantly.

'Give it to me. You will have more space.'

The sardar demurs.

Gopal is offended. 'You can trust me, sardarji. I am not a thief.'

Kartar Singh shifts uncomfortably inside the box, pushing the jhola further down. 'It contains clothes,' he says weakly. 'My wife's underwear. Panties, bras.'

Chastened, Gopal squats next to the box and lets the sardar be. He will wait until it is safe for the man to go. But how will he know when that moment has come? He can still hear scattered sounds in Chandni Chowk. When he emerged from Kucha Mahajani, he was told of the riot outside Gurudwara Sisganj where a sardar, backed by two dozen Sikhs, had charged down an army of Hindus. There is little doubt that the sardar was planted by the gurudwara to incite trouble. The riot has only just burned itself out, leaving three people with head wounds. No one knows how long this will last.

Gopal rolls up the tarpaulin above the junction box. Footsteps echo down the kucha – someone is walking toward them in the darkness. He has a flashlight. 'Quick!' whispers Gopal. 'Get into the box!'

'I am already inside it,' protests Kartar Singh.

'Your head, sardarji! Your turban!'

Gopal pushes down on the turban with all his might, then snaps the lid shut, climbs on to the box and squats on it, just as a constable appears in the kucha with the clickety-clack of police boots. As he walks, he lets his baton hop along concrete platforms on his left, creating a noisy beat. Gopal cannot contain his joy. 'It is a policeman,' he whispers to Kartar Singh. 'He will take you home safely.'

Inside the box, Kartar Singh makes a violent attempt to lift the lid and fling Gopal to the ground. Above all, he does not want to be revealed to the police. He has heard too many stories about them. 'Don't tell him!' he cries. 'Don't tell him!'

The constable is almost upon Gopal now. He stops and considers, then taps the chest. 'What is this?' he demands.

'Stall, sarkaar,' says Gopal with folded hands. 'Chai stall.'

Inderlal Jha weighs his options. As head constable, he is conscious of his status as the enforcer of permits among businessmen. A chai stall is beneath his purview, or should be. But all other shops are closed, so the chai stall must bear the full burden of his vigilance. 'Do you have a permit?' he asks Gopal.

Gopal nods. He does not know what a permit is.

Inderlal can tell, from years of looking into people's faces, that Gopal is lying. He clucks in irritation. He has spent fifty thousand rupees getting himself transferred to Chandni Chowk, where people buy and sell material worth a hundred crores every day. But of all the places that could have fallen within his beat, he has been dumped in Kucha Bansilal and the lanes around it. A few saree shops, paan stalls, tea stalls, a massage master, a seller of virility potions and an ear-cleaner. The saree shops are the only candidates for a little income. The rest – like this balding chaivala – are no better than beggars. Look at him! His shirt has buttons missing, his dhoti is torn, and his spectacles have so many scratches that you cannot look into his eyes. What is the point of asking such a man to produce a permit? You cannot squeeze juice out of a dry lemon. He will let the man be and continue to look for the sardar who caused the riot. It occurs to him, suddenly, that the chaivala's stall is closed. So why is he still loitering in the kucha?

'Why are you sitting here?' he demands.

'Waiting, sarkaar.'

Inderlal arches a brow. He will not humour the man with the obvious question.

'I am waiting for my son, sarkaar. Then I will go home.'

Inderlal nods. Fair enough. An irrelevant man busy with inconsequential affairs. Kucha Bansilal is full of them. He has heard that they do more than ten crores of business every day in the bullion market of Kucha Mahajani, and fifty crores in the Khari Baoli spice market from which, he hears, peppers and cardamom are sent all over the world. There must be a river of money in those areas! No matter how large a percentage the SHO skims off, there must be enough for the head constable and all junior constables. Why, even police-station sweepers probably earn a hundred rupees every month in Khari Baoli! In GB Road, where each whore brings no more than three rupees for every customer to the police check-post, there are at least eighty brothels: at forty whores per brothel, and seven customers per whore each night, the collection adds up to almost seventy thousand rupees. Then there are bais, pahalvans, recruiters . . . an endless stream of donors. That is fertile ground for a hard-working man like himself, because the money is to be shared by no more than six people – the SHO, the additional SHOs and the head constables. There are a dozen constables in the GB Road police chauki but they are Class IVs, and can be bought with ten rupees each. But how does a head constable get posted to a place like GB Road? He is a poor Jat from Bahadurgarh. He knows no one in the department. He has neither the connections nor the one lakh rupees you need to be posted to such places. His only sources of income are illegally parked scooters and stalls that encroach on public land. And superfluous, balding beggars like this one. 'How long have you been sitting here?' he asks irritably.

'Three hours,' lies Gopal.

'Have you seen that bastard sardar Satwant Singh?'

Inside the box, crushed into a bruised bundle, Kartar Singh grits his teeth at being called Satwant Singh. Ah! I am Beant Singh, I am Satwant Singh! I am the one who killed that whore! The gun may not have been in my hands but I wished her dead, and I will shed no tears over her dead body. You will live forever, Beant Singh, although they have riddled you with bullets. And you, Satwant, will never be forgotten, even after they have hanged you by the neck.

'I have seen no one, sarkaar,' says Gopal.

Some day I will repay you! thinks Kartar Singh, his heart overflowing with gratitude.

'He came running by here,' insists the policeman. 'I saw him with my own eyes, less than an hour ago. How could you have missed him?'

Kartar Singh senses Gopal's fear, and his heart sinks. The chaivala is a kind-hearted man, but he is a coward. He will not be able to stand his ground. Is this how it will end? What will the constable do to him, after he pulls up the lid and shines his flashlight inside, seeing him curled up like a shivering dog? Will all of Sukhbir's gutkas come to nothing? What would she say at such a moment? Should he recite the Japji Sahib? *Ek Omkar, Satnaam, Karta Purakh, Nirbho, Nir Vair, Akaal Murat Ajuni* . . . He does not know the rest. He is not a religious man. *Sachche Padshah*! He is an ignorant man, an ungrateful man, a man blind to the wonders of creation. But if he is spared today . . .

'What kind of man? Do you mean a sardarji?' asks Gopal.

'Yes, yes!'

'I saw him.'

Kartar Singh stops breathing, and hears the loud thumping of his heart.

'He came by an hour ago. A fat man with a jhola. He was running wildly, his turban was undone. A blue turban.'

'Where did he go? Tell me! Tell me!'

'That way, down the lane toward the railway station. He was too afraid to stop.'

Inderlal Jha's eyes glisten in the shadows of dusk. There is still time to catch the sardar. He could not have gone far, certainly not to the end of the lane, where the crowd would have attacked him immediately. He is hiding somewhere, perhaps inside one of these shops. He will catch the sister-fucking bastard. How often does a head constable in Kucha Bansilal get such an opportunity? He will catch the sardar and earn himself a medal. A commendation roll or, some day, even the president's police medal. And then he will somehow arrange the one lakh that will ensconce him in GB Road as additional SHO. But first he must catch his sardar, the murderer who incited the riot, the killer of Indira Gandhi. Not that he cares for Indira. She had short hair, cut like a man – not a woman whose morality was beyond question.

He saunters down the lane, letting his boots echo in the kucha, tapping closed shutters with his baton as if the sound will reveal the hidden sardar behind them.

Kartar Singh hears the footsteps recede and lets out a deep breath. The chaivala is more resourceful than he had thought.

'You will live a thousand years!' he whispers.

'Someone else is coming!' hisses Gopal. 'Stay quiet!'

Kartar Singh curses his luck. He cannot survive much longer in the suffocating confines of the box.

'It is Seth Sohan Lal,' says Gopal, happily. 'I will tell him about you and he will give you shelter in his shop.'

Suddenly Kartar Singh is alert. Should he reveal himself to Sohan Lal? The seth will have no choice but to help. Did he not say there was a committee meeting at six? Well! Here is Kartar Singh, present at the meeting, a little early, a little dishevelled, a little shaken, but still of sound mind.

Then he is thrown into doubt. Sohan Lal will notice the jhola, and take his money back. Perhaps that would be good for both of them. Good riddance to danger. He has not spoken to his contact in New York anyway. There has been no transaction. But he feels possessive about the money. He has sat with the jhola pressed to his legs for almost two hours. He has shared the box with it, felt its pressure, heard it crackling. Why, he has put his life in danger for this money! He deserves his commission. But Sohan Lal will give him no commission without a transaction. Very well, there shall be a transaction. It will be delayed by a day, but it will happen and he will get his commission.

'Do not tell the seth about me,' he commands Gopal.

'Why not? Sethji will help you.'

'I do not trust anyone but you,' pleads Kartar Singh. 'Let me stay here until it is completely dark. Then I will go.'

Sohan Lal is comforted to see the chaivala sitting on his box. At least the kucha is not completely deserted. Also, some tea will lighten the mood in the committee meeting. He nods absently at Gopal – wondering vaguely why he has closed his stall if he intends to sit in the kucha – then unlocks his doors.

Kartar Singh listens with bated breath, hearing bolts being drawn aside. The television inside the shop becomes louder when the doors are opened, its chatter borne to him on a whiff of fragrance. Then the doors are shut and the television is turned off.

'I will remember this!' whispers Kartar Singh, with feeling.

Gopal does not reply. His mind is on Mukesh. Perhaps he should go to the kholi in Khari Baoli, where he will find his son waiting for him. Ah, vain thought! Mukesh has not come to the kholi for months. Indeed, he has seen him only twice since the day, four months ago, when Seth Jhunjhunwala threw him out of his shop. In any case, going to Khari Baoli will involve a trek through much of Chandni Chowk, past Fatehpuri Masjid. The area around a mosque is never safe. For a Musalman like Ibrahim, perhaps, but not for him. And what is he to do with this sardar, who is too fat for the box? At this very moment he is pressing against sugar bottles, glass tumblers and milk pails, crushing them, spilling milk and tea on the floor.

'You can come out now,' says Gopal. 'There is no one in the kucha.'

There is no reply from the box.

'Did you hear me? You can come outside now!' Gopal wonders if the man has fallen asleep. 'Come outside, sardarji!'

A faint voice, insistent and urgent, answers him: 'Please do not shout. The seth will hear you.'

'I am going home now,' says Gopal stubbornly.

'Could you punch a hole in the box?' asks Kartar Singh. 'I need some air . . .'

I have helped him, and he wants to destroy my stall, Gopal thinks.

'Your son will come back to you,' says Kartar Singh, ingratiatingly.

Gopal shakes his head, refusing to find hope in the sardar's words. A thief never comes back. Even when he does, the tag sticks to him – the word 'thief' is imprinted on his soul. It is some consolation that Seth Jhunjhunwala is a kind man, easily mollified, unlike his sons. They clamoured for Mukesh's blood even after he had admitted guilt and returned the stolen diamond. Could they not see, as Seth Jhunjhunwala could, that the boy had merely over-reached, that he was a fool rather than a criminal? Everyone steals a little from the bullion market – bits of silver, an old coin, a figurine worth fifty rupees. It is a pity that the boy had to take a diamond. A foolhardy boy, a careless boy . . . Mukesh saw Seth Jhunjhunwala study the diamond with his magnifying-glass before he handed him the ring for refitting. The poor boy! He did not know that diamonds have impurities – even the Kohinoor is not perfect – and that carbon deposits in a diamond make it distinguishable from every other one in the world. So when Mukesh returned the ring – after reducing its diameter for refitting – the seth put his eye to the magnifying-glass and knew instantly that the diamond had been switched. 'I do not see marks at three o'clock and seven o'clock!' he had thundered. He already knew that the boy stole bits of gold whenever a ring was refitted, that he chipped off small pieces from silver bricks when he brought them from the foundry to the shop. The seth also knew that silver powder was siphoned off during titration in his laboratories, and that they scraped his tanks in the refinery after every electrolysis. Those were losses he could live with. But the foolish boy had stolen a whole diamond! Seth Jhunjhunwala was furious. Gopal shudders at the memory. He had had to plead – with Mukesh to return the diamond, with the seth to call off the police. He remembers the date, too, because Indira Gandhi had sent her army into Golden Temple the next day. 'Your son is a thief,' said the seth to Gopal, 'but he is not a terrorist like Bhindranwale, or a murderer like Indira. I will let him go but I do not want to see him again.'

Gopal wraps his arms round himself and lowers his face to his knees, sitting much as Kartar Singh does inside the chest below him. This was to have been an unfortunate day – marked by scorching heat, slow business and scooter accidents – not a terrible one. Why did Indira Gandhi have to die and ruin it?

Mukesh is relieved to find Kucha Mahajani closed for the day. After hearing the news, the traders have gone home early. He arrives at the shop and looks at the board, which has been repainted since he left – 'Jhunjhunwala and Sons, Jewellers and Bullion Merchants'. He knocks gently on the wooden shutters. There is no response. Assured, he lays down his sack, pulls out a crow-bar and crouches outside the shop, next to three slabs of concrete that form a causeway connecting it to the lane. He thrusts the crow-bar between the last two slabs, shakes them loose, then lifts out the second one. From the muddy grave below, he carefully extracts a metal box and opens it.

Everything is in place – bits of gold, stolen from resized rings, wrapped inside a newspaper ball, chips from silver bricks, silver dust from the titration lab and seven thousand rupees. He unravels the newspaper ball. 'Operation Bluestar,' screams the headline. 'Late edition, 6 June 1984.' Below the bold headline – 'Indira Orders Troops into Golden Temple' – lie a dozen pieces of gold. He eyes his collection greedily, then hurls a silent curse at Seth Jhunjhunwala. This is his entire treasure after three years of service. He was twelve when his father first brought him to the bullion market in the mistaken belief that a clerk who deals in gold and silver is destined for prosperity. Indeed, he has learned the trade. He can handle electronic balances, determine the purity of a silver brick to the tenth place merely by looking at it; he can almost do titration himself, having watched it done countless times; he has stood around when they set up electrolysis tanks. After all that, this is his entire hoard, with no prospect of accretion. No one will give him a job in Kucha Mahajani now. He does not care. He will manage, somehow – and without his father's silly chai stall. There is no shortage of employers for a resourceful man. He is glad he switched that diamond. What hope had he, with silver dust and bits of gold, of ever collecting anything that was valuable? Real money is in diamonds, not in gold or silver.

Mukesh counts out a thousand rupees, rolls the notes and stuffs them into his pocket. For today, a thousand should do. It is an investment. He expects Rajan Nahal to pay him three times this amount when he has finished.

A sound distracts him. A man is walking down the lane. He quickly collects the newspaper, stuffs it back into the box, buries it and lowers the concrete slab. He does not have time to pick up the crow-bar because the man is now within plain view. Mukesh shuffles into the alley between Seth Jhunjhunwala's shop and the next one, cursing inwardly. It is his father. Does he not know that Jhunjhunwala no longer employs him? What reason does he have to expect his son here? Has he got wind of the metal box? Hopefully, he will not notice the loose concrete slab, or the crow-bar, which lies conspicuously on it.

Gopal stands outside the shop for a long time, and Mukesh waits impatiently, lamenting the waste of time. He has important work to do. He must get back to Rajan Nahal before it is dark, and he has still to get the rods from a storehouse near Chawri Bajar. It will take him an hour to load them on to a ricksha and transport them, but he cannot leave Kucha Mahajani without pushing the slab back into place. It is his fate to be stymied by his father at every turn. His friends call him a Bihari, a Bengali, a Bhaiya. 'You may live in Delhi but you are not a true Dillivala,' they tell him. 'Just look at your father!' He tries to fight back but he knows he was born in Sasaria, even if his father brought him to Delhi when he was six. He never knew his mother: she died in childbirth, his father told him one night in the kholi. He had left it when he was twelve, as soon as he had some money – from his employment with Seth Jhunjhunwala – to spend on himself. He has lived in night shelters, kuchas, drums, drains and pavements since then. There is plenty of space in Chandni Chowk for a man who can take care of himself. Chandni Chowk is a dormitory, a battlefield, a home, a shit-pot, a urinal. He is comfortable here, released from the prescriptive confines of the kholi and the chai stall. And he likes his new friends. They walk with a swagger, speak of momentous events. They do not waste their time in the service of fat seths.

Eventually Mukesh hears his father walk away, deeper into Kucha Mahajani. He emerges, presses the slab into place, stuffs the crow-bar into his sack and leaves. He now has six thousand in his bank. Not much, but he hopes to replenish it tomorrow.

He hopes Rajan Nahal will keep his word about the money. For now, he must trust the man and hurry to Chawri Bajar for the rods, which are indispensable. Without rods, Rajan Nahal had said, you cannot crack open skulls, because even the most spirited man is too weak-hearted to wield an axe.

'You need a stronger heart, Sohan Lal, or how will you live through the earthquake that is on its way?'

Lala Surajmal, chairman of the IPP committee in Chandni Chowk, is seated comfortably on the gaddi in Sohan Lal's shop. His back rests against the wooden cabinet under the Lakshmi alcove, so his head appears to touch Lakshmi's silver foot. His right arm rests heavily on two bolsters, and his left leg is extended, creating distance between him and his audience of two, Sohan Lal and Jugal Kishor. His dhoti has ridden up his leg, exposing varicose veins that snake from his thighs to his shins. He has talked continuously for the last ten minutes, analysing the political situation in Chandni Chowk since the assassination. Neither Sohan Lal nor Jugal Kishor has interrupted him in deference to his superior position in the IPP committee. His shop, Bhagwan Das and Sons, is the oldest perfume business in Chandni

Chowk, perhaps the oldest in the country, predating the Mutiny of 1857, the British Raj and, some say, Red Fort itself. It is commonly believed – and prominently advertised on a plaque attached to the mahogany panels in the shop – that Bhagwan Das and Sons was established in Lahore in the early seventeenth century by one of Lala Surajmal's forbears. A hundred years later, after Nadir Shah's sack of Delhi, Lala Govind Narayan brought the business to Chandni Chowk, where land prices had dropped precipitously. He prospered with the blossoming of Chandni Chowk, serving the Mughal court, the British Resident and the Mughal emperor Bahadur Shah Zafar himself, who was known to have bottles of attar chameli delivered to Red Fort. Since then, the shop has witnessed momentous events in Chandni Chowk. It has seen the blinding of the Mughal emperor Shah Alam by Afghan Rohilla tribals, the hanging of Bahadur Shah Zafar's sons by the British after the Mutiny, and the bomb thrown at Lord Hardinge. It has heard the fiery speeches of Nehru and the rambling musings of Gandhi. Lala Surajmal himself saw the blood-letting of 'forty-seven, when bands of Hindus and Muslims roamed Chandni Chowk day and night while he sat inside the shop. A portion of it had been set on fire, and Surajmal had barely escaped being burned alive. The shop has since been rebuilt, but much of the polished oak interior was created by his great-great-grandfather.

That is the story on the plaque. A second version whispers that the business has never seen Lahore. When Jahanara Begum, Shah Jahan's daughter, laid out a shopping arcade in front of her father's Red Fort, she gave one of the first shops to her favourite perfumer, Lala Jamuna Prasad, another of Surajmal's ancestors. A third story, never told in Surajmal's presence, is that the shop is no more than fifty years old, built out of a warehouse by his father, who came to Delhi as a poor clerk from Rajasthan. But no matter what the antecedents of the shop, 'Of Lahore' is proudly affixed to its signboard. It is visited by prime ministers and film stars, and Lala Surajmal reigns over it like an icon, a monument to himself, familiar to half of Chandni Chowk gentry, a man of immense authority in the IPP committee, commanding grudging respect even from the Congress Party. At fifty-nine, he regularly reprimands councillors and has the ear of Members of Parliament, perhaps even junior ministers. He has never fought an election, but few understand the strings that tug at Chandni Chowk better than he does.

A sudden explosion checks Surajmal's harangue in a way Sohan Lal or Jugal Kishor would have never dared. Sohan Lal anxiously looks at his watch. It is past six, and people are still milling around the streets, exploding bombs! He shuts his eyes, folds his hands and murmurs the first few lines of Hanuman Chaalisa: '*Jai* Hanuman *gyaan gun saagar . . .*'

Lala Surajmal chuckles scornfully. 'It is only a ricksha tyre. When it bursts, it sounds like a bomb.'

'How do you know, Lalaji?'

'I have lived a long life, Sohan Lal.'

At this Jugal Kishor looks away, to avoid expressing agreement or disdain, but Surajmal does not look for confirmation. 'You have a weak heart,' he pronounces. 'Eat gooseberry every morning immediately after you wake up. Coat it with a thin layer of silver and swallow it whole without chewing. That will reduce your palpitations.'

He is almost sixty, thinks Sohan Lal, and he advises me on my heart. He will be dead long before I need to follow his prescription.

'This will all die down in a day,' predicts Surajmal. 'Here you are in Kucha Bansilal, shuddering at the blast from a ricksha tyre! What would you do if you had to sit in your shop for six days without food and water?'

Sohan Lal nods vaguely, hoping to change the subject from Surajmal's much-discussed ordeal in the riots of 'forty-seven. He suspects, in spite of Surajmal's affectation, that they are all afraid, more for their shops than their personal safety. He turns to Jugal Kishor and opens a safer conversation. 'We should prepare an obituary on behalf of the IPP committee. It will look bad if we don't offer condolences.'

'Do not worry about that!' snaps Lala Surajmal. 'They have not declared her dead yet.'

'The BBC says she is dead.'

'But All India Radio is silent. She is not dead until they say so.'

'Sixteen bullets!' protests Sohan Lal.

Surajmal has a knowing look on his face. He speaks softly, as if privy to a great secret: 'You do not know Indira. She has come back before, after we thought she was gone.' There is a moment of silence as he contemplates Indira's extraordinary strength. The other two wait politely.

'Her own security guards!' says Jugal Kishor in wonder. 'You cannot trust anyone . . .'

'They shot one of the assassins immediately,' whispers Surajmal. 'Do you know why?'

Sohan Lal nods, not knowing why but not inclined to hear Surajmal's conspiracy theory. 'It is time for sweets,' he says, to forestall the explanation, 'but we have to be discreet. You can have a few packets sent to us, Jugal Kishorji.'

Jugal Kishor Agrawal owns Mangat Ram Nawal Kishor, the largest sweet shop in Chandni Chowk. It claims, like Surajmal's shop, to have served Mughal emperors, but it is not quite as old and does not enjoy the same degree of prestige. Jugal Kishor is two years younger than Sohan Lal, but he has carefully cultivated his friendships and commands somewhat greater authority than Sohan Lal in the IPP hierarchy of Delhi.

'There will be time for sweets later,' grumbles Surajmal. 'The agenda of this meeting is to discuss the earthquake that will come now, just in time for elections.'

'That earthquake has already begun!' says Sohan Lal with a quivering voice.

Surajmal gives his host a cold stare. 'Do not be dramatic, Sohan Lal. I have asked Ramvilas to bring me a full report from every corner of Chandni Chowk.'

'Why is he not here already?'

'He is late,' says Surajmal.

'He must be caught up in the crowds,' says Jugal Kishor, soothingly. 'Let us wait. Perhaps we can have chai, Sohan Lalji. I saw your chaivala sitting around.'

Sohan Lal finds the request inappropriate. Is it polite to admit a chaivala into the shop when marauding killers are roaming the streets?

Surajmal has fallen into a reverie, which excludes the other two.

Jugal Kishor pulls nervously at his ear and tries to make a joke. 'Raam Raj was the age of milk. Krishna Raj was the age of ghee. British Raj was the age of beer. Indira Raj is the age of tea. Blow into it and drink up!'

'Indira Raj will end in a few hours,' says Sohan Lal, drily. It is clear, he thinks, that Jugal Kishor will not stop talking about tea until he places an order with the chaivala. He reaches out a hand, unlocks one door and opens it an inch. Kucha Bansilal is dark. The sounds of Chandni Chowk are dying out, perhaps because the police have cleared the street. Sohan Lal shouts through the crack. 'Nanak Chand! Chai!' Then he shuts the door firmly again.

Gopal, squatting on his box, nods on hearing the order.

'Now I will die!' Kartar Singh whimpers inside. 'You will open your stall to make tea and everyone will see me.'

Gopal sighs. 'Go to sleep, sardarji,' he says. 'You heard him call me Nanak Chand.'

'Isn't that your name?'

'That is code. Nanak, na na, means no, do not make tea. The seth does this when he has cheap customers on whom he does not want to waste tea.'

Even in his present condition Kartar Singh cannot suppress a perverse snigger. These are cheap customers all right, Surajmal and Jugal Kishor. Opportunists, self-aggrandisers, crooks who will not let him become a councillor in Chandni Chowk, although he contributes so much to the committee. He does not have the luxury, as they do, of walking up and down Chandni Chowk to offer gratuitous advice, meddling in everyone's affairs and playing off traders against each other. Some day, when Jasjit has taken over the store, he will become a mobile gossipmonger too. But where is Jasjit? His film will have finished by now.

'How many children do you have, sardarji?' asks Gopal.

'One,' whispers Kartar Singh. 'That is the one I am looking for. I hope he is safe.'

'Just one son!' Gopal wonders aloud. 'And you have such a big store.'

'Who told you I have a store?'

'I can see it in your clothes. And I can see you own a big house.'

Kartar Singh does not reply, thinking of his ground-floor flat in Trilokpuri – two rooms, a bathroom, a kitchen and a pocket-sized veranda just behind the front door.

'How many rooms does your house have?' Gopal asks.

Kartar Singh mumbles something.

'How much did it cost to build it?'

There is an impatient sound from inside the chest.

'Your wife must have brought a large dowry,' says Gopal.

From his wooden grave, Kartar Singh launches a counter-attack. 'How many sons do *you* have?'

'I have already told you!' Gopal says, in a hurt manner. 'Mukesh! He is fifteen. And your son?'

'Eighteen.'

'How old is your wife?'

'She is not as young as she used to be,' responds Kartar Singh, testily.

'Sushila would be thirty-five,' says Gopal. 'She died fifteen years ago.'

'What did she die of?'

'I went back to Sasaria when my father sent me a telegram, saying my son had been born. He was alive, but she was dead.'

'A woman gives her life for her son.'

'I did not know her very well,' says Gopal. 'After my wedding, my father sent me back to Delhi, but Sushila stayed in Sasaria with my mother. Where would I keep her in my small kholi? I went to Sasaria every year. Four years after our wedding, she gave birth to Mukesh. I now had a son but no wife. My father sent me back to Delhi while my mother took care of Mukesh. After my father died, I brought him here. "He is six," I told my mother, "so he can live with me in my kholi." Mukesh has never been back to Sasaria, so he is no longer a Bihari but a Dillivala.'

'What about you?' asks Kartar Singh.

'I don't know. A Bihari, a Bhaiya, a Dillivala – whatever my customers call me. As long as they drink chai.'

'Too many people have come to Delhi,' grumbles Kartar Singh. 'They do not belong here. It is a city of bastards!'

'Lower your voice, Satwant Singhji!' exclaims Gopal in alarm.

'That is not my name,' says Kartar Singh stiffly.

Gopal is befuddled. He clearly heard the constable call the sardar by that name.

Kartar Singh continues, raising his voice in spite of Gopal's admonition: 'All these Congress valas! Bastards! Who are they to hunt me down? My father was a brigadier in the war of 'seventy-one. He stood behind General Arora during the Pakistani surrender. My grandfather was a member of the Congress Party in Punjab. He was at the convention near the Ravi river, when Nehru declared that complete independence from the British, not dominion status, was the goal of the Congress Party. Who are these bastards to call me a traitor and a Khalistani? Have they fought any wars like my father?'

'Which war?' asks Gopal.

'The one in 'seventy-one,' repeats Kartar Singh.

'Fighting is terrible,' says Gopal vaguely. He is not sure which war the sardar is talking about. He has sat in his stall for as long as he can remember. He cannot recall a war, a victory or a surrender. 'You are a good man,' he says soothingly. 'But keep your voice down! Someone has just entered the kucha. Just a small man. You have nothing to fear.'

Inside Jamna Lal Kishori Mal, Sohan Lal gasps when someone knocks on the door.

'Stay calm, Sohan Lal!' Lala Surajmal scolds. 'It is probably the chaivala.'

Sohan Lal knows it is not the chaivala. The fool would not dare, after he was dispatched from the door earlier in the day. 'Who is it?' he shouts.

'Ramvilas!'

Sohan Lal reaches over and unhooks the clasp. The door swings open and Ramvilas steps into the shop.

'Shut the door behind you,' Sohan Lal says urgently.

Ramvilas fixes the clasp and stands with his back to it. The three of them survey him. He is haggard. His delicate features are drawn. His kurta and pyjamas, though still clean, are crumpled, but his appearance excites no interest because their minds are burdened with weightier matters.

'Why are you late?' demands Lala Surajmal.

'I was held up by the riot, Lalaji.'

'I asked you to come at six.'

'You also asked me to collect information.'

Surajmal looks away grudgingly, indicating by the merest nod that Ramvilas may sit down. He can never understand why Ramvilas always irritates him. He is not an inefficient or clumsy employee. On the contrary, he has learned quickly to identify more than fifty attars and oils, mastered the skill of pricing and packaging them, and learned how to pass off synthetic oils as natural. He is sharp and reliable. Surajmal can count on him to keep an eye on other clerks. In some ways, he prefers to leave Bhagwan Das and Sons in the care of Ramvilas – he himself is often busy with the committee – rather than Vimal, his eldest son, or Vimal's three younger brothers. His four sons – all grown-up, all somewhat wayward – are a disappointment to Surajmal, who still hopes they will take over the shop some day. Meanwhile, Ramvilas has proved himself invaluable outside the shop too, because he doubles as factotum to the IPP committee in Chandni Chowk – recorder of minutes, arranger of people, manager of disruptions, inciter of crowds, organiser of festivals, tents, ovens, cauldrons and anything else that is needed. No one likes him much but everyone finds him useful.

'All right,' says Surajmal. 'What have you found?'

'All India Radio has declared she is dead.'

'I already knew that,' says Surajmal irritably. He has not heard the All India Radio announcement but he feels instinctively that he must keep Ramvilas on the defensive. 'I did not send you to listen to the radio. Tell me what you have found in Chandni Chowk.'

'There was a riot outside Gurudwara Sisganj. A sardar attacked a crowd with a jhola. A few people were hurt but no one died. The Khalsa army launched a raid from the gurudwara – they had swords, kirpaans, even guns – but was pushed back by the police. A few other sardar shops have been attacked. A building was burned down in Ballimaran.'

'Is there any violence in Lajpatrai Market?' asks Sohan Lal, with bated breath.

'I did not go that far. There is not much violence anywhere yet.'

Sohan Lal is relieved. He had relayed his code to Ranjan in New York just before Lala Surajmal arrived. Ranjan was grumpy on the phone. 'Has there been an earthquake,' he asked, 'that you had to pull me out of bed so early in the morning?'

'It is more than an earthquake,' Sohan Lal said. 'It is Pralay – the end of the world!' Ranjan had not known about Indira. He had gone to sleep early the previous night. Sohan Lal told him to expect the money within twelve hours. Once it is safely with Ranjan, let the Congress Party destroy Kartar Singh's store in Lajpatrai Market, let them burn down Chandni Chowk itself . . .

'What is that on your face?' Surajmal asks Ramvilas.

Self-consciously Ramvilas touches the raw furrows on his cheek. The bai's Dettol still stings. He speaks mournfully, like a wounded soldier wedded to his cause. 'It is difficult to gather reports when there is violence. But you asked me to do this, Lalaji, and I did not flinch.'

Surajmal is embarrassed. 'I did not ask you to put yourself in danger,' he remonstrates.

'The committee comes first,' counters Ramvilas scathingly.

Surajmal is flummoxed. Reluctantly he allows his face to express sympathy. Jugal Kishor clucks. Sohan Lal stares at the red scars of war. Ramvilas sits comfortably, a martyr to the cause, his status enhanced.

'Rub a paste of neem into the wounds to disinfect them,' says Surajmal, solicitously.

'Let the war finish,' responds Ramvilas, with a sneer. 'Then we will take care of the wounded.'

'Are your men doing anything in this war?' asks Surajmal.

Ramvilas bestows a mysterious smile on his employer. He likes references to his 'men', though he never reveals to Surajmal who they are. He is not quite certain where they are right now. 'They are where I told them to go,' he says impressively.

Surajmal nods. He does not care to learn much about such people. It is a relief that Ramvilas is around to take care of them.

Ramvilas presses his advantage. 'My men have raised their rates,' he says. 'It is difficult to do business with them – there is too much competition. Even the Congress Party has approached them.'

Surajmal reluctantly motions to Jugal Kishor – who is treasurer to the committee – that this request will be accepted. 'Do you have anything else to report? If not, we can move on to other business.'

'One more thing,' says Ramvilas, casually. 'Gyani Zail Singh flew back from Muscat when he heard the news. He has just sworn in Rajiv as the new prime minister.'

Surajmal's jaw drops. 'You tell me this now! Rajiv is PM, and you have spent ten minutes talking about a sardar with a jhola!'

'I wanted to tell you right away, but you asked me about Chandni Chowk.'

'All right, all right.' Surajmal waves him away.

They remain silent for a while, overwhelmed by the news. Sohan Lal is unable to control his indignation. 'That sister-fucking sardar!' he mutters, in reference to Zail Singh. 'She made him president of India when he should have been her chaivala. Now she is dead so he has lined up behind her son!'

The obscenity causes a flutter among the seths. It is customary to disparage Gyani Zail Singh, but only as a buffoon. Surajmal turns a restraining frown on Sohan Lal. 'He is repaying her kindness, that is all.'

'This is not a country, it is a kingdom,' grumbles Jugal Kishor.

'What does Rajiv know about being prime minister? A pink-faced boy! A rich boy returned from England. Mummy gave him the Congress Party, and Mummy's doorman has now handed him India!'

Ramvilas is emboldened by such talk. He launches into a tirade of his own. 'Does the boy know what to say in Parliament? What will he discuss at summits with world leaders? Will he break down in tears when they pressure him? He was sucking at his mother's teats until yesterday.'

Surajmal expresses disapproval of such vulgar talk by interrupting: 'This is not a time to make speeches. Rajiv will certainly dissolve the Lok Sabha. There will be a general election soon.'

'In Chandni Chowk Naresh Babu will win again,' says Jugal Kishor.

His presumption irritates Surajmal. Naresh Agrawal is merely a first-term Member of Parliament. Why should the IPP adopt a self-defeating attitude toward him? 'Chandni Chowk is not the fiefdom of Naresh Agrawal,' he says excitedly. 'What is Naresh Agrawal? A spice trader who came to Chandni Chowk fifteen years ago, no more.'

'Who can defeat Naresh Babu now?' Jugal Kishor insists. 'There will be sympathy for Indira. No one will vote against Congress.'

'Musalmans and Scheduled Castes have always been with Congress,' grumbles Sohan Lal. 'Now even traders will go to Naresh Babu, as well as the illegal Bangladeshis he has been bringing here.'

'There are three new slums behind Red Fort. Do you know what they call the area? Naresh Colony! All illegal Bangladeshis, all his voters!'

'You do not speak like members of the Indian People Party,' says Surajmal, dramatically. 'Why do you sit on the IPP committee? So that you can hand Chandni Chowk to Naresh Agrawal?'

'We are being realistic, Lalaji,' Sohan Lal says.

'Sikhs will vote for IPP. They can no longer support Congress,' counters Surajmal.

'Who cares for Sikhs? There are too few in Chandni Chowk.'

'I telephoned Harilalji this afternoon,' says Jugal Kishor. 'He, too, felt there was going to be an election. He will issue a statement next week, asking all political parties to unite against Congress. I suggested he wait at least a week. It will look inappropriate right now.'

Lala Surajmal scowls at Jugal Kishor. Harilal Gupta is the IPP councillor from Chandni Chowk, and a potential candidate for Parliament against Naresh Agrawal. It is a breach of protocol for Jugal Kishor – a junior member of the committee – to discuss such matters with him. 'I will talk to Harilal,' says Surajmal stiffly. 'It is too early to discuss candidates and elections. Do you have updated voter lists?' The question is directed at Ramvilas.

'We can start next week,' says Ramvilas. 'But I already know what the lists will show. There are too many Musalmans in Chandni Chowk, all from Bangladesh, all with valid ration cards. The percentage of Hindus has dropped in the last four years.'

'That does not matter as long as we can consolidate the Hindu and Sikh vote.'

'Naresh Babu won on the Indira wave four years ago,' says Sohan Lal. 'What if there is a similar Rajiv wave now?'

'There will be no wave for the boy. He is inexperienced.'

'He is good-looking. From some angles he looks like a white man.'

'That is the problem with these chaivalas,' says Surajmal. 'They would rather vote for an Englishman than an Indian.'

'But we have the sardars,' says Jugal Kishor. 'I hope there is sufficient burning and looting tomorrow, after which no Sikh will ever vote for Congress.'

'We should have a Sikh candidate,' suggests Ramvilas. 'What has Harilalji done for Chandni Chowk?'

Surajmal frowns. The other two seths look away. Ramvilas is not expected to offer his opinion on anything. His formal function is to take down minutes – which are then edited to suit the purpose of the next meeting – and answer questions when asked. He is not officially a member of the committee, being neither a trader nor a member of any higher party council.

'These are important matters, Ramvilas,' Surajmal says coldly. Then, turning to the two seths, he continues: 'Hindus will not vote for a Sikh. The candidate must be a Hindu Bania. Only a trader can get trader votes from both Hindus and Sikhs. Do not forget this is Chandni Chowk – no one can win without the trader vote.'

Sohan Lal lays a silent curse on destiny. He himself is a Bania, as are Surajmal and Jugal Kishor, but there is little doubt that Surajmal has cast his vote in favour of Harilal. It is not clear what understanding exists between the two, but the pact has held for years. There will be a committee vote, of course, but it is a whitewash. Surajmal is the most senior member of the committee, and the IPP candidate – whether for local posts in the Municipal Corporation of Delhi or a national post in Parliament – is always a nominee of Surajmal. He has never stood for office, but favours people with a long history in Chandni Chowk. Surajmal's own antecedents – as spelled out on the plaque in Bhagwan Das and Sons – make him a 'history vala' without equals. Harilal Gupta comes from an old paper-trading family in Chawri Bajar. When Harilal dies – and that is not unlikely, considering his enormous girth – Surajmal's benign gaze will probably fall upon Jugal Kishor, whose shop claims 'two centuries of sweet success'. Only after Jugal Kishor has relinquished his hold on worldly matters – which is unlikely, considering he is younger than Sohan Lal – will it be the turn of the proprietor of Jamna Lal Kishori Mal. Sohan Lal bitterly wishes he was older, or that his father had seen fit to fold up the shop in Bikaner and move to Delhi before Partition, when land was cheap. To be called a newcomer, having lived in Delhi for more than thirty years! To raise ineffectual objections and then acquiesce before a man like Surajmal, who leaves his shop in the care of clerks because his sons are too lazy!

'A Bania candidate is all right,' agrees Jugal Kishor. 'We must not fall into the trap of the central committee, where they are talking about Musalman candidates just to get the Musalman vote.'

'Even IPP now talks of Musalman candidates,' sighs Sohan Lal. 'It is the Indian People Party, meant for the people of India! Where will Hindus go once IPP turns into Congress?'

And where will I go, wonders Ramvilas, if these Banias take over the IPP committee? The only difference between these old hogs and me is that I am young and my father has no capital.

He knows he is resourceful and industrious. In some ways he is indispensable to the committee. Yet he does not have a vote because he is not a trader. He will just have to get by until they realise what they have on their hands. He does not mind his employment at Bhagwan Das and Sons. Surajmal is a bore, but he spends much of his time politicking, leaving Ramvilas in charge of the shop. The four sons are fickle characters. Sometimes one or other of them sits cross-legged on the gaddi – right next to the cash-box – with a proprietary air, and pretends to be busy. Most days, they steer clear of the shop. Surajmal has made his disgust with them quite plain to the world. They are for ever scarred with guilt – heirs unworthy of their great lineage. All this puts Ramvilas in a comfortable position. He can boss around the other clerks, and present himself with a bottle of attar whenever it suits him. And, God knows, he needs those bottles to keep Gulmohar happy. She was delighted with the mixture of bela and chameli he gave her. He will keep mixing and inventing new fragrances for her – jasmine, kewra, khus, hina, monsoon, shamama, champa, harshringar, kadamba, chandan, mahua, motia – as long as she does not tire of it. And some day, if he can get Surajmal to go away for a few days, he will give Gulmohar the most precious of them all, ruh gulaab.

'What happened to the chai, Sohan Lalji?' asks Jugal Kishor.

Sohan Lal clucks impatiently, apparently defeated by the laziness of the chaivala. 'Nanak Chand!' he screams. 'Chai! Chai!'

'That chaivala is wrong in the head,' says Ramvilas. 'I saw him talking to himself when I walked down the kucha.'

Gopal hears the call for chai and chafes at the lost business. If he takes three cups of tea to Sohan Lal – in expensive china meant for good customers – the seth will not dare to refuse it, in spite of 'Nanak Chand'. But that will require him to open his stall.

'Please go now, sardarji,' he begs his prisoner.

The box below him remains silent. Gopal gets worried. Could the sardar have suffocated on his own beard? Is he stuck with a dead sardar? 'Wake up, sardarji! It is time to go!'

'All right!' says Kartar Singh, from inside the box. 'Pull me out and burn me alive!'

'I am a poor man,' says Gopal. 'I cannot sit with my shop closed all day.'

For a while Kartar Singh is silent. 'Is there a bathroom here?' he asks.

Gopal is horrified. 'Now you will shit and piss inside my stove! There is a bathroom behind sethji's shop. Should I ask him? He is a kind man. He will help you.'

'No!' says Kartar Singh, firmly.

Gopal shakes his head in resignation. The sardar will likely stay in the box until he is dead.

'Maybe I will go,' says Kartar Singh.

Gopal begins eagerly to undo the latch.

'Wait! Can you do something for me?'

'Anything!' says Gopal. 'Just go home.'

'I want you to go to Trilokpuri. To my house. My wife's name is Sukhbir Kaur. Tell her I am safe.'

'How can I go anywhere, sardarji?' asks Gopal, helplessly. 'It is too dangerous!'

'But you are not a sardar. Who will harm you?'

'I am a poor man.'

'You are my brother!' says Kartar Singh, emotionally. 'I feel I can ask you to do anything because you have a son too.'

Gopal finds himself unable to counter this.

'Tell my wife Jasjit was in Vishaal cinema four hours ago. She should telephone Harmeet Bhai to go and look for him.'

'Who is Jasjit?'

'My son! Tell my wife to lock all doors and windows and open them to no one. Tell her the store has been looted. I am going to Faridabad to my brother. I will be back in two days, after things settle down. She must stay in the house until then, with all the windows shut.'

'All right, I will go,' says Gopal.

'I will not forget this, Gopal Bhai! Sector Three, flat number forty-four, ground floor. You can take the three hundred and sixty-five, if the buses are still running. Get off in Sector Three and turn left into the first block. Or take an autoricksha and my wife will pay the fare.'

'What if she does not? Don't you have any money with you?'

Kartar Singh reflects on the jhola crushed under him. 'She will certainly pay you.'

'All right. Will you leave once I am gone?'

'Yes,' avers Kartar Singh. 'Tell me how to get to the railway station from here without going back into Chandni Chowk. Where does this kucha end?'

'The lane opens out into a park,' says Gopal. 'You can see the railway station from there. It is dark, so no one will bother you. But inside the railway station . . .'

'I will do what I can.'

'Be careful when you come out of the box. Shut it after you. You are too fat! The box is meant for a poor man like me.'

'You are not a poor man!' gushes Kartar Singh, in a surfeit of gratitude. 'You have the wealth of kindness!'

'I will go to your house now, Satwant Singhji.'

This time Kartar Singh does not protest at the name. What is the difference between the men who pulled the trigger and the millions who have mentally murdered Indira? Who cannot but feel some vindication in the bullets that riddled her body this morning?

'I hope you are in Faridabad when I come back,' says Gopal.

Five minutes after Gopal has gone, Sohan Lal opens the door gingerly and surveys the darkness in the kucha. 'That chaivala is unreliable,' he says, with satisfaction. 'He has gone home. I think we will have to manage without tea.'

Jugal Kishor appears crestfallen. 'I am going home then,' he says. 'We have nothing more to discuss. It is Rajiv's country now.'

'I wish Sanjay Gandhi was alive!' says Sohan Lal. 'If Indira had not had him killed, he would be PM now, not Rajiv. And he knew what to do with the mullas! He chased them out of Turkman Gate.'

Surajmal turns to Ramvilas. 'Kartar Singh did not come to the meeting,' he observes. 'Did you not tell him?'

'I tried to telephone him three times this afternoon. There was no connection.'

'Something must be wrong with the line. Why did you not go to his store?'

'I cannot stroll through Chandni Chowk at such a time!' protests Ramvilas.

Surajmal sourly accepts this, looking hard at Ramvilas's inscrutable eyes. He reminds himself to be wary of his head clerk. He has noticed that many attar bottles come half empty out of storage. Someone is dipping into them. A bottle of chameli went missing last month. Attar bottles break and leak often, but not with the consistency they have displayed in the last month. What use can Ramvilas have for so much attar? Everyone takes a whiff or two – that is understandable: the fragrances are difficult to resist. People like Sohan Lal – connoisseurs – can consume a full bottle every two weeks. But Ramvilas has been stealing with a passion unhealthy in a man, if understandable in a woman. Could his wife have suddenly discovered the fragrances of the Mughal empire? That man has a knife in his hands, says Surajmal to himself. I must never turn my back to him.

A vein throbs in Sohan Lal's forehead at the mention of Kartar Singh. It is normal for Kartar Singh not to answer the telephone unless he expects a call. A havala trader must always be cautious. But Ramvilas had said he could not connect at all. Perhaps it had not been a good idea to show such haste with his money. Hopefully Ramvilas hadn't bothered to telephone Kartar Singh and is now lying. Yes, that is the most likely explanation. Ramvilas has said that not much happened in Lajpatrai Market. There was a near riot outside Sisganj, but no one was killed. And Ramvilas should know, because his men are in the middle of it all.

'Turn on the television,' says Ramvilas. 'They may be telecasting Rajiv's oath-taking ceremony.'

'Leave it alone!' thunders Surajmal. 'I cannot bear to see the boy become prime minister. I would rather swear allegiance to the Queen of England.'

'What is there to see?' sneers Jugal Kishor. 'The bitch is dead and her puppy is king.'

'Watch your tongue, Jugal Kishor!' warns Surajmal. 'You are a member of the committee.'

Chastened, Jugal Kishor stands up and slips his feet into chappals. 'It is dark,' he says. 'I want to be home before it is too dangerous.'

'There is a curfew in Chandni Chowk,' warns Ramvilas.

'We will find our way through the lanes,' says Surajmal.

II

Kartar Singh has been stuck in an unnatural position for four hours. I am squatting for an endless shit, he thinks with self-pity. The air inside the chest is stale and putrid, and his body hurts. He has no room to relieve the weight on his haunches, or the pressure on his back. He seems to be getting fatter by the hour. The lower half of his leg feels numb. He has sent the chaivala away for two reasons – to inform Sukhbir about his whereabouts so she will not worry, and to prevent him seeing the jhola. *Sachche Padshah*! Let Jasjit be safe! Hopefully Harmeet Bhai will help. As soon as he reaches Faridabad he will telephone Sukhbir, and he will come back in two days to look for Jasjit. But it is time now to go to the railway station before the last train leaves for Faridabad. All he needs is a train to get him out of Delhi. Then he can catch a bus from wherever the train takes him. He knows he should get out of the chest, but a strange inertia has taken hold of him. I will die here, he thinks. The chaivala will find my body when he returns from Trilokpuri . . . Kartar Singh drifts into sleep.

He wakes with a start to the sound of a door being pulled open. Then he hears Sohan Lal, Surajmal and Jugal Kishor. They have emerged from their meeting. There is some talk of a curfew in Chandni Chowk, so they are going home through the kucha. He will open the lid as soon as he is sure they have gone far enough. It is too dark for anyone to notice him so he will certainly be safe in the lane. He cannot bring round his forearm to look at his wristwatch, but he thinks he has slept for no more than fifteen minutes.

He waits until the kucha is silent, then gently pushes up the lid with his turban. It rises with a creak that reminds him of a coffin being opened. Here I am, he thinks, a giant sack of jaggery in a wooden crate for every bastard to come and take a bite.

His arms are pressed to his sides. He is not an athletic man. It is impossible for him to raise himself merely by straightening his legs, which are wedged tightly under his body. He manages to raise one arm and, with the elbow pushing down on the rim of the chest, pushes up the rest of his trunk with a groan. Now he is kneeling. He rests for a while to catch his breath. Then he stands up and his turban hits the junction box. He bends sideways, climbs out of the chest and examines himself. His shirt is torn and his arms are bruised where they scraped against the chest. He scolds himself for such self-indulgence. What is a scratch to a man whose life has just been spared? He will come back from Faridabad to reward the chaivala. Ah! He forgot to ask the chaivala his name. It does not matter: he knows where the stall is. But what if the chaivala describes the incident to Sohan Lal? He will reward the man handsomely, for saving his life and for keeping his mouth shut.

He pulls out his jhola from the bottom of the chest. Its five cloth belts are crushed, but safe and dry. What should he do with them? It is not safe to take the money with him on the train. Perhaps he should have returned it to Sohan Lal when he had the chance. But this is no longer Sohan Lal's money. He has risked his life for it, and has the right to his commission. No, he will not return it, but hide it somewhere and come back for it.

The kucha is deserted. A naked bulb hangs from the peepul tree where the kucha opens into Chandni Chowk, throwing long shadows into the lane but doing little to illuminate it. Kartar Singh studies the chaivala's stall. There is a blue tarpaulin above it, bunched up, rolled carelessly and supported on wooden sticks cantilevered off the junction box. The chaivala's bicycle sits on the box, secured by hooks. Kartar Singh shuts the chest, squats on it and opens the box. It contains an array of switches and fuses, perhaps a junction for the entire kucha. There is a ledge at the bottom, upon which sits a glass tumbler with some chai in it. What would he not give for a cup of tea? But he must get rid of the jhola. The switches are arranged in neat columns, between which he squeezes one of the cloth belts. It fits snugly and looks like insulation padding. Is it safe to put his hands among those switches? The belts are cloth and the money is paper – both dry, both insulators – but he must be careful to keep the metal buckles away from the switches: the ceramic coating is broken in places, so the metal may cause a short-circuit and burn the entire box. What an expensive fire that would be!

When he has pressed four belts into the box, he pauses. They look neat, indistinguishable from the insulating ceramic round the switches, but there is no space for the fifth. He shuts the box to see if the bundles block the door. It clicks into place. He is still wondering what to do about the fifth one when a shadow falls across the kucha. He turns. A police constable stands three feet away.

'Here you are, Satwant Singh!' says Inderlal Jha. 'I have been looking all over Chandni Chowk for you.'

Kartar Singh steps off the chest and sinks to the ground, hands folded. He has tears in his eyes. The constable's face is dark, but he can see the white teeth. He is grinning.

'I am a reasonable man, sardarji,' says Inderlal, 'but you have committed a crime.'

'I have done nothing, sarkaar!'

'You have killed my mother, you bastard!'

Kartar Singh does not reply. He raises his folded hands higher and lowers his head, so his turban presses against the constable's knees. Perhaps his humiliation will soften the man's heart. What else can he do?

'What is that on your finger?' asks Inderlal.

'My wedding band, sarkaar. Twenty-two-carat gold.' He tries to pull it off. It has been in place for years, during which he has gained considerable weight so his finger has swollen round it, locking it in place. He licks his finger frantically, hoping to smooth the ring's passage, and yanks it off, scraping his knuckle. 'Take it! And take my watch! And this amethyst on my little finger!'

Inderlal slips the trinkets into his pocket and points to the jhola. 'What is inside that?'

Kartar Singh trembles. 'My wife's underwear, sarkaar! Panties, bras . . .'

Inderlal laughs. '*My* wife needs expensive bras too.' He sweeps the jhola off the wooden chest with a swish of his baton. 'What is this? A belt?'

Kartar Singh watches the policeman's hands as they squeeze the belt to get a feel for its innards, like a snake-charmer throttling his king cobra. His eyes have adjusted to the darkness, so he notices the change in the man's expression when the fingers divine what the jhola contains.

'You are a rich one, Satwant Singh! Why did you not tell me, you bastard?'

Inderlal shoves his hand into the belt and pulls out a bundle. His eyes shine in the dark. 'Is this genuine? Fake?'

'Genuine,' says Kartar Singh, softly.

Inderlal is suddenly aware that he must hurry. It is not a good idea to waste time in pulling out the other bundles, because there are other constables about. He looks threateningly at Kartar Singh. 'How much?'

'One lakh.'

Inderlal is breathless with excitement. He gives Kartar Singh a contemptuous look. 'I have seen your face, sister-fucker. If this is less than a lakh, or the notes are fake, I will come for you.'

Kartar Singh nods, eager to please. Inderlal casts a quick glance backward to ensure that the kucha is deserted, then bends to whisper: 'You are a good man, Satwant Singh. I will sacrifice the medal they would have given me for your capture. Do not whisper a word to anyone. The SHO will dismiss me for letting you go, but I am ready to make the sacrifice.'

Kartar Singh's tears flow freely.

'Indira was a whore,' says Inderlal. 'You have saved the nation by murdering her. Now, go quickly.'

Kartar Singh stands up with a trembling heart and walks away as quickly as he can, without seeming to hurry, expecting the constable to call him back at any moment. He is grateful that the kucha is dark. He can lose himself in it and forget about that bastard constable. Perhaps he really is Satwant Singh. He must be a killer if he has to suffer the consequences. They have probably destroyed the store. They must have taken away all his mixers, fans, purses, belts, toasters, ovens and gift cards. They will have torn up the mattress in the back room and opened the safe . . . But the safe will not open easily, and there is not much inside it. He grits his teeth. How he would love to come face to face with those bastards. And Bishan was with them!

The lane turns into an alley no more than six feet wide. He squats on the side and urinates. I am no better than a beggar or a dog, he thinks bitterly.

The alley opens into a park, beyond which he can see the brick-red Victorian railway station. I have had enough of this city, he tells himself, and enough of this country. This is a sign, if ever God could give one, that he must get away. This country does not belong to him, and he does not belong to it. He will telephone his cousins in Canada right away, perhaps even from Faridabad, and prepare to leave. Let the bastards make away with everything in the store. Who cares? It makes hardly any money. It is merely a front, a respectable façade for his havala business. He has enough stowed away to last him many years, and he will use a portion of that money to go to Canada.

'Today is the last day of my suffering,' says Kartar Singh to himself.

Beyond the park is a busy street, which he crosses hastily, wishing his large head – with its shamelessly prominent turban – could somehow disappear into his collar. He runs through the car park, avoiding eye-contact, taking comfort in the stench of beggars, shit, piss, dogs, horses, cow-dung, coolies and damp luggage. But then he passes under the giant arches and enters the station, lit with indiscriminate intensity by a thousand fluorescent tubes. Here, everyone stares at him. He stands in a line that winds its way to the ticket counter, aware that the line is full of sardars. There is a riot of turbans, beards, bangles and fleshy, hirsute bodies, as if the entire Sikh population of Delhi has turned out. Next to them, amid large bundles of hastily packed luggage, hundreds of women and children are waiting for their men to buy them tickets. The children – those too old to be wailing in their mothers' arms – play hopscotch in the lobby, having marked their courts with pieces of luggage. Kartar Singh takes solace from the numbers. There are too many of us to be in any real danger, he tells himself. Let the first man approach! We will skin him alive. What is it the Khalsa says of itself? One of us is equal to more than a lakh of them . . . As Guru Gobind Singh fought the Mughal armies three hundred years ago, so we will fight this army of beasts, this mother-fucking country full of bloodthirsty people!

Yet he is conscious of his turban. He should have worn a dull colour today, an innocuous grey, not a brilliant blue that screams its presence. But what is the use? He cannot hide it, no matter what its colour. If he could cover his head with a bag or a box, he could pass as a fat Bania. Come and see the Bania who has a box for a face! He must chop off his long hair as soon as he reaches Faridabad.

There are a few policemen in the station. The dogs! They will share the loot the constable took from him. They walk about as if nothing has gone wrong. It is a usual day, with the usual number of sardars buying tickets to get away. But a silent storm rages in the station. Why does everyone stare at the queue? This is Delhi – surely they have seen hundreds of sardars before! Are they waiting for something to happen? Do they know something that the sardars do not? I am a newly arrived monkey in a zoo, he thinks. *Sachche Padshah*! Let me somehow get out of this vile city.

The line seems stationary. The men at the front are engaged in an argument with the ticket clerk. Kartar Singh cannot wait any longer. He rushes to the counter and pushes the men aside. 'Faridabad,' he says.

The man behind the counter adjusts his spectacles and looks coldly at him. He has handled thousands of queue-jumpers in his long career at the counter. 'Train number eleven,' he says.

Kartar Singh is confused. 'There is no train number eleven.'

The man fixes a patient, tired, tolerant eye on him. 'Number eleven, sardarji.' He wiggles his index and middle fingers, letting them execute a dance on the counter, indicating that the train is Kartar Singh's feet, which must take him to Faridabad.

Kartar Singh is furious. He leans as far forward as he can until his face hits the metal bars behind which sits the man, unperturbed. 'I want to go to Faridabad!' he screams.

A murmur of disapproval arises from the sardars in the queue. 'We are all trying to go somewhere,' someone says. 'Why don't you get into the queue? Why must you waste everyone's time?'

Kartar Singh looks at them in dismay. They are his partners in misery, yet they side with this weasel! Very well, he will jump on to the first train that moves and then find his way to Faridabad once he is outside Delhi. He turns to the clerk. 'Give me a platform ticket.'

'Two rupees.'

Kartar Singh realises his pockets are empty. Ashamed, he leaves the counter – to a ripple of laughter from other sardars – and runs up the stairs that will take him to the platform, suddenly aware of the incongruity of buying a ticket when he is fleeing for his life. Why are those other sardars queuing anyway? What are they afraid of? That they will be caught travelling without a ticket? Perhaps they do not know how far things have gone. They have not had their stores attacked. They are travelling merely as a precaution, almost turning this into a family vacation. This thought gives him pause. Should he have tried to bring Sukhbir and Jasjit with him? No, he was right to leave them where they are. Hopefully the chaivala will deliver his message. They are safer in Trilokpuri – in the locked flat – than they would be in Faridabad. Everything will settle down in a couple of days. Then he will make preparations to leave this city and this country.

He arrives on a platform in time to see a train begin to creep away. It is packed to the point of exploding, with heads and arms hanging out of every window. He shrinks for a moment. Is the situation really so dire that he must squeeze himself in with these animals? Perhaps he should wait for the next one. But then he casts a look about him on the platform, where dozens of sardars are scrambling to board the train, which is picking up speed. He leaps on to the footboard of a passing carriage and immediately finds himself pressed against a wall of flesh, which will not let him into the carriage. The train has now overshot the platform, so the ground beneath the footboard is five feet away – too far for him to jump off. With one hand, he clutches a steel handle. With the other, he holds back the human mass that seems ready to spill out of the door and hurl him to the ground.

He wedges himself into a small niche formed in the human wall, frees his other hand and runs it over his body. The hand bumps reassuringly over the folds of his heaving chest, travels smoothly down his trunk and comes to rest on his belly, which shakes uncontrollably with the swaying of the train. His body hurts from crouching for four hours in the box, his clothes are crumpled, his turban is askew, his beard unkempt – the netting he uses to keep it orderly has slid off – and his arms are scratched, but he rejoices. He is at one with the stench of people packed into the train like fish. He is exposed to the stars of heaven, the winds of summer and the song of evening. And he is safe. The train clatters happily on its tracks, taking him further from the murderous dogs of Chandni Chowk. He does not know, and does not care, where the train is bound.

12

The bus is crowded and noisy. Gopal is in a seat near the aisle and tries to avoid every eye. He is afraid that people will read his mind if they look at him. They will know he is an accomplice, a man on a mission for a sardar. For now, they appear uninterested in him, as they jostle for space in the aisle. The bus conductor screams, again and again, that people should move to the front of the bus, as if the front contains infinite room for the limbs at the back.

I will leave my seat and find my way to the front at least ten minutes before Trilokpuri, thinks Gopal. That way, I will never have to see the conductor again.

He begins to plan the trip ahead. In twenty minutes he will stick a foot out and squeeze into the space between two men who stand near his seat. One of them wears a thick leather belt, whose metal buckle nudges Gopal's face. He looks up, and is shocked to find the man staring down at him, hatred in his eyes. They all know! They can see in his eyes that he has a sardar hidden inside his stall. Ah, he will leave the bus at the next stop, and may the sardar burn alive for putting him in such danger.

The man with the leather belt taps the back of the seat in front of Gopal, pointing to a freshly painted sign. 'Ladies' seat,' he says.

Gopal scrambles to his feet, vaguely wondering which seat is reserved for ladies – the one that carries the sign on its back, or the one that looks upon it? But this is not the time to argue with a leather-belted man who appears impatient. Gopal ducks through the crowd and pushes ahead, eager to become invisible to the man, and his wife, who will presumably take the ladies' seat.

The bus stops. Someone gets off and Gopal miraculously finds a seat near the front door. He shares it with a pudgy ball of flesh pressed against the window. A Bania, thinks Gopal, almost certainly from Chandni Chowk. He asks the man about Sector Three in Trilokpuri. How far is it from the bus stop?

'Trilokpuri!' repeats the fat man, meaningfully. He pronounces the word with pleasure, chewing it, dwelling upon it as one might on the name of a famous hill station. Darjeeling! Simla! Ootacamund!

'Sector Three,' repeats Gopal.

'Trilokpuri will burn!' declares the fat man dramatically. The effort of opening his mouth sends ripples down his throat, chest and belly.

'But I am going there,' protests Gopal.

The fat man turns lazy eyes on him. 'Bastards! Khalistanis!'

Gopal shrinks from him, then realises the abuse is meant for sardars.

'They were distributing sweets in Trilokpuri to celebrate her death!' says the man.

'There was a riot in Chandni Chowk,' says Gopal.

'Chandni Chowk!' exclaims the fat man. 'I hear a sardar wrapped a bomb inside a jhola and lobbed it at the crowd. It did not explode, but he managed to pick up the jhola and run away with it, after knifing a police constable.'

'Was this a sardar with a blue turban?' asks Gopal, with a pounding heart.

'The colour of his turban does not matter!' snaps the fat man. 'They are all Pakistanis! They have a whole arsenal buried under Gurudwara Sisganj. We should bring out the sardars one by one and behead them. They have a sent a trainload of Hindus from Punjab. All dead!'

Gopal gasps. When did this train arrive? The man leans closer to Gopal and whispers, 'I do not want to cause panic, but I will tell you, do not drink water from a municipal tap. The sardars have done something to the water supply. Have it tasted by a sardar first.'

Gopal looks around him in horror. No one in the bus has taken any notice of the fat man's announcement.

'We should wipe them all out!' says the fat man, his dewlap shaking violently. Before the quivering can stop, he agitates it again with a fresh torrent of threats. 'Chase them out of their houses and shops and send them to Pakistan! Burn down a few to set an example. You should have seen how they ran in Chandni Chowk, the cowards!'

'Where were you in Chandni Chowk?'

'I was in Paratha Gali, where a sardar asked his servant – a one-handed boy – to throw stones at the crowd. The boy tried to tip griddles but someone spotted him, so he ran away with a paratha. There were some NGO-type people who tried to calm everyone. They helped the sardar get away and locked up his shop. But who can stop such a crowd? Within two hours the shutter was broken and the shop emptied.' The man is calmer as he contemplates the sack of the shop. 'I took a television set from there,' he says. 'Small, but colour, not black and white.'

'Did you hear of any trouble in Khari Baoli?' asks Gopal.

'No one wants sacks of cardamom,' says the fat man.

Gopal sits uncomfortably in his small share of the seat, pulls up his dhoti to his knees and places his hands in his lap. Such horrible stories. He hopes Mukesh is not in Chandni Chowk. Anything can happen if you stand near those rioters. A stone could hit you, a brick could catch you as it fell from a wall, a burning plank could set your clothes afire. Why will Mukesh not come back to him? Sohan Lalji has promised to do something – perhaps replace Chotu with Mukesh. If only he knew where Mukesh was!

'Trilokpuri,' announces the fat man. 'Sector Three is the next stop.'

Gopal rushes to the front door, hoping to avoid a taunt from the conductor. As he steps off the bus, he looks back and sees the leather-belted man sitting in the ladies' seat.

Trilokpuri is quiet. A police jeep cruises by, announcing that a curfew will be imposed in thirty minutes. 'There is no cause for fear,' it says. 'Sikhs should stay in their houses and not panic'. A van follows the police jeep and comes to a stop, not far from where Gopal stepped off the bus. A man wearing a kurta-pyjama emerges from the van, hands glued together in the permanent gesture of a politician. A crowd forms round him, chanting slogans, which he tries to control with outstretched hands. 'Rajan Nahal *zindabad*!' shout the men. 'Long live Rajan Nahal!'

'We must remain calm,' says Rajan Nahal, to the men around him.

Gopal passes them quickly and turns left into a block of three-storey houses. The lane is deserted, except for a man who approaches from the other end. When asked, he points out number forty-four to Gopal, who wonders why the man has a bundle of sticks and a jerry-can in his hands.

Number forty-four is a ground-floor flat, set behind an iron gate, unlocked. The gate creaks. There is a small patch of grass, and a scooter parked beside the door. Gopal knocks. There is no reply. Then, remembering that such a modern flat might have an electric bell, he looks for a switch. He cannot find one. He knocks again. A man responds from within in a harried, uncertain voice: 'Who is that?'

Gopal is not prepared with an answer. He had expected the sardar's wife. 'Gopal Pandey.'

There is a pause.

'I do not know you.'

'Sardar Satwant Singhji has sent me,' says Gopal.

There is silence behind the door. Then it is unlocked and opened an inch, but no one is behind it. Gopal pushes it open and steps inside. A sharp blow to his head fells him.

'Do not kill me!' he screams. He shuts his eyes and braces himself for another blow. He hears the door being shut behind him and lays a curse on the blue-turbaned sardar, who sent him here to be lynched.

'Who are you?'

Gopal opens his eyes tentatively. His head hurts. A young man – another sardar – stands over him, cricket bat in hand – a muscular young man, the type he associates with army privates and security guards outside banks.

'Tell me who has sent you,' says the terrible sardar.

'I am here to meet Sukhbir Kaur,' pleads Gopal. 'Her husband has sent me.'

'Where is he?' asks the young sardar.

'He is on his way to Faridabad. He sent me to tell you this.'

'Why should I trust you?'

'He told me to come here. He gave me the address!'

'Tell me what he wore today.'

'A blue turban and a checked shirt.'

'Did he name his son?'

'Jasjit.'

'Has anyone followed you?'

Gopal shakes his head. Jasjit draws aside a curtain and looks out of the window – barred with steel rods – then lets the curtain fall back into place and stands the cricket bat against the wall.

'He looks like a good man,' says a woman, coming out of a room.

'All right.' Jasjit sighs. 'What did he say?'

'He has gone to Faridabad to his brother. He will telephone you from there.'

'Let the poor man stand up,' says Sukhbir. 'He has put himself at risk for our sake.'

Gopal struggles to his feet with a fluttering heart and shaking legs, his dhoti crumpled round his thighs, spectacles askew, shirt open at the front where two buttons have been ripped off by the fall. He wonders if this is a good time to ask for his bus fare.

'Sit down,' says Sukhbir, kindly, indicating a settee. Gopal settles down with a sigh. The veranda is so small that the settee touches opposite walls at either end. Gopal can see two rooms opening off the veranda. A third door opens into the kitchen.

Jasjit continues to look at Gopal suspiciously: it has been a tense day for him. He had gone to see the late-morning show at Vishaal cinema, hoping to save money on the cheap morning ticket, but they stopped the film half-way – even before the intermission. The audience erupted in howls of protest. Outside, he discovered the cause. He had thought, at the time, that the management was over-reacting. Why should people stop watching the film merely because the prime minister had been shot? He wanted a refund, but was told that was impossible: the show had been stopped for 'security reasons' for which the cinema could not be held responsible. He thought of going to the store in Lajpatrai Market, but he does not like sitting behind the counter, so he took an autoricksha home. Now he realises, as the radio speaks of a riot in Chandni Chowk, that this may have saved his life.

For the last four hours, he and his mother have waited anxiously for some communication from Kartar Singh. They have telephoned the store repeatedly but have been unable to get through. Meanwhile, police vans have been coursing through Trilokpuri, asking Sikhs to stay in their homes, reinforcing Jasjit's fears. A few men came to the house, saying they had been sent by Rajan Nahal – the local Congress leader – to reassure Sikhs of their safety. But Jasjit has heard of a robbery that took place two hours ago in Sector Two. The victim was a Sikh. They beat him senseless and took his wristwatch. No one attacks a man for a wristwatch! Jasjit turns over in his mind, again and again, the maxim which slips in and out of his daily conversation – one man of the Khalsa is the equal of savaa lakh; a single Sikh can fight more than a lakh of them! Perhaps he should have gone to Lajpatrai Market and brought his father home with him? But he could not have predicted the riot. And now this balding fool, breathing heavily on the settee, says that Kartar Singh has gone to Faridabad.

'Where did you meet Kartar Singhji?'

'He is safe,' says Gopal. 'He was attacked outside Gurudwara Sisganj and ran into Kucha Bansilal. I will tell you everything, but—'

'Let the poor man have some water,' says Sukhbir. She goes into the kitchen and comes back with a steel tumbler. Gopal eyes it hesitantly, his worst fears realised. *Have it tasted by a sardar first*, the fat man on the bus had said. 'I am not thirsty.'

'Should I make you some lemonade? Tea?'

Gopal shakes his head. He wishes he had not come all this way. He asks Sukhbir, who looks like a kind woman, more approachable than the young man, if he can go to the bathroom.

Sukhbir is embarrassed. '*Haay rabbaa*!' she says. 'Why do you have to ask me?'

Jasjit points to the room on the left. Gopal walks into it. There is a bathroom at the far end. After he has shut the door he realises it is a Western-style commode. How can he piss in a bowl like that? He hitches up his dhoti carefully and tries to squat on the seat.

*   *   *

Jasjit, who had followed Gopal all the way to the bathroom, returns to the veranda, flops down on the settee, and waits impatiently.

There is a knock on the front door. Jasjit springs up and grabs the cricket bat.

'Do not do anything rash, Jassi!' warns Sukhbir. 'They are probably Rajan Nahal's men, come to see if we are fine.'

'Be quiet!' whispers Jasjit. 'They do not know we are home.'

'Open the door, Jasjit Singh!' says a voice. 'We know you're there! We just saw someone go into your house.'

Jasjit recognises the voice. 'Is this Prabhu Lal?'

There is a brief lull in the knocking, as if Prabhu Lal is not sure of his own identity. Then it returns, and the voice: 'I told them to bring me along, knowing you would trust me. Open the door. I have a message from Kartar Singhji.'

Suddenly Jasjit is aware of grave danger. Why would his father send two messengers? He looks at Sukhbir, who covers her mouth with a trembling hand and glances fearfully at the bathroom door. 'And I offered to make him tea!' she says, outraged.

Jasjit grasps the cricket bat loosely and tiptoes toward the bathroom. He will bash the balding skull in. But the knocking on the outer door is frantic now.

'Can you wait?' Jasjit shouts at the voices outside. 'I need to take care of someone first.'

A cry goes up outside the door: '*Kachchhaa karaa aur kirpaan, bhej denge* Pakistan!'

Jasjit stops, mid-way to the bathroom, suddenly understanding the situation. He turns calmly to his mother. 'Run,' he says to Sukhbir. 'Go into the bathroom.'

'That man is in there!' she protests.

'He is harmless,' says Jasjit.

'I will not leave you alone!' says Sukhbir, trembling.

The front door is wrenched off its hinges and falls to the ground with a crash. Jasjit turns to face the men who charge through the opening. There are many of them, carrying rods, knives, sticks, axes and jerry-cans. Jasjit swings the cricket bat viciously, finding skulls and hearing them crack. He charges through the men and rushes out of the front door, where he is blocked by more men waiting near the scooter. He flings the cricket bat at them and runs round the house to the small garden at the back, where a ladder leans against the wall. He climbs it furiously and puts one foot over the top of the wall. As he prepares to jump off on the other side, he pauses, wondering if his mother is in the bathroom and if its door will hold. A cry goes up anew among the men chasing him.

'Indira Gandhi *amar rahe*!'

An axe flies through the garden and lodges itself in his back, tearing through his heart. He stands still for a moment, balanced on top of the wall, where shards of glass designed to thwart burglars cut his feet, turns back to see the terrible face of Prabhu Lal, then falls to the ground on the other side.

Gopal hears sounds outside the bathroom and climbs down from the commode. He has forgotten to lock the door. He pulls down his dhoti hastily just as the sardar's wife races in and locks the door. She gasps on seeing him, then runs to the window, pulls it open and puts a leg through it. 'Help me get out!' she pleads.

Gopal is still struggling with his dhoti. There is a loud banging on the bathroom door.

'Indira Gandhi *amar rahe*!' shouts a voice.

A single voice of terror, not a chorus of frightful sounds. It seems a familiar voice, but Gopal is not sure. With trembling hands, he slides the latch downward. The bathroom door is flung open and Ibrahim stands before him – yellow teeth, unkempt hair, flaming beard, bloodshot eyes, steel rod in hand.

'Ibrahim Mian!' exclaims Gopal. 'You look like a corpse!'

'Where is the sardar?' asks Ibrahim.

'He is not in the house.'

Ibrahim sighs in relief and lets the rod fall to the ground. Sukhbir, who is trying to squeeze out of the window, lets out a squeal. Ibrahim looks at her listlessly, then turns to Gopal. 'I have come from Ballimaran to see if you are safe,' he says.

Gopal is confused. 'Who told you I was here?'

Ibrahim does not reply. He shuts and locks the bathroom door.

'Who are these people?' asks Gopal.

'Murderers! I sent them round the house to chase that young sardar so you would be safe.'

'But who told you I was here?'

Ibrahim looks irritably at Gopal. 'Does it matter? I have saved you, and that is all you need to remember. Let them do what they will with that young sardar! He killed Indira, our mother.'

'You said she was a whore.'

'She was alive then,' says Ibrahim. 'Now she is dead. How can I speak ill of the dead?'

Stuck in the window, Sukhbir screams.

'Quiet!' says Ibrahim. 'Or you will die!'

There are sounds outside. Ibrahim opens the door and calls out that the bathroom is empty. 'We saw a sardarni!' say the voices.

'She must have run out of the front door when you went chasing after the sardar,' says Ibrahim. 'Did you see a television in this house?' he asks.

Gopal shrinks into a corner, afraid. It is my own sins, he tells himself, that have now come to devour me. Let me wither away and vanish in this bathroom like a puff of powder in the air, like a pinch of sugar in a cup of tea.

'I must go now,' says Ibrahim. He hesitates, then looks straight at Gopal. 'To protect people from these murderers.'

Ibrahim opens the bathroom door and is gone. Gopal wonders what to do with the sardarni, who is wedged in the window like a fat cow. Should he push her out, or try to pull her back in? Why have the feet stopped kicking? Is she dead? He squats on the commode and listens to the silence.

13

Kartar Singh has been on the footboard for more than an hour, waiting anxiously for the train to pick up speed. It has crawled out of the station, but has moved erratically since then. Every five minutes it blows a heartwarming whistle, strains, shakes its rusty underside loose, creeps, then screeches to a halt. At every stop, the pressure of limbs relieves itself and the carriage disgorges its human cargo. Kartar Singh is forced to jump off the train with the others, only to scramble aboard again when the whistle blows. On none of these reshuffles has he managed to get beyond the footboard. The inside of the carriage is reserved for more agile, or more aggressive, people.

In complete darkness, the train crosses the Yamuna bridge,

rumbling ominously over dark waters. Then they are in the wilderness, where distant lights on the horizon speak of small villages, and he breathes freely. The train is now more assertive, and he has time to analyse his situation. They are more than ten kilometres from Delhi. The wall of flesh presses constantly against him, threatening to expel him. His feet hurt. He is a heavy man, unused to standing for hours. Perhaps he can sit where he now stands. He tries to sink down on the footboard, one buttock overhanging the ledge, but the train sways dangerously, and the others will not move to clear sufficient space. He wonders if he should jump off now that he is safely out of Delhi. But where will he find his way in the wilderness? He can head for one of the lights and ask for help. But the train is moving faster now. He will have to wait until it pulls into a station. Until then he will keep himself glued to the bundle of people, exposed to the wind, eyes shut, awaiting deliverance. He must not fall asleep and loosen his grip on the metal handle.

'Come inside, sardarji! You will plunge to your death!'

Kartar Singh wakes and realises, to his horror, that he had dozed off. The words that have woken him, and perhaps saved him from a fatal fall, are the first kind ones he has heard in hours. He peers into the compartment, bathed in mournful yellow by dim bulbs screwed into the ceiling, and spots a dark turban. Another sardar in this aloof mass of short-haired people! His eyes fill with tears. He indicates to the sardar, with a nod at the crowd, that there is no way for him to squeeze through.

'Give me your hand.'

Kartar Singh tightens his grip on the handle, and extends the other hand inward. It is grasped and pulled. A chorus of protest issues from the door but he is dragged through yielding bodies. The opening closes behind him, and he is suddenly inside the carriage, pressed on all sides by people, facing the sardar who has rescued him. His saviour is a man of forty-five with a well-groomed beard, neatly combed whiskers and an immaculate turban. He surveys Kartar Singh with some amusement. 'You look like a beggar,' he says.

And you, thinks Kartar Singh, do not look like a man whose store has been looted.

The sardar tells Kartar Singh he is a captain in the army, just arrived in Delhi.

'You are the first Sikh I have seen on this train,' says Kartar Singh, in a rush of gratitude.

The captain throws a glance inward. Kartar Singh looks beyond him, and realises that the compartment is full of Sikhs. He had not been able to see them from the footboard.

'They are all soldiers in civilian dress,' says the captain.

'Why are they on the train?' asks a bewildered Kartar Singh.

'There is going to be trouble in Delhi. Everyone is going away for a few days. I just came back from Siachen myself. I did not know what I was getting into.'

'But why are you not in uniform? You could have controlled the crowd!'

The captain does not reply. He looks around anxiously. 'Have we crossed the Yamuna yet?' he asks.

'Yes. Do you know where this train will take us?'

The captain shakes his head. In spite of his neat appearance, he seems tense. 'Do you think we are slowing down?'

'We have started and stopped so many times,' says Kartar Singh, soothingly.

Even as he says this, he knows the train is indeed slowing down. There is a sick finality to this deceleration, coming half an hour after the last one, beyond the Yamuna bridge. It does not feel like the usual start-and-stop motion of a train pulling out of a great city. Then he consoles himself. It is merely another stop in a village – a red signal, or a blocked track, or an illegal yanking of the emergency-stop chain.

The train comes to a screeching stop. The crowd, standing as one body, sways and recoils. Silence falls. Every ear strains to decipher the sounds of the night. Kartar Singh wonders if the chaivala has reached Trilokpuri and met Sukhbir. She should call Harmeet Bhai about Jasjit . . . From the darkness outside comes a cry he has heard all day.

'Indira Gandhi *amar rahe*!
Neelee peelee rahane nahii denaa
sat sri akaal kahane nahii denaa.'

Indira will live for ever indeed, thinks Kartar Singh, once they have exterminated Sikhs from the world. He turns to the captain with peace in his heart. '*Sat sri akaal*, Captain Sahib. Truth is eternal. This is how we say farewell.'

The captain has a fearful gleam in his eyes. His lips tremble and his shoulder – pressed against Kartar Singh's arm – clenches with rage. There is panic among the Sikhs in the carriage. Everyone wants to get away, but there is nowhere to go. They are boxed in, possibly surrounded by enemies. Outside the carriage, the cry is repeated. A rip appears in the crowd, where a column of Sikhs pushes through and jumps off the train. Outside, the darkness erupts into battle, waged with rods, sticks and bottles. The Sikhs realise they have made a mistake and retreat. A few rush back into the carriage.

'Shut the doors!' shouts someone.

'Keep it open, you mother-fuckers! We do not want to die with you!'

Hindus rush to get out, fighting their way through sardars who try to get as far away from the doors as possible.

'If you go outside you will be slaughtered,' warns the captain.

'They are about to come in anyway,' says Kartar Singh.

'Come with me.' The captain takes Kartar Singh by the arm, and the two men force themselves through the bodies – Hindus and Sikhs – to the end of the carriage, where they lock themselves into a toilet.

The men outside carry torches. Through the toilet's frosted window-pane Kartar Singh can see dark shapes that wield rods, spears and axes. He can hear sardars being pulled off the train, he can hear their cries for help, and he can hear stones raining down on the carriage, miraculously missing his window. Sometimes he fancies he can hear the sounds of steel penetrating flesh. Who are these people? Is Bishan among them? Is that dark mass the bald head of the chaivala?

The captain squats on the pot and looks at Kartar Singh with mournful eyes. 'This is how they repay me,' he says. 'And I have just come from Siachen glacier where I was defending their fucking country.'

'We should have jumped off the train as soon as it crossed the Yamuna,' says Kartar Singh.

'Have you been to Siachen?' asks the captain gloomily. 'It is bitterly cold. Leave your hands in the open for a while and you get frostbite. Do you know what they do then?'

Kartar Singh does not reply.

'They cut them off.'

'Keep your voice down, Captain Sahib! Maybe they will move on to the next carriage.'

'Why should I speak softly?' yells the captain. 'I have been to Siachen!' A hammering sound startles him from below. Then his body clenches and he is silent.

'Captain Sahib?' Kartar Singh leans closer. The captain, squatting above the toilet hole that opens on to the tracks, is transfixed, impaled on a steel rod that has entered his anus, travelled through his gut and emerged near his heart. Directly below him, lying on his back on the tracks, a man sneers.

'Go shit in Siachen, not on me, mother-fucking sardar!'

Kartar Singh steps back with a cry and wraps his arms round himself. *Sachche Padshah*! This is the end! He presses himself against the wall, trying to avoid the blood that spurts out of the captain's chest, until he realises the wall is hot. A carpet of smoke slides into the toilet. He pulls off his turban, tears out its pins, unrolls it and places it against the crack under the door, but the smoke finds other openings. The carriage is on fire. He opens the door an inch and greedily sucks in the outside air. A shout goes up. 'Toilet! Toilet!'

He shuts the door quickly. A hailstorm descends on it. With each blow the door cringes, bends and prepares to yield. The heat becomes unbearable and the smoke begins to suffocate him. Kartar Singh pulls out of his hair the small kirpaan he always carries. It is a ceremonial kirpaan, almost a toy dagger, but it is sharp and strong.

The door swings open with a crash. Kartar Singh throws himself upon the men, slashing as hard as he can with the tiny kirpaan. His sudden frenzy and his great bulk cause the faceless figures with sticks and rods – smaller men in vests and lungis – to scatter. Kartar Singh uses both arms to push them aside and charges frantically toward the door, almost overcome by the smoke, heat and the smell of burning flesh. He hits the metal bar near the door, loses his balance and falls over the edge to the ground, five feet below. The fall breaks his left leg, but he picks himself up and runs. The train track runs on a gravelled causeway. He loses his balance again and half slithers down the embankment. At the base of the slope, in a ditch full of rain water, his broken leg gives way under him, and he falls face first into the ditch. With the pain in his leg and the fear in his heart, he experiences an odd moment of peace. He can hear them coming up behind him, but suddenly he does not care. Jasjit is certainly safe, in one of two worlds. The chaivala perhaps did not go to Trilokpuri at all. Sukhbir is sitting over her gutkas, fretting about his safety, unaware that he will never come back. He feels disembodied, as if he is soaring above himself and looking down on a drama in which someone plays him.

Mukesh comes running behind the sardar, determined not to let this one get away. His cheek smarts from the cut the sardar inflicted with his dagger. The bastard! He should have been allowed to burn inside the toilet. 'A hundred rupees for each corpse,' said Rajan Nahal, 'in addition to a lump sum for the day'. But no one told him the sardars would be armed with knives. For such people you need guns, not rods or kerosene canisters.

He stands over the fallen sardar, partially submerged by water in the ditch. Fat and prosperous! He squats next to the man and turns him over to study his hands. No wristwatch. No ring, no wedding band, not even a stone! What kind of a sardar is this? No wallet in his pockets, not a single rupee on him! And this on a man whose fat belly hangs obscenely to the side! Perhaps a secret pocket in his underwear? A pouch sewn into his vest? Ah, nothing. Mukesh stands up in disgust and kicks the sardar. A plucked chicken. A beggar. He can claim his hundred from Rajan Nahal, but perhaps he should run back to the train and find himself a bigger prize, as the others are doing. One gold chain is worth more than ten of these beggars. Maybe the one whose arse was speared in the toilet will yield richer pickings . . . It has been a rough day. There were the men on television, chanting around the body of Indira. *Khoon kaa badlaa khoon*! Blood for blood, blood for blood . . . They seemed to look at him from the screen, almost as if they were speaking directly to him, telling him what to do. He has no doubt of what they would want him to do now. This bastard must be punished. Here he lies shamelessly, half naked, penniless, so tender and juicy even in the dark. Look how he sleeps after killing Indira!

Mukesh turns the sardar on to his stomach. He does not want to see the face when it burns. He pours kerosene over the body, lights a match and throws it. It hits the sardar's heaving buttocks, sizzles, raises a little smoke and slides into the water. Mukesh douses the body with more kerosene and throws more matches at it, but the flesh refuses to catch fire. It is soaked.

'The bastard will not go easily!' He laughs.

He thinks of that strange white chemical Rajan Nahal handed out. It does not need a match to catch fire. But he has nothing left except canisters and matches. Someone brings him a rod of steel. 'Stick him on a pole! Like that Siachen bastard!'

'He is already dead,' laughs Mukesh.

'Stick him anyway!'

A shudder arises far to the right where a second train has been stopped. With a great cry, they charge at it.

'India is Indira, Indira is India!'

1990

I

Gauhar has learned that, by letting his muscles relax, he can reduce the sensation that accompanies the thrust. This man is his fourth client in four days, his oldest so far. He huffs and puffs as he ploughs back and forth, desire competing with exhaustion. By the time he is finished, thinks Gauhar, he will be dead and I will have a dead prick inside my arse. A small prick, perhaps, from the mild sensation it causes. Either that or these old men are loosening me up.

It is late morning. The sun penetrates in strips of light through a window in the cupboard where Gauhar stands with the man. The cupboard stands in an abandoned haveli, tucked under the main staircase, which rises from the courtyard in a sweeping curve that was once graceful, but it has long lost its ability to bear weight. Now it has melted back into the greyness that surrounds it, although its cast-iron rail still stands in a display of flowery patterns. The two-hundred-year-old haveli is owned by the government of India, which has affixed a new brass plaque outside it, designating it a national heritage site, like the scores of other such buildings around Jama Masjid. The cupboard itself, painted bright green and built of plywood, is not owned by the government. It belongs to the paanvala who has a stall next to the haveli, and who had it constructed ten months ago. For the privilege of owning a piece of the haveli, he pays a hundred rupees every month to the Jama Masjid area SHO. He rents it out by the hour, at the rate of two rupees. Most of his customers need no more than fifteen minutes, so he is able to quadruple his hourly earnings, to the extent that the cupboard pays more than his stall.

Gauhar stands with his face to the window, left hand clutching the iron bars for support, while the old man harrumphs behind him, seemingly in rhythm with the song playing on the paan-stall radio. Pushpa Rani's sweet voice floats into the haveli:

> *'You are the melody my heart sings*
> *You are the rhythm of my heartbeats*
> *You are the breath I breathe today*
> *You are the life I live for ever . . .'*

The stream of light that spills into the cupboard brings with it the scene of a pigeon fight behind Jama Masjid. The birds' wings have been clipped so they cannot fly, and their beaks and claws have been artificially sharpened. The owners – men wearing achkans, shervanis and caps – watch the fight eagerly and look for signs of weakness in their charges. Each has a man in the crowd, whose function is to maintain decorum, keep the audience at a safe distance and collect bets. When no one is willing to put money down, each factotum sets up a cheerleading session for his master's pigeon. The two birds – one white, the other with a mottled grey head – flap furiously and try to mount each other in violent pantomime, unmindful of cheers, stakes and the odds.

Four weeks ago, Mussabir Hussein shook Gauhar awake in the middle of the night and took him outside the Sparrows building. 'Pull down your pants,' he said. Gauhar refused. Mussabir laughed. 'Chitra Didi has asked me do this!' he said. At first Gauhar did not believe him. But Mussabir Ustad was the oldest boy at Sparrows and the secretary of Baal Bank, into which all of them deposited the money they earned in Chandni Chowk. He was almost Didi's assistant. He was also the strongest among them, and had been known to beat up boys who interfered with his gang. Even those not in his gang called him 'Ustad'.

'Why did Didi not tell me this herself?' asked Gauhar, hesitantly.

'She is shy!' laughed Mussabir.

Then, before Gauhar could say anything, his penis was enclosed within Mussabir's bony hands.

'What a small prick you have!' said Mussabir Ustad.

'Let me go!' laughed Gauhar, but his penis had begun to harden.

'Do you like it?' asked Mussabir.

'Yes, but I want to hold it myself,' said Gauhar.

'You will, you will! But the first time is mine. I must teach you.' Mussabir closed his fingers tightly round Gauhar's penis and moved the skin back and forth.

'Why did Didi ask you to do this to me?'

Mussabir laughed. 'So you will do it to yourself, not to other boys.'

Two weeks after Mussabir Ustad had taught Gauhar to masturbate, he asked for a progress report. Gauhar could not contain his enthusiasm at the new pleasures he had learned. 'Why do you want to do it alone?' asked Mussabir. 'If you do it with a client he will pay you.' So Gauhar had let three men watch him. For an extra two rupees he allowed them to touch his penis. For another five he watched films with them – dirty films, in which creamy white heroines with dirty yellow hair sucked large pink penises. He liked the films. He did not like the men who fondled him as they watched, but they paid five rupees each and the film was free. Then, a week ago, Mussabir asked him if he would like to have those men fuck him.

The man behind Gauhar is flagging. Why does he insist on going on until he is spent, wonders Gauhar, when he can withdraw now and pay half the money? 'The oldest ones are the worst,' Mussabir had warned him. 'They will grind and heave and not let go until they have ejaculated, but their pricks are small and their ejaculations weak.' Gauhar looks back contemptuously, and discovers that the man is in the throes of an orgasm that looks likely to kill him. He convulses violently, then sinks to the ground. Outside, the pigeon-watchers explode in an orgy of applause.

Gauhar stands over the man, who now squats in relief and exhaustion. He pulls up his shorts, thrusts his stump casually into his pocket and holds out his left hand. Pay up. The man looks up innocently – spent, defeated, clearly the weaker one – and holds up a hand, indicating that he needs a moment to catch his breath. Gauhar waits impatiently. The man senses his urgency, unties a knot in his dhoti, carefully counts out two ten-rupee notes and holds them up for Gauhar to see. 'Fifty,' he says.

Gauhar's eyes gleam. Chitra Didi has taught him to read, write and count. 'That is twenty, you bastard!'

The man is unnerved. He had assumed the boy was illiterate. He hastily returns the ten-rupee notes to his cloth pouch and pulls out a fifty-rupee one.

'We agreed on seventy,' says Gauhar.

'I said seventy if you were tight,' objects the man.

Gauhar takes a step forward and stands over the man. He is sixteen, thin but agile. 'You have the power over them,' Mussabir has told him. 'They will haggle – before and after – but they are weak in both instances, first with desire and then with orgasm.' And this one, being so old, is certainly diseased too.

'Give me seventy, arse-fucker!'

In the chiaroscuro light thrown by the sun into the cupboard, Gauhar sees fear in the man's eyes and presses his advantage. He places his left hand on the other man's shoulder and squeezes hard. A chorus of exhortation rises outside the haveli. The grey pigeon has gored the white one, whose blood now scatters in fluttering drops every time it attempts to fly. The crowd is calling on the grey one to finish the fight. The victor stands, one leg raised, head cocked, eyes blinking rapidly, looking to left and right with quick, jerky motions. He is about to make his final swoop on his quarry and peck him to death.

'All right,' says the man, with a wan smile.

He hands over the fifty and brings out the two crumpled ten-rupee notes again, looking away. Then he gets up, as quickly as exhaustion allows, and rearranges his dhoti. 'I will never come to you again,' he says sullenly, as he vanishes into the corridors of the haveli.

'Fuck you, mother-fucker!'

Gauhar unties a handkerchief from his right arm and extracts a two-rupee note. Then he rolls the fifty and a ten carefully into a cylinder, using his left hand and the wall of the cupboard, wraps the handkerchief round it, and ties it back on his arm. He locks the cupboard and strolls out of the haveli, where he hands the key and two rupees to the paanvala. With the remaining ten-rupee note in his hand, he heads for the pigeon fight. It has ended and the crowd has dispersed. The white pigeon lies dead, its plumage sullied with blood. Mussabir Ustad is counting money and grinning. Gauhar holds out the ten-rupee note. Mussabir looks suspiciously at him.

'The old bastard!' says Gauhar. 'Gave me fifty.'

With a quick motion Mussabir tears the handkerchief from Gauhar's arm and exposes the lie. Gauhar makes a feeble one-handed attempt at defence, but Mussabir is two years older. He gives himself another ten, wraps the fifty back in the handkerchief and flings it at Gauhar. 'Didi has made a thief of you,' he scolds. 'Did she not teach you honesty?'

Gauhar struggles with shame and annoyance. He does not dare fight Mussabir Ustad, but he feels the twenty-rupee commission is unjustified. Ustad is only two inches taller than him. 'Don't bring me any more men,' he says.

Mussabir laughs contemptuously. 'What will you do? Work at a chai stall? Sell apples? Collect paper? Pick rags? Pull a ricksha?'

'Didi says there is nothing wrong with pulling a ricksha,' retorts Gauhar.

'Has Didi never looked at your hand?'

'I can drive a ricksha with one hand,' says Gauhar. 'I have practised.'

'You will fuck ricksha pedals all day with a fat seth sprawling behind you, watching your arse hanging in mid-air. And after ten trips

– Red Fort to Fatehpuri, Fatehpuri to Red Fort – you will have fifteen rupees in your pocket. Why not let an old man fuck you for five minutes?'

'Because it hurts!'

'A ricksha hurts too. Your legs will become spindly, your arms will ache, your buttocks will shrivel up, your hands – your one hand – will have calluses. In this business, only your arse hurts.'

'There is too much haggling over the rate.'

'The rate will keep going up, and the times will get shorter. Old men get older. They have a difficult time keeping their pricks hard for a full five minutes.'

Gauhar does not reply. He has learned a trick that he will not share with Mussabir. Fix your eye on Jama Masjid. Watch the southern minaret and try to forget what is happening to you, and soon you will not be present in the cupboard. There will be a slight pain in the back of your stomach every time the man thrusts, but it will be in another body, another space, another time . . . 'I will not give you any commission from tomorrow,' he says defiantly.

Mussabir seizes him with both hands, traps his head in the crook of his arm and bends over until Gauhar's head is pressed against his side. 'Will you cheat your ustad, you thief?'

'All right! I will not!'

Mussabir releases him. 'I have always liked you,' he says reassuringly. 'Didi wants me to take other boys under my wing, but I have selected you. I have seen you steal notebooks and pencils but I will not tell her.'

Gauhar is caught unawares by this threat. He did not know that Mussabir knew. He nods vigorously, fully tamed.

Mussabir studies his face. 'Has Didi asked about me?'

Gauhar shakes his head. Mussabir looks disappointed.

'She has not noticed that I left Sparrows a week ago? That I no longer come to the class? That I don't even sleep there?'

Gauhar does not know if Didi has noticed.

'But who is running Baal Bank?' demands Mussabir.

'She made me the secretary,' says Gauhar, shyly.

Mussabir is crestfallen. Ever since Didi began Baal Bank, he has been its secretary, its imperious master. He is lax when children deposit money, and fastidious when they want to withdraw it. 'Why do you want it?' he asks fussily. 'Is it for food and clothing, as Didi has stipulated? Or is it for something else? For a film, perhaps? For some ganja? Other drugs?' He likes his role as taskmaster. He also knows that Didi will not notice if the interest on the money is twelve per cent, rather than the fifteen she asked him to add every month. None of the children – even those like Gauhar who can count – can differentiate between twelve and fifteen per cent.

'You have only one hand!' he protests. 'How can you be the secretary?'

'Didi says you need a mind to run Baal Bank, not hands,' counters Gauhar.

The boy has grown up, thinks Mussabir, angrily. His confidence grows every time he gets fucked. Today he has become secretary of Baal Bank. Tomorrow the entire gang at Sparrows will switch their allegiance to him. Perhaps he was wrong to think he could control them from outside. He needs Gauhar because his own business is drying up. At eighteen, he is too tall, too lean, too muscular. The men want fresher stuff, younger boys. 'You are not soft and tender,' they say, 'you are diseased . . .' The arse-fuckers! But the boy is beginning to grudge his commission, and this was only his fourth customer! 'It is my arse,' he said yesterday. 'Why should you get the money?' And today he tries to lie about the rate! This is why Mussabir has become involved in pigeon fights, where the only challenge is to convince the owners that he should collect the bets. Pigeon owners look for assertive men who can use a mix of coercion and persuasion with the crowd, and Mussabir is a master of both. He extols the virtues of his pigeon, swears on Allah that victory is pre-ordained, and uses a system of squeezes, holds and stares to intimidate people. At the end of the fight he slips a wad of bills into his pocket and hands the rest to the pigeon owner. No business, however, is safe in Chandni Chowk. Last month a few city women, dressed in trousers like men, came in an Ambassador car to watch the fight. They took photographs. The crowd posed happily for them. Mussabir pushed his way into the pictures, holding his master's bird and twisting its neck so it would face the camera. The next day, the police broke up a pigeon fight and said they would be regulated; every match is now watched over by a policeman, who can stop it at whim. 'The city women were appalled by the cruelty to the pigeons,' says the policeman. As if a pigeon can talk, walk and hurt like a man! And who told those city women about cruelty? Did the pigeons write them a letter?

Mussabir looks at Gauhar with greater understanding. He must be kind to the boy, or he will soon have to make his living by queuing to

pay people's telephone bills or showing white tourists round Jama
Masjid. 'You will make a good secretary,' he says, in a conciliatory
tone. 'You are Didi's favourite boy now. But remember, there are only
two jobs that have dignity in Chandni Chowk – collecting bets on
pigeon fights and getting fucked by old men.'

'All right,' says Gauhar. 'I will go now.'

Mussabir grabs Gauhar by the arm and pulls him close. With his
other arm, he slaps Gauhar on the back, letting his hand linger.
'What's the hurry?'

Gauhar draws back. In the last few days he has sensed Mussabir's
increasing urgency. But Mussabir is not an anonymous old man
spilling his guts in the darkness. He has a face, a name and a voice.
And Mussabir will not pay. 'I have to go to Didi,' says Gauhar.
'Suleman Mian is coming to Sparrows today.'

'Ah! Suleman Mian! He will talk about the Mandal Commission.'

'What's that?'

Mussabir laughs. 'From now on, every time you fuck three men of
other castes, you will have to fuck an OBC! Twenty-seven per cent of
all fucks are reserved for them!'

'Who says so?'

'V. P. Singh! And he is the prime minister, so you will do as he says.'

'What is an OBC?'

'Other Backward Class. You are one too.'

'But we are Musalmans,' says Gauhar. 'Can a Musalman be an
OBC?'

'Anyone, anywhere,' says Mussabir, carelessly, and pulls Gauhar
close again. 'I am an OBC too. You have to give me my quota.'

Gauhar angrily shakes himself loose. For years Mussabir has been
friend, guide and teacher, providing a counterweight to Chitra Didi's
colourless instructions – wash your hair, clip your nails, wear clean
clothes, wash off your shit with the left hand and eat with the right
. . . Mussabir and Chitra Didi have been his two tutors, each negating
the other. 'Wash your arsehole with the right hand and eat with the
left,' says Mussabir. 'Identify a man with a large prick before making a
deal with him. Stare down a niggardly customer because you know he
is weak with lust. Speak respectfully to Didi because you cannot bite
the hand that feeds you . . .' But now he feels impatient with
Mussabir's presumption, and his aggressive defence of his rights. 'I
am going,' snarls Gauhar.

He hops out of Mussabir's reach and walks away. His dirty brown hair, which reaches his shoulders, flops into his eyes. At sixteen, his chest and arms are still thin, but he has developed a habit of shoving his stump into his right pocket, which makes him look almost whole.

Mussabir calls, 'Tell Didi I can come back if she needs me.'

𝄢

It is past eight in the morning, but the kholi sees little light since Seth Sushil Jain installed a wooden partition wall six years ago. This also blocked off the ventilators and their fluttering curtains, so the smell of turmeric is strong. It is hot. It should rain in August, but Delhi is dry this year. Gopal crouches in the darkness and forces a steel wire into the lock that guards the partition. Behind the plywood wall steel trunks are buried under tins of asafoetida. Once the lock has been picked, he will go through the wall, remove the tins, open the trunks and withdraw his money.

He pauses, exhausted, and considers what happened during the night. For three months, he has tried to pick the lock gently, afraid that a forceful assault would wake the watchman. He has asked Ibrahim, indirectly, how locks may be opened without keys, and received only indirect answers. Last night, after an hour spent wrestling with the keyhole, he picked up a steel spoon and ran it back and forth on the lock. The edge of the spoon was sharp, and he managed to create a shallow groove. It lit a fire in his heart. Here, lying less than three feet away, were those belts of cloth, stuffed with countless bundles of hundred-rupee notes! With time, he might break the lock in two. All he had to do was cut through the offending neck . . . He began to file with renewed energy, chastising himself for years of caution, until a sudden tapping of the watchman's stick, deep down in Katra Badami, stopped him. He waited for the man to climb the ladder, but no one came. He threw away the spoon – shuddering as it clattered across the kholi – and went to sleep, heart filled with dread. The watchman would not forget, he knew.

The spoon lies on the floor where he threw it. He dare not use it again. If only the lock would pop open without breaking . . . He hears a sound and springs away from it, hiding the wire behind his back, grateful for the darkness.

'There you are!' says Hameed, coming up the ladder. 'Sethji wants to know who came into the building last night.'

'You frightened me.'

'Nothing frightens you,' retorts Hameed. 'The watchman heard sawing in the night. He thinks someone was trying to break into rooms in the katra. Did you see anyone?'

Gopal hesitates.

'Perhaps you were sleeping soundly,' suggests Hameed, scornfully.

'I was awake all night,' responds Gopal. 'I saw no one. The watchman imagines thieves to justify his job.'

'Sethji is thinking of changing the locks in every room for bigger, stronger ones.'

'There is no need for that,' says Gopal quickly. 'There are no thieves.'

Hameed laughs and disappears down the ladder. Gopal lies down on a sack of turmeric, crestfallen. He was foolish to put his money in those trunks. He should have guessed that the seth planned some construction when he hung the curtains over the ventilators.

He no longer wonders who left the money in the junction box. He is almost certain the cloth belts were always there. There were times, when he was a boy of fifteen, when he saw padding round the switches, but he never gave it much thought. Perhaps his father had put the belts there, meaning to tell his son where his savings were hidden. And it was not merely a stroke of good fortune that he had found them when he did. That discovery was the result of his selfless defence of the sardar. There are so many instances, in *Ramayan* and *Mahabharat* and perhaps the Bible – is not the Bible like a *Ramayan* for Christians? – when a good man finds himself enriched in spite of himself. He made a great sacrifice that day in agreeing to shelter the sardar and going to Trilokpuri, for which he was never even reimbursed the bus fare. How could he ask the sardar's wife for it when she was stuck in a window? 'Do not leave me,' she had cried, when he ran out of the bathroom. He was trembling like a leaf thrown to the winds. Ibrahim and the other men had all gone to some other house, and the only sounds in the flat were the screams of the sardarni. 'I will call the police,' he had shouted, as he left.

He ran all the way to the bus stop, jumped on to the first bus he saw, and had to change many times because the first took him in the wrong direction. Every time he bought a ticket he felt the pain of his sacrifice. Surely the sardar could have given him ten rupees for travelling expenses, especially as he was charged with such an important message.

He arrived back at the stall late at night, when all of Chandni Chowk had gone to sleep and the pavements were snoring with beggars. The sardar was gone, thankfully, and he had not stolen the stove, the cardamom or the milk. The only damage to the stall was a few squashed plastic bottles and sugar tins where the sardar had pressed against them. He decided to wash Ibrahim's tumbler, opened the junction box, and saw cloth padding lining the switches, filling what should have been empty space. Puzzled, he pulled out some of the padding, and the crackling of those bundles was wonderful! He squeezed the belt to extrude a bundle, examined it as well as he could in the darkness, caressed it, patted it, smelled it, pressed it against his cheek . . . Yes, it was money, all right! He tore out all the padding from the junction box and ran his fingers over it, heart fluttering, counting, adding up, until the numbers became too large. At least two lakhs, three lakhs, four, ten, twenty . . . To hold twenty lakhs in his own hands!

That was when he first paused to wonder how the money had come to be there. It was an inconvenient matter, a frivolous distraction, soon pushed aside. He would worry about that later. He shuffled through Chandni Chowk with cloth belts hanging over his shoulder like bandoleers. He stepped over beggars on pavements, careful not to disturb them, breathless with excitement at the load he carried. He did not stop to think until he had climbed up the ladder to the kholi and thrown the belts on to the floor, next to sacks of turmeric. He was not sure where he could hide them. Sushil Jain rotated his stock every few days, before the turmeric could eat into and melt its plastic sacks. Hameed came daily into the kholi to move them in and out. Imported turmeric was kept in plastic tubs, where it lasted much longer, and it was inside those tubs that the money spent its first night. The next morning, Gopal found the belts stained and took the money out. That night, he scoured all three floors in Katra Badami for spices that would hold his treasure. He needed whole spices, which could retain their flavour indefinitely and were unlikely to be sold for many months. He looked at peppercorns, cumin, cinnamon sticks and nutmeg. He considered dry dates, betel nuts, cloves, cassia, gambier, long pepper, raisins

. . . But where could he hide the money and rest assured that Hameed would not carry it away?

He decided to explore the steel trunks that Sushil Jain had transferred to the kholi over the last three months. He removed the tins of asafoetida, opened all three trunks and found stacks of binders covered with red buckram, their yellow pages smeared with vermilion swastikas. These were the seth's accounts. Why had he transferred them to the kholi and buried them under asafoetida tins? In any case, Hameed was unlikely to open those trunks, so Gopal placed all four belts in the bottom of two of them. He rearranged binders over his belts, shut the trunks and replaced the tins.

He slept peacefully that night. He was a wealthy man, enriched by the sacrifices he had made in saving the sardarji. The stories they told were true after all – Lakshmi did wander about Chandni Chowk, bestowing money on devotees. He thanked her from the bottom of his heart and pledged his everlasting devotion.

Five days after the terrible morning when they killed Indira, the sardarji reappeared in Kucha Bansilal. He came just after Seth Sohan Lal had finished his puja and Gopal had made his first pot of tea. He looked haggard and tired. He walked with a limp and wore a plaster cast on his left leg, throwing nervous glances behind him, as if afraid of being followed. The bruises on his face had partially closed his right eye and his lips were cut, making him almost unrecognisable. But it was the sardarji.

Gopal was appalled. Had this happened to the sardarji from being crushed inside the stall? He should not have shut the lid, and certainly not sat on it! The box was large enough for a poor man like him, but for a fat man like the sardarji it must have been torture!

'Namaste, Gopal Bhai,' the sardarji had said. 'I have returned from Faridabad.'

Gopal was thrown into confusion. To have the sardarji say namaste to him! He squinted through his spectacles and pretended not to recognise him. He extended a nervous tumbler of tea toward him – a customer, nothing more.

'You are a good man, Gopal Bhai,' said the sardarji.

'I delivered your message,' said Gopal fearfully. 'I tried to hold those men back, but I am a weak man. Your wife . . .'

'She is safe,' said the sardarji. 'But they took my son.'

Gopal covered his mouth with both hands, overwhelmed.

'You did what you could,' said the sardarji. 'I have to ask you something. Who was that man?'

Gopal looked at him, uncomprehending.

'The man in the bathroom,' said the sardarji.

Gopal gasped, thinking of the yellow teeth, the flaming beard, the steel rod raised high in the air.

'My wife could not see him because her face was toward the garden,' said the sardarji. 'She saw the axe enter her son.' His voice seemed to dissolve.

Gopal shuddered, about to mention the name. Ah, a friend, an old friend. *I have come from Ballimaran to see if you are safe*, Ibrahim had said. 'I could not see properly. My spectacles were on the ground.' He poured milk into the pan, added water – thrice as much water as milk to save money – and set it to boil for his next pot of tea.

The sardarji seemed to recover his poise. 'You have a nice stall, Gopal Bhai,' he said.

Gopal threw a fistful of sugar into the pan.

'It is good to have an electrical junction right above your head,' said the sardarji. 'You will never worry about power cuts. How often do you open the box?'

Gopal's heart sank. Somehow the sardarji must know about the money! Perhaps it was his! 'It is not my junction box,' said Gopal, flustered. 'It belongs to the Corporation.'

'The Corporation is a thief,' said the sardarji, through bruised lips.

Gopal found the sardarji scrutinising him, suspicion radiating even through the drooping eyelid, and wondered if he should tell him about the cloth belts. But what if the money was not really his? Wouldn't he still confiscate it? 'I went straight to my kholi when I returned from Trilokpuri,' he sputtered. 'It was late, and there was a curfew in Chandni Chowk. So I got off the bus at ISBT and took a ricksha to Khari Baoli. And I did not come to the stall for two days because of the riots.'

This lengthy explanation seemed to disappoint the sardarji. 'Have you looked inside the junction box?' he asked suddenly.

Gopal then prepared to reveal all. He could not look into the eyes of a bereaved man – even one whose eye was half shut – and lie.

'There was a glass of tea in there,' said the sardarji. 'I drank some. I thought you might want me to pay for it.'

Gopal chided himself for being foolish. The sardarji had been talking about tea all along. He knew nothing about the money. 'I left it for you. It was free, for your trouble.'

'Ah! Then I owe you nothing. This has weighed on my mind for five days.'

The words disappointed Gopal. It still rankled that the bus fares remained unpaid. He had changed buses so many times, making the trip almost as expensive as an autoricksha. 'I took an autoricksha to Trilokpuri,' he said softly.

The sardarji brought out a twenty-rupee note from his pocket and proffered it. 'What is an autoricksha, Gopal Bhai? Had you taken an aeroplane, I would have gladly paid you back.'

Gopal quickly took the money. It was not wise to play shy when the other man might change his mind at any moment.

The sardarji leaned closer, making him very uncomfortable. 'That was a painful day for me, Gopal Bhai. You must not tell anyone about it, especially Sohan Lalji. He is a good friend of mine. He might think you were responsible for my plight and tear down your stall.'

'This will remain between you and me, sardarji,' swore Gopal, fervently.

As Kartar Singh limped away, Gopal thanked Lakshmi, certain that it was not the sardarji's money after all. If it was, why had he not asked about it?

Gopal spent the next few weeks in suspended disbelief, waiting for someone to claim the money. The thought of giving it to the police passed through his mind, but what if they accused him of theft? And who could trust them to hand it to the rightful owner? It was best to leave it where it was, safely buried under asafoetida tins. After a few weeks, he was convinced that the money was a gift from Lakshmi herself, and it would be a sin to refuse it.

Then the problem of how to spend it rose in his mind. He could not possibly buy new clothes, new stoves, new bottles of sugar, new glass tumblers. A dhoti cost very little, a checked shirt could be stitched for eighteen rupees, a stove could be had for fifty. How could a man spend four lakhs in one lifetime? Every morning he walked through Khari Baoli and imagined himself reclining behind mounds of pistachios, almonds, gulbandi, apricots, figs, raisins and walnuts. Here sits Gopal Pandey, proprietor of Gopal Pandey and Sons, the finest dry-fruit shop in Khari Baoli! It would be a shop on the corner, perhaps, where Khari Baoli swerved to meet Fatehpuri Masjid, or a shop in Katra Peran, Katra Ishwar Bhava, even Katra Badami. Imagine the look on Seth Sushil Jain's face if he were to present himself in Katra Badami one morning, washed, wearing a clean checked shirt and neatly pressed dhoti! 'Have you been sleeping at night?' Sushil Jain would scold.

'Yes,' Gopal would reply, 'because I have a shop to open in the morning.' Then he would sit cross-legged on the gaddi to have chai with Sushil Jain – just as other seths did – and discuss rising prices. 'There is a supply shortage from Afghanistan,' he would tell Sushil Jain, 'so almonds have gone to three hundred and eighty rupees, and Afghani figs are at three hundred and sixty.' And Sushil Jain would bemoan the old days when Khari Baoli seths handed out almonds as loose change and beggars popped them into their mouths.

The dry-fruit market was too competitive, though, and Gopal quickly abandoned that idea. Instead, he imagined himself sitting behind mountains of sugar and jaggery, selling briskly and losing count of the money in his cash-box. But sugar and jaggery are difficult to store, and he would certainly not make the mistake of dealing in turmeric or pepper – too many problems with insects. Pulses had higher margins and no insects touched them. Yes, he would deal in pulses. Ah! To be sitting cross-legged next to a pair of scales, listening to the cricket commentary, watching carts and rickshas in Khari Baoli, filling polythene bags with grains of urad, moong, gram, masoor, rajma, chitra, lobia . . . He would not give up the chai stall. He would have someone sit there for him and serve frothy tea to his customers, and he would take a cut. Would there be money left over for cows and buffaloes? It was cheaper to produce your own milk, and that would teach Banwari a lesson for the water he mixed with his. Perhaps he could keep his cows behind the old post office in Khari Baoli where he went daily for his shit. He would no longer shit there, of course. He would get himself a shiny new toilet with tiles and lights and mirrors and stainless-steel faucets. He would have it constructed at the back of his new cubicle, only for himself. Customers would have to fend for themselves. His boy – he would hire a boy like Chotu – would have strict instructions not to indulge petty customers.

'Can we use your bathroom?' customers would ask.

'Nanak Chand, take babuji to the bathroom!' he would say.

'I cannot find the keys,' the boy would reply. He would be a nice, gentle boy, younger than Chotu – a boy who could be trusted with the keys to a shiny toilet.

Within a few days, the name Gopal Pandey and Sons proved itself inadequate. How could a shop boast of a son when the son was never visible at the cash-box? Also, Gopal Pandey was an ignominious name, betraying its Brahmin origins. Who had ever heard of a Brahmin becoming rich in business? The great shops of Khari Baoli bore the tags of venerable Banias who had died a hundred years ago. He abandoned Gopal Pandey and Sons, and turned over in his mind the names of weighty ancestors that might speak of impeccable Bania lineage – Balmukund Murarilal, Kanshiram Kanjilal, Baburam Moolchand, Nathumal Chunnilal – and settled on Kanjilal Moolchand. He sat next to the trunks in the kholi and imagined those old men to be his uncles, great-uncles, great-great-grandfathers, who had started the business to serve the British and bequeathed to him a family heirloom.

Once the name Kanjilal Moolchand had suggested itself, Gopal saw no impediment to his quest. He approached Ibrahim about buying a shop in Khari Baoli.

'Have you won the lottery, Gopal Bhai?' Ibrahim had scoffed.

'I have saved for years,' replied Gopal, unconvincingly.

'There is no fixed price in Khari Baoli,' said Ibrahim. 'How much money do you have?'

'Two lakhs,' said Gopal, with casual indifference. 'Maybe three – or four. Twenty.' He hoped, with his vagueness, to hide the value of his treasure, which he did not know anyway. There were four bundles, and each probably contained a lakh, but he was not sure.

Ibrahim continued to look at him incredulously. 'I will get you a dealer,' he said. 'He will register a shop in your name without asking where you got the money.'

Gopal was stung. 'It is my money!'

'It is yours, of course.' Ibrahim winked. He arranged a meeting with Khandelwal Seth in Ballimaran. They went up many flights of stairs, then into a small office divided into two halves by a Sunmica-topped counter, behind which sat Khandelwal Seth. Above his left shoulder was an alcove for Lakshmi and Ganesh. On the wall behind him hung the picture of an ancestor – perhaps his father – with its garland hanging down to graze the seth's bald head. A fan was mounted on the right wall, aimed at the seth, who was ensconced in a fat leather chair that flowed round his body. He leaned away from them until the chair touched the back wall, then motioned Gopal to one of the two chairs facing him across the counter. Ibrahim made a move to occupy the other, but a cluck from Khandelwal Seth stopped him.

The seth reached out, without taking his eyes off Gopal, and adjusted the fan to point more directly at himself, causing the diamond studs on his kurta to tremble on his chest. For a few moments he was silent, savouring the cool air. When he finally spoke, he was brief.

'Size?'

'A small khokha, sethji. A very small shop.'

'Ground floor? Upper floor?'

'Ground floor,' said Gopal, eagerly.

'Corner?'

Gopal shrugged.

'Bad times,' said the seth.

Gopal looked at Ibrahim. Was this a bad time to buy, or a bad time to sell? From his position at the door, Ibrahim motioned toward the seth, encouraging Gopal to continue. 'How much will it cost, sethji?' asked Gopal, with a sinking heart.

Khandelwal Seth turned down the left corner of his mouth a degree to indicate his displeasure at the question. Gopal was confused. Was it naïve to ask the price? The seth, after expressing his displeasure, ruminated with eyes shut. As a partial answer, he pressed a button on the fan, causing it to swing right and left in a periodic motion. Every fifteen seconds, Gopal's shirt fluttered happily when the fan swung toward him, then left him in a cloak of sweat for the next fifteen.

'Five hundred,' said Khandelwal Seth.

Gopal shot a sidelong glance at Ibrahim, afraid to ask – five hundred what? Crores? Lakhs? Thousands? Could a small shop in Khari Baoli cost five hundred crores? 'That is too much!' he protested weakly, not knowing what was too much.

Khandelwal Seth was offended. 'Five hundred rupees! This is the best rate I have ever quoted. This man has brought you with good introductions, or I would not give it for five hundred to anyone.'

Now Gopal was at a loss – a shop, a full shop, a corner shop, perhaps, for only five hundred rupees?

'Rent is due in advance for one full year,' said Khandelwal Seth. 'Six thousand rupees.'

Rent? thought Gopal. Ah, there was a misunderstanding. 'I mean to buy the shop, sethji, not rent it.'

Khandelwal Seth sighed with avuncular patience and leaned forward. 'What is the difference between buying and renting? You can sell what you want in the shop – spices, table fans, motor-cars, aeroplanes. It is yours. You can come and go as you like.'

'But the registry?'

'The registry is just a piece of paper. No one will ever ask you to leave the shop.'

Gopal considered this, pleasantly surprised at the prospect of renting a shop for a mere five hundred rupees a month. What need had he to buy one? Who knew how many shops in Khari Baoli were actually owned by their owners? And did it matter? Four lakhs would perhaps pay for a lifetime of rent! He dwelled lovingly on the serpents of currency notes sleeping peacefully in the steel trunks, and the decision was made. 'When can I see the shop, sethji?'

'As soon as you pay the pagari.'

Gopal turned to Ibrahim, who grinned. 'Pagari, advance rent,' he explained in sugary tones.

'All right,' said Gopal. 'For how many months?'

'Twelve lakhs,' replied Khandelwal Seth, speaking just as the fan found his diamond studs and set them dancing.

Gopal felt cheated. Why had Ibrahim brought him to this crook of a seth? Why had he not been told about this before he came up the three flights of stairs? 'I do not have twelve lakhs.'

'Then you cannot rent even a box in Khari Baoli,' said Khandelwal Seth.

Gopal fell silent. The seth looked mildly annoyed, but then continued: 'Tell me how much money you have, and I will suggest something for you.'

Gopal looked uncertainly at Ibrahim, who leaned forward in the door, visibly alert, his neck taut with stringy muscles.

'Tell the chaivala downstairs to bring me tea,' Khandelwal Seth commanded Ibrahim.

Gopal sighed in relief. The seth was a wise man. He understood.

'No sugar!' the seth called, as Ibrahim left.

'The pagari is lower in Musalman areas,' said Khandelwal Seth, helpfully.

'I cannot spend any money on pagari!' Gopal pleaded.

'A sale without pagari is possible only for registered deals.'

'Then I want a registered deal.'

Khandelwal Seth regarded Gopal coolly. 'A registered deal is possible only with white money.'

'I have white money!' protested Gopal, wondering what white money was.

'Can you show me a receipt for it?' asked the seth.

Gopal was flummoxed.

'Where did you get it?' demanded the seth. 'A gift? A sale of property? Business profit? Donation? Show me the receipt!'

Gopal was defeated. The fan swung toward him but the rush of air brought him no joy.

The seth leaned forward sympathetically and offered suggestions. 'We can look for something in Dariba, Sadar Bajar, Paharganj or Daryaganj. Those are cheaper areas.'

Gopal shook his head. It had to be Khari Baoli. It had to be 'Kanjilal Moolchand, Sellers of Afghani Figs and Apricots'.

'You can rent a double ceiling,' offered Khandelwal Seth. 'Made of strong plywood. Five feet of vertical space above a godown. You can crawl comfortably. Short customers can walk. The godown stores long peppercorns. No leakage, no insects. You can enter your space without going into the godown because I will place a ladder outside the door. Strong steel ladder, which I will provide free.'

Gopal was silent.

'A box?' asked the seth. 'Seven feet by three, enough space for a stove and one person.'

'I already have a box.'

'But this will be in Khari Baoli. Good business.'

'I can spend three lakhs, at most four,' Gopal whispered.

'A cubicle in Katra Peran, third floor. Fifteen feet by twelve.'

'Facing the road?'

'At the back.'

Gopal sighed. 'All right.'

'Bring the pagari tomorrow. Four lakhs.'

Gopal nodded weakly, aware that his treasury had been depleted and he would have no rent to pay the seth.

'The chaivala has gone home,' said Ibrahim. He was breathless, having run up three flights of stairs.

Gopal rose from his chair and walked out of the office, head lowered in defeat. Ibrahim followed him close behind. 'Did you get something?' he asked eagerly.

'The rent is only one hundred and fifty!' Khandelwal Seth called, as they left.

That night, Gopal returned to the kholi to find that Seth Sushil Jain had drawn a plywood partition round the steel trunks and asafoetida tins, hiding them from the rest of the kholi. There was one door – three feet by two – in the partition, and it was padlocked.

'Ah, you have played a joke on me, Gopal Bhai,' said an offended Ibrahim the next day, when Gopal informed him he could not deliver the pagari to Khandelwal Seth.

'I will get the money soon!' he protested.

Ibrahim let his jaw drop in the manner of the wronged. 'I asked you again and again how much money you had, and you remained silent. You could have told me you had nothing and spared me the embarrassment. Now no one will trust my word. No seth will let me bring clients to him.'

For a few months, Gopal agonised over how to retrieve his treasure from behind the partition. He could perhaps break the lock with a hammer, but how would he explain what would look like a robbery to Sushil Jain? Slowly he realised that Lakshmi did not want him to spend the money right away. It was patrimony for Mukesh, to be kept carefully until his son could use it. And if Lakshmi had given so generously, she could take away with equal abandon. The money would vaporise instantly, he told himself, if he opened the trunks and violated it. Who knew? Perhaps the four lakhs diminished every time his mind dwelled on them. He allowed the money to fade from his mind.

Then, three months ago, under the peepul tree outside Kucha Bansilal, he saw a locksmith demonstrate how a lock could be opened easily with a steel wire, and he knew it was a signal from Lakshmi. Why would she place the locksmith there if she did not think the time was right? So he broke off the wire handle from a tea-strainer, straightened it and applied himself to the task. But the locksmith had lied – the lock would not yield. Once, he thought he heard a click, and he did manage to tilt the wire sideways as he was supposed to, but the lock did not open, and last night he had attacked it with the spoon . . . He has perhaps been too hasty. He should have kept trying with the wire. Three months of careful preparation has been undone in one night. The groove is clearly visible. Hameed will know the lock has been tampered with – should he care to examine it – and Sushil Jain will ask for an explanation. And what if he breaks through the wooden wall only to discover that the trunks are similarly locked? Even if he risked using the spoon again, how many more weeks would he need to cut through two more steel rods? Ah, here he lies, steel wire in hand, rich yet poor for six years, with Hameed hovering suspiciously below the ladder. And now, the pagari for a cubicle in Katra Peran is at least eight lakhs.

It is almost nine o'clock. He will be late at the stall . . . Ah, it can wait! Sohan Lal gives him two rupees for every cup of tea, while behind that partition his bundles of money are coiled like snakes under red binders . . . He looks at the spoon lying on the floor, then sits up resolutely. There is no going back now. He will no longer procrastinate. He will talk to the watchman tonight, perhaps make him a partner. Or he will speak to Hameed, who sometimes opens the partition doors to stack more asafoetida tins, and silence him with ten thousand. Perhaps he will take Ibrahim into his confidence. The lock, no matter how strong, will yield to a hammer. He will not have to explain the robbery to Sushil Jain, because once the money is in his hands, he will leave the kholi and never come back. He will vanish. He is owed that money, considering he has kept his promise to the sardarji – after six years, no one knows of the money, not even Ibrahim. Tomorrow he will walk out of here a rich man.

He crawls through the kholi and descends the ladder. The sudden rush of light momentarily dazzles him. He wears his chappals, collects his dhoti round his waist, caresses his teeth with his tongue and clears his throat. From an alcove above sacks of cinnamon, he pulls out his spectacles and adjusts them on his nose, shaking his head this way and that to find clear spots in the scratched glass surface. He goes down the staircase impatiently, passes Sushil Jain's cubicle, grateful that the seth is not seated at his cash-box, looking into the katra. He rushes along the passage, past sacks of jaggery, simbhauli and agota, past sneezing men and screeching carts, and out into Khari Baoli, where he unlocks his bicycle from the police post and turns into the lane behind the old post office. When Rajiv Gandhi was prime minister, he had the toilets behind it cleaned, and the plaster replaced with white and blue ceramic tiles. The sacks that filled them were flung into the long-abandoned post-office building, which filled up rapidly with mounds of pulses and lumps of turmeric. The toilets were inaugurated under the Sulabh Shauchaalay scheme. The councillor from Chandni Chowk cut a ribbon and allowed the first rickshavala to urinate inside it. The post-office building was boarded up with green plywood for the occasion. For a few months, Gopal squatted uncomfortably on a shiny new ceramic hole, looking down at his naked reflection and marvelling at the power of Rajiv Gandhi. But, gradually, the post office spread into the lane as its plywood boards were stolen. It now functions as a dump for discarded sacks, rotting pulses and insect-laden turmeric. And now that Rajiv is no longer prime minister, the plaster is reclaiming its toilets.

Gopal fills a can at the hand-pump, pulls up his dhoti, walks carefully round the toilet wall to the grass behind it, squats and shits. Then he comes round the post office and walks back to Katra Badami for his bath, trying not to look at the shops he passes. There may never be a Kanjilal Moolchand. Land prices have risen in the last six years. Who knows what four lakhs can buy, these days? He will tell Mukesh about the money the next time he sees him, if he ever sees him again. Perhaps Mukesh can use it some day, when a cup of tea costs four lakhs.

He finishes his bath at the hand-pump and cycles to Dudhiya Gali. A new banner has been tied at the junction of Khari Baoli and Chandni Chowk, where the road passes Fatehpuri Masjid. It is a very large one, spanning the street and fluttering dangerously in the wind. Under it a few young men are beating a drum and chanting, 'Mandal Commission, *murdabad*! V. P. Singh, *murdabad*! Death to V. P.!'

He turns into Chandni Chowk, then swerves left into Dudhiya Gali, where he gets off the bicycle and wends his way through vats of curd and paneer, watching the curd tremble, as he always does when his bicycle hits a vat. Good business, he thinks enviously. One day Banwari will hand over a sprawling shop to his son. He himself should be sitting behind a mound of cardamom . . . At the end of Dudhiya Gali he stands his bicycle against a drum and taps the counter in Banwari's shop.

'You are late,' says Banwari Lal.

Gopal replies mechanically, 'This is an unfortunate day.'

'Every day is unfortunate . . .'

Gopal thinks of the stubborn lock that will not yield, and silently agrees. He watches Banwari's boy clean large cauldrons of curd at the pump, surrounded by a cloud of flies. Banwari opens his refrigerator, withdraws three large polythene packs of milk and slaps them on the counter, where they settle after much shaking and quivering. Gopal touches the packs to ensure they are cold, then bends over to smell them. 'Stale,' he grumbles. 'How old is this?'

'You cannot smell it through the polythene!' retorts Banwari. 'This will last you all day.'

Gopal stuffs the bags into a basket that sits above the rear wheel of his bicycle, then sits down on Ram Bibek's chair near the pump. Ram Bibek runs a rough hand over his balding dome and asks jokingly if he would like a haircut with his shave.

'I am only forty-four!' says Gopal.

Ram Bibek turns Gopal's face upward and lathers his chin.

'It is not age but family that defeats a man. How many children do you have, Gopal Bhai?'

'I have no shop to hand over to my son, so what does it matter?' Gopal replies mournfully.

'I have twelve grandchildren. Sit still, Gopal Bhai, or the razor will cut you.'

'There is a protest in Khari Baoli,' says Gopal. 'Some boys are shouting slogans. What is the Mandal Commission?'

Ram Bibek laughs. 'You are a Brahmin, Gopal Bhai. If I shave you thrice, I will have to shave Banwari for free. One OBC free after three men of other castes!' In his excitement, Ram Bibek nicks the skin with his razor. Gopal screams. 'You are like a little baby!' scolds Ram Bibek. 'You cannot sit still.'

An idea forms in Gopal's head, now dangerously exposed in Ram Bibek's hands. 'Can your razor cut steel?'

'It will cut diamond!' boasts Ram Bibek.

'Can I borrow it?'

Ram Bibek laughs. 'What do you plan to do, Gopal Bhai? Murder a seth?'

'I have lost the key to a lock in my stall,' says Gopal weakly.

'You need a hammer. A razor will not do.'

A hammer is what I need, then, thinks Gopal. By tomorrow the money will be in my hands . . . Then his heart sinks when he recalls that Hameed has brought in many more asafoetida tins over the last few days. They are now stacked five deep on the trunks. How will he move them after he has broken the lock?

'Your ears are dirty,' says Ram Bibek.

'All right,' Gopal acquiesces. 'Clean them.'

Ram Bibek begins to loosen the wax inside Gopal's left ear with a needle. The hammer must wait, Gopal thinks wistfully, until Hameed has removed some tins or he has arranged for two men, who will each want their share . . . Ah, he has waited six years, he can wait a few more days.

Ram Bibek pulls out a gobbet of wax with a plucker. 'Now when the prime minister speaks from Red Fort, you will need no loudspeakers to hear him.'

Gopal runs a hand over the wound on his jaw.

'I have no fitkari today,' says Ram Bibek. 'Banwari will give you some ice.'

He throws a look of challenge at Banwari who indicates, with a shake of the head, that he is not inclined to oblige them.

'And maybe he will also bring out some ice-cream for you!' laughs Ram Bibek.

Banwari turns sullenly and walks to the back of his shop. Ram Bibek and Gopal watch his face glow when he looks into the open refrigerator. Soothing vapours, visible in the yellow glow, bathe his face. From the chair outside, Ram Bibek and Gopal emit a collective '*Aaah*'.

Posters of Gandhi, Nehru and Sardar Patel line the wall, with Mother India, in a map, holding a lamp, shining the light of knowledge on the darkness around her. A poster lists the virtues of honesty, integrity, industry and simplicity in English and Hindi, another names fruit and vegetables, birds and animals, followed by a description of the ideal boy, who wakes up early, prays, reads, eats well, works hard and obeys his parents. 'Hard work bears fruit,' says a plaque in Hindi. 'Union is Strength, Greed is Weakness. Do not give way to flattery. We are the leaders of tomorrow!'

Chitra studies her children while she awaits Suleman. This class-room is meant for the youngest, who are under five, but she has asked everyone to assemble here for his arrival. There are twenty-six, from the youngest unnamed boy of two to Gauhar at sixteen, the eldest boy now that Mussabir has gone. He sits cross-legged in the front, distant. A change has come over him in the last three weeks. He avoids her eye, shuffles past when she approaches him and stays out late every evening, before sneaking furtively into the building. Sheila and Jolly, both fourteen, sit at the front with him, giggling. Their puberty has been delayed by poor nutrition – perhaps they cannot claim their share of daal and roti among the stronger boys at Sparrows. Soon she will have to send them away to Naari Niketan where, according to the letter she has received from the Social Welfare Department, 'unfortunate women can prepare to rejoin society in a safe, friendly environment'. She is to dispatch them as soon as they 'have reached womanhood', says the letter, because the government believes their honour will be safer in Naari Niketan. Chitra knows this to be untrue, but has to comply.

Behind Gauhar, in small groups defined by their position in the Sparrows hierarchy, sit Amin, Robert, Babloo, Suraj, Raju, Sonu, Afroz, Salim, Akram, Hafiz, Shaukat and Nadir. Each is the nucleus of a small cloud of younger children. At the back of the room sits the little Nepali girl brought last night by her mother, while at the front, behind the wooden desk Chitra has recently installed, stands Shalini, schoolmistress-like, in a neatly pressed saree. She is her junior from college. Three months ago she volunteered to help with Sparrows, and Chitra accepted gratefully.

This room is the largest of the three in the red-brick building behind Jama Masjid. It is in disrepair, but much more spacious than the one room in which Sparrows opened six years ago. There is also a central courtyard where the children hold a Parliament-style meeting every week, which Chitra calls 'Baal Sabha', and the hallway is large enough for two steel almirahs, where the accounts of Baal Bank are stored. She owes the building, as she owed the single room, to Suleman Mian's capricious interest in Sparrows. She knows the building is illegal: it encroaches on government land, and extends into a cluster of tarpaulin structures that are also illegal. Like Sparrows, the people who live in them enjoy Suleman's favour, even if it is bestowed in a distant manner. After his initial assistance, he has shied away from Sparrows. He last visited years ago, preferring to deal with Chitra through his men.

Suleman's arrival is signalled by a police siren and a storm of excitement in the lane. Chitra goes outside to greet his Ambassador car, which has stopped at the front door. A flashing beacon denotes importance, as do the two men who spring from the front seat to let Suleman out. He is, however, too quick for them: he opens the rear door, steps out in one smooth movement and stands outside the building, regarding it with opaque eyes. A full twenty seconds pass before he notices Chitra, who stands with her hand extended, a smile pasted on her face.

'*Aadaab*!' he says coldly, shrinking from her.

Misplaced vanity, thinks Chitra, as she follows him inside. Even as he tried to make a point by using the Muslim greeting, his hands folded themselves into a Hindu namaste.

A retinue of three follows Suleman inside: two men in kurta-pyjamas, and a factotum in a dirty lungi, who hovers behind Suleman and grins at Chitra, showing yellow teeth. The factotum rushes ahead when they enter the room, pulls out Chitra's chair from behind the table and prepares it for Suleman with frantic swipes. Suleman ignores it. He faces the class and surveys it with care. The children stare at him curiously, their noisy clamour replaced by hushed animosity.

'I have divided them into three groups,' says Chitra, 'those above ten, those between six and ten, and those under five.' Of course, they are all assembled in this room now.'

Suleman indicates, with a nod, that he has understood what she said.

'They sleep in this room too,' continues Chitra, 'wherever they can find space. When they are not in a class, I encourage them to find work in Chandni Chowk – in restaurants, at tea stalls. They can bring back their money and deposit it in Baal Bank, for which I pay them interest. This protects them from theft, and fosters a spirit of responsibility . . .'

She senses, from Suleman's distant manner, that he is not listening. Chitra fidgets. She should ask him to make a speech, but she never knows exactly where she stands with him. He holds no position in the Corporation or the council. She is not certain where he gets the flashing beacon on his car, or his obsequious handymen, or even the car. How does he make a living? Now he stands, oblivious, chewing, she has just noticed, the remains of a paan. Perhaps his mind is on the next function he must attend in his whirl of social-political activities. She studies the sallow face in profile – a creature, perhaps, of the system she seeks to demolish, yet indispensable for space, money and protection from the police. She feels guilty, reminded of something she read about running with the hare while hunting with the hounds. What does this Philistine, uncouth master of demagoguery know of the grand vision she strives to bring true? Does he have any conception of the liberal world-view that drives her to seek a fair share for every child she sees? Could she ever explain to him the honesty of her purpose? And, should he understand it, can she gain his respect? Why is Chitra Ghosh, graduate of Delhi's most prestigious college, intelligent, articulate, moderately prosperous, student of Shakespeare and Marlowe, protester against beauty pageants, agitator for sexually integrated buses and dormitories, flattering a crooked, paan-chewing upstart?

The thought depresses her momentarily. She searches frantically for a nugget she can use in justification. 'To do a great right, do a little wrong,' said Bassanio to Portia. She is not sure this qualifies, but it will have to do. She will seek a higher authority than Shakespeare after Suleman has gone. For now, she will continue doggedly and disregard his inattention.

'The older children are taught English, mathematics, drawing and basic hygiene. I have asked a girl from my college to teach them knitting and embroidery. And I ask the children to watch the cook, in the hope that they will begin to help her. The food is simple – daal, roti and rice, twice a day, noon and evening.'

Suleman suddenly turns to her. 'Do they not eat anything in the morning?'

She is startled and pleased at his interest. 'It is not in the budget.'

Suleman sinks into the chair behind him. He runs a tongue over betel-nut fragments stuck in his teeth. He knows he is required to make a speech. This is tiresome but necessary. The children must understand who their benefactor is. Most are too young to be useful, but they will grow up. Some are old enough to stick posters and shout slogans. In two weeks, he will need many hands for his rally, and young hands are cheaper and more compliant than older ones.

He turns to Ibrahim, standing attentively behind the chair, and holds out his hand, into which Ibrahim delivers a handkerchief. He wipes the spittle from his mouth and hands back the handkerchief. 'You said you teach them English?' he asks.

Chitra senses his antagonism and responds quickly: everything must be made simple for the monkey. 'Yes. But I also teach them about our culture. Rajputs, Marathas and the Mughals.'

'Mughals,' Suleman says approvingly.

'They play cricket and football. And I am training them in parliamentary democracy.'

Suleman turns an amused eye toward her.

She continues nervously: 'They have constituted a Baal Sabha. They elect their officers and debate their problems in a parliamentary manner – the speaker must give them permission before they can speak. This will develop leadership skills.'

Suleman delivers a chuckle, which is magnified into a laugh in Ibrahim's face. Chitra stops, offended. Suleman holds up a restraining hand and Ibrahim falls silent. 'Do you think these children will go into Parliament?'

'They could,' she says defiantly. 'They bring out their own news-paper. They have their own labour union.'

Suleman sits up very straight. 'How can they have their own labour union? They are children.'

'But they work!'

'There is no child labour in India,' says Suleman mechanically.

Chitra is exasperated with this dogmatic officialese. Where does he think he is? At the United Nations?

Suleman leans forward and lowers his voice. 'Are there many Bangladeshi boys here?'

She nods.

'It is not important to teach them debating,' he says. 'I never went to school, and did not need to. You must prepare them for life.'

'That is not easy,' retorts Chitra in a whisper. 'The police treat them like criminals, shopkeepers cheat them. All I can do is try to save them from drug addiction, sexual exploitation . . .' She turns her back to the children, aware that they are straining to hear her.

'They are too young for all that,' insists Suleman.

'You do not know them. They subject each other to the treatment they receive from adults. The older boys force themselves on the younger girls.'

Suleman turns a cold, official eye on her. 'I did not know you allow criminals into the school.'

'They are not criminals, they are children. I try to educate them about sex.'

'And how do you do that?' asks Suleman, sarcastically. He turns an amused face to Ibrahim, who mirrors him enthusiastically.

Chitra hesitates. She does not think he will understand. She can feel the eyes of the children on her. 'I ask the older children to conduct . . . demonstrations.'

Suddenly Suleman is attentive. Chitra knows her answer must be more explicit for his benefit: 'I have older boys teach the younger ones how to masturbate,' she whispers.

Suleman says nothing, suddenly at a loss for words. Ibrahim busies himself with staring at posters of fruit and flowers. Suleman stands up and studies the assembly before him, transformed into a cesspool of debauchery. Such innocent children, engaged in such an unspeakable act! He is rarely shaken in his interactions with people – and he meets many people every day – but now he is uncertain of his own reaction.

He regards the children with a mixture of horror and awe, irresistibly drawn to them. He walks among them, watching them move aside to make way for him. They sit in disorderly clusters. At the far end, with her back to the wall, sits a Nepali girl, no more than five years old. He lifts her into his arms. She squeals, then falls silent and looks hard at his pencil moustache. He wants to smile, but cannot. In his confusion he turns to Chitra. 'What is her name?'

'Kiran,' answers the girl, looking at him with an inscrutable expression.

He holds her close, running a hand over her smooth, light brown shoulders.

'New girl,' says Chitra. 'About five. Her mother brought her last night, saying she would put her in an orphanage if I did not take her.'

Ibrahim clucks, expressing disapproval.

'The mother works in GB Road,' says Chitra quietly.

'Prostitution is illegal,' observes Suleman. 'What is the mother's name?'

'She did not tell me.'

'You should have asked,' admonishes Suleman.

Kiran begins to cry. Something about Suleman's manner disturbs Chitra. He is an energetic man, and the way little Kiran sits on his hairy forearm . . .

Chitra hastily takes the child from him. 'She is new. She is not used to strangers.'

Suleman walks back to the front, followed by Ibrahim.

Chitra continues to speak breathlessly, hoping to end the meeting on a happy note. 'We have come a long way. We started with one boy and two girls.'

'Where is that one boy?' asks Suleman.

'Mussabir,' she says. 'I have not seen him for weeks.'

'We would like to meet him,' says Ibrahim, with a grin.

'I will tell him if he comes back.'

Suleman is preparing to leave. 'Will you not make a speech?' she asks.

'They are too young,' says Suleman. 'Maybe some other day.'

'Naresh Agrawalji was here,' she says. 'He spoke to the children.'

Ibrahim's face expresses outrage.

'Who invited him?' Suleman is brusque.

'He came uninvited. I cannot turn him away.'

'Yes!' snaps Suleman. 'We all know he is the Member of Parliament for Chandni Chowk. But what has he done for Chandni Chowk in ten years?'

Chitra shrugs. It is not a matter that interests her. Suleman sits down, despondent. He is a weak man, thinks Chitra, easily felled by his own vanity. He is like a balloon, swollen until pricked.

'At least we have the V. P. Singh government,' she says, to placate him. 'Who else would dare implement the Mandal Commission report?'

Suleman's response is an arched eyebrow.

'Look at these children!' she says. 'It will open doors for them.'

'These children are not OBCs,' says Suleman drily. 'Most are Bangladeshi Musalmans.'

She hesitates. She has never mastered the bewildering complexity of 'social justice' policies. Ah, yes, there are Scheduled Castes and Scheduled Tribes for whom the government reserves jobs and college places because, she was told in college, they must be compensated for three millennia of oppression. She was vaguely aware that some girls in college, who looked different from the rest, had come in through 'SC ST reservation'. Now, it appears there is another layer of humans – fully fifty-two per cent of the population – slightly above SCs and STs in the chain of oppression but far below the 'forward castes'. These 'Other Backward Classes' must be compensated too, says the Mandal Commission. No one paid much attention to the report when it was released in 1980 until this government of leftists, Communists and 'secular parties' decided to dust off its pages. Suddenly OBCs have their own 'reservation', and millions of young men and women – doomed by their 'forward caste' status – have no job prospects. Chitra has no opinion on this matter, but wants to steer Suleman into a better mood. 'Some day the government will extend reservations and quotas to Muslims,' she says.

'What makes you think we want that?' he snaps.

She is flustered. 'I thought you supported the reservation policy. Have you not called for a pro-Mandal rally in two weeks?'

He gazes at her contemptuously. When he speaks, he is curiously calm. 'Do you think this Mandal Commission will bring these children jobs, even if there are some OBCs among them? Where do you think they will go when they leave you?'

'To work in restaurants and shops,' says Chitra, weakly.

'That boy, Mussabir. Can you tell me where he is?'

Chitra does not know what to say.

'Do you think he is working in a restaurant?'

She thinks of Mussabir, first citizen of Sparrows along with Jolly and Sheila, the boy she found picking rags in Daryaganj. Has he gone back to where he came from? She turns to the children, who have sat in restive silence for twenty minutes. 'Do you know where Mussabir is?' she asks.

A giggle runs through the assembly. Everyone has something to say about Mussabir. Someone saw him in Ballimaran, someone saw him in Chawri Bajar, someone saw him stealing from a sugar-cane stall.

'I saw him this morning,' says Gauhar.

He is louder than the others, so Chitra hears him.

'I saw him on the steps of Jama Masjid,' lies Gauhar. 'He looks for white women in shorts who try to enter the masjid, and rents them lungis so they can cover their naked legs. Twenty rupees for one lungi.'

The children laugh. Gauhar revels in his triumph, imagining the look of irritation on Mussabir's face when this finds its way back to him. To be renting lungis to foreign women!

'Who is this boy?' asks Suleman, intrigued.

'Gauhar Muhammad,' says Chitra. 'He is the oldest boy at Sparrows now. He became the secretary to Baal Bank when Mussabir left. You must have seen Gauhar before. He has been here almost as long as Mussabir.'

'Come here,' says Suleman, who does not remember the boy.

Gauhar walks up to him, defiant.

'How old are you?'

'Sixteen.'

Suleman considers. The boy is short and thin for his age.

'He earns five rupees in a chai stall every day,' adds Chitra. 'And he deposits it in Baal Bank so he can earn interest.'

Gauhar looks down at his toes. The chai stall is imaginary. He has no other way of explaining to Chitra where he gets the money, most of which he spends before he returns to Sparrows every evening.

'Maybe Gauhar can take my man to Mussabir,' says Suleman.

'Why do you need to see him?'

'To get him a job,' says Suleman. He looks at Gauhar, notes the wrist that ends in a stump, and runs his hand over the matted brown hair. 'And I will get you a job too. A proper job.' He stands up, ready to go.

'Thank you for coming,' says Chitra ingratiatingly. 'I know there is tension in the city with these anti-Mandal student riots.'

Suleman stiffens in mid-stride. 'Those are rich, upper-caste boys!' he says. 'These anti-Mandal demonstrators go around smashing government buildings. Have you seen any poor boys protesting alongside the rich ones?'

Chitra wishes she had not brought up Mandal again. 'It is only a small movement,' she says, in a conciliatory tone.

'A movement of the rich against the poor,' retorts Suleman, and storms out.

The Ambassador roars into life, the beacon flashes, doors are slammed, and he is gone.

The assembly breaks up. The children have sat and fidgeted for almost an hour, intimidated by Suleman, shifting uncomfortably on coir mats. Released, they pour outside boisterously. 'Do not forget to bring back your money and deposit it!' Chitra screams after them. They will collect rags and bottles, run errands, serve as guides at Red Fort. Some will beg, although she has asked them not to, and some will steal, although she lectures daily against it. In the evening they will return, lured by daal, roti and rice, and she will prevail upon them to deposit their earnings in Baal Bank. She is strict about not handing out free meals, hoping to inculcate a sense of responsibility in them. This is not a children's home, she often tells herself, because a home is merely another kind of imprisonment. This is a nest that nurtures them until they can sprout wings and fly away, giving the school its name of Sparrows . . . She arrests this train of thought. What use is her idealism – if it can be called that – when it must use as a crutch the prosaic ambition of a man like Suleman? She is thirty-three. She has reached the age where, according to the laws of her world, a woman must either settle down or settle the matter. In the midst of what she likes to call her work, she has no time to make friendships.

Gauhar watches Didi, who is deep in thought. He knows that Suleman Mian has had this effect on her. He does not care. He must seek out Mussabir and let him know that people are looking for him. Perhaps Mussabir can steer another customer toward him. But he must somehow shake off the man with yellow teeth, who is now approaching him. He knows the type – large, discoloured eyes, ingratiating manner, gentle touch, all in the hope of getting a good rate. The man looks him up and down. 'How old are you, son?'

I am always a son before I am an arsehole, thinks Gauhar.

'Fourteen.'

'But you just said you were sixteen?'

'Why do you ask, then?'

Gauhar presents his profile to the man. Two days ago, a customer was taken with it. But two days ago he had claimed to be fourteen.

'Would you like something to eat?'

Gauhar nods eagerly. None of his customers has been so generous. He allows Yellow Teeth to take him by the hand – he has thrust his stump into his pocket – to a stall behind Jama Masjid, where he buys a bowl of nahari. Gauhar has never tasted anything so good.

'There are thirty-six spices in this,' says Yellow Teeth. 'It takes fifteen hours to cook.'

Gauhar devours the juicy, boneless mutton, and drains the pools of golden marrow. The broth rings his mouth. Three rupees, he thinks. He will take three rupees out of the rate he will give to Yellow Teeth.

'Take me to Mussabir,' says the man.

Why should Mussabir Ustad get a cut for this one? thinks Gauhar. Why should Mussabir even know?

He leads Yellow Teeth round the corner to the paan stall, where he gets the key from the paanvala. He enters the haveli, unlocks the green cupboard under the staircase and ushers the man inside. He tugs at his kurta with easy familiarity, then lowers his trousers and assumes a professional smile.

'Seventy.'

The man's mouth falls open as he stares at Gauhar's penis.

'Sixty-seven!' cries Gauhar. 'Three for your fucking mutton!'

Yellow Teeth appears still, frozen in shock. Gauhar sighs impatiently. Who will now pay two rupees to the fucking paanvala?

'Sixty!' he cries in exasperation, like a reasonable man willing to be talked down.

Yellow Teeth draws back. Gauhar wonders if he should attack him. The window to his left throws some light on his shocked face. He looks thin, dirty, harmless. He is certainly smaller than Mussabir Ustad. There cannot be fewer than a hundred rupees in the wad he took out to pay for the nahari. In a swift motion, Gauhar grabs the man's crotch and pulls it toward him. 'Like it? Fifty-five!'

Yellow Teeth squeals in pain and runs out of the cupboard, hitting the green door and tripping over the steps that lead out of the haveli. He falls flat on his face in the street and is too stunned to get up. Gauhar curses, pulls up his trousers and locks the cupboard. He comes outside, flings the key to the paanvala with a promise to pay later, and stands over the man. 'What do you want?' he asks.

'Take me to Mussabir.'

'I do not know where he is.'

'Suleman Mian asked me to get you a job.'

'Fuck Suleman Mian!'

'Speak respectfully! He is soon going to be the MP for Chandni Chowk.'

'Will he pay seventy rupees?'

Yellow Teeth stands up haughtily and brushes the dust off his kurta. 'Not for this job. Who taught you this?'

'Suleman Mian!' laughs Gauhar. 'Who else can afford to give me seventy?'

'Come with me.'

Gauhar considers. He has tried his hand at many things. He has polished shoes, picked rags and pockets, even pulled carts. Nothing has paid as well as this. And he has it on the authority of Mussabir Ustad himself that the only step up from this is to collect bets at pigeon fights. There is nothing Yellow Teeth could offer that is more rewarding than what he already has. So he puts on the nonchalant look that Mussabir has taught him for when he must bid up his price. 'Where will you take me?' he demands.

'Kucha Bansilal.'

Gauhar looks at him. The man seems harmless. A violent shove would knock him over. He is perhaps a pimp for someone else. 'All right. But we will do nothing until the rate is settled.'

Kartar Singh watches as Sachin Tendulkar hits a cover drive. The umpire signals four runs, and the crowd claps. Kartar Singh shakes his head. India should never play in England, he tells himself. The English do not understand cricket any more – either the playing or the watching. Here is a beautiful cover drive and they clap politely, their manners intact, as in a seminar on the tribals of Orissa, delivered by

one of those tall, unmarried women who work with NGOs. Here is a
cover drive, and this is a talented boy! Why do they not shout and
scream and ask for more? A de-fanged race! But perhaps they do not
want to show their disappointment at impending defeat. Could it be
that this match will see an Indian victory to level the series? Ah, cricket
is not what it used to be. The game has been tamed, shorn of
excitement and reduced to a predictable draw.

A cart rolls into the field for the drinks break, and the match yields
to a Godrej advertisement. Kartar Singh grunts, lowers the volume on
his television, and puts on a headset with a microphone that floats in
front of his face. The room is dark, illuminated only by the flicker of
the screen. The telephone rings.

'Five three,' says the telephone.

'Five three, five three . . .' chants Kartar Singh, into his microphone. It is connected to twenty-six parallel telephone lines that send
the message to twenty-six people, who pass it on to other dibbas and
bookies. Within seconds, the latest odds in the India–England cricket
match go out to three hundred bookies across northern India. Kartar
Singh carefully replaces the telephone in its cradle – after listening for
a dial tone to ensure it is disconnected – then removes his microphone.
He turns to his left and studies a chart on a computer screen. In
luminous green letters, it lists all the rates he has transmitted, the time
of transmission and the likely volume of bets against that rate. He
adds the latest transmission to the chart, typing slowly, one key at a
time. The keyboard is too small for his fingers. It is a marvel, this little
machine. It adds up all the transmissions and rates so he knows almost
to the exact rupee the commission he expects when the match has
ended. The boy who set it up also showed him a combination of keys
that will make the chart vanish instantly, should someone come into
the room. Of course, there is not much to hide in this business, because
he is only a dibba, not a bookie. His function is merely to transmit
rates, not to take bets, and he collects a commission on every
transmission, calculated from the volume of bets against that rate.
A tenth of a per cent is not much, but if it is multiplied by the betting
volume and the number of rates . . . He will let the computer do the
calculation. Ah! He must be the most successful dibba in Delhi.

The room is hot. Because it is right inside the building, far from the
outer walls, it has no windows. His hand has come away damp and
clammy from the telephone. He loosens the upper buttons on his shirt,
opens a bottle of Thums Up, presses it against his cheek and relishes

the soothing touch of cool glass on skin. The break for drinks has finished in England. He raises the television volume. The telephone rings again, but this time it is Ramvilas.

'I have talked to the boy,' says Ramvilas. 'Do you want to meet him?'

'Not now. I am playing the match.'

Ramvilas's chuckle flows down the line. 'How many runs have you scored?'

Kartar Singh is annoyed. Ramvilas knows, or should know, that a dibba cannot quote a rate directly to a punter, but only to other dibbas or bookies. He also knows, or should know, that a dibba who is playing a match does not like to be disturbed, because rates change every ten minutes and his commission depends on quick transmission. 'You can get the rate from the market,' he says evasively.

Ramvilas laughs. 'Bookies do not give good rates.'

'I can send you to a good one,' offers Kartar Singh. 'I have a computer that ranks all bookies by the rates they quote.'

'Ah!' sniggers Ramvilas. 'Rajiv Gandhi's legacy to the game of cricket. A computer!'

'You should ask Lala Surajmal to get one,' says Kartar Singh, happy to change the subject.

'Yes,' says Ramvilas drily. 'Take India into the twenty-first century and all that . . .'

'I can see the boy when they stop for lunch,' says Kartar Singh.

'Should I bring him to the store?'

'Not here. Bring him to Gurudwara Sisganj in an hour.'

Kartar Singh hangs up and turns his attention to the game again, his mood soured by Ramvilas. A small man, he thinks, who places small bets in the market without fully understanding the game. He will not dare bet large amounts, even when the money he stakes is stolen from Lala Surajmal's cash-box – a petty clerk, petty in all his dealings, attitudes, opinions and ambitions. People like him should not be allowed into the committee. He is certainly useful – he can arrange for crowds, audiences, placards, slogans and rallies – but it was he who brought him Bishan. 'Keep the boy,' Ramvilas had said. 'He is only ten but he has lost his parents.' Kartar Singh was a fool to take Ramvilas's word. He had kept the boy, fed him, raised him, trained him to work at the counter – and where was Bishan now? No doubt sitting around with his friends, drinking perhaps, boasting of the leather belts, purses and mixers he stole from his master. The bastard!

He has been careful not to repeat his mistakes with Salim. The boy came from a school run by an NGO near Jama Masjid. 'It is called Sparrows,' says Salim, 'an English name for a bird.' Be that as it may, he has checked on the boy thoroughly. He sent enquiries to the woman who runs the school, he once followed Salim home to cross-check his story, and he has installed a camera over the counter – unbeknownst to Salim – which shows him what is going on in the store even as he sits in the back room. He has told Salim about the back room, of course, and the white door that is to be used at all times. But Salim knows little else. Buying and selling of purses, belts, electric fans, cooking sets, cups and plates, mixers, soft drinks – this is all the boy is privy to. And he thinks it is the store that has bought Kartar Singh's Maruti car and the new furniture in his Trilokpuri flat. The less he knows, the less harm he can do.

Kartar Singh switches on the closed-circuit camera: Salim is sitting primly behind the counter. He presses a button on the intercom. 'Bring me another Thums Up,' he says. 'And a new Rolex wristwatch.'

He watches Salim spring up and open the refrigerator, then switches off the camera and turns to the game. Tendulkar is out, and the match is heading for a draw. The telephone rings. 'The rate is five four,' says the voice.

'Five four, five four,' repeats Kartar Singh, into his microphone. He does not like this team – Azharuddin, Shastri, Tendulkar and Kapil. They are incapable of winning Test matches. True, they have won one-day matches, but they will lose the Test series. What is the point of playing for five days and have the match end in a draw? All bets are placed on a victory or a loss, so a draw leaves everyone unhappy because no one bets on it. Yet a rate of five four is only one point away from a rate that predicts a draw. Seven days before the match began, he received a rate of four to one in favour of India, because no one wanted to bet on Graham Gooch. The English team with a captain whose name begins with G can never win in the month of August. But a team whose captain's name begins with an A – which is the case for India – can win only even-numbered matches, and this is the third. It has caused much confusion in the rates. He received varying and uncertain quotes for seven days and at five four the rate has now settled on its final plateau of uncertainty.

He watches the match carefully. The fall of one more wicket will almost certainly move the rate to five five, making the match even. He should perhaps place a small amount of money on that guess. He knows most of the bookies in Chandni Chowk. They will not refuse to take a bet from him even if the amount is small. He picks up the telephone and begins to dial, but natural prudence stops him. The rate may widen to five three again. He slams down the receiver resolutely. He will be a dibba, nothing more. A dibba's work is done when he has passed on rates to other dibbas and bookies. It is a good business, as long as he does not succumb and become a punter. Punters have to put their capital at risk, and they have to reveal their identity to bookies. He need never meet any of the twenty-six people connected to his phone line. No one will ever track anything back to him. Let the police harass punters and bookies, and leave the dibbas alone! This is a risky business, much more so than havala . . . He turns to the television again, feeling secure in his abstinence.

Salim brings the Thums Up through the white door in the back. 'The Rolex?'

The boy withdraws a piece of cardboard from his pocket. A clear plastic case is stuck to it, with a wristwatch set inside it. Kartar Singh turns it over in his hand – imitation gold with a cheap polish that will soon wear off, and garish dials that move on an off-white face imprinted with the word 'Rolex'. The market for brand-name watches is lucrative. There are many stores in Lajpatrai Market whose inner rooms double as factories, churning out foreign-label watches, and Kartar Singh's shelves are stacked with them.

After Salim leaves, Kartar Singh tears off the plastic packaging and slips the watch on to his left wrist. Then he studies the cricket match for another hour until the players break for lunch, when he switches off the television, checks the UPS battery – to ensure his computer will not switch off if there is a power cut – and steps out of the room. He comes round the building into the store, tells Salim he will back in an hour, and strolls into Lajpatrai Market.

He walks with a practised limp that minimises the pain in his left knee. It is a constant reminder of the ward in Faridabad and the untrained orthopaedic surgeon who set his leg six years ago. Now he walks less than he used to because of the pain, and his body, never thin, has responded by adding girth to his trunk.

Nods comes his way from many stores. As a nominated councillor for Chandni Chowk, he has limited executive powers, but he maintains good relations with shopkeepers in Lajpatrai Market. He has helped them expand their stores, build urinals and rebuild shops that were gutted six years ago. His own store still bears scars from those days. The signboard is charred – a cover of soot partially obscures 'Jasjit General Store, Meraa Bharat Mahaan'. He decided not to do anything about it even as he organised funds for other shops: it hides the name he does not want disinterred. He has also discovered that it gives him a strange power over all visitors – customers, committee members and councillors. They walk into the store humbled, cowed by his injuries.

His scooter is parked in a small car park beyond the market. For its construction, he had to marshal the support of Naresh Agrawal, Member of Parliament. A councillor's writ extends only so far, but an MP is omnipotent, especially one who has represented Chandni Chowk for ten years. People had found the association odd – an IPP councillor in league with a Congress MP – but he was not a man to scoff at compromise. The car park is set against a backdrop of shops and stalls, squeezed in the middle against all protest. It had helped, when he selected the spot, that his legs could not carry him far. 'Where will a man like me park his scooter?' he had asked the shopkeepers. 'Would you have me walk all the way from Red Fort so that the rest of my leg can fall off?' The shopkeepers, united in their right to encroach on public lands, were disarmed by this cruelty to a limping councillor. Of course, he cannot compete in patronage with Naresh Agrawal, but he has a limp and a charred signboard – wounds that even a Member of Parliament would covet.

The pain is never absent when he walks. If he had not fallen off the train, he might have come away with a few scratches – but he might also have been impaled like the captain. He remembers waking up in the dark, lying in a heap of limbs. He pushed against the flesh wedged round him and realised that nothing moved, nothing breathed. He was lying among corpses drenched in a horrid chemical. His first thought was that he was dead, newly arrived in a heaven that was curiously full of prone sardars. He felt no pain. His limbs lay comfortably on the ground, immovable, uncontrollable, almost as if they did not belong to his body. Slowly, he began to distinguish other bodies around him – all sardars, all dead, in a dark, foul-smelling, windowless room. Was this what they called a morgue? Then he heard a door open. A shaft of light shot into the room and a shadow fell across the heap. He knew he must do something. His limbs did not respond. He collected all his strength into his buttocks and heaved himself into a sitting position, causing an avalanche of corpses, just in time to see a nurse hold her hand over her mouth, utter a cry and run out of the room.

'Rest it as much as you can,' said the orthopaedic surgeon in Faridabad who set his fracture and encased it in plaster. The nurse refused to come near him. She had been frightened out of her wits to see a formaldehyde-drenched sardar rising from the dead. The surgeon was less excitable but he bungled the setting – the fool! – leaving him with a twist in his leg that would keep alive the pain in his knee for ever.

He came back to Delhi two days later, his leg in a cast, to find Sukhbir immersed in her gutkas. He had spent the days trying to get news of her, begging the hospital staff to find him a telephone that worked. He limped around the hospital, watching and counting corpses, afraid to step out yet anxious to go back to Delhi. When he finally spoke to Sukhbir on the telephone, she told him all was well.

The next day, when he walked into his flat in Trilokpuri, everything did look normal. She sat on a coir mat on the floor, reading her gutkas. 'You look like you are already dead,' she had told him, half in horror and half in jest. That was the first occasion he had to look at himself in a mirror – blood-soaked strands of flowing hair, dark welts on his chest where iron rods had torn the skin and tattered clothes. 'I have come back for a second life,' he said.

'The guru has saved your life,' she murmured.

'They have looted the store,' he told her.

'No matter, we will build a new one,' she said. And it was then, only then, that she told him about Jasjit.

'Why did you not tell me on the telephone?' he asked, crying.

'I wanted you to come back safely,' she said. He sat still for a long time as she told him her never-ending story. His eyes were dry when she finished, his tears defeated by his loss.

A strange madness came over him. There was Sukhbir, so clean and calm, sitting behind her gutkas as if nothing had happened. Did she blame him for having run away to Faridabad? Should he put his arms round her and beg for forgiveness? Should he beat his chest, tear his clothes, let his flowing hair strangle him and put an end to everything? 'I am going to Chandni Chowk,' he declared.

'Your leg is in a cast!'

'I will tilt the scooter to the right.'

'How can you go anywhere at a time like this?' she pleaded.

'How can I stay?' he asked.

'You are not in a state to go anywhere!' she protested.

'I have fought a hundred rioters in this state,' he told her. 'What is a trip to tame Chandni Chowk?'

'It is dangerous.'

He turned calmly toward her. 'What could they possibly take from me now?'

'It is midnight!'

'Then I will be invisible,' he said.

He rode the scooter through deserted streets, letting the cool breeze catch his hair. He was now even more set on telephoning his relatives in Canada. Ah, he would swallow his pride and ask them to sponsor him, no matter how long it took and how much it cost. There was nothing to keep him in this inhuman country. All he needed was ready money, and he knew where it was.

Chandni Chowk was quiet and peaceful with the soft snoring of beggars. The only sound that tore through the night was that of his scooter, on which he sat awkwardly, his left leg extended in its cast. Fortunately, the brake pedal was at his right foot. He rode all the way into Kucha Bansilal and stopped outside the chaivala's stall. He sat down on the wooden chest and opened the electrical junction box with trembling hands – and knew, even before his eyes had fully adjusted to the dim light, that the money was gone.

It was late the next morning when he limped into the store. The front had been burned down, along with the counter. One wall had collapsed, bringing down the adjacent shop with it. They had taken away all fans, mixers and purses. They had not bothered with the tins of Bournvita and Horlicks, which rolled over the floor when he kicked them in passing. The Bournvita shelf had been wrenched off the wall. Behind it, the red door hung by one hinge, shredded. He walked into the back room. The linoleum was clean, although the mattress smelled of urine and the sheet was bunched up in a corner. All telephone lines had been yanked out, and the walls defaced with scrawls in chalk. Khalistan *murdabad*! Indira Gandhi *zindabad*!

The fluorescent tube had exploded, but a bulb still hung mournfully from the ceiling, casting an ochre glow. In the centre of the floor, with his body balanced on a stool, his hand resting on a walking-stick, and one foot firmly planted on the urine-soiled mattress, sat Sohan Lal.

'God has saved you, Kartar Singhji,' said Sohan Lal. 'I received word of your well-being two days ago.'

He has been sitting here for two days! thought Kartar Singh, terrified. How had Sohan Lal's vision penetrated a morgue in the hospital at Faridabad to check the pulse of a dying sardar?

'I must be getting old,' said Sohan Lal. 'I gave the wrong code to Ranjan in New York. Operation Bluestar! Was that not it?'

Kartar Singh leaned heavily on his monstrous leg, plastered from foot to thigh, and sighed, indicating with a shake of his head that he had not completed the transaction. He saw Sohan Lal's face fall, then recover as his eyes came to rest on the steel safe, battered, bruised but whole. The seth heaved his bulk up from the stool, walked across the mattress, without removing his shoes, and gave the safe two affectionate raps with his stick. The sound echoed in Kartar Singh's broken heart.

'Godrej!' beamed Sohan Lal. 'You can always trust it. Even on the day they kill Indira.'

Kartar Singh had sunk to his feet and burst out crying. He was not sure what troubled him most at that moment – the body of Sukhbir Kaur stuck like a fish in her bathroom window, the corpse of Jasjit Singh transfixed by an axe, the treachery of Bishan, the looting of his store, the cast on his leg, the bruises on his chest, the impaled captain squatting over a train shit-hole, or the loss of Sohan Lal's money. He cried for Sukhbir, Jasjit, Sohan Lal, Indira, the guards who killed her, the Sikhs killed in return . . . He was not sure whom he cried for, but he cried like a child.

Sohan Lal stepped back in horror. 'Get up, Kartar Singhji!' the seth said sternly. 'You are not yourself! You have been through a horrifying experience. I will come back later.'

Kartar Singh stayed on the ground, crouching on his right leg, left leg stuck out awkwardly in its rigid cast. The seth did not know this, but Kartar Singh had no way of getting to his feet. He wondered, momentarily, if he should tell the seth about the electrical junction box and put the blame on the chaivala, but decided against it. He would have to investigate before he revealed anything. Perhaps the money was safe, after all.

'What is the name of the chaivala outside your shop?' Kartar Singh sobbed.

Sohan Lal appeared annoyed. 'Gopal Pandey. Why?'

'He is a good man,' said Kartar Singh, clutching at straws.

Sohan Lal had frowned. 'Your mind is unsettled, Kartar Singhji. Go home and rest. You can give me the money tomorrow.'

With a last possessive look at the safe, the seth walked out through the white door, leaving as he always did, pretending not to notice the gaping hole where the red door had been, even though that would take him straight through the store into the street. The strength of a Godrej safe has ruined me, thought Kartar Singh. Had they broken the safe – it contained no more than five thousand rupees – he could have claimed the money had been stolen by the rioters.

Two days later, he mustered the strength to go to Kucha Bansilal. He went late in the morning, hoping Sohan Lal would be busy with his puja. The chaivala seemed agitated to see him, raising hopes in his breast that he had the money. The man offered him tea, and gasped on hearing about Jasjit – a kind man, after all. He swore he had delivered the message to Sukhbir in Trilokpuri. That nearly moved Kartar Singh to tears – of what use had it been to poor Jasjit? He wondered how he could bring up the matter of the money, and asked about the junction box. The chaivala mentioned the Corporation and Kartar Singh left it at that – saying something about a glass of tea – but the man was definitely trying to hide something. Shameless bastard! To be harping on his bus fare when a life was at stake! Hopefully, the twenty rupees he gave him would ensure that the fool did not talk to Sohan Lal about that evening.

For many months, Kartar Singh observed the chaivala for signs of increased expenses, but there were no new clothes, no shining scooter, no Maruti car, no repairs to the stall. Kartar Singh spent many hours reasoning with Sohan Lal, seated on the seth's mattress with the doors closed, invoking the wrath of Lakshmi and Vishnu upon his head if his words were not true. But the seth, who kept his figurines polished and dressed, lent no credence to an oath sworn upon their heads. He would shake his head, open the door an inch and scream, 'Nanak Chand! Chai!' then go back to brooding silence, awaiting the chai that never seemed to arrive. Finally, in an effort to patch their relations and salvage his business, Kartar Singh offered fifty thousand rupees as compensation. 'From my own pocket, sethji! It is a small amount, insufficient to make good your loss, but it is my gift to you.'

'I do not want your gifts,' Sohan Lal replied coldly. 'And I do not want your goodwill. I want my money, as you want my trust.'

That trust had vanished as surely as the money. Sohan Lal never forgave him, and never quite believed his version – that the money had been taken by Bishan and his accomplices. Sohan Lal was not discreet in his denunciation. Every seth in Chandni Chowk soon heard the tale of those five lakhs. Everyone heard the heartrending account of how

Sohan Lal telephoned his nephew in New York, how the nephew went to a grocery store and whispered, 'Operation Bluestar,' how he was refused the money, then thrown out when he insisted he had the right code. The other half of the story – the sacking of Jasjit General Store – was soon buried in the retelling. It had become, thinks Kartar Singh bitterly, a mere business setback in the greater tale of his treachery. A havala trader's greatest asset, his inventory and his capital, is trust, so the havala business dried up abruptly after Sohan Lal's calumny found its way into the kuchas and katras of Chandni Chowk. Traders from other markets, such as Naya Bajar and Paharganj, still come to Kartar Singh with small amounts meant for the Gulf countries. Someone there once sent money for his father's heart surgery in Bombay, and Kartar Singh ensured that the money reached the old man before the son himself flew in from the Gulf. Someone sent pocket money to his child studying in London. Someone transferred hard-earned wages from Dubai to India at the real exchange rates, which are one and a half times the official ones. But those were small amounts, sent by middle-class minnows. The big seths who park large sums abroad have stopped coming. He no longer gets hefty dollar deals involving America.

Kartar Singh regards this ostracisation as unfair. He had been fighting for his life! He should not be held responsible for acts of God and the Congress Party! And what is the chance that he will botch another transaction? How many times can Indira Gandhi get killed?

Sohan Lal still favours Kartar Singh with a greeting when they meet in IPP committee meetings – it is impossible to avoid each other there – but the old warmth is gone. Well, Kartar Singh is accustomed to hostility and indifference. He has no doubt that some of it stems from jealousy, because the IPP committee nominated him – not Sohan Lal, or even Jugal Kishor Agrawal – as councillor for the Chandni Chowk area soon after the 'eighty-four riots.

It is almost six, the time of day when the fading sun co-exists with newly illuminated lamps. Kartar Singh straddles the scooter and rides out of Lajpatrai Market, his mind still on the cricket lunch hour in England – four and a half hours behind. He has learned to apply pressure with his toe when using the left leg for support, thus sparing the heel, which would transmit pain to his knee. He arrives at Gurudwara Sisganj, parks the scooter on the footpath, then jostles with the crowd vying to wash the marble steps. He sinks to his knees – gently, because he must bend the left leg with care – and wets his fingers in the river of water that gurgles down the staircase. Then he cups his hands, scoops up the water and sprinkles it on the front wheel, like a devout sardar bestowing the blessings of Guru Tegh Bahadur on his scooter. He continues to do this, taking care not to dirty the seat, until he hears Ramvilas.

'Careful, sardarji!' says Ramvilas. 'You appear too excited. Is the match going well?'

Kartar Singh ignores the gibe and studies the boy who stands behind Ramvilas – young, very young, about twenty, tall for his age but thin and unmanly, showing sparse chest hairs through the open buttons of his shirt. It is bright yellow, offset by mud-coloured trousers that are too loose for the thin body. The boy looks hideous, but that is probably the fashion these days, thinks Kartar Singh. He has probably received the shirt from Ramvilas or a similar benefactor. He looks oddly out of place in the crowd of sardars, whose frantic washing of the marble staircase seems to knock him about here and there.

Ramvilas stands still amid the chaos, dressed in a spotless white, neatly pressed kurta-pyjama. 'I have brought him,' he says. He puts an arm round the boy, who shifts uncomfortably in acknowledgement.

Kartar Singh happens to glance down at his feet. 'He is wearing shoes!'

The boy looks askance at Ramvilas, who reassures him with a squeeze of the thin shoulders. 'That is all right. No one will chase him away.'

'You cannot wear shoes on the steps of Sisganj!' protests Kartar Singh.

'We are not here to discuss the Khalsa,' says Ramvilas.

Kartar Singh shakes his head. A few people have turned to look at them. He sprinkles more water on the scooter, and lets some roll down his face. 'What is your name?' he asks.

'Mukesh,' replies Ramvilas.

'Mukesh Pandey,' says the boy.

Kartar Singh nods. It is a reassuring name – Brahmin, therefore naturally opposed to the Mandal Commission and its quota recommendation for OBCs. But he is only a boy – the face of a child not yet a full man, the first growth of a moustache, the first thickening of the voice, a hesitant Adam's apple, a bony chest, sallow cheeks, thin arms not yet swollen with biceps, all wrapped inside the fearful eyes of a motherless boy.

'He used to work for Seth Jhunjhunwala,' whispers Ramvilas.

'Does Jhunjhunwala know?' asks Kartar Singh.

'The seth threw him out years ago.'

'A thief!' gasps Kartar Singh.

'Who else could I get for such a job?'

'All right,' says Kartar Singh.

'I have asked around,' Ramvilas says, under his breath. 'He is one of Rajan Nahal's best men.'

Kartar Singh shudders. He has always believed Rajan Nahal had had something to do with the men who broke into his store in 'eighty-four. Here stands the boy, too young to be a man. He could not have been more than fifteen then. Who knows what secrets his inscrutable eyes hide? Does he know of sardars with scars on their chests, axes in their bodies, blood in their hair? 'When a big tree falls, the earth shakes,' said Rajiv Gandhi, after Indira's death. Was this boy, now standing harmlessly among sardars washing the steps of Gurudwara Sisganj, one of those who moved the earth for Rajiv?

'We cannot use someone who works for Rajan Nahal,' says Kartar Singh stubbornly.

Ramvilas smiles and leans closer to him, so the boy will not overhear. 'He is flexible in his political views.'

Kartar Singh shakes his head insistently and turns to the boy. 'Where is your father?'

The boy looks away vaguely, which could mean he will not tell, or his father is dead, or he does not know who his father is.

'Do you live in Chandni Chowk?'

The boy nods.

'Do you go to any school? Any college?'

'No.'

'Where are your brothers and sisters?'

'No one,' says the boy, cryptically.

What a delicious fruit, thinks Kartar Singh, whose plucking will cause no tree to mourn! The ideal man for a job so delicate they only discussed it indirectly at the committee meeting. No one in the IPP will ever refer to it explicitly, and no one but Ramvilas will ever get his hands dirty. But the boy must be given the context, so he will not waver when tested.

'Our country is passing through a difficult phase,' says Kartar Singh with a serious tone. 'You know what V. P. Singh is trying to do. He will destroy our society just to remain prime minister. One day, every job in every government office will be reserved for OBCs, SCs, STs

. . . I have no objection to that! I say, give them jobs, give them security, give them every opportunity they deserve, but do it on the basis of merit. Aren't there upper-caste boys who are poor and deserving? Look at you! Don't you deserve admission to a good college? Shouldn't you get a job so you can make something of yourself? But no, says V. P. Singh. Mukesh Pandey must sleep on the pavements in Chandni Chowk because he is a Brahmin!'

The boy nods uncertainly. Kartar Singh pulls him closer. 'Would you like to be cut up by an OBC doctor who got his medical degree because of Mandal Commission reservations? Or sit in an aeroplane flown by a backward-caste pilot?'

The boy's face lights up, losing its manly façade. 'I have never been in an aeroplane!'

Kartar Singh instantly regrets the remark. 'Aeroplanes are dangerous,' he mutters. 'We need to concentrate on defeating V. P. Singh. But he is prime minister, so we have to make sacrifices.'

Ramvilas kneels and lays his head on the marble steps, eyes closed in devotion. Then he walks to Kartar Singh's left and kneels again, repeating the gesture. This brings him to the other side of Kartar Singh, away from the boy. 'You don't need to give him a lecture,' he says.

'All right, it is settled.' Kartar Singh puts a tentative arm round Mukesh's scrawny shoulders. 'Ramvilasji will tell you what to do. The rally is in two weeks.'

'Ten thousand,' says Mukesh.

Kartar Singh looks at Ramvilas quizzically. He had hoped to inspire a germ of idealism in the boy. Ramvilas shrugs. 'This is not a job, it is a mission,' says Kartar Singh sententiously.

Mukesh wonders if he has overstepped the mark. 'Ask for a large amount,' Ramvilasji had said. 'If you ask for five rupees you will get three. The more you ask for, the more important you will be to everyone.' Also, the sardarji looks prosperous. He leans awkwardly on his left leg, and his shirt – open at the neck – reveals hideous welts on his hairy chest. But no man who is so rotund can be poor. Sardars are never poor, no matter how decrepit they look. He does not much care for sardars. 'They are traitors,' says Rajan Nahal. He has lost count of the number of sardars he beat senseless in 'eighty-four. Perhaps this one is a good man, considering he wants to pay good money, but all sardars look alike under their turbans. Ah, he will stand his ground – ten thousand, not a rupee less. 'Ten thousand,' he repeats. He looks at Ramvilas out of the corner of his eye, but Ramvilas does not respond.

'I am not asking you to do this for me,' Kartar Singh declares. 'Do it for your country.'

Mukesh does not budge.

'Do it for India!' says Kartar Singh, in a last appeal.

'Seven thousand,' says Mukesh, reluctantly.

'Five,' counters Kartar Singh.

Mukesh again seeks out Ramvilas, but Ramvilas looks away. 'All right,' he says.

'They will sing songs about you!' exclaims Kartar Singh.

'It is settled, then,' says Ramvilas.

'Wait!' Kartar Singh slips off his wristwatch, takes Mukesh's hand and slides it over the thin wrist. The metal strap is too large and the watch hangs loosely. Mukesh looks at it, wide-eyed. 'You are almost like my son,' says Kartar Singh. 'This is not a payment, it is a gift.'

'You can go now,' says Ramvilas. 'The rally is in two weeks. I will come for you.'

Mukesh turns to leave. Suddenly Kartar Singh feels sorry for him, for the manner in which the yellow shirt disappears furtively into mud-coloured trousers at the thin waist. He pulls the boy close and embraces him, shocked at how skinny the frame is, and is reminded of Jasjit. This is how old Jasjit was when he last saw him six years ago. 'I am going to Vishaal cinema,' he had said in the store. He was as shy, as skinny, as uncertainly poised on the cusp of manhood.

Mukesh shakes himself free.

'Sardarji has given you a watch,' says Ramvilas, with a twinkle in his eye. 'When I come for you, I will give you much better gifts!'

'Do not waste money on him,' says Kartar Singh, after Mukesh has gone. 'The committee cannot afford it. We cannot show this in the budget.'

'Some gifts are not monetary,' Ramvilas says. 'You need to give me five thousand for the boy.'

'What is the hurry? You need it in two weeks.'

'He should have an advance,' says Ramvilas.

'I do not carry such large sums in my pocket,' says Kartar Singh sourly.

'Your scooter has been sanctified, sardarji,' says Ramvilas. 'Let us go to the store, where you can give me the money.'

They go back to Lajpatrai Market with Ramvilas riding on the pillion, and enter along the back corridor, thus avoiding Salim. Ramvilas takes off his chappals with great care, deposits himself on the mattress, rubs the soles of his feet together, then sits cross-legged. In his spotless kurta-pyjama, he looks like a natural extension of the white mattress. Such cleanliness hides such dirt, thinks Kartar Singh, contemptuously.

'It is hot,' says Ramvilas. 'A Thums Up?'

'I do not like Salim coming into the back room,' lies Kartar Singh.

'All right, let us settle the money.'

'I do not trust the boy,' says Kartar Singh, hoping to delay the handover.

'I know what I am doing!' retorts Ramvilas, sharply.

Kartar Singh sighs, crawls over the mattress to the battered steel safe, opens it, withdraws a bundle of fifty-rupee notes and slaps it down on the mattress. The safe whines when opened and shut. Ramvilas looks amused. 'Godrej,' he says. 'Lasts a lifetime! But it seems you have practised cricket batting on it, sardarji.'

Kartar Singh does not reply. He points to the money, wondering why Ramvilas will not pick it up. Ramvilas looks at him meaningfully and smiles. 'It is five thousand,' insists Kartar Singh.

'For the boy,' says Ramvilas smugly.

Kartar Singh tries to prolong the moment of incomprehension but he knows what Ramvilas means, and that Ramvilas knows he does. He sighs, opens the safe again and withdraws a thousand rupees.

'A thousand?' asks Ramvilas. 'That is only twenty per cent of what the boy will get.'

'The boy has courage,' says Kartar Singh, coldly.

'Sohan Lalji said two thousand,' says Ramvilas.

'For two boys! You brought one.'

Ramvilas's smooth face dissolves into an easy grin. 'What is money, sardarji? It is the dirt on your palms. It comes and goes, is washed off when you take a bath.'

Kartar Singh clucks at this philosophical diversion. It is not a good idea to give Ramvilas so much authority in the committee. Surely there are others who can arrange for boys. You cannot trust a man who looks so much like a thief, a bookie, a punter, a crook . . . He pulls out another thousand in ten hundred-rupee notes and places them on the mattress. Ramvilas pockets the money. Kartar Singh wonders how much of the five thousand will find its way to the boy. 'All right, you can tell Sohan Lalji it is settled,' he says.

Now that the transaction is complete he wants Ramvilas gone, because lunch will have ended in England. Rates often change after lunch, so he must be at his station, transmitting them as soon as they are relayed to him.

But Ramvilas makes no attempt to get up. 'Do you have a pocket mirror in your store?' he asks.

Kartar Singh is annoyed. He does not like giving free gifts from his inventory.

'The new type!' says Ramvilas, with inexplicable excitement. 'The one that can swivel on a stand.'

'For your wife?' asks Kartar Singh.

Ramvilas nods.

'You can choose one from the store. Salim will help you.'

'I will be in your debt,' says Ramvilas. 'That mirror is worth another thousand to me. I also need a VCR.'

Kartar Singh gets impatient. 'I have to watch the cricket match,' he says. 'Lunch is over.'

'How much does a VCR cost?' insists Ramvilas.

'It depends on the model.'

'Can you get me a second-hand one?'

'In a week,' says Kartar Singh drily.

'All right. I will remind you.'

Ramvilas stands up, slips his feet into his chappals and runs his hands down his kurta to remove wrinkles from it. 'You can watch your cricket now,' he says. 'Now that V. P. Singh is PM, there will be reservations for backward-caste punters. Their bets will get better rates.'

Kartar Singh ignores the joke. 'Will you tell Sohan Lalji it is fixed up?'

'Later,' says Ramvilas. 'First I must go back to Bhagwan Das and Sons. Lala Surajmal has asked me to pack some attar bottles for Sohan Lalji.'

'Why would Sohan Lalji want them packed?'

'They are for his son-in-law.'

'I hear the wedding will be expensive,' says Kartar Singh.

'Sohan Lalji is rich.' Ramvilas sniggers. 'He can afford the finest attars.'

'I will meet Sohan Lalji today,' says Kartar Singh. 'I will tell him the boy has been fixed up.'

'He may not pay attention,' warns Ramvilas, scornfully. 'Sethji is busy supervising the wedding.'

'I will tell him all payments have been made,' says Kartar Singh. 'Will you need more money for your gift to the boy?'

'That gift will be free, but he will get it in two weeks, not now.'

'What is it?'

Ramvilas has a look of amusement on his face. 'Something he will remember!' He smoothes down his kurta once more, pulls open the white door and leaves the room.

That man is a natural thief, thinks Kartar Singh, as he turns back to the television. The telephone rings. The rate is now five five. Kartar Singh transmits it mechanically, suppressing his bitterness at the lost opportunity. Had he placed his bet at five four . . . The next time, he tells himself, he will listen to his instinct and trust his money to it.

A giant electronic signboard spans the façade of Jugal Kishor Agrawal's shop. 'Mangat Ram Nawal Kishor,' it says. 'Two centuries of sweet success.' No one has been rigorous in counting the years, thinks Sohan Lal, sourly, as he enters the shop. The floor is elevated. A ledge runs along the front, ending in an arch of glass-fronted cupboards that display the sweets Jugal Kishor is so proud of. There are six flavours of halva, eight different barfis made of cashew, a dozen varieties of gulabjamun and mohan bhog and unending rows of rasmalai bowls, each with a pinch of saffron floating lazily on its creamy surface. Sohan Lal strides deep into the shop, ignoring the nods of Jugal Kishor's clerks, and goes through a door into the backyard, where three cauldrons are set to boil on coal-fired furnaces. A dozen men scurry about to obey the commands of a halvai, who squats on a bench and peers into a cauldron, watching sugar caramelise on the surface and give a dark red colour to the gravy. Far away from the cauldrons, in the shade of a thatched awning, Jugal Kishor sits with a cup of chai, supervising.

'Those are ready,' says Jugal Kishor, on seeing Sohan Lal.

He points to a pyramid of kachauris lying on a mat of newspapers to drain excess oil. It gives off the fragrance of fresh desi ghee, and

Sohan Lal's stomach churns for a bite. 'Have they come out fine?' he asks.

'A little too salty,' says Jugal Kishor. 'But they will be all right. It is a wedding, after all. Better to overdo it than have people say Sohan Lal has skimped on salt.'

Sohan Lal nods. He wants to taste the kachauris. He takes a step toward the heap, then stops on meeting Jugal Kishor's eye. What is the big deal? Why is it bad form for the bride's father to enjoy his daughter's wedding?

'Your diabetes, sethji,' says Jugal Kishor, tactfully.

Sohan Lal sighs and sits down on the bench next to Jugal Kishor. His body aches from three days of sleepless activity. There is so much to be done for a wedding, even after you have contracted out everything, from food and decorations to the brass band and tents. He would have preferred not to spend so much, but his hands are tied by the unspoken rule that the second daughter must receive a send-off no cheaper than that of the first. He was foolish enough to go overboard with the first wedding. At the time, it had seemed the right thing to do. Vimla was going to a wealthy home whose pedigree outshone hers. He had not wanted to appear niggardly to her in-laws, or for her to face taunts when she entered her husband's house. He had had a replica of Taj Mahal constructed for the wedding: everyone commented on the faithfulness of the tent, which was made of cloth and bamboo, to the marble monstrosity. He himself has never cared for Musalman mausoleums. Most guests pronounced the copy to be superior to the original. He remembers looking at the Taj and marvelling at his success. What was money, if not the dirt off one's palm? It came and went as it willed, and the wise used it when they could. He had stood before the grand Taj and gently pulled Vimla away from her mother so that her new husband could escort her to his Maruti car. She sobbed uncontrollably, which reaffirmed to him that he had fulfilled his duty. He had sent her away with a trousseau even Lala Surajmal would envy, and he could go back to his shop the next day and repair the loss with a contented heart.

He knew then, four years ago, that he had found a good match for Vimla. His belief was borne out by the grandson she gave him soon after. The boy is only three, but he can already recite the entire English alphabet. And now Sohan Lal has received word that Vimla is pregnant again. He has no doubt it will be another grandson.

Shakuntala is another story. Vimla has a light complexion. He described it as 'milky white' when he presented her case to the fathers of boys. Shakuntala has taken after her mother. He admits to 'wheatish' when describing her, but he has noticed the re-evaluation in young men's eyes when they first see her. It took him two years to find a husband for her, and the family is not as prosperous. They have a shop in Chawri Bajar, but he has discovered through Lala Surajmal that it is shared between four brothers, one of whom is Shakuntala's father-in-law. When the inevitable rupture happens, each brother will get a quarter. But he must not fret over Shakuntala. She will enjoy what Providence has in store for her. In age, the sisters are two years apart, but their weddings are separated by four. While, for the first he spent freely, for the second he has parted with money grudgingly, his hand forced by convention. He has counted the mounting costs with a sinking heart. He has had to compensate for his daughter's complexion with jewellery and flattery, and he will give her the best sarees from the inventory in his shop. But he knows, and he knows that her in-laws know, that the finest Banarasi silk cannot burnish a dull complexion. Ah, he will cushion the discomfort with generosity, and Lakshmi will shower him with largesse for doing his duty. He is not as rich as a Birla, but he can definitely afford to marry off his daughter with dignity.

A sizzling sound rises from a cauldron when the halvai sprays water into it. Sohan Lal notices that the man's hands are dripping with mud. 'Your man is filthy!' he complains to Jugal Kishor.

Jugal Kishor appears mildly annoyed. 'He knows what he is doing.'

'His hands are dirty.'

Jugal Kishor sighs with the resignation of a wise man who must deal with a child. 'That is sondhi mitti, the purest clay, washed clean of stones. A few drops give a unique fragrance to the bhujia.'

Sohan Lal is humbled. Magnanimous in victory, Jugal Kishor places an arm on his shoulders and chuckles. 'You are an expert in sarees, sethji. Give Shakuntala the best Kanjeevaram silk, and leave petty matters like bhujia and kachauri to me!'

Sohan Lal forces a smile and fans himself with his cap. He does not trust the fat halvai, and he feels the men are not working fast enough. They have been at their furnaces for two days, and it is doubtful that they will be done by tomorrow evening, when he expects more than seven hundred guests at the wedding. But he knows Jugal Kishor will defend his man. 'You cannot rush a halvai any more than you can rush the sun,' he will say, with the authority of one who owns Mangat Ram

Nawal Kishor. And Sohan Lal will look foolish, burdened as he already is with Jugal Kishor's favours. He has saved considerable expense by using Jugal Kishor's shop, and even more by using his men at reduced rates, but he has been saddled with a debt of gratitude, to be redeemed at the other's convenience.

The halvai smokes endlessly. Sohan Lal notices a wisp of ash fly into the gravy. He looks in horror at Jugal Kishor – who is staring intently in the same direction – but there is not a wrinkle on his forehead. 'We will have a grand menu for you,' declares Jugal Kishor. 'Aloo tikki, ragaraa chaat, gol gappas, paaparii chaat. And there will be ice-cream with falooda, mango juice, lassi flavoured with almonds . . .'

'What about samosas?' asks Sohan Lal.

Jugal Kishor turns a horrified look on Sohan Lal. 'This is your daughter's wedding, not a committee meeting! I would not dream of cheap samosas when I can give you raj kachauris!'

A sudden commotion in the shop announces Lala Surajmal. He strides into the backyard regally, preceded by a man and followed by another with a chair, leaning heavily on his walking-stick but making that dependence seem like a fashion statement.

'Sit down, Jugal Kishor!' commands Surajmal, as Jugal Kishor springs up from the bench.

The chair is placed at a secure distance from the furnaces and Surajmal deposits himself in it, letting the walking-stick fall to the side.

'Chai?' asks Jugal Kishor.

Surajmal nods indifferently.

'Chai!' barks Jugal Kishor, to the men. 'No sugar for Lalaji.'

'No sugar for me either,' says Sohan Lal.

Jugal Kishor gestures to the man, who goes into the shop.

'Is everything under control, Sohan Lal?' asks Surajmal.

Sohan Lal nods sourly. Surajmal's concern irritates him, especially because he is not certain whether he is referring to the wedding or some IPP committee business.

'I am worried about this pro-Mandal rally,' muses Surajmal. 'Who is this Musalman?'

'Suleman,' says Jugal Kishor. 'He lives behind Jama Masjid.'

'What do we know about him?'

'He has been doing social work for the last few years, has clout among Musalmans in Chandni Chowk and says he want to counter the anti-Mandal protests. He claims that they are being mounted by upper-caste boys, so he wants to show that the poor support Mandal.'

'Of course the poor support Mandal,' grumbles Surajmal. 'Would you not support it if it gave you free jalebis?'

'He has support among Musalmans and OBCs,' says Jugal Kishor.

'You said he does social work?' asks Surajmal.

'Helps with some school for Bangladeshi children.'

Surajmal arches an eyebrow. 'How is that social work? Bangladeshi children! Why has IPP not raised the matter?'

Jugal Kishor shrugs. 'He is popular among Musalmans.'

'What else do you know about him?'

'Small man, thin. Intense face.'

'I do not care about his looks!' snaps Surajmal. 'I do not want to marry off your daughter to him. Do you know which party he supports? Congress? Communists? Janata Dal? Independent?'

'His policies are aligned with Janata Dal and the Communists,' says Jugal Kishor weakly.

'His policies are of no interest to anyone. Do you know which party he supports?'

Sohan Lal is relieved that the burden of ignorance has fallen, inexplicably, on Jugal Kishor.

The chai arrives, borne in glass tumblers sitting on a plastic tray. Surajmal scowls at them. 'Bring me a steel bowl!' he scolds the man.

'How could you bring Lalaji's chai in a glass tumbler?' demands a horrified Jugal Kishor.

The man scurries back into the shop to amend his error.

'When is this rally?' asks Surajmal.

'In two weeks.'

'What is the IPP committee doing about it?'

'Kartar Singh has made arrangements,' says Sohan Lal. 'I will meet him in Kinari Bajar in an hour.'

'Why is Kartar Singh not here?' demands Surajmal.

'He is a councillor,' explains Jugal Kishor, smugly, as he exchanges a glance with Sohan Lal.

'Harilalji is a councillor too!' thunders Surajmal. 'He is senior to Kartar Singh yet he would have come right away, had I called him.'

Sohan Lal notes that Kartar Singh has not been called to the meeting either. Indeed, this is not a meeting at all. It has been turned into one by Surajmal's insistence on discussing politics when he should be reviewing wedding arrangements. Look at how blithely he sits on the chair, as if the wedding was not about to happen tomorrow night!

'This Mandal business is going to become an earthquake,' declares Surajmal. 'Even Naresh Agrawal is nervous. He has been an MP for ten years, and he still does not know which side of Mandal to stand on. If he speaks against Mandal, OBCs will turn away. If he speaks for it, the Banias of Chandni Chowk will desert him. He will get no help from his party – Congress itself is confused.'

'That does not make it easier for us,' says Jugal Kishor, with uncharacteristic courage. 'Which side of Mandal does IPP stand on?'

Surajmal turns deliberately to Sohan Lal. 'You look old and tired, Sohan Lal. What is a wedding? A wedding happens by itself.'

Sohan Lal produces a self-deprecatory smile. 'The bride's father does not sleep, Lalaji. My migraine has come back.'

'Migraine!' scoffs Surajmal. 'Take three drops of sweet marjoram with a lump of jaggery, and the migraine will fly away like a bird.'

'I will,' says Sohan Lal, not inclined to follow the advice.

'It will also chase away hangovers,' adds Surajmal, with relish. 'But no one can accuse you of that affliction.'

Jugal Kishor laughs dutifully, but Sohan Lal thinks the joke is in bad taste. In his fifty-five years, he has not once touched alcohol. To his knowledge, no one in his family has had a whiff of the vile stuff. To crack such a crude joke, one day before his daughter's wedding!

'You should not wear yourself out at your age,' continues Surajmal, with a solicitous air.

This, from a man who is ten years older than me, thinks Sohan Lal.

'Tell Ramesh to make the rounds. Tell him to arrange for the tent and check on the halvai. It is his sister's wedding. He should be running the length of Chandni Chowk, not you!'

Sohan Lal nods absently and reflects on the picture of Ramesh sitting in the shop. The boy is not flashy and smart like some young men, these days, but he has become very responsible. Every morning he is on the gaddi by nine, sitting cross-legged as a businessman should. He leaves Kucha Bansilal late in the evening, and then only after Rukmini has implored him – with two telephone calls – to come home for his dinner. By relieving Sohan Lal from the shop, he lets him concentrate on the wedding. 'How can you keep the shop open right through your daughter's wedding?' Rukmini had asked. But the shop is a businessman's reason to live. If the shop will not bring in money, how will he have the courage to spend it?

'Buy your daughter an extra necklace,' he said to Rukmini, 'but let the shop remain open.' Nevertheless, he will shut down Jamna Lal Kishori Mal for two days, starting tomorrow. He needs Ramesh to help with the tent arrangements.

Sohan Lal turns to Surajmal, who is in the middle of a discourse to which Jugal Kishor is listening raptly. 'All this country needed was a pink boy who looked good on television,' says Surajmal, scornfully. 'In five years, Rajiv signed dozens of accords, bought hundreds of Bofors guns, and took us into the twenty-first century ten years too early.'

Jugal Kishor laughs. 'Look what this twenty-first century holds for us! We are ruled by phoney Rajas and low-caste commoners. It was a mistake to kill Rajiv. We should have enshrined the entire Gandhi family in a museum, ensuring they would never desert us.'

Only a father of four sons can say that a wedding happens by itself, Sohan Lal thinks. True, he has married off all four, but what does a man without daughters know about weddings? Surajmal has seen brides' fathers fawn over him, and never had to fawn over anyone. He has never felt the burden of an unmarried daughter sit heavily on his chest, so what does he know of the anxiety of a wedding?

'Have you brought my attars, Lalaji?' asks Sohan Lal.

Surajmal stops short, annoyed. 'Attars? Ah, yes, I asked the boy to hand them to you.' Surajmal's servant, standing behind his chair, produces a package. 'Ramvilas has spent all night packing them for you,' he adds.

Sohan Lal wears an expression of grudging gratitude and turns the package in his hands. It is beautifully wrapped in transparent poly-thene, bearing the brand name of Bhagwan Das and Sons. Inside the cardboard box, visible through an opening, eight small bottles are arranged in two rows, each with its own label. The first four are natural attars – jasmine, kadamba, mahua and motia. The others are natural oils – citronella, patchouli, basil and aniseed. He has ordered them especially for his son-in-law.

'Your daughter is fortunate, Sohan Lal,' observes Surajmal.

They sit in silence for a few minutes. Sohan Lal dwells on the wedding, anticipation mixing with dread, until Chotu arrives in the backyard with a steel tiffin sent by Rukmini. 'Biviji has said you should finish the food before it grows cold,' says Chotu.

Sohan Lal has him unlatch the tiffin and studies his lunch listlessly – daal, two rotis, a spoonful of rice and boiled vegetables surrounded by modest gravy – colourless because it has no turmeric, and tasteless because it contains no salt. To be sitting amid heaps of kachauris, to watch the halvai tap his strainer with mountains of bhujia, and to eat this! So much is forbidden to him – ghee, milk, jalebis, sugar, salt, spices . . . Rukmini listens to the doctor too closely. She has made the life span of her husband her greatest project. In my quest for longevity, he thinks sadly, I have destroyed my enjoyment of life.

He shakes himself out of this momentary depression. There is no place for loose thought in a well-organised world. A man with a daughter must marry her off, and a man with diabetes must take care of his diet. He decides to settle his payments in Kinari Bajar, and meet Kartar Singh, then force his lunch down his throat. He stands up and hands the package of attars to Chotu. 'Come with me to Kinari Bajar,' he says. 'Bring the tiffin with you.'

'I will take care of everything here,' says Jugal Kishor, reassuringly.

'Remember the marjoram and jaggery!' Surajmal calls, as Sohan Lal leaves, followed by Chotu.

'Get me a ricksha,' Sohan Lal tells the boy.

He directs the ricksha to Kinari Bajar. Chotu trots alongside, bearing the tiffin and the attar package. The ricksha navigates through late-afternoon traffic in Chandni Chowk, crawling so slowly that Chotu has to wait for it to catch up, and enters Kinari Bajar. Sohan Lal's heart softens as he passes shops displaying everything a bride may need for her wedding, and everything she may desire for her groom – ghagharas, shervanis, embroidered sashes, silver-lined shoes, churidaar-pyjamas, silk turbans topped with feathers and fake diamonds, flower garlands, electric lights, milk-white fly whisks and sequined umbrellas . . . This is the moment a father prepares for when a daughter is born to him, he tells himself.

Kinari Bajar has changed a lot since his youth, when he first walked about its lanes and wondered which trade was right for him. Even the oldest shops have now torn down their brick and plaster façades and replaced them with glass walls, inside which stand mannequins in crinolened ghagharas that come down to their ankles. Such beautiful brides they would make, were they alive! But they are fair, almost white. Their clay skin contains no pigmentation. Shakuntala was going to wear a yellow ghaghara for her wedding, Rukmini decided, or a pink one to offset her dark complexion, but Sohan Lal was aghast when he was told of this. All his life he had carried in his mind the image of his daughters in bridal finery, and it was blood red. How could a bride wear anything but red? He prevailed, so Shakuntala will wear a crimson ghaghara filigreed with gold thread, as these mannequins do. Ah, she will be a wilted flower in it, not the bright blossom Vimla was in *her* wedding ghaghara, when the red made her skin look milky, making him think he had not exaggerated when he first described her to her in-laws.

He stops the ricksha at Baburam Harichand and walks into the shop, thankful that Rukmini has already bought everything so he need not sort through the laces, tassels and sequins that scream at him. That is the woman's department, he thinks playfully. His department is to pay the bills.

The seth in the shop brings out Sohan Lal's account and tots up the bill for Rukmini's purchases of the last few weeks – five lakhs, eighty-nine thousand and nine hundred rupees. The amount shocks Sohan Lal, dispatching all tender thoughts of the wedding. How can a woman spend six lakhs in Kinari Bajar alone? Does she have no sense of proportion?

The seth studies Sohan Lal's face and asks if he would like tea. Sohan Lal demurs. A cold drink, perhaps? 'No,' says Sohan Lal. He will settle the bill quickly and leave. He writes out a note to the seth, saying the money can be collected late evening from his shop in Kucha Bansilal. Before he hands it over, he turns it in his hand, feeling sad for himself and for money lost to the caprice of a whimsical woman. Of course, he has prepared for this wedding all his life. He knew, when he held the dark little baby in his arms – another girl! – twenty-three years ago that she would cost him money. But five lakhs, eighty-nine thousand merely in Kinari Bajar!

The seth notices Sohan Lal's drooping brow. 'A daughter is Lakshmi,' he says. 'The more you give to her, the more she gives back.'

Sohan Lal responds with a wan smile, and is suddenly seized with guilt. Although he is frugal in his own habits and has always encouraged economy in the home, he is a wealthy man. If her father does not open his heart for her, who will show generosity to poor Shakuntala? She deserves the same abandon he displayed with his purse and spirits for Vimla's wedding. They are sisters, born to the same father, and they deserve the same send-off! She will go away tomorrow night, lost to him for ever. He has satisfied himself that her in-laws are a decent family with no blemish on their name, but he does not know his son-in-law well, having spoken to him only once. Now, knowing how he feels about Rukmini's Kinari Bajar purchases, how will he embrace his daughter with a clean conscience when she stands sobbing before him, waiting to be taken away after the wedding? Will he be able to look her in the eye and tell her, in all honesty, that she could always come to him when in need?

Sohan Lal tears up the IOU. He points to the left wall of the shop, dressed with garlands made of banknotes. He will give one to his son-in-law so that he can look his daughter in the eye and weep when she weeps. 'Are these real?' he asks.

The seth nods vigorously, somewhat offended that Sohan Lal should ask.

'Ten-rupee notes, twenty-rupee notes, fifty-rupee notes, hundred-rupee notes.'

'Give me the one with hundred-rupee notes,' says Sohan Lal.

'How many notes?'

Sohan Lal makes a quick mental calculation. 'A hundred and one. That will bring your bill to six lakhs. A round figure.'

The seth frowns. Surely Sohan Lal should know better, being a businessman himself. 'That is inauspicious,' he points out.

'All right, then,' says Sohan Lal, expansively. 'Charge me one rupee for the making of the garland.'

The seth packs the garland into a brown-paper bag, and Sohan Lal writes out a note for six lakhs and one rupee. He strides out of the shop, contented, like a man tested and triumphant. Chotu makes a motion to take the paper bag, but Sohan Lal shoos him away. 'I will keep this.' Then he wonders if the garland is not safer with Chotu. Who will think of snatching a paper bag from a servant? He hands it over reluctantly. 'It contains money,' he warns. 'I will count it later.'

'Your tiffin, sethji?' asks Chotu. 'Biviji said you should eat before the food goes cold.'

'Take it to Kucha Bansilal!' says Sohan Lal, sharply.

Chotu melts away. With the attar package in hand, Sohan Lal proceeds to the waiting ricksha. He places the package on the ricksha seat, heaves himself up, adjusts his cap carefully on his head, and asks the rickshavala to proceed to the Shiv temple. Before the ricksha can start, he is interrupted. A man lunges to touch his feet. 'Sethji!'

Sohan Lal pulls back his legs in consternation and looks at the man – dirty beard, dirty pyjamas, crumpled kurta that hangs about skeletal shoulders, and a perpetual grin showing yellow teeth. It is the Musalman he has seen in the chaivala's stall.

'Get away!' scolds Sohan Lal. 'Have you been following me?'

'I will follow you as far as you want,' says the man, with folded hands.

'Who told you where to find me?'

He does not reply. The lower lip hangs a little looser in acknowledgement of guilt.

'What do you want?'

'I have brought you a boy, sethji.'

Sohan Lal now notices the boy standing right behind the Musalman
– not much shorter than him, dark, very dark, almost certainly from
Bihar or Uttar Pradesh, perhaps a Bangladeshi. There are thousands of
them in Chandni Chowk, crawling out of every drain like rats. And
they are all thieves. Naresh Agrawal is responsible for this! He has
been bringing illegal Bangladeshis to Delhi for years.

'I do not need a boy,' says Sohan Lal.

'He will work for nothing.'

Sohan Lal is annoyed at the man's presumption. How dare he
accost him with such familiarity? Even the chaivala would not dare
speak to him thus. What possible use can he have for such a boy? A
thin boy, unclean with matted brown hair. Fourteen? Fifteen, perhaps?
You cannot tell with these famished children. They look like little
gnomes even in their twenties. And the right hand has been cut off –
for stealing, no doubt.

'I thought that sethji might need a hand,' says the man.

A hand, literally, thinks Sohan Lal with disdain. Those yellow teeth
and that infuriating grin! 'Get out of my way,' he says with finality,
and prods the rickshavala with his finger.

The ricksha moves. The man and the boy step out of the way. The
boy raises his stump angrily and shouts with all his strength: 'Suleman
Mian *zindabad*!'

Sohan Lal is startled. He has a visceral fear of disturbances, slogans,
loud talk and violence. Such things interfere with quiet trade. They
disturb the careful balance of life that he regards as sacred. He looks
around frantically. Has the rally begun two weeks early? Is there a riot
in Kinari Bajar? But the one-handed boy is alone, drowned by the
tooting of ricksha horns. Where had the boy heard of Suleman? 'What
do you know about Suleman?' Surajmal had asked. 'Do you know
which party he supports?' Surajmal had asked, and Jugal Kishor did
not know. Congress? Communists? Janata Dal? Independent?

'Stop,' he says to the rickshavala.

The man sees the ricksha stop and runs up to it.

'Who is this boy?' asks Sohan Lal.

'A poor boy,' says the man, apologetically.

'How does he know of Suleman?'

'He heard someone shouting in the street. What can he know about Suleman Mian?'

Sohan Lal studies the boy. He is perhaps a year or two younger than Chotu. Every morning Chotu sweeps the shop, then stands in Chandni Chowk to lure customers. If those he brings buy something, Chotu gets a small commission. Perhaps the boy could do the same. It will cost Sohan Lal nothing. And the boy certainly knows Suleman, in spite of what the Musalman says. 'What is your name?' he asks the boy.

'Gauhar Muhammad,' says the man.

'Let him answer!' Sohan Lal scolds.

'Gauhar,' says the boy.

'Where is your family?'

The boy looks at the man, who grins. 'He has no family, sethji. He lives in a school run by a madam near Jama Masjid.'

Bangladeshi, thinks Sohan Lal. It is not a good idea to have the boy around. He will spy, as Chotu does. He will watch out for wealthy customers, put his ear to the door, listen to money being counted and inform potential thieves about when it is taken to the bank.

'Do you know his parents?' he asks.

'Suleman Mian,' replies the boy.

Sohan Lal is amused. If you keep the snake close to you in a deep basket, it cannot bite you. He will keep the boy. He will never let him inside the shop, so the boy will have no opportunity to steal anything. 'Can he read and write?' he asks.

'In English!' says the man. 'The madam in the school taught him.'

'Can he count?'

'Yes!'

'Let the boy speak for himself,' says Sohan Lal coldly.

Gauhar nods.

'All right,' says Sohan Lal. 'He can stand in Chandni Chowk and bring customers into the kucha.'

'Commission?' asks the man.

Sohan Lal considers. Chotu gets between three and five per cent, depending on the customer and the season, but Chotu is an expert. 'Two per cent,' he says. 'My boy Chotu will teach you what to say.'

'You have been sent by Allah.' The man moves to grab Sohan Lal's feet.

Sohan Lal pulls back his legs a second time. 'Where will the boy sleep?' he demands.

'He sleeps at the school.'

That will not do, thinks Sohan Lal. The boy must be on hand all day and all night if he is to be useful. Chotu sleeps behind the collapsible gates of the Hanuman temple. 'He must find a place to sleep in the kucha,' says Sohan Lal.

'Perhaps inside the shop?' asks the man.

'No!' says Sohan Lal sternly.

'I will find him a place. He will be available to you, day and night. Can I bring him to the shop tomorrow?'

'Not tomorrow. Bring him in three days. And give him a bath first.'

'He will look like Dev Anand when he comes to you!' The man recedes – walking backwards so he can continue to present his grateful face to Sohan Lal – followed by the boy, sullen and indifferent. Sohan Lal directs the ricksha to the Shiv temple for his meeting with Kartar Singh.

The Shiv temple in Kinari Bajar is just a crudely fashioned lingam – a phallus of black soapstone protruding from the ground – shaded by a banyan tree which stands at the junction of two lanes. It is surrounded by shops on three sides, and under it the Kinari Bajar Traders Association has placed a bench. Together, the tree, the bench and the lingam constitute the temple. Sohan Lal asks the rickshavala to leave him in the banyan shade, and sits down on the bench to wait for Kartar Singh. The attar package lies at his side.

They have chosen to meet in Kinari Bajar because it is one of the few areas in Chandni Chowk where Kartar Singh, being a councillor, can hope to remain anonymous. Ten years younger than me, thinks Sohan Lal bitterly, yet a councillor! It was *his* money, not Kartar Singh's, that had been stolen in 'eighty-four. It was *his* trust that had been betrayed. It was he who had been waiting by the Godrej safe when Kartar Singh returned to Delhi – in a shocking state but alive and whole. He had expected a measure of gratitude for having guarded the store. And, of course, he had expected his money.

Instead, what a charade of self-pity the sardar had staged! Imagine a grown man, especially one with a plastered leg sticking unnaturally from his body, squatting on the floor and crying like a child! What was there to cry about? Riots happen. Stores get looted. It is in the nature of disaster to strike. The wise man prepares for it. The unlucky man shrugs off the setback and continues. The lucky man escapes it altogether. Only a weak man displays such vulgar emotion.

Sohan Lal judges men by their fortitude, not by their passion or intensity. He admires balance and equanimity. He grants men their cold calculations and abhors their impulsive actions. Now, if Kartar Singh, having pocketed the money, had staged an elaborate drama of grief to absolve himself of guilt, there would be something to admire in the deception. But it was clear that much of his lament was honest. And that was inexcusable. At any rate, Sohan Lal will never trust havala again, and he has taken care to let everyone know of Kartar Singh's betrayal. Incompetence must invite its just reward.

Kartar Singh arrives late, on his scooter. He parks behind the bench, limps round it and sits down next to Sohan Lal. Sohan Lal notes that the limp is much more pronounced than it was when he last saw the sardar. It is carefully measured to suit the occasion, he thinks. Perhaps there is no limp at all when no one is looking.

'It is all fixed up,' says Kartar Singh. 'Ramvilas brought me a boy.'

'Have you talked to him?'

'Yes. He is twenty or twenty-one, has no family, used to work in Kucha Mahajani many years ago. Stole from the shop so the seth threw him out. Since then he has worked on and off for Rajan Nahal.'

Sohan Lal arches an eyebrow.

'Ramvilas tells me that does not matter,' says Kartar Singh. 'The boy is not interested in politics.'

'Why has he agreed, then?'

'Five thousand,' says Kartar Singh. 'And Ramvilas will give him a present.'

'Who will prepare the boy for the rally?'

'Ramvilas will take care of that. He has two weeks.'

'Who else knows this besides Ramvilas and you?' asks Sohan Lal.

'No one. I assume you will tell Lalaji and Jugal Kishor.'

'Yes.'

'And Harilalji?'

'Harilalji does not involve himself in all this,' says Sohan Lal sharply.

They fall silent. It is my duty to sully my hands, thinks Sohan Lal, while Harilal Gupta deliberates on weightier matters in the council. Yet everything will benefit Harilal's career. Ah, to be in a position not to know!

Kartar Singh stands up unsteadily. 'I should go now, sethji. People know me.'

Sohan Lal nods, noting the relish with which Kartar Singh says,

'People know me.' It is wonderful what a riot can do for a man. No one can deny a council seat to a sardar who campaigns with his arm in a sling and his leg in a cast. If the chaivala had some ambition, thinks Sohan Lal, he would have robbed my store in 'eighty-four and I would be chief executive councillor today.

'I will see you tomorrow at the wedding,' says Kartar Singh.

'Yes,' says Sohan Lal.

'I will dance tomorrow! Shakuntala is like my daughter.'

Sohan Lal nods, wondering how a limping man will dance. Would that not blow away the subterfuge?

Kartar Singh kicks the scooter into life.

'What is the name of the boy?' asks Sohan Lal.

'Mukesh, I think. Mukesh Pandey.'

Sohan Lal gasps as Kartar Singh drives away in a peal of thunder. Mukesh Pandey! The chaivala's son! He has not seen him for years at the stall, but he has watched him play in the kucha – a motherless child of six – and he has heard the chaivala speak of him. Ah, there must be hundreds of boys with that name. But a boy of twenty-one, who says he has no family?

He sits under the banyan tree for a long time, thinking of Shakuntala, the wedding, the six lakhs spent in Kinari Bajar and the boy named Mukesh Pandey, until he realises he must go back to Kucha Bansilal and help Ramesh lock up. They will close early today. They have a long, sleepless night ahead. The cares of a bride's father!

He decides to take a whiff of jasmine. It will soothe him. He looks for flaps on the polythene wrap. 'Ramvilas has spent all night packing them for you,' Surajmal had said. Indeed, he has packed superbly. There is not a wrinkle on the surface of the package, as if it had been machine-wrapped. He finds the flaps, and turns them up gingerly with his nails. It occurs to him that a father should not taste what he will give to his son-in-law. What will Rukmini say? And what will his son-in-law think when he sees that the package has been opened? Ah, he must indulge this one vice. He is lavishing on his son-in-law what he would deny himself, even as he knows his son-in-law is no connoisseur of attars. He will give Shakuntala another saree of pure Kanjeevaram silk to make up for it. He must remember to pull it out of his stock when he goes to Kucha Bansilal.

He tears open the package like a child presented with his first gift. The bottle of jasmine glistens in the late-afternoon sun. He removes the cork with trembling hands and presses his nose to the bottle. He frowns, sniffs again and mutters a curse. The attar is synthetic.

Kucha Bansilal has no customers in the evening. Most shops have closed for the day. Gopal can see Ramesh Babu seated inside Jamna Lal Kishori Mal, adding up numbers, sethji being away making wedding arrangements. It will be an expensive wedding, he has heard. More than seven hundred people have been invited. Gopal had asked Sohan Lal if he could set up a chai stall, but the seth said no: for such occasions he hires a caterer, who can provide cold drinks, espresso coffee and masala chai with steel machines, electric ovens, and an army of uniformed boys.

Gopal sips his last cup of chai. He will close the stall, go to the kholi and continue filing at the lock. Then, some day, he will remove the asafoetida tins. After that, if there are any locks on the steel trunks, he will file those away. It will take years, by which time he will be an old man.

He looks up to see Ibrahim walk into the kucha, his form silhouetted against the electric bulbs outside the lane. It is getting dark. Ibrahim is not alone – a boy follows him. Gopal shakes his head in irritation. He does not want to make any more chai, and he has stowed away Ibrahim's glass.

Ibrahim sits down next to him. The boy stands uncertainly on the other side of the lane, his back to the glass façade of Jamna Lal Kishori Mal, his head blocking the folded hands of a white mannequin.

'I have brought you a boy,' says Ibrahim.

'I do not need one,' says Gopal stiffly.

Ibrahim grins. 'Your stall is getting big.'

Gopal spreads his arms and touches the furthest jars on his left and right. 'There is no space for a boy.'

'He is a poor boy. Maybe he can sleep in the stall at night.'

'What will he eat?'

'He earns money,' says Ibrahim. 'He works in sethji's shop.'

'Why have I never seen him, then?'

'He just started.'

Gopal looks at the boy suspiciously. Fourteen, perhaps fifteen, no more than sixteen – thin, not unlike Mukesh was five or six years ago. Mukesh has cleaner hair, of course, not the unwashed brown mat that covers this shameless head. And he is much darker than Mukesh. 'Where is his father?'

Ibrahim points upward to indicate that the father is dead.

'His mother?'

Ibrahim's finger continues to aim skyward.

'So you know nothing about his family,' grumbles Gopal.

'A poor boy has no family.'

Gopal is chastened. He has perhaps been too harsh. At this very moment, somewhere in Chandni Chowk, Mukesh is probably seeking shelter, saying his father is dead. 'Where did you find him?' he asks.

'At a school run by a madam,' says Ibrahim.

'Where is this school?'

Ibrahim slaps Gopal on the back with a laugh. 'You are a police detective, Gopal Bhai! Suleman Mian owns a school near Jama Masjid. The boy studies there.'

'What is his name?'

'Gauhar,' says Ibrahim. He shoots a warning glance to the boy, discouraging him from saying more. Suleman Mian was particularly displeased when he heard about Mussabir. 'What is the point in feeding and housing these boys,' he had asked, 'if they will fly away as soon as they sprout wings? Keep this one under your nose so I can send for him when necessary. Do not leave him with that madam in the school! She will fill his head with silliness, teach him drivel about Nehru and Gandhi, and make him unfit for party work.'

'Is he a Musalman?' asks Gopal, suspiciously.

Gauhar inches forward to hear the conversation.

'Do not come so close!' Ibrahim scolds. 'Go and stand outside the kucha.'

Gauhar falls back to a safe distance.

'A Musalman,' whispers Ibrahim. 'Like me.'

'Bangladeshi!' exclaims Gopal.

Ibrahim is offended. 'Does it matter where he is from? He is a poor boy, like your own son.'

'What if he steals at night?'

'Why should he?' counters Ibrahim. 'He will guard your box, so no one can steal from you.'

Gopal shakes his head. His own arrangement with Seth Sushil Jain is exactly the same and he has not spent a single night guarding the sacks, which disappear with regularity – how can he keep watch over three floors? Perhaps this boy can help confront the thief. Perhaps he knows how to pick a lock. Then they can move the tins together in the dark and open the trunks . . . But he will want his share. Can a Musalman boy be trusted? And what would Sushil Jain, already on the verge of throwing him out, say if he saw the boy coming out of Katra Badami every morning? 'A Musalman boy should work for a Musalman,' he declares. 'Why can he not work in your shoe shop?'

'Sharief Mirza will not have him,' says Ibrahim, ruefully. 'I am not a big seth like you, who can choose to have his own boy in his stall.'

The flattery touches Gopal and softens him toward Gauhar. 'All right. Perhaps I can let him sleep here for a few nights.'

Ibrahim presses his advantage. 'Look at him! He is a small boy, as thin as a stick! He will easily fit inside your stall.'

Much more easily than a fat sardar, thinks Gopal. The boy is indeed thin. He could curl up next to the stove and wrap his arms round himself. 'What happened to his hand?'

Ibrahim sighs and points upward again.

'How can he work with just one?'

'Only one is needed to pull customers into Jamna Lal Kishori Mal,' says Ibrahim, with a chuckle.

Gauhar instinctively covers the stump with his left hand. Gopal feels guilt wash over him. 'He can sleep in the box at night. I will give him a blanket.'

'He will disappear as soon as you arrive in the morning,' says Ibrahim, 'and he will not come back in the evening until you are ready to go home. I knew you were too kind to throw him out, Gopal Bhai.'

This, thinks Gopal, is a good time to bring up the subject. 'Can you get me two men for one night?' he asks.

Ibrahim is surprised. 'What would you do with them?'

Gopal considers. He can break the lock himself with a good hammer, but he will need one man to move the tins. One can be posted as a lookout at the entrance to Katra Badami, and another to keep Hameed away, should he wake up. 'Three men. Strong. They should bring hammers and knives.'

Ibrahim laughs. 'Do you want to rob a house?'

'This is not robbery,' insists Gopal.

'What makes you think I can get such men?' asks Ibrahim.

'You know people.'

'Not such people.'

'Your Suleman Mian—'

'Suleman Mian is a leader!' barks Ibrahim. 'He will be the Chandni Chowk MP some day.'

'But I have seen you with such men.'

Ibrahim snorts dismissively, annoyed that Gopal cannot forget one little incident. 'I have told you a hundred times,' he mutters angrily, 'I came to see if you were safe.'

'I saw you, Ibrahim Mian! You had a rod in your hand! And the sardarni was stuck in the window, kicking like a cow.'

'Speak softly!' says Ibrahim. 'The boy is listening.'

'You told me he was trustworthy.'

Ibrahim gets up with hurt in his eyes. 'I bring you a good boy to help you forget about your son, and you attack me as if I am a criminal.'

I do not know where my son is, thinks Gopal. 'All right,' he says. 'The boy can sleep here. Sit down, Ibrahim Mian, and I will make you some chai.' He opens the junction box, places Ibrahim's glass before him, then pumps the stove. Ibrahim turns to Gauhar, who has crept closer on seeing the stove. 'Come back in an hour.'

The boy melts away.

'You have done a good deed today,' he comforts Gopal. 'A good deed never goes unrewarded.'

Gopal lights the stove and sets water to boil for Ibrahim's tea. Three strong men, he thinks, for no more than fifteen minutes. He must ask someone else.

Ramvilas slinks along the edge of the street, avoiding eye-contact and never looking directly into a shop. Too many people know him these days, given his position in the committee. The river of rickshas provides partial cover, as do truckloads of wash-basins, pumps and commodes that are stacked illegally on the road. He runs across an intersection, jhola in hand, eyes downcast, and across a metal plate screwed into the asphalt, announcing the old name no one now knows or uses – Garston Bastion Road. He prefers to come by day, when the market bustles with activity. If a man is careful not to draw attention to himself, nothing will distinguish him from the thousands buying bathroom tiles. He is another buyer from the states that surround Delhi, or even as far off as Bengal or Bihar, with his clothes in his jhola, scrounging for good deals on pumps that will fetch high prices back home. By night, however, GB Road is more sinister, because all visits have the same purpose, laid bare before touts, pimps, bais and pahalvans.

He passes Agrawal Pump House and turns into the staircase beyond it. On the landing he sees Parvati, visibly pregnant, in a plain salvaar-kameez. She returns his gaze, presenting her profile in the hope that he will notice her. He does, but only that she is getting old, and that she is at least six months pregnant. She does not like his patronage of Gita and has expressed her hostility on more than one occasion. He has considered sharing his largesse between the two, but Parvati does not have Gita's pale smoothness. Although she claims to be twenty-one, she is nearer twenty-eight. It is difficult to imagine her luring customers away from Gita.

He runs up two flights of stairs and bursts into Gita's room. It is simply furnished, with a four-poster bed, a dressing-table, a wash-basin, condoms and massage oils. There are no chairs or tables. He marvels, once again, at the functional efficiency of the furniture, most of which he has arranged – no more than absolutely necessary. Gita sits, and continues to sit even after he enters, at the dressing-table, studying her reflection in the mirror. At the door, Ramvilas paints an expression of suitable concern on his face. 'I know you are unhappy, Gulmohar.'

She does not reply. He steps into the room and stands behind her, regarding himself in the mirror, then answers her unasked question: 'I have been busy.'

She frowns. 'What could be so important?'

'A wedding.'

'Whose?'

'A seth's daughter.'

'Is she pretty?'

'Not as pretty as you.'

'But she got a handsome husband, no doubt.'

'Only a spineless rich boy too weak to stand up to his father, who made the match.'

'But a good man?'

Ramvilas shrugs. 'All men are good, until proven vile.'

The mirror shows him a reflection he does not dislike. He is thirty-six. His hair has always been too fine – on the verge of thinning – but it has not receded with age and is smooth, shiny and black. It is no match for Gita's, of course, but it does not need to be. He is constitutionally thin. No matter what he eats, he will never be fat. There is no trace of a growing belly, no flesh on his upper arms, no distasteful cow-like dewlap under his chin. He believes his slenderness is the source of his vigour in bed, and he is proud of his youthful looks. As a scrawny child he lost many fights to bigger boys. As a man, in a world where battles are won by wits, he hopes to defeat them all. His eyes, of course, are the crown jewels of his face – sharp, black, ever leering. That leer, combined with the slight droop of his lower lip, gives him the look of a sly man, a deceitful man, a man always hiding a card under his sleeve. He prizes it. It has secured him entry, with wealthy seths, to the IPP committee. How many men in Chandni Chowk, who are not traders or relatives of other members, can claim to have made such headway in the IPP or Congress committee? True, he is still not a member of the committee, but let them try to hold a meeting without him!

His kurta and pyjama are spotlessly white. As he regards himself in the mirror, it occurs to him that he does not look like a man who would condescend to visit GB Road. Indeed, she is fortunate that he is so presentable, considering she would have had him no matter what he looked like. Satisfied, he turns his attention to her reflection. She is still attractive after six years. There is a slight sagging of the shoulders, and the hint of a double chin when she tilts her face forward, but the skin is still pale, still smooth, still unblemished. He places both hands on her shoulders, but she brushes them away. 'Was the wedding grand?' she asks.

'As grand as the wedding of Noor Jahan! I danced for hours. That is why I am tired, my Roshanara Begum.'

She rises to her feet and walks away, stung by 'Begum'.

'You no longer come when promised,' she pouts. 'And you call me "Begum".'

Ramvilas sighs. He knows that the pangs of separation spring from necessity. Her prestige in the kotha owes much to his patronage. She is one of the few girls in Kotha 842 with her own room. It was constructed especially for her, after he had made more promises to the bai than he can possibly keep. It is at the top of the building, next to a water tank. It overlooks GB Road, and opens on to a terrace where she can see pigeons cooing over grains of millet. 'I must avoid many eyes in coming to see you,' he says lovingly.

'Why can you not come at night like the others? There was a time when you did not mind.'

There was a time, thinks Ramvilas, when his wife did not mind him staying overnight in Delhi. Now, as his daughters grow, so does her possessiveness. A man with two daughters – they will be marriageable some day – cannot spend a night outside his home. He must take the bus back to Bahadurgarh every evening and immerse himself in the boredom of responsibility. All pleasures, if he can afford any, must be reserved for the irresponsible glare of sunlight. But he cannot explain that to her. 'Because I am not like other customers!' he says, with a flourish. 'I am not a customer at all. I am an admirer.'

She snorts and runs to the other side of the bed, away from him. 'Parvati has six every night,' she says, 'even now that she is pregnant.'

'You are tender, unlike Parvati. You cannot handle more than one.'

He does not mind about her other customers, whoever they are. When she is not with him, she does not exist. But he has asked the bai to spare her a heavy load. He does not want her to wear out.

'The bai grants Parvati everything she asks for,' pouts Gita. 'Soon she will have her own room.'

'You will eventually prevail over Parvati, my Jahanara Begum. You have me!'

Gita tosses her head. 'Did she get much jewellery?' she asks.

'Who?'

'Sethji's daughter.'

'Sethji is rich,' says Ramvilas. He instantly regrets saying that. He can hear the thoughts in her head, as she fingers her necklace – sparkling but fake, his gift from last month – that compare him with the seth, to his disadvantage.

'How much was her jewellery worth?' she insists.

'I did not appraise it.'

'What did sethji give to his son-in-law?'

'A garland of currency notes. Fake!'

'Did she go away in a Maruti car?'

'Maruti Esteem.'

'What did sethji place in her hands when she stepped into the car?'

'A package of the finest attars,' he says provocatively.

She turns away, despondent. He pulls out an attar package from the jhola and holds it in front of her face. She brightens and snatches it. 'Is this what sethji gave to his daughter?'

'Better than that, infinitely better. These are the finest attars from Bhagwan Das and Sons, my Mumtaz Mahal! This is jasmine, this is kadamba, this is mahua and this, motia.'

'The other four?'

'Oils – citronella, patchouli, basil, aniseed.'

'Which is the most expensive?' she asks.

He laughs. 'You will smell sweet with any!'

She is pleased, but a thought clouds her brow. She looks at him threateningly. 'And this is what sethji gave his daughter?'

'I have never been more honest with you,' he says.

She tears the bottles out of the package and turns them in her hands, pulls out the corks, sniffs, then squeals with delight. He sits on the four-poster and watches her. Her gaiety subsides, and she joins him, suddenly forlorn. 'How old is sethji's daughter?'

'Your age. Twenty-three.'

Gita broods. Ramvilas wishes he had never mentioned the wedding.

'What will happen to me when I am thirty?' she murmurs.

He puts an arm round her. 'You will never be thirty. You have always been twenty-three, and you will be twenty-three for the next twenty-three years.'

'And when twenty-three years have passed,' she demands, 'will I suddenly turn forty-six?'

Ramvilas removes his arm and stands up. The attars have brought him no advantage.

'I can probably start a business of my own,' she says. 'You could give me some money. We can sit in the shop together. And I will never have to worry about my age again.'

He is exasperated. He has just given away attars worth a thousand rupees. Must he now offer career advice to a whore? 'Of course!' he exclaims. 'You are in Chandni Chowk, market to the world! What can you not hawk here? Would you like to sell gold coins? Or silver bricks? Diamond jewellery? Clothes, shoes, radios and watches? Or cotton, yarn, fruit, spices, leather, hardware, water-pumps, cardboard, pipes, bicycles, spectacles, kites, fireworks, fans? Or you can sell peacock feathers, make parathas in Paratha Gali, or churn out horoscopes on computers!'

She appears intimidated. 'I am a poor girl.'

Ramvilas decides the visit has been worthless. He gets up and folds his jhola. All right, he will try a diversion, even a distasteful one, to soften her mood.

'Call Kiran up to the room. I want to play with her.'

She eyes him suspiciously. 'You have never played with her before.'

'I feel a change in myself,' he says, making a desperate effort to sound sincere.

'Kiran is not here,' says Gita.

At first, he does not understand. He thinks Kiran is playing somewhere in the kotha, and is grateful for her absence. 'All right, I will bring her a talking car tomorrow. It is you I came to see, my Gulmohar.'

'I sent her away,' says Gita.

'To whom?'

'To a madam.'

Ramvilas stares at her, confused. He suspects, though he cannot be sure and will always chase the thought from his mind, that Kiran is his daughter. He finds her presence unsettling, but has not been able to discuss this with Gita. He is pleased that the matter has resolved itself, but why would Gita send her daughter to another whorehouse? 'Madam?'

'Not that kind of madam!' says Gita angrily. 'A madam who runs a school.'

'Ah,' says Ramvilas. 'Some NGO.'

'What is an NGO?' she asks.

'A business that never turns a profit.'

'Why would anyone do such a business?' she asks.

'Because you can have other people give you their profits.' The germ of an idea appears in his mind, and he cannot resist smiling. 'An NGO, my Jahanara Begum, is the perfect business for you, fit for an emperor's daughter with delicate hands.'

'I want a shop,' she insists.

He looks at her, seated on the bed, a child at twenty-three. What a wonderful experiment this might be. What interesting stories will emerge! 'Parvati does not have an NGO,' he says suggestively.

'What will this NGO sell?' she asks.

'An NGO sells nothing. It only buys, for free. It writes letters. It issues pamphlets and brochures.'

'What will I write in the pamphlets?'

Ramvilas spreads his arms wide. 'You live in a whorehouse, my Jahanara Begum. Surely you can find a cause?'

'I do not like the bai,' says Gita. 'Or the pahalvan.'

'So destroy them. The NGO is not for them. It is for you, for the girls in the kotha.'

'Except Parvati?'

'Except Parvati.'

Gita considers.

This is the most creative moment of my life, thinks Ramvilas.

'I will call it Dukhiya Naari Uddhaar Sabha,' she says.

He laughs. 'The great newspapers of the world will not write about your NGO, my Gulmohar, if the name is unpronounceable! It must have an English name that shortens to a Hindi acronym, or a Hindi name that shortens to an English acronym, or a—'

'You can choose it yourself!' she says impatiently.

'Self-employed Women's Association,' says Ramvilas. 'Child Relief and You. National Organisation for Women. Do you see what is wonderful about these names?'

She looks at him, uncomprehending.

'They contract into wonderful words in English or Hindi,' he says.

She still does not understand.

'Do not worry,' he says. 'I will find a name for you.'

'What must I do, then, for this NGO?'

'Once you have the name, there is not much to do.'

'Nothing at all?' She is incredulous.

'Learn to speak better Hindi, my Mumtaz Mahal.'

'I spoke Nepali at home!' She pouts.

'Your home, my Gulmohar, is where your NGO is. And the NGO will require you to talk a lot. It is too late for English, so Hindi will do.'

'Who will teach me good Hindi?'

'Ask your customers,' he says, with a laugh. 'You will have staff, an office, workers, publicity. Above all, you will have your own cause. A whore campaigning for the rights of whores. The right to free condoms. The right to medical check-ups. The right to refuse customers who will not wear condoms. The right to education for your children. You will be the most beautiful of them all! Your face will bring you what protests and rallies cannot. You will not take a delegation to the PM, you will go alone so the PM can appreciate your point of view!'

'Why will I go to the PM?' she asks.

He chuckles and walks to the door, borne aloft on the tide of imagination, fired by his own eloquence, dazzled by his own brilliance. She shall be his lump of clay — what a smooth lump of clay! — that he can mould at will. Perhaps she does have the capacity to amuse him in other ways.

'The bai is having trouble with the police,' she says, from the bed.

That stops him. He cannot allow the police to interfere with Kotha 842. 'Did she tell you that?'

Gita nods.

'The sub-inspector is an OBC,' he says, with a sigh. 'That makes it more difficult.'

'What is an OBC?' she asks.

He chuckles. 'There is a great rally for OBCs next week. They are demanding that every fourth whore be an OBC.'

'But what is an OBC?'

'You are not one, and Parvati is. This means Parvati will soon have customers reserved for her, so you must speak against this rally.'

She falls silent.

'But you must not worry,' he cajoles. 'I am reserved for you, and you alone, even after the Mandal Commission locks away the entire world for OBCs.'

He turns to go, but she stops him again. 'You have forgotten the VCR.'

'I am doing my best,' he says irritably. 'It will take time.'

'And the mirror?'

'Ah, the mirror! I have bought for you the mirror of Noor Jahan. It swivels on a stand! You can put it on the table and twist it any way you like. No matter where it points, it will show the most beautiful face in Delhi.'

She gurgles. 'Why did you not bring it with you?'

'It will be brought to you by a boy. A sweet boy in a yellow shirt, who has heard much about your beauty.'

'When will he come?'

Ramvilas winks. 'I will send him to you on Sunday. On Sunday night, give him what he wants because on Monday morning he will move the earth.'

'Every day is the same in GB Road,' she says, as he leaves. 'What will happen on Monday?'

He descends the staircase quickly and finds the bai asleep in the waiting room next to the landing. He shakes her awake. She groans on seeing him.

'Has Gulmohar been rude to you?' she asks wearily.

'Gulmohar is a flower in bloom,' he says. 'Tell me about the sub-inspector.'

The bai sighs. 'He has raised the police rate. Seven per customer.'

'You must have done something to provoke him.'

The bai shakes her head. 'He says prices have risen everywhere else. I cannot reason with him, and my pahalvans do not want to interfere with the police.'

Ramvilas wonders if he should offer to help.

'I will have to ask Gulmohar to raise her rates,' says the bai casually.

Ramvilas is annoyed at the threat. He has been constant in his patronage. Is it fair to treat him as if he were just any customer? But the bai has a question in her eyes that must be answered. 'The sub-inspector is an OBC,' he protests. 'You know how things are with this Mandal Commission business. You cannot fight an OBC these days.'

'Perhaps Gulmohar is an OBC too,' retorts the bai. 'She will have to charge accordingly.'

Ramvilas stalks out. At the front door, he waits in the dark stairwell until a particularly dense wave of rickshas floods the street, then steps outside and quickly puts distance between himself and the kotha. He makes his way to the police chauki at the end of GB Road.

It is deserted, but he has no trouble in locating the sub-inspector, Inderlal Jha, who sits in a room at the back, sipping tea, fanning himself with a piece of cardboard and doodling on a register marked 'First Information Report, August 1990'. 'The chauki is closed for lunch,' he informs Ramvilas.

'I have not come to file an FIR,' says Ramvilas.

'This is lunchtime,' repeats Inderlal.

'I am from the IPP committee in Chandni Chowk,' declares Ramvilas. 'I have been sent by Harilal Gupta and Kartar Singh, both councillors.'

Inderlal sits up carefully. He is not familiar with the names, and is not certain what interest the IPP committee might have in talking to him, but it is imprudent to display ignorance.

'Harilalji has decided to take up women's issues,' says Ramvilas.

Inderlal is annoyed. 'Do I look like a woman to you?'

'He was informed that the police in GB Road have dealings with kothas.'

Inderlal maintains a carefully neutral expression. He must ferret out more information before he can answer this man. 'You will have to come back when the SHO Sahib returns,' he says.

'When will that be?'

'He has gone on his rounds,' says Inderlal vaguely. 'You can try again in the evening.'

Ramvilas looks at the inscrutable face before him – beady eyes, folds of loose skin round the cheeks and a thick, well-groomed moustache that dominates every other feature. A man perhaps younger than him by a year or two, but not as well preserved. A man who lets his meanness show in his eyes, and does not know it. 'All right,' he says. 'I will discuss the higher rate with the SHO.'

He rises. Inderlal scrambles to stop him. 'Which higher rate? You can discuss it with me!'

'But the SHO?'

'He is on his rounds,' says Inderlal. 'Who knows when he will be back?'

'Harilalji has been discussing women's issues with kothas,' announces Ramvilas. 'At Kotha eight hundred and forty-two he was told the rate had gone up to seven.'

Inderlal frowns. 'Yes, that is the new rate.'

Ramvilas raises an eyebrow.

'Everything is more expensive these days,' says Inderlal, defensively. 'I have been in GB Road for six years. In that time, the price of a water-pump has doubled. Bathroom tiles cost three times as much so how can the kotha rate remain the same?'

'Harilalji is unhappy with this harassment of women,' says Ramvilas, gravely. 'He will discuss the matter with the SHO.'

Inderlal studies the man before him and weighs his options. He reflects with satisfaction on his own position in the police force, not forgetting the commendation roll he received from the commissioner of police in 'eighty-four, for bravery in saving sardars during the riots. 'Tell your Harilalji to go and discuss this with the police commissioner himself. He is a good friend of mine.'

'But Harilalji has no intentions of interfering with police work,' says Ramvilas. 'He feels a small revision is fair. Even a sub-inspector must eat. How about five and a quarter?'

'Six,' says Inderlal.

'Five and a half,' says Ramvilas, with finality.

Inderlal nods in resignation.

'There is no need to bother your SHO with such details,' says Ramvilas. 'Perhaps you could tell him the rate stays at five.'

'The SHO?' responds Inderlal. 'There is no knowing when he will be back.' He calls for two cups of tea, but Ramvilas rises.

'It is your lunch hour,' he says. 'The police must not be disturbed.'

The peepul tree outside Kucha Bansilal stands so close to the Hanuman temple that the wall has an opening to allow for the trunk. The temple is the real reason the tree has not been chopped down to make way for a stall selling jalebis. Twenty-five years ago, when digging to repair a power line, engineers from the Delhi Electric Supply Undertaking unearthed a small brass figurine of Hanuman, which an examination by the Archaeological Survey of India revealed to be more than five hundred years old. It depicted Hanuman as a boy, eyeing the sun in the sky – attached to the figurine by a fine brass wire – ready to leap and swallow it. The discovery created great excitement among archaeologists, who found themselves in rare agreement with local politicians from the Jan Sangh. They prevailed on DESU to dig round the site, and Jan Sangh politicians prevailed on the council to build a makeshift Hanuman temple. It was later noted by the Archaeological Survey that the figurine looked rather modern, that the fine brass wire could not have survived intact for hundreds of years, and that the foot of Hanuman was embossed with the symbol of a foundry outside Ghaziabad. Jan Sangh politicians refused to accept such politically motivated revisionism, and the temple stayed, turning from a wooden structure into a concrete kiosk, which is what it is today, with a red stone statue of Hanuman. It is not a replica of the disgraced figurine – that is not the usual image of Hanuman anyway – but shows him in his canonical pose as the faithful servant of Raam, on one knee, hands folded, eyes shut in devotional bliss, tail flaring up behind his head. The pujari lives next to the statue, in the squatting-room-only space between the statue and the wall. He bathes it every morning, places sunflowers at its feet, paints a vermilion tilak on its forehead, and pockets the coins thrown by passers-by.

Gauhar stands under the peepul tree, leans against the temple wall, scans every face and chants his lines: 'Mysore silk, Banarasi silk, Kanjeevaram silk! French chiffon, Indian chiffon, organdie! Silk blouse, rubiya blouse!'

'Look for fat men who walk slowly with wives in tow,' Chotu has told him. 'Look for women in pairs, walking with handbags slung from their left shoulders, chatting. Look for children holding corners of sarees in one hand and ice-cream in the other. Look for men with gold chains and women with jewellery. Do not waste your time on a thin man who strides purposefully – even when he has a slight paunch. He is going somewhere on business, not looking to buy anything. Do not bring the seth dirty men in crumpled kurtas, or dark, underfed girls who have never touched a silk saree.'

Gauhar watches anxiously, becoming increasingly uncomfortable in the afternoon sun. He tries standing under the tree. It has almost no leaves, but the signboards and banners on its branches provide good shade. It is set back from the street, however, so he cannot keep an eye on the crowd if he stands under it. He comes back into the sun. He will get one per cent of every sale he generates, says the seth. It seems a paltry amount compared with the fifty-five rupees he can earn for every customer brought by Mussabir Ustad, even after he has paid him and the paanvala. He does not know what to make of the faces that swim by. He can tell at a glance whether a man is an arse-fucker: he can see it in the eyes, the gait, the arm movement, the rhythm of a person's breath. But how can Chotu tell if a man is a customer for Jamna Lal Kishori Mal? Is it the woman who sits on a ricksha, or the one who peers out of an Ambassador car?

His attention is drawn to a couple approaching the kucha. The man delivers a bow to the Hanuman temple before moving on. He looks mean and cold but the woman is fat – as Chotu said she should be – and wears a necklace. The man walks briskly, but she dawdles, looking at the signboards. He puts an arm round her shoulders to urge her on. Gauhar looks around them for children but there are none. He steps forward. 'Mysore silk, Banarasi silk, Kanjeevaram silk! French chiffon, Indian chiffon, organdie! Silk blouse, rubiya blouse! Jamna Lal Kishori Mal!'

He looks at the woman, afraid to make eye-contact with the man, and gestures to the kucha. She glances at him uncertainly, then at the man. Gauhar steps in front of her to block her path. She gasps in horror, points to his stump – which he has raised to prevent her passing him – and shrinks back. The man screams, 'Step aside, you mother-fucking one-handed bastard!'

Hurriedly Gauhar clears the way and runs to the Hanuman temple. The woman wraps her saree tightly about her shoulders so that not an inch of overflowing flesh is exposed, and walks away. Her husband follows protectively, and turns to glare at Gauhar when he is out of reach.

Fuck them all, thinks Gauhar angrily.

He clutches the metal grille of the Hanuman temple and pulls hard. The pujari scowls at him. Gauhar glares back. He does not like any of them – the pujari, the seth, the chaivala, or Yellow Teeth who brought him here. 'Give him a bath first,' the seth had said. He will piss on the seth's shop! He will piss on his sarees and blouses, and then he will piss on the seth himself, so they will all be equally dirty. There will be no need for baths then! 'You said two per cent to Yellow Teeth,' Gauhar had protested on his first day.

'That was before I saw your one hand,' said the fat seth. 'A one-handed boy can work half as much as a two-handed one!' Very well, he will work for one per cent, because sarees are expensive. The seth does not know that he can add, subtract, multiply and divide. If he tries to cheat Gauhar, he will get a kick in the arse.

It has now been ten days and he has found no customers. Not a single fat kurta has agreed to be drawn into Kucha Bansilal. In that time, he could have had ten men fuck him in the green cupboard. All right, he will work here for a few more days, then go back to Didi and Sparrows. He does not like fawning over fat women, and he does not like sleeping in a box in Kucha Bansilal. 'Is he a Musalman?' the chaivala had asked Yellow Teeth. 'Is he Bangladeshi?'

'He is poor like you and me,' Yellow Teeth said.

Ah, how he would love to sock them all in the eye, Hindu and Musalman, Indian and Bangladeshi together! He has let himself be fooled by Yellow Teeth. Two hundred rupees a day, he was told. He should have known better when he first saw the man – straggly beard, perpetual grin, dirty pyjamas. Why does he grovel in front of the fat seth? Does he not know that one swing of the arm can bring the seth to the ground? Look how Yellow Teeth giggles when he begs the balding chaivala for a cup of chai! He could reach over and make himself a cup, or carry off the whole shop. The chaivala is perhaps half blind and will barely notice – his spectacles are scratched and foggy. Were he to notice, would he be able to put up a fight? Yellow Teeth is not a man. To be spurned like a dog by a seth and a chaivala!

Gauhar wonders if he should approach Suleman Mian directly – he looks self-assured, with his pencil moustache, shining cheeks, well-oiled hair and the mean expression of a man who knows his way about. He will get Guahar a good job that will pay more than getting fucked in the arse. He is a man of the world, even more so than Mussabir Ustad, though no one can beat Mussabir Ustad at collecting bets for a pigeon fight.

'Get out of here!' says the pujari.

Gauhar realises he is too close to the temple wall. 'It is hot in the sun,' he says. 'I want to stand in the shade of the temple.'

'What is your name?' asks the pujari, suspiciously.

'Gauhar Muhammad.'

'Ah! Get out of here!'

Gauhar releases the grille and jumps away from the temple door. The grille is hot – it has left a dark blotch on his palm.

'Fuck you, panditji!' he says, to the pujari.

He walks down to the next kucha and stands at the entrance arch, which is plastered with posters. The pillars that support it are rectangular, with a small alcove built into each. He crawls into one and falls asleep.

Hours later he is woken by a screaming siren. It is evening. A van passes the kucha and comes to a screeching halt near the peepul tree. The police, thinks Gauhar. He is not certain why they should be looking for him, but he jumps out of the alcove and prepares to run. Then he reads the letters on the van – DESU, Delhi Electric Supply Undertaking. Three uniformed men emerge and place a ladder against the tree. One climbs it. Their attention is on the branches adorned with dozens of electrical wires, which find their way through the tree and then jump off to the power line that leads into Kucha Bansilal.

Gauhar approaches the van. The man on the ladder holds a pair of gigantic clippers in his gloved hands and cuts the wires, one by one. The largest signboard, Jamna Lal Kishori Mal, melts into darkness at the first snip. The next throws the temple into darkness, including the decorative red lamps that ring Hanuman's image. The pujari storms out and hurls a curse at the DESU men, who pay no attention.

'Atheists. Musalmans!' he screams. 'How can you keep Hanuman in the dark?'

Chitra follows the boys from Chawri Bajar all the way to Fatehpuri Masjid. They turn into Chandni Chowk and head toward Red Fort in a procession. There are no more than a dozen, carrying banners and shouting slogans in support of the Mandal Commission. It is a sort of advance guard for the great rally tomorrow. She balances the camera on her shoulder and tries to capture their faces mid-slogan. She wishes they had begun sooner because soon it will be dark.

'Mandal Commission *zindabad*!'

She feels the warmth of adventure among the boys, and finds it exhilarating to be released from the red-brick building behind Jama Masjid. She is reminded of protests during her college days. 'Ours is the most prestigious women's college in Delhi,' said her principal, 'so we must not sully its reputation with politics and protest.' The very term 'women's college' seemed antediluvian to her, implying that a separate form of knowledge was reserved for women – home science, history, English, sociology – while men studied the masculine matters of economics, finance, engineering and mathematics. 'We have mathematics in our women's college too,' said the principal.

'But how many women are encouraged to study them?' Chitra had demanded. And what was home science but a euphemism for cooking, cleaning, sewing and knitting? To call it a science was a travesty.

'We must not belittle housekeeping,' said the principal.

'We belittle it when we place it exclusively in a "women's college",' countered Chitra. 'Why should a men's college, known simply as a "college", not teach its students housekeeping?'

The principal finally agreed to take her suggestion – to remove the prefix 'women's' from the name of the college – to the Board. But Chitra knew that a mere name change was insufficient, as was the introduction of classes unsuitable for housewives. How could a woman know what to ask for in the pursuit of equality? Chitra protested against beauty pageants, for allowing male faculty members into the newly unwomaned college, and for unisex dormitories, yet she was never certain these were women's causes. 'We are fighting Aids and prostitution,' said grave feminists to her. 'We cannot lend our names to your frivolous obsessions!' She knew then that hers were not women's causes. Indeed, in a world of true equality, was there any meaning to the phrase 'women's causes'?

When she opened Sparrows, she thought she had embarked upon a glorious career of social service. After six years, she suspects that 'social service' is not a career. It is a hobby for some and a calling for others, an obsession or even a compulsion for believers, but never a career. She has been fortunate to find Shalini, who brought in two other girls from her college who, as they told her, wanted to 'see the real world'. Together, they can manage Sparrows if she looks in from time to time. She knows the girls regard it as a project with a timeline, an indulgence to be quickly abandoned on marriage or at the start of a proper career, but she is grateful for their presence. They will look after her twenty-six children while she films these boys.

She does not think much of the boys. How could they possibly benefit from this Mandal Commission, which they defend with such intensity? Do they understand what it recommends? She will interview them after the march with Red Fort in the background. She will ignore the possibility that their protest is a farce – all protests are launched on a slight misconception of reality and relevance. This, after all, is the street of protests. The boys have passed a plaque that records a protest of eighty years ago. 'This is where a bomb was thrown at Lord Hardinge,' it says, 'when he rode into Chandni Chowk to mark the moving of the Indian capital to Delhi.' And that peepul tree, thinks Chitra, is where Captain Hodson may have hung the sons of Bahadur Shah Zafar after he shot them. The tree wears a beard of wires that hang from it like roots.

She smiles. Every few years, DESU launches a drive against power theft and cuts off illegal connections, which are promptly restored. The tree has a foliage of wooden signboards, none visible in the fading light. A dark form steps out from beneath it. For a moment, she thinks the man is going to attack her, but he says, 'Mysore silk, Banarasi silk, Kanjeevaram silk! French chiffon, Indian chiffon, organdie—'

'Gauhar!'

Gauhar stops chanting and looks embarrassed.

'I have not seen you for ten days,' she says. 'You missed Baal Sabha, and Baal Bank has been closed for all that time!'

He shifts uncomfortably. In his new life, he has almost forgotten her rules and systems, which now appear quaint. 'I work,' he says evasively.

'Where?'

He points to the tree. The largest signboard is impossible to miss even in the darkness of dusk: 'Jamna Lal Kishori Mal'.

Chitra is overwhelmed. This is the boy who came through her door six years ago, dirty, ragged, naked from the waist up, one hand clutching a paratha, the other arm flailing in the air, displaying the stump. For six years he has missed classes, broken rules, fought other boys and tangled with Mussabir. But here he stands, employed in a saree shop, making a living with skills she has taught him. A literate boy, exhorting customers to come to his shop, the personification of her success, the poster she will carry for ever in her mind. 'I want to speak to your seth,' she says emotionally. 'Take me to his shop.'

Gauhar does not like the idea. He is uncertain how his association with her will appear to the seth. 'I have just started!'

She relents. 'I will come back.'

'What is that on your shoulder?'

'A camera,' she says, 'to make a film.'

'Where is the hero?' asks Gauhar.

She laughs. 'It does not have one.'

She looks around to discover that the protesting boys have gone ahead. Two stragglers rush to catch up with them, but the rest are far away, shouting slogans. A thought strikes her. Why film this self-centred movement, this pro- and anti-Mandal farce, when she has a moving story right before her eyes?

'What is your film about?' persists Gauhar.

'It is about you,' she says.

Gauhar is overjoyed.

'And Mussabir.'

This irritates him.

'Do you know where Mussabir is?' she asks.

At the pigeon fight or getting his arse fucked, thinks Gauhar. But he says nothing. If he squeals and Mussabir finds out . . . He shakes his head.

'It is getting dark,' says Chitra. 'I will come back here tomorrow, at eleven in the morning. Look for Mussabir and bring him if you find him. Tell him he will be in a film. You will both be film stars, like Amitabh Bachchan! And tell your seth I want to speak to him. Tell him he will be in the film too.'

'Why should he be in the film?' grumbles Gauhar.

'You will have the largest role,' she assures him, and turns to go.

'Didi,' he says.

She stops.

'I am hungry.'

'Did you not earn anything today?' Gauhar remains silent. She sighs, pulls out ten rupees, and is shocked at the alacrity with which he grabs the note. Ah, he's just a child, a poor child. It takes more than a few days' employment to rid a boy of his sense of deprivation. 'Make sure you look for Mussabir,' she says, then walks quickly to catch up with the boys, who have almost reached Red Fort.

'I will have a bath tomorrow morning,' Gauhar calls after her. 'Can you bring me a comb?'

He looks at the ten-rupee note with contentment. Fuck Mussabir Ustad, he thinks. He will not waste his time looking for him, only to share the film with him. He runs through Chandni Chowk, walks into the lane behind Jama Masjid and spends three rupees on nahari. His stomach gurgling with the soporific broth, he wonders if he should seek out a client, then decides against it. Didi will give him something tomorrow, so why bother with an old arse-fucker?

He walks to the Sparrows building. Through the windows, he can see boys and girls lying on mats, asleep. Didi is strict about everyone being asleep by nine. 'You must not go back to the school,' Yellow Teeth had warned him ten days ago.

'Why should I sleep in a box when I have a room?' he asked.

'Suleman Mian wants you to stay in Kucha Bansilal,' Yellow Teeth had said, 'so he can send for you when he needs you.'

Who the fuck is this Suleman Mian? Gauhar wonders. And why will he send for him?

He decides to go back to Kucha Bansilal. He is not afraid of Yellow Teeth. He is not afraid of Suleman Mian either, but perhaps Suleman Mian can get him a better job. He will go back to the chaivala's box. He has made a couple of holes in it without telling the chaivala, so he can breathe better. In a couple of days he will place a mattress inside it, and then he will be as comfortable as if he had his own room.

He will spend the night in the box. Tomorrow morning he will become a film star, and Mussabir can go fuck himself and his pigeons.

The night breeze flaps against his yellow shirt and cools his chest as Mukesh turns into GB Road and finds his way in the ochre arcs of bulbs that illuminate signboards. Afraid of being followed, he turns frequently, and hurries past every man who approaches him, holding close to his chest the paper package that Ramvilas gave him. He must avoid pimps, pahalvans and touts, Ramvilasji said. High above him, on upper floors to his left and right, the whores giggle behind grilles. On either side of the street men in kurtas and lungis eye him carefully. He walks quickly until he arrives at Agrawal Pump House, announced by its flashing electronic sign. Ramvilasji has warned him not to go to the wrong kotha, so he reads the sign three times. Assured, he runs into the dark staircase that leads up to Kotha 842.

He crosses the dark landing like a thief, tiptoes into a waiting room and sits gingerly on a divan. 'Someone will come for you,' Ramvilasji had said.

The room is walled with bunks, covered with curtains that flutter unnaturally. He studies the endlessly repeating pattern on the lino-leum floor, then looks at the pictures of Nehru, Gandhi, Guru Nanak and Sai Baba on the walls. They make him anxious. Has he blundered into a temple? A religious meeting hall? Should he run away before he is discovered and thrown out? Suddenly the room explodes with laughter and the curtains shake. He sees bits of flesh – a thigh, a breast, a shank, a rump. He gasps, gets up and runs to the door, where he collides with a middle-aged woman. 'Ah, you must be Mukesh,' says the bai in loving tones.

She adjusts her saree – thrown askew in the collision – and studies him frankly, holding his face in both hands. The impact has seared him: he has not touched such soft female flesh before. But he shakes the thought from his head, ashamed – the woman is at least forty!

She takes his hand, leads him up two flights of stairs and knocks on a door. It opens, and before him stands a Nepali woman, the most beautiful woman he has ever seen.

He stares, afraid to look but emboldened by her beauty. Such a small, plump, delicious woman, shorter than him but so self-assured that she looks straight into his eyes. Pale, creamy skin without a blemish, as smooth as the cheeks of a film heroine. Lips that remind him of a pomegranate bursting with juice. Flesh-coloured blouse that melts into her creamy skin, long, straight hair, saree worn low on her waist to reveal a deep navel.

She smiles, letting her lower lip hang loose. He notices that her narrow eyes close into slits, and her teeth are stained with paan. This bothers him a little. Then she speaks: 'Come.'

He is drawn into the room. He does not know when the bai leaves and the door closes behind him. The woman puts a hand on his shoulder and giggles. She is short, no taller than his chest. She stands him next to the bed, climbs on to it and kisses his forehead. He is bathed in the fragrance of jasmine and mahua. Her blouse is thin – almost transparent – and cut so low that he can see the straps of her bra, the swell of her breasts and the thrust of her nipples. Ah, the smooth, smooth skin! A mango, an apple, a juicy orange ready to be peeled!

Suddenly ashamed of his lack of etiquette, he fumbles with the package and tears off its paper wrapping. With trembling hands, he extends a swivelling mirror toward her, presenting it face first so that she can see her reflection.

She clasps her hands over his and brings him closer. They stand still with the mirror between them. He looks again at the paan-stained teeth, and imagines himself sucking her skin to find blood oozing from it. In confusion, he takes a step back. The mirror slips from their combined hands and crashes to the floor.

She cries out in consternation and jumps away to avoid the glass shards that leap at her from the floor. He stands, forlorn.

She looks at the mirror, then at him, and laughs. He laughs too. She pulls him toward her and he lays his head on her breasts, pushing his nose between then. There is softness, there is comfort, there is smooth skin, and there is the wildly strong aroma of jasmine and mahua.

'Slow down,' says Sohan Lal, to his son. 'I am not as young as you.'

He withdraws a silk handkerchief from his kurta and wipes his forehead. It is early morning in September. There is not a cloud in the sky, and the sun beats down on him as if he were trudging through sand dunes in a desert. Perhaps these environmentalist NGOs have a point, he thinks. September, and not a drop of rain. What will happen to the poor earth? You would not know it was parched, he thinks with disgust, if you looked at the rolling lawns on your right. Look at these miles of green grassland along the Yamuna river, luxurious graves in a poor country, kept in immaculate condition by the living to honour the dead – Rajghat, Shanti Van, Shakti Sthal, Vijay Chowk. A tribute to itself by the Congress Party at the expense of businessmen like him. How much does it cost to keep this necropolis humming with life? Would Gandhi, that frugal Bania, feel comfortable in the splendour of Rajghat?

It was a mistake to let the driver drop them off so far from Chandni Chowk, thinks Sohan Lal. He would have preferred to take the car all the way to Red Fort, but the driver thought otherwise. 'There is heavy traffic near the fort,' said the driver, 'because of the rally. They have blocked off the intersection and we may get stuck at police barricades.' Sohan Lal had agreed that they would walk along a stretch of Ring Road and cut across to Red Fort, thinking the exercise would do him good, that he could go home and tell Rukmini he had followed the doctor's advice. But now he regrets his rashness. He cannot keep up with Ramesh, and he cannot bear to look at the symbols of waste that lie buried under sylvan hills to his right.

No such thoughts seem to hinder Ramesh. They pass the deep avenue that leads into Rajghat.

'Shaku telephoned last night,' he says.

'No one told me,' grumbles Sohan Lal.

'You were asleep. She is fine. She says everyone liked the Queen Victoria coins.'

Sohan Lal plants his stick in front of him and walks doggedly. He remembers the frown that swept the brow of Shakuntala's father-in-law when he first saw the coins at the wedding. 'These are small ginnis,' he had remarked. Sohan Lal's heart had fluttered. How had the man found out that Vimla had received larger ones?

'They are Queen Victoria brand from nineteen thirty-nine,' Sohan Lal had said brightly. 'They do not make them any more.'

The frown had eased. Also, Shaku's father-in-law appeared pleased with the wedding arrangements. Jugal Kishor's bhujia and kachauris were popular, though not as much as he had expected. When all was taken into account, Mangat Ram Nawal Kishor had cost more than it should have. With greater care, he might have saved unnecessary expense, but the wedding could be called successful. Shakuntala has telephoned every day for the last ten – not a good sign – but the news has never been troubling. She will soon settle down and call less frequently. Within a year, she will have a son and he can stop worrying about her.

'It was very nice of Nareshji to come,' says Ramesh.

'That was not Nareshji!' Sohan Lal snaps. 'That was one of his nephews.'

It was shameless of Naresh Agrawal to accept the invitation and send his nephew as his representative. Sohan Lal had wanted a Member of Parliament at the wedding, not his lackey. It was generous of him, as an IPP committee member, to extend an invitation to a Congress MP. Did he deserve the humiliation of having his offer accepted and then ridiculed so? And how the nephew had torn into the kachauris like a beggar with a bottomless stomach! Harilal Gupta had fawned on the young man endlessly, paying vicarious homage to Naresh Agrawal. Everyone knows Harilal wants to become an MP, and that he must defeat Naresh Agrawal to win in Chandni Chowk. What sense did it make to tie himself up in the tail of the elephant who must be slain? But Harilal is shameless. It was embarrassing to see him dance to the brass band. He has gained considerable weight in the last two years and looked like a drunken rhinoceros, or a buffalo under-going a seizure. His body parts shook with such violence that the bandmaster had stopped playing his clarinet to watch. The most pathetic display, however, was the one put on by Kartar Singh, who had insisted on ingratiating himself with the committee by making a heroic attempt to dance on his one good leg. What better way to remind everyone about the 'eighty-four riots?

'They should not hold rallies on Mondays,' says Ramesh. 'It is bad for the saree market.'

'Yes.' Sohan Lal sighs.

He approves of the concern implicit in that comment. In the last two weeks, he has been impressed by Ramesh's stewardship of the shop. Perhaps it was wise to have the driver leave them here. It is good to hear the boy speak his mind, and to say a thing or two himself. In the shop they are constrained to speak about business. The boy is twenty-six now, ready to settle down with a wife. He must find a match soon – a match worthy of a seth, unlike his own. He had had to wait until he was twenty-two, considered late in those days. He had hoped to find a Marwari girl of good family from Delhi, the better to settle in the city, but why would a rich Delhi seth choose for his daughter a clerk, whose only capital was the promise of a loan from Seth Ghanshyam Das? It was easier to talk up his career in Bikaner, which is how his uncles had found him a very good match there. The girl was sixteen, and her education consisted of the entire *Bhagavad Gita*, which she could recite by rote. Her family was told that he was a junior partner in a Delhi business – only a half-lie. It has now been thirty-three years, and who can complain of Rukmini? She is a little too short – which is why Ramesh is short – but she is frugal, cooked well in the days before they had servants, and is soft-spoken. Those are no mean attributes in a wife. He has seen sharp-tongued women destroy a man's peace of mind. It must be because of Rukmini that he has no blood-pressure problems, and his migraine cannot be blamed on her.

He must not waste a moment in looking for a daughter-in-law, thinks Sohan Lal, now that both daughters have been married off. He must speak with Lala Surajmal right away. That man has married off four sons, no small feat in an age when getting a good girl has become difficult. A suitable girl may be available in Bikaner, but who will explain the ways of Delhi to her? Ramesh is not a smart city boy, but he deserves better than a village bumpkin. He is a responsible, mature son, who dutifully finished his BCom. He is a boy without a vice – does not touch alcohol, smoke or speak disrespectfully; a boy given to moderation, industry and indulgence in the right proportions, who folds his hands when passing the Hanuman temple even if he is not given to flashy displays of religiosity; a boy who attends weddings and pujas, drops one-rupee coins into collection boxes and hums along gently – with mild devotion but not fanatical fervour – when he hears a song sung in a temple.

They have walked a great distance. Ramesh seems to pause near Shantivan. He looks at the green lawns, then turns into the grounds for a detour. Sohan Lal is tired, but acquiesces. The shop can wait. He hurries to catch up with his son.

'The flowers are beautiful,' says Ramesh.

Sohan Lal nods eagerly, although he disapproves of such frivolous interests. He points to a sea of roses – red, pink, white and yellow – then to clumps of gulmohar and jacaranda. 'This is not the season for flowers,' he says, 'yet the gardener can make them bloom in Shantivan.'

'Their fragrance is better than the attars you gave Shaku,' says Ramesh.

Sohan Lal winces. He must get back at Surajmal for the insult. How regally Surajmal had stood in his silver-lined shervani, blessing Shakuntala and his son-in-law, extolling the virtues of those attars when he must have known!

'But they were good attars,' says Ramesh soothingly. 'I had a whiff.'

Sohan Lal does not know what to say. It is a matter of some regret to him that Ramesh has shown no interest in olfactory refinement. The stench of Chandni Chowk drains has dulled the boy. He will never be a connoisseur.

'Attars are frivolous,' says Ramesh. 'Why waste money on them when you can buy a bottle of perfume for two rupees outside Kucha Bansilal?'

Sohan Lal feels chastened. The boy is probably hinting that his father has squandered money on the wedding. Then, suddenly, remorse floods him. Has he turned his boy into a prudent mule? Delhi girls want flashy young men, and their fathers are beginning to heed their demands. They seek boys with drive and ambition, with college degrees, boys who are fashionable and can speak English at such speed that it appears to be their own language. If Ramesh were taller, or projected an air of confidence, he would make a better match. It is not enough to be a God-fearing, stable man of good breeding with a shop of your own, thinks Sohan Lal ruefully. You must be able to eat comfortably in five-star hotels and upbraid the waiter in English if your Thums Up is not cold enough! He still believes he was right to insist that Ramesh sit on the gaddi with him as soon as he turned sixteen. This had meant that Ramesh spent less time in college, but what can a young man do in college after his classes have ended? Drugs, smoking, alcohol and loose women! If he has homework, he can do it while seated on the gaddi. Why should he waste time in the college library where he will fall in with irresponsible young men, whose fathers have no businesses to bequeath them and who loiter about the campus, recruiting impressionable young boys such as Ramesh into their nefarious schemes? One day, when he himself is incapacitated, Ramesh will take over the shop, and the transition will be smooth because of his training. If college has not left its mark on him, so much the better. He does not need one of those girls who insist on college boys. Such wives are unreliable, and such a daughter-in-law brings more trouble than comfort to a household.

Perhaps his son is a Philistine, but he is mature with sensible habits, which will serve him better in life than any refinement affected by the city boys.

Thus assured, Sohan Lal taps his stick on the ground and wanders among the flower-beds, watching Ramesh out of the corner of his eye. The boy steps away from the path to let three joggers pass. Then he walks up to the marble memorial to Nehru, folds his hands and bows his head. The boy is politically naïve, Sohan Lal mourns. After I am gone, he wonders, will he know how to handle sales-tax and income-tax inspectors? Will he be able to kick out boys like Chotu when they steal? Does he know that he must have the shop cleaned for Durga Puja, and that new account books are opened at Divali? 'You should not bow your head,' he chides Ramesh. 'He was only a man.'

'His spirit lives in me,' says Ramesh.

Sohan Lal smiles drily. When Ramesh was born, everyone said the spirit of Nehru was rekindled in him because the news of Nehru's death spread across Delhi just before his birth. How unfortunate to be saddled with the spirit of such a weak man! A man who fell for white women and grovelled before white men, who peddled unmanly, impractical and self-defeating pacifism with impunity, making India ridiculous in the eyes of the world, securing for himself a place in history even as he destroyed the future of his country. How he had pandered to Musalmans and danced with Naga and Mizo tribals! All of India was a cultural festival, a zoo, a circus, to be watched in wonder.

'Some day, IPP will undo the damage he has done,' Sohan Lal says. He is making a wish, not stating a belief. And he knows that it means nothing to Ramesh, who is oblivious of such matters. 'We should go now,' he adds. 'We cannot stay in Shantivan for ever.'

They walk back to Ring Road in silence. Sohan Lal slows to catch his breath, letting Ramesh put some distance between them. He does not want to continue the conversation. Perhaps father and son should be left in their spheres. The less he learns about his son's beliefs, the less their naïveté will bother him.

They cross Ring Road and walk up the street that leads to a pathway behind Red Fort. From there, it runs along the fort wall, passes Lahore Gate and opens out into Chandni Chowk. The path is blocked by a police check-post. A jeep stands guard, and three policemen bar their way. 'There is no entry into Chandni Chowk this morning,' says the constable.

Sohan Lal is irritated. 'How will I get to my shop?' he demands.
'You will have to go via the railway station,' says the constable.
'The rally will not begin for another two hours!' protests Sohan Lal.
The constable shrugs. They turn and go back to Ring Road.

'Let us take a ricksha,' says Sohan Lal. 'I cannot walk all the way to
the railway station.'

They sit silently on the ricksha as it crawls along Ring Road, turns
left and arrives at the railway station. Sohan Lal directs it through the
park at the front – through sleeping beggars – and into a lane too
narrow for it, so they continue on foot. Their walk has become much
longer than planned. Sohan Lal sets his jaw grimly and walks ahead.
The lane, after much winding, will finally connect to Kucha Bansilal.

'We cannot enter the kucha from this end,' says Sohan Lal. 'It is not
a good omen to approach your shop from the wrong direction.'

'All right,' says Ramesh. 'We will first turn into another kucha that
takes us to Chandni Chowk, then enter Kucha Bansilal from the
front.'

Gopal arrives in Kucha Bansilal to find Ibrahim waiting for him at the
stall. He steps off the bicycle, removes the milk bags he has bought
from Banwari, then hoists the bicycle above the junction box. He
raises the lid of the chai stall and kicks it twice, waking Gauhar, who
opens his eyes, then shuts them under the onslaught of sunlight. He is
surrounded by tins of cardamom, sugar and tea.

'The boy is small,' says Ibrahim, approvingly. 'He fits easily.'

'I cannot lock the box at night,' protests Gopal.

'The boy will guard it with his life,' declares Ibrahim.

Gopal kicks the box again, and Gauhar scampers out.

'Go!' says Ibrahim. 'You do not need to stand here.'

Gauhar points to the shuttered doors of Jamna Lal Kishori Mal.
'Sethji is not here yet.'

'Will you shit after sethji arrives?' asks Ibrahim. 'Do you never take
a bath?'

Gauhar withdraws.

'Has the boy given you any trouble?' he asks.

'Not yet,' says Gopal. He secures the lid to the junction box, crawls
into the stall and arranges his sugar and cardamom tins. 'There is a
hole in the box!' he complains.

'A rat,' suggests Ibrahim.

Gopal is unsure if rats eat wood, but not confident enough to challenge the theory. He pumps the stove, wondering if he will have to offer his first cup of tea to Ibrahim. It is bad luck to begin the day with a Musalman, especially one who will not pay. 'It is too early to make tea,' he says. 'I will not have customers until sethji arrives.'

Ibrahim turns his yellow-black teeth to Gopal and grins. 'I will pay you for your tea today, Gopal Bhai.'

This soothes Gopal. He pumps the stove vigorously.

'Twenty-five rupees,' says Ibrahim, casually.

Gopal is pleasantly surprised. 'Twenty-five for one glass of tea?'

'That is what Suleman Mian will give you. And you can eat for free. Aloo puri.'

'Has Suleman Mian opened a free hotel?' laughs Gopal.

'Yes. A hotel for poor people. He has called for a big rally today, near Red Fort. It will start in one hour. Everyone in the rally will get twenty-five rupees and aloo puri.'

Gopal shakes his head. 'I do not like all this politics.'

'Where else will you get twenty-five rupees?' demands Ibrahim.

'Get me a hammer, Ibrahim Mian,' says Gopal eagerly. 'A hammer, and three strong men whom you trust.'

Ibrahim is irritated. 'I have heard enough about your hidden treasure! Here I am, offering you twenty-five for walking up to Red Fort.'

'All right,' says Gopal. 'When does the rally start?'

'As I said, in one hour. Now let us have some tea.' He pulls out his tumbler from the junction box, rinses it with water and sets it next to the stove. 'Tie your dhoti carefully when we go,' he says. 'There will be a large crowd. And leave your spectacles in the stall. You cannot see much through them anyway. They may get lost in the lathi charge.'

'Lathi charge!'

Ibrahim is offended by this vulgar display of panic. 'Must I explain every detail to you? When you throw stones at the police they beat you with sticks and batons.'

'I am a poor man,' pleads Gopal. 'Should a stick fall on my head—'

'Stop snivelling!' says Ibrahim. 'This is a rally, not a Divali mela. We are going to protest against these anti-Mandal people. Who are these rich boys to deny us our quotas? We want justice for all OBCs, all Musalmans! Why should we clean up shit for upper-caste boys?'

'Bhangis clean up shit,' says Gopal. 'You told me Bhangis are SCs. But you are a Musalman.'

'Musalman, SC, ST, OBC. What is the difference?'

'But I am a Brahmin,' says Gopal.

'You are a poor man,' says Ibrahim firmly. 'You are no different from a Bhangi.'

They drink tea, Gopal from a cup and Ibrahim from his glass tumbler.

'I have never been beaten with a stick before,' says Gopal, mournfully.

'You said you were coming! I have already drunk your tea. How will I pay you now if you do not come?'

Gopal sighs in resignation.

'A little beating does no one any harm,' says Ibrahim. 'A doctor will tell you it hardens the bones. And tear gas is good for your eyes.'

'What is tear gas?'

'These rallies are like Muharram. People beat their chests and cry.'

'Why should they cry?'

'Do you see any reason to celebrate, Gopal Bhai? Do you not see rich college boys running all over Delhi, stoning buses and shouting slogans? And do you not want your son to become a clerk in the government, just as these rich boys do?'

'I want my son to help me in the stall.'

'And make tea?' says Ibrahim.

'Yes.'

Ibrahim shakes his head. 'You should not have been a Brahmin, Gopal Bhai! You should have been a Musalman, or an OBC. It is our government now, it is our party.'

'You used to say the Congress Party was your party.'

'Congress was not good for Musalmans,' says Ibrahim. 'In forty years, Suleman Mian has told me, all it gave us was Musalman presidents. We do not want to become presidents, we want to be clerks and peons. Come to the rally and Suleman Mian will tell you everything. One day, he will be the MP for Chandni Chowk. Then you can close your stall and become rich. Even you, who are a Brahmin.'

Sohan Lal and Ramesh pass the Hanuman temple, fold their hands and bow their heads. Chotu sees them and steps outside the temple – where he assists the pujari every morning in return for a place to sleep – takes the keys from Sohan Lal and runs ahead to open and dust the shop. Sohan Lal casts a habitual glance at the peepul tree, and notes sourly that the Jamna Lal Kishori Mal sign is askew, marred by wires that hang loose over it. 'DESU has come again,' he says grimly.

'I will ask Chotu to reconnect the wire,' replies Ramesh.

They turn into the kucha. Sohan Lal sees the chaivala and averts his gaze. He had hoped, somehow, that the stall would be closed today, thus lightening the burden of knowledge that he cannot shake off. The sight of the yellow-toothed Musalman, sitting so smugly with the chaivala, annoys him. He slips off his shoes on the concrete slab and walks on to the mattress, which Chotu is dusting.

Sohan Lal opens the alcove where Lakshmi sits, sprinkles a few drops of water at her feet, and puts a spot of vermilion on her forehead. Rukmini has packed halva in a polythene bag, to be given to the Hanuman temple. He loosens the knot and places it at the feet of Lakshmi. Then he folds his hands and sings aarti. From the corner of his eye he can see the Musalman talking to the chaivala, and his voice falters.

He is not a man given to inflexible stands in the name of principle. He understands, with the wisdom of fifty-five years, that sales-tax inspectors must be appeased and income-tax inspectors need not be told everything. A man has to live and prosper against the odds, and a few justifiable transgressions need not cause him to lose faith in his honesty and humanity. He has sometimes sold a rubiya blouse with a silk saree, told customers they did not need to iron silk, sold maroon chiffon to the darkest women – 'It looks so beautiful on you!' – and pastel colours to fair ones. He has even told plump women they look thinner in organdie. A man must run a shop, and he must rearrange the properties of fabric to become what they should have been in the first place. If he sometimes engineers under-voting in Musalman areas of Chandni Chowk, it is merely so that deserving candidates may sit in the council. If he has spread rumours about Harilal Gupta's health, it is only because Harilal's expanding waistline makes such stories seem true. Lakshmi is not a stickler for rules, when a slight bending of them can advance a just cause. Which is why, as he now concentrates on her form, he can think only of the chaivala and wonder if he should tell him about his son.

Sohan Lal concludes his aarti, opens his eyes and looks across the kucha. The Musalman is grinning, and the chaivala seems amused. Ah, the fool deserves no more than he has! Look at him! A balding man with hair flopping out of giant nostrils. A man with a ridiculous checked shirt, dirty dhoti and scratches on his spectacles. A man whose protruding belly makes him look much older than he is – how old *is* he? Forty-three? Forty-four? A useless man, who will never move one inch from where his father left him. It is not possible to imagine him setting out to buy a larger chai shop, turning it into a fancy general store with tea, coffee, ice-cream and chocolates, working day and night to extend the little life gave him, as Sohan Lal himself would have done. No, the chaivala is no entrepreneur. He is not a Marwari, not a man with trade and money in his blood. He is from Bihar or Uttar Pradesh or one of those states where they do not make men with drive. He is of no use to the gods, humanity or society.

Sohan Lal disengages a small lump from the halva lying at Lakshmi's feet, rolls it into a ball and drops it guiltily into his mouth. Sugar and ghee. Rukmini would be horrified, but these are the leftovers of Lakshmi herself. Surely a little halva will not exacerbate diabetes, especially when it is the prasaad of Lakshmi.

He unlocks his attar cabinet and selects two bottles, khus and kewra – two soft fragrances that mix rather well. A drop of each on the back of his hand, rubbed gently, invigorates his nose. He replaces the stoppers, puts away the bottles and relocks the cabinet. The chaivala is derelict in his duties as a father, he thinks. What else can come of a boy who does not sit with his father once he has turned sixteen? And if the father's neglect leads to the son's ruin, can anyone but the father be blamed? What can the world do about it anyway? Go on a fast unto death, as Gandhi did? What purpose would it serve if he, Sohan Lal, were to jeopardise his own position in the committee to fulfil some imagined duty to a chaivala? Everyone cannot be a Gandhi. Even Gandhi knew that a 'fast unto death' was a public stunt, that the British would intercept it by acceding to his demands, that one of his minions – Nehru or Rajagopalachari or Azad – would somehow contrive a situation that would enable him to end the fast without losing face. For the rest of us, a fast unto death means death. We must step away from the edge, every now and then, to stay on the path of life. A pinch of dishonesty teaches us the worth of being honest. We are only humans, and surely Lakshmi understands.

He considers offering some halva to Ramesh, then decides against it. Ramesh sits idly, cross-legged, awaiting the first customer. The rally is bad for business. And it is time that Bangladeshi boy sent customers into the lane. It has been ten days, and he has yet to find one. Sohan Lal was wise not to promise him any money, except as commission. A one-handed boy, and a dirty one! What possible success can he have?

He turns back to Lakshmi. The mould that cast her was rather intricate. Etched into her silver face are dimples, nostrils, eyes, eyebrows and even a frown. He has never taken a good look at the eyebrows, and it now appears to him that she seems displeased. The brows arch sharply, and the frown is deep. It is odd that he has never noticed this before. He cannot bear to look at it. He turns and calls to the chaivala, across the kucha, 'How old is your son, Gopal Bhai?'

'The seth is talking to you!' whispers Ibrahim.

Gopal looks across the kucha uncertainly. Sethji has never before addressed him as 'Gopal Bhai'. 'Twenty-one,' he says.

'The seth is looking straight at you!' hisses Ibrahim. 'He is wondering when you will die, so he can take over the plank you sit on. Look how he wipes his forehead with a silk handkerchief! Have you ever touched a silk handkerchief?'

'He is a good man,' says Gopal.

'He is worried about your son,' says Ibrahim sarcastically. 'Maybe he wants to make him a partner in his shop.'

'I have not seen Mukesh for two months,' says Gopal.

'If only you had listened to me when he was young,' says Ibrahim.

Sohan Lal feels the sweat pour from his forehead. It is not I who have made the arrangement, he reminds himself. I am only a witness, a bystander, an innocent spectator. Who knows how many boys are walking about Chandni Chowk named Mukesh Pandey? Not all of them are the chaivala's sons! 'Your son,' he calls to Gopal. 'Did he ever work in Kucha Mahajani?'

'Six years ago,' says Gopal.

'Why did he leave?'

'It was not his fault! Someone else switched the diamond!'

Sohan Lal's heart beats loudly, and his mouth is dry. Doubt was his last refuge. Is a man who watches a child drown less culpable than one who pushed it into the river? He is afraid to look at Lakshmi. She condones much, but he is no longer certain of the limits of her tolerance, now that he has noticed that frown on her brow. 'You should take better care of your son,' he calls.

'You know how young men are, sethji.' Gopal shrugs.

'Where is he today?' asks Sohan Lal.

While Gopal searches for an answer, Ibrahim slams down his tumbler. 'Don't tell the seth where Mukesh is!' he whispers. 'He must have a reason for asking.'

'But I really do not know,' whispers Gopal.

'Did he not sleep in your kholi last night?' asks Sohan Lal.

Gopal shakes his head.

'An unmarried son should always be within sight of his father. Look at Ramesh! I never let him go out anywhere without first letting me know.'

Gopal is flattered. The seth has compared his own son with Mukesh! 'I will do as you say, sethji.'

Sohan Lal turns his next words carefully in his mind before he speaks. 'This rally near Red Fort. It is not good for boys to go to rallies.'

'Do not listen to him!' whispers Ibrahim. 'He is a rich seth, a bloodsucker. He just wants the rally to fail!'

Gopal drowns his face in his cup of tea.

'Suleman Mian will become MP,' says Ibrahim. 'Then you will buy a large tea shop. I will go and find your son for you, Gopal Bhai. We will make him the seth in your new shop. Everything will be fine when Suleman Mian is MP.'

Sohan Lal wipes his forehead. It is now up to the chaivala to take the hint. No one can help a fool. So much happens in this world that will make a good man tremble, he consoles himself. Someone is raping a woman in America at this very moment. Someone is robbing a good man of his wallet in New York. This does not bother him because he does not know the good man's name. The only reason he knows this boy's name is the curse of his sharp memory. A lesser man may have missed the connection with the chaivala and gone to sleep in innocent bliss. Is it his fault, then, that he can recall the name of a boy he last saw years ago? In any case, he did not engage the boy. He is merely a God-fearing man taking care not to overstep the bounds of propriety.

'You will cry today,' says Ibrahim to Gopal. 'And you will get twenty-five rupees for it.'

IF

Chandni Chowk bustles with the excitement of morning, but most shops are closed. A barricade of metal fences erected by the police stretches along the length of the street from Fatehpuri Masjid to Red

Fort, separating both footpaths from the road, which itself is blocked off in sections. The footpaths are choked with onlookers while the road is deserted, police jeeps its only traffic. Inderlal Jha surveys his portion of the road with proprietary contentment. A Maruti Gypsy and twelve constables have been loaned to him for the occasion. The jeep has a beacon that he can flash at will, and a loudspeaker that he intends to use when the procession goes by. He sits in the front passenger seat, one foot placed confidently on the footboard, as if he is ready to spring out at a moment's notice. It is nice, this rally. It gives him a chance to organise security, which is far more interesting than sitting behind his desk in the police chauki and entering FIRs, most of which are fraudulent anyway. He has never seen such elaborate arrangements, and the premonition of violence has doubled his pleasure.

Mukesh staggers through Chawri Bajar and turns into Chandni Chowk near Fatehpuri Masjid. His head hurts and his eyes smart. His limbs feel weak and lifeless, so much so that each step requires effort. He does not know when this blanket of lethargy descended on him, but it has gripped him ever tighter since she brought him that cold brass tumbler. 'Drink it all,' she said. 'It is the elixir of love.' She stood close behind him, pressing her breasts to his back, and held the tumbler to his lips. 'It is going to be a hot morning and this will cool you,' she said. The drink was like the thandayi he has tasted at Holi – milk, walnuts, almonds, saffron and the strong smell of hashish. When he had drained the glass she turned him round, embraced him and gave him a long kiss. 'Now you can go,' she said. She escorted him downstairs. At the door she touched his cheek. 'Remember me,' she said. And he walked out into a swarm of rickshas in GB Road.

Chandni Chowk is quieter than GB Road today, empty, as if it has been awaiting his arrival. There are metal fences strung along the edge of the footpath. He does not want to walk along it: it is too crowded. He slides a fence outward and cuts through the wall. An avalanche of police constables descends on him. They grab his arms, shout excitedly and laugh at his vain attempts to keep his eyes open. A police inspector waddles out of a Maruti Gypsy and grips his jaw with one hand.

Inderlal frisks Mukesh. Another drunk with nothing on him, he thinks angrily. No gun, no knives, no wallet even. His eyes fall on the skinny wrist where a Rolex dangles loosely. 'Your wrists are too thin for this watch,' he says suggestively.

Mukesh shakes his head. Inderlal decides not to pull the watch off. He is in plain view of the constables. But perhaps he could hold the man in the lockup and approach him at a more opportune moment. He pulls the man's wrist toward him for a closer look, and notices a deep scratch running across the face, starting at ten and ending at four. Perhaps the prize is not worth the trouble. The man has a curious smell about him, not unpleasant but suggestive of flowers and womanly delicacy, or a perversion unsuitable for a man.

'Let him go,' he says to the constables.

They push him on to the footpath and close the gap in the metal fence. Mukesh flings silent abuse at them, smoothes down his yellow shirt and begins to walk away unsteadily. Last evening, before sending him to Gulmohar, Ramvilasji gave him two thousand rupees. 'We had agreed on five,' said Mukesh.

'You will get the rest tomorrow,' said Ramvilasji.

Mukesh wondered, for a moment, if he should kick him in the shins and walk out of the building. Rajan Nahal always paid in advance, and this Ramvilasji was holding on to his money for as long as he could. 'You did not say it was two and three when we agreed on the amount!' he protested.

Ramvilasji put an arm round his shoulders. 'What is money?' he said. 'And what harm can one day do to you? You may be robbed tonight. Is it not better for you to have less in your pocket when you are robbed? Rajan Nahal gives you money, but I will give you something better.'

Then Ramvilasji had handed him the package with the mirror and sent him to Gulmohar. On his way to GB Road, he had stopped in Kucha Mahajani, prised up the loose concrete slab outside Seth Jhunjhunwala's shop and stowed away the two thousand. He counted his hoard carefully before he left. Eight thousand rupees.

Mukesh wends his way groggily, enveloped in a cloud of jasmine and mahua. People swim by him in twos and threes, rickshas float in the air, and a jeep flies by at astonishing speed, horn beeping. He raises his eyes to the sun, shining brilliantly behind Red Fort, making silhouettes of its pillars and canopies. Three arches have been con-structed along Chandni Chowk to welcome the procession that will walk through, on its way to the rally in the Red Fort grounds. They frame the central ramparts of the fort. Banners hang from them – 'Mandal Commission *zindabad*! Reservation for OBCs! V. P. Singh *zindabad*!' More have been slung across the street, tied at either end to windows from which peer thousands of faces. Green bunting flutters noiselessly from the arches, forming a transparent ceiling under which police jeeps crawl, engines sputtering. The footpath is overrun with juice stalls, cobblers, bhujia counters, watermelon carts and stalls selling chappals.

'Walk toward Red Fort and he will spot you,' Ramvilasji told him last evening.

'What must I do?' he had asked.

'He will tell you,' said Ramvilasji.

'How will he know me?' asked Mukesh.

Ramvilasji had laughed. 'He will know you as surely as he knows his own brother,' he said.

'How will I know him?' Mukesh asked.

'Why do you need to?' retorted Ramvilasji. Then, perhaps sensing it was best to tell him, Ramvilasji had described the man: 'He is thin and short, and his upper lip is split down the middle, thus exposing his teeth. Look for a hare-lipped man with splayed upper teeth that have red paan stains on them.'

Mukesh cannot focus on the scene before him. Every lip appears cleft, every mouth has exposed teeth, every face carries the scowl of a rabbit. Is this the man, who walks briskly behind him? Or is that his accomplice, who leans heavily against the metal fence? He should have resisted when she gave him the thandayi. But she stood so close, and her breasts were pressed so warmly to his back!

He casts his fuzzy mind back to the night he spent in Kotha 842, and shudders with fear and delight. He remembers the room well – four-poster bed, dressing-table, stool, coir mat on the floor, a few children flitting in and out. He remembers noises in the corridors, quarrels, screams, giggles and arguments. Some time during the night, he woke to the sound of a crash – perhaps a cup of tea dashed to the floor. But, most of all, he remembers the soft embrace of her body, her breasts and buttocks, her smooth flanks. He could not see much in the dark, but she was like a ball of flesh wrapped round him. His memory of her is fragmented into the use of body parts – the sucking of breasts, the licking of flanks, the burying of his face in her plump navel. He wanted to tear her saree and assault her, but she held him off with curious self-assurance. Finally, she squeezed his trembling penis in her hands and guided it into a jelly-like space. He waited for the sensation of unparalleled delight, but he was weak with anticipation. She looked at him with a smile, visible even in the dark, waiting. 'You need to move back and forth,' she told him. Then she took out his limp penis, stroked it until it was erect again – he gurgled with pleasure at her touch – and inserted it again. He went limp. She made an impatient sound and drew him out. 'We will try some other time,' she said.

He was furious. He raised himself on his elbow and spat into her face. 'Are you saying no to me, you whore? How dare you deny me?'

She slapped him so hard that he fell back into the bed. Then he attacked her, trying to bite and kick. She jumped out of bed and ran to the door. He was penitent. He did not want a scene with those women on the first floor, and perhaps Ramvilasji would not be pleased. 'Come back,' he said. 'I will be kind to you.'

She crawled back into bed, and the sight of her swaying breasts aroused him again. She pulled his penis into her and rocked him to and fro, but he collapsed instantly. She hugged him, smothered his face in her breasts and cuddled him. He fondled her breasts, finding much more joy in them than in the sticky, jelly-like vagina. He was grateful that she did not try to direct him there again.

He woke up late to find the bed surrounded by children. Gulmohar arrived soon after. She led him down two floors to a bathroom, where she threw bucketfuls of water over him, in plain view of a dozen women, who giggled and pointed. They ran in and out of the bathroom – half naked – chattering, quarrelling and laughing. There was a moment that morning – a brief one – when he thought of abandoning the whole thing and saying no to Ramvilasji. Why not live here with this soft, plump woman with succulent breasts? They could play in bed every night and wake up before dawn to take a bath together. And the other girls could join them whenever they wanted. But then he saw other men in the corridors, and realised he was not alone. He was suddenly uncertain of his position, and grateful when Gulmohar led him back to her room. She took away the old saree in which she had wrapped him for the trip to the bathroom, and dressed him in his yellow shirt and brown trousers. She brought him parathas stuffed with gobhi. 'They are from Paratha Gali,' she said. He was surprised at her generosity. 'You can thank Ramvilas,' she said.

He ate voraciously. 'I will come back to you this evening,' he told her.

'You will have to pay,' she said.

This bothered him. Had she not been moved by the tender fondling of the night before? Was there not a special bond between them? 'I want to meet your parents,' he said.

She laughed, and her narrow eyes closed into slits. 'My parents are dead.'

'Where are your brothers? Sisters?'

'I do not have any.'

'Then no one can tell you to stay away from me!' he exclaimed.

'No one,' she said.

'I will come for you in the evening,' he repeated, 'and I will bring you a brick of silver.'

Her face brightened. She kissed his forehead. Then she brought him the thandayi, stood behind him and pressed her breasts to his back.

Red Fort looks like a giant insect, hovering ever closer as he walks toward it, poised to sting him with its minarets. The crowd that lines Chandni Chowk forms a wall alongside which he walks uncertainly, jostling people, using the metal fence to steady himself. 'Do not look directly into people's faces,' Rajan Nahal always told him. 'Think of them as masses of flesh that will attack you unless attacked first. Unfocus your eyes and swing your arm without hesitation. Throw, hack, burn and pierce before those creatures throw themselves at you!' Yet he must now scan all faces for the hare-lipped man.

The body that floats toward him is certainly that of a woman. What is she doing in this male domain? A tall woman in a flowing saree, carrying a large, electronic box on her shoulder. It looks like a camera, a giant eye, the largest camera he has ever seen. What does she want with him? Will she give him her breasts, as Gulmohar did? Even in the haze that now descends on his eyes, he can see that she is less womanly, less delicate, less inviting. She does have long, flowing hair, but he dislikes the large red bindi that covers a third of her forehead. Gulmohar had a small bindi that set off her smooth forehead and she was much fairer. This woman is too tall, too masculine. Even the way she holds the camera on her shoulders – which are muscular, not soft and rounded like Gulmohar's – is unattractive. That saree is not silk but some cheap material. But he has no interest in her. He must look for a man with a cleft lip. He studies his Rolex. It is past eleven! Or is it five thirty in the evening? Has he put on the watch upside-down? 'I do not want you, madam!' he whispers. He straightens up for the imminent assault but she does not stop, her camera brushing against him as she passes. She did not want me at all, he thinks.

Her face and body linger with him for a moment. A woman in Chandni Chowk! A woman with breasts, with everything Gulmohar had offered. He must find the man. He must go to Gulmohar this evening, perhaps this afternoon, and sink his face in her breasts again. He does not want more.

'Mysore silk, Banarasi silk, Kanjeevaram silk! French chiffon, Indian chiffon, organdie! Silk blouse, rubiya blouse! Jamna Lal Kishori Mal!'

Mukesh takes a step back, startled, but it is only a short, thin, dark waif of a boy, who gestures with an odd-looking hand. Mukesh looks carefully at the mouth. The upper lip is so horribly caked with dry skin that it will wither away soon. Surely this is not the man he is looking for. No, he's just a boy – but a boy as importunate as a beggar, who blocks the narrow footpath, daring Mukesh to pass through.

'Mysore silk, Banarasi silk, Kanjeevaram silk! Saree! Saree!'

In his muddled head, Mukesh knows instantly what Gulmohar needs. 'Yes, I will buy a saree! Not now . . .' A beautiful silk saree, thinks Mukesh. The colour of cream for her milky skin, with a matching blouse. A small cream-coloured bindi on the forehead between the narrow doe-like eyes. The sleeves on the blouse must be short, very short, to expose her smooth arms. It must be cut low at the back. And at the front . . .

The boy grabs Mukesh by a corner of his shirt and pulls hard. Mukesh looks down at him in annoyance, and notices the stump. 'Let me go! I do not have money. I will come tomorrow.'

The boy releases the shirt, but lingers hopefully. Eight sarees, thinks Mukesh, each worth a thousand rupees. He will ask her what she wants before he makes a purchase. Why not bring her to the shop so she can choose her own material? Or should he buy five sarees and silver jewellery to go with them? He should not have said 'brick of silver'. His box contains only chips that he has collected from silver bricks. What she needs is jewellery, silver jewellery – bangles, earrings, necklace and a bracelet. Can one get gold jewellery for eight thousand? Then he can buy three sarees with the three thousand Ramvilasji will give him tonight.

The boy grabs his shirt again. 'Are you coming into the kucha or not?' he asks.

'Get away, sister-fucker!' shouts Mukesh.

He shakes off the boy and walks away, nearly colliding with a cart carrying air-conditioners. He turns swiftly to study the man who pushes it, but he now has his back to him. It could not be this man. 'He will know you as surely as he knows his own brother,' Ramvilasji had said. Mukesh walks on.

Gauhar stands despondently as the man in the yellow shirt walks away. Although he looked poor, he had the smell of wealth about him. A man who can afford perfume must have money in his pocket. He will have to try another sister-fucker. He does not know what words will make them change course and enter the kucha behind him to buy sarees. Chotu brings in three customers every day. The seth is getting impatient. Fuck the seth! How can he expect people to buy sarees when a rally is about to start? He is tired of pulling at shirts, dhotis, sarees and kurtas, and having everyone shake him off, abuse him, shoo him away like a dog. He does not like sleeping in the chaivala's box either. At night, pigs rummage through the heaps of garbage in Kucha Bansilal, and poke their snouts through the air holes he has bored. They lick him all night before deciding he is not tasty enough. Mussabir Ustad was right. It is much easier to get fucked for seventy rupees than to cajole fat kurtas into Kucha Bansilal.

Today will be his last day, decides Gauhar. He will wait for Didi to come and make her film about him. Afterwards, not beforehand, he will tell her he wants to come back to Sparrows. She may not make him the hero in her film if she finds out he does not want to work in the kucha. He walks to the peepul tree, sits down, and spots her coming along the footpath with the camera on her shoulder. She is so much taller than the men around her, he thinks.

'Gauhar! Look this way!'

He pretends not to hear. He does not want her to think he saw her before she saw him.

'Gauhar!'

He looks at her. She points to the camera, indicating he should look there, then switches it off and lays it carefully on the ground. She puts another electronic box on the street, draws a wire from it and squeezes a foamy bulb on to his collar. 'This is a microphone,' says Chitra. 'It records what you say.'

'Hello! Hello!' he shouts gaily.

'Did you bring Mussabir?'

'I could not find him,' he lies.

'All right, I will film just you for now.'

She brings her face close to Gauhar so she can speak into the microphone. 'This is Gauhar Muhammad,' she says. 'He ran into Sparrows six years ago, clutching a paratha. He has learned to read and write at Sparrows, and replaced Mussabir Hussein as secretary of Baal Bank. Two weeks ago he moved to Kucha Bansilal and found employment as a clerk in a saree shop. We will now learn more about Gauhar.' She steps back, picks up the camera and aims it at him. It looks like a gun. 'Say something!'

Gauhar is silent, unsure what can be said to a camera. The lens winks at him, alive, omniscient, unfriendly.

'Say something, Gauhar!'

He watches the lens, wide-eyed, and words roll out of his head. 'French chiffon, Indian chiffon, organdie! Silk blouse, rubiya blouse—'

'No! No!' interrupts Chitra, laughing. 'Talk about yourself – about Baal Bank.'

He shifts uncomfortably, tongue-tied, wishing she would point the camera somewhere else.

She wonders if a replay of what she has recorded will give him confidence. 'Let me show you what you look like.'

She brings the camera to him, rewinds a little, and plays it back on a small screen. Gauhar is amazed to see his own face, saying, 'French chiffon, Indian chiffon . . .' He is in a film – a star! He laughs, stands up and steps back from the camera, ready to act.

'All right now, tell us what you do,' says Chitra.

'My name is Gauhar Muhammad,' he says. 'I live in the school and Didi takes care of me.'

'Tell us about the job you have found.'

'I work for a seth in Kucha Bansilal.'

'What do you do for the seth?'

Gauhar dwells on his own image, chanting 'French chiffon' on the screen. The left side of his face looks a little better, he thinks. He should thrust the stump into his pocket. And he should square his chest and push it out. Perhaps he should take a deep breath and hold it. But then he could not speak! At the very least he should flex the muscles in his arms.

'Gauhar, you are making faces!' says Chitra.

'I am the manager of sethji's shop. I look after it when he is not there.'

Chitra stops filming and looks at him suspiciously. 'Is that true?'

He does not reply. She turns on the camera again. 'Do you like your job, Gauhar?'

'Yes,' he says.

'Why are you smirking?'

She sets aside the camera, wondering how the footage will look. She cannot understand why his shirt, which she has always known to be dirty, is clean today. There is nothing of the Sparrows boy in him. He is alternately awkward and cocksure, never serious. She must edit out his lies. He is not the perfect mascot for the film. Perhaps she should have stuck to her Mandal Commission film. A documentary about destitute children makes no sense if the children do not look destitute. She hopes to have it screened at the great festivals of the world – Cannes, Toronto, Fort Lauderdale, Sundance . . . Sparrows has provided her with wonderful material, but how can she use it if the boy strikes ridiculous poses and grins shamelessly for the camera?

'This is not a film,' she tells him. 'This is your life.'

Gauhar laughs, happy to be in the film. He will look so handsome when the video is played back!

'Sing a song!' she says wearily, picking up the camera again.

He tilts his face upward, looks carefully into the lens and sings. '*Saare jahaan se achchhaa, hindosataan hamaaraa hamaaraa . . .*'

He is drowned by the slogans of the rally.

'Mandal Commission *zindabad*!'

'Backward-caste reservation!'

'V. P. Singh *zindabad*!'

The procession is charging down Chandni Chowk, headed for Red Fort where Suleman will address the gathering. Columns of policemen walk up the footpaths on either side, separated from the procession by metal fences. There is a sudden scramble as the police clear the way, pushing onlookers into kuchas and katras. Hushed faces peer from windows high up on either side of Chandni Chowk, awed by the flood of people. At times, it looks as if the police are marching with the procession.

Gopal walks hurriedly behind Ibrahim, afraid he will get lost in the crowd. His dhoti is doubled up and tied tightly round his waist, just below the cantilevered projection of his belly. He has buttoned his shirt all the way up. On Ibrahim's advice he has not brought his spectacles, so he is in a half-blind haze. With one hand he pulls

continually at Ibrahim's kurta to steady himself. In the other he holds
a saucepan. A cry goes up somewhere at the front: 'Mandal Commission!'

A thousand hands are thrown skyward, carrying sticks, knives,
spears, crutches, axes and lathis. On cue, Gopal raises the saucepan
and bellows with everyone: '*Zindabad*!' He looks at Ibrahim and
mutters, 'I need a stick.'

Ibrahim, who holds a spear, cannot hear Gopal above the noise. He
turns back, nods reassuringly and resumes marching. Gopal is embarrassed to raise the saucepan, when everyone around him is better
equipped. He has never seen such a large crowd in Chandni Chowk, or
so many banners, placards, policemen and barricades. He brings his
face close to Ibrahim's ear. 'Are these Suleman Mian's people?'

'Villagers!' scoffs Ibrahim. 'From Haryana and Uttar Pradesh. They
have never been to a city before. They have never seen a traffic light.'

'V. P. Singh!' someone shouts.

'*Zindabad*!' the crowd chants.

'That policeman is coming straight at me!' says Gopal, urgently.

'You are in a rally, Gopal Bhai. No policeman will dare touch you.'

'We do not need to shout. We can just mouth the words. No one can
tell.'

'They can,' counters Ibrahim. 'For every twenty-five men there is a
monitor, who is watching how loudly you shout. He will not bring
you for the next rally if you don't. And no aloo puri if you whisper!'

Gopal walks on unhappily. They are next to the Hanuman temple.
Perhaps he can duck out of the procession and hide inside Kucha
Bansilal? He will forget about the twenty-five rupees, which are likely
to get him trampled to death in this crowd.

'Do not think of leaving,' says Ibrahim. 'Suleman Mian's monitor is
watching.'

Gopal glances wistfully at the peepul tree, now almost behind them.
Beneath it he sees a familiar face – that of a dark boy with dirty brown
hair. He cannot make it out clearly at such distance. 'Ibrahim Mian! Is
that the Bangladeshi boy under the tree?'

'Your boy,' smiles Ibrahim. 'He is trying to get customers. For the
next rally I will bring him instead of you. You are too weak.'

'There is someone else with him,' says Gopal.

'Yes,' replies Ibrahim coldly.

It is the madam who runs Suleman Mian's school. Ibrahim decides
he will have to discipline the Bangladeshi boy. After all that Suleman

Mian has done for him, and after the nahari he himself fed him, how dare the boy talk to the madam when he has been asked not to? How can Suleman Mian trust him if he continues to associate with her? She seems to be making a video of him. But now she swings quickly toward the crowd, eyes glued to the camera. Ah, she is filming the crowd! This mollifies Ibrahim. He paints a look of stern resolution on his face and slaps Gopal hard on the back. 'Look straight ahead, Gopal Bhai. Straighten up and march proudly. You are going to be a film star!'

Chitra studies the faces as they file by through the eyepiece of the camera, inside which they lose all colour and definition. One electronic blotch is indistinguishable from another, making the procession more powerful in its anonymity. In spite of her ambivalent attitude toward the rally and the Mandal Commission, she is breathless with excitement. The faces in my camera are enemies, she thinks. If she was in college right now, she would be among the students stoning buses in protest against the Mandal Commission, assuming female students were allowed to infringe upon the male domain of violence. These faces – having come from their villages and towns hundreds of kilometres away – would be marching against her, reviling her, spewing their venom against people like her. What is this Mandal Commission anyway but a ruse to prolong their misery? Who among these marchers – all backward castes, OBCs and other presumed beneficiaries – will benefit from it? And who cares? Will Gauhar get a better job because of the Mandal Commission? Will Mussabir? Will Jolly and Sheila? Or the little Nepali girl, Kiran, brought in a few days ago by that prostitute?

She recognises the face at the lower edge of her camera frame. The colours are indistinct, but she has seen the grinning man with his threadbare beard and long teeth. She has met him at some uncomfortable moment, during one of those humiliating obeisances she must make periodically to the political class in the form of functions, speeches, seminars and exhibitions.

Gauhar watches the procession with rising excitement. He has no doubt Mussabir Ustad is in the crowd somewhere. Everyone knows about the twenty-five rupees and aloo puri. In spite of his preference for pigeon fights, Mussabir will not pass up a chance like this. Twenty-five rupees are less than seventy, but you do not have an old man oiling his prick inside you. All you have to do is shout slogans and clap when Suleman Mian makes his big speech. True, aloo puri does not have the fragrance of nahari, but it is mouth-watering when it's free. Perhaps *he* should have arranged to go to the rally instead of waiting for Didi. She lured him with the camera, but now her attention is on the crowd. The eye of the camera no longer points toward him. And now, she has begun to move with the procession. Whatever happened to the film in which he was to be the star? 'Didi!' he calls indignantly.

She keeps walking with the crowd, drawing disapproving stares from policemen, watching everything through the eyepiece, moving inexorably away from him toward the Red Fort grounds, where a large stage has been erected for Suleman Mian.

Mukesh stands in a kucha, facing the rabbit-man. He is very small, no taller than a boy, dark, with colourless clothes and eyes that are almost closed by the crawl of a thousand wrinkles. Mukesh notices none of this because his eyes are riveted to the naked teeth, which hang shamelessly behind lips drawn aside like a stage curtain. As promised, the man has found him, and now holds him at arm's length, studies him carefully and sniffs. A frown appears on the narrow forehead. He is wondering about the perfume on my body, thinks Mukesh. This reminds him of Gulmohar, and he shuts his eyes. When he opens them the rabbit-man is smiling. He is so short that he has to tilt his head up to talk to Mukesh. He reaches up and pats Mukesh's shoulder. When he smiles, his lips are drawn aside completely, and Mukesh stares at a monstrous array of paan-stained fangs.

He frisks Mukesh, taking particular pleasure in patting down his pants. Mukesh flinches, and the man laughs. Then he points toward the deep recesses of the kucha and walks quickly. Mukesh staggers after him in a heady swirl of hashish. From behind a counter, the rabbit-man brings out a jerry-can. 'You need a bath!' he says, with a glint in his eyes. He climbs aboard the counter, stands Mukesh next to it, and turns the jerry-can over his head. The fragrance of jasmine and mahua is overwhelmed by another, much stronger one. 'Now you are clean,' says the rabbit-man. 'Listen carefully to me.'

Suleman sits impatiently inside a tent in the Red Fort grounds, sipping a cold bottle of Thums Up. A gigantic stage stands next to the tent. Behind it is the dry moat that separates Red Fort from the invader. In front of it is the entire stretch of Chandni Chowk, from Red Fort to Fatehpuri Masjid. From his chair in the tent, the masjid is faintly visible through a maze of electrical wires, poles and banners. The stage will have a commanding view when he mounts it. Two canvas flaps have been pulled away in the tent wall so he can see that the procession is still a few hundred metres from the fort. He drains the Thums Up and walks outside the tent, where a dozen men eye him intently.

'They are moving too slowly,' he grumbles.

'You must be patient,' says someone.

Suleman sighs. He does not like the man's patronising tone, or the Communist and leftist parties that have provided support for the rally. He walks round the tent so he will be invisible to them, and studies the vast, empty grounds before him. The Communist parties have paid for a network of bamboo fences that will break the crowd into compartments so a stampede can be controlled. They have also paid for loudspeakers that hang from poles, and flower garlands that swing under the faces of political leaders. And they have paid for the stage itself, bedecked with sunflowers, with space enough for twenty men. From that sea of sunflowers, he will address his army. But it will be more than an hour before the bamboo partitions are full enough for him to ascend the stage in a crescendo of applause. Until then, he must remain imprisoned in the tent. A leader cannot be seen waiting for people to come to him. He must arrive after they have already noted his absence.

At the far end of the field, where the wall of Red Fort turns away at a sharp angle, he can see hundreds of buses, parked haphazardly, in which his supporters have been brought from their villages. Twelve lakh rupees, he remembers, to bus all these people from Haryana and Uttar Pradesh. Comfortable vehicles with deep cushions for people who have never sat on anything softer than the bamboo reeds of a bullock-cart. Twenty-five rupees and aloo puri for every mouth, for men who have been taught to chant, 'Zindabad,' after every challenge. They raise their spears on cue, bark on cue, then relapse into awe-struck contemplation of Chandni Chowk. An uninspiring army, yet how else can a man turn himself into a general?

These grounds, he thinks, are filled with the blood of Musalmans. This is where British officers watched Musalmans being blown from cannons. They sipped Cognac, gave the signal by tipping their glasses, and a Musalman was fired from a cannon, to fall deep inside Chandni

Chowk. People speak of Mangal Pandey when they talk of the Mutiny in 1857, but everyone knows that the mutineers were Musalmans. It was they who were the real patriots, and the British never forgave them for it. They razed everything around Red Fort, creating a vast expanse of open land between it and Chandni Chowk. These were Musalman shops, no doubt. The open ground made the British feel safer. It emphasised their role as rulers, separate from the ruled, and the people who paid the price for this assertion of imperial power were Musalmans. It is no coincidence that when they left, the British handed over the country to Hindus.

Suleman looks beyond the stage to the ramparts of Red Fort, where the prime minister delivered his Independence Day address less than a month ago. A Hindu, who has earned his right to fiery speeches, bitter denunciations and grand visions on the back of Musalman sacrifices.

His eyes drift back to the stage. He is not the prime minister, perhaps never will be, so the ramparts are closed to him. He will have to rely on these Communists – crusty, bookish old men – to erect stages for him. And he will have to hope that this one commands a clear view of all Chandni Chowk, so he can see his entire army.

A police dog is nuzzling round the tent, held on a leash by its trainer. Suleman feels the animal sniffing at him and kicks it away. It snarls and strains at the leash. The trainer scowls, then leads the dog toward the bamboo partitions. The Communists did not pay for the dog, thinks Suleman sourly, so I can afford to kick it.

He walks back to the other side of the tent, from where he can see the procession. It seems to be where it was ten minutes ago. He is annoyed. 'Have they stopped?' he asks.

'Someone is making a speech,' says a man.

'It is not a speech, it is a skit,' says someone else.

'This is not the time for drama!' exclaims Suleman.

'Those are not our men. They are college boys.'

Suleman grits his teeth and goes back into the tent.

Gopal trembles every time the crowd roars. They are still more than five hundred metres from Red Fort and the villagers have turned aggressive. A few stones have been thrown at shuttered shops. One shattered a glass façade, and he saw the police charge into the crowd, then take some people away. A few men, who wear green badges on their chests, are arguing with the stone-throwers, who demand their twenty-five rupees right away. 'We are hungry!' they say. 'It is noon and the sun is upon us. We want our aloo puri! We will not move another inch without twenty-five rupees!'

But the procession moves anyway, pushed along, pulled along. Gopal shivers on seeing the dome of Gurudwara Sisganj coming up on the right. It awakens dreadful memories of 'eighty-four. He pulls frantically at Ibrahim's kurta. 'Are they going to attack sardars? We must leave before that happens.'

Ibrahim points to the men in green badges. 'Nothing will happen to sardars,' he says. 'The monitors will control everything. We will keep moving until we reach Red Fort.'

'But we are not moving,' says Gopal.

'There is some disturbance at the front,' says Ibrahim. 'It will be cleared soon.'

A hundred metres ahead of the procession, policemen wearing helmets stand in its path. Each carries a baton in one hand and a cane shield in the other.

'Why are the police dressed like that?' asks Gopal.

'Riot police,' whispers Ibrahim. 'Stay here, behind others.'

'But we have thrown no stones!' protests Gopal.

'They do not like us,' says Ibrahim. 'They are all upper caste.'

The procession has stopped for its leaders to weigh the situation. The police deploy their shields to form a wall. With a cry of defiance, a few men charge forward. The front lines of the procession press against the police, who push back with their shields. Their wall extends across the street, from one line of metal fences to the other, allowing no passage for the procession.

'Ibrahim Mian, don't push me!' cries Gopal.

'The police are pressing us back.'

'You told me the rally had a permit.'

'It does. But the anti-Mandal college boys who are blocking our path haven't got one.'

'Why have they come?'

'They are doing a skit, a show,' says Ibrahim, angrily.

Beyond the police, in a square created by the intersection of Chandni Chowk with another street, thousands of students squat on the road in a ring six or seven deep. The clearing at the centre has become a stage. A raucous street play is in progress, in which a college girl in jeans is singing an obscene song about V. P. Singh, followed by three college boys who are the supposed beneficiaries of the Mandal Commission. They try to tear her clothes but she keeps eluding them, at which the audience claps wildly. The students wear T-shirts, jeans and sneakers, and squat comfortably on the road. Every time they clap and whistle, they raise banners. 'I am ashamed I voted for V.P.!' say the banners. 'V. P. Singh is a dog! Fuck you, V.P.! Mandal is a scandal! Mandal *ko maaro sandal*!'

It is impossible to cross the intersection without cutting through the students. They sit with guitars, harmoniums, drums, cymbals and cameras, and cry in unison, munching peanuts, potato chips and roasted grams.

Inderlal presses hard with the cane shield and tries to push the men back, cursing the day he was deployed on riot-control duty. He had imagined he would direct traffic, frisk men and issue commands through the loudspeaker in his Maruti Gypsy. Who thought he would be part of a human wall, in a pitifully thin helmet, without a bulletproof vest, tossed about by two opposing crowds! Should he face the students or the villagers? The two rallies are very different. The students are in festive mood and hawkers sell peanuts among them. They laugh and cheer. The crowd on the other side is much more ominous. He knows they do not belong to Delhi, these sweepers, farmers and Bhangis brought from somewhere. In a few minutes the dam will burst and the two waters will mix in a bloody swirl. He should keep his face toward the villagers during the breach, because they are more dangerous.

'This is *our* rally!' says Ibrahim to Gopal. 'We should charge through them.'

Gopal is squeezed between bodies. He is being pushed forward from behind, but Ibrahim, against whose back he is firmly pressed, will not yield because he himself is sandwiched between Gopal and the men in front of him. It is very hot, and Gopal is shorter than those around him. He feels the men are like walls, closing gradually over him. Soon their heads will meet in the sky and he will be entombed. With a burst of strength he stands on tiptoe and places his chin on Ibrahim's shoulder. He can now see into the clearing.

The skit has ended. In the brief pause before another can begin, a young man walks unsteadily toward the centre of the ring. A watch flops round his wrist. His clothes appear drenched and define the contours of his skeletal frame. His yellow shirt disappears into mud-coloured trousers. The buttons at the neck are open, exposing a skinny chest that struggles to sprout hairs. His damp trousers hang helplessly round his bony legs. A rumble runs through the crowd. Who is he? A student at Dinanath College, comes the answer. No one knows who first shouted it, but it is soon on everyone's lips. 'Dinanath College is for babus!' says a student. Someone laughs. 'What is a Bhaiya doing here? Go back to your little town!' Other students laugh.

'College for clerks!' says someone else.

'Shut up,' says a voice. 'We are united against V.P. today!'

A cheer goes up for the young man from Dinanath College, who reaches the centre and stands still.

'Get him out of here!' shouts someone. 'He smells!'

Gopal sees the man in a blur, and is soon enveloped in the powerful stench of kerosene. The yellow shirt disturbs him. 'Who is that man?' he asks, in his semi-blindness.

Ibrahim stares, stone-faced, at the apparition before him. Gopal's chin digs painfully into his right shoulder, and the hand that holds the spear is slippery with sweat. He blinks hard, but the image before his eyes will not fade. 'Just a boy,' he whispers. 'A boy, one of them . . .'

The man stands still. A silence falls on the crowd. He looks like an unlikely mascot for their crusade. Too oddly dressed. Too black. Too thin. Too sallow. Too poor . . . They would have jeered him off their stage but there is a seriousness behind his thin face that makes them take notice. He seems to be preparing for a speech, a demonstration, a dance. Then he shakes himself out of his daze and draws a box of matches out of his shirt pocket. He pulls out a matchstick, lights it, holds it in front of his face and lets it fall on to his extended leg. His trousers burst into flames.

'Who is that man?' asks Gopal. 'He is on fire!' He watches the yellow shirt carefully, trying hard to focus on the face. He knows the movements of that body as it writhes in agony. In the instant that he recognises Mukesh, Ibrahim turns and places his hands firmly on his shoulders.

'Let me go, Ibrahim Mian! Can you not see he is burning?'

'There is nothing we can do,' Ibrahim mutters, so softly that Gopal cannot hear. But he holds Gopal firmly. A few others have closed round them to prevent Gopal springing into the clearing.

'Stop him! Stop him!' Gopal screams, but the words die in his throat. He is struggling against the hands that pin him down, imagining that a strong man will walk up to his son, blow out the flames that engulf him and sweep him up in his arms. He does not see such a man, but he knows Mukesh will be safe as soon as this is over. It is a joke, a game, a trick, a ploy to amuse the crowd. His son has always been a prankster. The stones thrown at buses, the rickshas stolen for fun, the silver misplaced at night, the diamond switched inadvertently, and the flames that now crawl over his flailing limbs.

Five hundred metres away, Suleman's Thums Up is long finished, and he is looking impatiently into the distance for the crowd that shall listen to him. He can see a mass of people but they are not moving.

Careful, very careful! Chitra says to herself, her eyes glued to the camera. She prays she has remembered everything – batteries, focus, exposure, colour balance, sound levels – because nothing can be changed now. A ball of fire rolls before her lens, surrounded by a stunned mass. A thousand eyes watch it spin round the clearing but only one records it for eternity. Forgive me, says Chitra, to her conscience. Forgive me this voyeurism not of my own making. The fires of Pralay dance before my very eyes and my fingers are glued to the button, letting the tape run on and on . . .

Mukesh thinks of the eight thousand rupees, chips of silver and pieces of gold under his slab in Kucha Mahajani. With the three thousand he will get this evening, he will buy ten sarees for Gulmohar. He wonders how much the silver dust is worth, and if he can have it melted and fused into a figurine. A figurine of Gulmohar!

   In the instant before his mind switches off, he wonders why the rabbit-man has not sprung upon him with a blanket to douse the flames, as he said he would.

1992

Rain slides silently over a wooden cut-out of the prime minister that looms over GB Road. He stands three storeys tall, cardboard smile fixed on his face, pink lips touching the steel grilles behind which stand whores in their best sarees. His face is smooth from chin to bald head, and his hands are folded in benign greeting. His shoulders are draped with a grey shawl, at which point he is attached to a wooden electric pole with hundreds of nails. From these, bunting stretches across the road to hooks and pillars near shopfronts on the opposite side. Decorative awnings have been slung outside shops selling commodes and wash-basins, and a large hoarding has been erected where GB Road connects to the main stretch of Chandni Chowk. 'STREE, Sex-workers Training, Rehabilitation and Education Endeavour, greets all guests to its Women's Day function,' says the hoarding. It also thanks the Chandni Chowk committee of the IPP for its sponsorship of the event. Above the messages there are pictures of Harilal Gupta and Kartar Singh, each bearing the description 'IPP councillor for Chandni Chowk', then a smaller rectangle featuring Lala Surajmal, 'Chairman of the IPP Chandni Chowk Committee'.

A stage straddles the street, blocking access to vehicles for the day. It is decorated with garlands and hung with banners that proclaim in English and Hindi, 'STREE wants equal rights for Sex-workers! Legalise Sex-workers of GB Road. Aids is a problem inside your home, not in GB Road!' and has a canvas ceiling, presciently arranged by Ramvilas so the leaders will not be drenched as they speak. Gita stands on the stage, arms akimbo, directing last-minute efforts to set up microphones and loudspeakers. She looks up anxiously at the balconies on either side of the road, full of whores in bright yellow sarees, with nose-rings that shake flirtatiously and silk blouses that expose cleavage, shimmering with sequins. Of the eighty brothels in GB Road, only seven have agreed to declare this a holiday. The bais in the rest have resisted all pressure from STREE, and have remained open for business. Their whores are looking forward to a busy day, while those given a holiday stand sullenly in the street, unhappy at missed opportunities, shivering in the chill brought by the rain to the August air. Some whores have taken a voluntary day off, with or without the approval of their bais. Both groups – on- and off-duty –

have decided to wear their best clothes, so Gita cannot tell which face behind the balconies is soliciting customers, and which is merely watching the function in the street.

The chairs on the stage are occupied by members of the IPP committee, but the most prominent seat, meant for Harilal Gupta – the senior councillor from Chandni Chowk – is vacant. Gita walks to the back of the platform, where Ramvilas is sprawled on a chair. 'When will Harilalji arrive?' she asks. 'All the other leaders have taken their places.'

Ramvilas shrugs.

'We cannot begin until he arrives,' she says.

Ramvilas points to the area in front of the stage, where no more than a hundred whores stand, clustered together, drenched in spite of a garden of colourful umbrellas. 'I will telephone him after you get an audience,' he says.

'They do not want to come out in the rain!' protests Gita.

'I promised five hundred whores to Harilalji,' replies Ramvilas.

Gita turns to Nasreen and Manju, who stand at either end of the stage, wearing new sarees and pink badges with 'STREE' on them. 'Can Parvati help?' she asks.

'She is working today,' says Nasreen.

Parvati will make good money, thinks Gita, bitterly. 'I do not like this politics,' she had said, when asked.

'This is not politics but support for your sisters!' countered Gita.

'I have a son to take care of,' said Parvati.

'It will be only a few hours,' pleaded Gita.

'I prefer to do my duty,' said Parvati.

Gita could not tell whether she meant her son or her business. Parvati will have no competition in Kotha 842 today because the other whores are all members of STREE.

Ramvilas walks to the front of the stage and conducts a quick head count. If the whores who stand behind grilles in the balconies are included, the total number awaiting Harilalji is around four hundred. This is embarrassingly small, considering there are at least three thousand in the eighty kothas of GB Road, but Harilal Gupta does not know this, and a number greater than four hundred is probably beyond the resources of STREE. 'I will telephone Harilalji,' he says.

Gita heaves a sigh of relief, then recedes to the rear of the stage, away from the chairs. She is used to speaking with customers, bais, pahalvans and pimps, each of whom has a clearly defined desire she can satisfy. What can she offer to these traders and politicians? What should she say to them? She can speak sufficient Hindi to communicate with her customers, but that does not require an extensive vocabulary. These men intimidate her with their glib talk of elections and committees. She will avoid conversation with them, and wait for Ramvilas to return.

The leaders on the stage sit in three rows of chairs arranged round the seat of honour – front row centre – that awaits Harilal Gupta. Next to it Lala Surajmal sits in a silk kurta and carefully pleated dhoti. A year ago, at the age of sixty-six, he had a stroke that paralysed the right side of his body. This has curtailed his political activities in the Chandni Chowk IPP committee, though he has lost little of his vigour. Slowly, he has regained strength in his right arm and leg. The only concession he makes to infirmity is the new walking-stick that stands beside him, balanced perfectly on its steel ferrule. When he walks with it, he cups its ivory head with casual authority, and seems not to notice that his right leg drags behind him. He has perfected the art of walking on one strong foot, and pulls along the other in such a way as to make his limp nearly unnoticeable.

Kartar Singh, being the junior councillor from Chandni Chowk, sits to the left of Surajmal. Jugal Kishor Agrawal is beside him, looking over his shoulder toward Surajmal and talking to him through Kartar Singh. Sohan Lal sits in the second row, head bowed, spectacles low on the bridge of his nose, his cap folded in his hands, which lie in his lap. He can see the back of Surajmal's decaying scalp, bare of cap and hair; the skin behind the ears is mottled and loose. Sohan Lal fears he may yet arrive at that state of physical decline, but hopes to age with more dignity. He can feel the chill through his thin sweater, and wonders why he is here. It is not appropriate for the IPP leadership in Chandni Chowk to be consorting with such women, whom he has never seen before in such proximity. He is afraid to look straight ahead lest his eyes meet theirs. What expression should he assume when his eyes look into the painted face of a prostitute? And there are so many of them that they look almost normal, as if a regular crowd in Chandni Chowk wears brightly coloured sarees and vulgar lipstick! As if it was not enough that they look half naked, the rain has plastered their sarees to their skins, displaying their shameful bodies. He shudders. He tries to look away, but the women are visible in every direction. He looks skyward but is horrified to find prostitutes pressed against the grilles, their body parts carelessly flattened against the steel bars, bursting through them, overflowing them. He hastily lowers his eyes to his feet, trying to wipe the images from his mind, admonishing himself for looking as long as he did.

Kartar Singh and Surajmal are talking about the assembly elections in Delhi, which are likely to take place next year. Sohan Lal feels a stab of anger. The assembly elections will be the first ever to take place in Delhi, and he does not even have a seat in the front row! Kartar Singh is ten years his junior, but is two seats away from Harilal's chair because they are both councillors. Surajmal's stature has never been in dispute: he is the chairman of the committee, and a hundred strokes will not separate him from that position. Jugal Kishor is the chief acolyte who will do his best to deny Sohan Lal the position of chairman, should Surajmal abdicate.

Sohan Lal hears a rustle to his left, and notices that Ramvilas has taken the chair next to him. He shrinks involuntarily.

'You look worried, sethji,' says Ramvilas.

The cheerful tone offends Sohan Lal. Must he now contend with Surajmal's clerk? Ramvilas has not made proper arrangements for this function. What an absurd idea to erect a giant cut-out of the prime minister at an IPP function, making it look like a Congress achievement! Perhaps it is just as well. Ramvilas has been imprudent to drag the IPP committee into this prostitute fair. 'It will bring us the women's vote,' he said. But who cares for the votes of a few hundred whores, whose support will likely put off people from good families? It is fitting that the function is marred by rain. Prostitutes have no right to sunshine, or there would be no reason to maintain a morally upright character.

'You did not have to put up a cut-out of the PM,' he says.

'I did not,' says Ramvilas. 'It has been put up by Naresh Agrawal's men for the fifteenth of August.'

Sohan Lal shakes his head angrily. It is typical of Naresh Agrawal to take advantage of 15 August and erect a cut-out so far in advance of the date, knowing everyone will notice. 'Why don't we start?' he asks.

'I just telephoned Harilalji. As soon as he comes, Gita Didi will welcome him to the stage and we will begin.'

'Who is Gita Didi?' asks Sohan Lal.

Ramvilas appears surprised. 'She is the convener of STREE, the NGO that has organised this function.'

Sohan Lal follows Ramvilas's gesture and notices, for the first time, the woman who stands at the edge of the stage, looking anxiously into the crowd. A Nepali woman, almost certainly a prostitute. She is very young, perhaps no more than twenty-five, but she is plump and mature. There is something masculine about a woman who strides with such confidence in the presence of men, head uncovered, short-sleeved blouse and – what is that? Fashionable sandals! She is attractive, yet she is sexless in that she is unaware of her sex. She does not hug her saree close to her as women do in respectable households. She lets it hang so that it swings open when she walks, to reveal the contour of her midriff. He has a glimpse of full breasts, squeezed into a flesh-coloured blouse, and is suddenly outraged. How dare such a woman call herself 'Didi'? Who could think of her as a sister? The fact that Ramvilas knows this woman is scandalous in itself. After today, they will all be counted as her acquaintances! He watches her bend to talk to someone below the stage. An involuntary image of her drenched with rain passes through his mind and he quickly lowers his head in anger and shame. Ramvilas will make lechers of committee members.

Ramvilas gets up and goes to her. Sohan Lal notes the familiarity with which they speak, and his anger turns to wistfulness. He considers the weight of what he suspects, then shakes his head. He will not make vile assumptions about anyone.

A car horn shatters his meditation. Harilalji's Ambassador car is trying to get through the whores. It comes as close to the stage as it can and stops. Ramvilas runs to open the door, umbrella in hand. Harilalji emerges to a shower of applause, and is escorted up six steps to the stage by Ramvilas, who holds the umbrella over his head until he is safely under the canvas ceiling. Everyone on the stage stands up. Even Surajmal struggles up from his chair and supports himself unsteadily on his walking-stick. Ramvilas hands out garlands to everyone, and Harilalji suffers his neck to be encircled repeatedly, raising his hands in a communal namaste each time. The leaders take their seats after Harilalji has been ensconced – with some pushing and pulling – in his chair.

Harilal Gupta is a relatively young man, barely past fifty, the scion of a great paper-trading family in Chandni Chowk. A combination of wealth, ancestry and political acumen has served him well in his quest for councillorship. He wears with ease the khadi kurta and pyjama that he was seemingly born in, and his Gandhi cap sits comfortably on his head, almost as if he belongs to the Congress Party, which indeed he did until the Emergency of 'seventy-five. In the elections that followed, he switched to the Janata Party, then found his way into its more aggressive incarnation as the IPP. In the Congress Party itself, the Gandhi cap went out of fashion with the coming of Rajiv Gandhi, but Harilal derives a feeling of seniority from it. For as long as he has been in politics – his entire adult life – he has thought of himself as a senior leader, even when he was merely chairman of the Chawri Bajar Traders Association. His political career has seen him on the winning side in most battles, even if that meant changing sides as often as battles were fought. These principled swaps, which would be called opportunism in other people, have never frayed his energies, his confidence or his reputation. He walks, sits, looks, listens and speaks slowly but deliberately, like a man fortunate enough to have known no adversity, and sharp enough to avoid any that may come his way. His speech is usually confined to subjects he understands, and if he sometimes wades beyond them, no one points this out. Nuances do not trouble him, and he has never felt the need to qualify an opinion. He feigns ignorance when names are listed and affects comprehension when ideas are broached. If Jawaharlal Nehru were to be mentioned, he might ask, 'Who?' then nod in weary recognition. His calm confidence extends to the great bulk of his body, which has expanded generously in his years of political ascension. Now, squeezed into his chair, he spills over to touch Surajmal's paralysed hand, and flicks off the few drops of water that have sullied his khadi jacket in spite of Ramvilas's careful shepherding.

Ramvilas, standing near the second row of chairs, signals to Gita, who walks to the left corner of the stage and taps the microphone. Instantly the whores fall silent. Ramvilas notes with approval that they seem to recognise her, if only because she goes to their kothas to distribute condoms. She is too short for the microphone. Two men struggle to lower it for her. She withdraws a piece of paper from inside her blouse, unfolds it and reads in faltering Hindi. 'My sisters!'

The whores clap.

'We are part of the largest family in India,' she declares. 'There are three thousand of us in GB Road, four thousand in Calcutta, five thousand in Madras, six thousand in Bombay and lakhs in countless towns and villages. Yet this family has no home, no doctors, no security, no protection.'

The whores applaud in agreement.

Ramvilas watches her, smug at having placed a whore in the midst of Chandni Chowk traders. He is, however, irritated by her uncertain delivery of his speech. After eight years in Delhi, she still speaks with a Nepali accent, which can be cute in her room but sounds crass in public. He is not one to surrender to foggy sentiment, yet he is proud of the facts and figures he marshalled for the speech, the emotions expressed in florid Hindi. Perhaps he is meant to be a feminist, if only because he can write so well. And now his speech stutters in the mouth of one who speaks pidgin Hindi with a Nepali accent, and even slips into Nepali phrases. He has asked her not to extemporise. Is she doing this to show off to other Nepali whores?

'There is much talk of liberalisation these days,' says Gita.

Ramvilas chuckles. He put in that line as a dig at the prime minister, hoping to offend Naresh Agrawal, who has chosen not to come, perhaps because this is an IPP function in which the place of honour belongs to Harilal Gupta, a mere councillor, while he himself is a Member of Parliament. His chair, at the edge of the front row, has been taken by someone else.

Gita holds her script high in the air and continues: 'By liberalisation, does our prime minister mean that it will be easier to bring poor Nepali girls across the border into India, without paying Customs duties?'

The whores laugh. The IPP committee members seem amused.

'More than one lakh Nepali girls have been sold as sex-workers in India,' Gita goes on. 'There are men who comb the towns in Nepal every day, looking for new girls. Thirty years ago, when Arab men came to Bombay with lakhs of rupees in their pockets, they wanted fair Nepali girls, not dark Indian ones. And men, Arab or Indian, still want Nepali girls.'

A cheer goes up among the Nepali whores – a quarter of the audience – while others look around wistfully.

Harilal Gupta twists round uncomfortably and fixes Ramvilas with an angry look. 'What is this?' he demands. 'There are newspaper people here! They will say Harilal Gupta encourages prostitution!'

Ramvilas walks quickly to Gita, snatches the script, turns the page and hands it back to her.

'There is nothing shameful in what we do!' says Gita. 'Today is "Women's Day", they say, so they must acknowledge the sex-worker, and the child forced to become one. It is not our privilege, it is our right to be accorded honour and dignity, to have the same status as clerks, typists and secretaries.'

The whores clap politely, confused by the sudden change of tone.

Nepali whores look about themselves, confronting hostile glances from others.

'We need doctors and clinics. We need condoms to protect us from Aids!'

Sohan Lal is shocked. He was not aware that the speech would be so explicit. To mention condoms in public! He studies the back of Harilal Gupta's head, which has fallen forward on his chest. Surajmal also appears to be asleep. Jugal Kishor watches the Nepali woman wide-eyed, and Ramvilas, standing at the edge of the stage, has a mysterious smile on his face. Sohan Lal wonders if he should get up and walk off. There are people from the newspapers in this crowd. What if this speech is printed with a photo that shows him on stage? What would he say if Ramesh questioned him? The indignity of having a woman like this speak in front of so many people! Words like 'Aids' should not be uttered casually in public. He should have known better than to let Ramvilas drag him into this.

'The government says it gives out condoms,' says Gita, 'but the man who distributes them wants a commission of two rupees per box. How can a sister afford that? We need our own agencies, such as STREE, to distribute them. We need doctors who will examine us without sniggering or insulting us. We need sex clinics, not *near* GB Road but *inside* GB Road. We need an office for STREE. And for all of these we need funds – not money collected from the meagre earnings of our sisters but from the government! I would like to thank the IPP committee of Chandni Chowk for donating ten thousand rupees to STREE.'

Sohan Lal, whose head has sunk deeper on his chest with every thrust of the word 'condom', looks at Ramvilas helplessly, aware that reporters will note down the donation. Has Surajmal lost his mind to be authorising such a payment?

'Now I request Shri Babulal to read a message from Shri Naresh Agrawal, Member of Parliament for Chandni Chowk.'

The man sitting in Naresh Agrawal's chair rises. Ramvilas approaches the microphone and raises it for him. How clever of Naresh Agrawal to send a lackey to represent him, he thinks.

Sohan Lal looks up in time to see Gita fold her speech and stuff it into her blouse. It is all right, he tries to console himself. Rukmini keeps everything there – keys, pins, hair-clips, jewellery – but to do so in full view of hundreds!

Babulal is a tall, wiry man, dressed in khadi and Gandhi cap. A

Congress Party flag is affixed to his chest. He reads Naresh Agrawal's message without passion or inflection, using the same even tone for rousing exhortations and mundane announcements. 'In five days India will celebrate Independence Day,' he says. 'The prime minister will speak from Red Fort and outline government programmes for the empowerment of women. He has already declared today, the tenth of August, Women's Day, to be celebrated every year. The Congress Party has always honoured women in keeping with our ancient Indian tradition.'

Sohan Lal looks at Ramvilas in quiet protest. 'This is not a Congress function!' he whispers.

Ramvilas shrugs. Babulal, eyes glued to the page, continues: 'This is the only country, my sisters, where a woman inherits a man's position on his death. Whenever a great leader dies, we ask his wife or daughter to take his place. Did we not make Indira Gandhi prime minister after Nehruji left us? And did we not ask Soniaji to be our leader when Rajiv Gandhi was taken away from us?'

The whores clap.

'Naresh Agrawalji is dedicated to women's issues. To demonstrate his commitment, he has issued a cheque of fifty thousand rupees for STREE, from his local area-development fund.'

Gita lets out a whoop of joy. Nasreen and Manju cover their mouths in disbelief. The whores let out a collective sigh. Ramvilas is annoyed. Surajmal turns irritably to him. 'You did not tell me about this. Now who will notice our ten thousand?'

They speak as if it is their own money, thinks Sohan Lal.

Babulal recedes amid the excitement generated by his announcement, nods briefly at Harilal Gupta and takes his seat. Gita approaches the microphone again. 'Now I request Lala Surajmal to introduce our chief guest, Shri Harilalji Gupta, councillor for Chandni Chowk.'

Surajmal tries to raise himself from his chair but proves unequal to the task. Harilalji gallantly heaves him up and helps him to the microphone. It is a well-drawn picture, thinks Sohan Lal – the firm leader holding the frail grandfather in a manly embrace. The gesture is lost on the whores. They clap impatiently and set up a chant in Hindi: 'We want respect, we want dignity, we want honour . . .'

They say we are living in Kaliyug, thinks Sohan Lal in horror, and now there is no doubt this is the Black Age. If prostitutes shall have respect and dignity, will the women in our homes have to be worshipped?

Harilalji bows his head politely to one side, a sign of good-natured fatherly indulgence toward unruly children. He has heard them, the bow seems to say, and will accede to their demands in good time.

Surajmal, balanced on one strong leg and one ivory-topped walking-stick, raises his right hand impatiently to silence the crowd. In his entire political career he has never held elected office. His experience is limited to servile committee members and docile clerks, and does not extend to intractable crowds. So, while Harilalji waits patiently for the inevitable abatement of the chant, Surajmal scowls when his raised hand goes unnoticed.

The whores, after a minute of raucous chanting, lapse into bored silence. Surajmal seizes the opportunity to limp forward. The micro-phone emits a squeal and, unaccustomed to public speech, he takes a step back in horror. This sets off a flurry of activity among the technicians responsible for the audio system. When the squeal has been tamed, Surajmal finally finds his voice. 'My brothers and my sisters,' he says, in his best Hindi.

A titter runs through the crowd. 'There are no brothers here!' shouts a whore.

'My sisters,' he begins again.

The whores laugh. 'We are not your sisters!' one shouts from a balcony. 'We are your mistresses!'

Surajmal is flustered. He would like to tell them to shut up but they are not committee members. Over the din of whorish joy he hurriedly introduces Harilalji, the senior councillor from Chandni Chowk, and withdraws from the microphone. The ivory walking-stick taps loudly on the wooden stage as he walks back to sink gratefully into his chair.

Harilal is welcomed to the microphone by more chanting. He looks benignly at his constituents and begins. The microphone is co-operative, as if it senses his superior station in life. 'My sisters!' His voice glides smoothly over GB Road.

The whores fall silent, intimidated by the fuss Gita and Surajmal have made over Harilal.

'There have been no municipal elections in our city since 'eighty-three,' says Harilal. 'Delhi is the capital of our democracy, yet the people of Delhi have been deprived of self-representation! For years, IPP has fought for statehood. In January, our Parliament has finally granted it to Delhi!'

Harilal's voice reaches a crescendo, which the whores take as a cue to clap politely.

A half statehood, thinks Sohan Lal. In another corner of his mind, he wonders how this subject is relevant to the occasion.

'We will have elections to our own state assembly by next year,' declares Harilal Gupta. 'Next year, my sisters, all your problems will be addressed by your own MLA.'

All Harilal's problems too, thinks Sohan Lal sourly. Harilal's is the most recognisable face of the IPP in Chandni Chowk and he will certainly be the IPP candidate. Should the IPP win the assembly election, he will perhaps become a minister.

The whores shuffle uncomfortably.

Harilal, thinking they have not understood him, explains. 'MLA – Member of Legislative Assembly.'

Surajmal turns to Sohan Lal and winks. 'What will Harilalji do when he is a minister?' he mutters. 'Provide husbands for whores?'

Ramvilas wishes he had written a speech for Harilal too. He goes over to him and whispers that he should speak about Women's Day. Harilal covers the microphone with one hand. 'What can I possibly say to prostitutes?' he asks irritably, and turns back to the microphone. 'When I was a child, my teachers taught me that in this great country called India every man is as courageous as Raam and every woman as pure as Sita. Every one of you, my sisters, is as pure as Sita Maiya. Do not be fooled by men who cast a slur on your character. You have my support, my sympathy and my forgiveness. I say to the Indian Woman, "It is better to let them kill you than let them soil your honour."'

The whores listen in hushed silence. Then a giggle bubbles up somewhere, and soon they are all laughing.

Harilal Gupta takes this as a sign of approval and warms to his subject. 'Forty years ago, an image of Raam Lalla appeared in our temple in Ayodhya. It was a miracle, my sisters! I ask you, why are we still waiting for our temple? Why do Musalmans claim this structure, which they call Babri Masjid as if it were really a mosque, when Raam Lalla himself chose to walk into his temple? We will build our temple there, my sisters, we will build it on that very inch of land!'

Harilal Gupta stops, confused. The whores have begun to disperse. He turns to Ramvilas. 'Why are they leaving?'

'Because of the rain,' says Ramvilas.

It is an obvious lie: the rain has stopped. Harilalji is annoyed. He has faced indifferent crowds before, and he knows not to yield to its lethargy. He draws himself up and screams a pledge into the microphone. 'We will build the temple at the very spot, my sisters! *Kasam Raam kii khaate hain mandir vahii banaayenge!*'

Gita claps furiously. Her enthusiasm travels to the whores and arrests their departure. The entire assembly bursts into applause. She beckons Nasreen and Manju, who are in opposite corners of the stage, and the three present a plaque of appreciation to Harilal Gupta. Reporters rush to capture the moment. Harilalji stands transfixed, holding the plaque, smile frozen for eternity, until the cameras have finished clicking. Then he stalks back to his chair and lowers himself into it with the contented smile of a man whose mission is accomplished. Surajmal nods absently at him, and Jugal Kishor greets him enthusiastically.

Harilalji leans over to Babulal. 'Why did Nareshji not come?'

'He does not want photos of himself with whores,' says Babulal.

Harilalji is incensed, and suddenly aware that he is at a disadvantage. He looks angrily at Manju and Nasreen, now talking to reporters, and then at the crowd of whores, who have begun to disperse again.

Ramvilas makes a signal to Gita. She regains the microphone and pulls out her script. 'We will now walk to Kotha eight hundred and forty-two, the headquarters of STREE, then through Chandni Chowk to raise awareness of Aids.'

Harilal turns angrily to Ramvilas. 'You did not say there would a visit to a kotha!'

'I did not know,' says Ramvilas, weakly.

'What is this Aids?'

'A new disease from America.'

'I cannot march through Chandni Chowk with prostitutes!'

'I will have you escorted away,' assures Ramvilas.

'You can tell this Nepali lady I had to go on important council business,' says Harilal.

'She will understand.'

'Do you think people in Chandni Chowk will watch this march?'

'It will be impossible not to notice it,' says Ramvilas.

'Why has IPP never organised a march?' demands Harilal.

Ramvilas says he is not sure.

'We keep protesting against this and that,' continues Harilal, petulantly. 'Why has the IPP committee never organised a goodwill march? Something to celebrate the heritage of Chandni Chowk. The traders would like it. It would look good in the newspapers.'

'I will note it down for the next committee meeting,' says Ramvilas.

'We have a surprise guest today!' announces Gita.

The whores stop and look back at the stage with curiosity.

'A sister like us, but one who has used her beauty for good causes.'

She turns, and the crowd follows her gaze to a little screen that stands at the back of the stage. From behind it a lithe, slender woman wearing a long, flowing saree emerges. She smiles and waves at the whores. 'The former Miss India, Miss Amita Sharma!' declares Gita.

The whores cheer. Harilal Gupta, on the verge of departure, waves away the man approaching him with an umbrella. Miss Amita Sharma glides down the stage, hips swaying rhythmically, in a swirl of legs, smiles, eyelashes, curls, heels and bangles, and stands with her hands folded in namaste, displaying impossibly long nails. She wears a sleeveless blouse, and her saree is draped carefully over one shoulder to leave the other bare. A communal sigh emerges from multi-coloured whores in yellow and red sarees. Their admiration floats to the stage in bursts of sound. 'Thin! Smooth! Earrings! Necklace! Heels! Aaah!'

Gita then announces that Miss Amita Sharma will lead a march through Chandni Chowk for Aids awareness. Whores line up.

Sohan Lal walks back to his shop in lonely despair.

Harilalji walks a few steps with Miss Amita Sharma before being spirited away in his Ambassador car, accompanied by Jugal Kishor.

Ramvilas walks all the way until the march returns to GB Road. So does Gita, and a dozen whores who are volunteers for STREE.

Chitra presses the camera's shutter with no regard for economy, capturing every possible moment in the scene before her. It is wise to be indiscriminate, she has learned. From amongst these thoughtless snapshots will emerge a poignant portrait of the chaivala that will perfectly illustrate her article. It will be published in the September issue of *India Now*, and the caption will read, 'The Father, Two Years Later.'

'You must be rich, madam,' says Gopal. 'How can you take so many pictures?'

She laughs, then realises she must not be cruel to the chaivala. He is too easily distracted. He appears too afraid, too vulnerable, which is perhaps why he refused to talk to her until she paid him. 'Your life is important to the country,' she says.

Guilt stabs her. Is this not shameless voyeurism? But the picture is harmonious. The chaivala stands next to Mukesh Minar in Chandni Chowk, with Red Fort in the background. Now, too far away for her to see, the prime minister is on its ramparts behind a bulletproof screen, delivering his Independence Day address. The crowds – black heads in a sea of white kurtas, pyjamas and dhotis – begin beyond Gurudwara Sisganj and extend to the Red Fort grounds, and the heads of politicians seated on a raised platform near the fort are just visible.

'Touch the minar,' she says to Gopal. 'Put your hands on the poster.'

'I have never come here before,' says Gopal, uncertainly.

'It is a memorial to your son!'

She clicks away, asking the chaivala to lean against the electricity pole, to touch the garlands that hang round it and place his palms on posters of Mukesh. Two years ago, when the students of Dinanath College first converted this pole into a memorial called Mukesh Minar, they laid fresh flowers at its base every morning. They scrawled their names in blood, plastered the pole with posters berating V. P. Singh and Mandal, and wrote slogans on them. 'Mukesh Pandey's immolation is the cremation of India!' said one. 'This is the pyre of Indian youth!' said another. 'Never forget Mukesh Pandey!' said a third. Since then, the Mandal Commission has lost its sting – especially because V. P. Singh is no longer prime minister – and the students of Dinanath College have gone back to their classes. The posters abusing V. P. Singh have been torn away. Someone stuck up a few pictures of Mukesh – newspaper photographs – and painted a moustache on them. Occasionally, a few garlands are thrown at the minar by passers-by, most of whom take it to be a Hanuman temple in the making.

She is not certain that the story still carries appeal. Two years ago, *India Now* sent reporters to interview the chaivala. They came away with his name, age and that he had hardly known his son, and mentioned him in passing in their articles. It had been difficult for anyone to notice the father amid the flames that had consumed the son. Why had she, who had taken the only known picture of that terrible conflagration, paid no attention to the chaivala? If she can now extract something from him beyond his name and age, perhaps she can live her moment again. She remembers, of course, the famous lines of her article, beginning with the bald statement – how courageous she had been to shed all hyperbole! – 'Mukesh Pandey, a student of Dinanath College, burned himself to death in Chandni Chowk in protest against the V. P. Singh government's decision to implement the Mandal Commission report. His death set off a wave of self-immolations across the country . . .' She had described the event in detail, never stooping to drama or eulogy. However, as the anti-Mandal agitation gathered momentum, her language had become more florid. 'How many more young men must burn to ashes before V. P. Singh realises he is a murderer?' What memorable rhetoric! 'There will come a day when V. P. Singh finds himself in an operating theatre, and the surgeon wielding the knife is a boy who got his degree through the Mandal Commission quotas. "I do not know how to cut you up," he will say, "but I was born a backward caste and surely that is enough?" Will V. P. Singh fly in an aeroplane whose pilots are Mandal Commission appointees? V. P. Singh is a Thakur, not a backward caste. Why is he the prime minister?'

The last few articles had not enhanced her status, she believes, but she was only responding to the passions of the moment. It is challenging to report on a revolution when it is under way. She could not find admission records for the yellow-shirted boy in Dinanath College. Ah, a mere typo, a confusion of college names. He was probably from Deenbandhu College, or Ramlal College. Did the details matter? A boy had burned himself to death in pursuit of an idea. Was that not revolutionary enough? She herself had resigned from the presidency of her student union to protest against beauty pageants. It was a post that brought her neither wealth nor power, so her self-abnegation was bought cheaply. How much more noble was this boy's sacrifice! Why should she not have used poetic words to describe it? It was sharp of her to dig up the old line 'When you go home, tell them that for your today I gave up my tomorrow' . . . A slight modification of text and context, but most people would not have heard the original line anyway.

Then there were the awards for fearless journalism. Others, of course, had written sententious articles on the subject, but she was the one with the right tone, and she was the one with that unforgettable picture . . . Whoever thought she would end up calling herself a journalist? She had imagined herself as a dogged reformer bringing slow, inevitable change, but she had been reincarnated. In press circles she is known as the Mandal Woman, the Self-immolation Woman, the woman who brought the anti-Mandal agitation into middle-class homes, whose articles sparked – and then chronicled – a nationwide spate of immolations, the woman responsible for the fall of the V. P. Singh government two months after the Mandal agitation. That famous photograph was printed in countless magazines over two full pages. She had extracted it from her video footage – a young man writhing in a ball of fire, yellow shirt flaring outward, left hand thrown up in agony, wristwatch sliding down a skinny wrist, face contorted with an indescribable emotion that was somewhere between terror and surprise. And a crowd of stunned onlookers, students and policemen, holding back a swarm of villagers, among them a frantic, balding man.

She will live that moment again, of course. She will find in the chaivala the father those reporters from *India Now* could not. 'Tell me about your wife,' she says.

Gopal does not want to talk to this madam, but she has given him fifty rupees. He wishes he had not accepted the money, which he has spent on parathas in Paratha Gali. Now he watches two sprocketed wheels turn inside her tape-recorder, demanding that he satisfy them. 'She is dead,' he says.

Chitra is taken aback. 'What was her name?'

'Sushila.'

'When did you get married?'

'I was nineteen,' says Gopal.

'How old was she?'

Gopal does not remember. 'My father took me back to Sasaria for the wedding.'

'In Bihar?'

Gopal nods. 'I had no space for her in Chandni Chowk so I left her in Sasaria with my mother when I returned to Delhi.'

'When was Mukesh born?'

'Four years after we were married – the day she died.'

Chitra decides not to ask more about Sushila. It is clear that he does not know much about her. Whatever he says he will construct out of his imagination. If fantasy must inform her article, she trusts her own. 'Tell me about your father.'

'Manohar Lal Pandey,' says Gopal. 'My father was from Sasaria.'

'When did he come to Delhi?'

''Forty-seven.'

Gopal is not certain of this, but 'forty-seven is the only date that stands out in his mind when he thinks of the past.

It amuses Chitra. It fits snugly into the picture she has constructed. Here is Manohar Lal Pandey, a Brahmin who sets out from remote Sasaria to make his fortune in the great city of Delhi. He leaves behind his wife and a year-old son named Gopal. His train pulls into Delhi – the Old Delhi railway station – after a journey of forty-eight hours. He steps on to the platform at the stroke of midnight. A few miles away, Mountbatten watches the Union Jack slide down a pole, to be replaced by the tricolour fluttering against a dark sky. Manohar Lal Pandey, a young man of thirty-two, walks the great streets of Chandni Chowk while the new emperor of India recalls a tryst with destiny. The picture is complete, the coincidence startling, the dramatisation perfect! Chitra commits it to memory. How fortunate that one person should yield such reams of material! 'When did your father bring you to Delhi?' she asks.

'I was seven. We lived in Seth Sushil Jain's kholi in Khari Baoli, where he guarded the sacks of turmeric at night.'

Gopal does not have many clear memories of his childhood, but he does recall taking tea tumblers round Kucha Bansilal as a boy of ten, and bringing money back to his father. They did not say much to each other. Every evening, after his father had locked up the stall and washed out the tumblers that stood inside the electrical junction box, they would walk to the kholi in Khari Baoli. Seth Sushil Jain stayed up late in those days, checking his accounts, making telephone calls and drinking tea. He watched them walk into Katra Badami, asked after his sacks and tins, and had Gopal sweep the shop downstairs.

'When did you bring Mukesh to Delhi?' she asks.

'He was six.'

'Why not leave him with his grandmother in Sasaria?'

'My father died when Mukesh was five. I lived alone in the kholi for a year. Then Seth Sushil Jain said it was all right to bring Mukesh.'

'What did your father die of?'

'Age.'

'He was not even sixty!' says Chitra. 'There must have been another reason. Heart-attack? Accident?'

Gopal shakes his head. He does not remember. Chitra watches the sprockets rotating in her tape-recorder. The death of Manohar Lal Pandey must have been more dramatic. Can a chaivala go to sleep one night and not wake up the next day? There must have been a reason for his refusal to face another morning. Poverty? Loneliness? Debt? Something that illustrates the story, makes it more complete. Something that might even connect with the immolation that happened sixteen years later. She must spend more time on this.

'So you brought Mukesh to your kholi,' she continues. 'Did he help you in the stall?'

'Yes, he took chai to the seths.'

'Did you send him to school?'

'There was a government school near Chawri Bajar. He went there for a few years until the school shut down.'

'Then?'

Gopal shrugs.

So it is true, she thinks. Mukesh never studied in Dinanath College or any other. Who in the crowd first chose that label for him? Dinanath College is one of the less fashionable colleges in Delhi. It is where the sons of newly arrived villagers go with their pidgin English and dirty clothes. Perhaps the skinny, yellow-shirted boy looked the type. He had sallow cheeks, and eyes that had died long ago in the aisles of Delhi buses. On a normal day the boys and girls of Delhi University would not associate with a clerk-like boy from Dinanath College, but that had been no normal day. 'Did he tell you anything that morning? Perhaps he gave you a hint in the night.'

'He did not live in the kholi,' says Gopal. 'He stopped sleeping there when he was thirteen. I saw him only when he came to the stall every few months.'

How odd, she thinks, that I saw him but his father did not. She has not shown that footage, taken a few minutes before the immolation, to anyone. Amid the crowd of onlookers, bicycles and carts on the footpath, Mukesh walks beside the metal fences erected by the police, in a yellow shirt and mud-coloured trousers. He looks frequently at his watch. He notices the camera and stares at it in wide-eyed despair. He shuffles nervously, buffeted by the crowd, searching for someone or something. He passes the camera hastily, looking as if he is holding his breath. 'Do you know if he was a member of a political party?' she asks.

Gopal shakes his head.

'Did you know he was against the Mandal Commission?'

'He was pro-Mandal!' says a man, who has suddenly appeared beside the chaivala.

It is Suleman's bearded factotum, looking much the worse for wear and tear. He wears a scandalously dirty kurta. The yellow of his teeth has spread to his skin, nostrils and even his eyes. The lower lip hangs loose, and the gums – ever exposed – have been blackened by the constant company of tobacco. A few teeth are missing from the gaping mouth. Chitra is annoyed. What is he doing here?

'He was a pro-Mandal boy,' insists Ibrahim. 'He was a saint, a pir! The seths in IPP turned his head.'

'And what did *you* think about the Mandal Commission?' she asks Gopal.

'Gopal Bhai has always been pro-Mandal,' says Ibrahim.

Chitra looks angrily at Ibrahim. She does not like his condescending manner, but he has injected himself into the interview. That grin! His face is permanently disfigured by it. He grins even when he frowns. He will be buried grinning. And what is his relationship with the chaivala?

'Gopal Bhai is my brother,' says Ibrahim, as if she has voiced her question. 'I was with him when they burned his son.'

'Burned him?'

'Yes,' says Ibrahim. 'I saw IPP men set fire to him with a cigarette lighter.'

There may be a story here, she thinks. Gopal Pandey's associates claim that the self-immolation was a lynching. But she was there, she saw it happen, as did a thousand others. She has travelled the world to describe it to wide-eyed audiences. And who cares any more? V. P. Singh was dethroned two years ago, and Mandal is merely a name in the vocabulary of politics.

'They murdered Gopal Bhai's son,' screams Ibrahim. 'And they killed five hundred Musalmans! And now they want to damage Babri Masjid in Ayodhya! IPP will stop at nothing!'

Chitra sighs. There is no story here. The plot is known, and the protagonist is too colourless to fire anyone's imagination. He is unequal to the position thrust upon him by his son. She had hoped for an ideologue, a fire-breathing dragon, or at least a vengeful father. 'The Father, Two Years Later' may never be written. She would like to write on other subjects but she is the Mandal Woman, the Self-immolation Woman. The great newspapers of the world will condescend to print her articles on this subject alone. What can a woman do, if not follow up on the one story she is allowed to tell?

She stops her tape-recorder. Perhaps she will come back later when Suleman's man has gone. For now, she must go to Sparrows to attend the Independence Day function organised by Shalini. Suleman will be there as the chief benefactor. Periodic attendance at Sparrows is a tiresome duty. She went there last almost a year ago.

At Red Fort, the prime minister has still not finished his speech. His voice floats to her indistinctly, mangled by a hundred loudspeakers. As she leaves, she turns to the chaivala and his companion. They squat at either side of Mukesh Minar. They could not be more dissimilar. One is rotund, balding and slow, the other thin and energetic. One wears on his sagging face the slow agony of life, the other sports a passionate hatred of all living things. One hides his eyes behind foggy spectacles, while the eyes of the other burn with fiery intensity. Yet they sit like brothers, their hands touching the pole.

'You should listen to the prime minister's speech,' she says to Gopal.

'Why should he?' retorts Ibrahim. 'The PM is a Hindu! He wants to demolish Babri Masjid.'

'I may come back later,' she says to Gopal.

'Take a picture of the two of us,' calls Ibrahim, as she leaves.

As soon as Chitra is out of sight he turns on Gopal. 'You are a fool, Gopal Bhai! Why did you have to talk to her?'

'She only asked about my father,' says Gopal.

'Do not tell her about him.'

'What harm can come of it?'

'This is what reporters do! They find out about murders, thefts, debts, and then they blackmail you.'

'My father did not murder anyone.'

'How do you know?' demands Ibrahim. 'And how do you know they did not murder your son? You cannot even see properly!'

Gopal falls silent. He no longer remembers the incident with any clarity. For days after, he stayed among the sacks in Khari Baoli, too afraid to venture out. He lay in perpetual darkness, staring at the partition Seth Sushil Jain had built round his asafoetida tins, moving higher and higher in the mountain of sacks until he could touch the ceiling with his hand. Hameed came to move some sacks and was frightened to see a ghost haunting the kholi. Three servants climbed up the ladder and crawled in with sticks and brooms, determined to frighten it away. When they woke him up, he was lying in a pool of shit and piss. Seth Sushil Jain was furious. Faced with immediate eviction, Gopal helped them move the sacks, then cleaned the kholi. He had destroyed three sacks of turmeric with his piss. 'You will have to pay me nine hundred rupees,' the seth said.

'Where will I get it?' he had cried. He thought of telling the seth about his money belts behind the partition. But the seth would have taken it all, claiming it as his own. He staggered to Kucha Bansilal and opened the stall after a hiatus of four days.

'Where have you been?' asked Sohan Lalji, in a kind voice that soothed him.

He took the first cup of tea to the seth. 'Can I borrow nine hundred rupees?' he had asked.

'Why do you need nine hundred rupees?'

'I need to pay Seth Sushil Jain for damaged sacks of turmeric,' he said.

'I will talk to Sushil Jain,' promised Sohan Lalji.

That evening, a small man stopped him near Fatehpuri Masjid when he was on his way to the kholi. His upper lip was cleft in two, making him look like a rabbit. 'Are you Gopal Pandey?' he asked. He drew from his pocket a burned and twisted wristwatch. 'They found this on your son. Keep it.'

He had recoiled. He had not known that Mukesh owned a watch. It was bought, perhaps, with the silver stolen from Seth Jhunjhunwala. Even if the watch had belonged to Mukesh, why should he keep it? Its blackened face showed nothing, its dials were broken, and it had been inside the fire that had consumed his son.

'I found it on the body,' said the man.

Gopal had wondered if he was laughing, or if his upper teeth were permanently ranged in a vicious smile. How had he come so close to Mukesh's body, with police swarming everywhere? They had not even let Gopal touch him, so how did a buck-like man rob his dead son? What else had he taken?

The man held out an envelope. Its flap was open. 'Two thousand,' he said.

'Was the money in his shirt pocket?' asked Gopal. 'Why did it not burn?'

'It was not on his body,' said the rabbit-man. 'It is for you.'

'From whom?'

'He was a good boy, your son. He sacrificed his life.'

Gopal cycled furiously to Katra Badami. Over the next few days, he waited for Sushil Jain to bring up the subject of his money, but Sohan Lalji must have paid him because he never mentioned the nine hundred rupees again. Who would have known that Sohan Lalji was so kind? He has a son of his own and perhaps understands the pain of losing one, thought Gopal. When it became clear that Sushil Jain was not going to ask for his money, he bought himself a wristwatch with the money the rabbit-man had given him. And he never tried again to pick the lock in the kholi. There was some connection, no doubt, between his attempts to do so and the flames that had consumed his son. Perhaps Lakshmi had not meant to give him the money. Only great seths ever stumble upon lakhs of rupees. The poor man must satisfy himself with two thousand . . . What would he do with the money anyway, now that his son was dead?

A flood of applause interrupts the prime minister's speech. Gopal rises, using Mukesh Minar for support. 'I am going back to Kucha Bansilal,' he says.

'Who will drink your chai today?' asks Ibrahim. 'All the shops are closed for Independence Day.'

'Someone has put posters on my stall. I need to remove them.'

They walk to Kucha Bansilal. Ibrahim's eyes brighten on seeing the posters. 'Where is the Bangladeshi boy?' he asks.

'Working,' says Gopal, with pride. 'He earns a lot of money!'

'How much does he give you?' asks Ibrahim sarcastically.

'It does not matter. A son owes his father nothing.'

'Who made him your son?'

Gopal sighs. 'He has slept in my box for two years. Perhaps he was sent in exchange for Mukesh.'

'He is a Musalman,' objects Ibrahim.

'He is a hard-working boy.'

'You cannot trust him! He may vanish any day.'

'I see him more often than I saw Mukesh. Help me tear off this poster.'

'Leave it,' suggests Ibrahim. 'It is a poster for Suleman Mian's hunger strike in Rajghat. All secular Indians support it.'

'I have nothing to do with politics!' protests Gopal.

'Your son was murdered by upper-caste people,' says Ibrahim. 'Your father may have been murdered too. If you are not in politics, who is?'

Gopal searches for an answer.

'Politics is like a cricket match,' Ibrahim tell him. 'After you have watched it for some time, you are playing it, whether the ball is in Kapil Dev's hand or yours.'

Gopal sighs and opens the stall.

'We are committed to the principles of secularism,' says the prime minister. 'We will await a decision by the courts on the matter in Ayodhya.'

Chitra walks briskly toward Red Fort. She can see the prime minister's head bobbing up and down as he speaks. Passing Kucha Bansilal, she notes that the peepul tree outside is dying, burdened with signboards and advertisements. Next to the Hanuman temple, the pujari sits cross-legged on a mat, brushing his teeth with a stick of babool. The mat is littered with soap, brass utensils, a lantern, two pillows and a sheet. He has moved his bedroom outside: the mat is surrounded on three sides by wooden planks that form a fence. A section of the temple wall has been removed so it opens into the fenced courtyard. A tarpaulin forms a ceiling fifteen feet square, and a figurine of Hanuman as a boy stands on a pedestal in one corner. Chitra has heard of this figurine. It was the subject of a rift between archaeologists, who wanted to examine the embossed symbol of a Ghaziabad foundry under its left foot, and members of the IPP committee in Chandni Chowk, who thought it offensive that atheistic hands should prod and probe the left foot of Hanuman himself. She wonders if the rift has been healed, because Hanuman appears permanently stuck to the pedestal by the soles of his feet. The offending symbol, whatever its origin, has been for ever obscured. The lower part of the pedestal bears a plaque describing the unearth-ing of the figurine twenty-seven years ago and the rejoicing that followed. The pujari comes up behind her and waits for her to finish reading. He offers her prasaad. She refuses. 'One day we will build a brick wall round Hanuman,' he says. 'It is not proper that a servant of Raam should stand in the open with a mere tarpaulin over his head and a wooden fence round him. When the wall has been built, and a ceiling spans the courtyard, this Hanuman will enjoy the same status as the red one inside the temple.'

Chitra nods absently and steps out of the courtyard. A bearded man stands next to the pujari, loitering. He is tall, thin and dark. Her gaze travels down his long arms to his wrist, and she realises he is Gauhar. She has not seen him since that terrible day two years ago. He looks self-assured and comfortable, and his beard, although wispy, transforms his face into that of an adult.

'Didi!' he calls.

She is not pleased to see him. 'You have grown taller,' she says.

He acknowledges this proudly. 'They will not recognise me now!'

'Who?'

'Those who watch my film!'

She looks away in confusion. The film lies in the back of her mind, unedited, untouched, forgotten in the storm that has borne her aloft on wings of success into parlours, committees and functions for the last two years. Yet here he stands, looking at her expectantly. He is her child, after all. She cannot turn him away.

'I am still shooting,' she says, half believing it. 'I will come back and take more pictures of you.'

She walks away before he can respond, crosses Bhai Mati Das Chowk, runs past the dry fountain and Gurudwara Sisganj, then turns into a kucha that will take her into the lanes behind Jama Masjid. The prime minister's drone is drowned by rickshas and bicycles. She stops by a paan stall – deserted – and studies herself in a large mirror that is open to the street. She is proud of her long hair. A broad, clean forehead, given focus by the large red bindi centred in it. Her eyes, lips, nose and chin seem to be arranged round the bindi in perfect symmetry. Strong, broad shoulders, perhaps too masculine for some. A long-sleeved blouse, with the saree wrapped harmoniously round her body. She does not remember when she began to wear these handloom sarees with a tribal weave. She has travelled and been interviewed in them so much that they have become her journalistic uniform. Overall, the effect is not bad. She is thirty-five, past her prime in any society. In this one, some would consider her past redemption. Perhaps her height is a disadvantage, or her shoulders. In college, she heard a boy say there was no 'feminine delicacy' about her. She did not know whether he meant her frame or her opinions. But what is that? A streak of white! An unmistakable strand shining offensively in the mass of black! She turns away from the mirror and resumes her walk. Some women are married to time, she thinks, with a sigh.

She is surprised to find that the lane inside which Sparrows sits is closed permanently to traffic, and now serves as one of the class-rooms. A walkway spans the drain outside the red-brick building, while a tarpaulin provides partial cover, and work is in progress to convert it into a concrete ceiling. There is also an open-air kitchen, of which two sides already have brick walls. On the upper floor, she can see children peering down. She wonders how Shalini wangled a permit to build a second floor or to erect the tent that holds up the tarpaulin, or if she has a permit at all. Outside the blocked lane she sees the beacon-flashing Ambassador car that has brought Suleman to the function. She quickens her steps.

She sees him as soon as she enters the building through a glass door. He is dressed in a white kurta-pyjama and Gandhi cap. He greets her with an expansive namaste, and she is shocked – as always – by the intense pinpoints of his eyes. He has aged slightly in that his face is fleshier. But the moustache is still narrow, sharp and close-clipped.

'Madam is late today,' says Suleman ingratiatingly.

She tries to gauge the level of sarcasm in his voice. 'I have been interviewing someone,' she says.

'Ah!' says Suleman. 'You have many stories to write. A famous reporter!'

She is embarrassed because he is half sincere, and also because he is wrong. She is a familiar figure in press circles, but she is not a film star, a cricketer or a politician whose face is known to rickshavalas and rag-pickers. Hers is a different kind of fame, an understated notoriety, a position in history known only to history students. It is the most a woman like her can hope to achieve; she must carry the burden of her education, the restrictions of her class and the shackles of her upbring-ing – and observe the bounds of decent human behaviour, which do not restrain people of Suleman's tribe. To achieve a more earthy fame, the kind when living souls tremble in your presence, she would have to be far more simple-minded, and fortunate, than she is.

'Which story are you writing, these days?'

Knowing his interest is disingenuous, she shrugs and changes the subject. 'The prime minister is still speaking. Were you not invited to Red Fort?'

'I would not go if I had been,' he says. 'The PM will not say what I want to hear.'

She raises an eyebrow.

'The state government in Uttar Pradesh should be dismissed,' he says. 'Everyone knows that Babri Masjid is not safe with it. I want the PM to say, "Do not try to damage the masjid or you will be riddled with bullets, as you were two years ago."'

'I heard him say he will wait for the courts.'

'Musalmans want their masjid back,' scoffs Suleman. 'No court has authority over them.'

'The PM said he is committed to secularism,' she says.

Suleman fixes his sharp eyes on her. 'He is a Hindu.'

Chitra does not reply. Suleman has turned to greet Shalini, who has entered the main hall from the corridor beyond. She brings with her a long line of children, walking in orderly columns, who take their places on coir mats. An open area at the front serves as a stage.

Suleman walks up to Shalini, beaming. Chitra notes that she looks attractive in her light blue saree, which leaves large areas of her midriff exposed. When she smiles, her face dissolves into dimples, the same ones that had earned her much ridicule in college but now add to her charm. Chitra senses Suleman's interest in her, his relief at seeing her. Shalini extends a hand to him, and Chitra sees him freeze. He is given to the passions of ordinary men, but he has developed many airs that are particularly his own. He has perfected specific greetings for man, woman, constituent and animal. He will not condescend to shake hands with a woman. It is a gesture that defiles the image he has built for himself. Shalini pauses, then brings her hands together in a namaste. He nods his forgiveness, taking care to stay at least four feet from her.

'You have not visited us for more than a year,' she says sweetly.

Chitra watches Suleman. He finds Shalini more attractive than me, she thinks wistfully. Shalini turns to the children and asks them to greet Suleman Mian.

'Good morning, Suleman Mian!' say the children, in a musical chorus.

Chitra knows the English greeting bothers him, in spite of the tolerant smile he has pasted on his face. He sits down on the chair Shalini proffers.

It is only then that Shalini notices Chitra. 'Welcome, Miss Ghosh.'

Miss Ghosh – formal, distant, reverential, and insultingly reminiscent of maidenhood. From a callow, fumbling girl in college, Shalini has turned into a self-assured woman. When Chitra chose her for

Sparrows, she had relied on Shalini's passion, sincerity and honesty, not her self-assurance or skill. Chitra would feel embarrassed by that passion now. She suspects, even if she will not admit it, that these children were never meant to have a home but to live and die in the lanes of Chandni Chowk, unkempt, unlettered, unloved and un-wanted. Now, house-broken, they are domesticated dogs who cannot survive among the wild ones in the street, where they must inevitably find their way when the curtain comes down on this conceit. What will happen if, or when, Shalini herself begins to question the passion? Will she pass the torch of unquestioning belief to someone else, or shut down Sparrows and throw out the children, who are unprepared for Chandni Chowk?

The thought worries Chitra, and the image of Gauhar returns to her mind. 'They will not recognise me now,' he had said, with pride. He could not have included her in 'they', yet she had turned away quickly . . . At least he did not appear to be hungry, unlike some of these children. What will happen when Shalini abandons them? She brushes the idea aside. At twenty-four, Shalini is too young for doubts: she has many years of productive social work in her before the first seeds germinate. Many years, thinks Chitra wistfully, reminded of her own. Shalini extends a hand to her. Very manly, thinks Chitra, as she clasps it, then takes her seat beside Suleman.

'I thought we would dispense with speeches,' Shalini whispers excitedly, 'so I wrote a skit for the children.'

'What is a skit?' asks Suleman.

'A play.'

Suleman appears annoyed.

'It is not just a play,' says Shalini, quickly. 'It is social commentary.'

Suleman seems to acquiesce. Chitra smiles in encouragement. She wonders what comments Shalini could make about social issues with which Suleman would agree. She is a rich Delhi girl whose parents have shown her the world through the tinted rear windows of a car. But then she realises that Shalini is not too different from her, and is mortified by the revelation. She sighs and prepares for the long hour ahead. The happiest actors in this great skit – the skit of Sparrows, not the skit inside it – are the children, she thinks, because they understand it least.

Shalini arranges her actors in a line. The children stand awkwardly, casting furtive glances at Suleman, who sits with gentlemanly poise, right leg folded over left, right foot beating a rhythm, leather sandal flapping against his foot. His hands lie in his lap, his face is composed, and his eyes are fixed on the children with keen interest. Beneath the pencil moustache, his lips are blood red with paan, and curved into a permanent half-smile.

'Do not fear Suleman Mian,' says Shalini, to the children. 'He will give you chocolate.'

The effect he has on the children goes unnoticed by Suleman, whose face continues to project a benign blessing. Chitra watches the scene with some amusement, aware that Shalini, who now pushes a Nepali girl to sit inside a plastic bucket, is oblivious of Suleman's menace. The child, who is about seven, clutches the sides of the bucket and screams for help. 'Who will get me out of this ditch?' she calls.

A boy dressed as a mendicant stops on hearing her cries. He has long unkempt hair, a fake moustache that juts awkwardly from his upper lip, and a ten-year-old face smeared with holy ash. 'You suffer now,' observes the holy sadhu, 'but you will reap dividends in the next life.'

Suleman chuckles. Chitra notes that the boy and the girl have chosen to perform closer to her than to Suleman. Suleman continues to stare ahead, although much of the action takes place to his right.

'What about this life?' asks the girl.

The sadhu produces a packet of holy ash from the folds of his saffron dress, and holds it out to her. 'Smear a little vibhuti on your brow,' he says.

'Perhaps you will rub it in,' she asks.

'I do not want to touch you,' he replies. 'How do I know you are a Brahmin?'

He throws the packet at her and departs in a hurry, drawing laughter from the children and an approving nod from Suleman, who looks with interest at the little girl.

'Nepali?' he asks Chitra.

'Yes. Some are from Bangladesh, others from Nepal.'

'Pretty girl,' he says.

It is an innocent remark, but Chitra shivers. It seems to come from the depths of indescribable debauchery. The child is indeed pretty: her skin is brown and smooth, her eyes light. In a few years she will be a beautiful woman. Who will protect her then?

'What is her name?' Suleman asks Shalini.

'Kiran. She is only seven, yet hear how confidently she speaks.'

Kiran's next saviour, after the sadhu's desertion, is a politician in a white kurta-pyjama, and a Gandhi cap too large for his little head. The resemblance to Suleman, if only in dress, is unmistakable. Chitra casts a curious glance at him but he looks blandly through the boy.

'Help me!' screams Kiran.

The politician pauses and studies the girl. 'She looks like a Hindu,' he declares to his audience. 'I will pull you out of this ditch,' he tells her. 'Then you and I will build a great Raam temple in Ayodhya.'

'But there is a masjid in Ayodhya,' Kiran says.

'Babri Masjid? It is only a structure. We will tear it down.'

Chitra looks sideways at Shalini. Has she written these lines with an eye on Suleman? Perhaps she has a better perspective on her position than Chitra thought. When she had opened Sparrows, she had thought of it as her final destination. Has Shalini always known that it is a first stop on a long journey?

'Why will you tear down Babri Masjid?' asks Kiran.

'Because Babur tore down a temple to build the masjid,' replies the politician.

'Will you also tear down Qutab Minar?' asks Kiran.

'Yes. It represents the shame of defeat.'

'Will you tear down Taj Mahal?'

'Yes. It is a cruel tyrant's monument to himself.'

'Will you tear down Jama Masjid? Fatehpuri Masjid? Red Fort? Agra Fort?'

'Yes, all masjids, all monuments and all minars built by Musalmans.'

Kiran's innocent face is alight with mockery. 'What will I do with the ruins?' she asks.

'You and I will build great temples among them,' says the politician.

'But I do not go to a temple!' protests Kiran.

'You look like a Hindu,' says the politician.

'I am not a Hindu.'

'Are you a Musalman?' asks the horrified politician.

'I do not go to a masjid.'

'Are you a sardarni, then?'

'I do not go to a gurudwara.'

'A Christian?'

'No.'

'Parsee?'

'No.'

'Buddhist? Jain?'

'No.'

'What are you, then?'

'An Indian!' declares Kiran, grandly.

The children burst into applause.

The politician stands humiliated. He adjusts his Gandhi cap, and realisation dawns. 'Yes, we are all Indian,' he says, with sombre finality. He extends his hand to help Kiran out of the bucket.

Shalini cheers and claps. The children applaud enthusiastically.

Suleman leans toward Chitra. 'The girl in the bucket should have been a Musalman,' he whispers, 'not a Nepali Hindu.'

Chitra wonders whether he is passing artistic judgement or making a political point.

'Only a Musalman understands these things,' explains Suleman.

Chitra tuts, not inclined to humour him. Then, fearing she has been rude, she gives him a tolerant smile that may mean anything from 'What an idiotic suggestion' to 'You are absolutely right.'

He assumes the latter and chuckles. 'I am going to stand in the assembly elections next year,' he confides.

She wonders why he has chosen to tell her this.

'You could write an article about it.'

His deference is explained.

'Foreign magazines like pictures of local politicians,' he declares. 'They want to know about grass-roots workers. Who is Suleman Mian? A man of the people, a son of Chandni Chowk, a child of Jama Masjid! You can be the journalist who discovers him.'

Arrogance refers to itself in the third person, she thinks. At the same time, she cannot help feeling gratified, aware of herself as his gate-keeper to foreign magazines. A two-page spread flashes before her eyes: a man in a yellow shirt, flailing inside a ball of fire, reaching out a Rolex hand for help . . . So many articles, interviews, photographs, and the magic names of CNN, *Time*, *Newsweek*, have stoked the hunger of an animal behind Jama Masjid! She no longer has the access she once had to those magazines, but he does not know that.

'Where will you stand?' she asks.

He points in an expansive gesture that includes her, Shalini, the children, the small crowd that has formed in the lane outside the building and the entire race of humans and animals who live around Jama Masjid. 'Here!' he says. 'Matia Mahal constituency.'

'You have never been a candidate in any election.'

He chuckles. 'I have worked in this area for eight years. Can you find one person in these lanes who does not know me?'

Some of that work is Sparrows, Chitra thinks sourly. It will be listed as an achievement when he campaigns.

'Seventy per cent of people in Matia Mahal are Musalmans,' he points out.

She knows his presumption is justified. Even now, when he occupies no post in any council or assembly, his demeanour is that of a representative of the people. The flashing beacon on his car – certainly not his own car – is a symbol of his power, as is his ability to raise funds for Sparrows, have pensions approved, secure employment for his wards, ask banks to write off loans to his favourites, and provide protection to Sparrows, which sits on illegally acquired land and extends into the lane.

'Which party will give you its ticket?' she asks.

He points to his constituency again. 'These are my people. Why do they need a party? I will be an independent candidate.'

That makes political sense, she thinks. As a party candidate he will be hamstrung by the party hierarchy. As an independent he can vault past the lower rungs of a party ladder and offer himself as a member near the top of it.

'We will now sing our national anthem,' declares Shalini.

The sadhu, the politician and Kiran stand in a line, glowing with the success of their performance. They begin, and the other children follow.

'"*Jana gana mana adhinaayaka . . .*"'

Chitra and Suleman stand to attention. In the middle of the song, she notices the reluctance with which Suleman mouths the words.

'We welcome all Musalmans to join the national mainstream,' says Lala Surajmal to the reporter. 'People say Hindutva is against Musalmans, but Hindutva is not a religion; it is a way of life, a nationalist philosophy. We are happy to let Musalmans be Musalmans. It is their burden to bear. We do not want them to convert to Hinduism – in this we are more tolerant than Musalmans – and we do not want them to renounce Allah. We merely ask, "Can you not dissolve yourself in the culture of this country? Can you not support the Indian cricket team during India–Pakistan matches?" '

The reporter scribbles furiously. Surajmal pulls a handkerchief from his kurta pocket and wipes his mouth, which has begun to dribble. He leans heavily on his walking-stick outside the east gate of Fatehpuri Masjid, surrounded by two servants and Ramvilas. His forceful harangue is directed as much at the reporter as at Sohan Lal, Jugal Kishor and Muhammad Salauddin Qureshi, a young man in a spotless achkan who hovers shyly at the edge of this circle.

'Lalaji looks very ill,' whispers Jugal Kishor to Ramvilas.

'Another stroke,' says Ramvilas. 'He will not admit it.'

Why must the old fart insist on speaking? thinks Sohan Lal. This is a walk, not a rally.

After handing his soggy handkerchief to a servant, Surajmal continues, 'This Heritage Walk was conceived by our beloved leader, Shri Harilalji Gupta. We will begin here, at Fatehpuri Masjid, walk through all the places in Chandni Chowk that represent our cultural heritage and end at Town Hall. IPP has great respect for historical buildings, even when they remind us of Musalman and British atrocities.'

The reporter, a diminutive man of sixty with a camera slung over his shoulder, cocks a bold eyebrow and senses an opportunity for good copy. 'Does not Babri Masjid represent our cultural heritage?'

Surajmal makes an intense effort to turn to the reporter, fails, and begins to collapse. The servants prop him up. He breathes heavily. Angry glances are cast at the reporter for his impudence. Surajmal thrusts an index finger at him, lower lip trembling in excitement. 'That is a structure, not a mosque. No one has worshipped there for decades. We have nothing against mosques – such as the one outside which we stand – if they are not built out of Hindu temples. We have offered to move that structure at our own expense. We will place it anywhere the Musalmans want. They can have any spot in India – and one spot is as good as another to Musalmans – so why must they insist on the exact spot where our Raam Lalla was born?'

Ramvilas bends to whisper in Surajmal's ear: 'Harilalji said we should not discuss Ayodhya and Babri Masjid on this walk.'

'Why should I not discuss Ayodhya?' asks Surajmal, irritably. 'Raam Lalla himself walked into his temple and claimed it.'

Jugal Kishor shrugs. Sohan Lal turns away. Surajmal clears his throat and calls the reporter closer. 'Congress says IPP is anti-Musalman. Ask those pseudo-secularists how many Musalmans they have in their committees.'

'How many Musalmans does IPP have?' challenges the reporter.

Surajmal gestures triumphantly at Qureshi, opens his mouth and falters. Ramvilas realises that Lalaji has forgotten his name. Qureshi shifts uncomfortably.

'Lalaji is not well,' says Jugal Kishor.

'Qureshiji has joined the IPP committee in Chandni Chowk,' declares Ramvilas.

Sohan Lal, Jugal Kishor and Surajmal's servants clap. The reporter – whose energy belies his age – hastily turns to Qureshi. 'Do you think Babri Masjid should be moved from its site?'

Qureshi runs a finger along the collar of his achkan, which is wrapped tightly round his wiry frame, and makes a gesture deploring the heat, which has already dissolved the early-morning chill. He speaks in a reedy, uncertain voice, so softly that the reporter leans closer to catch his words. 'We favour consensus, not a decision by the courts, because this is a matter beyond the jurisdiction of courts.'

Surajmal nods approvingly and continues his announcements: 'Harilalji Gupta has announced the setting up of a Heritage Council, which will meet in a month to draw up a plan to preserve the historic buildings in Chandni Chowk.'

'How many people do you expect on this Heritage Walk?' asks the reporter.

Surajmal looks around angrily. Attendance is abysmal. He can see two traders from Kucha Sugandh – he summoned them last evening – advancing toward him. Even with them, there are only eleven people, including the two servants, the reporter and the second Musalman whom Qureshi has brought with him.

'Where is Harilalji?' grumbles Sohan Lal. 'It was his idea.'

'Harilalji cannot come to every little function,' Surajmal responds irritably.

'He has time for prostitutes like that Gita Didi,' whispers Sohan Lal to Jugal Kishor.

'We should set off now,' suggests Ramvilas. 'People will join us as we go.'

'We will begin the Heritage Walk with a visit to Fatehpuri Masjid,' says Surajmal, to the reporter. 'From here, we will carry a message of communal harmony and peace all over Chandni Chowk, even to Musalman areas of Matia Mahal.' He gestures to Qureshi, whose designated duty is to point out Muslim landmarks on the way. However, being somewhat ignorant of buildings in Chandni Chowk because he is from Lucknow, Qureshi has brought along a Kashmiri scholar who has studied Mughal and pre-Mughal architecture for years. Sheikh Noor Muhammad is a delicate man with fine features, dressed in a grand achkan that chokes him in the oppressive August heat. He is given to speaking with relish about minars, mausoleums and mosques. He holds the monuments of Delhi in great esteem and the traders of Chandni Chowk in great contempt, and has agreed to serve as guide only because Qureshi has made him vague promises of a government appointment. Now he stands, lips compressed in consternation, awaiting Qureshi's signal. Qureshi walks up to him and nods. Noor stands straight, tilts his head slightly and speaks in a theatrical, high-pitched voice.

'Fatehpuri Masjid was built in the year sixteen fifty by Begum Fatehpuri, which may explain its feminine charm and cloistered look.'

What charm? Sohan Lal asks himself, looking up at the worn red walls. He firmly disapproves of such fuzzy sentimentality over decrepit buildings.

'The eastern gate of the masjid faces Red Fort,' says Noor Muhammad. 'Khari Baoli lies to the north and Katra Baryan to the south. Notice the lotuses on either side of the gate.'

Lotuses! Sohan Lal is seized with horror. Was this mosque, too, built atop the ruins of a Hindu temple like the structure in Ayodhya? Then why is the IPP playing a heritage charade when it should be bringing it down with hammers? Perhaps Harilal Gupta is enamoured of his old party. Perhaps he wants to please the pseudo-secularist press so it will write wonderful lines about him in English newspapers. Why else would the IPP behave like the Congress Party and pander to Musalmans?

'We will now enter the masjid compound,' suggests Noor Muhammad. He looks at Qureshi for confirmation. He is not certain the seths are to be invited into the mosque.

'It is a Monday,' says Qureshi, softly. 'Except on Jumma, there is never a crowd.'

Noor Muhammad leads his unsympathetic audience into the

mosque. There are shops selling wristwatches under the gate. Narrow stairs lead up to doctors' clinics, announced by wooden boards hung under the grand arch. If a Hindu tried to set up his stall here, thinks Sohan Lal, they would accuse him of being a fundamentalist.

Qureshi and Noor Muhammad step into the flagstone compound and remove their shoes. Jugal Kishor and the other two traders follow suit. Surajmal, at the head of the procession, has been led far into the compound by the two servants, his shoes in the hands of Ramvilas. Sohan Lal bends over with difficulty, slips off his galoshes and finds, to his annoyance, that there is no rack where he can deposit them.

'Did you telephone Kartar Singh?' Surajmal asks Ramvilas.

Ramvilas is happy to provide bad news. 'Kartar Singhji is playing cricket. He has been up since three in the morning.'

'I did not know there was a match today,' growls Surajmal.

'England versus Pakistan in Sydney,' says Ramvilas. He has a small financial stake in the match, in the form of a bet placed with Kartar Singh. He has had good luck when two countries play in a third.

Surajmal shakes his head. 'It is not even an Indian match! A councillor should be present when the party organises a march.'

'The masjid served as a battleground against the British,' says Noor Muhammad. 'After the Mutiny of eighteen fifty-seven, the British auctioned it to Lala Channa Mal for nineteen thousand rupees. Twenty-five years later the government wanted to buy it back for a lakh and twenty thousand rupees, but Lala Channa Mal refused.'

Noor Muhammad looks round to see if anyone has noticed the irony – a Hindu Bania trying to make a profit out of a masjid! But Surajmal stands in moribund bliss, Sohan Lal frowns at a signboard and Jugal Kishor watches the water tank, around which a dozen men are seated on stone slabs. Noor Muhammad is unhappy to be in the masjid with seths. They are uncouth and uncivilised, he thinks, Philistine traders whose daughters dance to vulgar Hindi film music, whose wives sing toneless bhajans, who have no conception of art, architecture or aesthetics. He has no doubt that Kashmiris were the original rulers of India. Why, even in this cauldron of Hindus, the prime ministers come from Kashmir! They call themselves Hindus, but when did a Hindu have such fine features, such a sharp nose, such glistening skin? Has no one looked closely at the aquiline features of Nehru, Indira and Rajiv? They call themselves Kashmiri Brahmins but they are really Kashmiris, no more. It is a pity Qureshi Sahib is not with the Congress Party where he belongs and where he will certainly find himself in the future. Until then, he must pander to seths and Banias.

'This is how Musalmans wash themselves,' says Jugal Kishor to Sohan Lal, pointing to the water tank.

A congregation sits inside the masjid, listening to a speaker who is not visible from the water tank, but whose voice echoes from loudspeakers placed throughout the compound, its different sounds mixing to form an unintelligible drone.

'Can we not put our shoes away somewhere?' Sohan Lal asks Qureshi.

Qureshi shrugs. Sohan Lal is irritated. It is all right for a Musalman to walk about with leather shoes in his hands, but a seth has dignity!

Noor Muhammad turns to his audience and resumes: 'The dome is built of lime mortar but plastered to look like marble from a distance. The tank in the courtyard was once fed directly by the Yamuna river. The main mosque is on a platform three and a half feet high, and the pulpit is pure marble . . .'

'A little water!' gasps Surajmal.

Qureshi rushes to the water tank, scoops up water in his hands and runs back to Surajmal, who has almost fainted in the arms of his servants.

'That water is dirty!' thunders Sohan Lal.

Qureshi steps back, mortified. Ramvilas produces a bottle of Bisleri from his jhola and tips it over Surajmal's face. Surajmal breathes heavily and shuts his eyes in relief. Sohan Lal turns to read a wooden plaque affixed to the wall, beyond which stretches an open corridor. A dozen children in skullcaps sit on coir mats, reciting the alphabet, swaying with each syllable, watched over by a mulla.

Alif se Israfeel, Be se Jibraeel, Te se Izraeel, Se se Mikaeel . . .

'The Madarsa Ali Arabia Fatehpuri,' says Noor Muhammad, thoughtfully, 'founded as a centre of Islamic education more than a hundred years ago, when Lord Northbrook was viceroy. It functions today much as it did in the last century.'

'That is the problem,' Sohan Lal whispers to Jugal Kishor. 'Who knows what poison it spews?'

Jugal Kishor admonishes Sohan Lal gently. 'Harilalji has said that IPP will no longer accuse Musalmans of anything without proper evidence.'

Noor Muhammad leads the way out of the masjid. The servants lift Surajmal's legs, one at a time, slip on his shoes and lead him out behind Noor Muhammad. Sohan Lal gratefully throws his shoes to the ground and slips them on. They emerge from the eastern gate and turn right, away from Khari Baoli. Surajmal's gaze falls on a cauldron of jalebis outside a stall. He is mesmerised. Sohan Lal notices the look in his eyes. 'They are not good for your diabetes, Lalaji.'

'That is what English doctors tell you,' scoffs Surajmal. 'They know nothing about naturopathy. Do we still have lemon oil in the shop?' His question is directed at Ramvilas, who nods.

'Sniff a little lemon oil regularly,' counsels Surajmal. 'Ramvilas will give you a bottle.' He makes a valiant attempt to look cheerful and radiant. 'A few drops of lemon oil will cure diabetes, asthma, boils and varicose veins.' With this nugget, he orders jalebis for everyone.

Sohan Lal refuses one. 'You can continue your tour,' he says coldly to Noor Muhammad.

Noor Muhammad, savouring the sweetness, speaks through a stuffed mouth. 'To our left, a short distance away, is Dariba Kalan, where Nadir Shah slaughtered ninety thousand people.'

'Ninety thousand Hindus,' corrects Sohan Lal.

'Was he the Persian?' says Surajmal.

Noor Muhammad crushes a juicy jalebi with a crunch and nods.

Surajmal calls the reporter to his side and directs him to take notes. 'Tell us what he took away from India,' he says with childlike curiosity to Noor Muhammad.

Noor Muhammad takes another bite of his jalebi – can a jalebi really be larger than his hand? – and feels gratified. Perhaps the seths are not so vile after all. 'Nadir Shah carted away a hundred million pounds sterling, a thousand elephants, seven thousand horses, ten thousand camels, a hundred and thirty writers, two hundred masons, three hundred stone-cutters, two hundred carpenters—'

'We do not need an exact list!' says Qureshi, indignantly.

Surajmal, dribbling jalebi juice, raises a restraining hand. 'Let him speak! This is history.'

But Noor Muhammad remains silent, aware that he has crossed Qureshi, his primary benefactor. The jalebis finished, they wash their hands and commence the Heritage Walk. In the first steps, Lala Surajmal stumbles. Qureshi rushes to steady him but he recovers by himself, leans on his stick and snarls, 'I am still alive. Wait until I am dead!'

Qureshi is embarrassed. After the display of bravado, Surajmal realises he cannot walk all the way. He stands pitifully. His joints hurt, his right leg is still paralysed, and he is ashamed to mount a ricksha. Ramvilas studies his face from the corner of his eye, well aware of his discomfort. Every day, in Bhagwan Das and Sons, he sees servants help the seth sit down on the mattress and stand up from it. He savours his master's humiliation for a moment, then signals to the two servants, who run to a ricksha and pull down a wheelchair. Surajmal sinks into it with shame on his mottled face. His defeat is complete.

It is only a matter of time, thinks Sohan Lal, before a second stroke finishes off Lala Surajmal. The old man refuses to change his diet to control his diabetes, trusting in his knowledge of obscure oils and attars. 'The left hand still writes,' he says, 'the left leg still walks. God would have taken both if he wanted me to stop! He takes you when you have lost the will to live . . .' And Surajmal certainly has the will to live, thinks Sohan Lal, considering the relish with which he devours jalebis and makes announcements. Yet he seems to be speaking from far away. He cannot concentrate. His words trail off. Every sentence has a finality to it, as if it might be his last. Does he know that his four sons are already fighting for pieces of his carcass?

It is undignified to hang on like Surajmal, thinks Sohan Lal. When he himself found out about his cholesterol and blood pressure two months ago, he immediately went on a regimen of Atenolol. A man must do what he can to live meaningfully.

The walk begins. Surajmal is still at the head in his wheelchair, pushed by one servant while the other clears the way. Three other traders have joined them with placards. The procession cuts a straight line through Chandni Chowk, bringing rickshas and scooters to a halt, aiming for Red Fort, a dark smudge in the distance. Sohan Lal pushes past the others and arrives at Surajmal's wheelchair. 'I will take care of Lalaji,' he says to the servant.

He grips the wheelchair and gives it a gentle tug, to let Surajmal know that his chauffeur has been replaced. Surajmal, now fully recovered but afraid to try walking again, turns and speaks grudgingly: 'You are not so young yourself, Sohan Lal.'

Sohan Lal pushes harder, aware that the others have fallen behind. He decides to dispense with a preamble. 'I need to speak to you about the assembly elections next year.'

Surajmal frowns. 'What is the hurry? The Election Commission has not set a date.'

'I would like a ticket this time,' says Sohan Lal.

'You?' asks a shocked Surajmal. 'What will you do as an MLA?'

Sohan Lal is annoyed. After thirty years of public service, why is it still a matter of surprise that he should have ambitions toward office himself? Must he always work to elect others? Of the four assembly segments in the area, Chandni Chowk will obviously go to Harilal Gupta, and Paharganj to Surajmal's nephew. Why could he not have the IPP ticket for Ballimaran? 'I can stand for Ballimaran,' he says defiantly.

'Kartar Singh has already expressed interest,' says Surajmal.

'Why was I not consulted?'

'Kartar Singh is a councillor,' says Surajmal. 'I cannot turn down his request.'

'You can give Matia Mahal to Kartar Singh,' says Sohan Lal.

'You are too impatient! The election is more than a year away. Nothing will be finalised until the Commission sets a date.'

'You can call a committee meeting tomorrow and finalise it,' insists Sohan Lal.

Surajmal sighs deeply. 'You do not need to win an election to be in politics,' he says. 'Look at me! I have made a dozen people councillors. What is an MLA, or even an MP? A servant of the people. Such posts are for servants, not for established businessmen like you. You are the kingmaker. You pull strings in the background while they dance to your wishes. They are puppets!'

Ah, to be a puppet in my waning years! thinks Sohan Lal wistfully. It is all right for Surajmal to speak like this. He enjoys unparalleled influence. The entire committee defers to him. He can get his nephew the ticket for Paharganj, and perhaps ensure his victory. When Harilalji becomes a minister in the Delhi assembly, will Sohan Lal be allowed inside his government bungalow? Will the guard even recognise him?

'Call Ramvilas and Jugal Kishor,' Surajmal commands.

Reluctantly Sohan Lal stops the wheelchair and signals to Ramvilas and Jugal Kishor. Surajmal twists round and grabs his hand. 'I am getting old. After me, the committee will need a new chairman.'

Sohan Lal tries to decipher the look on his wrinkled face, which turns opaque when the others join them. Ramvilas takes over with the wheelchair.

'Push faster,' says Surajmal.

Sohan Lal and Jugal Kishor walk briskly to stay abreast of the chair. Qureshi and Noor Muhammad fall behind, walking silently because the only monuments in this part of Chandni Chowk are shops for garments, shoes and wristwatches. Surajmal tilts his head up and signals to Ramvilas.

'I have arranged for twelve boys,' says Ramvilas.

'A training camp needs a hundred, not twelve,' reprimands Surajmal.

'We need to hurry,' says Jugal Kishor. 'We have only two months before the boys must leave for Ayodhya.'

'Who will pay them?' challenges Ramvilas.

'That is not your concern,' Surajmal snaps.

Ramvilas huffs and struggles with the chair. He is vain about his slender frame. It looks presentable in a mirror but is unsuitable for tasks such as this, and Surajmal is a heavy man even as he withers away. 'We have fourteen members on the committee,' he says casually.

'What about them?' demands Sohan Lal.

'They can go to the training camp,' says Ramvilas.

'Hold your tongue,' says Surajmal coldly. 'We will provide money. We will provide meals for the training camp, people to run it, space to house it. You cannot expect committee members to run round with sticks in their hands. Do you take us for hoodlums?'

In that case, who do you think I am? wonders Ramvilas.

Sohan Lal bristles, disappointed with Surajmal's mild response to Ramvilas's proposal. How dare a clerk suggest such a thing?

But Surajmal speaks with a palliative note. 'Arrange for more boys. We will raise your rates. Do whatever is possible because Babri Masjid cannot remain where it is. Have you not seen what they did to our men in Ayodhya two years ago? I have watched the video. The waves of Saryu were flowing with Hindu blood. This is Kaliyug, when a Hindu sheds the blood of Hindus in a Hindu land, all for trying to reclaim a temple from Musalmans. What kind of a democracy is that?'

The last words are spoken with rising passion, causing Qureshi and Noor Muhammad to look up. They are aware that they have been excluded from the discussion and are afraid to barge in. They take the loud talk as an invitation.

Qureshi speaks: 'IPP will bring real democracy to this country, Lalaji.'

Sohan Lal fixes him with a cold glare. A bad idea, adding these Musalmans, even if we do want to broaden our base.

Ramvilas hands control of the wheelchair to the servant and drifts away from the group to get a paan. At the stall he listens to the radio, which is playing a live commentary of the cricket match in Sydney. England is batting in a storm of fours and sixes, and it appears that Pakistan is heading for defeat. He chuckles inwardly. He has heard rumours – not from Kartar Singh, who will never tell him directly but from someone who heard Kartar Singh say so – that the match is coloured, that Pakistani bowling will rip England apart to win at the last moment. This is a good time to place a bet on a Pakistani victory – when it appears unlikely – because the odds will be good.

He rushes to Mangat Ram Nawal Kishor, where the staff know him and will let him use the telephone. 'Jugal Kishorji has sent me,' he says. 'Pack a box of barfis for the Heritage Walk.'

Then he picks up the telephone from the glass counter, pulls it with its cord into a corner and calls Kartar Singh.

Kartar Singh is behind an array of telephones that ring every few minutes. Two accountants and three boys sit cross-legged on the white mattress. The first accountant answers calls, quotes the latest rate and notes bets in pads bound with red cloth. As soon as a bet is entered, one of the boys leaves to collect money from the punter. On returning, they hand it to the second accountant, who counts and enters it against the punter's name. Kartar Singh is propped up against a mountain of bolsters, Thums Up in hand, legs comfortably splayed. A microphone attached to a phone line comes alive from time to time when the dibba announces the latest rate for an English victory.

'Four one for England!' he calls, in response to the dibba's voice.

'Four one for England,' says the accountant, into the telephone. He writes a number on a chit and hands it to a boy, who leaves immediately. A second telephone rings. The accountant listens to the caller, then repeats loudly, 'Banwari Lal?'

Kartar Singh thinks hard but cannot remember anyone by that name. The bookie business can be dangerous if a man is not careful. There are sting operations by the police, punters connected with gangsters, frauds posing as punters . . . He cannot accept a bet from someone he does not know. He shakes his head.

'Sardarji is not in the store,' the accountant tells the caller. The caller insists. 'What bet?' asks the accountant, and hangs up.

Suddenly the television screen explodes. It is a boundary. England looks likely to end the series with a four–one record over Pakistan. The dibba's voice responds to the boundary.

'Seventeen four for England.'

'Seventeen four,' repeats Kartar Singh.

Five telephones ring simultaneously. The accountant struggles with them, two at a time. These are old punters, whose names he does not bother to verify. Kartar Singh watches him take frantic notes. Once England goes past two hundred, the match will become too predictable and he will stop taking bets. Punters are rushing to put down money before the odds go out of control. Kartar Singh takes the notepad from the second accountant and asks him to assist the first. He runs his finger down the entries. More than ten thousand rupees have been collected in the last three hours. He makes a quick calculation of his three per cent commission and is gratified at the result. He will have to give a twentieth of that to the dibba, sitting somewhere in Punjab. Half of the dibba's share will be absorbed by the anonymous channels that transfer this money to him. That is the price the dibba pays for anonymity. A dibba, thinks Kartar Singh with satisfaction, will remain safe but poor.

'Ramvilas Sharma?' repeats the accountant.

Kartar Singh nods.

'Seventeen four for England,' the accountant speaks into the telephone.

The accountant listens, then holds out the telephone to Kartar Singh. Kartar Singh grunts. It is not good practice for him to take bets. Punters should talk to his accountants. Ramvilas usually places small bets – too small to command Kartar Singh's time – and is given to frivolous talk, which Kartar Singh cannot afford while playing a match. He takes the telephone with an expression of annoyance.

'Sat sri akaal!' says Ramvilas's breezy voice. 'What is the rate?'

'You have already been told,' says Kartar Singh, coldly. 'Seventeen four for England.'

'Put down five hundred,' says Ramvilas.

'I do not accept anything less than a thousand.' He savours the pause and imagines greed competing with prudence in Ramvilas's deliberations.

'Put down a thousand,' says Ramvilas. 'For Pakistan.'

'But that rate is four seventeen!'

'I know,' says Ramvilas.

Kartar Singh smiles. 'You are my friend. I should warn you, Pakistan will certainly lose.'

Ramvilas laughs. 'To choose between Pakistan and England, the brother and the master! I hate my brother and love my master, but I cannot confuse money with love.'

'One thousand on Pakistan,' says Kartar Singh, loudly. 'Ramvilas Sharma.'

The accountant jots down the figure and glances around, but all three boys are out collecting money.

'I do not have a boy handy,' says Kartar Singh. 'You will have to wait.'

'Send Salim,' suggests Ramvilas. 'I am in Mangat Ram Nawal Kishor.'

'Salim is in the store.'

'How is business?'

'Slow,' says Kartar Singh.

He knows why Ramvilas has brought up his business. People derive satisfaction from the decline of Lajpatrai Market. The margins in the store keep dropping, driven down by competition from cheap Chinese goods. Who can make money selling light bulbs in such a market? He can afford Salim, the three boys and two accountants – all officially employed by the store – only because they spend much of their time in the back room taking bets, reconciling them, collecting from punters and paying them. The store is no more than a front. A man can no longer earn a living in Chandni Chowk unless his family has been in business for generations. Havala is dead, killed by foreign banks where beautiful girls in starched sarees greet you and transfer your money in full view of the police. They even give you a piece of paper to account for the transfer, and their rates are lower than those of most havala traders, who have lost their reputation for trustworthiness. There was a time, barely ten years ago, when a man could leave a few lakhs with a trader and be assured that it would be handed over the next day, anywhere in the world. Now no one trusts anyone in this city of thieves and politicians. One day, after he has set aside a tidy sum, he will close down everything – the store and the bookie business – and take Sukhbir to Canada where they will grow old in peace . . .

The dibba's voice crackles again in Kartar Singh's ear. The odds are now nine to two for England. Kartar Singh decides not to bother giving Ramvilas that piece of information. He quoted the rate at the time the bet was placed. He owes Ramvilas nothing more.

'Don't tell Lalaji I have bet on Pakistan,' chuckles Ramvilas. 'He will throw me out of Bhagwan Das and Sons!'

This is not the time for idle chatter, thinks Kartar Singh. He must keep the phone lines free for other punters. 'Good luck,' he whispers into the phone, then hands it back to the accountant. 'Send Salim to Mangat Ram Nawal Kishor.'

Kartar Singh knows Ramvilas's bet is doomed. He himself has spread the rumours on whose basis Ramvilas has bet on Pakistan. Two days ago, Kartar Singh placed two hundred rupees on Pakistan, when the odds were four to two for England, knowing that his accountants sell information to punters, leading to rumours that the script is coloured in favour of Pakistan. They reason that if Kartar Singh, master bookie, has secretly placed money on Pakistan, the match must be fixed in Pakistan's favour. Punters in the know, who are in contact with his accountants, have been betting heavily against the odds. The lower the rates for a Pakistani victory – currently two to nine – the more they stand to gain when, as they believe, Pakistan will win. They do not know, of course, that the accountants have been misled by Kartar Singh, and the script runs counter to the information given by them. Pakistan will lose, and by a wide margin. Kartar Singh will forfeit most of his two hundred rupees, but will earn many times that from the hundreds of losing bets made by people like Ramvilas.

This is a good business, he reflects with satisfaction, as long as they keep playing coloured matches. Why allow the vagaries of chance to determine the outcome when you can write it in advance? The trick, of course, is to know the script beforehand. A thought clouds his mind. What if his contact has not given him the right script and Pakistan indeed emerges victorious? Anything can happen in cricket. The fall of another two wickets may transform the game . . . Ah, he must not worry. A bookie never loses money – he merely earns less from winning bets. He has been wise to resist the temptation of placing his own bets other than those designed to start ultimately lucrative rumours. Sometimes even when you know the script it can go wrong. And only an idiot will bet on a match whose script he does not know. Worse still, there exist punters who bet on straight matches, whose script is known only to God!

'Five one for England,' says the dibba.

'Five one for England,' repeats Kartar Singh. He watches the faces of his accountants carefully as they digest the new odds. They have brought in cups of chai, which they sip with inscrutable faces. Their hearts are beating fast, thinks Kartar Singh, malevolently. They will have a lot to answer for when they step out of the room and confront the punters who acted on their information. Or are they privy to information he does not have? Could it be that Pakistan is poised to make an impossible recovery? But England has now crossed two hundred. The odds are prohibitively in its favour. Even the most imaginative script must respect the logic of the plot.

'We should stop putting down names now,' says Kartar Singh, casually, 'unless the figure is very high.'

He fancies he sees a twitch in the faces of his accountants, but he cannot be sure.

The Heritage Walk has now covered a third of its distance and advanced beyond Bhai Mati Das Chowk. Surajmal has nodded off in his wheelchair. Qureshi has fallen behind, demoralised, aware that he has been added only to 'secularise' the walk. Noor Muhammad forges ahead gallantly, trying to find historic associations wherever he can. The reporter follows with a perfunctory expression, disappointed at the lack of fanfare.

'We are now passing Gurudwara Sisganj,' declares Noor Muhammad, and falls silent. He has been called to speak about Mughal buildings and knows nothing about Sikh temples. Surajmal wakes up with a start and begins to cough. 'Was Kartar Singh supposed to talk about Gurudwara Sisganj?' asks Sohan Lal.

'He is watching his cricket match,' says Surajmal sourly.

'A councillor should know his duty,' grumbles Sohan Lal.

'We should keep walking,' suggests Jugal Kishor. 'We can go back and rest in my shop.' He spies Ramvilas approaching the group. He has a box of barfis in his hand and a barfi in his mouth.

'Where have you been?' snaps Surajmal.

'Mangat Ram Nawal Kishor,' says Ramvilas. He holds out the box of barfis. Qureshi and Noor Muhammad take one eagerly. The two traders from Kucha Sugandh take two each. Surajmal takes a small piece. Sohan Lal demurs. Jugal Kishor refuses angrily, aware that Ramvilas will not have paid for them.

Surajmal appears pleased. 'These barfis are incomparable, Ramvilas!'

Jugal Kishor grits his teeth. They are from *his* shop, paid for by *him*! 'I keep only the best halvais in my shop,' he says pointedly.

'I have been talking to Harilalji,' says Surajmal, without context. 'He would like to highlight ladies' issues. Some were raised in that function on Swami Shraddhanand Marg. There was that Nepali lady . . .'

Ramvilas chuckles inwardly. It is typical of Surajmal to call it Swami Shraddhanand Marg – the official, sanitised name for the street – when everyone in Delhi calls it GB Road. And to refer to Gita as a lady!

'We must build a network among the ladies,' continues Surajmal.

'Harilalji made a good speech at that function,' Jugal Kishor says ingratiatingly.

'The committee needs to give more than ten thousand,' says Ramvilas. 'What can you do with ten thousand?'

Surajmal looks up in surprise. 'For what? They can take money from their husbands!'

There is muffled laughter. Jugal Kishor grabs the handles of the wheelchair, turns it round, and pushes it resolutely toward Mangat Ram Nawal Kishor. The reporter, worrying that he will have nothing to show for the day, closes in on Surajmal's chair, which he senses to be the nucleus of the walk. On seeing him, Jugal Kishor begins an enthusiastic narration. 'We are now passing Mangat Ram Nawal Kishor, two centuries of sweet success! A hundred years ago, nawabs came to my shop in palanquins and buggies, not these polluting cars and scooters. No licence was required to drive those buggies! My great-great-grandfather fed halva first to the nawabs and then to their elephants, who saluted him with painted trunks. No one cared for Western-packaged sweets in those days. Everything was made in desi ghee.'

The reporter takes copious notes.

'The building was clean and the road was wide,' continues Jugal Kishor. 'Now there are hawkers on every pavement. There are crowds, stalls, Bangladeshi immigrants. And there is pollution! We need to preserve such buildings.' He points to the reporter's camera. 'Perhaps you can take a photograph here?'

'I need a historical building in the background,' says the reporter.

'This is a historical building!' Jugal Kishor protests.

Surajmal watches Jugal Kishor's attempts with rising impatience. 'We must turn into this kucha here,' he says.

'Kucha Sugandh?' Jugal Kishor asks indignantly. 'We did not plan this detour for the walk. The kucha leads neither to the Baptist Church nor to Gaurishankar Temple.'

'It is a historical kucha,' says Surajmal.

It is Surajmal's turn to show off Bhagwan Das and Sons, thinks Sohan Lal. In that case, why could they not go to Kucha Bansilal?

Could he not say that nawabs and emperors had bought his sarees for their wives?

Reluctantly Jugal Kishor pushes Surajmal's chair into the kucha. It bounces roughly over stones and planks. The entourage squeezes into the narrow lane and scatters in its semi-darkness.

'How will we get out of this kucha?' fumes Sohan Lal. 'It does not open into anything.'

'We will turn round to go to the Baptist Church,' says Surajmal, calmly. 'What is the hurry? Call the newspaper boy.'

The reporter falls back, thinking Surajmal means someone else because he himself is sixty, but he is pulled forward to the wheelchair by the servants. It bumps along the rough lane, so he is now forced into a gentle trot to stay alongside.

'Write something about Kucha Sugandh,' commands Surajmal.

'What is the purpose of this walk?' asks the reporter, in a formal tone.

'I have already told you!' scolds Surajmal. 'It is a Heritage Walk.'

The reporter writes, chastened.

'Also, it promotes communal harmony!' says Surajmal in English. The reporter nods. Surajmal switches back to Hindi. 'My perfume-makers are Musalmans. The men who grow my flowers, the men who boil them, the men who distil them are all Musalmans. After all, ruh gulaab was discovered by a Musalman queen, Noor Jahan. Perfume-making is a Musalman art, yet it is Hindus who bottle and sell it to other Hindus. Yes, Qureshi Sahib?'

This sudden mention of his name startles Qureshi. He has caught up with Noor Muhammad, and they have outpaced the procession. 'Yes, yes, Lalaji!' he replies.

Jugal Kishor brings the chair to a sudden halt. The kucha has become too narrow and uneven. 'It is not safe to take the chair any further,' he says.

'We must get to Bhagwan Das and Sons,' insists Surajmal.

'We do not have time, Lalaji.'

Surajmal looks round for support but is disappointed. The traders from Kucha Sugandh had abandoned the procession when it went by their own shops. Sohan Lal stands in hostile indifference. 'All right, we will go to the Baptist Church,' Surajmal declares grimly.

The servants turn the chair with difficulty and wheel it back into Chandni Chowk. Jugal Kishor falls back. Sohan Lal walks alongside Surajmal. 'This Heritage Council,' he says, 'who will be in it?'

'You can be a member,' says Surajmal. 'It does not matter to me. My goal is to preserve the heritage of Chandni Chowk.'

Sohan Lal moves away from the chair, humiliated. It would have been better if he had rejected me, he thinks.

'Do we really need to go to the Baptist Church?' asks Jugal Kishor. 'We have already covered a masjid and a gurudwara. That takes care of Musalmans and Sikhs. There are no Christians in Chandni Chowk.'

Sohan Lal points to Qureshi and Noor Muhammad. 'Let those two go on to Gaurishankar Temple. After all, we went to their masjid. The reporter can go with them.'

'I will not abandon the walk half-way,' says Surajmal, angrily. He tells the servants to push him faster. The reporter, Qureshi and Noor Muhammad quicken their pace to follow Surajmal's chair. Sohan Lal falls behind and makes his way to Kucha Bansilal.

Ramvilas slinks away to a public booth and telephones Kartar Singh, to learn that England has won the match. He curses. He has lost thirteen hundred rupees – three hundred in a bet placed two days ago, a thousand in the one he just placed.

Sohan Lal walks into Kucha Bansilal in a bad temper to find Ramesh waiting for him. 'Your tiffin arrived an hour ago,' he says.

'The walk was slower than I anticipated,' replies Sohan Lal.

Chotu spreads newspapers on the gaddi, opens the tiffin and lays out its parts in a semi-circle. Sohan Lal surveys his lunch approvingly: daal, beans, roti, pickled green pepper, slices of tomato and cucumber. The daal has only a pinch of salt, and the roti is clean, crisp and dry without a trace of ghee – a spare diet dictated by doctors, but prepared lovingly by Sushma. 'Do not put your daughter-in-law to work right away!' said Rukmini, after Ramesh's wedding. He himself was not keen to have her cook in the first week, but Sushma is no ordinary daughter-in-law. She has been in the house less than six months, and she has already taken over its management. It is not enough that she cooks, supervises servants, lays out his kurta on the bed every morning, has every room swept and scrubbed twice a day. On hot evenings – and there are so many, these days, with the frequent power cuts – she sits beside him as he eats his dinner, fanning him tirelessly while Rukmini sits on a mat in arthritic stillness.

Sohan Lal nibbles his food delicately, savouring its perfect balance of taste and nutrition, and congratulates himself. He must have done something right – in this life or his past ones – to deserve such a daughter-in-law, although he senses listlessness in Ramesh when the boy is in the shop. It is not healthy for a man to spend too much time in the embrace of his wife, but he will indulge the boy for now. Let him enjoy marital bliss and produce an heir! At twenty-eight, Ramesh has only a few years before middle age brings its aches and pains. And it will not be long before Sushma loses the soft face that pulls her husband into her arms. She is already twenty-five, somewhat old for a newly married girl. Rukmini had acquired a mature, stodgy demeanour within two years of marriage, when she was only eighteen. It was both comforting and unattractive. In the first few years after Ramesh was born, she managed the house with a combination of self-assurance, thrift and predictability. With advancing age, weighed down by two daughters, she has become sloppy and inept. He had to sit up nights with her when there was a problem with her uterus last year, which nearly derailed the plans for Ramesh's wedding. 'It is normal in women of her age,' said the doctor, although Rukmini was only fifty. Since it was removed, she has developed some annoying habits, including a slight moustache. Her voice has become hoarse, and she spends considerable time finding fault with Sushma, who is thankfully soft-spoken. It is Sushma, not Rukmini, who ensures there is peace in the house.

Sushma's soft face drew many compliments at the wedding. It was the face that lowered the dowry she brought with her. How can you ask for a fortune when the girl has a face like Lakshmi's? He could not possibly expect to recoup what he spent on Shakuntala's wedding, but Lakshmi should be thanked for what she gives. A man with two daughters and only one son cannot expect much more.

He thinks wistfully of Surajmal's four sons – all married – then reminds himself with satisfaction that they are irresponsible and incompetent. He will watch those four with interest. There shall be fratricide when the father dies. Jugal Kishor's two sons are already talking of dividing Mangat Ram Nawal Kishor into two. No such cares afflict a man with one son, who can hand over the keys when it is time to leave for the peace of Hardwar and Hrishikesh. Lakshmi has her ways. She takes and she gives.

Shakuntala gave birth to a daughter last year. The girl is dark, as expected. She looks like a perfect mix of Shakuntala – large nose – and Shakuntala's husband – small eyes. Well, a granddaughter is always lovable, no matter her appearance. Perhaps the next child will be a son. Vimla's can form entire sentences in English and her daughter can crawl at such speed that Vimla worries about accidents. Lovely children, every bit as fair as Vimla, perhaps even fairer. They seem to get their complexion from their grandfather, or to have reached further back in their ancestry to find the handsomest forefathers. The lines of his two daughters seem to diverge, one getting fairer and the other darker, but he cannot complain about his grandchildren: two girls and one boy in all. Tolerable.

He casts a grateful glance to the alcove where Lakshmi sits, and is astonished to see a television under it. He looks at Ramesh, who is slumped against the wooden cabinets in late-afternoon somnolence. 'You can watch cricket at home,' grumbles Sohan Lal.

Ramesh brightens. 'That is a computer,' he says.

'Ah,' says Sohan Lal. He feels cheated. He has told Ramesh countless times that they will wait to see how this machine fares with others. There is much talk – he is half afraid it is true – that a computer can do everything automatically and do it better than a human being. It can add, subtract and multiply faster than any seth could imagine, no matter how many years he has been in business. It can turn on lights, switch them off, adjust the volume on radios, diagnose diseases, play cricket, drive cars and fly aeroplanes. What will it do next?

'I will enter transactions every evening, and it will update the inventory for me,' says Ramesh.

'I have done that for thirty years,' says Sohan Lal coldly. 'I needed nothing but my mind.' He is rather proud of his ability to add numbers. He can sell three sarees for six hundred and thirty-five each, offer a fifteen per cent discount on the first saree, ten per cent on the second, then combine that with two pieces of rubiya cloth at sixty-five each, and quickly determine the total bill. A good trader has numbers in his mind. He knows his exact stock of sarees and blouse-pieces, he knows how many sarees he sold last year, how many he sold last month, how many he will sell tomorrow, and how many he should order at what price . . . It is somehow improper to hand over that task to a television-like machine with a mind of its own.

'How much did it cost?' demands Sohan Lal.

Ramesh hesitates. 'I will tell you tomorrow when the boy comes round to start it.'

Sohan Lal finishes his lunch, signals to Chotu that he can remove the tiffin, lays his head on a bolster and sleeps for two hours. When it is dark Ramesh wakes him. 'We will close early today,' he says. 'Sushma asked us to be home by seven.'

'Tell the driver to bring the car round,' says Sohan Lal with a sigh. He goes to wait outside in the kucha while Chotu shuts the shop. The boy throws a switch, and darkness descends on the clay mannequins that stand behind the glass façade. He slides into place the wooden planks that protect the panes.

'Who did this?' asks Sohan Lal irritably, pointing to the planks. They are plastered with posters – the same one, repeated endlessly. A grand dharna at Rajghat on 2 October. Organised by Suleman, local leader in Chandni Chowk, and sponsored by the Babri Masjid Defence Committee. 'Come and implore the Father of the Nation to protect the rights of Musalmans! Come to fight Hindu fundamentalism! We will not let the sons of Hitler rule India!'

'I cannot control who slaps on which poster at night,' says Chotu. It is his way of putting himself in the clear.

Sohan Lal looks around angrily but cannot find a target for his ire. 'Remove the posters,' he says to Chotu.

'Mysore silk, Banarasi silk, Kanjeevaram silk! French chiffon, Indian chiffon, organdie! Silk blouse, rubiya blouse!' Gauhar watches the ricksha that slows down as it passes Kucha Bansilal, its passenger craning his neck, obviously looking for a shop. 'Jamna Lal Kishori Mal!' screams Gauhar.

The man shakes his head and the ricksha moves on. 'Sister-fucker,' says Gauhar without emotion. He has already made three sales today, at two per cent, seven per cent and ten per cent – a total of three hundred and sixty rupees. Whatever he gets in the afternoon will go toward his latest indulgence, a cassette-player.

He sits down on the mat next to the Hanuman temple, after pushing aside pillows and utensils that belong to the pujari. The mat is cool, lying in shade cast by the tarpaulin above it. The pujari, inside the temple, observes Gauhar with care. 'Business is good today,' he remarks.

Gauhar nods, pulls out a ten-rupee note from his pocket and extends it to the pujari, who grabs it. Then he pulls a pillow closer, reclines on the mat and idly watches the street. Two men walk by, hand in hand, wearing dirty shirts over flapping trousers. They wear broad leather belts with gigantic metal buckles. Too thin, too poor to buy, thinks Gauhar. A man passes in a ricksha, looking about frantically. A businessman, not a shopper. A team of beggars – man, woman and crying child – approaches the temple. Gauhar shoos them away. A large bear-like man drinks orange juice at a stand, pays with change, then crosses the street briskly, out of reach. Gauhar continues to watch – a fat woman buying rubber slippers, a sardarji on a scooter with a large bag strapped to the pillion, a sudden rush of three-wheelers with buzzing horns, three Christian nuns in white robes who won't need sarees, an old man with a young woman, advancing slowly along the footpath. Wife or daughter?

Gauhar stands up and begins to speak: 'Mysore silk, Banarasi silk, Kanjeevaram silk! French chiffon—'

'Georgette?' asks the young girl.

Gauhar sighs. Sohan Lalji does not like georgette customers, saying on most occasions that he has none in stock unless the customer is also buying something else. The old man looks too ragged to afford much. 'No georgette,' he says tersely.

The old man begins to leave. Gauhar stops him and points to a signboard on the other side of the road. 'Arora Emporium,' he says. The old man begins to cross with the young woman. 'Do not forget to say Gauhar sent you!' Gauhar calls. He has an arrangement with Arora Emporium, where he gets a small amount for blocking customers from Jamna Lal Kishori Mal.

The rays of the sun are now slanted so the tarpaulin provides little protection. His watch shows it is four. He spies a clay pot in the temple and asks the pujari for a drink of water. The pujari makes an impatient sound. 'Shave your beard!' he says peremptorily.

Gauhar laughs and turns away. The beard is a memento from Madarsa Ali Arabia Fatehpuri, where Ibrahim Mian took him two years ago. 'I do not have clothes to go to the madarsa,' Gauhar had said. In response, Ibrahim Mian bought him a clean kurta-pyjama, and presented him with a gold and white embroidered cap. His stump made him an instant celebrity at the madarsa: he told them his hand had been blown off in a bomb blast during a riot. Then he had taught the boys everything he had learned from Mussabir Ustad. For a few days he continued to go back to Shalini Didi and the school, to learn how to read and write in English, to be told to shit in the Sulabh Shauchalay, hear her talk about personal hygiene and civic duty and exhort him to become a rickshavala or a clerk. He also remained, for some time, the secretary of Baal Bank, but Shalini Didi became a source of distraction, annoyance and, finally, irrelevance. He could not reconcile her presence with life in the madarsa. He let the school fade from his mind.

He found the routine in the madarsa too rigorous. They rose at four in the morning and studied the Qur'an until their first prayer at six thirty. Then they studied for another two hours until breakfast, after which they studied until noon, then stopped for a second prayer, ate, and took a short nap until two. They studied until four, prayed, did mathematics, prayed again, studied until eight thirty in the evening, prayed, ate roti and onions and slept at nine. 'You will live and sleep with the others,' Ibrahim Mian said, but Gauhar never lived in the madarsa, and never followed its routine faithfully. He came back to the chaivala's box almost every night, where he had made himself very comfortable with a blanket and the air holes. He was unsuccessful at memorising the Qur'an, and surprised when, after a long session in which he failed to read the alphabet, the mulla told him he was suitable to become a mulla himself. 'I have already been here for fourteen months,' said Gauhar. 'How much longer will it take?'

'Twelve years,' said the mulla.

'I will be an old man by then!'

'Or you can memorise the Qur'an in three years and get a shahaadat,' offered the mulla.

That night, Gauhar decided never to return to Fatehpuri Masjid. There were a hundred boys in the madarsa, he reasoned, and any of them could become a mulla, or get a shahaadat, instead of him. He still has the gold and white embroidered cap, but Sohan Lalji saw him wearing it one afternoon and ordered him to remove it. He complied. He cannot afford to lose his commissions. He is somewhat ashamed of his moustache – too sparse – and of the straggly beard, but it is a badge of honour.

The afternoon is grey and dull in Chandni Chowk. Gauhar watches a trio of women waddling along in silk sarees that keep slipping off the mountainous folds of their bodies. Ah, prosperous women, wrapped in silk sarees, hungry for more. He shakes himself out of his lethargy and springs toward them. He thrusts his stump into a pocket, salutes the women with his hand, and speaks in his most charming manner. 'Namaste, madam! Banarasi silk, madam? Kanjeevaram? Organdie?'

The women waddle into Kucha Bansilal behind him. He slows down so they will not be left far behind. Such fat women! 'Another two steps, madam! A little further!'

The convoy arrives, in maddening slow motion, at the glass façade of Jamna Lal Kishori Mal. They stop to admire the clay mannequins wrapped in perfect sarees. Gauhar stands guard, ready to bar the way should they change their minds. Finally, the women take off their chappals and step on to the mattress. Sohan Lalji looks up with a wide smile.

'Mangal Dasji, namaste,' says Gauhar. He watches the seth's smile turn into a frown. Fuck his stinginess, thinks Gauhar. He will insist on his 'Mangal' commission of twelve and a half per cent.

'It is already five in the evening!' protests Sohan Lalji.

Gauhar is annoyed. Five per cent is an unfairly low commission for this sale. These are not regular customers. The smoothness of their skin, the abundance of their flesh, their silk sarees, all speak of 'deep' clients who have money and are willing to spend it. These are mothers and aunts shopping for a wedding, not housewives authorised to buy one chiffon saree as a favour.

'Mangal Dasji!' insists Gauhar.

He turns to go away, so as to leave the seth no choice. Fuck all this! If the seth thinks the commission is too high, he can turn the women away by saying all silk sarees are out of stock, or plead a Divali closing – though Divali is still two months away – or quote outrageous prices for everything they like. Let him do as he pleases! The rate shall not come down.

The seth nods toward Gauhar and hastily repaints the smile on his face. 'Namaste!' he says to the women.

'Namaste, Mangal Dasji,' repeat the women, thinking it to be Sohan Lal's name.

Gauhar slinks away from the shop, but does not go outside the kucha. He stands next to the mannequins, separated from them by the glass pane, and watches the women. He is afraid Sohan Lalji will conclude a sale quietly, have the sarees delivered by messenger, and tell him that no sale ever happened.

The women settle down on the mattress after many missed attempts, with much clinking of bangles and adjusting of sarees. This will be a long session, thinks Gauhar. Fat women in groups are impossible bargainers, but they always buy, and Sohan Lalji knows it. The seth calls out to the chaivala. 'Nanak Chand! Chai!'

Gopal gets busy in his stall. Gauhar walks across to Gopal and says he would like a chai too. 'Not for Musalmans,' says Gopal.

'You have a tumbler for Ibrahim Mian,' says Gauhar. 'You can use that for me.'

He walks back to the glass façade and the mannequins. A clerk flits about the shop, pulling packets from cabinets in the wall and throwing them at the seth, who opens them for the women, who turn the sarees over in their fleshy hands, pointing out flaws and shortcomings. This is not good organdie, this has too much polyester, and this is not Banarasi silk at all.

'We are not looking for silk,' says one. 'We want chiffon.'

'Chiffon?' repeats a disappointed Sohan Lal. 'We sell that in April. Why would you want to wear chiffon in winter?'

'We want it for summer,' she says.

'But you said the wedding is planned for January,' objects the seth.

'Silk is too slippery. The girl cannot walk in it. She slips and falls.'

'She needs to practise,' proclaims Sohan Lal. 'Young girls must be taught how to handle silk sarees. You walk so easily in it!'

Gauhar watches the woman gurgle with pleasure.

'We have heavy silk,' continues the seth. 'You must never wash it. Dry-clean only! And you have to iron it before you wear it. We don't sell cheap synthetic silk.'

'She is too thin,' says the woman.

'Silk will fill her out,' insists Sohan Lal. 'For informal occasions she can wear organdie. If you starch it properly she will look fuller and rounder.'

The women whisper to each other.

'Is she as fair as you are?' asks the seth. 'Maroon will look good on her. Maroon Kanjeevaram silk!'

None of the fat cows is fair, thinks Gauhar. The seth must be colour-blind!

Sohan Lal reaches out his hand and dislodges an entire wall of sarees packed into cabinets. He opens each packet and throws it on to the mattress, quickly obscuring each saree with the next.

'The chai, sethji?' asks one of the women.

They are determined to get their tea, thinks Gauhar. The seth sighs and calls.

'Gopal Bhai! Chai!'

Gauhar smiles inwardly. Although he will lose his commission, he hopes the sale will be unsuccessful. The fat buffaloes have seen more than a hundred sarees, examined every warp and woof, held them against their skin, tried to see if they are wrinkle-free, wondered if the colours are fast, asked for colours in which sarees are never made . . . but they have not committed to a single one.

'Saffron! Do you have saffron sarees?'

Briefly, the seth appears unnerved. Are these women IPP activists? wonders Gauhar. Who wears saffron sarees except political women? The thought makes him chuckle.

'Saffron will look good against fair skin,' says Sohan Lal.

The clerk unloads a few packets whose saffron shades do not satisfy the women. The chaivala brings tea in the four china cups that are kept especially for good customers. Gauhar accosts him when he returns to his stall. 'Pull out that tumbler from the electrical box,' he says. The chaivala refuses.

The women sip comfortably, taking an interminably long time to finish their tea. Gauhar understands the look in their eyes. They are on the verge of making a decision. He knows they will buy one of the silk sarees from the way they held it – all three at the same time. And they may go for an organdie too.

'This is not saffron,' says the woman.

'It is orange!' protests the seth. 'What is the difference between saffron and this colour? A shade or two, known only to experts.'

Gauhar knows the women need a nudge as greed wrestles with tight-fisted meanness. Why is the seth so slow to offer his discount?

'Today is the first day of September,' sighs Sohan Lal. 'We have everything on sale. Five per cent.'

Gauhar chuckles silently at the agony in his voice. That five per cent, added to his own twelve and a half, will cut steeply into the seth's margin. The five per cent will be deducted before his commission is determined, so he stands to lose a little too, but he has already factored that in his twelve and a half per cent.

The woman in the middle appears to soften. It is the language of a customer who has just decided to buy. She pulls the corners of two sarees, lying buried in the mountain spread before her. 'How much will these two come to?' she asks.

Ramesh Babu, who has been watching with a solicitous air, opens the alcove where sethji keeps his gods and starts up a television-like machine to add the numbers. Gauhar notes that he is beginning to get fat, now that he is married.

Suddenly Sohan Lal turns to Gauhar. 'Who asked you to stand around?'

Gauhar steps back from the glass pane.

'Go and wait outside the kucha,' commands the seth.

Gauhar withdraws from the shop and walks back into Chandni Chowk. It is getting dark. Ramesh Babu has just switched on the Jamna Lal Kishori Mal sign, which has lit up the peepul tree. The old wooden sign was removed a few months ago and replaced with this electronic one. It is much heavier, so it cannot hang from the branches. It sits in a fork in the trunk, and is lashed to the tree with steel wires. Another wire emerges from the sign and snakes up the branches, flies over the kucha and joins the power line. When DESU engineers made their annual trip last month to snip it, Gauhar sent them into the kucha to meet Sohan Lalji. They seemed satisfied with what he told them because they snipped all the wires except the one that led to the neon sign.

He decides he has worked enough for the day. Four sales, and the last one at twelve and a half per cent. He will go and eat aloo puri outside Kucha Sugandh. It is tiring to look for customers in the dark, even in the dull glow cast by the neon sign. The evening belongs to beggars, not to rich customers.

A ragged, frail old beggar approaches, hand outstretched. 'Get away from me, sister-fucker!' screams Gauhar. The beggar gasps. Gauhar bends down to look closely and his lips tremble with fear and excitement. It is Mussabir Ustad.

'I have looked everywhere for you,' says Mussabir.

It is a ghost, thinks Gauhar. It cannot be Ustad himself! So small, so weak, so pitiful! He has not seen Ustad for two years. He is some-where else . . .

'You are so tall,' says Mussabir. 'And when did you grow a beard?'

Gauhar does not reply. The man who stands unsteadily before him is already dead. Yellowness has seeped into his skin and eyes.

'Mussabir!' he says, unable to utter the word 'Ustad' with it. 'What has happened?'

'It was the yellow man,' sighs Mussabir.

'You are getting fucked again?'

Mussabir nods.

'Ibrahim Mian fucked you?'

Mussabir shakes his head. 'He is not in this business. It was another man, much yellower, with yellow eyes and yellow skin. He kept vomiting even as he fucked. With every thrust of his prick there was a spray of vomit. There was vomit all over the cupboard, all over the floor.'

'You should not have taken him,' scolds Gauhar.

'He offered a hundred,' says Mussabir. 'I have been vomiting every day since then, and the pain in my stomach is sometimes so severe that I cannot stand up.'

'I thought you had stopped taking customers. What happened to pigeon fighting?'

'Stopped,' says Mussabir. 'The government banned it after some city people complained that it was cruel. Bastard NGOs! Who told them it was cruel? Can they speak to pigeons and understand their feelings?'

'City people cannot be trusted,' says Gauhar.

'Chitra Didi was with them,' says Mussabir, in a hurt voice. 'She stood with them and held up signs behind Jama Masjid. Then the police came and broke up the tournament. What could I do? They still have tournaments, but quietly, inside havelis. Only the rich go there to place large bets. There is no room for Mussabir Ustad now.'

Gauhar watches him with pity.

'I will never forgive didi!' says Mussabir. 'I went and threw stones at the school building.'

'Chitra Didi does not go to the school any more,' says Gauhar. 'There is a new didi in charge – much prettier!'

Mussabir shakes his head, not interested in her, no matter how beautiful.

'Chitra Didi has changed,' says Gauhar. 'She came to me two years ago and told me I would be in a film.'

'I know nothing about a film,' says Mussabir suspiciously.

'I wanted to tell you about it,' says Gauhar. 'But she refused. She said I was to be the sole hero in the film.'

'Sister-fucking bitch!' shouts Mussabir.

'She was lying,' says Gauhar, reassuringly. 'There was no film. I looked for posters in every cinema hall in Chandni Chowk for almost a year. I thought I would see myself somewhere. I wore a clean shirt for the shooting, but I saw nothing. And now the film is too old, even if she did make it. Who will watch it?'

'I cannot get old men any more,' says Mussabir.

'Perhaps I can find you some other job,' suggests Gauhar.

'I have been paying bills – telephone, electricity. Two rupees for each one.'

Gauhar is shocked. This is how low Mussabir Ustad has sunk: queuing to pay bills for others!

'But now they shrink from me at counters. They say I smell, and everyone is afraid to look at my face. I vomited in the DESU office yesterday, and they threw me out.'

Gauhar looks away, embarrassed. When he turns back, Mussabir is smiling. Gauhar is reminded of the old insolence, of the ustad who knew everything. 'What is so funny?'

'I was right,' says Mussabir. 'There are only two ways to make money in this world, pigeon fights and getting your arse fucked!'

They both laugh, and Gauhar thinks of Mussabir Ustad, king of Chandni Chowk, ruler of Jama Masjid, now shrunken into a yellow-brown monkey, with watery eyes and runny nose, torn shirt and loose trousers, flies circling his head like vultures over carrion. He is suddenly aware of being a man confronting a child. 'I will make you my boy,' he says grandly. 'I will be your ustad!'

Mussabir says nothing.

'No more arse-fucking for you,' declares Gauhar.

Mussabir laughs and rubs his face against Gauhar's clean shirt. Gauhar takes a step back. The seth will be angry to see him standing with this corpse.

'Have you seen any pictures of women?' asks Gauhar. 'They are nicer than wrinkled old men. White as milk, completely naked, smooth, sucking pricks and getting fucked in their arseholes!'

'I have seen pictures,' says Mussabir, eagerly. 'But they will not pay me . . .'

'No! No!' Gauhar laughs uncontrollably. 'Women will not pay you. You must pay *them*!'

'Where will I get the money?'

'It is much more fun with women,' says Gauhar, authoritatively. 'Have you been to GB Road? I will take you.'

'But where will I get the money?'

'It rains from the sky, Mussabir Ustad. It grows like fruit on the trees!'

'Where?' asks Mussabir, with a wild look in his eyes. 'Where is that tree?'

'Right here,' says Gauhar, pointing to the neon sign above him.

'I could see this board all the way from Gurudwara Sisganj,' says Mussabir.

'That is my shop,' says Gauhar. 'When I take customers to the seth, he pays me. When I stop customers going to his shop, the other seth in Arora Emporium pays me. When I take customers to Arora Emporium, that seth pays me, and when I block customers from Arora Emporium, Jamna Lal Kishori Mal pays me. No matter what I do, I get a commission.'

'Can the seth not cheat you?'

'He will not try,' says Gauhar. 'I know the price of every saree, every material, every blouse-piece. And I know my commission.'

'You are smart,' says Mussabir, admiringly.

'Sometimes I forget which seth I am working for,' laughs Gauhar. 'I do not know which customers to block and which ones to take into the kucha!'

'I want this job too,' says Mussabir, eagerly. 'You can teach me, be my ustad!'

'You will need a lot of practice,' says Gauhar.

'Anything you say!'

'Come to me tomorrow. I will give you five hundred posters. You have to stick them all over Chandni Chowk. Five rupees for a hundred.'

'Give me a thousand posters,' says Mussabir enthusiastically. 'Two thousand!'

'I have only five hundred left. I will ask Ibrahim Mian to bring more in a few days. But do not cheat! Ibrahim Mian will go into the kuchas and count the posters you have stuck. He will only pay after he has counted.'

'Why don't you do the job yourself?' asks Mussabir.

'I have already put up thousands,' says Gauhar. 'I have plastered Kucha Bansilal, and all the kuchas from here to Fatehpuri Masjid.' He looks at Mussabir and delivers his final insult. 'It does not pay well enough for me.'

Mussabir snarls, but recovers. 'Five for a hundred?' he confirms.

'That is how much Ibrahim Mian pays me,' says Gauhar. 'I will give you three.'

Mussabir is miffed. 'Go and stick your fucking posters yourself! Why should you keep two?'

'I am the ustad.'

Mussabir stands sullenly.

'I will also get you into dharnas and rallies,' offers Gauhar. 'Thirty-five rupees and food.'

'All right,' says Mussabir. 'I can take the posters now.'

'Not now,' says Gauhar. 'You cannot stand here. The pujari will see you, all dirty and yellow. And if my seth sees you he will throw me out. Come tomorrow morning, early.'

Gauhar flicks his head to indicate that he should leave, but Mussabir continues to stand there. Gauhar lays two crumpled ten-rupee notes on Mussabir's outstretched palm. 'Keep this.'

Mussabir breathes heavily and inches closer. Gauhar shrinks away in horror from his strong smell. 'No! Not now. I am earning, making money.'

Mussabir grins, and his eyes glitter in the dark.

'I told you I would show you women,' insists Gauhar.

Mussabir stands his ground. Gauhar sighs. 'Tonight. Where do you sleep?'

Mussabir smiles a tired smile. 'I sleep where I get fucked . . .'

'The green cupboard?'

Mussabir nods.

'Go now,' says Gauhar.

Mussabir lumbers away and Gauhar sits down under the tree, burning with the excitement of being an ustad.

Suleman steps out of the Ambassador car, adjusts his achkan and walks briskly through the gardens outside Town Hall. He passes the statue of Swami Shraddhanand – noting with satisfaction that it is bathed in bird-shit – walks past waving security guards into the wide passages of the Victorian building and enters the central committee room. It was designed to be naturally air-conditioned with cleverly placed air-ducts that generate a draught, but they also admit the smells of Chandni Chowk, so that truck fumes mix with the odour of shit inside the committee room. The smell is at variance with the stately mahogany desks laid out on a blood-red carpet, arranged in a semi-circle round the speaker's ornate chair.

Suleman pauses at the door and runs his eyes over the room. From the balding heads and caps, he can tell these are seths, traders and local leaders. There are two Musalmans, seated in the back row and therefore inconsequential. He is disappointed. Everyone knew that the IPP would nominate seths to the Heritage Council, but he had hoped that Congress and the Communists would send larger Musalman contingents. The second row from the front is dominated by IPP members, and the front row is empty.

He pulls out a paper cone from his pocket, stuffs a paan into his mouth, then advances into the room. He walks past the seths and lowers himself into a seat at the front, aware that the eyes of others are trained on him. He feels a tap on his shoulder and turns. A face is frowning at him – a fat seth with heavy jowls that remind him of a cat, and beady eyes that expose his foxy mind. Suleman arches his eyebrows.

'This is a Heritage Council meeting,' says the seth. 'Only members are allowed.'

Suleman chews his paan. 'I am the Communist Party nominee,' he says casually. 'I have a voting membership.' He continues to look straight at the seth, daring him to cross-check the claim.

'The front row is reserved for city-council members,' says the seth sullenly. 'Harilalji Gupta is on his way. And Kartar Singhji will come as soon as he can.'

Suleman makes a great show of looking about him, then asks, 'I don't see any city-council members. Where are they?'

A murmur runs through the back rows at this revelation.

'Perhaps they are late,' he adds. 'We should begin without them.'

The seth appears crestfallen. Suleman presses his advantage. He flashes his paan-stained teeth and asks innocently, 'Which party has nominated you, sethji?'

The seth is too dumbfounded to reply, but Suleman continues to look at him, waiting for a reply.

'IPP,' whispers the seth viciously. 'I am Sohan Lal Agrawal!'

The name means nothing to Suleman, and he indicates his indifference by looking away. 'We should begin,' he proclaims.

'We must wait for Lala Surajmal,' objects Sohan Lal. 'He is the chairman of this Heritage Council.'

But Suleman senses that the other seths are tired of waiting. 'We can begin the lecture,' he says. 'Lala Surajmal will be here by the time we vote on proposals.'

This meets with general agreement, and a man adjusts the microphone near the speaker's chair. It discharges a shriek. A woman in salvaar-kameez approaches the speaker's chair, sets down a sheaf of papers and makes preparations to speak. Suleman turns to the seth behind him. 'Who is she?'

'Researcher,' says Sohan Lal. 'Archaeological Survey of India.'

'Ah,' says Suleman.

The woman adjusts her spectacles and reads carefully. 'Shri Harilalji Gupta, councillor from Chandni Chowk, has provided inspiration for the setting up of this Heritage Council, whose goal is to preserve the heritage of Chandni Chowk. We would like to start by thanking him for his foresight and leadership.'

A smattering of applause greets this.

'Where is Harilal Gupta?' challenges Suleman.

A sudden silence falls on the room. Suleman savours it. He signals to the woman that she can continue. She does so with sudden intensity.

'If we set out to preserve the heritage of Chandni Chowk, we will not know where to look because every second building has a story behind it.'

A Musalman story, thinks Suleman. The heritage of Chandni Chowk is a gift from Musalmans. The street was laid out by Jahanara Begum, yet the Heritage Council is full of Hindu seths. There are only three Musalmans, two of them someone's toothless dogs.

'We will start with our own office,' says the woman. 'It is now the Archaeology Department of the Delhi administration, but was the library of Dara Shikoh three hundred and fifty years ago. Dara created his library in Agra, where he had an early-morning view of the Yamuna river. When Shah Jahan moved his capital from Agra to Delhi, Dara moved with him and brought his library in dozens of carriages. Even in Delhi he chose to stay close to the Yamuna, which flowed near Kashmere Gate. The library contained invaluable books from Turkey, Greece, Egypt and Iran. Dara was a mystic. He mingled with Sufi saints, Vedantists, Jesuits and Jain ascetics. He had the Upanishads translated into Persian . . .'

Suleman stares at her with intense dislike. She speaks of Dara Shikoh as if he were a scholar! Dara was a heretic, unlike his devout brother. Must a Musalman deny his faith before Hindus will talk of his libraries? Ah, but the woman is neither Hindu nor Musalman. She passed years ago into an unidentifiable state where she can dissect both Hindu and Musalman history with equal carelessness. Women like her cannot find husbands, he tells himself. She is no less than thirty-six — his own age — and well past the bloom of youth, rapidly descending into the middle age that bears no children. She is thin — what is a woman without flesh on her body? — and her features, if she has any worth noting, are hidden behind gargantuan spectacles. To top it all, she is dark in a helpless sort of way. Such women turn to books in despair, or dig up old bricks and pottery to spend years cleaning and photographing them. No wonder she wastes time deliberating on Dara Shikoh!

On finding Suleman's eyes on her, she falters and shuffles her papers.

'Why must this culture-talk always be about Musalmans?' whispers the seth behind Suleman. 'Do Hindus have no heritage to protect in Chandni Chowk?'

The researcher overhears this and is thrown into nervous indecision. 'Shall I move on to Gaurishankar Temple?' she asks.

'Let us finish the Dara Shikoh library,' insists Suleman.

The woman looks uncertainly at him, then the seth, adjusts her spectacles and continues: 'After Shah Jahan's death, Dara was defeated by Aurangzeb and fled to Sindh, where he was betrayed by his Baluch host, Malik Jiwan. Aurangzeb had Dara's head cut off and displayed at the Khooni Darvaza. Aurangzeb destroyed most of his books because he considered them heretical. In the Mutiny of 'fifty-seven, the British Resident and troops made the library their home, and a few of the books may have found their way to England.'

'We will get them back!' declares Sohan Lal, with passion.

The researcher appears confused by this sudden enthusiasm. 'Most are lost,' she says.

'Let us move a resolution to bring Dara Shikoh's books back from England,' says Sohan Lal.

'We cannot move resolutions until Lala Surajmal arrives,' says someone from the back.

Suleman places another paan in his mouth and considers what to do next.

'Talk about Gaurishankar Temple until Lalaji comes,' commands Sohan Lal.

'No,' says Suleman. 'Tell us about Fatehpuri Masjid.'

'We visited it during the Heritage Walk,' protests Sohan Lal.

'Red Fort, then. Or Jama Masjid.'

'They have already been preserved. We are here to discuss endangered landmarks.'

'All right,' says Suleman. 'We'll hear about Babri Masjid.'

Sohan Lal glares at him.

'It is part of our heritage,' says Suleman, defensively.

'It is not in Chandni Chowk,' says Sohan Lal, 'or even in Delhi.'

'But as we cannot pass any resolutions until Lala Surajmal comes,' counters Suleman, 'why not enlighten ourselves?'

The assembly murmurs in general approval, and he knows the seth will back down.

'Two minutes,' allows Sohan Lal.

The researcher appears unprepared for the new intensity with which her audience listens to her. She speaks softly, almost in a whisper: 'Babri Masjid was built in Ayodhya around fifteen twenty-eight. It has three domes made of burnt bricks, supported on fourteen pillars of schistose stone. The pillars have figures of Hindu gods and goddesses, a vishkanya—'

'Ah!' says Sohan Lal, triumphantly.

'Two tablets at the entrance announce that the masjid was built by Mir Baqi, a Mughal governor, on the orders of Babur . . .'

There is a flurry of activity at the door, announcing the arrival of Lala Surajmal. He plods into the committee room, his cane prodding a rhythmic measure on the carpet. A servant walks behind him, ready to spring to his aid. The traders in the back rows rise to greet him. Suleman notes that Sohan Lal heaves himself up as quickly as he can.

'You look hot, Lalaji,' says Sohan Lal. 'You should not be walking.'

Beads of sweat roll down the old man's forehead. He fingers the lining of his kurta collar where it chafes his neck. 'September used to be cool in Delhi,' he says irritably. 'Now we need fans until the end of November.'

Everyone expresses ready agreement. Sohan Lal steps forward to guide him to his seat in the front row. Surajmal wards him off with a jab of his stick, then plants the stick hastily on the floor to preserve his balance. 'I have walked all the way from Kucha Sugandh to Town

Hall.' He casts a challenging look at the servant, who nods to confirm the claim.

'Aromatherapy!' says Surajmal triumphantly. 'Attar gill is made from sondhi mitti, the finest clay. It has the flavour of the first monsoon showers. Perfect for nosebleeds and blood-pressure problems!'

Sohan Lal acknowledges the effect of the remedy.

'I feel like a young man!' says Surajmal, looking very old. He hobbles to the front row and stands over Suleman.

They are all holding their breath, thinks Suleman, with pleasure, because I have taken the central seat. He chews his paan with renewed intensity and looks at the woman, as if she is still speaking. Surajmal gazes down at him, incredulous, then angrily deposits himself in the seat next to him, brushing off the servant who rushes to help.

Suleman asks the woman, in a loud, clear voice, 'There is no record that Mir Baqi destroyed a Hindu temple to build the masjid, is there?'

He watches Surajmal's jaw drop. 'What is this? What is she talking about?'

Suleman turns politely to him. 'Babri Masjid, in Ayodhya.'

'That is not a masjid!' fumes Surajmal. 'It is merely a structure!'

'Whatever it is,' says Suleman drily, 'she is describing it.'

'We should not discuss buildings in other towns,' Surajmal says, before turning round to challenge the back rows.

A general murmur of assent travels to the front. 'Let us speak only about buildings in Chandni Chowk,' someone says.

The woman at the microphone purses her lips.

'We will have a twenty-minute recess,' announces Surajmal.

The woman realises that her lecture is finished. She appears disappointed, but collects her papers and leaves. Sohan Lal comes to the first row, sits beside Surajmal and whispers into his ear. 'Have you thought about that matter?'

Surajmal appears irritated. 'What matter, Sohan Lal?'

'The assembly elections . . .'

Ah, thinks Suleman. They have already begun preparations.

'I have told you it is too early,' scolds Surajmal.

Sohan Lal stares at the mottled folds of flesh on Surajmal's neck. He catches Suleman's eye, withdraws and waits for the recess to end.

After the recess, Surajmal sends a trader from the back rows to the microphone to speak on his behalf. 'Shri Harilal Gupta has proposed that a revolving fund of one hundred crores be set aside,' says the trader. 'It will be used for the preservation of buildings such as the Dara Shikoh library.'

'Does the Heritage Council have such a budget?' asks Sohan Lal.

'Not yet,' says Surajmal, 'but Harilalji will propose it to the city council.'

Suleman chuckles. It is typical of the seths to vote for large sums that do not exist. 'Why do we need a hundred crores to preserve a library?' he asks.

'For the library, and many other buildings,' says Surajmal.

'Which ones?'

'We will publish a list,' says Surajmal evasively.

A generally affirmative muttering indicates that the proposal is acceptable.

'The next item is a proposal by Babulalji, the Congress nominee.'

Babulal stands up from his seat in the back row and reads. 'Shri Naresh Agrawal, Member of Parliament for Chandni Chowk, has nominated me for the Heritage Council. Nareshji has proposed that Bhai Mati Das Chowk, where Indira Gandhi addressed a large rally in 'seventy-five a few days before her illegal arrest, be renamed Indira Gandhi Chowk. It can be declared a heritage site, and some funds allocated for the erection of a statue of Indira.'

'We will consider this item at our next meeting,' says Surajmal.

'Why not now?' demands Babulal.

'It is not on the agenda,' says Surajmal.

'The next item is the Heritage Festival,' says the trader at the microphone. 'Harilalji has proposed that we celebrate a Heritage Festival every year to highlight the culture of Chandni Chowk. In honour of Chandni Chowk, it can be called Moonlight Festival.'

'Is there a budget for this?' asks Sohan Lal.

'We will allocate one after the motion is passed,' says Surajmal.

The motion is passed quickly.

'The next item is property-tax exemption,' the trader at the microphone announces. 'Shri Harilal Gupta has proposed that all buildings more than a hundred years old be exempted from property tax. The proprietors can use what they save to maintain them.'

Suleman is suddenly alert. 'Not every old building is a heritage site,' he protests.

'How many do you know of?' asks Surajmal, contemptuously.

'Take Mangat Ram Nawal Kishor. The store is more than two hundred years old, and the wall was erected a hundred and five years ago.'

He does not mention Bhagwan Das and Sons, thinks Suleman, angrily, because it is located in a nawab's haveli that is even older. Most buildings in Kucha Sugandh were built a hundred and fifty years ago. They have chosen the hundred-year ceiling carefully. 'The limit should be at least two hundred years,' he insists.

'Let us take a vote,' says Surajmal.

Suleman realises that the seths have discussed this already and their votes will carry it. He leaps to his feet. 'We do not have a quorum!' he exclaims.

'Sit down!' scolds Surajmal. 'This is not a rally.'

Suleman looks straight into his sixty-seven-year-old eyes. 'Harilal Gupta is not here. Neither is Naresh Agrawal. No more than one member may be absent for a quorum.'

'They do not have time to come to every meeting,' says Surajmal. 'Quorum rules do not apply to them.'

The trader at the microphone calls for a vote, which leads to considerable confusion because most Heritage Council members are not eligible to vote. Babulal, the Congress nominee, and Surajmal vote yes. So do two traders at the back, but they are cancelled by the two Musalmans, who vote no, as does Suleman. Surajmal turns to Sohan Lal with a broad smile.

'You are the last one, Sohan Lal.'

'The hundred-year limit seems low,' suggests Sohan Lal.

Suleman twists in his seat, surprised. Perhaps the seth is not such a bad man, after all.

Surajmal wipes his forehead with a silk handkerchief. 'I am not sure what you mean, Sohan Lal,' he says threateningly.

'The hundred-year limit seems low,' repeats Sohan Lal.

'We can raise it to a hundred and twenty-five,' says Surajmal, with barely disguised fury.

So, he has abandoned Mangat Ram Nawal Kishor, thinks Suleman. Now Surajmal is worried about himself. This Sohan Lal is a man of substance!

'We should set the limit at forty years,' says Sohan Lal.

Surajmal trembles with rage. 'Every building in Chandni Chowk is forty years old! Do you think the city council will agree to exempt the entire area from property tax?'

'In that case the limit should be at least three hundred years,' Sohan Lal declares.

'It is unfortunate that you think so,' says Surajmal coldly.

'The proposal is defeated,' says the trader at the microphone.

'It is not defeated, it is tied,' says Surajmal. 'We will bring it up again at the next meeting when Harilalji Gupta is present.'

'A tie is the same as defeat according to the rules,' says Suleman.

'It is a tie!' screams Surajmal.

His face is blotchy. Sweat pours down his loose cheeks. He points angrily at the microphone with his cane, then plants it on the floor as he attempts to stand up. He splutters in fury, his tongue apparently stuck to the roof of his mouth as words emerge in grunts and snorts.

'Lalaji is ill!' shouts Sohan Lal.

The seths rush to the front row, protocol forgotten. Surajmal falls forward on to the carpet, semi-conscious, tongue lolling, still trying to utter imprecations. The servant holds his head in his arms.

'Lalaji! Lalaji!' yells Sohan Lal.

Suleman stands still, unmoved, while the crowd of seths shake and slap Surajmal and look into his dying eyes.

'A man with four sons cannot find moksh after his death,' says Ramvilas to Gita. 'He must suffer the indignity of another birth, because his last rites were not performed properly. The oldest son must cremate the body, while the youngest may step in if the oldest is dead, diseased or unfit. Where does that leave the two in the middle? How do they display filial love? Ah, you should have seen the hotch-potch they made of everything. They fought over who would wash the body, who would place pearls on the pupils of its eyes – only two for four sons – and who would carry the body for how long on its way to the banks of the Yamuna. They took turns reciting the Gayatri. One lit the pyre, a second circumambulated it, a third poured ghee into his father's mouth, the fourth crushed the skull, and all came away dissatisfied. For the next twelve days, they took turns doing puja.

You can imagine the fights they had on the thirteenth day! The youngest won, so he had the honour of having the largest number of days under his belt.'

'What will he get from it?' asks Gita.

'Nothing,' replies Ramvilas. 'The man who reaped the reward was the pandit. He received everything four-fold, once from each son – four gold rings, four electric fans, four beds, four sets of pillows and sheets, and four cows, each with its own calf.'

'Lucky man!'

'Lucky Lala Surajmal. Four sons to whisper four sets of instructions into the ears of four cows. Take my father safely across the Vaitarani river! Bring him back in three days! Ask him if he has left the business to me! Tell him to divide Bhagwan Das and Sons fairly before he crosses that river and finds his way to the court of Yamaraj!'

Gita laughs.

'I wonder which of the four cows served as Lalaji's guide across the river,' chuckles Ramvilas.

'You should not speak thus of a dead man,' she scolds.

'I am a Brahmin too.' He sighs. 'I should have been a pandit instead of a clerk.'

'What will happen now?'

'Have you not heard the story of the monkey and the cats?' he asks. 'Two cats fought over a piece of roti and asked the monkey to divide it equally between them. The monkey broke it in half and said, "One piece is larger!" He took a bite of it to even things up, but then the other piece looked bigger. So he took a bite out of that, and then the first piece . . . until there was no roti to divide up. The sons of Lala Surajmal are like four cats.'

'Who is the monkey?'

'His head lies against your warm thighs, my Gulmohar!'

Gita giggles. 'Have the sons come to the shop since Lalaji's death?'

'It has been closed for fifteen days,' he says. 'By now, Lala Surajmal is safely across the Vaitarani river, and it is time for decent people to go about their business. Bhagwan Das and Sons will reopen today under the guiding hand of Ramvilas Sharma.'

Gita pushes him off her lap and walks to the dressing-table. He raises himself on his elbow and studies her. When she was younger, her fleshiness pleased him. It rounded her into a woman, even at seventeen. Now she is merely plump, tending to fat. Her narrow eyes are sunk into full cheeks, and tend to close when she laughs. Her chin has a fleshy pad beneath it. Her shoulders are full, and her breasts are fuller, in a matronly way. She is no more than twenty-five, but she looks mature, worn, dowdy. Her Hindi is still poor, but she has developed a manner of speech that allows words to flow freely, even if fluency is achieved through uncertain grammar and awkward pronunciation. With it, she has even acquired a degree of self-confidence that is very unattractive.

Gita studies herself in the dressing-table mirror, then walks to the television, turns it on, studies a video-cassette, and slides it into a VCR. 'What have you brought today?' she asks.

'*Mother India*,' he says.

She comes back to the bed with extra pillows, stacks them against him and presses down on them. He likes this familiarity. 'What is it about?' she purrs.

'The greatest film of the fifties,' he says.

'I was not born then.' She pouts. 'Why don't you bring newer films?'

He is irritated. Who is she – an ignorant twit – to pass judgement on such things? 'That is when they made good films,' he snaps. 'Everyone who watched *Mother India* left the cinema in tears.'

'I prefer happy films,' she counters. But she watches raptly, never taking her eyes off the screen. 'The heroine looks Nepali,' she says of Nargis.

Ramvilas laughs. 'Yet she speaks good Hindi. Maybe you can learn from her.'

'I know enough to manage STREE,' she retorts.

'Ah, STREE,' says Ramvilas, distantly.

Nargis has broken into song.

> '*This is the world we are in, so we must live*
> *If life is indeed poison, we must drink it*
> *A woman is a woman when she guards her modesty*
> *She has but one religion: her honour*
> *One who lives with dignity dies with dignity.*'

Gita's eyes are glued to the screen. They are moist. Ramvilas waits until the song finishes, then gets up, walks to the VCR and turns it off. 'I should never have given you this,' he says. 'You spend too much time watching films.'

'I cannot go to a cinema as you can!' protests Gita. 'The bai does not like me to leave the kotha.'

'I thought she had little control over you.'

'I still live in her kotha,' says Gita. 'As long as it is hers, she controls me.'

'Who would take it from her?'

'Parvati is going to Bangladesh next month,' says Gita. 'To get more girls.'

'The bai does not mind?'

'The bai thinks it is good – more girls, more money for her. She does not know that Parvati's girls will be loyal to Parvati, not to her. Some day Parvati herself will become a bai.'

Ramvilas comes to the bed and embraces her. 'One day you will be a bai too. Then you can throw Parvati out.'

She disentangles herself and moves away from the bed. 'I do not want to be a bai.'

'Ah! Then you can be a kotha regulator. An inspector of kothas! Bais like Parvati will kiss your feet to get their papers signed.'

'She is right,' says Gita, vehemently, 'that Nepali woman.'

'Nargis?'

' "A woman has but one religion: her honour." '

She has gone to the large desk in the corner, covered with STREE paraphernalia – posters, banners, announcements and placards.

Ramvilas regards her with consternation. He does not approve of this train of thought. 'There is more honour in this kotha than in all the kuchas of Chandni Chowk,' he says grandly. He turns to observe himself in the dressing-table mirror. For a moment, he almost believes what he has said. His right hand is raised for emphasis, his head tilted, his kurta hitched up over the left hip. I could be a Member of Parliament some day, he thinks. 'You have more shame than the wives and daughters of seths,' he continues with a flourish.

'I think you have forgotten,' says Gita, caustically, 'that I am a whore.'

He falls silent, irritated. He woke up early this morning to catch the first bus from Bahadurgarh. He needs to prepare for the reopening of Bhagwan Das and Sons. In spite of his bravado, he is nervous about the four sons, and whether he will be able to navigate through their internecine wars. It is not easy for a man – a man with two daughters who are twelve and ten, and a wife who grows increasingly slovenly – to handle so much in one day. He had hoped for a quiet morning, an idyllic interlude before his day began in earnest. They could have lain in bed, naked, while watching Mother India, a long film to be accompanied by hours of pleasure.

'You can get me an air-conditioner,' she says.

He is outraged.

'Not for me,' she says, 'for STREE.'

'I've already given you an air-cooler. Why don't you turn it on?'

'Coolers work only in dry heat,' she says. 'They are useless after August.'

'But no one needs air-conditioners in October. I feel perfectly cool.'

'It is only eight in the morning. Wait until noon. The room is on the third floor and it gets sunlight from three sides.'

'Move your STREE office downstairs.'

'I will, as soon as the bai lets me. I have asked for the waiting room, but she receives new customers there. She has said I can sit in it when no one is using it for business. I will soon have a new desk installed. I need money for that too.'

He kneads the pillows. 'The IPP committee gave STREE ten thousand! Naresh Agrawal gave fifty thousand! What have you done with it all?'

She grabs a sheaf of papers, pamphlets and placards from her desk and thrusts them into his face. 'Do you not see these?'

He jumps off the bed and rushes to the desk, strewn with Aids pamphlets, literature on trafficking, pictures of local leaders and posters for STD clinics. Next to the desk stand three stacks of cartons, full of condom boxes. Another contains copies of a brochure describing the activities of STREE. 'This is not worth sixty thousand,' he says.

'Look around you,' she challenges him.

Suddenly he notices new furniture – tables, chairs and lamps, a large desk, a new coat-stand next to the dressing-table, a rug, doormats, tablecloths, a coat of varnish on the four-poster bed, new taps on the wash-basin, pelmets and curtains, except at the window with the unused air-cooler. Photographs of Gandhi, Nehru, Mother Teresa and Swami Shraddhanand line the wall, mounted in gilt frames. He has been so wrapped up in her that the room has escaped his notice. Where does she get these expensive tastes? Has she an admirer?

'You have been taking too many customers,' he says.

She laughs. 'I refuse them all! You are the only one even allowed into my room.'

'And the bai does not mind?'

Gita tosses her head. 'Fuck the bai! Does she want Kotha eight hundred and forty-two to remain open for business, or does she want it shut down?'

A woman's charm, thinks Ramvilas, is in direct proportion to her assertiveness. He presses her close. 'You do not look happy today,' he says.

She disengages herself. 'You must go now.'

'What? Is the emperor to retire from his harem so soon?'

She does not reply. 'There was a time when you enjoyed my emperor role,' he says.

'You are too old for whoring,' she says brutally.

He gasps. For some time now, he has thought of himself as a lover, an admirer, a connoisseur, a somewhat irregular husband to her. He is not certain he always felt so, but at this moment he has little doubt that he is sincere. How could he, a respectable man, be a mere customer? 'I have loved you for years!'

'You have not loved enough,' she says softly.

A wave of self-pity washes over him. 'Do not turn away, my Gulmohar! I will arrange for the air-conditioner.'

'You are a stingy man.'

He is furious, no longer feeling like the rejected lover. Such ingratitude! 'Where would you be if I told the bai I was no longer interested in you?' he asks. He lunges and encircles her in his arms from behind. She yields easily. He laughs, maddened with desire, and walks slowly toward the bed with her. She is too heavy for him. He pants wildly as he loosens his grip to heave her into bed. She hits him hard in the stomach, and he doubles up on the floor. She walks to the VCR and turns it on again. He gets up unsteadily, trying to preserve his dignity.

'Take your attar,' she says.

He picks up a package from the bed and moves toward the door. Nargis pours her heart into song again. 'Do not fear sorrow, my heart, the Master is with you! To a person who strives, no task is difficult!' 'I will not forget this,' he says ominously, from the door.

He runs a hand over his kurta to smooth it, brushes back his hair and runs down the staircase.

On the first-floor landing he sees Parvati, lounging against the steel banister. 'Ramvilas Babu!' she calls.

He stops, embarrassed. She knows.

'You are leaving early today,' she taunts.

Ramvilas looks carefully at her – dark, snub-nosed, short like Gita, fleshy but not invitingly so. Unlike Gita, who wraps her saree seductively around herself and leaves much of her midriff exposed,

Parvati is in plain salvaar-kameez. Perhaps she does not expect customers at eight in the morning. Then he notices her makeup. She has chosen a light foundation quite unmatched to her complexion, so her face looks odd in comparison with her neck and arms.

'Gita Didi has taken a vow of abstinence,' says Parvati, breezily. 'At least for a week. Tomorrow is Gandhi Jayanti. It is not appropriate for a woman to indulge herself on the birthday of the Father of the Nation.'

Ramvilas turns away. He does not want her to see his shame.

'She is a social reformer now, like Gandhiji,' continues Parvati.

'What is that to you?' he mutters.

'I am still an ordinary worker, living off students and truck drivers. I have no NGO.'

He is horrified, but cannot tear himself away. When she speaks, she rolls her fleshy lips. Her mouth is clean. He is reminded of Gita's paan-stained teeth. It is odd that he has never noticed Parvati before. She is at least thirty – five years older than Gita – but a woman can be attractive well past that age. Why, he is thirty-eight! Perhaps he should spend his time with more mature women now. She is not pretty like Gita, but she has a certain appeal. She is a woman of skill and calm self-assurance.

'You should be on your way,' she dares. 'It is broad daylight.'

'I was coming to you,' he says suddenly.

'You have been coming for eight years, and you have never said that before.'

'It took me time to become wise,' he pleads.

She giggles and walks away. He follows, drawn inexorably toward the waiting room. She beckons him inside. He pauses at the sight of the linoleum floor, the bunks and their curtains. 'Don't you have your own room?'

'The bai has been promising me one for three years.'

He sits gingerly on the divan and stares at the picture of Sai Baba on the wall.

'Perhaps you can talk to her about a room for me,' she says. 'Why not this one?'

'It will soon be the office for STREE,' he says.

Parvati looks annoyed. 'Has the bai agreed?'

Ramvilas nods.

'Let her have it!' says Parvati. 'I will take care of both Gulmohar and the bai!'

Ramvilas notices how her chin trembles when she is angry. He finds it attractive.

'Can you lend me fifteen thousand?' she asks.

He is taken aback. 'Why?'

'I am going to Bangladesh next month. I have not been home for eight years. There are so many girls there . . . Imagine their envy when they see me dressed in beautiful sarees!'

'Where will you get them?'

'That is why I need the money. Think of your fifteen thousand as an investment. You can have thirty rupees every month for each girl I bring, for the next ten years.'

'I can try getting you sarees instead of money,' he says.

'How would you know what to buy?'

'I have bought many gifts for many women,' he says wearily.

'Kanjeevaram and Banarasi silk,' she commands. 'Four each. And two nylon sarees. I have heard nylon is still in fashion there.'

'It is not easy to bring girls across the border,' he warns. 'There are laws. The government is thinking of sending back Bangladeshis.'

'But I won't bring them at all,' she declares triumphantly. 'I have five men who will marry them. Five wives will come from Chittagong to Delhi with their husbands.'

'How much will you pay the men?'

She ignores his question. 'I already have their divorce papers. The bai had better be careful. If she does not keep me happy, I may take my girls to another kotha. Do you know how much money I could make with them?'

He takes a deep breath. He does not want to know. She points to the paper package in his hands. 'What is that?'

'It is for you,' he says, with relief. He tears it open and holds up a little attar bottle, his spirits restored at the sight of it.

'It looks like water,' she says contemptuously.

He laughs. 'This is ruh gulaab!' he declares grandly. 'It is the most expensive attar in the world, discovered by Noor Jahan. Do you know who Noor Jahan was?'

'How should I?' she asks petulantly.

Unable to restrain himself, he leans over, brushes the hair off her face and kisses her passionately. 'Noor Jahan was the empress of India, the most beautiful woman in the world.' He fancies a threat in her eyes. 'In her time,' he adds quickly. 'Now it is you.'

She gives him a cryptic look that unsettles him. Does she prefer not to receive the compliment?

'She was the wife of Jahangir,' he explains. 'On a cool morning, she found an oily film on the rose-water in her bath. She had it distilled, and the result was ruh gulaab, the purest, most sublime attar of all!' He holds the bottle to the light. The fluid is wonderfully clear, but he feels the story is lost on Parvati. She appears bored. 'A hundred kilograms of roses yield only two grams of attar,' he goes on. 'Half a teaspoon costs nine thousand rupees.'

Parvati gasps, flattered beyond imagination. 'Where did you get so much money?' she whispers.

'For you, my Noor Jahan, the attar takes wing and flies into my hands.'

Parvati gives a cry of delight, then twists her mouth as she has seen heroines in films do when they are angry with their lovers. 'So I am worth nine thousand. Is that all?'

'Ah! Your worth cannot be measured, my Noor Jahan! Nine thousand is for the delight in your eyes.'

Parvati snatches the bottle from him. In her plump hands, thinks Ramvilas indulgently, even a harmless bottle looks like a penis. He kisses her passionately again. She pushes him away.

'There will be many attars,' he promises. 'And bangles, earrings, necklaces, vanity kits . . .'

'Money?'

He paints hurt on his face. 'The attar is worth nine thousand!'

'I cannot pay the bai with attar. And what about the pahalvan, the kotha owner and the inspector?'

'Inderlal Jha?' asks Ramvilas.

She nods. 'He was just promoted to additional SHO, so he has raised his rate again.'

'I will pay you in kind,' he says. 'I have no money right now.'

He pulls her close to plant his lips on her neck and chest.

'You will break the bottle!' she cries.

She places it in an alcove, rises from the divan and leads him to the lowest bunk. He hesitates. She pulls aside all of the curtains to show him that they are alone. 'No one will come in at this time,' she says. 'Most men leave by six in the morning, or their wives will find out and beat them.'

He climbs into the bunk. She throws herself on to him and pulls the curtain shut. He is pleasantly surprised by her violence. He tears away her blouse and sinks his teeth into her chest. She cries out in pain.

'Mummy!'

Parvati shrinks away from him and pulls back the curtain. A child stands next to the bunk, peering inside with frightened eyes. He holds up a tiny hand – encased in a condom – to touch Parvati.

'Bittu!' exclaims Parvati. 'Go away!'

Bittu stands his ground, weighing the security of his mother's body with the presence of a stranger.

Parvati notices the condom. 'Who gave you that?' she asks.

Bittu looks at her in confusion. Parvati covers her chest with her saree, steps out of the bunk and picks him up. Bittu begins to cry when she pulls off the condom and throws it away.

Ramvilas sits up with a weary sigh. 'How old is he?'

'Two,' says Parvati. 'We will have a birthday party next month.'

He waits for a few moments, then gets impatient. Bittu continues to cry, and she shows no urgency in dispatching him. He knows she has no idea who the father is. 'You should not keep a child in the kotha,' he says.

'What else can I do with him?' she retorts. 'Throw him away?'

'There are government homes.'

'They beat boys,' she says. 'They starve them, let them go naked. He will stay here. He is a boy, so the bai cannot turn him into a whore.'

'He will become a pahalvan or a pimp, depending on whether he grows up to be strong or weak.'

Parvati plants kisses on Bittu's creased forehead. 'Pahalvan or pimp, I don't care, as long as he stays with me.'

She carries him to the alcove, pulls the stopper out of the ruh-gulaab bottle, and daubs the tip of Bittu's tiny nose with a minuscule drop.

'No!' protests Ramvilas. 'Use it sparingly!'

'It is mine,' she says. 'I can do as I please with it.'

'That drop on his nose was worth five hundred rupees.'

'I know where to get more when it runs out.'

The attar diffuses into the boy's nostrils. He struggles with the cloying scent and sneezes, spraying two hundred rupees' worth of attar – mourns Ramvilas – on to the linoleum. Parvati kisses him again and sets him down. Bittu, wrapped in the fumes of the attar, appears dazed. He has stopped crying.

'Go to Gulmohar Aunty,' Parvati commands.

The child looks blankly at her. Parvati points upward – to Gita's room on the third floor – and pulls the skin at her temples to form narrow Nepali eyes. 'Gulmohar Aunty,' she repeats.

Bittu wanders off, still lost in the envelope of attar.

'You just wasted five hundred rupees,' Ramvilas grumbles.

'Gita will recognise the fragrance and know where I got it from,' says Parvati smugly. 'That is worth a thousand rupees to me!' Then she laughs and hugs him. 'Come, let me show you what Gulmohar cannot!' She pulls him into the bunk and does not bother to close the curtain.

Thirty minutes later he staggers out of the bunk, shocked and pleased by what a woman can do. It is not her looks, the smoothness or fairness of her skin. Parvati possesses none of these. In the semi-darkness of the bunk, he could see nothing. It was her desire to please, her willingness to pay attention to him. He has forgotten, in the dull embrace of his wife and the listless favour of Gita, what pleasures are to be had in bed.

Parvati sits up in the bunk with a haste that disturbs him. He had imagined that he would stalk out of the room and leave her lying there, exhausted.

'Remember the sarees. Eight silk – four of each type – and two nylon.' She steps out of the bunk and adjusts her blouse.

'I do not want to leave right away,' he protests.

'I have to go to the clinic,' she says.

He does not understand.

'Aids clinic,' she explains. 'Organised by STREE with your money. The doctor comes to the kotha every month.'

She pulls out a crumpled piece of paper from her bra. 'My Aids-free certificate is about to expire.'

Suddenly Ramvilas is afraid. 'You should have shown me that before, not after!'

Parvati laughs. 'Do not worry! The doctor is government-approved.'

That is what I am afraid of, he thinks with a shudder. He walks out of the waiting room and runs down the stairs, shaken.

Parvati wraps her saree carefully about herself and walks to the other end of the kotha where STREE volunteers have put up a poster: 'Sexually Transmitted Disease Clinic – Prevention, Detection and Cure. Free, sponsored by STREE, Sex-workers Training, Rehabilitation and Education Endeavour.' Manju and Nasreen stand at the door, wearing STREE badges. Three whores await their turn to be inspected by the doctor, who has set up his clinic inside the room. After they have left, Parvati steps forward but is stopped by Manju. 'Gita Didi says there is a fee,' says Manju.

Parvati points to the poster, which announces that the clinic is free.

'It is indeed free,' says Nasreen, smoothly. 'You pay only what we have to pay the doctor.'

Parvati sighs and withdraws a twenty-rupee note from her blouse. It vanishes into Manju's hands. 'Can I go in now?'

'The doctor has already examined you,' says Nasreen, as she thrusts a piece of paper into Parvati's hands.

'Now you are Aids-free,' laughs Manju.

'Does Gulmohar know this?' demands Parvati.

Manju shrugs.

'How much do you pay the doctor?' Parvati asks.

They giggle. 'He does not accept cash!'

'This is good business,' says Parvati, admiringly.

'We have had only seven visitors,' says Nasreen. 'Bad day!'

'I thought STREE put up hundreds of posters about the free clinic.'

'We put up five hundred all over GB Road,' says Manju, indignantly. 'But someone stuck other posters over them. Thousands!'

'For another clinic?'

'For a hunger strike in Rajghat tomorrow. About Babri Masjid.'

Parvati stuffs her new Aids-free certificate into her bra and walks back to the waiting room to secure her bottle of ruh gulaab.

Chitra directs her cameraman to pan over the placards and wonders why they are all in English. None of these people – villagers, rickshavalas, porters, cart-pushers and stall owners from Chandni Chowk – will be able to read them.

'Babri Masjid Defence Committee,' say the placards

'Indefinite Hunger Strike in Rajghat on Gandhi Jayanti!'

'Stop Hindu Fundamentalism!'

'Protect the Rights of Muslims!'

'Protect Our Cultural Heritage!'

'Stop IPP terrorism in Ayodhya!'

'Babri Masjid will not move an inch!'

She is glad to have the cameraman – she can interview people without that heavy gizmo on her shoulder. The television company will pay his fee and she can take stills from the film for her magazine article.

'Enough of the placards!' she says to him. 'Catch their faces.'

She is surprised by the civility of the crowd. They have been instructed, perhaps, not to do anything that would result in unsympathetic reports. They have unfolded white bed-sheets on the grass, at a respectful distance from the smooth granite platform of the Gandhi memorial, and sit cross-legged, surrounded by flowerpots with placards stuck into them. It is a silent obeisance to the Mahatma: the grass has not been violated. The atmosphere is relaxed, almost festive. There is none of the anger and passion she would have associated with an indefinite hunger strike in which, presumably, some people will starve to death. The men chat and crack jokes. A few singers chant 'Raam Dhun' – she notes their choice of Gandhi's favourite song – to the music of a harmonium and a tabla.

There has been little rain this year, but the grasslands of Rajghat form a lush green carpet, kept so by a network of generous sprinklers. The grounds are landscaped to slope down from the entrance. From where the hunger-strikers sit, the rolling grass seems to hug the entrance, where a posse of policemen keeps onlookers at bay.

It is early in the afternoon. The singers have now switched to devotional tunes from films. The crowd chants with them, and some have begun to clap. The cameraman, mesmerised, lingers on the harmonium and the tabla.

'Stop filming the singers,' she says. 'Try to find serious faces in the crowd.'

She irritated with the demeanour of the hunger-strikers. Here is a story made for the front page. Two hundred activists of the Babri Masjid Defence Committee will starve themselves to death unless the IPP calls off its campaign for the destruction of Babri Masjid in Ayodhya. They will sit here in Rajghat, at the feet of the master starvationist, and let cameras capture their gradual death. What wonderful copy it will make! What unforgettable images! This is perhaps her best chance to escape the Mandal Woman prison. But here sit the starving protesters, bedizened in new dhotis, kurta-pyjamas and

Gandhi caps, exchanging frivolous talk, oblivious of the gravity of the moment, cheapening this marker in history with flippancy.

'I am getting hungry,' Gopal complains to Ibrahim.

'A dharna is not for women,' retorts Ibrahim.

'But we have already been here an hour!'

'I said three hours for thirty-five rupees.'

'Can we go home in three hours?'

'We must wait and see,' says Ibrahim vaguely. He does not specify what they must wait for. The sun bears down on them, even though it is October.

Gauhar squats behind Ibrahim, bored. This morning, he combed and oiled his beard, and washed his face. He put on a clean kurta-pyjama and covered his head with the gold and white embroidered cap that Ibrahim Mian gave him when he first took him to the madarsa. Two hours ago, he drank deeply from the hand-pump in Dudhiya Gali, and now his bladder is bursting. He must piss soon, or he will have to piss on the clean white bed-sheet spread out by Ibrahim Mian. He curses his poor judgement in agreeing to come. It is one thing to put up posters for a dharna – he has made three hundred rupees, most of them from Mussabir – and another to participate. Mussabir was eager to come, but Gauhar refused permission. The stink would put everyone off. Also, he does not want Ibrahim Mian to meet Mussabir, because he will likely draft him for rally tasks, and Gauhar will lose future commissions. 'Stick up some more posters', he told Mussabir.

'What posters shall I stick up now that the dharna is upon us?'

'Go get yourself fucked a few times!' Gauhar had advised.

Mussabir is probably getting fucked right now and earning seventy rupees, thinks Gauhar, wistfully. But who will fuck a stinking yellow man who vomits with every thrust? In any case, half his clients are here. Gauhar recognises many from the green cupboard. He has not been there for two years and he only saw them in semi-darkness, but how can he forget the face of a man who has fondled him? Unmanly sister-fuckers, whose pricks barely penetrated him! Now they are all going to earn their thirty-five rupees by sitting on the sheets for three hours. At this rate, they will need two dharnas to get a fuck. Gauhar shifts from one foot to the other, desperate to piss. He bumps into Ibrahim.

'Sit still,' Ibrahim scolds.

'Fuck you!' mutters Gauhar.

'Do not speak like that in front of the Mahatma!' whispers Ibrahim.

'Who the fuck is the Mahatma?'

Ibrahim points impatiently toward the Gandhi placards.

'Why is he naked?' asks Gauhar.

'He is wearing a dhoti.'

'Is he sitting with a bicycle? A sewing-machine?'

'A spinning-wheel.'

Gauhar laughs. 'He looks like Gopal Bhai.'

Gopal turns angrily. 'I am forty-six! He was at least seventy.'

'You will be bald like him in two years,' says Gauhar.

'He is the Father of the Nation,' admonishes Gopal.

'He must have fucked a lot to have so many children!' laughs Gauhar.

Horrified, Gopal puts a hand over Gauhar's mouth. Gauhar shakes it off.

'Yes,' says Ibrahim, seriously. 'He fucked a lot. And he fucked everyone.'

Gauhar lapses into uncomfortable silence. He wonders if any of these men will buy organdie sarees. Or even salvaar-kameez, which Sohan Lal does not like to sell because of low margins. Every minute he spends here, he is losing commission. He looks around unhappily, and sees Chitra and her cameraman. He grits his teeth. She is making a film again! Ah, he will not be fooled this time. He is glad he is wearing his cap and kurta, not the shirt in which she wants him when she is making her films. If she happens to notice him, he will look away or pretend he does not know her. The cameraman has already panned over them. Perhaps it is a ruse. Perhaps his camera is turned off. Perhaps she is really interested in that naked Mahatma who is buried under the stone platform. Fuck her film! She will not get him for a hero. She can stand Ibrahim Mian against the Mahatma's stone grave and ask him to grin with his yellow teeth, and she will have to be content with that. He must piss soon . . .

'I am hungry,' says Gopal.

Ibrahim casts a stern look at him, then unties a bundle that is wound tightly round his waist. It contains crushed grams, mixed with salt and minced onions. Ibrahim pours a fistful into Gopal's cupped hands. He stuffs it into his mouth, smearing his face, and chews noisily. 'Lower your head,' Ibrahim commands.

'It tastes horrible.'

'This is Rajghat,' says Ibrahim. 'You must eat simple food, as Gandhiji did.'

'Why is everyone looking at me?' asks Gopal.

'We are on a hunger strike,' Ibrahim reminds him. 'I told you to eat well this morning. What if that television madam sees your mouth stuffed with food?'

Gopal stops chewing, hides his hands in the folds of his dhoti, and glances around uncomfortably. 'Will I go to jail?'

'I will not tell anyone,' says Ibrahim.

'How long must we sit here?'

'Until we die,' says Ibrahim, brightly.

Gopal gasps. Crushed-gram powder puffs out of his mouth.

'Put down your head before the television madam sees you!' commands Ibrahim.

Gopal swallows. 'I don't want to die!' he yells.

'Lower your voice!'

'But I don't want to die!'

'Gopal Bhai,' says Ibrahim, through clenched teeth, 'the television madam is looking at you.'

Chitra, scanning faces in the crowd, sees Gopal gesticulating wildly with his mouth half open. Something foamy drools out of it. So, the chaivala has decided to take up a cause, after all. But why would he join a hunger strike in defence of a mosque he has not seen? He is not even a Muslim! Now that *is* a wonderful story – a Hindu starving himself to death to preserve a four-hundred-year-old mosque!

'Let me go,' pleads Gopal.

'Do not worry. Suleman Mian will stop this dharna before things get bad.'

'What does he have to do with it?' asks Gopal.

Ibrahim looks scornfully at him. 'Suleman Mian is the convener of the Babri Masjid Defence Committee.'

Gopal looks about him. None of the men looks like Suleman. 'Where is he?'

'Turn to your left, Gopal Bhai,' declares Ibrahim grandly.

'Turn to your left,' Chitra commands the cameraman.

She does not want to miss Suleman's entry amid a colourful procession of people shouting slogans, television cameras and microphones. The cameraman walks backwards to capture it, and the sound men scramble to thrust their boom poles into the centre of the circle that moves haphazardly toward the hunger-strikers. At the epicentre of this hurricane, visible when the circle breaks, Suleman is in a spotless white kurta-pyjama, with a rakishly tilted Gandhi cap. He holds aloft his folded hands, acknowledging friend, admirer and underling, even as he advances to pay homage to the man whose gesture he has borrowed. A slight smile plays on his lips, doing nothing to soften the determination behind his sharp eyes. The pencil moustache is stretched to accommodate the smile, which reveals clean white teeth, free of paan stains. There is a buzz among the hunger-strikers, and the moving circle breaks into chants.

'Suleman Mian *zindabad*!'

'Babri Masjid Defence Committee *zindabad*!'

Suleman seems unfazed by the mêlée, and arrives at the stone platform with bare feet – he has removed his shoes outside – falls on to his knees, then bends to touch the ground with his forehead. Chitra's cameraman captures the moment.

'It is Suleman Mian!' says Gauhar, excitedly.

'He walks so fast on a hungry stomach,' says Gopal, with admiration.

Gauhar shakes Ibrahim. 'It is Suleman Mian!' he repeats.

Ibrahim gives him a chilly look that seems to deny all association between them.

Suleman stands up, turns to face the crowd and holds up both hands to silence it, indicating, with a shake of his head, the stone platform. We must be respectful in *his* presence, he implies. Then he addresses the cameras, in a voice carefully modulated to be passionate yet controlled.

'I have come here as a beggar,' he announces. 'Today is Gandhi Jayanti! The Father of my Nation is one hundred and twenty-three years old. I have come to beg him for my rights – my right to be a Musalman, my right to believe there is no God but Allah, my right to protect and preserve my masjids, just as Hindus have the right to protect their temples, Sikhs their gurudwaras and Christians their churches. I am here to beg, and I have two hundred beggars with me!'

'Why does he call us beggars?' asks Gopal.

Ibrahim raises an angry finger to his lips. Suleman points to the granite platform.

'Two hundred men will starve themselves before *his* eyes,' he declares. 'They will neither eat nor drink unless IPP fundamentalists are stopped, unless the Supreme Court issues an order that restores Babri Masjid to Musalmans.'

Chitra watches breathlessly, aware that footage is being lost because the crowd obstructs her cameraman's view. Is it possible to get a shot of Suleman with the chaivala? The prince and the footman!

Suleman finishes his speech. The shouts of 'Zindabad' begin anew as he walks back across the green expanse. The entourage follows, the cameramen scramble, and the procession finds its way back to the gate and disappears. The hunger-strikers sink down on the bed-sheets again. Suleman's arrival had energised them, but his departure leaves them feeling abandoned, unappreciated and drained. The cameramen and reporters who arrived with him have gone. Only Chitra remains with her cameraman.

Gauhar, still excited by the sight of Suleman and his retinue, cannot contain himself. 'Why are we sitting around like eunuchs?' he asks Ibrahim. 'Let us all make speeches like Suleman Mian!'

'Shut up,' says Ibrahim.

'I need to piss,' says Gauhar. 'Can I piss in the grass?'

'This is Rajghat,' Ibrahim reminds him.

'Why did Suleman Mian leave so soon?' asks Gopal.

'He has other hunger-strikers to visit,' mutters Ibrahim.

Gopal is impressed. 'At his age, I could also go hungry for hours and still speak loudly.'

'He is not hungry,' says Ibrahim, irritably.

'But the hunger strike?'

'That is for us. People like Suleman Mian cannot go on hunger strike.'

Gopal looks confused. Ibrahim shakes his head, irritated, and explains, 'If everyone dies, who will ensure that our sacrifice is commemorated? Someone must stay back to talk when IPP seths come to listen to us. That is why Suleman Mian must live.'

Gopal lowers his head, chastened, and reflects guiltily on the grams and onion in his stomach. Perhaps he will live through the three hours, but he is very hungry . . .

'Quiet!' hisses Ibrahim.

His admonition is aimed not at Gopal, but the far edge of the white bed-sheet, where a quarrel has sprung up. Someone in Suleman's entourage brought a paper cone of peanuts and left it lying in the grass. It was spotted immediately on his departure, and the peanuts were retrieved. Now, those who do not have any have attacked those who do. In the struggle, the peanuts are being flung into the air and land on the sheet like raindrops. Men scramble for them. Gauhar watches them fight on all fours. This is better, he tells himself. We are like dogs! We should tear up the seths of the IPP, skin them and hang up their skins for sale! Why not burn down all the fucking shops in Chandni Chowk and piss on them? *He must piss!* He can piss on these dogs, piss in their eyes, piss into their mouths and charge them seventy rupees for the favour! Why is he sitting here anyway, in front of a black stone? Who is this bald man with his toothless smile, smiling down from every poster? How tall is this man that he needs to stretch his feet over an entire stone platform, when he himself sleeps in a box? And why does he need the entire field for shitting and pissing? A man can shit his whole life on a square yard of grass if he covers his shit every time like a cat . . . He must piss *right now*!

The peanut quarrel has escalated into war. The crunch of shells being chewed punctuates the abuse the hunger-strikers hurl at each other. Gauhar runs up to the platform and stands before it. What smooth stone! And what wonderful steel letters are stuck to its side! The Hindi that Didi taught him is now shaky, pushed out of his mind by the Arabic alphabet taught at the madarsa, but he can read the letters: '*Hey* Raam!' Smooth black stone and bright steel letters. He runs his hands over them.

Chitra directs her cameraman to capture the peanut fight. She hates to thrive on scandal when she could have reported on a pivotal moment in history. But who is that? A young man is standing at the memorial, wearing a gold and white embroidered cap. He's actually touching it! A one-handed young man . . . It is Gauhar! She did not know he was there – perhaps he was hidden behind Suleman's yellow-toothed factotum. But he is running his hands over the letters, so close to the memorial when all approach is forbidden. If the police see him he may be arrested. Is this a poignant moment? A young man from Bangladesh meets the Father of the Nation! But now he has unzipped his trousers. He is urinating on the memorial!

'Stop that man!' she screams.

Gauhar pisses, unfazed. He pisses in peace, in defiance, in joy, in relief. Fuck this Mahatma and fuck his grass. Watch the delightful stream of yellow as it hits the steel letters and flows down the smooth stone walls, forming puddles at the bottom!

A shout goes up among the quarrelling men. Suddenly their war ends as everyone watches the great urinater in shock. A horde of police constables charges down the knoll, screaming curses. Gauhar zips up his trousers and runs.

'Catch the sister-fucker! Don't let him get away!'

Two hundred hungry men swoop on Gauhar but he scatters them with the sheer force of his approach as he runs toward the main entrance. He rams himself into the advancing wall of policemen and cuts through them, stopping for a frantic moment to pick up his cap, which has fallen to the ground. The entrance is clear, and he streaks out. The head constable barks into a walkie-talkie as several give chase. A one-handed man wearing kurta-pyjama, he says, with a white embroidered cap.

'Sister-fucker!' screams an angry hunger-striker.

'Who was that man?'

'A boy, not a man!'

'One-handed bastard! Cut off his prick and attach it to his stump!'

'What a fool!' mutters Ibrahim. 'Suleman Mian will blame me.'

'Gauhar!' says Gopal, pitifully. 'My boy, my son! It cannot be him!'

'I have told you before,' says Ibrahim. 'He is not your son.'

A crowd collects around Gopal. 'He knows the boy,' someone says. His son? His nephew? Who the fuck is that boy to this man? And who is this balding man? He does not look like a Musalman.

'He is an innocent chaivala and I will vouch for him,' says Ibrahim.

'Can you vouch that he is a Musalman?' someone asks.

'Take off his dhoti and let us look at his prick!'

'This bastard brought that one-handed freak and ruined the hunger strike!'

The head constable asks Gopal if he knows Gauhar. Gopal nods sadly and looks for Ibrahim, but he has disappeared. The constable handcuffs Gopal.

At Chitra's direction, the lone cameraman shoots carefully. A small procession starts out of the grounds, very different from Suleman's triumphant entourage. This is an unhappy group: an officious head constable, a company of policemen, a frightened Gopal and a busy cameraman trailed by Chitra, who wonders what came over Gauhar. She has had little contact with him since she left Sparrows two years ago, and she knows he does not live there any more. He is supposed to be working for a seth in Kucha Bansilal. What was he doing in

Rajghat? And why has the chaivala become embroiled in this, when he could not possibly have any connection to Gauhar? Perhaps she is responsible. She raised Gauhar to manhood, and she should not have let him slip away from Sparrows even after Shalini took over. She must do something about it!

The white bed-sheets are rolled up and the hunger-strikers disperse. Ibrahim carries the placards back to Suleman Mian's headquarters behind Jama Masjid.

Gopal sits on his haunches, shivering. The cell smells of shit and piss. From a shaft of light that falls on the floor, he guesses it is early morning. The blanket they gave him last night is threadbare. He slept fitfully, turning over again and again to present different sides of his body to the cold floor. They gave him two rotis and a bowl of daal when they brought him to the police lockup, late in the afternoon, but nothing since.

Gauhar lies next to him, bundled in his own blanket, snoring. Gopal shakes him awake.

Gauhar moves the blanket off his face – the embroidered cap is still on his head – and curses. 'It is not time for you to open your stall,' he says.

'You are not in my stall,' replies Gopal.

Gauhar sits up and looks around. 'I wondered why there was so much space,' he says brightly.

'You should not have pissed there,' says Gopal, mournfully.

Gauhar looks blankly at him. 'That bastard constable runs fast,' he says, 'but I am faster! I had caught up with that bus on Ring Road. It would have taken me to Mehrauli, and I would have stayed there for at least a week. Before I could jump on to the bus, though, he caught my left hand.'

'He is the Father of the Nation,' continues Gopal.

'I could have grabbed the handle with my right hand if I had one,' says Gauhar. 'That bastard had my left arm.'

Gopal turns away unhappily. At this time, he should be waking up in the kholi to prepare for his morning trip to Dudhiya Gali. An hour from now, he would be sipping his first cup of tea in Kucha Bansilal. Every boy he calls his son brings him trouble. Perhaps he should never have allowed this one to sleep in his stall.

He feels a pain in his bladder. Before he was given the blanket last night, a constable escorted him to a latrine across the dark courtyard. Since then the cell has been locked and no one is in sight as far as he can see down the corridor. He waits uncomfortably, while Gauhar drifts back into sleep. After an hour, Gopal can no longer control himself. He shakes Gauhar awake again. 'Can you call someone?' he pleads. 'I need to piss.'

Gauhar laughs. 'Piss anywhere you like.'

'I am not an animal!' says Gopal.

Gauhar throws off his blanket, stands in a corner and pisses. Gopal sees the golden arc of his urine and turns away angrily. Gauhar finishes and wraps himself in the blanket again. 'I am hungry,' he says. 'Wake me up when they bring something.'

Gopal crawls uncertainly to the corner and squats. A mound of sand is stacked against the wall, soggy with urine. The stench is strong, but no worse than it is behind the old post office, now that plaster has reclaimed the ceramic tiles installed by Rajiv Gandhi. Gopal pisses tentatively into the mound. The sand catches the urine and tries to hold it but the hill is saturated. A stream flows down the slope almost as if it were made of glass. From behind him, Gopal hears Gauhar laugh.

'The piss-mountain no longer accepts offerings,' says Gauhar.

Gopal stands up hurriedly and lowers his dhoti.

'Why do you squat to piss?' asks Gauhar.

Gopal does not reply. He is wondering where he can shit in the cell. Is there a shit-mountain in another corner? And perhaps someone could bring a roti and a cup of chai . . .

'How can one man be the father of so many people?' Gauhar asks. 'My baba never told me about him.'

Gopal sighs. 'Your baba died when you were too young to remember what he said.'

'Who told you so?' demands Gauhar, angrily.

Gopal is confused. He thinks he remembers Ibrahim telling him this, but he isn't sure. 'Do you know where he is?'

Gauhar shakes his head. Gopal, overwhelmed, sits down near him. 'I am your baba now,' he says softly.

They hear footsteps in the corridor.

'Someone is coming,' says Gauhar.

'It must be Ibrahim Mian,' says Gopal. 'He has come to give us our thirty-five rupees.'

A constable appears outside the cell. 'Gopal Pandey!'

Gopal goes eagerly to the barred door. The constable unlocks the door and leads him out.

'Don't leave me here, sister-fucker!' yells Gauhar.

'You can come too,' says the constable.

Ibrahim Mian is here, thinks Gopal. Friendship as old as theirs cannot be forgotten in a day. Thirty-five rupees for each of them, and a safe return to his stall. It is all a mistake, he will tell them. But perhaps the boy will not be let go because he pissed.

The constable takes them into an office on the upper floor of the police station, where two inspectors await them. The older one is sprawled in a chair behind his desk, sipping chai. Chai! Gopal looks longingly at the wisp of steam drifting up from the cup. The second inspector stands to attention near the first. The constable pushes Gauhar forward.

'Why have you not handcuffed the bastard?' asks the SHO.

The constable holds up Gauhar's stump. The SHO laughs, as does the additional SHO.

'Fuck you, sister-fucker!' says Gauhar.

The constable slaps him hard across the face. Gauhar takes a swing at the constable but misses. The constable traps his head in the crook of his arm and holds him immobile.

'That will teach him,' says the additional SHO.

'Handcuff the bald man,' says the SHO.

The additional SHO bends over to whisper into the SHO's ear: 'I know the bald man, sir. He is a dangerous chaivala.'

The SHO nods indifferently. The constable snaps handcuffs on Gopal's wrists with a practised hand, without releasing Gauhar's defeated head from its prison.

'Has Ibrahim Mian arrived yet?' asks Gopal, timidly. 'He will explain everything.'

'Even the PM cannot get you out of here,' says the constable.

The SHO motions the additional SHO to draw closer. 'Why have you brought these two here? Take them to Daryaganj police station.'

'Special prisoners, sir,' says the additional SHO. 'National security!'

'So why are they in GB Road?' insists the SHO.

The additional SHO communicates, with his eyes, that the prisoners will pay well for their release, but the SHO does not seem to agree.
He resumes drinking his tea. Gauhar struggles in the vice that clasps
his head. His cap falls to the floor. The additional SHO scoops it up
on the end of his baton and deposits it on the desk, adducing this as
evidence of the importance of the prisoners. The SHO studies it
without touching it.

'So you are a chaivala,' he says, casually, to Gopal.

Gopal nods, eager to resolve the matter and be on his way. Could it
be that Ibrahim did not see the constables take him? Perhaps they have
captured him too.

'What else do you do?' asks the SHO.

Gopal does not know what to say. The SHO exchanges a knowing
look with the additional SHO. Gopal attempts a smile. He cannot see
the SHO's face clearly through his scratched glasses. Is he smiling
back? Or is that anger on his face? But now the SHO is staring into his
cup. Ah, he has picked it up and taken two loud sips. Finally, he grasps
a sheet of paper, reads it slowly, and looks at Gopal with a bored
expression. 'Gauhar Muhammad! Your boy?'

Gopal shakes his head.

'You said he was your boy in front of a hundred people.'

'He sleeps in my stall, sarkaar,' says Gopal.

'Do you have a permit?'

Gopal considers. A permit for the stall, or a permit to let Gauhar
sleep in it? He is afraid to answer either question. The SHO sighs and
points to Gauhar. 'Is this the terrorist boy?'

'Mother-fucker!' yells Gauhar. The constable places a hand firmly
over his mouth.

The SHO points to the embroidered cap. 'Musalman militant!
Pissing on the Mahatma! Where did you get this cap?'

'Madarsa,' says Gauhar, defiantly.

'Ah! Who pays for this madarsa? Foreign terrorists? Saudis?
Pakistanis?'

'It runs on zakat, sister-fucker! There are many good families in
Chandni Chowk, unlike yours! They support it.'

The SHO and the additional SHO exchange a look. 'How much is
this zakat?'

'Two and a half per cent,' says Gauhar.

The additional SHO laughs. 'He can count!'

The SHO shifts in his chair to face Gopal, who folds his handcuffed hands in supplication. 'You are a Hindu.'

'Yes, sarkaar.'

'Yet your son is a Musalman.'

'He is not my son. He sleeps in my stall at night, when I am not there.'

'Did you tell your boy to piss on the Mahatma?'

Gopal shakes his head in horror. The SHO leans forward, places his elbows on the desk and looks straight at him. 'I will give you one chance. Tell me the truth. Do you work for ISI?'

Gopal ruminates. Is ISI a seth the police do not like? Then perhaps the correct answer is no.

'Or is it CIA?' asks the SHO. 'RAW? Mossad?'

The constable inches closer to Gopal, striking terror into his heart. Are they going to beat him now? He knows Gauhar works for Seth Sohan Lal and Hameed works for Seth Sushil Jain. He himself has run errands for Sushil Jain. Is there someone else he works for whom he does not know? What would Ibrahim Mian do? Should he explain to them what the rally was about? Should he talk about Babri Masjid?

The SHO stands up, pushes past the additional SHO and comes round the desk. He is short and rotund. He lands a thwack on Gauhar's trapped head, and stands so close to Gopal that their noses almost touch. At this distance, Gopal has a clear view of his face, and of the heavy jowls that give him the expression of a bulldog.

'Tell me who you work for, mother-fucker!'

Gopal breathes very hard, thinking of the hunger strike, Suleman Mian and Ibrahim, and recalling a song from his childhood. 'We are all *her* sons, we live for *her*, we work for *her* . . .' He collects himself and answers, in a loud voice, 'Mother India!'

A sudden silence falls on the three policemen. The SHO turns to look at the additional SHO, then turns back to the constable, bewildered. Then he slaps Gopal's shoulder and breaks into raucous laughter. The additional SHO giggles. The constable, unable to control himself, guffaws. Even Gopal laughs. Hope springs in his heart. We are all brothers together! Sons of Mother India!

'Fuck you and fuck Mother India!' screams the SHO, still laughing. He puts a friendly hand on Gopal's shoulder. 'If you need to piss, it is all right to piss on the Mahatma. But why did you have a Musalman do it, you sonofabitch?'

There is a knock on the door, which swings open. Chitra stands outside. A constable runs up behind her. 'You cannot go inside, madam!'

The constable who holds Gauhar's head leaps to the door, dragging Gauhar with him, and tries to shut it in Chitra's face, but she has already stepped inside, followed by the constable. Her flowing hair and carefully worn saree, and the manner in which she stands firm, intimidates him. He has seen many such English-speaking women who spend their time among men doing men-like things. He has learned to fear their invisible power. In his village in Haryana, he would have dragged her by the hair and handed the bitch to her in-laws. But here in Delhi he must watch his actions. This is a strange city with strange ways. It is safer not to tangle with women, especially those who strut among men.

'I have come to post bail for Gopal Pandey,' says Chitra, to the SHO.

She speaks in English, so the constables do not understand her.

'Bail?' responds the SHO. 'He is being held under TADA. Non-bailable.'

Chitra starts, then begins to laugh. To think of Gopal Pandey as a TADA detainee! A master terrorist! 'I know him. He is just a chaivala,' she says.

'That is what you think,' says the SHO, mysteriously.

'Can I see the FIR?' she asks.

The SHO walks back to his desk and sits down with an air of solemnity. 'I cannot show you anything, madam. National security. ISI links!'

'I want to see what charges have been filed. Have you produced him in court? Habeas corpus . . .'

'Madam! Why do you trouble yourself over a chaivala?'

'Because you are harassing an innocent citizen,' she says grandly.

'Five thousand rupees,' says the SHO.

'I will deposit it in front of a magistrate,' says Chitra.

The SHO sighs. He knows, and knows that she knows, that the bail will be set by the magistrate, not him. He would love to throw this madam into the lockup with the chaivala and the terrorist boy, but that is the problem with Delhi. Newspaper people infest the city like flies. If you shake one off they come back in a swarm. He must now make a trip to the court and hand over the chaivala. Until then, she will stick to him like a leech. 'Let me do the paperwork,' he says.

Chitra seats herself opposite him. 'I will wait until you finish,' she says.

'What about the Musalman boy?' asks the SHO.

Chitra looks away from Gauhar, guilt overpowering her. This is the child she has raised to manhood! Where did she go wrong? Was hers an impossible quest to turn the boy into a respectable clerk?

'I will post bail for Gopal Pandey,' she repeats, wishing Gauhar was not in the room.

Bitch, thinks Gauhar. He makes another attempt to be released from the constable's grasp but fails. First she cuts him out of her film, then she stops Mussabir's pigeon fighting, and now she will send him to jail. He should tell her what he thinks of her.

The additional SHO approaches Chitra obsequiously. 'Madam! I am Inderlal Jha, additional SHO. Some chai?'

Chitra shakes her head, overwhelmed by what she has just done. With a great effort, she brushes away her doubts. What can she do for Gauhar anyway? Hundreds saw him commit the crime. It is Gopal Pandey to whom her future is tied. His son provided her with that first photograph, bringing her to the point at which she can request and be granted an interview with the home minister of India. And now he can provide her with the next few frames. He *must* be the right man to do so! She feels the pride of ownership when thinking of him. An ordinary chaivala, she has told the SHO, but he need not know. He cannot see the entire story as she does. Perhaps she will exaggerate a little in her article, but surely no one confuses minor embellishment with untruth. This story, the story of Rajghat, must be about Gopal, not Gauhar. The truth must be presented in the right light if it is to be visible at all.

Inderlal leads Gopal to a far corner of the room, where neither the SHO nor Chitra will be able to hear him. He knew the chaivala the moment the constable brought him into the room. The man has changed little. He is fatter, his shirt is torn, his dhoti dirtier and he has lost some more hair round the ears, but it is the chaivala from Kucha Bansilal. 'You said this Musalman boy sleeps in your box?' he asks.

Gopal nods fearfully.

'So you keep both sardars and Musalmans in it. Do you always harbour terrorists?'

Gopal watches him, open-mouthed. When they brought him into the room, he knew he had seen that sinister moustache before. All policemen look the same, he had told himself, and driven the idea from his mind.

'Do not worry!' says Inderlal cheerfully. 'I will not tell them about your terrorist activities.' He slaps Gopal on the back and turns to face the SHO, who is finishing his paperwork. They will write about the terrorist Musalman in the newspapers, he thinks. And they will mention him, not the SHO, because he has been careful to let madam know his name.

Bhagwan Das and Sons retains the understated elegance of a perfumery from another age. The walls are lined with mahogany panels, and the stools for customers are antique with velvet cushions. A Victorian grandfather clock keeps time with majestic regularity. The floor is old linoleum, kept scrupulously clean by a servant. There is an oak cupboard with arched panelled doors, drawers, bracket feet and beautifully shaped apron, an intricately carved pine cupboard from 1850, and three cupboards over drawers with recessed doors, a deep wax sheen and mellow colour. The oak counter is lined with decanters and cut-glass bottles, filled with attar and synthetic oils that display the seven spectral colours in delicately etched contours.

Sohan Lal sits at the counter, unimpressed. Ramvilas, standing on the other side, taps it with his knuckles. 'Solid oak!' he says. 'More than a hundred years old, polished in England.'

'It is too dark here,' complains Sohan Lal. 'How do you see the attars?'

Ramvilas laughs. 'This is not a paan stall. Why do you need to see anything? Your nose will tell you good from bad.'

'I like to see what I am buying,' Sohan Lal retorts.

'You cannot sniff ruh chameli, worth six hundred rupees a bottle, while seated under the glare of fluorescent tubes on a steel folding-chair manufactured in Noida.'

Sohan Lal pulls a face and drums on the counter. He is impatient with such talk, but Ramvilas has been in high spirits since Lala Surajmal's death. He now points eagerly to the grandfather clock. 'That is the largest oak case I have seen, made from a single trunk, with mahogany cross bandings. Have you seen a clock seven feet tall? Meant for a tall Englishman. The dial is hand-painted.'

'Does it work?' asks Sohan Lal.

'Of course,' says Ramvilas. 'It has worked continuously for the last one hundred and eighty years!'

The clock looks newer than that to Sohan Lal, but he does not argue.

'You can still see the clock-maker's name,' says Ramvilas, 'written in brass.'

Sohan Lal is disinclined to step down from his stool and walk to it, but Ramvilas saves him the trouble. 'T. Cook of Loughborough, in England.'

Sohan Lal nods absently.

'That housekeeper's cupboard,' says Ramvilas. 'It was specially commissioned by Lala Bhagwan Das more than a hundred years ago to fit exactly into the space between the pine cabinets. Do you see how well its polish has held?'

'I do not much care for old wood,' says Sohan Lal. 'I prefer stainless steel and Sunmica for counters.'

Ramvilas laughs and busies himself with the attars. Such enthusiasm for your master's shop is unseemly, thinks Sohan Lal, as he studies Ramvilas, watching his hands move over decanters, mixing and sniffing attars. The clerk appears too comfortable behind the counter. He has not yet dared to sit on the gaddi – the mattress where Surajmal sat for as long as anyone can remember – tucked away in a recess to the left. The white bed-sheet on the gaddi is clean. Perhaps the servant still changes it every day. The bolsters lie in perfect formation, awaiting Surajmal's shrivelled arm, although he has been dead for two months. The cash-box lies next to the bolsters, undisturbed.

Ramvilas notices Sohan Lal's eyes on it. 'The sandookcha is antique too,' he says. 'Someone could make a lot of money just by selling the furniture.'

He has already made plans for pillaging, thinks Sohan Lal. 'Lalaji knew how to keep an elegant shop,' he says. 'Will the sons keep it like this?'

'The sons are with their wives,' says Ramvilas, 'being coddled. What do they know about attars and oils? You could fill a bottle of ruh gulaab with Morarji's urine, and they would not know the difference.'

'Will they divide up the shop?'

'They will not be able to agree on terms. They fought even when Lalaji was alive. Now they are the four sons of Shah Jahan, ready to kill for the empire of Hindustan.'

'What will you do?' asks Sohan Lal, with affected indifference.

'I could wait until the four have settled matters and one Aurangzeb has emerged among them. But you know what a disaster Aurangzeb was for the Mughal empire. I will not allow history to repeat its fumbles. I have selected a Dara Shikoh and I will install him as emperor of Bhagwan Das and Sons. He is the gentlest, best-mannered of the four.'

And the most pliable, thinks Sohan Lal. Perhaps Vimal, the eldest, as Dara was. 'I am worried about the future of Vimal's children,' he says, watching Ramvilas carefully.

Ramvilas laughs and points to the calendar that hangs on a mahogany panel. 'Today is the fourteenth of November, Children's Day. Nehru decreed that we worry about our children today!'

The servant ushers in a customer. He appears to have stepped out of the last century – a grand turban, crisp whites, ornate slippers that are pointed at the front, churidaar-pyjama and gold-inlaid shervani. 'The shop is closed,' says Ramvilas, with an exaggerated display of annoyance.

The man does not withdraw. Ramvilas casts a glance at Sohan Lal. The man – whom Ramvilas seems to know – withdraws stacks of hundred-rupee notes from the folds of his shervani. Ramvilas produces a sealed aluminium flask. The man wraps it in a piece of cloth, stows it in his shervani, and leaves without a word. Ramvilas winks at Sohan Lal. 'We have decided not to sell attar until all inventory is divided among the sons. But who can turn away old customers? That man was from an export house.'

Sohan Lal nods. He knows, of course, that all clerks steal, and has no sanctimonious scruples about it. They have wives and children to feed. He always pays them less than he should because he knows they will make up the difference for themselves. It is difficult to steal much in a saree shop. You can put away a rubiya blouse, a salvaar or a dupatta, or stash away a lining in your kurta pocket. None of these is expensive. You cannot pilfer an entire silk saree. Where would you hide it? In a jewellery or attar shop, however, the clerk can wreak havoc. Surajmal, aware of this, paid his clerks even less than Sohan Lal does. A clerk's kleptomania is a business expense, to be tolerated by the seth as long as it remains within the bounds of decency and discretion. And that is why Ramvilas's anonymous customer troubles Sohan Lal. Ramvilas should not be siphoning off the attar inventory in his presence. It is a breach of etiquette for a seth and a clerk to be united in crime. Clerks talk to each other about gullible seths and seths give each other unscrupulous clerks, but they cannot both be on the same side. Now that he has witnessed the phantom customer, Sohan Lal has no choice but to inform the sons of Surajmal, if only to enforce propriety. But which of the four sons should he take into his confidence? Should he tell Vimal because he is the eldest? How can he be sure Vimal is not the chosen accomplice of Ramvilas? Well, he will let the matter rest. It is Surajmal's misfortune that he has no well-wishers. I would have mourned him with all my heart, thinks Sohan Lal, and protected his sons if he had given me Ballimaran before he died.

'Don't the sons count their attar vials?' he asks.

'I guard those with my life,' says Ramvilas, a naughty look in his eyes. 'Let me show you.'

He brings out an attardan of ivory from the pine cupboard, and carefully pours a viscous dollop into a crystal decanter on the counter. Then he dips a swab of cotton into the decanter, lets it soak, and presses the swab to Sohan Lal's right wrist. 'Ruh chameli,' he says softly. 'English sahibs loved it. The viceroy said it reminded him of an Indian summer evening. He did not know what he was saying, of course, because he went away to Simla in the summer.'

Sohan Lal rubs the attar into his skin and raises his wrist to his nostrils. Ramvilas watches his reaction with interest. Then he brings out a vial and lets a drop fall on Sohan Lal's left wrist. 'This is ruh chameli too, but it is synthetic. The first is made from essential oils, steam-distilled from herbs, spices and the sweet scent of the chameli flower. The other is made from . . . who knows what?'

Sohan Lal brings each wrist to his nose, one by one.

'You are an expert, sethji. I would never try to fool you. But my customers . . .'

'Yes, yes!' says Sohan Lal. He is flattered but humiliated because he cannot tell the difference. He regards himself as a connoisseur in the matter of attars, but lately he has allowed his senses to be dulled. How long can a man continue to show fine discrimination, sitting amid the odour of drains in Kucha Bansilal? And the horrible smell of over-brewed tea leaves that continually floats to him from the chaivala's stall, and the stench of that yellow-toothed Musalman, and the cheap scents that Ramesh buys for Sushma . . . Ah, to be lectured by a Philistine clerk! Yet the clerk watches his face carefully, so he must betray no trace of weakness. He must put each wrist to the test, in turn, and assume appropriate expressions – bliss on the right wrist and horror on the left.

'This is between you and me,' says Ramvilas, confidentially. 'The two attars are identical, are they not?'

Sohan Lal chuckles. Ramvilas laughs inwardly. The attar from the ivory attardan is synthetic while the vial contains the purest ruh chameli. I have fooled everyone today, he thinks with satisfaction: the export house, the sons of Surajmal and Sohan Lal. He feels enormous brotherly love for Sohan Lal, now that the seth has shown himself to be a weak man. One day, he himself will be a seth. Then they can sit on the same gaddi and exchange jokes. 'Unlike you, people cannot tell the difference,' he says. 'Give them synthetic attars in cheap plastic bottles – gill, kewra, molshri, harshringar, motia, hina, kadamba, patchouli . . . they take a whiff and say, "*Subhaan* Allah!" And I am satisfied with that.'

Sohan Lal shifts nervously, aware of the swab soaked in raat ki raani wedged behind his right earlobe. He must not lean close enough that the clerk can analyse it, for fear of what that may reveal. But he cannot disregard his own judgement so quickly. Perhaps chameli is too subtle a fragrance. What of jasmine, kadamba, motia and mahua, his four favourites, which he can sniff out even in the truck fumes of Chandni Chowk? He believes the bottles delivered for Shakuntala's wedding were synthetic. Perhaps this is the time to find out.

'I once ordered jasmine and kadamba from Lalaji,' he says carefully. 'I do not think the quality was very good.'

He notices the quick motion of Ramvilas's sharp eyes. Ah, the clerk is guilty. 'For Shakuntala's wedding?' asks Ramvilas, officiously. 'Lalaji packed those himself.'

'He said you packed them.'

Ramvilas tries a self-deprecatory snigger. 'Lalaji was a selfless man. Only he had the nose to select good kadamba, but he wanted me to collect the credit.'

Sohan Lal stares directly at Ramvilas, who calls the servant with sudden urgency. 'I am a poor host,' he says. 'Do you take sugar in your tea?'

Sohan Lal shakes his head. Ramvilas instructs the servant and sends him away. 'Lalaji never allowed us to have tea at the counter. Its smell mixes with the attars.'

Saying this, Ramvilas ushers Sohan Lal into another room, revealed by pushing one of the oak panels. It is windowless. A mahogany wardrobe forms one wall, and an oak-framed bergere sofa, upholstered in leather, takes up much of the floor.

'Lala Bhagwan Das did not like sitting on the gaddi because of his arthritis,' says Ramvilas, 'so he ordered this sofa from London. It arrived by ship in Bombay, then travelled by train to Delhi. Seven men were required to cart it into the shop. The leather is still as soft as it was a hundred years ago. The cushions are filled with feathers.'

He flops down on the sofa and crushes the cushions under his weight. Sohan Lal remains standing. 'I did not come here to admire the furniture, Ramvilas.'

Ramvilas freezes mid-bounce, then rises from the sofa. He has been waiting anxiously for the seth to state his purpose. He is relieved to be discussing business at last. 'Sit down, sethji.'

Sohan Lal lowers himself on to the sofa gratefully. He is tired of standing, and the doctor has advised him against it. 'The committee needs to elect a chairman,' he says.

'Ah!' Ramvilas sighs. 'Lalaji cannot be replaced.'

They allow a perfunctory caesura at the mention of Surajmal. Then Sohan Lal speaks firmly: 'We will continue the tradition of electing senior members. You should discuss this with Jugal Kishor. It will look nice if he proposes my name.'

'I can propose it,' offers Ramvilas.

Sohan Lal hesitates. It will not look good to have his name put forward by a clerk. 'I was going to ask you,' he says, 'but you are not a voting member. It is appropriate to have a voting member nominate me.'

'What a coincidence,' says Ramvilas. 'Jugal Kishorji spoke to me about this yesterday. We asked ourselves, "What does the IPP committee need at this stage? Consider a man like Suleman. What does he have that we do not? He is nothing, not even a councillor! He owns no shop, has no education that we know of, no money – at least, not his own. No one knows where he was born, who his parents are, where his family is. Yet he has a quality our committee lacks – youth!"'

'Suleman is a poisonous snake,' says Sohan Lal. 'No one can trust a man with a pencil moustache. And his eyes!'

'He is no more than thirty-six or thirty-seven,' continues Ramvilas. 'A little younger than me. And here we are, packing our committee with grandfathers.'

'Age brings wisdom!' Sohan Lal thunders.

'Of course,' says Ramvilas. 'A son cannot prosper without his father's guiding hand. But must the father sit on the committee? It is hard work.'

Sohan Lal runs his tongue over his teeth and suppresses the desire to spit. Where has he erred that this minion should offer him advice? Surajmal kept the man in check. Who will restrain him now? The task must fall upon him, since Jugal Kishor has abdicated his responsibilities. What poor judgement Jugal Kishor has shown in discussing such matters with a clerk over the heads of committee members! He is only two years younger than Sohan Lal. Surely he cannot be planning to mount a challenge for the chairmanship. Does he not have troubles of his own in Mangat Ram Nawal Kishor? His two sons are planning to divide it while he still lives.

'Kartar Singhji was of the same opinion,' adds Ramvilas.

I have been too slow, thinks Sohan Lal, with bitter regret. I thought a decent interval should be allowed to elapse after Surajmal's death, but not everyone has a sense of shame. Does Kartar Singh have designs on the chairmanship? He is forty-eight, not a young man. And this clerk is no teenage boy to be speaking of the passion of youth. True, he looks somewhat delicate and youthful. He is slender and has smooth skin stretched across his bony cheeks, but he is not far from forty. Perhaps he wants to become a full member of the committee, forgetting that he is not a trader and owns no business. 'If we want young men in the committee, let us find those under thirty,' he suggests. 'We no longer have the energy we once had.' He emphasises the 'we', and continues before Ramvilas can interrupt: 'This is a time for sacrifice, not discussion. I will let Ramesh be nominated to the committee. Every time I look at him, I am reminded of how vigorous I was at twenty-eight. I know it is not good for Jamna Lal Kishori Mal to have him on the IPP committee. He will waste time in meetings, he will get into politics when he should be sitting in the shop. But I have no choice, if the committee wants to increase representation by the youth.'

Ramvilas frowns. 'Vimal has shown interest too,' he says. 'And the other three sons. Each is eager to replace his father on the committee.'

Sohan Lal considers this new obstruction. He does not know the four sons of Surajmal very well. He has perhaps been amiss in not cultivating them. At the very least he should have commiserated with them after Surajmal's death.

'We need not bring mere boys into the committee,' offers Ramvilas. 'I have seen how foolhardy Vimal can be. Ramesh Babu is the same age.'

'Ramesh is a steadfast young man,' says Sohan Lal coldly. 'He has even bought a computer for the shop. We need boys who understand these things.'

'Like Rajiv Gandhi?' sniggers Ramvilas. 'He spoke of computers all the time.'

The insult is unbearable to Sohan Lal. He considers storming out of the room, but the servant brings tea and he grudgingly accepts a cup.

'I should not be telling you this,' says Ramvilas, 'but I value our friendship. Jugal Kishorji told me, in private, that many committee members feel you are responsible for the death of Lala Surajmal.'

Sohan Lal stares, aghast, at Ramvilas. Who has spread the canard, and why?

'They feel you should not have opposed him on that vote about property-tax exemption for heritage buildings. It looks bad for an IPP committee member to be on the same side as Suleman. If that vote had not been defeated, Lalaji might still be among us.'

Sohan Lal grits his teeth. 'Jugal Kishor said that?'

'It is not his opinion,' says Ramvilas. 'He was worried when he heard these stories from others.'

Sohan Lal raises the cup to his mouth with trembling hands. Sipping, he reaches a decision. 'We will add two new members to the committee,' he declares. 'One under thirty, and one under forty. That will give us both passion and maturity.'

Ramvilas drains half his cup and says, in a conciliatory tone, 'We must combine passion with patience, energy with experience. These young members will need guidance, so we should respect tradition when it comes to the chairmanship. That is where we need the stability that comes with age.'

Sohan Lal leans back on the bergere sofa, feels the feathers yield beneath him, and decides the arrangement is reasonably balanced. He will ensure that Ramvilas joins the committee as a voting member. Ramesh will join too, and he himself will become chairman, as he rightfully should. But he needs more from Ramvilas than a vague assurance of support. 'I will rely on you to speak to Jugal Kishor, Kartar Singh and others.'

'Kartar Singhji is on his way here,' says Ramvilas.

'Why?'

'Ayodhya,' says Ramvilas softly.

'Ah,' says Sohan Lal. Ayodhya is far from his mind. As chairman, his first task will be to assign constituencies for the assembly election next year. It has not been notified by the Election Commission but it will certainly take place now that Delhi has become a full state of the union. He will take Ballimaran for himself. It is still a Hindu majority area – traders, clerks, people he understands, patriotic people who mean well and know that their interests are aligned with the IPP. Although there is a sizeable Musalman population, it will be divided between Congress and the Communist parties. He knows Kartar Singh had discussed Ballimaran with Surajmal, but how long can he live off the riots of 'eighty-four? There are sardars whose entire families were wiped out. What is one son when weighed against an entire family? Why was Kartar Singh foolish enough to have no more children? Should not a prudent man produce two sons, in case one meets with an accident? Moreover, there was not a scratch on his wife when they pulled her out of the window, even though she was screaming and crying. True, his store was looted, but the loss was really Sohan Lal's. Even on that score, the Ballimaran ticket belongs to him. Yes, he will take Ballimaran. Harilal Gupta will certainly want Chandni Chowk, and no one can stop him. Paharganj offers no opportunities to the IPP. Anyone can have it. That leaves Matia Mahal, the last assembly segment in Chandni Chowk, where seventy per cent of the votes are Musalman. Everyone knows Suleman plans to stand for Matia Mahal. Only a fool would try to challenge him there.

'More chai, sethji?'

Sohan Lal realises he has been holding an empty cup for some time. He looks for a table and, finding none, sets it on the floor. It is a chilly, overcast day. The tea has warmed him and lifted his spirits.

'I have to ask you for a favour,' says Ramvilas.

Sohan Lal nods.

'My wife has been needling me for some sarees.'

'I just had a Divali sale on my silk ones,' says Sohan Lal. 'Why did you not buy then?'

'You know how women are. They must buy only when their husbands cannot afford it.'

'Send her to Kucha Bansilal,' says Sohan Lal, with a wave of his hand. 'I will ask Ramesh to show her the best we have, and give her a twenty per cent discount.'

'She cannot come all the way from Bahadurgarh,' says Ramvilas. 'I will trust your judgement. Who knows sarees better than you?'

Sohan Lal tilts his head sideways to accept the compliment.

'Eight silk,' says Ramvilas. 'Four each of Kanjeevaram and Banarasi. And two nylon.'

'Nylon is not in fashion any more.'

'She is old-fashioned,' says Ramvilas, with a sigh.

Kartar Singh arrives before Sohan Lal can make his getaway. The servant ushers him into the room. He strides forcefully through the door, a magazine in one hand and a briefcase in the other.

'Chai!' commands Ramvilas. 'Sugar?'

Kartar Singh laughs. 'Yes! Two spoonfuls. I have no diseases yet.' He sinks down heavily on to the sofa with a nod at Sohan Lal, who marvels at this cheerfulness. The sardar has become fatter and certainly more prosperous in the last few months. The diamond studs in his sleeves are real. That money has not come from the general store, thinks Sohan Lal. Everyone knows about the declining state of Lajpatrai Market. He has heard the lament about Chinese goods, and the prediction that the market may die a slow death. No one would think so, to look at Kartar Singh. This cricket business must be lucrative!

'You look tired, sethji,' Kartar Singh notes.

Sohan Lal nods. First the sardar arrives in offensive good cheer, he thinks, and now he insults me.

'Your chaivala is becoming quite famous,' says Kartar Singh. He riffles through the magazine and holds it open for Sohan Lal.

'It is in English,' grumbles the seth. 'If I could read English I would be in Nehru's Congress Party.'

'A little English is necessary in these times,' says Kartar Singh.

'Especially for the chairman of the committee,' adds Ramvilas, ingratiatingly.

Sohan Lal is mollified. He casts a look at Kartar Singh, but gets the impression that the sardar already knows of his plans to become chairman. 'Read it,' he says.

Kartar Singh holds the magazine close to his face and reads slowly and carefully, running his finger along the lines. ' "The Lone Protester, by Chitra Ghosh. The guardian of free speech and secularism is not a great leader addressing mass rallies through the length and breadth of

India. He is a simple chaivala standing handcuffed inside a police station in GB Road . . .'''

Sohan Lal stops Kartar Singh with a raised hand. He does not fully understand what he has heard, but has gathered the drift of the article. 'Is this the same chaivala? Gopal Pandey?'

Kartar Singh chuckles and nods.

'There must be a mistake,' Sohan Lal insists. 'I know him well.'

Kartar Singh turns the page and holds it out to Sohan Lal, who recognises the man in the picture. 'Who would have thought such a man would go to a rally?'

'Perhaps you should ask him to join the committee!' laughs Kartar Singh. 'Then this madam will write about you too.'

'Why must she waste time on a chaivala when she could write about the work done by the committee?' Sohan Lal demands. 'IPP launches cleanliness drives, organises blood-donation camps and provides pensions to widows. Why does someone not bring her to witness all that?'

'She is interested in free speech, not social work,' says Kartar Singh.

'Did you say her name was Ghosh?'

'Chitra Ghosh.'

'I know her,' says Sohan Lal. 'She came to talk to me about the boy who used to work in my shop.'

'The boy who pissed on Gandhi!'

'I will not let him into the kucha again,' says Sohan Lal. 'He did not tell me he was Bangladeshi. And if I had known . . .'

'She wrote nothing about the Bangladeshi boy.'

'She wore a georgette saree, so I knew she was not of a good family. An unmarried woman. I wanted to show her my silk sarees, but she insisted on talking about the boy. What could be said about him? Musalman with one hand, almost certainly a thief if given the opportunity. She called him by his name. And she wanted to know if I saw a bright future for him!'

'She is famous,' says Kartar Singh. 'Her picture has appeared in America's biggest magazine.'

'She will get nowhere if she keeps talking about Bangladeshis.' Sohan Lal shakes his head. What a waste – a woman who never possessed the delicacy of womanhood and is fast losing her only redeeming feature: her youth. It is a mistake to educate women – they cannot find husbands once they have learned to read English magazines.

'Let us finish the Ayodhya business,' says Ramvilas.

Kartar Singh opens his briefcase, brings out a sheaf of papers and points to a diagram. 'There are three domes,' he says. 'The central one is the largest. A ladder will be needed to scale it.'

'What is it made of?' asks Ramvilas.

'Burnt bricks, plastered with a paste of lime and coarse sand.'

'The walls?'

'Coarse-grained sandstone blocks, plastered like the domes.'

'Pillars?'

'Fourteen, made of black schistose stone with silica grains. But we can concentrate on the four located in the main door that opens into the central dome.'

'What is schistose stone?'

'Kasauti. Not too strong, but strong enough to support the arches.' Kartar Singh folds the diagram and puts it away.

'This will require at least a thousand people,' says Ramvilas.

'We have been asked to send fifty,' says Kartar Singh.

'I cannot get fifty people in Chandni Chowk!' protests Ramvilas.

'How many boys have you arranged for?' asks Sohan Lal.

'Twelve,' says Ramvilas, uncertainly. 'Each wants two thousand rupees.'

'We do not have twenty-four thousand,' says Sohan Lal.

'This is not a rally where they can shout slogans, eat aloo puri and go home. This is dangerous! The police no longer use tear gas. What if they open fire? When they do, they no longer aim for legs.'

'The police will not fire,' says Sohan Lal.

'They fired the last time we marched in Ayodhya,' says Ramvilas. 'Every boy I speak to has seen the video – bodies lying in heaps, limbs scattered in the street, the Saryu river red with Hindu blood . . . They will not settle for less than two thousand.'

'That was two years ago,' says Sohan Lal. 'Now the chief minister is ours. I have information that the police will not fire.'

'I cannot tell the boys that!' protests Ramvilas. 'They assume the police will fire, so the rate cannot be lowered.'

'And what of their religion?' taunts Sohan Lal. 'Have they no desire to protect it?'

Ramvilas studies Sohan Lal's face for traces of sarcasm but finds none. 'It is for their religion that they have agreed at all,' he says slowly. 'No one will consent to be shot for two thousand rupees.'

'Young men want money for everything,' complains Sohan Lal.

'How does Suleman get them for free? Two hundred people came for the hunger strike in Rajghat on Gandhi Jayanti, ready to starve.'

'It is easy to get people to starve,' says Ramvilas. 'Death comes gradually. But a bullet ends it all in a second, before you have time to change your mind.'

'We also need hammers, axes, ropes and ladders,' says Kartar Singh.

'Those are easy to arrange,' says Ramvilas.

'Have them sent to Ramkatha Kunj near Ayodhya in a week. That is where the volunteers will practise.'

'People will see them,' protests Sohan Lal.

'It is a hilly area. Not too many people live there. And it is close to Babri Masjid.'

'Masjid?' Sohan Lal says mechanically. 'Call it a structure!'

'Ah, yes,' says an embarrassed Kartar Singh. 'The structure.'

His evident discomfort puts Sohan Lal in a better mood. 'We must be careful what we call it,' he says gravely. Then he heaves himself up from the sofa and turns to Ramvilas. 'Summon a meeting of the committee next Tuesday. We will have a puja in the Hanuman temple. Then we will nominate the new members and transfer the chairmanship.'

Sohan Lal turns to go, pleased that Kartar Singh did not interrupt him. The chairmanship now seems to belong naturally to him. Warming to his new role, he unburdens himself. 'We will also use this meeting to assign constituencies for the assembly election. We need to find four candidates for the four segments.'

'The assembly election has not been notified yet,' says Kartar Singh.

'We should start early,' says Sohan Lal. 'Lala Surajmal wanted to finalise this by November. Who am I to question his judgement? The committee owes its existence to Lalaji.'

Ramvilas and Kartar Singh exchange a look. Sohan Lal turns to go.

'Lalaji has already finalised the four candidates,' says Ramvilas softly.

Sohan Lal pauses mid-stride. Can a dead man wield power from beyond? Has he not crossed the Vaitarani? Does he not stand at this very moment before Yamaraj, trembling while the list of his sins is recited?

'Lalaji was always afraid he would die before the election,' explains Ramvilas. 'This will be the first assembly election in Delhi. He did not want to take a chance with such a historic event.'

'How do you know?' asks Sohan Lal, tartly. 'Where is the list of candidates?'

'In a sealed envelope with Jugal Kishorji,' says Ramvilas. 'Signed by Lalaji.'

Sohan Lal is furious. 'It is no longer valid. We will choose four candidates when the new committee meets on Tuesday.'

'But the list includes you, sethji,' says Ramvilas.

'Ah,' says Sohan Lal, confused.

'And Harilalji Gupta, of course. And Kartar Singhji. And a trader for Paharganj.'

'Harilal Gupta gets Chandni Chowk?' asks Sohan Lal.

Ramvilas nods. Sohan Lal stands with his back to them and asks softly. 'Who gets Ballimaran?'

'Kartar Singhji.'

Sohan Lal turns viciously to face the two of them. 'Do I have Matia Mahal, then?'

Ramvilas nods.

'It was the only open seat,' explains Kartar Singh, with a shrug. 'I told Lalaji I would gladly sacrifice Ballimaran, but he said, "Sohan Lal's shop is nowhere near Ballimaran. How can he stand there?"'

Nor is Kartar Singh's store, thinks Sohan Lal. Measured in a straight line, Lajpatrai Market is even further from Ballimaran than Kucha Bansilal. But, of course, distance was not a consideration. Ah, Yamaraj shall listen to a very long list indeed!

'Ask Jugal Kishor to bring that envelope to the meeting,' says Sohan Lal, in a measured tone. 'We will see what to do about it.'

'Harilalji has already seen the list and approved it,' says Kartar Singh.

Sohan Lal walks slowly through the shop, past the oak counters and mahogany cabinets, helpless with fury. Matia Mahal means a sure loss to Suleman. And Kartar Singh will win Ballimaran to become an MLA. Kartar Singh, with his affected limp and his diamond studs! What does he, Sohan Lal Agrawal, chairman of the IPP committee in Chandni Chowk, get after thirty years of public service?

Ramvilas calls to Sohan Lal: 'Do not forget to set aside those sarees, sethji! Eight silk and two nylon!'

'I may not have any in stock,' says Sohan Lal, through clenched teeth. 'I will ask Ramesh to order some for you, but the new stock will be expensive.'

He steps out of Bhagwan Das and Sons and walks through Kucha Sugandh, just as the clock manufactured by T. Cook of Loughborough begins to chime, announcing that it is three o'clock in the afternoon.

IP

Gauhar pulls hard at his cigarette and reminds himself for the hundredth time that he must bring Mussabir Ustad to Tihar Jail. He will get an entire corner of a room to himself, an army of grandfathers to fuck – though they will pay in coupons – and guards to feed him roti and daal twice a day. What more can an ustad want for the rest of his life? His only fear is that, by the time he gets out, Mussabir Ustad may have left the green cupboard and gone somewhere else. There is no telling when Gauhar will get out of jail, says the rabbit-like old man, his new friend. He calls himself Bobby, which is not his real name, of course. When Gauhar asked why he was inside, he laughed and said he had stolen a car, which Gauhar knows to be untrue. One look at the man's face – his split lip and his exposed front teeth – and you can tell he has never sat in a car, let alone driven one.

Gauhar decides to roll another cigarette and digs under his blanket for the Bible. It is gone. He turns angrily to Bobby, seated on his own blanket, rolling a cigarette. 'You took my Bible, you mother-fucker!'

Bobby grins, and the split lips fall away to expose his remaining teeth. 'Father Noronha has not come for a week,' he says. 'I will return yours when I get a new one from him.'

'Ten rupees,' says Gauhar. Bobby sighs, digs under his blanket and hands over a sheaf of grey-blue coupons. Gauhar counts them, taking care not to tear the thin paper. Fifteen. 'Three more,' he insists. 'The rate is eighteen ten.'

'Give me a discount,' pleads Bobby. 'We are friends.'

'Three more, mother-fucker!'

Bobby brings out his coupons again. Gauhar helps him tear off three and stows them under his mat. Bobby rolls a cigarette.

'What will I smoke until Father Noronha comes?' asks Gauhar. 'Give me one page.'

'Two rupees!' says Bobby, triumphantly.

Reluctantly Gauhar hands over two coupons. Bobby pulls out the Bible from under his blanket, tears out a page and hands it to Gauhar. Gauhar folds it in half, pulls out a tobacco bag and rolls the page into a cigarette. Bobby has tricked him again. The bastard!

'Jesus has saved me again!' cries Bobby. 'Father Noronha said he would.'

It is a good thing Bobby cannot count, thinks Gauhar, or he would have made a beggar of me by now. He does not care much for Bobby, who is indistinguishable from the twenty other grandfathers in his room, except for his upper lip. The last two months have been comfortable. The grandfathers are so frail that he fears he might kill them by speaking too loudly. He does not fear them: it is the men in their forties who are dangerous. In the first few days they approached him with menacing eyes. He did not know what they wanted – his kurta, his pyjama, his cap or a fuck. He gladly offered himself for seventy rupees, but soon found out that the rates were different in jail. The men wanted to fuck him without payment. So he told them about yellow Mussabir, and that the two of them fucked together all the time. 'I am soon going to be as yellow as your shit. I am going to vomit on the floor and get terrible stomach pains.' The men left him alone after that. He has been given his own corner in the room – five times as large as Gopal Bhai's box – and only the grandfathers venture into it. Even they are wary of him. His only regular visitor, and constant companion, is Bobby, who is everywhere all the time. Bobby has certainly been in Tihar Jail before. He knows the guards, he knows the superintendent and claims he can get out whenever he wants. When asked why he will not leave, he says he will wait until he is needed outside.

'Who needs you outside?' Gauhar has often asked.

'Different people from time to time,' he answers cryptically.

Gauhar has no doubt Didi has something to do with this jail business. She was talking to that bastard policeman in GB Road. She used words in English. She has been careful not to teach him much English, so she can lock him up when she wants and he will never know. When he was taken in the police jeep with Gopal Bhai he thought they were going to be released. In the courtroom he stood silently. He was on his best behaviour, afraid to offend the judge, assured that Didi was doing whatever was necessary. She is very well known – that was obvious from the way the judge spoke to her – so he was shocked when the constable pulled him away from Gopal Bhai, who left the court with Didi. Had she not paid the police for both of them? He cursed and abused her, but he was alone in the lockup. He should never have trusted her. There is little doubt he would have been released had she spoken to the black moustache in GB Road. What harm can come from pissing on a stone? It has been beaten by rain for years and the letters 'Hey Raam' are made of steel. It is not as if they will be wiped off by the piss.

After Didi had left with Gopal Bhai, they put him into a large van and brought him here. Tihar Jail, said the constable, where beggars too old to beg are brought to die.

'I am only eighteen,' he told the officer.

'Who allowed you to live until eighteen? You were meant to die a long time ago in the shit and piss of Chandni Chowk.'

He socked the policeman in the eye. In return, he was slapped and put into a room with these grandfathers. And they did not give him a blanket for the entire month of October. In November, when nights became really cold, Bobby gave fifty coupons to someone and brought him a mat.

He does not mind the jail. They took away his kurta-pyjama and gave him a uniform, but he managed to hide his cap, and wears it when he can. The guards are friendly. Now and then, one of them may kick someone or beat a grandfather with a baton, but they soon relent. Bobby knows them all, and Gauhar has befriended them. They have to be given a few coupons every day to ensure their good humour, but Bobby has an inexhaustible supply. It is wise to remain on the right side of the guards. Many of the younger men have begun to eye him suspiciously because he has not turned yellow as he promised. He can ward them off for a few more weeks, but then he must let them fuck him at whatever rate applies inside the jail. 'You will live here for the rest of your life,' Bobby has assured him, 'so there is no point in continuing with the yellow scare.'

At night he rolls himself up in the mat to keep warm. Twice a day the guard gives them daal and roti. Once a day they go out into the compound to play kabaddi, and every fortnight a barber clips his hair for free. He has allowed his beard to grow, but is disappointed that it is patchy and uneven, not the lush growth of Suleman Mian or even the straggly brush on Ibrahim Mian's dirty face. On balance, he is comfortably settled: he has never been so certain of his meals; he has never had such a large space to sleep in, and he does not have to stand in Chandni Chowk looking for fat women in silk sarees. We should all piss on the stone in Rajghat and come to Tihar Jail, he thinks.

The only adjustment he has had to make is in the matter of shitting. He cannot shit in the grounds of Red Fort any more, or in the park outside Old Delhi railway station. There are no fields inside the jail and he cannot leave the compound. If he shits there the guards beat him, so he must squat on a bucket inside a tin shed. There is a tap inside the shed, so there is no need to take a lota of water there, but he must ask the guards' permission to go to it. When they first told him about this he wondered how a man could shit in a shed. Once, it rained – there were only three rainy days in October and this was one – and he sat in the shed, shitting. Then he realised what a wonderful thing it was to shit inside a shed. You could shit while it was raining! In two months he has become an expert at this type of shitting. He can now aim his piss and shit to fall into the bucket. He does not mind missing, but the guards beat him if they see that he has when he emerges from the shed.

Bobby coughs. His cigarette is finished. He tears a page from his Bible and holds it out to Gauhar. 'Another?'

'I cannot waste my coupons,' says Gauhar.

'This one is free!' Bobby grins.

Gauhar takes the page. There is a clatter outside and the guards bring in daal-roti in large cauldrons. Gauhar watches them slap three rotis and a ladle of daal on his aluminium plate. He eats quickly, before Bobby can interfere. There is a fixed amount of daal-roti set aside for everyone in the jail, Bobby has told him. 'You will stay here your entire life and you are still young,' says Bobby, 'so you must make your daal-roti last fifty years. It is better that you fast now so you can stuff yourself when you are older because that is when you need food. A young man can go hungry and still remain strong, but an old man will shrivel up like a grape without food.'

Bobby eyes Gauhar's rotis. Gauhar hands him the third, and pours the remaining daal into Bobby's cupped hands. He slurps it greedily. Gauhar does not know if the fixed-amount story is true, but Bobby is knowledgeable and it will not do to have him shrivel up like a grape and die: as well as his unlimited supply of coupons, he is the only one in the room who knows where to get tobacco.

'You will live a long life,' says Bobby, gratefully, as he devours Gauhar's food. 'Think of this roti as having gone into your stomach.'

'Fuck you!' says Gauhar.

He rolls himself up in his mat and turns his back. One of these nights, he will strangle Bobby and take his blanket, which is much thicker than his own mat. Also, he has seen large lumps of tobacco sewn into the lining. He has seen Bobby's double-soled shoes, full of coupons and wires. The bastard has treasure buried under his blanket. But once Bobby is dead, who will replenish the hoard? Perhaps it is wiser to keep him alive, feed and fatten him, and rob him periodically. Better still, he should put a hand on his chicken throat and extract his secrets, because Gauhar must live here long after the rabbit-man is dead.

He sleeps fitfully. It is bitterly cold. The guards will not tell him the date, but by his count he has been here sixty-one days, which makes this December.

Bobby shakes him awake early the next morning.

'It is still dark,' protests Gauhar.

'I have found you a client!' says Bobby, breathlessly.

'Have I not told you I am about to turn yellow? Does your client want to vomit every day?'

'He does not mind,' says Bobby. 'If he falls sick they will send him to the hospital, where they will give him milk.'

'Why should I not go and get milk myself?' asks Gauhar.

'He is a good man,' insists Bobby.

'He can put onions in his armpits,' suggests Gauhar. 'That will give him a fever and he can go and drink milk. Now, let me sleep.'

Bobby brings his rabbit-mouth close to Gauhar's face and whispers, 'He has given me a Gandhi!'

Gauhar is suddenly alert. He sits up, shivering, excited. 'Show me!'

Bobby springs back, out of Gauhar's reach, and opens his palm like a flower. He has not lied. The note stuck to his palm is crisp and new. Five hundred rupees – real money, worth at least nine hundred coupons. Gauhar stares at it, then raises his hand to touch it. The palm snaps shut.

'Give it to me!' says Gauhar.

'What is my cut?' asks Bobby.

'Why should you get a cut, you bastard? Who will get fucked, you or I? Do you think you are my ustad?'

'I will return it,' threatens Bobby.

Gauhar considers the scrawny neck of the rabbit-man. Should he reach out and end the business? But a Gandhi, even a Gandhi, does not last for ever. Perhaps the rabbit-man can arrange more . . . He sighs. 'Twenty per cent.'

'How much is that?' asks Bobby, suspiciously.

'Twenty rupees.'

Bobby shrugs. 'All right. Come. The client is in another room.'

'Right now? The doors will not open until six.'

'I will have them opened,' laughs Bobby. 'The guard will need a cut too.'

'I will not give a cut to the guard.'

'All right. Maybe I can ask the client to wait until six.'

'Ask him to wait until eight in the morning.'

'Why?'

'Do you want him to fuck me before I shit?' laughs Gauhar.

Bobby sniggers.

'Give me the Gandhi,' says Gauhar. 'I need to sleep.'

'Why should you keep it?'

Gauhar snatches the note from Bobby and rolls himself inside his mat. Before he drifts into sleep again, he warns Bobby, 'If you touch me while I sleep, I will sock you in the face!'

Two hours later, Gauhar is shaken awake by a guard. 'Gauhar Muhammad?'

Gauhar nods. The guard pulls him upright. He hastily stuffs his cap and the five-hundred-rupee note into his groin. The guard leads him out of the room.

Bobby springs up and pulls at Gauhar's right arm, but the stump slides through his hands. He runs after the guard. 'Where are you taking him?'

The guard does not reply.

'Give me the Gandhi!' Bobby whispers.

'I will when I come back,' says Gauhar.

He has no doubt that Didi has finally taken pity on him and come to take him away. Ah, he will forgive her everything, even the film from which she cut him out. He might even go back to Sparrows and help with Baal Bank.

The guard leads him down a corridor and pushes him into the superintendent's office. It is not Didi who has come for him. It is Yellow Teeth, dressed in a churidaar-pyjama. He looks curiously respectable with a combed beard, but then he grins on seeing Gauhar, and Gauhar sees the teeth.

'You look dirty,' says Ibrahim Mian.

Gauhar shrugs, thinking he looks no different from other men in the jail, but perhaps they are all dirty. Ibrahim Mian himself is no film star like Amitabh Bachchan.

'I have come to take you away,' says Ibrahim.

Gauhar looks at the superintendent and receives no rebuttal. Perhaps his jail term is over. But Bobby has told him he will be here for the rest of his life. 'What date is it?'

'The fourth of December,' says Ibrahim.

The superintendent gives Gauhar a piece of paper and an envelope that contains fifty rupees. Ibrahim slips the envelope into his own pocket. A constable brings his kurta and trousers. Gauhar changes into them and puts on his cap. Ibrahim Mian walks out of the office and Gauhar follows him gleefully, looking back to make sure they will not be stopped. They walk out of the gates and take a bus. Gauhar considers the sudden turn of events. Jail was comfortable, but perhaps this change is for the better. He was beginning to get bored. He would like to see Mussabir Ustad, unless he is dead. He would like to go to GB Road where they have those creamy women. He will have to work for Seth Sohan Lal again, but at least he has the Gandhi, now tucked in his kurta, and he is for ever rid of Bobby. He is glad he did not exchange the money for coupons, which are worthless outside the jail. It is just as well that he is going back to Chandni Chowk. But if this Ibrahim Mian knew how to get him out, why did he not do so sooner?

'Where were you for two months?' asks Gauhar angrily.

'The time was not right until now,' says Ibrahim Mian.

'For what?'

Ibrahim does not reply.

'Give me my thirty-five rupees,' says Gauhar.

'Why?'

'You are the one who took me to the dharna! You said thirty-five rupees.'

'I said thirty-five rupees for three hours,' scolds Ibrahim. 'You pissed and ran off within an hour.'

'It was hot!' protests Gauhar.

'You ruined Suleman Mian's dharna,' says Ibrahim, 'and he has spent a lot of money to get you out.'

Gauhar grudgingly drops his demand. 'I will get off here,' he says.

'I have ten thousand rupees waiting for you,' says Ibrahim.

'Fuck you!' says Gauhar. 'You have been promising me money for two years.'

'Ten thousand,' repeats Ibrahim.

'What do I have to do? Piss on the prime minister?'

'Suleman Mian wants to see you.'

'Fuck Suleman Mian!'

'Speak respectfully of him!' scolds Ibrahim. 'He is the one who got you out of jail.'

'I have to go back to sethji,' says Gauhar. 'He will throw me out of his shop if I do not go to him.'

Ibrahim grins, revealing his dwindling stock of yellow teeth. 'Your duty is to Allah. Have you learned nothing in the madarsa?'

'Allah does not pay.'

Ibrahim places a restraining hand on Gauhar's right shoulder. They stand in the bus, steadying themselves by gripping the bar overhead. Gauhar thrusts his stump into his kurta pocket, where he can feel the five-hundred-rupee note. They get off the bus at Red Fort and walk down Chandni Chowk. Gauhar has an impulse to desert Ibrahim and go to Kucha Bansilal. He is sure the seth will take him back. Ibrahim Mian can hardly stop him. A hard punch will knock him to the ground, and he will never get up again. But he has mentioned ten thousand rupees and he is a Musalman. They turn off into Paratha Gali and Gauhar's stomach churns at the smells. 'I want to eat,' he says.

'I will buy you nahari,' offers Ibrahim.

But Gauhar has already stopped at a signboard in Urdu. 'Arya Restaurant. Prove our parathas are not made with pure desi ghee and get a reward of one thousand rupees!' The man behind the griddle eyes them suspiciously. Gauhar points to the fattest paratha lying at the top of the stack.

'Mattar paneer paratha,' says the man. 'Twenty-two rupees.'

Gauhar fishes out the five-hundred-rupee note from his kurta and throws it at the man. 'Five mattar paneer parathas!'

Ibrahim's jaw drops. Gauhar throws a glance over his shoulder and turns his back to Ibrahim. Let Yellow Teeth drool. He will not get a single bite.

With four parathas in a paper bag and one in his stomach, Gauhar allows Ibrahim to take him to the lanes behind Jama Masjid. He seems to be heading toward Sparrows, where they had first met, but he turns into a narrow lane where children are playing cricket. They enter a haveli and climb up its narrow staircase in almost complete darkness. The staircase groans under their weight. Pigeons coo in dark recesses on upper floors. On the third floor he can see the outline of a door on the landing. A cloud of pigeons rises and flies away in a grey storm. Ibrahim leads Gauhar to the door, pushes it open and ushers him inside. Gauhar finds himself in the most luxuriously appointed room he has ever seen.

'Take off your dirty chappals,' commands Suleman Mian.

Gauhar slips them off and stands on the stone floor, which is cool. It is a calm day, without the slightest suggestion of a breeze even here on the third floor. Curtains hang still in the windows. They are made of a thin material and light filters through them. In this light Gauhar sees dazzling maroon sofas arranged carefully round a coffee-table, and tall lamps with beautiful shades in two corners. Neither is switched on. The walls appear to be smooth, cream-coloured, very different from the peeling grey of the haveli. The floor round the sofas is covered with a bright red carpet that transforms the room into a set from a film. He imagines a heroine sitting majestically on the sofa, inviting the hero into her boudoir. He plants himself in the hero's body, then remembers that Didi has cut him out of her film.

Suleman sits on the sofa wearing a Nehru jacket and a kurta-pyjama, holding a cigarette in his right hand. The left lies carelessly on a side-table next to a tumbler from which he has just taken a sip. Gauhar stands uncomfortably. He has never stood so close to Suleman Mian, and never been alone in his presence. It is one thing to talk of him with Yellow Teeth, a decaying man who can be socked in the face without much trouble, and another to stand in his presence. His eyes are sharp and stare too frankly at him – they can almost see the four parathas lying inside his paper bag, or bore through his kurta pocket to count the three hundred and ninety rupees that lie folded inside. Although Suleman Mian is now smiling, his face speaks of violence and fear. His moustache is too thin, too neatly combed, and his hair is so black that it merges with the dark cupboard behind him. If Suleman Mian wanted a fuck, thinks Gauhar, he could get it whenever he liked at any rate, or even if he did not pay at all. Unlike Yellow Teeth, he is a man. A full man.

'You are Gauhar Muhammad,' says Suleman.

That is not a question, thinks Gauhar.

'You have to go to Ayodhya,' says Suleman.

Gauhar gets tired of standing under such scrutiny. He takes the stump out of his pocket and steadies the paper bag in his left hand. A frown crosses Suleman's face. 'Is this the boy from the school?' he snaps at Ibrahim.

Ibrahim nods.

'A one-handed boy for work that needs a thousand hands?' whispers Suleman.

'I could not find anyone else I trust,' says Ibrahim, defensively.

Suleman shakes his head. Gauhar stares at the sofas and wonders if he could steal and sell the lamps to someone in Chandni Chowk.

'Who will suspect a one-handed boy?' points out Ibrahim. 'He can pass through easily.' He turns to Gauhar. 'I trust you. Do you trust me?'

'Fuck you!'

Suleman smiles, evidently pleased with Gauhar's spirit. 'Why did you piss in Rajghat?'

Gauhar looks suspiciously at him. The interrogation reminds him of the black moustache in the police station.

'Do you know whom you have pissed on?'

Gauhar knows very well, having been told countless times. 'The Father of the Nation!' He laughs. 'The man who fucked so many women that he has eighty crore children!'

Suleman is pleased with the answer. He beckons Gauhar closer. 'Listen carefully and I will tell you a true story,' he says. 'There was a great Musalman emperor named Babur, who built a grand masjid in Ayodhya and ruled over the kafirs in this country for three hundred years. But people from England – white men – lured Babur's children out of Red Fort and imprisoned them through trickery and deception. Babur's children defeated the white man and recaptured Red Fort, but they found that the white man had filled Red Fort with kafirs. That is why a kafir speaks every fifteenth of August from the ramparts of Red Fort, where Shah Jahan once stood to gaze upon Jama Masjid. And now the kafirs want to destroy the great masjid built by Babur. Fifty years ago, they broke into the masjid and put their idols inside it. Now they want the entire masjid. They are training in camps all around the country with lathis, rods, axes and hammers. They will go to Ayodhya in two days. They will come from Delhi and Rajasthan, UP and Bihar, Gujarat and Maharashtra, Punjab and Haryana . . . In two days, thousands of them will march upon the great masjid. They will castrate Musalmans and rape their women. They will force Musalmans to eat pork and worship idols. Will you allow that?'

Gauhar finds the imagery familiar. He has heard it countless times in the madarsa, but he is uncertain of his own role in it. 'If thousands will march on the masjid, how can I protect it?'

'Protect the masjid? No, you have to destroy it.'

'Fuck you!' says Gauhar. 'I will not destroy a masjid.'

'But you must,' says Suleman Mian. 'Hindus are unmanly and effeminate. They will strike against the walls and they will fall to the ground. Do you think they will so much as scratch a masjid protected by Allah? And if they do not, who will punish them for the sin? A Musalman must bring down retribution on their heads. Once the masjid has fallen, the Musalmans of India will not sit still. Do you think they will let their sisters be raped? Do you think they will let Hindus fill their mouths with pork? Before the dust from the masjid settles, our armies will crush the kafirs who have come to attack. But unless the masjid falls the Musalmans will not be aroused. It is important that the masjid fall – it is necessary!'

'It is a great sin,' says Gauhar.

'Do you know what WT means?' asks Suleman.

'Without Ticket,' says Ibrahim, helpfully.

'If you are caught WT in a Delhi bus, the conductor will throw you out of the bus. Before he does, he will fine you fifty rupees for not buying a one-rupee ticket. And because you do not have fifty rupees, he will kick your arse and knock your teeth in. Then someone will throw you into jail. You are the worst type of WT. You do not fetch him fifty rupees but you take up space in the bus and interfere with other WTs who have the money.'

'I have never taken a bus until today,' says Gauhar.

'But you have,' says Suleman, seriously. 'You have taken the bus and you are WT. Every Musalman is WT in this country of kafirs. You are WT in Chandni Chowk. You are WT in the seth's shop. You are WT in Rajghat. You are WT, no matter where you shit and breathe in this country, because you are a Musalman.'

'Try to get fifty rupees out of me,' says Gauhar.

'For you, the fine is a hundred rupees because you are a Bangladeshi. A Musalman and a Bangladeshi!'

'I am not a Bangladeshi!' says Gauhar. 'I am from Murshidabad.'

'You think you have a ticket to the bus but you don't! That bus left for Pakistan forty-five years ago. You are WT and the conductor is not far from you. He is inching toward you, advancing through other WTs in the aisle. He will find you and kick you in the balls. Look at me, sitting here on this sofa with a cigarette in my hand. I am WT. Ibrahim Mian is WT. Every Musalman boy in the madarsa is WT, as is the mulla in the madarsa. All fifteen crore of us in this country are WT. We are an army of WT passengers in the bus and the conductor is coming toward us!'

Gauhar is frightened by Suleman's intensity.

'And if you are WT, isn't it good for you if a man in the bus has a heart-attack? When the conductor is fussing over him, do you think he will notice you? Will he even know you exist? Perhaps you could snatch his satchel while he is busy with the heart-attack man! That is why you need to bring down the masjid.'

'How can I bring down an entire masjid?' asks Gauhar.

'I will give you a package,' says Ibrahim. 'Take it to Ayodhya. I will also give you a diagram that shows you where to place it. All you have to do is flick the switch.'

'Fuck you!' says Gauhar.

'You will leave for Ayodhya tomorrow night,' says Suleman. 'When you come back the next day, Ibrahim Mian will give you ten thousand rupees.'

Gauhar gasps. When Yellow Teeth said it, the ten thousand rupees seemed elusive. Coming from Suleman Mian, the promise cannot be broken.

'You must shave your beard,' says Suleman.

'Why?'

'Give your cap to Ibrahim Mian.'

Gauhar reluctantly removes it, fingers the gold embroidery one last time, and hands it to Ibrahim.

Suleman smiles. 'You must become a Hindu for two days.'

He motions to Ibrahim, who pushes Gauhar out of the room.

'I still do not like that one hand,' says Suleman.

'It is the hand of a Musalman,' swears Ibrahim, fervently, as he steps outside. 'Can you get another boy?' he asks Gauhar.

'I can get a hundred,' boasts Gauhar.

'I need one. A good Musalman.'

'It will cost you another ten thousand.'

'Five,' says Ibrahim. 'But if you mention this to anyone, you get nothing. Meet me at Old Delhi railway station tomorrow night. Bring the other boy, but do not tell him where he has to go. The train leaves at nine. Remember, do not speak to anyone about this, not even a Musalman!'

I2:

Gauhar turns into Dudhiya Gali and eats another paratha from his bag. He finds his way through shivering vats of curd and arrives at Banwari's stall, where he drinks water from the hand-pump. Then he asks Ram Bibek to shave his beard.

'I do not shave Musalmans,' says Ram Bibek.

Gauhar flashes a twenty-rupee note at him. 'Musalmans pay well.'

Ram Bibek hesitates.

'I will be a Hindu when you are done!' laughs Gauhar.

'I do not even know your name,' says Ram Bibek.

'Chotu,' says Gauhar.

'That is not a Musalman name.'

'That is my name after you finish shaving me.'

'Who is your father?' insists Ram Bibek.

'Gopal Pandey,' says Gauhar.

'I know him!' Ram Bibek threatens. 'His son is dead.'

'I am the son that lived.'

Ram Bibek covers the chair with an old towel so the Musalman will not touch anything, then seats Gauhar. 'What happened to your hand?' he asks.

'A train ran over it,' says Gauhar.

When Ram Bibek has finished, Gauhar runs his hand over his newly smooth cheeks and looks at himself in the glass front of Banwari's ice-cream stall. Not bad! He will go to GB Road when he is back from Ayodhya. For now, he must seek out Mussabir Ustad.

He arrives at the green cupboard in the dull glow of dusk. The door is wide open. Mussabir lies in a pool of vomit, sprawled on the floor. Blood oozes from dozens of cuts in his legs. Gauhar wonders, for a fleeting moment of horror, if Ustad is dead.

'Mussabir Ustad!' he calls.

He kicks the body on the floor. Mussabir stirs and sits up with a curse. Gauhar is shocked by his appearance. His eyes are deep yellow and his skin looks like a membrane wrapped over his ribs, which form deep ridges that are visible through his shirt. Slowly, his eyes focus on Gauhar and a smile of recognition swims on his face. 'Seventy-five! Eighty!'

Gauhar is amused to think of himself as a customer for Mussabir.

He still has three hundred and seventy rupees in his pocket. At a rate of seventy, he could fuck Mussabir five times, but he will save that money for GB Road tonight. Mussabir is hard and stringy. Gauhar wants the soft flesh of a woman.

'You look like a Hindu,' groans Mussabir. 'Where have you been?'

'They pay me to be a Hindu.'

'Business is bad,' says Mussabir, and lies down again.

Gauhar points at the dribbling sores on his legs. 'Who did that to you?'

'The doctor. Can you take me to him again?'

'Does he see patients late in the evening?'

'Do you have fifty rupees?' asks Mussabir.

Gauhar nods.

'Then he will see me.'

'Can you walk?' asks Gauhar.

Mussabir stands up with great effort, using Gauhar's arm for support. They find their way through Meena Bajar to shop number 460. Muhammad Ghayas's clinic is on a quadrangle of jute sacking outside. 'The clinic is closed,' he says.

'I have fifty rupees,' replies Gauhar.

Ghayas insists on seeing the money. Gauhar steps back and twirls a note in his hand. Ghayas relents and asks Mussabir to sit down on the jute mats. He turns Mussabir's legs and examines the neat array of cuts, all of which he has made over the last seven days. 'Do you feel better?' he asks solicitously.

Mussabir shakes his head. Ghayas is displeased. 'I told you to let the bad blood seep out,' he says, 'but I see you have tried to plug the wound.'

'The bleeding stopped on its own,' says Mussabir.

Ghayas sighs, disbelieving him. 'I will make new cuts today, nearer the ankle. This time, you must not interfere.' He gets busy with his blades and bowls of water.

Gauhar studies the framed photographs arrayed on the jute sacks behind Ghayas, all testimonials from cured patients. Ghayas notices his gaze and cannot resist braggadocio. 'White people,' he says. 'They come from all over the world – England and America – after their English doctors have given up.' He indicates to Mussabir that he is ready. Gauhar holds Mussabir's leg over a bowl of water. Ghayas makes two swift incisions above the heel and lets blood dribble into the bowl. He holds the leg still for almost a minute, studying the colour of the blood that spreads in a cloud inside the bowl. Then he moves another bowl into position, sets the leg down and washes it, watching the continued bleeding with approval.

'Come again in two days for the last bleeding,' he says.

Gauhar hands over his fifty-rupee note and helps Mussabir to his feet.

'Step away from the mat!' scolds Ghayas. 'You will dirty it.'

Mussabir hastily steps on to the street and rests his leg daintily on the asphalt. Gauhar holds out his right stump. 'Can you fix this?' he asks Ghayas.

Ghayas studies the stump with professional disdain, then looks Gauhar in the eye. 'Anything is possible if you have money.'

'How much?'

'Ten thousand,' says Ghayas.

'I will come back,' promises Gauhar.

They walk back to the old haveli, Mussabir leaving puddles of blood in his wake. 'I already feel better,' he says.

'Does the paanvala not mind your use of the cupboard?' asks Gauhar.

Mussabir laughs. 'The police came for him. He no longer collects rent for it. It is mine now.'

They come back and sit outside the cupboard, so Mussabir's leg will not sully the floor inside, although it is already smeared with vomit.

'You have not told me where you were for two months,' says Mussabir. 'I lost my postering business.'

'I have found a hotel for you,' says Gauhar. 'It is free. A large room to sleep in, tin sheds for shitting, daal and roti twice a day, and grandfathers to fuck you. They will pay in coupons but you can buy tobacco with them, and you can get Bibles to roll cigarettes in. I also have a friend who will get you clients.'

'When can we go there?'

'As soon as we come back from Ayodhya.'

Mussabir looks at Gauhar suspiciously. 'I have never been to Ayodhya.'

'Would you like a thousand rupees?'

Mussabir's eyes grow wide as his groggy mind retrieves the arithmetic he learned at Sparrows. A thousand rupees! Is that ten fucks or fifteen? Or twenty? Who cares? The amount is large – very large. But he must stake out a negotiating position before Gauhar gets into details. 'I will not fuck vomiting men,' he says.

Gauhar laughs. 'You must become a Hindu.'

'That is all?'

'Come with me. Tomorrow night we will take a train to Ayodhya where no man will fuck you.'

Mussabir is suspicious again. 'What must I do?'

'I need your hands to tie wires and flick switches.'

'A thousand rupees for tying wires?' asks Mussabir. 'Who will pay that much?'

'Do you not trust me?' counters Gauhar. 'Did we not agree that I was your ustad?'

Mussabir nods.

'Can you walk to the station, or do you want me to come for you?'

'I can walk,' says Mussabir, with renewed energy.

Gauhar stands up. 'Tomorrow night, then, at eight. Old Delhi railway station. Meet me in the park outside.'

'Where are you going?'

'I have business to take care of.'

'Do not leave me alone! You can sleep here.'

Gauhar thinks of the soft, warm bodies in GB Road. 'I do not want to get your disease,' he says uncertainly.

'You can sleep in the cupboard. You can have my blanket. I will stay outside.'

'It is cold,' says Gauhar. 'Sleep in your blanket. I will see you in the park tomorrow night.'

He leaves before Mussabir can say more. He runs all the way to GB Road, anxious, eager, impatient. His visit to Kotha 842 is unsuccessful. The whore asks him to wear a condom. He is baffled. 'What am I paying you for if I must wrap my prick in a bag?' he asks angrily.

'It is the new rule,' she says.

'Who made it?' he demands.

'Our sisters in STREE have told us to require all clients to wear condoms,' she says.

'Who the fuck are these sisters?' he screams. He jumps out of his bunk, scaring the other clients in the room. 'Why do you have *sisters* in GB Road? Is this not a whorehouse? What right do those bitches have to interfere with a good whore trying to do her job?'

The pahalvan comes into the room and asks if there is a problem. 'She wants me to cover my prick!' roars Gauhar. Five minutes later he

is outside the kotha, lying on his face in GB Road. He managed to get
in a few kicks but the pahalvan is a large man and has two hands.

He stands up and spits toward the kotha. The pahalvan continues
to stand at the foot of the staircase, arms crossed. 'I will come back to
burn down this kotha!' Gauhar shouts.

It is bitterly cold now. He must sleep somewhere, but not on the
pavement. He is not a beggar. He could go to the night shelter next to
Fatehpuri Masjid, but he knows they will ask him to write down his
name in a register and deposit money, then give him a small bunk to
share with two snoring grandfathers. Perhaps it is better to go back to
Mussabir. But he is sure to get the disease Mussabir has if he sleeps in
the cupboard with him. And Mussabir has only one blanket, soiled
with blood and vomit. Gauhar misses his comfortable corner in the
large room in Tihar Jail. Fuck Ibrahim Mian! Why did he have to
pluck him out of there, where he had his own blanket and his own
corner? Very well, he will go to Kucha Bansilal and sleep in Gopal
Bhai's box. He may have to break the lock, but he can explain to
Gopal Bhai. He will pay to have the lock repaired.

In Kucha Bansilal, Gauhar is pleasantly surprised to find the box
unlocked and a blanket folded neatly among bottles and tins. He
opens the lid, arranges himself inside the wooden chest – he has to fold
his legs to fit properly – and lets the lid fall back into place.

13

Gopal raises the lid of his box and is baffled to find Gauhar curled up
inside, fast asleep. He looks around fearfully to make sure no one else
has noticed. Sohan Lal sits quietly on his gaddi, absorbed in puja.
Chotu wipes down the glass panes of Jamna Lal Kishori Mal. Ramesh
Babu sits next to the cash-box, writing in a register.

Gopal shakes Gauhar awake. 'Have you broken out of jail?' he
whispers.

'No! They let me go when I turned myself into a Hindu.' Gauhar
steps out of the wooden chest and stretches.

Gopal watches him curiously. 'You look different.'

Gauhar runs a hand over his cheeks.

'You're thinner,' says Gopal.

'I have been fasting like a good Hindu,' says Gauhar.

Gopal is impressed and confused. 'A young man should not fast. Fasting is for wives.'

'Make me some tea,' says Gauhar, as he takes out Ibrahim's tumbler.

Gopal opens the stall, arranges chairs, opens his tins and pumps the stove. Gauhar hauls the bicycle on to the junction box and secures it, with one expert hand. Five minutes later, they squat on the wooden planks and sip chai contentedly.

'I knew you would come back,' says Gopal. 'I left the box unlocked every night, with a blanket for you. I knew Madam would get you out of jail, as she did for me.'

'The bitch!' mutters Gauhar.

Gopal is shocked. 'Don't call her that! She followed the van from the police station to the court in a taxi. She stood with me when the magistrate asked my name, and she brought me back to Kucha Bansilal in her taxi. She never once asked me to pay the fare. I do not even know what she paid the magistrate to have me released.'

'So why did she not bring *me* back in the same taxi?'

'I told her, when she brought me from the court, that we should go and fetch you too. She said she would do that as soon as time permitted. And here you are, only two months later.'

'It was Ibrahim Mian who got me out,' says Gauhar.

'He is a good man,' says Gopal. 'He told me he could do nothing about it. I asked him to seek Suleman Mian's help. He said that was impossible, but his heart is not made of stone. Old friendships never die.'

Gauhar shrugs.

'I know you could not hold your piss,' says Gopal, mildly. 'I told Ibrahim Mian it was not your fault. He has forgiven you.'

Gauhar says nothing, and sips his chai. Gopal watches him with pride. With his smooth cheeks, the boy looks ever more like Mukesh. He is darker, of course, and his hair is still dirty, but he has grown tall and assertive. The stump at his wrist is not visible from most angles. He can almost imagine that this boy is Mukesh, restored to him. 'You are my son,' he says.

Gauhar looks embarrassed. 'I have come for a short while. I will be gone for two days.'

'Where will you go now?'

'On business. When I come back I will be rich. I will not sleep in the box then.'

'Poor boys like you do not become rich.' Gopal sighs.

'I will show you ten thousand rupees in two days,' insists Gauhar. Gopal shakes his head.

'Wait for me!' challenges Gauhar. 'When I come back from Ayodhya I will show you ten thousand rupees.'

'Why will you go to Ayodhya?' wonders Gopal.

Gauhar looks around furtively. 'On business. Do not tell Ibrahim Mian I told you.'

'I do not understand your business,' says Gopal. 'And you have a good job with sethji. Why do you not ask him to take you back?'

'What will I do with his ten per cent commission? I am going to be rich.'

'You do not have any money right now,' points out Gopal.

Gauhar laughs. 'All right! I will stand in Chandni Chowk one last time and bring customers for sethji. One last time, before I become rich.'

Sohan Lal watches Gauhar sitting with Gopal and looks away. He is back, the thief! It is impossible to get rid of Bangladeshis once you let them enter the country. They come, they stay and they breed like insects! No jail can hold them for ever. He does not much mind the pissing act in Rajghat. It was time someone pissed on the Mahatma, even if it had to be a one-handed Bangladeshi. Who was the Mahatma anyway? A fornicator, a dirty old man with scandalous ideas, a man gone soft on Musalmans, a man endowed in senility with a dangerous degree of power, thankfully stopped before he could lay waste the new Indian nation with his constant appeasement of Musalmans. Worst of all, he was the man who foisted Nehru – a Musalman in Hindu garb – on the country. Perhaps the one-handed boy should be rewarded for pissing: it is a more Indian way of killing the Mahatma than the pistol Nathuram Godse used in 'forty-eight. He even looks like a Hindu now! He was a good salesman in spite of his one hand. He learned to hide the stump and spoke smoothly. But his commissions were too high, sometimes up to twelve and a half per cent. He was no good for business.

Sohan Lal watches Gauhar stand up and walk toward Jamna Lal Kishori Mal. Why must the boy come this way? He is crossing the kucha now, approaching the shop with an ingratiating smile on his

face. No, he will not give him work. How can he take back a vandal, a
terrorist, a militant? Will it look good in the committee, especially
with the upcoming assembly election? How will Kartar Singh react to
the chairman of the committee employing a terrorist?

'Namaste, sethji,' says Gauhar.

Sohan Lal looks at him with a mixture of horror and annoyance.

'Should I stand in Chandni Chowk?' asks Gauhar, from the doormat.

Uncomfortably, Sohan Lal adjusts the cotton swab behind his ear –
molshri, a gift from Ramvilas – and runs a handkerchief over his moist
forehead. It is hot inside the shop, even in this brutal winter. He must
pretend to be busily employed and not notice the Bangladeshi. But the
boy continues to stand. He must say something to him. 'Step back!'
says Sohan Lal. 'Who allowed you inside?'

Gauhar, shocked, takes a step back and regards Sohan Lal with
hostility.

The boy is bold, thinks Sohan Lal. Too bold.

Gopal sees Gauhar back away and wonders if the boy has said
something inappropriate. 'It was not his fault, sethji,' he calls. 'They
forced him to piss there. He can start again in two days, as soon as he
is back from Ayodhya.'

Gauhar turns angrily on Gopal. 'I am not going anywhere!'

'Why are you going to Ayodhya?' asks Sohan Lal.

'I am not going anywhere,' repeats Gauhar.

'Ah, are you Gauhar?' Sohan Lal asks.

'Yes, this is my boy!' says Gopal eagerly.

'I did not recognise you,' says Sohan Lal. 'What happened to your
beard?'

'I shaved it,' says Gauhar, defiantly.

'You have allowed your boy to starve,' Sohan Lal scolds Gopal. 'He
is much thinner. But what a difference a beard makes. You're such a
good-looking boy without it!'

Gauhar is softened by the praise but held back by his suspicion of
the seth.

'The boy has no father,' says Sohan Lal, solicitously, to Gopal.
'Who took care of him in jail?'

'He has two fathers!' chimes Gopal. 'Ibrahim Mian and Gopal Pandey!
Ibrahim Mian got him out of jail, and I will take care of him now.'

'I have been waiting for you,' says Sohan Lal. 'My customers keep
asking about you. I tried many other boys but none of them was as
good as you.'

'You are a kind man, sethji,' says an overwhelmed Gopal.

'Come inside and tell me what they gave you to eat,' says Sohan Lal. 'You must have been hungry.'

Gopal's jaw drops. The seth has invited the boy into his shop! A one-handed boy and a Musalman, even if he has shaved his beard! Ibrahim Mian says many things about the seth, but a good man cannot be tarnished by a foul mouth.

Gauhar stands stubbornly. He does not need the fucking seth and his commissions, which will never add up to the ten thousand rupees Ibrahim Mian will give him. He will give five hundred to Mussabir – not the thousand he promised – and the rest should last for years. No one can spend nine and a half thousand rupees in GB Road, even with whores who do not insist on condoms. But why does Gopal Bhai keep pushing him into the shop? Perhaps he hopes to get a share of the commissions as rent for his box. Maybe he can spend a few weeks more with the seth after he is back from Ayodhya. He will set his own commissions. Now that he has shaved, he will get customers even more easily than he did before. He is too good-looking not to. Even the seth realises that.

'I have been thinking of a twenty per cent commission for you,' says Sohan Lal.

The seth calls Chotu and asks him to draw shutters over the mannequins. Then he asks Gopal to make two cups of chai. Gauhar slips off his chappals and steps inside the shop.

Gopal sits uneasily, hands moving mechanically over the stove – a dash of tea leaves, a sprinkling of sugar, a shake of the pan, two violent heaves and the final pouring. Ibrahim's tumbler for Gauhar and a cup of fine china for the seth. That boy is going places! Here he is, taking chai for a one-handed boy who is not quite twenty but sits cross-legged on the gaddi, facing the seth himself, hidden behind wooden shutters.

14

Ibrahim lugs a sack up the stairs, crosses a bridge over the railway tracks and goes down to the platform. He stands the sack against a spittoon and catches his breath. Suleman Mian did not tell him the contraption would be so heavy. How will a one-handed boy cart it all the way to Ayodhya? At least he is strong and resourceful. Hopefully, the second boy he brings is strong too.

The platform is crowded. Many trains run along this route. That is a good thing, he tells himself. The sack will mingle unobtrusively with the pots, pans, bags and bedrolls of others. But it is well past eight! Has the boy forgotten?

Gauhar arrives at eight thirty, running, and bumps into Ibrahim.

'I thought you had backed out,' says Ibrahim coldly.

'Where is my train?' asks Gauhar.

Ibrahim points to the line of carriages standing at the platform. 'It will leave at nine. We need to load the sack into it. It is heavy. The train will take you to Faizabad. From there, you can take a bus to Ayodhya. Where is the other boy?' asks Ibrahim.

Gauhar points at Mussabir, sitting unsteadily under the staircase, surrounded by islands of luggage.

'Is he also from the school?' asks Ibrahim, suspiciously.

'Yes. Mussabir Hussein.'

'Ah.' Ibrahim nods, recognising the name. 'But he looks like a corpse.'

'He has two hands,' says Gauhar, 'and he is a good Musalman.'

'How much does he know?' demands Ibrahim.

Gauhar shrugs.

'Have you told anyone else?' asks Ibrahim.

Gauhar thinks about Sohan Lal. But the seth is a grandfather, a soft old man who will give him twenty thousand when he comes back. It cannot do much harm that he knows. In any case he does not know much, just a little more than Gopal Bhai. And Gopal Bhai could not possibly have understood. And who does Yellow Teeth think he is, interrogating him like the black moustache in the police station? 'Shut up,' he says. 'Just tell me what I have to do.'

Ibrahim pulls Gauhar under the staircase where Mussabir sits, dragging the sack after him. 'No one will bother you in the train,' he says, 'but when you take the bus to Ayodhya, the police will stop it to look inside. There is tight security round the town. You must make no trouble in the bus.'

He hands Gauhar a piece of paper. 'This is a picture of the compound. You will need it once you get to Ayodhya. I have also provided some clothes and two shawls in the sack. Put them on when you enter the compound. You must look like a good Hindu. No

Musalman can strike a blow against a masjid.' Ibrahim points to Mussabir. 'He should have shaved too.'

'I will find a barber on the railway station in Faizabad,' says Gauhar, carelessly. 'We will make his cheeks as smooth as silk.'

'The marchers will collect outside the compound by eight in the morning,' continues Ibrahim. 'You must stay at the front.'

'What if the police fire at us?'

'They will not,' says Ibrahim. 'You must run through the compound and enter the masjid. Do not worry about others, they will fall back. Hindus are unmanly. Some will circle it, some will climb the walls, some will shout slogans, but you must run straight into the masjid. If anyone tries to stop you, shout slogans and push them out of the way.'

'What slogans?' asks Gauhar.

Ibrahim brings his mouth close to Gauhar's ear and whispers, '*Jai Shri* Raam!' Gauhar grins. In the yellow gloom under the staircase, Ibrahim opens the sack and Gauhar peers inside to see a bedding roll. Ibrahim unwraps it partially to reveal a battery tied to a box. 'Place the box in a corner of the masjid, as close as possible to the main dome. It must touch both walls. Stick it with Plasticine, here. You must splice these two wires together. For this, you need two hands.' Ibrahim casts an uncertain look at Mussabir, who appears to have fallen asleep. 'Can he do this?'

'I will take care of him!' says Gauhar, sharply.

'This is a safety lever, and this is the switch. The lever must be pulled hard with both hands but the switch can be flicked easily. Unless you do both, nothing will happen. Once you have engaged them, you have one minute to get out of the masjid.'

'How do you know it will work?'

'The masjid is more than four hundred years old,' says Ibrahim. 'If you ensure the box touches the walls properly . . . You have one full minute. Ensure that the switch is properly thrown before you run away.'

'What if they stop us?'

Ibrahim smiles. 'They will be too busy.'

'Where should I go when I am back in Delhi?' Gauhar asks.

Ibrahim appears momentarily confused. 'Go to Kucha Bansilal. No, come to Suleman Mian. No, not Suleman Mian! Come to me in Ballimaran. No, do not go anywhere. I will contact you and tell you what to do next.'

'What if something happens to the sack in the train?'

'It is safe,' says Ibrahim. 'For anything to happen, the wires must be spliced together, the safety lever must be pulled and the switch thrown. It is impossible for all three to happen by accident.'

They drag the sack to the train and heave it on. Gauhar and Mussabir jump inside, push the sack under a seat, and find their way through the crowd to the window, where they can see Ibrahim on the platform. Gauhar leans out and beckons. 'Do I have to engage the lever and the switch at the same time?'

'One after the other,' says Ibrahim. 'You will need all three hands. Remember, you have one full minute after that.' Ibrahim brings his face close. 'Do not leave Mussabir alone with the lever. Stand next to him and watch him.'

'Give me my advance,' says Gauhar.

'There is no advance. You will get everything when you return.'

'Who the fuck will pay for my food tomorrow?'

'I will give you a hundred rupees when the train starts,' says Ibrahim. 'Buy some aloo puri. When the TT comes round to see your ticket, give him fifty.'

'Fuck the TT,' says Gauhar. 'And let me see the hundred.'

'But Suleman Mian said you must get a ticket—'

'Tell him how we went to Ayodhya – WT!' laughs Gauhar.

Sohan Lal tells the driver to park where Rajpath intersects Janpath: he has decided to walk the rest of the way. He has been told by the doctor to exercise four times a week. It is advice he usually ignores unless it fits in with his other activities. In the last two years he has noticed an increase in his girth. His arms have become beefy, his belly hangs over the knot of his dhoti and his chin has sunk down to his chest. He is not displeased by this development. He has always felt that thin, athletic people are not well fed. A seth and a politician must not look famished. Moderate rotundity is the mark of prosperity, and the onset of obesity signifies wealth. He is comfortable with his expanding body, but he fears the inconveniences that come with it. Over the last year he has been besieged by backaches that arise, says the doctor, because of the strain on his spine, which must now support his bloated belly. So a light walk cannot harm him, especially because Suleman will not arrive for twenty minutes.

It is a cold night. Rajpath is brilliantly lit by rows of golden lamps. To Sohan Lal's far right, thrust upward against the night sky, shines the dome of Rashtrapati Bhavan. To his left India Gate is illuminated by dozens of powerful lights placed on the ground. In spite of the cold, traffic on Rajpath is heavy. Sohan Lal walks slowly toward India Gate, a hand holding the corner of his dhoti. He has resisted Ramesh's attempts to buy him a walking-stick, but he feels he may have to yield soon. A stick would have been handy tonight. He pants as he nears the India Gate complex and walks past the point where cars are stopped by police barricades. The road loops into a circle here, creating three expanses of green grass, which have evolved into family parks. It is almost nine but they are swarming with people – fathers, mothers and children, women in sarees and salvaar-kameez, peanut-sellers, hawkers of toys, balloons and Kwality ice-cream. That is cheap organdie, thinks Sohan Lal, and that is georgette. That is satin, not silk. Who wears chiffon in winter? Sohan Lal sighs. When Ramesh has children, he will probably bring them to India Gate on Sunday evenings. He should buy a new car for Ramesh, better than his own Maruti 800. They will tell the driver to park nearby and they will spend Sunday evenings here. Ramesh will sit on the grass with Sushma, watching the lights on India Gate as they share a cone of peanuts, and the children will run around. Little will they realise how fortunate they are to be within a kilometre of Rashtrapati Bhavan and Parliament, to be folded within the very bosom of India, the seat of its power, the nucleus of eighty crore human beings. And they will not know, at least not at that age, that they are the grandchildren of a mere Sohan Lal Agrawal, runaway youth from Bikaner in Rajasthan, chairman of the IPP committee of Chandni Chowk. By the time they are born, he will perhaps be an MLA in the first assembly of the state of Delhi. From Bikaner to India Gate is no mean journey . . .

He reaches the great arch of India Gate, and approaches the Amar Javan Jyoti beneath it. Of the four gas pipes on the platform, one is aflame. Next to it Suleman is partially shaded by the arch. He wears a thick overcoat that hides half of his face. Above its collar his pinpoint eyes flicker with the flame. Sohan Lal notices, as he comes closer, that the eyes dart about, unable to settle. Suleman is tense. There is even a little panic in his manner, even though he is trying to appear cocksure. They stand at opposite ends of the Amar Javan Jyoti, looking down at the flame, each reluctant to acknowledge the other's presence.

Finally, Suleman looks up and sighs. 'The eternal flame of the Indian soldier,' he says, with irony. 'Have you wondered, sethji, how many of these Indian soldiers were Musalmans?'

'The British preferred Pathans, Jats and Sikhs,' says Sohan Lal, drily. 'They were more reliable.'

'Even here you deny our sacrifice.'

Sohan Lal points to the sides of the arch. 'Their names are written all over those walls,' he says. 'Read them for yourself.'

'I know something about this,' counters Suleman. 'Thirteen thousand five hundred and sixteen names because no more would fit. What of the other forty-four thousand who died in the war of the English? Would it surprise you if most of those forty-four thousand were Musalmans? The white man did not trust us after the Mutiny of 'fifty-seven. We paid for our patriotism.'

Sohan Lal shrugs.

'We are still paying,' says Suleman.

Sohan Lal does not reply. He dislikes such banter. Suleman points to the families on the grass. 'I apologise for calling you out to this part of Delhi, sethji. I myself hate this city, this so-called *New* Delhi. This is not Dilli, this is not India, this is Englistan. Look at these people! Poodles of the English sahib. These are the people who should fear me because it is them I shall first destroy.'

'I have no doubt of that,' says Sohan Lal. And I have no doubt, he thinks, that Suleman is exactly the type of opportunistic, uneducated, crass human being that the IPP was created to obstruct.

'These are the people who have oppressed the working classes,' says Suleman.

Borrowed terminology, thinks Sohan Lal. It is all to be blamed on the Communist parties. When upstarts like Suleman begin to speak their dialect, the corruption of Indian politics is complete. As if Marx could be transplanted into Hindu society!

Suleman pulls the overcoat closer round him. 'We have to meet in this foreign land only because too many people recognise me in Chandni Chowk. Even here I prefer to stand in the shadow of India Gate.'

Sohan Lal knows this is mere vanity. Which of these families in red

Maruti cars – Punjabi yuppies, or Puppies as the press calls them – has heard of Suleman? He is a local politician, a rising star in the firmament of Chandni Chowk, but until he becomes an MLA – that will not happen until next year – no one outside Old Delhi will become aware of his existence. This hide and seek is more farce than drama.

Suleman points to the vacant pavilion behind India Gate. 'There shall be a statue of Jai Prakash Narayan under that canopy. Not Gandhi, your goat-milk-drinking Bania!'

'I have no interest in statues,' says Sohan Lal. 'Do you know why I wanted to meet you?'

'I was told it is a matter of great urgency,' Suleman hedges.

'A matter that cannot wait another day,' says Sohan Lal. 'It must follow that this concerns something that will happen tomorrow.'

Suleman nods nervously.

'I happen to know of your involvement in tomorrow's events,' says Sohan Lal, softly.

Suleman considers this challenge. It could mean one of many things. He cannot allow a Bania to lead him on. 'I choose to involve myself in events that benefit my community, not those that bring me personal profit.'

Sohan Lal shakes with rage at the insult. A cipher! A Musalman from nowhere, with no known family or lineage, casting a slur on the proprietor of Jamna Lal Kishori Mal! But he must remain unperturbed. It is not with passion that prosperity is shepherded ever higher through the generations. A shopkeeper has no pride, his father often said. Insults slide off his round shoulders like water off the wings of a duck. He must keep his eyes focused on the sale as did the great Arjun, who saw nothing but the eye of the bird that his arrow would pierce. 'I am here to save you, not myself,' he says.

'Unless you are more specific, sethji, we cannot have a conversation.'

'I can promise to tell no one of Gauhar Muhammad's trip to Ayodhya.'

'Who is Gauhar Muhammad?' asks Suleman.

Sohan Lal sighs. 'I do not know how you found out about the plans for the sixth of December,' he says, 'but it is easy for news to travel when ten thousand people are involved. Everyone knows that a crowd can get out of hand. Everyone knows the police will not fire. But everyone does not know of the one-handed Musalman among the marchers.'

'It is good to see you befriending Musalmans,' says Suleman. 'I still do not know what you are talking about.'

'You will, when Gauhar Muhammad returns from Ayodhya and comes straight to me to claim his twenty thousand rupees.'

Suleman gapes at him. His eyes have lost any composure they may have had. Behind the collar of the overcoat he breathes deeply, discharging furious clouds of fog. 'The mother-fucker!' Suleman mutters, under his breath. 'The sister-fucking bastard!'

'The boy is on the train,' says Sohan Lal. 'There is nothing you can do to stop him.'

'He will not live beyond tomorrow,' says Suleman. 'The bomb will destroy both the masjid and the bomber.'

Sohan Lal frowns. He had not considered this. If the masjid buries the boy, no one can pin this on Suleman . . . But he must not let details defeat him. 'The boy will be arrested before the act,' he lies. 'He will be brought directly to me, after which I will advise him to hold his tongue. Or talk to the police.'

'Who will find him in the crowd?' challenges Suleman.

'He is being followed to Ayodhya.'

'He does not know my name! He has nothing to do with me!'

'But he does. He told me so himself.'

Suleman falls silent. He has fought many battles and knows when he has lost. He also understands that the victor calls the vanquished for a parley for only one reason. 'What do you want, sethji?'

'There is word that you will stand for Matia Mahal next year.'

'In the assembly election? It has not even been notified yet.'

'But it will be,' insists Sohan Lal.

Suleman makes a vague gesture. It is not a good idea to lay out his cards. 'I may stand for Matia Mahal or I may stand for Paharganj. I may not stand at all. My goal is to serve my community, not become an MLA.'

'There is no need for a speech!' says Sohan Lal sharply.

Suleman shrugs to cover up his deep confusion.

'You must move to Ballimaran,' says Sohan Lal.

'But people love me in Matia Mahal! I have spent ten years working there!'

'There are many Musalmans in Ballimaran too. You will still win, if you ensure that the Musalman vote is not divided with Congress and the Communists.'

Suleman is pleased at this tribute to his power over the Musalman

vote. 'Let me tell you, sethji,' he says eagerly, 'no one can defeat me in
the Chandni Chowk area, not even Harilal Gupta. I will win any of
the four assembly segments I choose. In fact, if I stood for Lok Sabha
elections I would defeat Naresh Agrawal himself.'

Sohan Lal ignores this. 'You will stand for Ballimaran in the
assembly election,' he repeats.

'But why do you want me to vacate Matia Mahal? It is more than
seventy per cent Musalman. They would rather vote for a dog than for
a Hindu IPP candidate.'

'In that case, ensure that not even a dog stands against me,' says
Sohan Lal, drily.

'You! You will stand for Matia Mahal? Why?'

Sohan Lal does not reply but he can sense, from the smirk that
replaces bafflement on Suleman's face, that he has guessed. 'Lala
Surajmal was a prescient man,' says Suleman.

'I want to represent the people of Matia Mahal,' says Sohan Lal. He
quickly looks away, unable to meet Suleman's eyes. The man is a
poisonous snake. Let him make what he will of this.

'I cannot promise,' says Suleman.

'You must,' insists Sohan Lal.

'Why would you trust the word of a Musalman?' taunts Suleman.

'You are not a foolish man, I hope. If Gauhar Muhammad were to
talk, where would that leave you? Even if you are able to stay out of
jail, no Musalman will vote for you.'

'You ask too much.'

'We can meet again,' says Sohan Lal. 'I will bring the boy with me.'

'All right.'

Sohan Lal inhales a deep breath of victory. The man is not
unreasonable. He knows when to retreat. It is a quality that will
take him far. 'Come to Kucha Bansilal some day,' he offers. 'I have a
new stock of silk sarees.'

'I am not married,' says Suleman.

'For your sister, then.'

'I have no sisters.'

'Surely you have a mother?'

'I do not like coming into these kuchas and katras,' says Suleman.
'They remind me of the Musalman havelis they once were – soaring,
gigantic havelis, now partitioned into shameful little cubicles to
accommodate shops like yours.'

'But my kucha has no old havelis,' smiles Sohan Lal. 'Kucha

Bansilal was built merely forty years ago, after Partition, by refugees from Punjab.'

'Ah,' says Suleman. He is reminded of his alliance with Sohan Lal in the Heritage Council. This explains the seth's curious position on that property-tax exemption bill. What they say is true: when a Bania appears altruistic, he has found profit in his altruism. 'I may come,' he says grudgingly.

'So it is settled, then,' says Sohan Lal. He is pleased with the outcome – a tangled matter resolved amicably. Suleman, in Ballimar-an, will become Kartar Singh's headache. Surely the ashes of Surajmal cannot reach out from the waves of the Ganga and foil this! But there is still a loose end to be tied up. Suleman is not a forgiving man. 'One more thing,' says Sohan Lal.

'What now?' Suleman says irritably. 'Do you want me to disappear from Chandni Chowk?'

'That boy, Gauhar Muhammad.'

'I have told you I do not know him!'

'Nothing must happen to him after he returns to Dilli.'

Suleman smiles. 'Why are you so concerned about a Musalman? He is a Bangladeshi, the kind your party is determined to expel from India.'

'Give me your word.'

'You hold my word in great regard,' says Suleman. 'You have it.'

'You should also know that he will prepare a sworn statement as soon as he arrives, in front of a witness. It will remain safely with me. For ever, I hope.'

Suleman shrugs and turns to go.

'You need not have sent the boy at all, you know,' says Sohan Lal.

Suleman stops. 'Babri Masjid . . .'

'The structure,' corrects Sohan Lal. 'A Hindu army can be very dangerous, even without the aid of a one-handed Musalman. Who knows what will happen tomorrow?' He turns and walks away, his mind busily preparing for the night ahead. He will now place telephone calls to IPP officers in Faizabad, Ayodhya, perhaps even to the Uttar Pradesh police . . . He cannot tell them much, of course, and they are unlikely to pay heed unless he does, because they are preparing for the army that is already converging on Ayodhya. Yet the boy will be found, he will be arrested, he *must* be brought back to Kucha Bansilal for a sworn statement.

Once that statement is under lock and key, thinks Sohan Lal, he will honestly mourn Surajmal's death. He will shed a tear and light a joss-stick in the Hanuman temple.

He walks down Rajpath toward his car. Rashtrapati Bhavan flings its lustrous dome high into the night sky. He takes bigger strides. The walk will do him good.

16:

'Give some more panditji to me!' says Gauhar to Mussabir.

Mussabir pulls another ganja-soaked cake from his pocket and stuffs it into Gauhar's open mouth.

'*Jai Shri* Raam!' yells Gauhar, through a full mouth.

The crowd takes up the cry and it skips along. A sea of saffron marches down the lanes of Ayodhya. There are saffron towels, shawls and turbans with 'Raam Raam Raam' printed on them in red letters, saffron scarves, saffron bandannas, saffron dhotis, saffron banners and placards. There is a profusion of tridents, spears and sticks, sandalwood paste and Holi colours. No one knows who is leading the crowd, but everyone seems to know the general direction.

'Look at this, ustad,' says Gauhar. 'This is the greatest army of Raam ever assembled. This is the best the Hindus can do!'

Mussabir stuffs more cakes of panditji into his mouth and laughs. Someone at the front raises a trident and yells, '*Kasam* Raam *kii khaate hain mandir vahii banaayenge*!'

'Do you hear that, ustad?' laughs Gauhar. 'We swear on Raam's head that we will build the temple on that very spot! Let us swear! Let us swear, all sister-fucking kafirs . . .'

'Keep your mouth shut!' whispers Mussabir. Then he raises his trident and cries, '*Jai Shri* Raam!'

'You are a regular pandit, ustad,' says Gauhar, admiringly. 'Give some more panditji to me.'

'You have had too much,' laughs Mussabir.

Gauhar is dressed in a saffron kurta and pyjama, thoughtfully placed by Ibrahim in the sack. Mussabir still wears the shirt and trousers he brought from Delhi. Their shoulders are covered with large saffron shawls emblazoned with 'Raam Raam Raam'. Their faces are clean-shaven, and they have been to a temple in the morning where a pujari smeared their foreheads with sandalwood paste.

'Do not vomit when we get there,' cautions Gauhar.

'That Muhammad Ghayas is a magician,' says Mussabir. 'I am fully cured!'

'Your forehead still looks yellow.'

'That is the sandalwood mark the pujari gave me. A Hindu is always yellow.'

'Has the bleeding in your leg stopped?'

'On its own! I will swear to Muhammad Ghayas that I did not try to stop it. I will write a letter for him saying he cured me of the vomiting disease. Perhaps he will frame it and put it in his clinic, as he did for those white people. With my photograph!'

'But you will look like a Hindu in it,' taunts Gauhar.

'I will grow my beard as soon as we get back to Dilli.'

'You should also have shaved your head,' jokes Gauhar. 'With a bald head, you will become a regular pandit!'

'Raam Lalla is listening to everything you say, you sister-fucking Musalman,' returns Mussabir.

'Bastard mulla!'

'Mother-fucking son of Babur!'

They subside into laughter, drowned by the cries of the crowd. The lanes are becoming narrow as they come closer to the Babri Masjid complex. Gauhar carries the heavy sack hidden under his shawl, tied tightly to his chest and steadied by his hand. They have shared the burden most of the way. One carries the trident, the other carries the sack. The trident helps clear their way to the front of the crowd.

'The armies of Raam Lalla are watching us,' says Gauhar, pointing up.

On either side of the lane, the rooftops are choking with people, who shout encouragement, and sometimes taunt the procession as if they are watching a cricket match. Khaki-clad policemen are interspersed with them. Bunting has been strung across the lane – saffron flags, posters of the chief minister, the national leaders of the IPP, the Vishwa Hindu Parishad and pictures of Raam in majestic stance with Sita standing at his side and Hanuman kneeling in sublime devotion. Policemen line the lanes along the way, watching the crowd and evidently awaiting orders. A van with loudspeakers exhorts the crowd to remain calm.

The army finally arrives at the police barricades that cordon off the area. The sea of saffron buffets the iron levee. Small breaks are created here and there and closed off quickly by the police. Gauhar and Mussabir push through until they are pressed against the barricade.

'Who is that man?' asks Gauhar.

In the centre of the crowd, behind them, there is a white jeep. On its roof stands an elderly man. His forehead is smeared with sandalwood paste, his kurta is of white silk, his dhoti is a dazzling white, and he wears a saffron bandanna on his head. He is making a speech but at first his words are lost in the roar of the crowd. He seems to be telling them to take positions in different lanes that converge on the masjid. Gradually, they fall silent, and his words can be heard.

'Twenty men from every town in India!' he screams. 'Twenty men from every corner of our great Bharat have come to Ayodhya! If two hundred march, you can stop them with barricades. If a thousand march, you can block their path with police. Five thousand can be scattered with tear gas, ten thousand with live bullets. But fifty thousand cannot be stopped by any force in India, and seventy crore Hindus cannot be stopped by Allah himself!'

'*Jai Shri* Raam!' roars Gauhar.

The crowd responds.

Gauhar looks up at the rooftops and sees hundreds of pink identity badges, with cameras and microphones pointing down. 'Look at those birds staring at us,' he says to Mussabir. 'We will be in a film after all!'

'This is bigger than Didi's film. It will be shown all over the world!'

'Shout! Do something so you will be in the film!'

Mussabir raises the trident and yells at the top of his voice. Then there is an ominous silence. Policemen behind the barricades have taken firing positions and pointed their guns at the crowd.

'They are going to fire!' whispers Mussabir.

'Stand still!' says Gauhar. 'Duck if they shoot!'

'But we are right at the front!'

'They will not fire, they will not fire!' chants Gauhar.

He looks up again at the rooftops. The pink badges and cameras have been pushed back and the roofs are now full of policemen with guns, pointed straight at the street below. This is not what Yellow Teeth told him. 'We are going to be killed,' he says calmly, 'and there will be no one to make a film of it.'

'Suleman Mian is a bastard!' screams Mussabir.

'He is not a Musalman, to send another Musalman to death,' says Gauhar.

They are pressed against the barricades. The barrels of police guns look directly into their faces. Gauhar brings up his left hand and looks at his wristwatch. It is ten o'clock. He tells Mussabir that they should pray before the bullets fly. Mussabir breathes heavily, looking straight at the barrels pointed in his face. 'Allah will protect me!' he whispers.

He pulls out a stone from his trouser pocket and hurls it with full force at the line of policemen. It hits a helmet and bounces off. Suddenly a shower of stones descends on the police line. Gun barrels are lowered and riot shields raised. The crowd moves another inch, and it appears the barricades are about to yield. A man in a saffron headband confronts Mussabir and asks him to stop throwing stones. Mussabir knocks him down with a thrust of his trident. 'Let's go!' he screams.

They push their way through the crowd, sideways, toward a tree near the barricade. As they approach, a flood of pink identity badges descends from the rooftops.

'White people!' roars Gauhar.

'Fuck them all!'

Mussabir grabs a camera and smashes it to the ground. The swarm of cameras is scattered in all directions. 'Hit anyone who stands in the way,' says Mussabir, as he leads Gauhar toward the tree. He clambers up the branches and jumps off on the other side of the barricade, shedding gouts of blood from the reopened wounds in his legs. With both hands, he lifts a steel fence and lets Gauhar inside. They run frantically into the compound, Mussabir still carrying the fence and Gauhar lumbering behind with the heavy sack tied to his body.

'*Jai Shri* Raam!' yells Mussabir.

'Run faster!' pants Gauhar. 'If you stop now they will shoot you!'

Hundreds of bodies rush to fill the breach in the dam. Others crash against the barricades and turn them over, then tear through police lines, scattering the guns. Mussabir and Gauhar charge through the compound, ahead of the wave. Mussabir places the metal fence against the masjid wall and, using it as a ladder, climbs the right dome. Standing atop it, he raises both arms and screams a challenge to the sky: '*Jai Shri* Raam!'

Someone tosses him a pickaxe. Mussabir begins to hack at the bricks in the dome, sending flecks of plaster flying into the air.

Gauhar stands at the base. 'Come back, ustad! We have not come here to peck at domes!'

Mussabir stumbles down the ladder in a ganja-induced stupor, slips, falls to the ground and laughs. 'Muhammad Ghayas will now have to fix my broken leg.'

Gauhar drags Mussabir away, and dozens of men rush up the ladder to the domes with ropes, pulleys, hammers and axes. 'Come with me, ustad. We must go under the main dome.'

Mussabir opens his eyes, staggers to his feet and watches the men rushing past him. 'I want a hammer too.'

'We have no time for that.'

'I want a hammer!' insists Mussabir.

They follow the crowd to an arsenal inside the complex, where two volunteers hand out axes, ropes and hammers. Gauhar grabs an axe, Mussabir a hammer, and they run back to the masjid. They enter through the central archway. Framed photographs of Raam, Lakshman and Sita are placed in a makeshift shrine in the courtyard. Mussabir wants to urinate on the photographs, but Gauhar urges him on because an army of men is pushing behind them. They stand in a recess and watch three men take away the photographs.

'They are removing the kafir gods!' says Gauhar triumphantly. 'The masjid is now clean!' He strikes the door with the axe, and hacks frantically until it is in pieces. He drags Mussabir through it and wedges the wood back into place as best as he can. Behind them, the roar of ten thousand people grows louder. Mussabir collapses under the main dome. A spray of vomit issues from his mouth, and a yellow stream flows down his trousers.

'You are pissing!' laughs Gauhar. Then he sees that Mussabir's eyes are yellow and expressionless. 'I will kill Muhammad Ghayas when I get back,' he mutters.

He pulls Mussabir away from the pools of vomit and urine, then takes off his own saffron shawl, unties the sack and pulls out the box inside it. It is very heavy. He drags it to the wall with his hand and tries to push it into a corner, but is unable to manoeuvre it. Outside the walls, he can hear announcements from loudspeakers, exhorting the men to use all their strength. 'Another push and the masjid will collapse! This is our answer to Jinnah! This is our answer to Babur! This is our answer to Pakistan!'

They will never bring it down with pulleys and axes, thinks Gauhar.

'This is Shiv Kumari from Meerut!' screams someone, over a loudspeaker. 'The first woman to climb the right dome! And here are Sharad and Ram Kothari! Their sons were killed by the police two years ago when they tried to march on Babri Masjid! Look at them! They have tears in their eyes! Their sons' murders have been avenged!'

Gauhar pulls out the wires and tries to splice them by holding one end pressed under his elbow. It slips out when he needs to twist it against the other end. Then he holds one end in his mouth and tries to thread the other but the wires are too short, requiring him to bend over so he cannot see what he is doing. He runs back to Mussabir and shakes him violently. 'Wake up, ustad! You need to splice the wires!'

Mussabir laughs hysterically but does not move. The fog of ganja descends on Gauhar's eyes, so Mussabir's laugh appears to echo through the chamber. It rises to the high dome and comes back in cascading trills. 'Fuck you!' laughs Gauhar. 'Fuck Suleman Mian!'

He lies down beside Mussabir. The sounds of hammering, the cries of triumph and the exhortations of the microphone all fall silent as he drifts into sleep.

He wakes up to the sound of a great crash. The main dome rises high above him. To its right, the sun streams through a gaping hole where he can see the sky, heads, tridents and hammers. They have brought down the right dome!

'*Jai Shri* Raam!'

Gauhar sits up in panic and looks at his watch. It is almost three in the afternoon. The left dome shudders under the hammers, ready to cave in at any moment. It is a marvel that none of the men has entered the area below the main dome. Gauhar kicks wildly at Mussabir.

'Get up, Mussabir Ustad!'

Mussabir opens his eyes, stares blankly at Gauhar and laughs. 'Muhammad Ghayas has cured me,' he says.

'Do you want your thousand rupees?' demands Gauhar.

'Yes!'

'Get up, then, and help me wedge the box into this corner.'

Mussabir reluctantly walks to the corner and struggles with the box. The left dome thunders to the floor, adding a stream of light from the left to the one on the right.

'Now we are in the open,' says Gauhar. 'Hurry up! Splice the wires!'

But Mussabir is clumsy with the box. His hands are stiff with the after-effects of ganja. Gauhar can hear sounds outside the main door. He slings the axe over his shoulder. 'I will kill anyone who tries to enter,' he says.

He runs to the shattered door and takes up a position just behind it. Mussabir mutters that the box is wedged as tightly as it can be.

'Stick the battery with Plasticine,' commands Gauhar.

The loudspeakers outside are urging people to block highways that lead into Ayodhya. 'They have sent the great Indian Army against us! Let us show this army what fifty thousand Hindus can do!'

'Hurry up!' shouts Gauhar. 'Once they block the highways we will not be able to get away!'

He hears a sound beyond the door and swings the axe. The door, held in fragile balance, falls apart. A man lies in a pool of blood on the other side. Gauhar steps through the opening and hacks wildly. This is for being a kafir, you sister-fucker! This is for bringing down the right dome! This is for bringing down the left dome!

'I have stuck the battery,' calls Mussabir. 'There is no more Plasticine.'

'Splice the wires,' calls Gauhar. He looks at his watch. The army will be here soon, and then all exit routes will be closed. 'Are your hands made of wood?' he taunts.

'The wires are too thick,' complains Mussabir.

The hammering on the main dome is louder. There must be a hundred people up there, thinks Gauhar, and they still cannot bring it down! Mother-fucking kafirs! But what is taking Ustad so long? Ibrahim Mian was right. He has brought a corpse with him, not a human being. And whose idea was it to buy those cakes of panditji? He could not resist them, but now Suleman Mian will back out of the ten thousand when they go back to Dilli and the main dome still stands in all the newspaper photos.

'I think the wires are spliced,' says Mussabir from inside.

'Flick the switch,' says Gauhar, trembling.

Mussabir comes running through the opening in the wall and crashes into Gauhar.

'What is the hurry?' laughs Gauhar. 'We have one full minute to get out.'

They run out of the masjid but Gauhar suddenly remembers. 'Did you throw the safety lever?'

'What is that?'

'Mother-fucking fool!'

'Go and throw it yourself.'

'It needs two hands,' says Gauhar. 'Go back and pull hard! It is almost five, and we need to get out!'

Mussabir runs back into the masjid. Gauhar watches the horde on the main dome, hacking like maniacs, smashing giant jackhammers against the bricks with pulleys and ropes. The plaster has come off most of the dome. Wide cracks are visible in its surface.

'Hurry up, ustad!' screams Gauhar.

Three men with tridents descend on him, trying to pass through the shattered door of the masjid. He brushes them off and raises the axe to bring it down on the man closest to him.

A great shudder lifts Gauhar and the three men off their feet and flings them to the ground. The main dome collapses in an earthquake that sends dust and debris high into the air, and brings down with it the dozens of men who had climbed on to it. Plaster rains on Gauhar, who rolls on to his side and drags himself away from the debris — wood, bricks, hinges, brackets, stones, dust, sand, all the detritus of a four-hundred-year-old building. The region where the dome stood is a thick cloud of dust. Somewhere in that cloud is Mussabir Hussein.

'Ustad!' screams Gauhar. 'Ustad!'

A cry of triumph goes up from the ten thousand people in the compound.

'*Jai Shri* Raam!'

Gauhar hears the cry very faintly. The crash has punctured his eardrums. He crawls toward the cloud of dust, aware that hundreds of cameramen are running greedily through the compound, drinking the dust-laden air. Feet scamper past as he inches closer to the mountain of plaster. He sees a leg, an arm, an entire body, but none looks like Mussabir. He props himself up against a fallen soapstone pillar. Far away, behind the haze of dust, he can see rows of police officers on rooftops, their caps silhouetted against the evening sky. What are they waiting for? Can they not come and extricate Ustad from this rubble? He will not be able to breathe in the dust!

He turns back to watch the mountain behind him. People in saffron bandannas dance on the rubble, throwing their tridents into the air, mashing the bodies that have come down with the dome. They seem to dance silently, and their movements are slow and smooth. They jump in wide arcs, land softly, then jump again. He wants to tell them to be careful because Ustad lies buried somewhere beneath them. He imagines that the dome is still sinking, in slow motion, every time they stomp upon it, and that it will soon be level ground. He turns back to rest against the fallen pillar, pulls his 'Raam Raam' shawl round him and waits. Ustad is here somewhere. Mother-fucking ustad! He will come round soon, taking bets for his pigeon fight and bringing him clients for seventy rupees.

1996

F

How do I describe your love when I am not overwhelmed by it?
How do I speak of your tenderness when I cannot touch your heart?
How do I mourn our separation when we have not had a tryst?
How do I complain of your cruelty when I still yearn for it?

The radio perches on Gopal's counter and Pushpa Rani sings blithely, mellifluous voice dancing down Kucha Bansilal, punctuated by the swishing sound of Chotu's broom. Gopal and Ibrahim squat behind the counter on high stools and finish their first cup of tea. Ibrahim chomps unsuccessfully on a biscuit. Drops of tea cling to his straggly beard.

'You drool like an old man, Ibrahim Mian.'

Ibrahim grins, displaying the remains of his yellow-black teeth. 'Look at yourself,' he replies. 'You have a missing tooth. And the hairs on your head can be counted on one hand.'

'I counted them,' retorts Gopal, 'and my head has more hairs than your chin.'

Ibrahim strokes his straggly beard. 'How could you count through your foggy spectacles?'

'Even a blind man can see you are withering away.'

'I am a poor man,' says Ibrahim, mournfully, 'but you are beginning to look like a seth.' He prods Gopal's heaving belly, contained with difficulty by his checked shirt. 'How does a man like you grow a paunch like that? You have no wife to stuff you with ghee, no son to earn money for you, no servant to bring your tiffin, no daughter-in-law to fan you while you eat.'

'It is the chai,' says Gopal, solemnly.

'Your chai does nothing for me,' sighs Ibrahim.

He rinses his tumbler and stows it in the junction box. Gopal washes his cup and replaces it in the rack. Ibrahim readies pen and paper and waits, pen poised, for Gopal to begin.

'Six benches,' says Gopal.

Ibrahim writes.

'Eight stools, three stoves, fifteen cans,' says Gopal.

Ibrahim transfers them to his list.

'Do I also call out sugar and tea?' Gopal asks.

'Of course! Everything is part of the stall.'

'Ten kilograms of sugar, seven kilograms of tea, five hundred grams of cardamom, a packet of cloves, two hundred and fifty grams of ginger, six packets of milk.'

'Bicycle?' asks Ibrahim.

'One bicycle, one radio, three mirrors, twenty-four packets of biscuits, ten yards of jute sacking, six yards of tarpaulin.'

'You are a rich man,' says Ibrahim, admiringly.

The image of four cloth belts buried under asafoetida tins flashes in Gopal's mind. He is a rich man indeed! He shudders and dismisses the thought. Those four white snakes took his son from him . . . He points to the wooden banner that runs across the front. 'One signboard. Mukesh Tea House.'

Ibrahim adds the banner to the list and says, 'Now that you are rich, you should get new spectacles.'

'What is wrong with my spectacles?' Gopal demands. 'They show me what I need to see.'

'When a man has money,' says Ibrahim, 'he buys things he does not need.'

'Where will I get money?' asks Gopal, nervously. He points to the stools and biscuit jars. 'This is from selling chai. Seths in Chandni Chowk drink a lot of tea.'

Ibrahim asks, 'What about the junction box?'

'It belongs to the Corporation.'

'They do not even know it exists!' scoffs Ibrahim. 'It is yours now.' He adds the junction box to the inventory, then points to the wooden planks that bridge the drain straddled by the stall. 'How many boards do you have underneath?'

'Seven.'

Ibrahim writes that down. 'One television,' he continues. 'Black and white.'

'I do not have a television,' protests Gopal.

'You will have one before the festival. It is still two months away.'

'Where will I get the money?'

'They will give you money to paint your stall. Buy a television with it.'

'What if they find out the junction box is not mine?'

Ibrahim folds the inventory list and looks impatiently at Gopal. 'This is the Moonlight Festival, not an Independence Day parade! You have to list everything possible or they will not include your stall in the festival.'

'Will they also include your shoe store? Did you not say it is a hundred years old?'

'Ballimaran is too crowded,' sighs Ibrahim. 'Too many rickshas. The lanes are narrow. No one will go there for a festival.'

'Kucha Bansilal is narrow too,' says Gopal.

'Sharief Mirza is an old man,' says Ibrahim. 'He does not even have a son to take over the shoe store when he dies. He is not connected to important people as you are.'

Gopal is pleased. He glances across the lane at Jamna Lal Kishori Mal. Chotu has finished sweeping. The boards that hide the manne-quins have been removed, joss-sticks have been lit in the alcove of Lakshmi, the computer has been started, and Ramesh Babu sits behind his Sunmica counter, staring aimlessly down the kucha, looking back when the computer beeps.

'Did you get a letter from Sohan Lalji?' asks Ibrahim.

Gopal produces a plastic-wrapped document from under the coun-ter. Ibrahim holds it up to read it, and is instantly annoyed. 'Why is it in Hindi?' he demands, as he hands it back.

Gopal is at a loss. It had not occurred to him to specify a language.

'Such letters should always be in English,' says Ibrahim.

'Perhaps sethji cannot write in English,' suggests Gopal.

'He has a son! Or he could have asked someone.'

Gopal fidgets uncomfortably with the document. Ibrahim snatches it from him. 'I do not like reading anything that is not in Urdu,' he grumbles. He reads the document anyway, murmuring so softly that Gopal has to lean closer to hear him.

' "Sohan Lal Agrawal, MLA, Matia Mahal. I have known Gopal Pandey for more than twenty years. He is a man of good character, and I will support the inclusion of his stall in the Moonlight Festival." ' Ibrahim shakes his head. 'He should have mentioned that the stall is very old, or they will not accept your application. Ask him to rewrite it.'

Gopal makes a gesture of helplessness and points across the lane. 'Sethji is not here. He rarely comes to Kucha Bansilal.'

Ibrahim puts away the letter and they sit silently, dejected.

'He did not even mention Mukesh,' muses Gopal.

'Why would he do that?' Ibrahim asks contemptuously. 'It is he who murdered Mukesh.'

'I should get another letter for Mukesh Minar,' suggests Gopal. 'It should be shown in the Moonlight Festival.'

'It is just an electricity pole,' says Ibrahim.

'Mukesh is a martyr! He is part of Chandni Chowk!'

'No one puts pictures on that pole any more,' says Ibrahim, with finality.

Gopal falls silent. Perhaps he should dissuade Ibrahim Mian from the entire plan. Stalls included in the festival will be repainted, Ibrahim Mian has told him. They will be visited by newspeople, they will have pictures published in magazines and they can charge three rupees for a cup of chai! But without a proper letter from Sohan Lalji, who will consider his stall a heritage site? What if they laugh in his face and ask him to shut down the stall during the festival?

'This festival is for rich seths,' he suggests. 'It is not for us.'

'Suleman Mian supports it,' says Ibrahim, wistfully. 'But he does not support the involvement of IPP seths. Why should they celebrate Musalman heritage? Why should Harilal Gupta call himself chairman of the festival committee?'

'He is the MLA for Chandni Chowk,' points out Gopal.

'He is the MLA for traders and seths,' says Ibrahim. 'And to say that the festival is in memory of Lala Surajmal! Where was Surajmal when Shah Jahan built Red Fort?'

'They will not include my stall when they have Red Fort,' says Gopal. 'My father came to Dilli in 'forty-seven, less than fifty years ago.'

'Never say that to anyone!' scolds Ibrahim.

'But I told the madam,' says Gopal.

'That was years ago.'

'She printed it in the newspapers.'

'I warned you not to tell her anything. You cannot trust these newspaper people. Now everyone in America knows that your father came to Dilli in 'forty-seven. Who will believe you are a Dillivala?'

'Maybe I should not apply for the festival,' suggests Gopal.

'Those were English newspapers,' says Ibrahim, soothingly. 'Who reads English newspapers in Chandni Chowk? You are a pure Dillivala.'

'But I was born in Sasaria.'

'Who said so?' challenges Ibrahim.

'That is what my father told me.'

'You have a poor memory,' says Ibrahim. 'How could you be born in Sasaria when your father himself was born in Chandni Chowk? It was your grandfather who came to Dilli.'

Gopal searches his mind to exhume memories of his grandfather, and fails. 'Where did he come from?' he asks.

'Sasaria, perhaps. No one is ever certain where his grandfather came from.'

Gopal nods, uncertain how Ibrahim knows this but relieved that he does.

'Your grandfather was active in the freedom movement,' continues Ibrahim. 'He went to jail for the Congress Party. He once met Nehruji, touched Gandhiji's feet, and was at Birla House when Gandhiji was shot. He was murdered by RSS hoodlums a few days after they killed Gandhiji.'

'What is RSS?' asks Gopal.

'Hindu murderers. Friends of IPP. They hate secular leaders like your father.'

'My father never told me this,' protests Gopal.

'He did not want you to know, but it runs in your blood. That is why you are a supporter of secular parties.'

Gopal nods gently.

'And that is why IPP murdered your son,' says Ibrahim.

'I saw Mukesh die!' protests Gopal.

'What can you see with those spectacles?' taunts Ibrahim. 'I saw IPP men set fire to him with a cigarette lighter.'

'All my sons die,' mourns Gopal. 'Even Gauhar.'

'At least he was Bangladeshi,' Ibrahim says, in consolation.

Gopal has never understood why Gauhar went to Ayodhya and did not come back.

Sohan Lalji, too, asked after Gauhar. 'Where is the boy?' he asked one morning. 'I need a good man like him to bring in customers.'

'He is dead,' Ibrahim Mian told Gopal, without explanation. 'What an irresponsible boy to die when he had a seth waiting to take him back!'

For two years Gopal left the stall unlocked at night, hoping that he would find Gauhar curled up when he opened it in the morning. What he found instead were three magazines he had not noticed before. What horrible images! Naked women with yellow hair and paper-white skin, in poses Gopal had never imagined. Why would a good one-handed boy bring those magazines to the stall, and where had he found them? Perhaps he was ashamed of them, and that was why he had not come back. In any case, the stall is now too large to be left unlocked. There are benches and stools and cushions, which can be stolen. He cannot leave everything to the mercy of thieves. If Gauhar were to return, he would not know where to sleep.

'That boy was a snake,' says Ibrahim.

'How can you say so?' demands Gopal. 'You were the one who found him for me.'

'A man comes to regret his kindness. But you should be glad he is gone. How would you include your stall in the festival with a Bangladeshi man sleeping in it? It must be an Indian jalebi stall, not a Bangladeshi one!'

'Jalebi stall?' wonders Gopal.

'Your father was given a jalebi recipe by Nawab Tahir Hussein Sahib. His was the most famous jalebi stall in Chandni Chowk.'

'I remember a chai stall,' says Gopal. 'And my father never mentioned a Musalman nawab.'

'How can a jalebi shop in Chandni Chowk start without a Musalman?' Ibrahim asks rhetorically. 'The jalebi mix was a secret – a recipe known only to Nawab Tahir Hussein before he told your father.'

'But I do not know the recipe—' begins Gopal.

Ibrahim covers his ears with his hands. 'Do not tell me!'

'But I do not remember my father ever mentioning a jalebi stall.'

Ibrahim turns on him angrily. 'Do you want a certificate for the festival or not?'

Gopal does not reply. Ibrahim stands up, letter in hand. 'Let us go and submit your application,' he urges. 'The sooner we do it, the sooner they will give you money to paint the stall.'

Reluctantly Gopal pulls in his stools, boards up the counter and locks it, then follows Ibrahim into Chandni Chowk. They walk briskly to Town Hall. On the way, Gopal suggests that Ibrahim's recollection of his grandfather's exploits may be inaccurate. Perhaps Ibrahim is confusing Gopal's grandfather with someone else.

'No one knows anything about his father or grandfather,' Ibrahim assures him. 'What you remember is what you know.'

In the corridors of Town Hall, they find a queue that doubles up on itself and continues for half a kilometre. Everyone who sells anything in Chandni Chowk seems to be in line for a certificate – paratha stalls in Paratha Gali, bookstores in Nai Sarak, shoe stores in Ballimaran, garment stores in Maliwara, paper godowns in Chawri Bajar and spice shops in Khari Baoli. Ibrahim chuckles. 'They do not have letters like you,' he consoles Gopal.

But Gopal can see their letters rolled carefully in their hands. His own does not appear so exclusive any more. 'How could they each know an MLA?' wonders Gopal. 'There are only four in the Chandni Chowk area.'

Ibrahim curses. 'There are four MLAs, eight councillors and hundreds of seths on the festival committee.' He challenges the man ahead of them in the line – a milkman from Dudhiya Gali – and finds that he has a letter from Naresh Agrawal himself.

'Your MLA letter cannot compete with his MP letter,' he confides in Gopal.

'How many people have MP letters?'

Ibrahim does not know.

'We should go back,' suggests Gopal.

Ibrahim's eyes are on a man who walks casually down the line, looking furtively at the letters in people's hands. He stops at Gopal and scrutinises his plastic-wrapped testimonial.

'MLA letter?' he asks.

'Yes!' says Gopal eagerly.

'The MLA letter line is inside.'

Gopal hesitates, but Ibrahim takes his hand and they follow the man inside a room, where another sits behind a desk.

'Two hundred rupees,' says the second man.

Gopal turns to Ibrahim for help. 'It is a fee for the certificate,' explains Ibrahim.

'Why is it two hundred rupees?' demands Gopal.

'You will earn much more when rich people come to your stall in the festival.'

Gopal, seeing that Ibrahim makes no protest, loosens a knot in his dhoti and pulls out his bundle of notes.

As they leave Town Hall, Gopal hands his certificate to Ibrahim. 'This is in Hindi too,' says Ibrahim sullenly.

'When will I get money to paint the stall?'

'You have to apply for it in four weeks.'

They walk back to Kucha Bansilal, Gopal forlorn and Ibrahim contented. 'They should display me in the festival,' chuckles Ibrahim. 'I am the heritage of Chandni Chowk!'

'I thought your father came from Bihar?' asks Gopal.

'What Bihar?' Ibrahim snorts. 'My ancestors have always lived in Ballimaran. My great-grandfather was a silver-beater for a seth. So were my grandfather and my father. I decided to work in Sharief

Mirza's shoe store only because I cannot beat silver. The hammers are too heavy for my hands.'

'Will you help me paste the certificate in the stall?' asks Gopal.

'I am only a poor clerk, Gopal Bhai, not a seth like you,' says Ibrahim. 'If I do not go back to the store right away, Sharief Mirza will throw me out.'

2:

Gauhar throws the next pellet on to a new sheet of paper and hits it hard with a sledgehammer. The pellet flies sideways and lands in the far corner of the room, lost.

'Sister-fucker,' grumbles Faquira.

Gauhar crawls to the corner, presses his palm to the floor and moves it in ever-widening circles until he finds the pellet. He sweeps it up and puts it back on the paper. This time, the sledgehammer catches the ball of silver on its head, flattening it brutally against the sheet. Now that the initial spherical shape is lost, the next twenty blows are easy. Each *thukk*! increases the radius of the circle. The pool of silver expands until it is as thin as the sheet of paper it sleeps on. The varq is ready. Gauhar slides the sheet out of reach, where Alimuddin cuts it into two – silver foil and paper together – scoops it up and stacks it on other foils in the box.

Faquira begins to tell his story for the day. He is full of anecdotes, some true and some not. Gauhar and Alimuddin are in the habit of listening with feigned enthusiasm, both because it passes time and because the Musalman who owns the silver-beating shop is Faquira's father.

'There was a henpecked silversmith,' says Faquira, 'who went into the forest and found fairies beating wisps of silver in the moonlight, and blowing them like thistle into the night air. He spent the night watching those wisps and, before morning, he had learned the secret of beating silver from the fairies. Then he returned to Chandni Chowk to start his silver business and become a rich man. His silver foils now adorn all sweets – gulabjamuns, barfi, kalakand – and fruits like loquat, pomegranate and mangoes, turning humble fruit into grand fare, served with pride at the weddings of kings, nawabs and seths.'

'What was the secret the silversmith learned?' asks Gauhar.

Faquira smiles and brings down his sledgehammer on a pellet.

'Was the silversmith your ancestor?' asks Gauhar, dutifully.

Faquira, sledgehammering, allows himself a modest nod.

Ah, yes, thinks Gauhar, he will now talk of how his family has beaten silver for fifty generations. That is where all his stories lead to. What secret could the fairies have revealed? What secret, indeed, lies in hammering a pellet into a thin sheet? Squat on your haunches and hit the pellet hard on the head. *Thukk, thukk, thukk . . .* The secret is repetition, the secret is never tiring of the *thukk, thukk, thukk* and discovering in it the silver-beaters' song. He picks up another pellet, positions it on a sheet of paper foil and viciously crushes it.

After three hours, when Faquira is not looking, Gauhar stuffs some varq into his pocket and stands up. Faquira senses a break in the song of the sledgehammer and turns. 'You have three more hours.'

'I will leave early today,' Gauhar says.

Faquira smiles indulgently in the manner of the kind master. 'I have not finished my story.'

'Fuck you!' says Gauhar.

A frown clouds Faquira's brow. 'I will pay you for a half-day,' he says. 'Sweep up all your cuttings before you go.'

'That is Alimuddin's job!' protests Gauhar.

'But you are leaving early,' retorts Faquira.

Angrily Gauhar collects the discarded pieces of silver – left-overs from foils and wasted pellets – and crushes them into new balls, then throws them into the box of pellets. Faquira comes and stands beside the box, places a friendly hand on Gauhar's shoulder and grins. 'Come back this evening,' he says gently.

Gauhar jerks the hand away.

'A hundred rupees,' says Faquira.

'Fuck you!' says Gauhar.

'Someone told me you used to do this,' Faquira says.

'I will crush your skull like silver if you touch me again,' warns Gauhar.

Then he stalks out of the room and into the lanes of Ballimaran. He passes Ghalib Shoe House. Deep inside the store, in the semi-darkness, he can see Ibrahim Mian squatting before the rexine settee, sliding a shoe on to a customer's foot, grinning. Gauhar collects all the paan juice in his mouth and spits. Ibrahim looks up, shoe in hand, then away, pretending not to notice. Gauhar allows a moment to elapse, then moves on. 'Sister-fucker,' he says, under his breath, hoping Ibrahim will hear him yet afraid that he might.

It was Ibrahim Mian who got him this silver-beating job three years ago. 'What will I eat?' he had asked.

'Show me your hands,' said Ibrahim Mian. He had held them out – the hand and the stump. 'One hand, but it is strong,' said Ibrahim Mian. Then he took him to Faquira's father and he got the job.

My one hand saved my life, thinks Gauhar. Two-handed Mussabir is dead while one-handed Gauhar lives. He had planned, as he lay on the ground near Babri Masjid, that he would crawl under the rubble to dig out Mussabir after darkness had fallen and they had all gone. But the crowd stayed all night, removing the rubble, levelling the area and washing it with buckets of water. He lay still, covered with his 'Raam Raam' shawl. By night, under the glare of lights, he saw Hindu idols on a washed mud floor, standing under a saffron tarpaulin held up by bamboos driven into the ground. He crawled away from the compound and ran into the lanes, where every house seemed to be on fire and everyone was running away from something. In panic, he took a bus to Faizabad, then a train to Banaras. At Banaras railway station, as the fog of ganja cleared from his mind, he became aware of his situation. Perhaps the police were after him, and some of the horde he had hacked to death. It was not clear how Suleman Mian would receive him. Sohan Lal might help, but it was not wise to trust a seth. He went into the city and entered a ghat along the river. It was early morning. People were bathing, washing clothes, singing. He descended the stone steps of the ghat, placed a foot in the water and looked down at his reflection in the Ganga. And remembered that he was a Hindu.

He stayed in Banaras for a year, living near the Ganga, trolling the ghats for old women who were too weak to bathe in the river. They came from all over the country, desperate to take one last dip in the Ganga, then die in Banaras. Gauhar, beardless, held their hands and led them down the stone steps, sometimes carrying the ones who were too sick to walk. They paid five rupees, and usually gave him a few rotis. On slow mornings, he sat on the ghat steps and thought of Mussabir Ustad, the ten thousand Suleman Mian owed him, and the twenty thousand promised by the seth in Kucha Bansilal. As winter approached, the stream of old women dried up. He helped one last woman bathe in the Ganga and took a train to Delhi.

It was late in the evening when the train pulled into Old Delhi railway station. He passed Kucha Bansilal, saw the Jamna Lal Kishori Mal sign on the peepul tree, and knew he would not stop there in spite of the twenty thousand, because the word of a seth carried no more weight than the wind. He walked all the way to the haveli behind Jama Masjid, where he had met Suleman Mian, ran up the trembling staircase and knocked on the door. The first knock raised an angry squadron of pigeons that scattered upward with noisy fluttering and startled him. He shrank back into the staircase. He had heard stories of haunted mansions behind Jama Masjid, and anything was possible after that terrible earthquake in Ayodhya.

When the fluttering died down he tiptoed to the door and knocked again. The door opened, and it was Ibrahim Mian. In a flood of relief Gauhar collapsed on to the floor, with the events of the last year, the shuddering masjid, the dancing hordes and Mussabir Hussein in his mind.

'Why did they let you go?' asked Ibrahim Mian.

'Mussabir Ustad!' sobbed Gauhar.

'Who is that?'

'You saw him at the railway station. He was under the dome . . .'

'Which dome?'

'It was he who brought it down! Babri Masjid . . .'

'Why did they let you go?' Ibrahim repeated. 'Or have you run away from jail? Is this some trick by the seth? Has he sent you?'

Gauhar looked up into yellow, opaque eyes, and his heart trembled. He noticed, only now, that Ibrahim Mian had not stepped aside to let him into the room. 'I have come from Banaras.'

Ibrahim Mian appeared to be confused. 'Did they not arrest you in Ayodhya?'

Gauhar shook his head. 'I have been in Banaras. Alone.'

'Why did it take you a year to come back?' asked Ibrahim, irritably. 'Suleman Mian thought they had locked you up. Now I must tell him you ran away.'

'I was afraid . . . Mussabir Ustad was under the dome. He saw the dome fall on him!'

'You should have come back straight away,' said Ibrahim. 'Suleman Mian will be furious when I tell him.'

'Tell him about Mussabir.'

'Did Sohan Lal make you sign anything? A piece of paper, perhaps?'

'I have told you I was in Banaras. I have not seen the seth for a year.'

'Go back to Banaras,' said Ibrahim. 'You are in great danger here.'

'From whom?'

Ibrahim leaned forward conspiratorially. 'Sohan Lal wants to have you arrested. He says you stole twenty thousand rupees from the shop. Had you come back right away, Suleman Mian would have protected you.'

'I am here now!' said Gauhar, fearfully.

Ibrahim sighed and began to shut the door. 'Go.'

Gauhar sobbed and grabbed Ibrahim's knees with his hand. 'I need to see Suleman Mian!'

'He is not here,' said Ibrahim.

Gauhar put his face – his clean-shaven Hindu face – against Ibrahim's pyjama and wept. Something about the gesture, perhaps the mere fact that his tears were wetting the pyjama, caused Ibrahim to soften and put a hand on his head. 'Where is Mussabir?'

'Dead, dead . . .' Gauhar continued to cry.

For a few panic-stricken moments, Gauhar wondered if his imagination had galloped away with him. Was he in the wrong haveli with the wrong man? Had he not come here and met Suleman Mian? Was there not an ustad named Mussabir who had stuck a battery with Plasticine and spliced two wires together, selected for the job because of his two hands? 'Mother-fucking fool,' Gauhar had said, 'go back and pull hard!' So Mussabir had run back into the masjid to throw the lever. 'Hurry up, ustad,' Gauhar had shouted. And then he was thrown to the ground. But had not Ibrahim Mian said there would be a delay of one minute between the flicking of the switch and the explosion? Ah, it was all clear now!

Gauhar stood up, suddenly furious, and thrust a finger at Ibrahim. 'You killed Mussabir Ustad!'

'Killed whom?' asked Ibrahim.

But of course, thought Gauhar, they were both supposed to be inside the masjid when the switch and lever were engaged. 'Do not leave Mussabir alone with the lever,' Ibrahim Mian had said. 'Stand next to him and watch him . . .' Poor two-handed Mussabir! And here stood Yellow Teeth, appearing to grin even when trying to look innocent. A sock in the face would knock out those yellow teeth, strew them all over the haveli, and wipe out that infuriating grin for ever.

'You wanted to kill me.' Gauhar stood over Ibrahim and looked down at him, seeing him shaken by his sudden ferocity.

'It was a mistake,' Ibrahim said. 'Bad bomb . . . But Suleman Mian has forgiven you. It is best I do not tell him that you are back.'

Gauhar blocked the door with a hand. 'And the money?'

'What money?'

'Ten thousand rupees. And five for Mussabir Ustad. To be given after the masjid came down.'

'To be given if you brought down the masjid,' Ibrahim corrected him.

'Well, the masjid is rubble now.'

'It was brought down by Hindu fundamentalists,' said Ibrahim.

'Mussabir flicked the switch!'

'How do you know?' asked Ibrahim. 'You were outside. There were a hundred people on the main dome. How do you know it did not come down by itself?'

'I saw the bomb go off!'

'You saw the dome collapse, that is all. Did you not hear the news on television? Did you not read the newspapers? Was there any mention of a bomb?'

'How do you know those men brought it down?'

'If there was a bomb, why did it take seven hours?' countered Ibrahim.

Gauhar had no answer to this. He decided to come back the next day and meet Suleman Mian himself. Why waste time with Yellow Teeth?

'Go,' said Ibrahim again.

'Where will I go?'

'Anywhere,' said Ibrahim. 'And do not come back.'

'I will go back to Gopal Bhai.'

'No!' said Ibrahim. 'Not Gopal Bhai.'

'Sohan Lalji, then.'

'No, no. Wait!'

Gauhar sensed a sudden strength in his position. Ibrahim's bluster had vanished.

'Yes, Gopal Bhai,' he said. 'And Sohan Lalji will want to see me. After all, he is my sethji. I will tell him where I was.'

'If you go back to Kucha Bansilal again, you will be arrested,' warned Ibrahim. 'Even Suleman Mian cannot help you then.'

'Where shall I sleep?'

'Go back to the school. I will talk to the madam tomorrow.'

Gauhar felt emboldened. 'And the money?'

'I will give you something tomorrow. But remember, never show your face to the seth or Gopal Bhai.'

'Do not forget the money,' warned Gauhar.

He turned to walk away, scattering the pigeons again. This time he was indifferent to them. When he had reached the staircase, Ibrahim called him back. 'You have to be careful what you say about Babri Masjid,' Ibrahim whispered. 'Suleman Mian is a kind man, but he has many friends. No one knows what they can do. And do not worry about Mussabir. He was a corpse anyway.'

Gauhar shivered. He went down the staircase in silence. He had a hold over Ibrahim, for some reason, but he was petrified of being on the wrong side of Suleman Mian. It was a cold night. He walked quietly to the Sparrows building, found an open window and crawled into the main hall. In the morning Shalini Didi found him curled up on the floor. Ibrahim Mian came in the afternoon. She seemed reluctant to keep him, but Ibrahim Mian said something that seemed to satisfy her. Gauhar was relieved. Shalini Didi made him the Baal Bank secretary again. 'You can help with the children,' she said, and she told them that Gauhar had come to give back the love he had received from Sparrows. He shrugged when she said this.

Two days later Ibrahim Mian came again. 'You must stay here for a few years,' he said.

Gauhar had imagined this was to be a temporary stop. And where was the money? After a few days, he went angrily to Ghalib Shoe House to confront Ibrahim Mian. He still remembers how Ibrahim Mian studied his face, and how vulnerable he felt with his clean cheeks. A man without a beard is only a boy. 'There was no bomb,' Ibrahim Mian told him again. 'Suleman Mian does not know you, and you must not go to Gopal Bhai or sethji. It is better for you to stay away from Ghalib Shoe House, Suleman Mian's haveli and Kucha Bansilal. The friends of Suleman Mian are dangerous people. Do you know how many young men disappear from Chandni Chowk every day?' The yellow eyes bored into Gauhar's flesh and made him tremble. 'Besides, money not claimed for a year goes back into the bank,' said Ibrahim Mian.

Gauhar was not certain he understood this, but the spectre of Suleman Mian, raised by Ibrahim, was fresh in his mind. 'How about eight thousand?' he offered.

Ibrahim Mian shook his head.

'Seven? Six?'

'It will have to be withdrawn from the bank,' said Ibrahim. 'But where will you keep it?'

'Baal Bank.'

'Your didi will not allow such a large sum in the cash-box.'

Gauhar pondered this complication.

'Also, there is the problem of identification,' continued Ibrahim Mian. 'The bank will not release the money until you come and identify yourself.'

'I can do that right away!' said Gauhar eagerly.

'I cannot take you. You are a Bangladeshi. They will put you in jail. I will see what can I do about it.'

'What will I eat until then?' Gauhar had asked.

'Show me your hands,' said Ibrahim Mian.

Gauhar presented his arms – the hand and the stump.

'One hand, but it is strong,' said Ibrahim.

Then he took him to Faquira's father and got him the silver-beating job.

It has been three years, and Gauhar does not like the work. It pays fifteen rupees every day. All day long – his tongue stained blood red with paan – Faquira tells his tales of Hatim Tai, Alif Laila, Rustam and Sohrab. These are stories Gauhar has never heard before and does not believe. He tilts his head to the side, pretends to listen and swings the hammer. Fifteen rupees every day – except for the days he has missed through laziness – for three years. He has been careful not to spend much – nahari, chai, a new wristwatch, the cinema, a pair of sunglasses, velcro-strapped sandals and a leather belt with a heart-shaped buckle. He bargains hard when he buys, and he takes good care of these things. It is GB Road that is becoming more and more expensive, and the whores offer less and less. With the condom rule, they are hardly worth the price. Even so, he has at least five hundred rupees stowed in Baal Bank – not much after three years of *thukk, thukk, thukk* but more than anyone else at Sparrows. He knows, because he is the Baal Bank secretary.

He hates Faquira, dislikes Alimuddin, and detests the dark room they sit in every day, but he is safe from Suleman Mian, and the police whom Sohan Lal has set on his trail.

He has spoken to no one about Mussabir. There is no question of going to Sohan Lalji or Gopal Bhai after what Ibrahim Mian said. He could meet Gopal Bhai in secret, but the chaivala cannot keep any-thing to himself, and whatever he tells him is sure to find its way to

everyone in Chandni Chowk. It is best if they think he is dead. In the
beginning, he went a few times to the haveli to plead with Suleman
Mian, but the door never opened to him. He hears Suleman Mian is a
big man now. His Ambassador car has a large red beacon on it and
two jeeps follow him wherever he goes. He hears that Sohan Lalji is a
great leader too. Ramesh Babu sits behind new Sunmica counters, he
has been told, and Sohan Lalji goes around in an Ambassador car with
a flashing beacon, just like Suleman Mian. He once saw Chitra Didi at
Sparrows. He tried to tell her about Mussabir but she seemed not to
listen. The shadow of Suleman Mian hung over her all the time. There
he was, standing beside her, smiling like a snake, his eyes piercing
Gauhar's heart and seeing its deepest secrets, yet refusing to talk to
him. How could he have told Chitra Didi the whole story in Suleman's
presence? When he did whisper a few words to her while Suleman was
looking away, she just smiled indulgently. She almost turned to
Suleman and told him what Gauhar had said! He knew then that
he could never confide in her.

A silver-beater is what Allah has made him, and a silver-beater he
will be when he dies, although the hammering hurts his hand, his back
hurts from the strain of squatting, and his teeth chatter from the thuds
of heavy hammers falling on the foil.

He walks out of Ballimaran and approaches Sparrows. Faquira will
steal half his money today because he has left early. He is surprised at
Faquira's interest in fucking him. He is twenty-two. Mussabir Ustad
was already too hard at eighteen. Or maybe Faquira cannot find
younger boys. Perhaps he will lead Faquira on and squeeze a little
money out of him tomorrow. Today, he will spend his time in
Sparrows watching Shalini Didi. She is much prettier than Chitra
Didi. And at night, when Shalini Didi has locked up and all the
children are asleep, he will go to GB Road. He thrusts his hand into his
pocket and fingers the rolled-up varq he has stolen. He has heard from
Faquira that it is an elixir. A few silver foils drive a man's potency to
infinite heights. He will put it to the test in GB Road tonight. Let us
see if those whores can accommodate a man as vigorous as him! He
passes through the Sparrows kitchen in the lane, then enters the
building. A double glass door separates the kitchen area from the main
building.

Shalini Didi is surprised to see him at this time of day. She says he
should open Baal Bank now that he is here. He walks into the
corridor, unlocks an almirah and brings out the Baal Bank register

and cash-box. The children swarm round him until he orders them to form a queue before his desk.

They bring him their deposits – five rupees and ten rupees – and he adds the sums to their accounts in the register. He asks, as instructed by Shalini Didi, where they came by the money, and notes down the answers – rag-picking, pushing carts, selling wristwatches, shining shoes, serving as waiters . . . He has no doubt some of them get it the way Mussabir and he did, and wonders what the going rate is for a tender young boy. If he can command a hundred rupees from Faquira at twenty-two, how much more might these boys be making? They deposit it in small amounts, no doubt, to avoid arousing suspicion.

'I want to close my account,' says a little boy.

Gauhar looks up in surprise. No one ever closes an account at Baal Bank. The first accounts, opened ten years ago – Mussabir's and his own – are still open. He checks the register. Shalini Didi is strict about withdrawals. The money must remain in Baal Bank for a year before it is taken out.

'What is your name?'

'Bobby,' says the boy.

Gauhar starts, but this is just a little boy, he's nothing like Gauhar's friend in Tihar Jail. Bobby's money, says the register, has been in Baal Bank for less than two months. 'You cannot close your account for another ten months,' he informs Bobby.

'I want it now!' Bobby insists.

Gauhar holds up a hand as if to slap the boy, and Bobby scurries away. The other children laugh. Gauhar winks at them. A Nepali girl, next in line, empties her skirt pockets on the table, sending hundreds of coins rolling over the surface. He is surprised when it adds up to almost twenty-four rupees. 'Where did you get so much money?'

She shrugs. He knows she has been begging. Shalini Didi will not like that. 'What is your name?' he asks.

'Kiran.'

What a pretty name, he thinks. Kiran is eleven, says the register. Perhaps it is her prettiness that makes her such a successful beggar. Why should a girl work when she can collect twenty-four rupees just by holding out her hand? Such cute little eyes, such tender brown skin, such a smooth, oval face! 'All right,' he tells her. 'Your money has been deposited.'

'Receipt?' Kiran asks.

Gauhar gives her one.

'What is the rate?' she demands.

'Five per cent every month,' he says.

She tries to calculate. He laughs at the furrows that form on her forehead as she concentrates. 'This will become fifty rupees next month,' he lies.

He is pleased with the look of content that comes into her eyes. She skips off down the corridor. There are six more children with deposits. He makes a final tally, counts the money and arranges it in the cash-box, which he locks. Then he stows it away in the steel almirah and locks that too. As always, he struggles to shut the almirah – he must hold the handle with his left hand while he kicks the door with his right leg, so it will snap into place.

The cash-box now holds more than three thousand rupees, five hundred of which are his. In some sense it is all his, but Shalini Didi studies the register every evening. She has told the children to keep track of how much money Baal Bank owes them. As secretary, Gauhar is responsible for discrepancies. He does not care about making a good impression on Shalini Didi, but he is comfortable at Sparrows: the children spring to do his bidding, the kitchen gives him food, and he sleeps comfortably in the hall in a corner of his own, which is larger than the space in Tihar Jail. In return, he must help Shalini Didi with some lifting and pushing, and keep the accounts in Baal Bank. He is safe from Suleman Mian, though Suleman Mian certainly knows where he is. Hopefully, Sohan Lal does not.

The children file out of the corridor when Shalini Didi rings a bell. It is time for her moral-science class. He stands at the door, leans against the wall and watches. She begins to talk to the children about honesty, discipline and politeness, but he does not hear what she is saying because he is marvelling at how pretty she is. So unlike the whores in GB Road! He would give anything to have her embrace him . . . It bothers him that the little Nepali girl sits alone at the back. Most desks are for two children, so why is Kiran by herself? Does she have no friends? How can such a defenceless, innocent girl be left alone?

When the class has ended and most of the children have run out of the building, he approaches Kiran and tells her that her deposit has already climbed to thirty rupees. She chortles with delight. He can tell she is flattered that he has singled her out. He is something of a legend at Sparrows. 'There is a prize for the largest deposit of the day,' he tells her.

She looks disbelieving. He fingers the roll of varq in his pocket. Ah, the whores in GB Road do not deserve him! They must make do with what vigour he has on his own, without help from the elixir. He pulls out the roll and holds it out to her.

She eyes it suspiciously. 'What is it?'

'Silver!'

She takes it, squeezes it in her hand, breaks off a piece, puts it into her mouth and spits it out. 'It is tasteless,' she groans.

He laughs. 'Your spit is worth fifty rupees! This is silver varq. When stuck on sweets, it enhances their taste.'

'Take it back,' she says.

He puts out his hand. 'What are those marks?' she asks.

He studies the ridges hardened by three years of sledgehammering. 'I used to stand on every street corner, begging. This is what happens to your hand if you beg for money.'

She is wide-eyed, mesmerised by his hand. He cannot resist stroking her cheek. It is so smooth, so soft, so chubby! She stands still for a moment, letting him slide his hand to her chin. Then, with a sudden snort, she snatches his hand with her teeth and sinks them into his flesh. He screams and pulls away. She giggles.

'You have bitten off my hand!' he cries. He pulls his stump out of his pocket and thrusts it into her face. She stops laughing. Her lips tremble with shock and she begins to cry, which makes him feel sorry. He brings out his left hand and shows it to her. 'This was the hand you bit,' he says. 'Look at the bruise! It matches your teeth perfectly.'

She stops sobbing, but her cheeks still run with tears and she cannot stop looking at the stump. 'What happened to it?' she asks.

'There was another beautiful girl like you,' he says, 'but she bit much harder.' Kiran laughs. She looks so pretty when she laughs, he thinks.

Kartar Singh wakes up when the television erupts. It is a four, a six or a wicket. Or the gods who watch over cricket have noticed that he has dozed off and created a noisy moment to wake him. He runs a tired hand down his face from brow to beard and is embarrassed to find his cheeks moist. He must have allowed a tear to escape before he fell into Johnnie-Walker-induced sleep. A man should not cry. He should absorb setbacks stoically, down a drink or two and go about his life. What kind of a life is it, though, when a man is alone at fifty-two?

'Liver cancer,' said the doctor about Sukhbir.

'Can we not do anything at all?' he had asked. 'Can we not take her to Canada or America, spend untold amounts of wealth, and have the animal extracted without damaging her body?'

'It has metastasised,' said the doctor, 'and spread all over her body.'

How could that be, Kartar Singh had demanded, when she was walking about two weeks before this animal reared its head? Had not a hundred people seen her eat prasaad in the gurudwara? Had not two hundred seen her beaming when they first entered the new house in Vasant Vihar? Could a woman who regularly read her gutkas suddenly complain of weakness, run a slight fever, turn pale yellow and announce she was on the verge of death? How had he been negligent? 'It is not your fault that the cancer was asymptomatic,' said the doctor. 'It has been growing for many months, but there was no way you could have known.'

The doctor is right that the animal had been growing for a long time, but he does not know how long. How can a woman retain the will to live after seeing her son murdered before her eyes? Poor Sukhi! That was when this cancer was born, Kartar Singh believes. That was when she made up her mind to die. If she had kept herself alive all these years, it was merely for her husband's sake. She read her gutkas, spent time in the gurudwara, and let the animal grow inside her until she turned fifty. The chaivala had not saved her life: he had merely postponed her death by twelve years.

A disturbing thought makes him sit upright. Could it be that she was not fated to live in the new house? She had expressed her indifference in the last year as often as he told her of progress on the new plot. 'We are old,' she said. 'Why do we need such a large house? Why must the entry have marble? Must the bathrooms have Italian tiles? No daughter-in-law will enjoy that cavernous bedroom, no grandson will frolic in the spacious hall. Why can we not continue to live in the flat in Trilokpuri? Why waste all our money on a new house when we have no son to support us? Is it not wise to save our money for our old age?' she had asked.

Kartar Singh sighs. He lied to her every time she asked. She never found out where the money came from, thinking to her dying day that the store had been profitable. She did not know that a punter must necessarily turn his earnings into stone and cement, or such earnings do not exist. She noticed but did not comment on the stones that adorn his fingers – amethyst, emerald and pukhraj. She had expressed surprise – almost disappointment – when he insisted on a diamond necklace for her. 'It is unseemly at my age,' she said. But where else could he keep his money safe, away from the prying eyes of the CBI? 'We will build a grand house,' he told her, 'far away from Trilokpuri where they took our son away from us. We will spend winters in Delhi and summers in Canada. As the years pass, we will sell the house – it will appreciate – and spend the rest of our lives in Canada, safe from this city of murderers and thieves.'

Because she did not know about the bookie business, she did not know that he had sold it and become a punter. He became one almost by coercion, after the dons in Bombay and Dubai discovered the bookie business and decided to enter it. He began to get phone calls that asked him to call off all bets on certain matches in Sharjah, and received threatening letters when some punters lost large sums because they did not know the script. These were not regular gamblers but dons of a betting Mafia that extended from India to Pakistan and into Dubai, the Emirates, Kenya, South Africa and Morocco. They played for large stakes and could harm him if they wished. So when he received an offer to buy him out – from a man he had never met – he sold off the business gladly, on vague assurances that he would receive tip-offs about the scripts of future matches. The tip-offs did come. They were infrequent and irregular, but always accurate.

He discovered, to his surprise, that the bookie business had been a millstone round his neck, a trap to keep him in the middle class below seths like Sohan Lal. Real money lay in betting, not in collecting a measly commission on others' bets, if he could control himself. He usually stuck to coloured matches whose scripts he knew well. He stopped receiving threatening phone calls as he slipped off the dons' lists. He had no direct contact with them any more, except in the form of anonymous letters that told him the script, when it pleased someone in Dubai to do so. The letters arrive rarely now. Sometimes he puts down a few thousand on a match he knows nothing about. He can afford to lose the money. The first three years of active betting were very successful. It is only now that the CBI is looking closely at the business.

Sukhbir also did not know that he has a shed in Mangolpuri, in case

prices rise when industrial units move out of the Chandni Chowk
area. He had also planned to buy a shop in Khari Baoli as soon as the
cricket betting season ended. That is the best time to buy property in
Chandni Chowk: those who have lost money sell their shops to cover
their losses. But the betting season will end after these five matches in
Toronto, and he will let it slip by.

He leans back in the sofa and wonders if he is responsible for
Sukhbir's death. Has the wrath of a higher being reached down and
touched him? Should he sell the house, every brick of which has been
baked with punting money? Can he enjoy the sinful marble that has
taken his Sukhi's life? But he is not a superstitious man. The animal
inside her would have grown regardless, he tells himself.

He tries to concentrate on the match, beamed live from Toronto.
Ah, he could have been sitting in the stadium – on the other side of the
world – if Sukhbir had lived! How beautiful it looks, how green the
grass inside, and how clear the sky above it! He can still go to Canada,
alone, and wrap himself in the obscurity of another world. But a man
goes to Canada to give his children a brighter future, or to retire in
comfort with his wife. He has been denied both, so he must live on as
he is.

He collects himself, determined to pay attention to the match, so he
can place a proper bet. Pakistan has made a hundred and seventy runs,
an easy target for India, given the Indian batsmen's good form. India
lost an early wicket, but the batsmen now control the game. Tendulkar is playing well as usual, heading for a comfortable half-century.
Kartar Singh knows, through old channels which have not yet dried
up, that this match is not coloured, and no tip has arrived from Dubai,
but anyone can see that the odds on an Indian victory are high.
Perhaps he can place an easy bet on India, which will bring back his
stake and a small amount over it.

Then he is overwhelmed by desolation. How can a man occupy
himself without his wife and children? Perhaps he should give up
punting and concentrate on the store. After all, it has Jasjit's name on
the front. He can dedicate himself to it, thinking of it as a tribute to his
son. Yes, that is what he will do – the store and the gurudwara. The
first to set things right with his son, the other for his wife to rest in
peace.

The weight of his resolution intimidates him. So much of his life has
been spent watching cricket, as dibba, bookie and punter. Perhaps one
last bet? A well-placed guess to cap a successful career? No, that will

desecrate Sukhbir's memory. It is a mockery of his resolve. All right, he will place a perverse bet, one that bets against India, which he is likely to lose. A man who needs the stick is not easily persuaded by arguments, so a loss will serve him right! It will rid him of his dangerous addiction. How much should he place on a Pakistani victory? A lakh? Five lakhs? Twenty? Jasjit General Store? The Vasant Vihar house? He picks up the telephone.

'Manoj STD Service,' says the boy in the telephone booth.

'I need to place a call to Dubai,' he says.

'The phone is not working,' says the boy.

'Tell Sitaram Babu it is Kartar Singh.'

In a few seconds, Sitaram is on the line.

'What is the rate on Tendulkar's century?' asks Kartar Singh.

'Seven two,' says Sitaram.

'Put me down at two seven,' says Kartar Singh.

Sitaram is slow to understand. Then he is incredulous: 'You are betting against Tendulkar's century?'

Kartar Singh laughs. He knows Sitaram is concerned by his lack of patriotism, not his foolhardiness, which can only benefit the other man should he lose. Even bookies are sentimental when India plays Pakistan.

'How much?' asks Sitaram.

Kartar Singh takes a deep breath as large sums sail through his mind. 'Twenty thousand,' he says weakly.

'Twenty thousand at two seven,' Sitaram repeats, and hangs up.

Kartar Singh puts the phone down and sinks deeper into the sofa, defeated. He has failed to live up to his own expectations. At the last moment, with a large sum on the tip of his tongue, he was not able to destroy himself. Twenty thousand is a sum he wins and loses in a matter of hours. He is a weak man, and must live with the shame. He will not wait for the match to end. He has an account with Sitaram, so there is no immediate need to pay the boy. He will settle in a few days, whatever the outcome. He switches off the television and falls asleep on the sofa.

The next morning, he rises early and asks the driver to take him to Chandni Chowk. He gets out at Lajpatrai Market, far from the store, and tells the driver he will not be needed for the rest of the day. When the driver and the Maruti are out of sight, he drinks chai at a stall and walks through the market. Not many people recognise him since he gave up his seat on the council, and that is a good thing. He does not want them to remember that he was here on the day before the demolition.

All these stalls will be gone tomorrow, he thinks, with satisfaction. These are the shops that have flooded Lajpatrai Market with cheap Chinese goods and destroyed his store. They sit on stilts that straddle drains, with a wooden table for glass displays and a tarpaulin overhead – row upon row of matchbox stores, selling dinner sets for thirty-five rupees, trousers for thirty, sweaters for twenty-eight, T-shirts for fifteen, needles and noodles and shoes and toys and lipsticks for prices even a beggar can afford. Never mind that the china in the dinner set is from an oven in Naraina, the Reebok shoe really says Reebak and the Rolex logo has been crudely hand-painted, because it is cheaper to buy, throw away and buy again than waste money in Jasjit General Store. Is it his fault, then, that he has taken to selling some of these so-called brand names? What else is a man to do if he runs a proper store, pays rent and electricity and a dozen government inspectors? All the matchboxes pay is a flat fee to the SHO. They encroach on government land, block the footpath, hide the legal stores and take their business. Chandni Chowk has become China Chowk – Chinese fans, fibres, bicycles, shoes, semi-conductors, batteries . . . Dry-cell batteries from China sell for two rupees! In India, the lead alone inside the battery costs two rupees. It is another matter that an Indian dry cell lasts fifty minutes while the Chinese lasts twenty-three, if that. Who cares? People want the satisfaction of buying cheap.

These shops must go, thinks Kartar Singh. He notes their numbers and location, and commits them to memory. 'Concentrate on Musalman shops,' Sohan Lal told him, 'especially Bangladeshi ones. It is those we want to clear away from Chandni Chowk.'

'How will I know who is a Bangladeshi?' Kartar Singh asked.

'Put down the names of all Musalman shops that appear illegal,' said Sohan Lal, 'and we will see who is a Bangladeshi after we have demolished them.'

Kartar Singh notes with satisfaction that many of these Chinese shops are owned by Musalmans. He will have no trouble justifying them to Sohan Lal. Some shopkeepers sitting behind Chinese-made counters appear to be Hindu. He writes them down anyway. These people cause as much damage to the country as Musalmans, he thinks. Sohan Lal may object, but will he notice a few Hindu names in the long list of Musalman ones?

Then he stops. What is this? A stall full of Chinese fans, all whirring soundlessly, bathing passers-by in cool air! The owner is surrounded by them – a raja with his trophies after a great hunt – and smiles beatifically. His hair flaps happily in a Chinese breeze, the loose ends of his kurta wave at customers, and even his moustache hairs wiggle to advertise the power of his product. It is a hot, clammy morning. Kartar Singh cannot tear himself away from the benevolent draught. The monsoon gods have long abdicated, which means the fans will sell ever more quickly. 'Eight hundred rupees,' says the sticker on the fan closest to him. 'Six hundred and fifty,' says another. Who will buy the thousand-rupee fans in Jasjit General Store? The shopkeeper asks if he wants to buy anything.

'Give me a pen and a notepad,' says Kartar Singh.

He will mark the stall for demolition. This row will be the first razed by the bulldozers.

'Chinese,' says the shopkeeper, as he presses a notepad into his hands. 'Two rupees.'

It is cheaper, crisper, whiter and shinier than the Indian notepad Kartar Singh sells. He knows, without being told, that the ballpoint pen thrust into his hands is also Chinese – smooth, clear, clean with no leakage. He pays the shopkeeper, then asks him the name of this row of stalls, and notes it on the pad. The shopkeeper raises an eyebrow.

'Municipal Corporation survey,' mutters Kartar Singh.

The shopkeeper asks if he would like to buy a fan.

'Why should I?' asks Kartar Singh. 'I will buy an Indian one. A Khaitan!'

'But this is much cheaper,' says the shopkeeper. 'It has a built-in inverter that allows it to continue running for three hours after a power failure. And notice how quiet it is! Do you not know that Khaitan will soon close down its own production plants and market Chinese fans instead? Smooth, soundless fans from China . . .'

All this for eight hundred rupees, thinks Kartar Singh, ruefully.

He moves on before the man can offer him a bicycle. He knows they are made of stronger alloys and cost five hundred rupees less than the steel ones he sells. And who will buy his toasters, mixers and sandwich-makers? The Nepal corridor, he thinks angrily, is like a sieve. We should build a wall three storeys high along the India–Nepal border, and shoot down these touts and smugglers when they try to scale it.

He stalks out of the kucha. He will use the day to visit every kucha and katra in Chandni Chowk. If the kucha is too narrow for bulldozers, he will ask the demolition crew to go inside on foot and do its work with sticks and hammers. All signs of China Chowk must be obliterated. Some day, when these illegal stalls have gone, he will nurse Jasjit General Store back to profitability.

On his way to Kucha Bansilal, where he must present the list to Sohan Lal for approval, he passes the telephone booth in which he placed his bet last night. It is legal, he knows, even if the business it supports for Sitaram Babu is not. He resists the urge to go inside and find out how his bet fared. A punter should never enter a telephone booth such as this. Everyone knows they are watched by the CBI. He walks on.

He passes the Hanuman temple and notices the neon sign on the peepul tree: 'Jamna Lal Kishori Mal – Sarees and Blouses.' He has not come this way for years. He remembers a sign made of tin and wood, not this electronic one, which flashes in different rhythms. The lights have danced and hopped all night, it appears, and they continue to dance even so late in the morning. Sohan Lal has been redecorating, thinks Kartar Singh wryly, ever since he became an MLA.

He turns into Kucha Bansilal with a shudder. He has not forgotten that dark evening in 'eighty-four. But where is the chaivala's box, which was so small he could barely squeeze inside it? There is a large stall in its place, and at its centre the junction box he remembers. In fact, it is the same stall – it has simply grown, like a fungus sprouting from the drain. Now it extends two metres on either side of the junction box, with benches and stools for customers, glass jars full of biscuits sitting in neat rows on wooden counters, and a light bulb swinging in the centre. And who should be sitting behind the counter, his head almost touching the bulb, but the chaivala! The man is much changed. Kartar Singh remembers sunken cheeks, a balding head, unclean stubble and a shirt with missing buttons. The head is now naked, except for scrubby growth where it connects to the neck and hairs that sprout from the man's ears, but the face is fuller and rounder. The shirt still lacks buttons – the same one, perhaps? – and the spectacles are still foggy, so he does not know if the chaivala, while looking straight at him, has recognised him. There is a seth-like quality about him that disturbs Kartar Singh. He seems to be sitting on a small cushion tied to a stool. A customer will now have to look up at him, instead of looking down to order tea. He is at the same height as Ramesh, seated at his Sunmica counter across the lane, somewhat higher than Sohan Lal, whose little gaddi occupies the far corner of his shop. Kartar Singh has come to see Sohan Lal, but he moves instinctively toward the stall, where the chaivala has stood up, hands folded.

'*Sat sri akaal*, sardarji.'

Kartar Singh is irritated. Who does the chaivala think he is? A politician? But he must be careful not to antagonise him. He must set things right with Sukhbir. She is certainly watching over him, and will approve. He sits on a stool, leans over the counter, and whispers, 'I have not seen you for years, Gopal Bhai.'

Gopal had recognised the sardarji as soon as he walked into the kucha. He had noted that he was thinner and looked worn, as if he did not care much for his appearance. Gopal could tell that he was unhappy. If he were chased now by Congress hoodlums, he would perhaps not run so hard, or force himself into a box – though he would fit much better – or plead with the same urgency. His face is so close that Gopal can study the checked design on the expensive shirt, and he has placed a hand on the counter, so Gopal can see the stones on his fingers. Also expensive, no doubt.

'My wife is dead, Gopal Bhai.'

Gopal shuts his eyes. 'She was a brave woman,' he says, with fervour.

'She should have died in 'eighty-four,' murmurs Kartar Singh. 'You gave her twelve more years.'

'She lived as long as God wanted her to live,' says Gopal.

'But it was you who saved her,' insists Kartar Singh.

Gopal remains silent. Kartar Singh looks down at the counter. 'You never told me whom you saw in the bathroom,' he says suddenly.

'Your wife,' replies Gopal. 'Stuck in the window.'

Kartar Singh shakes his head. 'There was a man,' he says, 'who attacked her with a sword. You fought him off with your bare hands. She told me so.'

Gopal's mind is a maze of confusion. He does not remember a sword, but his memories of that moment are clouded. What should his answer be?

'Who was that man?' presses Kartar Singh. 'Congress? Musalman? Hindu? Sikh?'

'I did not know him.'

'You did!' says Kartar Singh, emphatically. 'She said you called him by name! A Musalman name, but she was not sure.'

Gopal quakes. The scene replays itself indistinctly in his mind. He hears that one voice above all others. 'Indira Gandhi *amar rahe*!' says the voice. He recognises it. And then Ibrahim Mian stands before him, looking like a dead man with a rod in his hand. 'I have come from Ballimaran to see if you are safe . . .' The sardarni screams. 'Quiet,' says Ibrahim Mian, 'or you will die!' And the fat woman is wedged in the window, thick thighs encased in a brown salvaar that bursts at the seams, legs flailing as she tries to squeeze out. He cannot see her from the waist up, but he can somehow discern terror in her eyes. From beyond the window he hears her squeals for help, which frighten him to his very bones. He cannot decide if he should push at her thighs so she can fall into the garden – possibly to her death – or pull her back into the room to be beaten by Ibrahim Mian. But Ibrahim Mian had come from Ballimaran for him . . . Had it been Ibrahim or another Musalman?

'She was frightened, sardarji,' he says. 'She could have heard anything. There were more than twenty people in your house.'

Kartar Singh looks at Gopal sceptically. 'How did you fight them all? You do not look like a pahalvan to me.'

Gopal lowers his gaze. I will be punished for this deceit, he tells himself. This is why Mukesh was taken from me, and this is why those snakes of money will lie curled up for ever. He leans back in exhaustion, and his head knocks against the junction box.

Kartar Singh points to it and smiles. 'How do you go from this side of the stall to that?'

Gopal swallows nervously. Why has the sardarji mentioned the junction box? Was that money his, after all? Those belts have given him nothing but pain! He cannot use them, cannot return them, cannot admit to owning them and cannot forget about them. But, of course, the sardarji has nothing to do with them, or he would not have waited twelve years to ask.

'I crawl under the box,' Gopal replies, watching the sardarji's face carefully.

'Perhaps you should have it removed,' Kartar Singh suggests.

'I have asked sethji,' says Gopal. 'He will tell the Corporation to remove it for the festival.'

'Is your stall part of the festival?'

'I have applied. Sethji wrote me a letter. It will not look good to have a junction box when the newspeople come and take photographs. Look at the wires that hang from it!'

Kartar Singh feels the urge to reach out and jerk open the box, but he knows it is useless now. He should never have put the money there.

The sense that he was been wronged – by illegal stalls, junction boxes, Sohan Lal and betting dons – attacks him with renewed violence. Why would a good man bet on cricket if he had not been chased like a dog in 'eighty-four, if the chaivala had not spirited away his money, causing him to lose his havala business? Look at the chaivala now, straddling the drain like a don, letting his stall spill into Kucha Bansilal so that people can barely pass! What can he be thinking about now, except the money he has stolen from a sardar in distress? It may explain the benches, counters and glass jars. They have been bought with *his* lakhs. Why, much of that money might be hidden under these counters!

'You should clean your stall,' he suggests.

'I have not cleaned it for years,' says Gopal self-deprecatingly.

'Who knows what you will find?' muses Kartar Singh.

Gopal wishes he could curl into a small ball and bounce off the counter, down the kucha, away from Kartar Singh's penetrating gaze. The sardarji knows!

'Do you have a permit?' asks Kartar Singh.

Gopal wonders if the sardarji has joined the police. 'Permit, permit . . .' he repeats, turning the question over in his head like a philosophical argument, but not answering it.

Ingrate! Kartar Singh berates himself. Here is the man who saved you from the Congress mob. Here is the man who saved Sukhbir from a Musalman murderer. Does it matter that he has four lakhs hidden away? Four lakhs is a trifling sum, these days. He wins and loses such amounts weekly at the height of the cricket season. The emerald and pukhraj on his fingers alone are worth a lakh! Does it matter that the chaivala does not have a permit, when Kartar Singh spent his darkest hour inside this box, praying for his life? But he is asking only for what is rightfully his. The four lakhs are hidden somewhere among these planks, stoves, jars, cans, tins and pieces of sacking. Where else could the chaivala keep them? Kartar Singh made some enquiries in 'eighty-four. There is little space in Sushil Jain's kholi, where the chaivala sleeps at night, and it is regularly inspected by the seth's men, so the chaivala would never keep anything there. No, the stall must be searched. And it is a stall without a permit.

'It is very hot these days,' says Kartar Singh, breezily. 'You need a table fan.'

Gopal is relieved at this change of subject. 'I am a poor man. Fans cost money.'

Kartar Singh lets his eyes rove over the stall. 'You do not look poor to me.' He pulls out his notepad and makes an entry.

'What are you writing?' asks Gopal.

'An order for a table fan,' says Kartar Singh. 'It will be delivered tomorrow.'

'I cannot afford it,' says Gopal, regretfully.

'It is free.'

Gopal sighs in guilt and repentance. Here is the sardarji, come to buy him a table fan, and he had assumed that greed pulled him into the kucha. What a kind man, he thinks, as he watches the sardarji turn away, take off his chappals outside Jamna Lal Kishori Mal, wipe his feet on the mat, go round the Sunmica counters and sit down on the gaddi near Sohan Lal.

'Chai!' calls Sohan Lal.

Gopal gets to work.

'You do not come to Kucha Bansilal any more,' says Sohan Lal to Kartar Singh, in mild reproach.

'Even you do not spend time here,' he replies. 'That is what Jugal Kishorji told me at the last committee meeting.'

Sohan Lal casts an approving glance toward the Sunmica counter, where Ramesh sits in deep concentration. 'It is my son's shop now,' he says. 'I am merely the relic that cannot be demolished. Ramesh is here at nine every morning. I come when I can get away from public service. A man with three grandsons has little time on his hands!'

Kartar Singh laughs to acknowledge the new baby born to Sushma. 'How is she?'

Sohan Lal leans toward him, but whispers so loudly that everyone can hear: 'I keep worrying for her! She is a machine. Three boys in four years!' Three boys born in quick succession, he thinks. With Vimla's son and daughter, that is four boys and a girl. Even after adding Shakuntala's daughters, the balance is fair, with four boys and three girls. Vimla's daughter will surely be spoilt. She will be indulged by her parents and her doting brother, and her wedding will be planned with great care. His only concern is Shakuntala. Two daughters are always a cause for concern, if not panic. Perhaps a son will come along and set the matter to rest. He has no cause to worry about his daughters yet. 'Sometimes I think it is time to go to Hardwar with Rukmini,' he says.

He is lying, thinks Kartar Singh, even as he chuckles in agreement.

An MLA does not think of retiring to the Himalayan foothills and bathing daily in the Ganga, he plots to become a minister in the state government. The seth is past sixty, the age when a man begins to affect a desire for renunciation. He will continue to speak of it until Yamaraj, thinking him to be sincere, catches him unawares and fulfils his wish.

'This is the match from last night,' Kartar Singh says, noticing the television.

Sohan Lal disapproves of the television sitting on the counter, much as he disapproves of the counter itself. A shop is a temple, a place of business, an arena in which a man must discharge his duty, then lock up and go home to discharge the duties that await him there. A temple should not be polluted with vulgar entertainment, sullied with film music or defiled with cricket matches. Granted, Ramesh is a father of three, a responsible family man who should enjoy some authority in the shop, but must the television be on all the time? It is scandalous how Ramesh is absorbed in cricket when customers await his attention. And the staff take their cue from the master: they glance at the screen when they are cutting cloth, folding sarees and taking inventory. When Ramesh is not around, they are glued to it like flies to a jalebi, oblivious even of Sohan Lal.

He had protested when Ramesh installed the counters and moved the gaddi to its present corner. 'It does not look good to have a mattress lying in the middle of the shop,' Ramesh had said. 'A shop with counters has a more modern look. Customers – even those who wear dhotis – prefer to sit on stools,' said Ramesh. 'They do not like to take off their chappals and make the effort of sitting down cross-legged.'

It is humiliating enough that the gaddi is squeezed into a corner near the Lakshmi alcove: now Lakshmi must share her temple with wires from the computer that sits below it. He wonders, sometimes, if Sushma has something to do with Ramesh's assertiveness. She was pleasant and soft-mannered when she first arrived. He watched with approval as she assisted Rukmini in the house, and fanned him while he ate his lunch. Her cooking was always beyond reproach. She is still polite when she speaks to him, but perhaps she does not accord the same respect to Rukmini. He has overheard comments and remarks that disturb him. Rukmini's hands have begun to tremble when she lifts things. He is afraid it is early Parkinson's, but the doctor says it is merely a sign of weakness. Her blood pressure is too low. He does not feel Sushma takes adequate care of her. She is preoccupied with her sons, and he suspects she carps about him behind his back. Ramesh is too mature to listen to frivolous talk, but how long can a boy – even one as dutiful and obedient as Ramesh – ignore incessant chatter from a wife who has given him three sons? He dreads the day when she might speak directly with him without even the modest cover of a saree over her hair. But he will go to Hardwar long before that. He must!

On the counter, the television roars. Tendulkar has just hit a six, taking his score to sixty-three. Ramesh turns to Kartar Singh. 'I do not like watching live matches. I prefer recordings, because I already know that India won the match.'

Kartar Singh does not ask him what Tendulkar's final score will be. At sixty-three, he is inching toward a century. Let him score a hundred, he wishes silently, and let that put an end to my habit!

'But, of course, you know all this better than I do,' says Ramesh.

'I thought you had stopped that business,' interjects Sohan Lal.

'I have,' says Kartar Singh.

'India will win the Friendship Cup,' declares Ramesh.

'What friendship?' snarls Sohan Lal. 'Will Pakistanis become our brothers by playing cricket with us in Canada?'

Kartar Singh turns away guiltily from the television.

'What about the terrorists they send over the border?' demands Sohan Lal. 'What about the riots they instigate in our cities, the large families they produce? Is this how we will solve our Musalman problem?'

Kartar Singh, eager to get on with his business, places the notepad on the gaddi where Sohan Lal can see it. 'I have made a list,' he says. 'Harilalji wants it by this evening. I thought you could review it before I send it on.'

Sohan Lal frowns. 'I do not like this demolition idea,' he murmurs.

Kartar Singh shrugs. When he was first told of it, he had not cared for it. But now, having walked through Lajpatrai Market, he is determined to have those stalls removed. If Harilal Gupta had a stall of his own, he would put it on the list.

Sohan Lal whispers: 'If Harilal Gupta wants to demolish Musalman and Bangladeshi stalls, let him do it quietly! A police jeep, a couple of vans, a few arrests, detentions. Why must he launch a full drive? Half of Chandni Chowk is illegal. Will he uproot half the street? Did he become transport minister so he could cause such upheaval?'

'Harilalji is powerless,' says Kartar Singh. 'This is a Supreme Court order.'

'That is what Harilal says.'

'It is necessary for the Moonlight Festival, sethji.'

Sohan Lal snorts. 'The festival was Harilalji's idea, too.'

'IPP has been talking of broadening its base,' says Kartar Singh, defensively. 'Our national policy is to include Musalmans, Christians, OBCs, SCs and STs. How can the Chandni Chowk committee disregard national party policy?'

'So must we recreate Mughal history in this orgiastic festival?' retorts Sohan Lal. 'They were sodomising, opium-addicted lechers! We should hide them under mounds of earth, not put them on display. Harilalji wants to preserve heritage? Very well, why not preserve the heritage of Hindus? Has no one heard of the Tomar kings, Raja Anangpal, or Prithvi Raj Chauhan? Did the Pandavs not build the city of Indraprastha, where Chandni Chowk stands, thousands of years before there was anything called Islam? And those university girls in thick spectacles who speak of Dara Shikoh's library – do they not want to locate the spot where Shri Krishna stood when he recited the *Bhagavad Gita*?'

Kartar Singh looks silently at the Lakshmi alcove. It will not do to contradict the seth: as chairman of the IPP committee, he will determine candidates for the next council elections. Kartar Singh resigned his council seat to stand for MLA in 'ninety-three. His loss to Suleman in the assembly election left him without an office, appointed or elected. He never found out why Suleman switched from Matia Mahal to Ballimaran. Why would he abandon a constituency he had nurtured for a decade to take his chances in unfamiliar territory? But who can predict the mind of a snake? Ballimaran has a sizeable Musalman population, even if it is not as large as that of Matia Mahal, so Kartar Singh had known he was doomed when he heard of the switch. Why, if Suleman had stood from the Chandni Chowk segment, he would have made Harilal shiver.

'This festival is merely Harilal's way of ingratiating himself with Musalmans,' says Sohan Lal. 'He is not satisfied to be an MLA. He wants to become an MP. For that he will have to defeat Naresh Agrawal, and who can do that in Chandni Chowk? Nareshji is everyone's candidate. Traders vote for him because he is a trader, Musalmans because he is from Congress, and others because they have voted for him all their lives.'

Kartar Singh sighs in agreement. In the general election three months ago, Naresh Agrawal won his fifth successive term in Lok Sabha. 'He is sitting in Parliament right now. He will be the MP for Chandni Chowk until he dies.'

'And he plans to live for ever,' says Sohan Lal wistfully.

The next general election is almost five years away, thinks Kartar Singh. 'Harilalji is planning too far ahead.'

'No one thinks this Lok Sabha will last more than two years,' says Sohan Lal.

Kartar Singh nods. This is common wisdom, but it sounds even wiser coming from Sohan Lal. He has underestimated the seth in the past. He will not do so again. They still talk of the seth's assembly victory at Matia Mahal – the triumph of a Marwari seth in a Musalman area. He pushes the notepad closer to Sohan Lal, as a way of indicating that they should finish the task at hand. Sohan Lal puts on his gold-rimmed glasses with great care and scans the list. This list, of course, is secret and unofficial. It bears no relation to the lists being compiled by the Corporation, but this is the one that will be followed when trucks and bulldozers come in the morning. Sohan Lal reaches the end of the page and looks up. 'Why is the chaivala on the list?'

'He does not have a permit,' says Kartar Singh, neutrally.

'He has been in the kucha for more than twenty years.'

'He does not have a permit,' repeats Kartar Singh. 'We must be fair.'

Sohan Lal takes off his spectacles and studies Kartar Singh. To be lectured on fairness by a man who lost his five lakhs! He should cross off the chaivala's name without explanation. The demolition drive is meant to ferret out illegal Bangladeshis, not innocent men like the chaivala. The man has suffered enough; he saw his son die in a ball of flames.

'The chaivala shelters Bangladeshis,' points out Kartar Singh. 'Did not that boy – the one who pissed in Rajghat – sleep in his stall? Perhaps he still does.'

'He went away,' says Sohan Lal vaguely, eager to change the subject. He does not want to discuss the one-handed boy, whose disappearance nearly derailed his assembly election. He tried hard, but was unable to locate the boy in Ayodhya. Fortunately, he was able to convince Suleman that he had the boy in custody. Perhaps the thief has been dead all these years. No, they must not discuss the boy.

'I have given the chaivala a letter recommending his inclusion in Harilal Gupta's festival,' says Sohan Lal firmly. 'And now you want to demolish his stall? Remove the chaivala from your list.'

He hands it back to Kartar Singh, who makes a vague sound signifying neither assent nor demurral. Sohan Lal pulls out a handkerchief and wipes his moist forehead. 'Dilli is fast becoming like Rajasthan,' he grumbles. 'September, and not a drop of rain! We called it dry heat in Bikaner. My grandchildren will not know what the monsoon looks like.'

Kartar Singh responds with an obligatory chuckle. His ears are tuned to the television set, where Tendulkar is marching inexorably toward his century, and India toward victory. The crowd has ratcheted up its response to every run, and Ramesh has turned up the volume. Kartar Singh watches with a mixture of dread and anticipation. I have done this for my Sukhi, he tells himself. All I need now is a century, and I will never bet again. He is aware that Sohan Lal is watching him. Well, this is his last bet, the last time Sukhbir will see him stoop so low.

Suddenly, Ramesh lets out a loud whoop and the staff claps. India has won. 'Beating Pakistan is always more delicious than beating others,' says Ramesh.

Yes, thinks Kartar Singh, but Tendulkar has been left not-out at eighty-nine, short of a century. Sitaram Babu will now be returning his money three-fold. Either someone is watching over him or he has a knack for this. He places a bet any punter would consider foolhardy, on a match that does not even have a script, and he wins! What shall he tell Sukhbir now? That he is doomed to remain a punter all his life?

He still bets, thinks Sohan Lal, as he studies Kartar Singh's face. Why else would he appear crestfallen? The traitor! He must have bet on a Pakistani victory.

Gopal brings two cups of tea on a plastic tray.

'Chinese cups,' mutters Kartar Singh.

'A good man,' says Sohan Lal of Gopal, as he sips his tea. 'I once loaned fifty thousand to his father. He returned every rupee. Some men can be trusted with money.'

So that is why the seth is so hostile toward me, thinks Kartar Singh. It is not concern for the chaivala, it is the matter of the money which he has neither forgotten nor forgiven, even after twelve years. If they find those four lakhs somehow – or whatever is left of them –

in the chaivala's stall, he might be reconciled with the seth. The stall will stay on the list. Mistakes can easily happen in an extensive demolition drive. Who will remember the one chai stall included accidentally?

'I have given him my word about the festival,' stresses Sohan Lal.

He has given his word, thinks Kartar Singh, but he will gladly retract it for a few lakhs. It is his word or his money.

He drains his cup and rises from the gaddi, notepad in hand. As he slips into his chappals, he says, 'You forgot to switch off the sign outside the kucha.'

Sohan Lal frowns, then scolds Chotu for the waste of electricity.

'I will hand over the list to Harilalji,' says Kartar Singh. 'He is concerned that there may be some interference by Suleman.'

'Let the dog bark,' says Sohan Lal. 'The elephant will walk on.'

Kartar Singh savours the seth's annoyance. Everyone dislikes Suleman because no one is oblivious of his growing influence. He is merely an MLA like Sohan Lal, and not a ruling-party MLA at that, but his name throws even Harilal Gupta – an MLA and a minister – into fits of agony.

As he walks out of the kucha, Kartar Singh casts a quick glance at the chaivala, who is busy with another pot of tea. The seth's ire at Chotu is a feint, of course. Anyone can see the wire spliced into the transmission pole, from where it girdles the branches of the peepul tree and finds its way into the neon sign. A seth never pays for the electricity that powers his signboard. But Kartar Singh has the list in his hands, approved by Sohan Lal. Surely a few additions will not be noticed? Sohan Lal himself advised him to be thorough.

He passes the peepul tree. The sign is now switched off. Perhaps it casts its neon glow on the Hanuman temple every night. No engineer, from DESU or anywhere else, will dare turn out the lights on Hanuman. Hanuman can never be illegal, and the sign that illuminates him is as legal as he is. But the sign sits on a tree, and no one worships the tree. It has no legal right to stand in Chandni Chowk.

42

Ramvilas crosses the wide expanse of asphalt outside Red Fort, walks past stalls selling mineral water and biscuits, and enters the Lahori Gate. The *son-et-lumière* show, at eight that evening, is being advertised on a wooden board placed at the entrance. A tout offers tickets at half-price. He waves him away scornfully. Two tourists have propped up a sadhu against a hedge and are photographing him. He laughs to reveal decayed teeth; they ask him to stop grinning if he wants his ten rupees. Ramvilas walks past them, turns into the archway under which lies the Red Fort Meena Bajar, and pauses at the rows of stalls selling trinkets at outrageous prices. He looks at earrings, beads and wind chimes, then selects a cheap Chinese necklace – imitation gold that will come off with a little sweat and a plastic pendant masquerading as emerald. He haggles hard and brings down the price from thirty-five to twelve. 'I am not a white man, so stop trying to steal from me,' he scolds the stall-owner. With the necklace encased in a polythene bag and curled like a snake in his kurta pocket, he walks through Meena Bajar to the vast Red Fort grounds.

It is afternoon. He should be sitting in Bhagwan Das and Sons, assisting the four sons, but he will let them cut each other's throats for a day. The shop has reopened today after a hiatus of two months, when it was closed by a court injunction. It was the first time in living memory that the shop had remained shut for more than two weeks. Surajmal never tired of describing the last time the shop suffered this fate – eighty-four years ago, when the British closed down Chandni Chowk and cordoned off Kucha Sugandh after a bomb was thrown at Lord Hardinge. Chandni Chowk reopened, but the kucha remained sealed to ferret out the bomber they believed was hiding there.

No bomber has shut the shop this time. And now that it is open, the four brothers sit side by side on the gaddi, eyeing the cash-box, watching every rupee that comes in. Customers are uncomfortable to see four seths in the same shop – four seths who communicate only through Ramvilas. He is the go-between, the chief negotiator and the chief arbitrator. The youngest is thirty-three, while Vimal, the oldest, is almost the same age as Ramvilas but still calls him Ramvilas Kaka.

He chuckles at the thought: Ramvilas Kaka will soon give his ruling, and three of the sons will not like it.

He heads for the red sandstone pavilion of Divan-i-Am. Gita Didi stands at the eastern edge of the hall, wearing a white saree, leaning against a column, looking up at the white marble balcony where Shah Jahan himself might once have stood. She is chubbier than he remembers. Her hair is tied in a tight bun behind her head. Her blouse, also white, has long sleeves, and a black handbag swings from her shoulder. Still pretty, he thinks, in spite of the plain white saree and the bulge at her midriff. It is late afternoon. Divan-i-Am is virtually deserted. She senses his arrival and turns to him.

'You look like a film heroine,' he says, as he approaches, 'begging for the emperor's mercy, your eyes full of tears.'

Instinctively she covers her head with a corner of her saree.

'Now you look like Mother Teresa!'

'You have put on a little weight,' she says softly.

Ramvilas shrugs. 'Being on the IPP committee does that to you. I am almost a seth now!'

She ignores the boast.

'I have brought you a little gift,' he says. He produces the polythene bag, extracts the necklace and holds it out to her. She wraps thumb and forefinger round the pendant and hands it back.

'Ah!' he mutters 'Gita Didi, emancipator of GB Road!' She shakes her head and he notices that she is wearing no makeup or jewellery. Mollified, he stuffs the necklace back into his kurta. 'Why did you ask me to come here?' he asks. 'I could have met you at a STREE meeting.'

'To preserve your reputation,' says Gita. 'You are a committee member.'

He is pleased by her forethought. 'But why Red Fort?' he asks.

'The sisters of GB Road are not interested in old sandstone buildings,' she replies. The sisters of GB Road, she thinks, know Ramvilas too well. They know of his visits to Parvati and her girls. How can she justify a tryst with a man like him? The reputation to be preserved is hers, not his. She notes that his appearance has declined. He is fleshier. The skin that once stretched tightly across his cheek-bones is tired. He must be forty-two now. An old man! The kurta-pyjama is still spotlessly white, but it cannot hide his sins. Soon the plastic pendant will swing from the seventeen-year-old throat of Parvati's prettiest girl.

She takes out a bottle of Bisleri from her handbag and drinks. Ramvilas is irritated by this. Why should a GB Road whore worry that her digestion will be ruined if she drinks tap water at Red Fort? Who does she think she is? The Queen of England?

She finishes drinking and holds out the bottle to him. He refuses. 'Why me?' he challenges. 'I have seen you three times in four years, and only at STREE functions. Surely you don't expect anything from me. Why not go to your powerful patrons? Harilal Gupta never tires of talking about STREE. And if an MLA is too small to do your bidding, try Naresh Agrawal. He will gladly give you a lakh from his MP funds.'

'I do not need money,' she says.

'Ah.'

'Only you can give me what I need.'

He wonders if she is being naughty. The old passion stirs. This is his Gulmohar, after all. This is his lump of clay, shaped by his will, given form and function as he desired. She may be plump, without a trace of jewellery, wrapped in a white saree that destroys all sexuality, locked behind an unattractively self-assured, manly demeanour, but the skin is still smooth and soft, the body still lush. 'I have never denied you anything,' he says softly.

Suddenly she turns and walks away. He follows. She steps out of Divan-i-Am and walks across the gardens, evidently disturbed, then finds her way into the ornate pavilion of Rang Mahal. 'A beautiful building,' she says listlessly.

'The zenana,' he smirks.

She does not understand. He cannot resist the comparison. 'This is the emperor's GB Road.'

She does not appear amused, and walks to the end of the hall, away from him.

'You might have enjoyed working here.' He laughs. 'Imagine these columns plastered and painted and draped in silk. Imagine ornate balconies, carved marble and ceilings of gilded stucco. Imagine the frolic of Yamuna water, the music of a dozen instruments, the sounds of a hundred peacocks! And then imagine an impotent old man, the emperor of Hindustan, limping slowly toward you, leaning heavily on his cane . . .'

She laughs, but cuts herself short. 'Even that is denied to me,' she says.

He wonders, not without amusement, if she misses her whoring ways.

'The bai does not let me enter the room upstairs,' says Gita. 'She has taken everything – the four-poster bed, the dressing-table, the bottles of attar, the mirrors.'

'That is your room!' protests Ramvilas.

'It is Parvati's now.'

'But the gifts were yours,' he says. 'I gave them to you, not the bai.'

He knows, even before she answers, that the gifts are attached to the kotha and the bai. When the bai first demanded her share ten years ago, he threatened to abandon Gulmohar if she was not allowed to retain her gifts. The bai retreated, preferring regular crumbs to a windfall. Her defeat was Gulmohar's triumph, but that was before Parvati had brought her girls from Bangladesh.

'Ask the bai to have another room constructed for you.'

'I am not her favourite whore,' says Gita.

'You bring national attention to the kotha,' he assures her.

'But I bring in no money. I bring scrutiny – from other NGOs, police, politicians, newspapers. The only reason the bai puts up with me is fear of what I can reveal if I am kicked out. She and I are a team, each afraid of the other.'

'At least the waiting room belongs to you.'

'It is my prison,' she says bitterly. 'My life – as is proper for Gita Didi, the NGO woman – is open to all. Because it is the STREE office, the waiting room has no doors or locks. There sits Gita Didi at her desk! She owns the divan, the linoleum, the STREE boards against Aids and the pictures of Sai Baba and Nehru. Everyone knows what she says, when she says it and how she says it. Everyone knows she has no thought in her head except the welfare of whores!'

'They are your daughters,' says Ramvilas. 'You say so yourself in your speeches.'

She turns viciously on him, lips trembling. In spite of himself, he is moved. This is Gulmohar, twenty-nine years old, Nepali girl from Sindhupalchowk district. How can those GB Road girls be her daughters? In another life they would be her sisters and friends, in this one they are competitors. She is not Gita Didi, after all. Beneath that exterior lies the troubled spirit of Gulmohar – a child trapped in the body of an old hag.

'It was your idea,' she says angrily. 'While I was printing pamphlets, Parvati went to her village wearing expensive jewellery and perfumes. Someone gave her silk and nylon sarees. She was the talk of the village – the successful garment exporter and boutique owner from Delhi. Do you know how many girls queued up to become garment exporters? She brought back the prettiest five, the ones with the best flesh on their bones.'

'I thought you enjoyed your work,' he says defensively.

'Parvati is the best-paid whore in GB Road,' continues Gita. 'She flounces around in beautiful sarees, wears flashy jewellery, flaunts leather purses and wafts fragrant clouds of attar wherever she walks. I spend my time distributing condoms and pamphlets.'

She has become increasingly agitated. A mid-life crisis ahead of itself, thinks Ramvilas, scornfully, perhaps because of the loss of her looks. She looks even more pathetic now that she is plain Gulmohar. The sloughing-off of Gita Didi has deprived her of poise. As Gita Didi she was the picture of dignified womanhood, standing mother-like in a white saree against a column in Rang Mahal. As Gulmohar she is a whore worn down with use. Now he can see flaws he did not notice before. She is too plump to be attractive – too much flesh bursts out of the sleeves of her blouse – and . . . what is this? A few lines round the edges of her eyes and mouth! The skin is still smooth but the flesh is sagging at the waist, under the chin, on her upper arms, her thighs . . . A cricketer and a whore are too old at twenty-nine.

'How old are the girls Parvati owns?' he asks.

He knows, of course. He has asked Parvati countless times, and received the same answer for four years – twenty-three.

'The oldest is seventeen,' says Gita.

He gasps. So they were thirteen when they came from Bangladesh. Parvati has fooled him. Gita looks at him oddly. 'Men are ignorant when it suits them,' she says. 'They will believe a seventeen-year-old girl when she tells them she is twenty-three.'

Does she know? wonders Ramvilas, with a shudder. He has been very careful, visiting the kotha on lazy afternoons, rushing past the STREE office and up to the room on the third floor. Parvati is sworn to secrecy, and her girls do not know his name.

'Seventeen is too young for a girl to be in GB Road,' says Gita.

He looks hard at her. She cannot be unaware of the irony. But he will say nothing to inflame her.

'Someone has been giving sarees and jewellery to Parvati and her girls,' says Gita.

She suspects! thinks Ramvilas. But I will not give myself away.

'Parvati gets eight rupees for every girl,' says Gita. 'Eight rupees for sitting on the divan and chewing paan! She pays a cut to the bai, but it is only a matter of time before she sets up her own kotha and becomes one herself.'

'You are the convener of STREE,' he reminds her. 'How can you compare yourself to a bai?'

'A bai earns money without doing anything,' she says defiantly. 'It is a good life.'

Ramvilas laughs. An MLA wants to become chief minister, an MP wants to become prime minister, a whore wants to become a bai!

'She will soon have her own pahalvans, her own agreement with the pimps and owners,' continues Gita, 'and pay her own commission to Inderlal Jha.'

Ramvilas frowns. Every time he hears that name, he hears of an increase in police rates.

'He just became SHO,' says Gita, with a sigh. 'When a man is promoted, he raises his rates.'

This cannot be why she called me here, Ramvilas thinks. He should not have shown her Rang Mahal. The emperor's debauchery has reached out from three centuries ago and touched her.

'Let us see Divan-i-Khas,' he suggests. He holds out his hand.

She does not take it. 'I have heard of this Moonlight Festival,' she says suddenly.

He brightens at the change of subject. 'Yes! On the fifteenth of October. It is Harilal Gupta's idea, to celebrate the heritage of Chandni Chowk, in memory of Lala Surajmal.'

'I do not care in whose memory it is being organised,' she says.

He wonders why she is interested in the festival. Surely she does not want a stall to recruit whores. 'GB Road is also part of our heritage,' he says playfully. 'As is STREE.'

She does not appear amused. 'There is a rumour that the festival is an excuse for a demolition drive.'

He is taken aback. 'Who told you that?'

'GB Road is mute,' she says. 'It is not deaf.'

He hesitates. Anything she learns will give her power over him. 'There are too many illegal structures in Chandni Chowk,' he says evasively.

She stares angrily at him. He looks at his wristwatch. It is almost five. She cannot use anything he tells her now because the demolition begins early tomorrow morning. 'Come with me,' he says.

This time, she takes his hand. He leads her to a brick staircase beyond the north-eastern edge of Rang Mahal. The door to it is shut, but the lock is rusty and comes undone in his hands. He removes it carefully and they climb the stairs, taking care to stay away from the crumbling edges.

'Is this allowed?' she asks.

'Shah Jahan is no longer emperor!' He laughs.

They go up the octagonal tower, testing each step before placing their weight on it, until they reach the top, where they stand high above the ground, overlooking the fortress walls.

'Mussuman Burj,' declares Ramvilas. 'This is where the emperor stood every morning, so his people could see that the lecher was still breathing. From here, he saw the Yamuna flowing by the fortress walls. He saw dances and celebrations, trials of strength and endurance, duels between elephants and lions . . . What do you see?'

Gita looks around her. Far out near the horizon she can see the asphalt ribbon of Ring Road. To her right there is a great moat and an expanse of grass, then Chandni Chowk and, rising above the clutter of grey-white rooftops, the domes and minarets of Jama Masjid.

'Look down there, to your left,' says Ramvilas.

Gita turns to the north-east where, sprawling along the fortress wall and stretching as far as she can see, there is a great slum – tarpaulins, canvas, cooking fires, pots, pans and thousands of children. It is a giant city, thrown into early-evening shadow by Red Fort, preparing for the onset of darkness.

'Naresh Colony,' says Ramvilas. 'The kingdom of the reigning emperor of Chandni Chowk. Fifty thousand illegal Bangladeshis, fifty thousand votes!'

Gita squeezes Ramvilas's hand, afraid that the wind will blow her off her perch.

'We will wipe it out,' he whispers. 'Bangladeshi Musalmans and all the rest. Every stall, every platform, every stake they have dug into ground that does not belong to them. Can you imagine how much more beautiful Chandni Chowk will be?'

She stands silently, overlooking the scene of impending destruction. He wonders if he should have told her so much, but she's only a whore. Whom can she tell? It is not STREE business anyway. And it will all be over before she wakes up tomorrow.

'It is not safe to stand here,' she says suddenly.

She turns and descends the stairs, leaving him to scramble after her. At the foot she turns north and walks through Khas Mahal, passing another board that advertises the *son-et-lumière*.

'Buy me tickets for this show,' she says indifferently.

'Yes, so they may stuff your head with lies,' he replies. 'They will tell you Shah Jahan built the fort.'

'Didn't he?'

He points to a carving on the wall – two swords laid hilt to hilt, a kalash above them, a lotus bud and the scales of justice balanced over it. 'That is the royal emblem of Raja Anangoal,' he says. 'He built Red Fort six hundred years before Shah Jahan was born. Do you see that Hindu kalash? And the Hindu conches that lie at the sword tips? Do you see the letter *om* carved in the arch above your head? Did you see the giant lotus carved on the floor of Rang Mahal?'

'I did not know there were Hindu symbols in Red Fort.'

'Because you did not look. There are elephants, statues, doorknobs, lattices, banana leaves, sun motifs . . . Even the name Rang Mahal is Hindu.'

She considers him with renewed interest. 'Who told you all this?'

'I am a committee member of IPP,' he says, with dignity. 'It is my duty to know about the cultural heritage of my country.'

She laughs and walks out of Khas Mahal.

'Let me show you where the PM stands on the fifteenth of August,' he says, in a rush of enthusiasm. He leads her across the gardens to the front wall. He would have liked to ascend the ramparts and see Chandni Chowk laid out before him, but the staircase is barred with a metal chain.

'I did not know you were law-abiding,' she taunts.

'I choose which laws to obey,' he replies.

'Show me the exact spot where the prime minister stands,' she insists.

He shrugs. 'The man who stands there on the fifteenth of August is a cipher. I will show you where real emperors sit.' He leads her to the marble pavilion of Divan-i-Khas. They walk on the cool marble floor.

She looks up at the ceiling and gasps at the gilt patterns. 'Gold and silver!'

'That is painted wood,' he says. 'The gold and silver are gone. Look there!' He points to an inscription that runs on the wall above the arches.

'I cannot read Urdu,' she says.

'Persian,' he says. ' "If there is Paradise on earth, it is this, it is this, it is this." '

'Ah.' She is unimpressed.

'The poet was carried away by his own rhetoric,' says Ramvilas. 'Or he was trying to please the emperor who employed him. Perhaps Shah Jahan himself selected the inscription. It is an old Indian habit. Do you know the first thing Harilal Gupta did when he became transport minister of Delhi? He had "Green Delhi!" hoardings put up all over the city, as if that would turn Delhi green and pollution-free.'

'Harilalji is a generous man,' says Gita.

Ramvilas ignores her comment. He points to the marble pedestal at the far end.

'I see nothing there,' she says.

'What you do not see is the most important seat in the empire of Hindustan,' he says. 'That is where the Peacock Throne stood. Thousands of diamonds, sapphires, rubies and emeralds, watched over by two peacocks. Enough to build entire cities, equal to the revenue from entire provinces! And this man – this wasteful lecher – is whom we call the greatest builder of all. His sons fought over the Peacock Throne. When one finally sat on it, he was the worst of all four!'

'Where is it now?' she asks.

'All over the world. Persia. England. Who knows? It still stands here and everyone wants to mount it. The prime minister, the chief minister, ministers, MPs, MLAs, councillors, Naresh Agrawal, Harilal, Sohan Lal, Parvati, every whore and every chaivala in Chandni Chowk. He who sits on the Peacock Throne rules the empire of Hindustan.'

'And you?' she asks.

He sighs. 'I was born to stand behind the throne and fan the emperor with a fly-whisk.'

She remains silent for a while, staring at the pedestal. Then she turns to him resolutely. 'Will this demolition extend to the lanes behind Jama Masjid?'

He is caught unawares, but recovers. 'Jama Masjid? Yes, behind it. It is a nest of Bangladeshis. Every building, every stall is illegal.'

Gita starts. The saree slithers from her shoulders. As she struggles to wrap it round her, Ramvilas notes with distaste the flesh that hangs and shakes under her arms. In spite of her agitation, she speaks slowly and deliberately: 'Do you know which buildings will go?'

'There is a list,' he says carelessly. 'I have not seen it.'

'There is a children's home in those lanes – a school run by a newspaper woman. Her name is Chitra Ghosh.'

'I have heard of her, but I don't know of a school.'

'It has an English name. Sparrow, I think. It is a red-brick structure, not a legal building, constructed by an MLA. Who is that Musalman MLA?'

'Suleman?'

Gita nods.

Ramvilas smirks. 'In that case, it will certainly be demolished!'

Gita breathes heavily. Ramvilas notes the rise and fall of her chest. Her breasts are beginning to sag. The rhythm is pleasing but the sight is not.

'Can you ask them not to demolish it?' she pleads.

He is puzzled at her interest in Suleman. Has she been bitten by the pseudo-secularists? 'Why do you care?'

She does not reply, but her eyes repeat the plea.

'There is not much I can do,' he hedges.

'Aren't you a committee member of IPP?'

'A minor one,' he says, with exaggerated humility. 'Perhaps you should ask Sohan Lalji. He is the committee chairman. Nothing will be demolished without his permission.'

'How do I contact him?' she asks desperately.

'He will first ask you why,' replies Ramvilas.

She takes a deep breath. 'Do you remember that I sent Kiran away?'

Ah, thinks Ramvilas. 'I told you it was a bad idea.'

'She is safe,' Gita responds.

'If so, why have you called me here?'

Gita looks away.

'How do you know she is still there? That was six years ago.'

A tear rolls down Gita's plump cheek. 'I know.'

Ramvilas is irritated by her self-assurance. He knows that, on STREE business, she frequently travels outside GB Road. Where the bai would rarely allow a whore to set foot outside the kotha, Gita sometimes leaves Chandni Chowk to travel to New Delhi to attend functions. She has sources of information other than him.

'There is nothing I can do,' he says.

Gita looks at him sadly. She has not lost her whoring ways, he thinks. Those soft eyes would melt any heart. This is Gulmohar, his prize after years of scouting ugly whores in GB Road. He was the first man to touch her, the one she will remember when she is old and haggard. Perhaps he owes her one last favour. But what can he do? Go to Sohan Lal and beg for this one building?

'I am your Mumtaz Mahal,' Gita says dreamily. 'Shah Jahan built Taj Mahal for her. Will you not save one little building for me?'

He turns away in disgust – a cheap Nepali whore comparing herself to a cheap Musalman whore!

'You are just a junior committee member, after all,' she taunts.

'I cannot stand in front of the bulldozers,' he retorts.

'All right, then. Bring her to me.'

'I thought you did not want her in the kotha,' he says sarcastically. 'The bai will turn her into a whore.'

'She will not dare,' says Gita. 'I have no choice anyway.'

'What about Inderlal Jha? Does he not collect a fee for every new girl?'

'She is not coming to work there.'

'He won't care.'

'She is only eleven!' says Gita.

Ramvilas cannot suppress a smile. 'Old enough.'

Gita trembles in outrage, but subsides. He looks at her with approval. This is how he likes to see her, not pious in a sanctimonious white saree. She almost reminds him, as she stands now, of the Gulmohar in her third-floor room in the kotha.

'I will take care of it, Jahanara Begum! And I will take care of Inderlal. What is a mere SHO before a Chandni Chowk IPP committee member? I will send someone to that Sparrow building tonight. How will my man recognise her?'

'I will go with him,' she says eagerly.

'No.'

'I will cover myself from head to toe. No one will know who I am.'

He looks at her playfully. 'What if my man wants a taste of you?'

Gulmohar stomps her foot, losing all traces of Gita Didi. Then she makes a strenuous effort to smile and acknowledge the joke. She knows she must not offend him.

'My man will be at the kotha in three hours,' he says. 'It will be dark by then. He will come to the waiting room and ask about STREE. "What are your programmes for sex-workers in Agra?" he will ask. Ask him who sent him. He will say, "Arjumand Bano Begum." That is your cue. Go with him, and cover your face. Do not enter the school. Stand at the door and point out the girl to him. He will bring her outside and hand her to you, and accompany you as far as GB Road. If Inderlal notices anything, ask him to talk to me tomorrow.

Tears flow down Gita's face. 'I will never forget this, Ramvilas Babu.'

He is flattered at being called 'babu'. His Gulmohar! His Delhi wife! 'For you, my Jahanara, my life!'

'She may even be your daughter,' says Gita.

He turns on her. 'Don't ever say that! A whore fucks five customers every night. One hundred and fifty men in a month!'

He pushes the thought from his mind and thinks of his daughters – the younger is too tall for fourteen, the older a full woman at sixteen, both clamouring silently to be married off. Ah, the responsibility and the expense! Perhaps he will sell the flat in Bahadurgarh. But where will his wife – a woman who has never left Bahadurgarh in fifteen years – live then? He cannot bring her to Delhi. She has never seen Chandni Chowk. She has no understanding of its scale, its magnitude . . . He must speed up the division of Bhagwan Das and Sons.

'I must go,' says Gita.

'Wait! We have not discussed payment.'

She appears offended.

'Surely you did not think I would do this for free,' he says.

'I thought you were a seth now,' she says.

'I have four sons to deal with.' He frowns. 'Like Shah Jahan's four sons, they are engaged in fratricide. Aurangzeb has moved the court. Shuja and Murad are his allies, but it is Dara Shikoh who shall be my partner in the oldest perfumery in India.'

'You are a partner?'

'I will be.' He chuckles.

'I thought Aurangzeb won the war and became emperor.'

'In *that* century, yes. Dara will win in this one. Simple, sweet, studious Dara, eldest of the brothers, the mildest, gentlest, most gullible, most malleable . . .'

'I have no money to give you,' she says. 'You know I do not work any more.'

'Do not tell me you spend everything you collect for STREE. More money can be earned through it than Parvati can make with an entire harem of whores.'

'I am too poor to give anything to a seth,' says Gita.

'But you can.'

Gita wraps her saree round herself. 'Come to the kotha tomorrow evening,' she mutters. 'The STREE office.'

He chuckles.

'I promise nothing,' she warns. 'Now I must go and prepare a feast for my daughter. Your man will come in three hours?'

He nods. She turns to go. 'Who was Arjumand Bano Begum?' she asks.

'The whore who is buried under Taj Mahal.'

Gauhar dreams. With his stump in his pocket, he throws the left arm round Kiran's shoulders as they walk into the cinema. He is wearing new black trousers, a new cream shirt, a new leather belt, black rexine shoes, and his hair is oiled . . . Kiran looks so beautiful in her new saree! A full woman, plump and fleshy. The sleeves of her blouse are short, the saree is tied low on her hips – below the deep navel – and her creamy skin is so alluring at the midriff. Where did she get that fragrance? Does someone give her perfumes and attars?

They reach the ticket counter and he makes Kiran stand in the female queue because it is shorter. The men are envious of him, because he need not stand in the long queue with them and because the girl he has brought to the cinema is the most beautiful of them all – more beautiful than the heroine on screen! Kiran reaches the counter and turns to him for money. He reaches absent-mindedly for the pocket at the back of his new trousers. He pulls out his wallet, bursting with crisp notes, unfolds it and hands her a hundred rupees. 'Get us the softest seats,' he tells her. Kiran throws the note on to the counter and buys two dress-circle tickets at twenty-five rupees each.

'Here are the tickets,' she says. Only then does she notice his right hand and squeals in delight. 'What happened to your hand?' she asks.

'Muhammad Ghayas cured me,' he says. 'He made cuts and let the bad blood seep out, so the hand has now grown back. It has been trying to grow back all my life, but the bad blood would not let it. I will write a letter for Muhammad Ghayas so he can get more customers!'

Kiran holds up his right hand, rolls it into a fist, spreads out his fingers, turns it upside-down, pinches it, but it really is a hand. 'I will go and thank Muhammad Ghayas,' she says.

'Laila and Majnu!' shouts a woman in the female line. 'Get out of the way now that you have your ticket! You can warm each other inside the cinema!'

Gauhar and Kiran walk to the entrance, laughing. He puts the first two fingers of both hands into his mouth and lets out a loud whistle that echoes through the hall, sounding like a police siren. He wakes up.

There are loud knocks on the Sparrows walls that cause the entire building to shake. Gauhar is curled up on the floor in the hall. The children in the room are screaming. They run here and there, approach the windows, then rush into the room when they see men in the lane. Gauhar gets up and races to the window. He peers outside. There are twenty men with pickaxes, hammers and long sticks, accompanied by a dozen police constables and an inspector. They bring their hammers down, again and again, on the brick wall of the Sparrows kitchen. It runs across the lane but they have already loosened a few bricks. They shred the tarpaulin, uproot the wood-burning oven, and tear up the planks on which the cook squats. They toss chairs and tables from the kitchen over the brick wall. Behind them, advancing steadily with an increasing roar, a bulldozer is coming straight toward Gauhar.

Suleman Mian has sent men to kill me! thinks Gauhar. He should not have stolen from Faquira, who enjoys Ibrahim Mian's protection. He must run before they enter the building. He ducks back into the hall and races to the corridor outside, which is a sea of scampering children, stampeding out into the street through a side-door. A crash resounds through the hall, and he knows they have broken down the glass door that separates the hall from the kitchen. A loudspeaker announces that all occupants of the building should evacuate immediately because it will be brought down in a few minutes. He must escape before they come in, he tells himself. Where is Kiran? She will not be able to run as fast as him.

He hurries into the smaller room next to the hall where the girls sleep. They are all awake, crying, collecting their clothes, running about, but there is no sign of Kiran. 'Where is Kiran?' he asks the girls. But they do not hear him. They run away from the room, the building and the loudspeaker. She is not in the room, not in the hall, not in the passage that connects the two. He kicks in the door of the latrine in the backyard, and frightens a little naked girl who squats in fear. 'Get out of here or you will be killed!' he says. But she is not Kiran. Why did Kiran run away instead of coming to him? He will have a last look. He comes back into the passage and peers into the girls' room again. The left wall has yielded to the bulldozer. It has a gaping hole in it, through which five men pour with hammers, swinging carelessly at the remaining bricks. Gauhar runs back into the passage, brushes against the Baal Bank almirah, and is reminded of the cash-box that sits inside it. More than three thousand rupees . . . Those men will find it, he thinks. Why should they have it? No one will know where it is once the building is razed.

He pushes hard against the almirah. It tips over and crashes in a cloud of dust. He kicks the warped door until it breaks. He picks up the cash-box – it is locked but he can open it later – and runs through the crowd of men who have now swarmed into the passage, and leaves through an opening in the wall.

Inderlal Jha stands – hands behind his back – outside the crumbling building. He sees a man jump through the broken wall with a large box pressed between his chest and his left hand. Instinct causes him to raise his baton, but he lets the man go unchallenged. It is not his business. It is awkward enough for him to provide escort to these Corporation coolies, to be shouted at by the municipal commissioner. As SHO in GB Road, his job is to apprehend crooks, beat up thieves, extract confessions and collect commissions from bais. He has worked hard to get where he is. Not everyone who starts out as a head constable becomes SHO in less than fifteen years. Then there is the commendation roll he received from the commissioner of police for the sardars he saved in 'eighty-four, the out-of-turn promotion from ASI to SI, the quick move from SI to full inspector, then SHO, and the police medal for meritorious service he hopes to receive. After all this, must he stand with his hands crossed – like a bank security guard – while coolies tear down buildings?

They had started early in the morning with Naresh Colony, along the north-eastern wall of Red Fort. How those Bangladeshis had resisted! They had formed rowdy armies, hurled abuse and stones, cried, brought down the wrath of Allah on the crew, and finally had run for their lives. He had had to bring out riot shields. Thousands of shelters were torn down, tarpaulins removed, cans overturned, stoves destroyed and sacking shredded. The entire stretch of land between Red Fort and Ring Road is now a graveyard of pots and pans.

The procession, which consists of two bulldozers, twenty Corporation workers and a dozen policemen, has now found its way to the Jama Masjid area, destroying everything in its wake. The municipal commissioner rides in a jeep alongside, beaming as if this was his wedding procession, poring over files and lists, pointing to this or that shop. Then, the demolition squad goes to work. Inderlal's duty is to guard against untoward incidents. He does not much mind demolitions in this area. This is not his stamping ground: it pays him nothing. But he knows they will eventually find their way to GB Road. If they destroy all encroachments there, he will be left with nothing but the dwindling cuts from whores and bais. Yet he must stand and help the bastards destroy his livelihood. How is a man with a wife and children to live on his SHO salary? He has paid many lakhs on his way to this or that posting, so where are those police officers now, when he needs them to protect his territory?

The red-brick building is a heap of rubble. Corporation workers stow away chairs, tables and other furniture in trucks, with a large steel almirah. Its door swings open and a shower of files descends to the ground. The procession moves on. Inderlal marches with it, seething. They wind their way through Urdu Bajar and the fish market, hammering, jabbing, tearing down, carting away. As soon as they approach an area – announced by police loudspeakers and sirens – men scamper to collect what they can and disappear into the lanes like rats, carrying ovens, baskets, wooden planks, lanterns, electric fans, stoves, canvas covers, sticks, chairs, mattresses, cauldrons, sieves, knives, spoons, glasses, pavement mirrors, barber bowls, head-massage basins . . . and the demolition squad reduces the rest to dust. The workers have begun to enjoy their task. Even Inderlal's men join in, and he begins to think it is not such a bad day after all. He fills his pockets with small trinkets from a shop – fake necklaces and earrings – until they overflow. He uses his baton to deliver lethal blows. Biryani stalls, haleem shops, halva cauldrons, attar baskets, rose-water canisters, fish heaps . . . A labyrinthine store reveals closely packed walls of music cassettes – Noor Jahan, Mehdi Hassan, Ghulam Ali and Iqbal Bano. It is very narrow, almost like a tunnel, and juts outrageously into the street. Inderlal slashes at the cassettes, which cascade down to thunderous applause from his constables. 'Listen to the music of Noor Jahan!' he declares. 'Break them all, turn them all into dirt and rubble!'

'Go to Meena Bajar,' orders the municipal commissioner.

Inderlal hesitates. Meena Bajar is a Musalman region. 'It is a sensitive area,' he says.

'It is on the list,' says the stone-faced commissioner.

Inderlal walks alongside but stays in the background while they uproot Meena Bajar. He wants to be able to say later that he was not involved with this. 'Muhammad Ghayas, proprietor,' says a board on the pavement. There is a quadrangle of sacking, an array of blades, bowls of water and large blotches of dried blood on the pavement. 'Heart disease, asthma and impotence cured by blood-letting,' says the board in Hindi. Three framed pictures still stand – testimonials from happy patients, white men and women, their names signed in English below letters written in Hindi. 'I tried doctors all over the world but my asthma was cured by Muhammad Ghayas,' says the smiling woman. 'May Jesus bless him! I now live happily in America, and will come once every year to meet Mr Ghayas.'

A clattering sound distracts Inderlal. The demolition men have spotted the clinic. He steps back. The men raise their sticks and cut a wide swathe through the water bowls and framed pictures, obliterating Muhammad Ghayas's past record. The sound draws frantic protests from a bearded man, who comes running and hops round the demolition crew, flinging curses, bringing down the wrath of Allah on their heads. He picks up his scattered blades and throws them at the bulldozers. 'I have been on television!' he screams. 'There was a madam who made a film about me!' The bulldozers advance indifferently. He scoops up two picture frames – the longest testimonials from his patients – before the giant steel rollers can crush them to dust. Then he runs, hugging the frames close, crying, screaming.

They leave Meena Bajar a full hour later. Inderlal casts one look back before he steps into his jeep, and sees mountains of bangles, mirrors, laces and trinkets. He wishes he could let his wife loose here for a day. What a wonderful time she would have!

The procession storms through Ajmeri Gate, Kamla Market, Nai Sarak and Chawri Bajar, leaving stacks of books, cardboard boxes and cartons in its wake. Passing through Ballimaran, the bulldozers tear through a dozen illegal rooms and send hundreds of silver sheets flying into the air. The demolition crew rushes to capture the silver varq, some of which is flung over buildings into adjoining lanes.

Inderlal heaves a sigh of relief when they rush through GB Road, making only two stops to smash some commodes and wash-basins, and destroy a paan stall. Whores watch curiously from third-floor grilles as the bulldozers move on. The kothas are the only legal structures in this shameless city, Inderlal chuckles to himself.

In Khari Baoli, the crew overturns stalls and carts, depositing mountains of red pepper in the street. Blinded by pepper, they make their way through, sneezing repeatedly, stamping on sweet-smelling cardamom, kicking sticks of cinnamon, and finally emerge to gasp for fresh air.

They rush out of Khari Baoli sooner than planned, relieved to be free, and smash the watch shops outside Fatehpuri Masjid in a fit of pique. 'Those are not on the list,' says the annoyed commissioner, but the glass panes are already shards, and a few watches have already been strapped round demolition-crew wrists.

Ramvilas stands in the recesses of the doorway to Fatehpuri Masjid, and watches the squad with amusement. It is the horde of Nadir Shah, he thinks, converging on Dariba, having slaughtered the Mughal army near Karnal. 'Until I put my sword back into its sheath,' said Nadir Shah, 'the life of every man, woman and child in Delhi is forfeit . . .' What sublime destruction the horde leaves in its wake!

The procession moves up Chandni Chowk and makes a detour to Dudhiya Gali. Bulldozers crush the milk pails and vats of curd that lie in the lane. Ram Bibek throws his razors, mirrors and shaving brushes into a sack, slings it over one shoulder, his chair over the other, and runs. The bulldozer operator, in over-zealous discharge of his duty, aims for the running barber, misses and hits the hand-pump instead, releasing a spray of water into the air. The men arrive soon after and smash the glass front of Banwari's ice-cream shop because it juts into the pavement. When they leave, the drains of Dudhiya Gali flow with milk. Curd lies in trembling pieces all over the lane, like a colony of floating icebergs.

As the bulldozers approach Town Hall, they find the first signs of resistance. A dozen traders stand in their path, raising slogans against Naresh Agrawal and Harilal Gupta. The municipal commissioner steps out of his jeep and announces, through his loudspeaker, that the drive has been launched by order of the Supreme Court, that he is powerless to stop it, that he himself is facing contempt-of-court charges for not implementing it sooner. 'We will not let you destroy our shops so you can stay out of jail!' shout the traders.

'Only illegal structures will be destroyed,' the commissioner assures them. The traders do not budge. The bulldozers wait, engines whirring ominously.

Harilal Gupta arrives with a cavalcade of cars, assures the traders that their shops are safe, and invites them to a meeting inside Town Hall. They file inside, and the demolition resumes.

Inderlal's jeep drives behind the bulldozers, using them for cover while providing protection to the demolition crew who follow it. It is almost noon, and he is hungry. The bulldozers rumble past Mangat Ram Nawal Kishor, where fresh laddus and kachauris lie displayed behind glass walls. 'Stop the jeep,' he says. He hops out and runs up the stairs into the shop. A wall is being constructed right down the middle. Illegal, he thinks, just like the ornate façade of plaster and marble, built recently, that straddles the drain to project into the street. The shop has extended itself by a yard. Even the pavement at the front – municipal property – has been resurfaced with white marble.

He knocks on the façade with his baton, signalling to the workers with hammers. The municipal commissioner, whose jeep has stopped with Inderlal's, walks rapidly toward him.

'Not on the list,' says the commissioner, frowning.

Three men sit behind the counter, watching Inderlal suspiciously. On seeing the commissioner, they smile. Inderlal shrugs. The seth, who had been supervising the construction of the wall, hurries toward the commissioner.

'Namaste, Jugal Kishorji,' says the commissioner.

Jugal Kishor looks tired and haggard. Servants bring chairs for the commissioner and Inderlal, followed by chai, kachauris and laddus.

'My sons have finalised partition terms,' says Jugal Kishor, in a voice that mixes relief with resignation.

The comment is directed at the commissioner but Inderlal nods anyway, including himself in the seth's circle. He likes to be in such company, exchanging confidences. He can see two signboards stacked against the wall – Rajesh Kumar Jugal Kishor and Pavan Kumar Jugal Kishor – waiting to be put up once the dividing wall is complete.

'Did you get a permit for the wall?' asks the commissioner, tentatively.

Jugal Kishor shrugs and spreads his hands helplessly. 'I have been trying to mediate between them for two years now, but they are bent on going their separate ways.'

'But the wall?'

'What can you do about family matters?' Jugal Kishor asks rhetorically.

'But a permit . . .'

'This shop has been a perfect example of communal harmony for the last hundred years,' mourns Jugal Kishor. 'All cooks are Hindus, and all patrons once were Musalman nawabs and emperors.'

'The permit . . .'

'We still serve Hindus and Musalmans alike,' says Jugal Kishor. 'What is a wall? It is a family matter, an internal matter. The façade is temporary. And the ledge is for convenience. If I remove the ledge, where will my customers stand when they look at the samosas and kachauris?'

'Another kachauri?' asks the commissioner, his mouth full.

'Give Commissioner Sahib another kachauri!' Jugal Kishor commands his staff. 'Give one to SHO Sahib too. And give samosas to the bulldozer drivers and everyone else.'

Thirty minutes later the demolition squad, bellies full, resumes its journey and makes its way toward Red Fort. Half-way down Chandni Chowk, they arrive at a large peepul tree that rises along a temple wall.

'We cannot destroy a temple,' says the commissioner.

Inderlal folds his hands, invokes the name of Hanuman for his trespass and carefully removes his shoes. He pushes aside the collapsible gates amid much screeching, and steps into the concrete kiosk. The temple wall has an opening to allow for the tree, which was evidently full-grown before the temple was constructed. He folds his hands again toward the red statue of Hanuman, who is on one knee, eyes lowered in devotion, hands folded, tail raised, vermilion tilak on his head and sunflowers at his feet.

The left wall of the temple is breached, opening into a courtyard. In the middle of this sits the pujari, oblivious of the noise, surrounded by his brass utensils, pillows, bed-sheets, soap, a lantern and a radio, engaged in brushing his teeth with a twig of babool. Inderlal tells the pujari that the tree is on the demolition list because it does not have a permit.

'What tree?' asks the pujari.

He appears surprised when it is pointed out to him, visible through the gap in the temple wall. 'Cut it down,' he says, 'but leave the big electric sign in place because it lights up the temple at night.'

Inderlal comes out and tells the commissioner that the pujari has no objections. The commissioner looks carefully at the tree, burdened with its many signboards – 'We accept torn money'; 'Try not to follow the crowd'; 'Full body massage'. In a fork between the two thickest branches sits a gigantic neon sign: 'Jamna Lal Kishori Mal – Sarees and Blouses'. 'Cut down the peepul,' he tells the crew.

They swing their axes at the tired trunk. The tree shakes, lets go of a few signboards, swoons and crashes on to the Hanuman temple, levelling it to the ground. The pujari crawls out of the rubble, flings his babool twig at the crew and hurls imprecations at the bulldozers.

'What is next on the list?' Inderlal asks the commissioner.

'Kucha Bansilal.'

Inderlal remembers the kucha well. This was his regular beat as head constable, before he got himself posted to GB Road. The kucha is too narrow for bulldozers, so the commissioner orders his workers to enter it on foot, wielding hammers and axes. Then he follows them. Inderlal is behind him, but the commissioner stops him. 'Stand guard here,' he says. 'There is no need for police protection in a narrow lane.'

Inderlal twirls his baton and loiters round the fallen tree, picking up objects, watching the crowd that has formed outside the kucha. We should demolish all of Chandni Chowk, he thinks, in a moment of clarity. We should tear down its havelis, kuchas, katras, shops, cubicles and cubbyholes, and we should build a beautiful city in its place, with wide roads, large police stations and great kothas full of whores.

The STREE office is on the first floor of Kotha 842, at the end of a flight of stairs that leads up from the street door. The passage that leads to it has been brightly illuminated by three naked electric lights that swing from the ceiling. Paan stains have been removed, the walls painted, and a whore sprays air-freshener every morning to eliminate the smell of urine and semen. Boxes of condoms are stacked six feet high outside the office. A board says, 'STREE – Empowering the Sex-worker in GB Road.' A clean curtain flutters at the door.

On the walls, between pictures of Gandhi, Nehru and Swami Shraddhanand, posters declare the objectives of STREE and exhort sex-workers to assert their rights. 'Sex-worker Training, Rehabilitation and Education Endeavour,' says the largest poster, and the text runs round a circular logo showing a woman holding a pen. 'STREE, giving women the dignity they deserve!' says a second poster. 'Legalise prostitution!' demands a third. 'Punish the customer, not the shop-keeper!'

'Our honour is your honour,' declares a woman in a saree. 'Every woman is someone's sister, mother or daughter! Safe sex: in your home and in the marketplace! Use a condom, save a life!'

A picture of Amitabh Bachchan hangs among the slogans, perhaps a remnant from the old days when the bai used the room to offer fresh virgins to regular customers.

There is a framed picture of Gita Didi receiving a plaque from Harilal Gupta, MLA for Chandni Chowk and transport minister in the Delhi government. A divan stretches along one wall, with a mirror above it, another relic from the past when it offered a complete view of the whore being advertised. The opposite wall is partially hidden by a desk and a chair. Cartons of condoms are stacked, four high, next to the desk. Three chairs are scattered around the room. The floor is old linoleum, frayed in places. The walls, where they are not covered with posters, bear the imprints of bunk beds that have been removed and sent across the landing to another room.

The divan is covered with a floral bed-sheet and two neatly arranged pillows. Gita Didi sits on it in a plain cotton saree. It is late in the evening. The entire kotha – indeed, all of GB Road – has been in uproar as word of the demolition drive has spread. Most shops had already shut down before the bulldozers arrived at noon. They rumbled through in a stately procession. A paan stall was removed, some awnings were torn and the wash-basins under them smashed. The men had a romp with ceramic commodes, throwing them into the air and watching them crash into smithereens. A few taps, pipes and bathroom tiles were stolen. Gita saw it all from the balcony, standing far behind the grille in case they looked up and whistled at her – irritating during the day, when the kotha is closed for business.

When the bulldozers had gone she went back into the waiting room and tried to complete STREE records, but could not concentrate. She bathed, washed her clothes, combed her hair, cleaned the waiting room, spoke to Manju and Nasreen, had a tiff with the bai, and spent much of the day waiting for Kiran to wake. Late in the afternoon, when the heat became unbearable, she placed a table fan next to the cot behind the curtain where the girl slept. She spent the afternoon wondering if she should wake her daughter. How could she sleep straight through the day? She had had a rough night. Let her sleep! She will have to find Kiran a bed for tonight when she will need the cot herself. Perhaps a second cot could be placed near the desk. She will have to ask the bai, and tolerate some sniggering. Their relations have been frosty ever since she asked the bai to move her reception room across the landing.

She knows that the bai's retreat is tactical. The woman cannot afford to alienate STREE, especially with the increased scrutiny of kothas by the government and NGOs. There is no dearth of meddling women, all dressed in flowing sarees and chattering in English, who hover about, trying to talk to the pahalvans and the whores. Having STREE inside the kotha – as a sort of homegrown NGO – causes NGO women to turn their attention to other kothas when they preach against under-age girls and Aids. The bai knows this, and Gita knows she knows, and that she uses STREE as a shield against government doctors. There is not much Gita can do. Should STREE turn its gaze inward, it will find itself summarily evicted.

Kiran makes a sound behind the curtain, and Gita looks at the clock on the wall. It is seven. She pulls the curtain aside and holds her daughter's small, oval face in her hands. She could not look at her carefully last night, and was afraid to look all day while the girl slept. This is the child she last saw six years ago, and she has changed so little! Age never destroyed the innocence of a beautiful girl. The skin is light brown – a shade darker than Gita's but no less rich and smooth. The lips are thin and unformed, as yet. The arms are soft and defenceless, the frame is lithe and underfed, but it is the eyes that make her Gita's daughter – almond-shaped eyes that close delightfully whenever she tries to concentrate. There is nothing of her father in them. They are beautiful Nepali eyes. But where had they acquired their hunted, shell-shocked look? Perhaps in that dreadful home, where she was surrounded by boys who intimidated her.

Gita has seen such a vulnerable face before. She is reminded of a boy of twenty seated on the edge of a plastic chair, in a shocking yellow shirt and ill-fitting mud-coloured trousers. On seeing her, he stands up with an embarrassed smile – desire competing with emotion. He looks at her wide-eyed, then looks away, and she knows his mind has frozen on an image that will not leave him. She had destroyed that innocence.

She will not let her daughter be violated as she herself violated that boy. She will protect the stainless face before her. Kiran is not a woman yet, but there is a suggestion of breasts. The new frock – bought in a hurry last evening – is too large for her. Gita had imagined a taller, fuller girl than the one she saw in Sparrows. She had anticipated an outpouring of love rather than pity. No matter, Kiran will fill out now under the care of a loving mother. You are the fruit of my youth, thinks Gita, and I will wipe that frightened look from your eyes. I will fill them with joy and radiance. 'You have not eaten all day,' she says.

Kiran shakes her head. She is not hungry.

'Say something! Anything! Call me Ma . . .'

Kiran looks around uncertainly. Her eyes close again. 'Where is Didi?' she asks.

Gita sighs and brushes a strand of hair off Kiran's cheek. She will have to work hard to bring her daughter back. My daughter, mine, even if not mine yet . . . It was perhaps a mistake to send her away, but Nasreen was adamant. 'She will grow up to be a whore,' she said. The bai, who seized every opportunity to send children away from the kotha, gave her approval, and everything was arranged quickly. Now Gita realises she should not have listened to Nasreen. She has watched Bittu grow up in Parvati's care. He is six, a little older than Kiran was when she sent her away. It is easier to keep a boy, of course. As much as she dislikes Parvati and finds the boy obnoxious, she cannot resist fondling him, kissing him. How much more should it mean to have her own daughter in her arms! Yet here sits a girl of eleven, lost to her, asking for another woman.

'Let me comb your hair,' says Gita.

Kiran resists, but Gita turns her and runs a comb through it anyway. It is unhealthy hair, lumpy and brittle. The comb finds a knot and yanks her head back. Kiran screams in pain. Gita laughs and continues.

Kiran submits to the grooming, but she is torn with suspicion of this woman who claims to be her mother. She remembers the building, the landing and a room upstairs. She remembers wandering in and out, hearing her mother called 'Gulmohar'. And she remembers a woman far more beautiful and less plump. Who is this Gita Didi, and why does she tell her repeatedly that she is her mother? Didi has warned everyone about kidnappers who take girls and keep them locked up for days without food. Perhaps this Gita Didi is one of them, but she is kind even if she is not gentle, and she is solicitous, not indifferent. Although she is no substitute for Kiran's mother, she is mother-like in her attitude, and her eyes and skin resemble Gulmohar's. She would like to go back to Didi and ask her about this woman. And she would like to meet the man whose hand she bit. She hopes the hand is all right. Perhaps he can tell her who this new mother is, and rescue her if necessary.

The curtain shakes. A man stands at the door, smirking. A man with smooth cheeks and cruel eyes. 'Who is that?' She points.

Gita turns quickly, anticipating the bai, but it is Ramvilas. She stiffens. 'The kotha is not open yet,' she says. 'Did the pahalvan not stop you at the door?'

'He knows me from the old days,' chuckles Ramvilas, as he advances into the room, looking at Kiran.

'Go!' she commands Kiran. 'Nasreen Aunty will comb your hair.'

Kiran rises from the divan, comb in hand, and leaves the room. Gita watches her every movement. How modestly she smoothes down her frock after she gets up! As she approaches the door, she steps aside to avoid Ramvilas, who makes no attempt to get out of her way. 'A beautiful girl,' he observes.

'You are early,' says Gita sharply.

'I am almost a seth now,' he says. 'I like prompt payment when the goods have been delivered.'

She remains on the divan, silent. He sits at her desk, noting the scattered registers, notebooks and stationery with derision. 'So, this is where Gita Didi maintains records of condoms distributed.' She looks away. He reads from a list. 'STD-awareness campaign, a case of Aids, the matter of under-age girls . . .' He laughs. 'I thought every whore in every kotha was twenty-three?'

'I cannot change the world overnight,' says Gita.

Ramvilas chuckles. He points to the cot, exposed behind the drawn curtain. 'Is this where you sleep?'

Gita nods.

'It does not look like a four-poster bed,' he says. 'Did you have any trouble last night?'

'You can see I did not.'

'Does Inderlal know?'

Gita makes a contemptuous sound. 'He came here this morning, saying he had to leave with the Corporation bulldozers but he would be back to collect his share. I wonder who told him.'

'How much did he want?'

'I never asked,' said Gita. 'I told him to collect it directly from Harilalji. To claim his share for a girl of eleven! She is not here for business! You should have seen his face when he left.'

'He will be back,' says Ramvilas. 'What about the bai?'

'She wants money too. And I cannot say no to her.'

'She should be grateful her kotha was spared,' says Ramvilas. 'Did you see the bulldozers?'

'They hardly stopped in GB Road,' she says.

'The children of Shah Jahan have been thrown out of Chandni Chowk,' he exults, 'all fifty thousand of them. Now we can have a festival to celebrate our cultural heritage, the heritage of the whores, pederasts, sodomising psychopaths whose children we are! We can illuminate every garden in which the emperor fornicated, every palace in which he raped, every dungeon in which he tortured!'

Gita says nothing.

'I will ask Harilal Gupta to give you a STREE stall,' Ramvilas jokes. 'Do not bring Bangladeshi whores to the stall. You can distribute condoms. Talk about Aids, under-age girls, legalisation, police harassment. You are part of our heritage too, Gulmohar. You were here before Red Fort, before a single ray of the moon glanced off the waters in Ali Mardan's canal. You are Chandni Chowk itself!'

'What happened to that school, Sparrow?' asks Gita.

'Razed to the ground,' says Ramvilas, with satisfaction. 'Like all other structures erected by Suleman. More than nine hundred shops and stalls have been removed, with thousands of chairs, benches and tarpaulins, all the hovels of sin infested with Bangladeshis, the cauldrons where Suleman's men breed and fester.'

'Why did he allow it?'

'There are three IPP MLAs from Chandni Chowk,' says Ramvilas, 'and only one Suleman.'

'Where are the other children?'

'Children?'

'From Sparrow.'

'How would I know?' he says peevishly.

Gita remembers the girls in fraying frocks and the boys in fraying shorts – thin, small, underfed, lost to the world – when she went there last night. They looked so much like Kiran that she had to strain hard in the poor light to recognise the one that was hers. She briefly entertained the thought of bringing them all to the kotha, then saw the impatient look in the eyes of Ramvilas's man and thought better of it. She was consoled that the children did not look unhappy. Even Kiran was not eager to leave the red-brick building. She brushes aside the images of the other children. Kiran is in the kotha, sitting in Nasreen's room, having her hair combed. That is enough for now.

Ramvilas withdraws a paper bag from his pocket. 'Keep this,' he says.

She shakes out the necklace on to her palm – imitation gold, green plastic pendant. 'I have already said I don't need it.'

'It is not for you,' he says gently. 'It is for Kiran.'

She hurls it into his face. 'You cannot buy her with a cheap necklace!'

He is annoyed. 'Have you not heard of the Chinese invasion of Chandni Chowk?' he asks scornfully. 'Everything is cheap now. Why should a whore cost more than twelve rupees?'

'She is not here for business!'

'None of them comes here for business.'

'She is your daughter!' Gita screams.

Ramvilas grits his teeth, then leers. 'But I am Shah Jahan! Do you know what Shah Jahan said when he saw his daughter Jahanara standing in the gardens of Red Fort? He said, "A gardener has first rights to the fruit of the tree he planted . . ."'

She slaps him hard, and he is suddenly silenced. She takes a step back, horrified, watching him carefully as she would a wounded dog. She must placate him. She can ward him off today, but he will come again and again . . . 'Give her time,' she pleads. 'A week – a few weeks.'

He nods slowly, caressing his cheek. He must tread carefully, now that Harilal Gupta has promised him a prominent role in organising the Moonlight Festival. It is not a good idea to visit the kotha frequently. Many shopkeepers in the water-pump market recognise an IPP committee member. Some may still be sitting in their shops, even so late in the evening. He would have abandoned GB Road altogether, at least for a few months, but he has noticed blisters in his groin. He is afraid to go to a doctor for fear of what he may say, but he has no doubt he caught them from Parvati or one of her girls. He has heard about the curative powers of virgins, known to heal hundreds of diseases, perhaps even Aids. He only half believes the theory but there is no harm in trying, especially when the trial will be so enjoyable. Meanwhile he must exercise discretion and be patient, applying gentle pressure until Gita yields. She cannot shield Kiran for ever. A whore is a whore, after all, and he will pay mother and daughter quite well. Kiran looks too Nepali to be his daughter. Obviously the bai offered Gulmohar to others in those days without seeking his permission. The girl could not possibly be of his blood, or he would certainly have been moved by her. He remembers encouraging Gita to send her away. Of course, she was a child then and is almost a woman now. A beautiful woman. 'I will see her before I go,' he declares firmly.

'She is tired. She has not slept for twenty-four hours, and it is past ten.'

'She looked well rested a moment ago,' insists Ramvilas. 'Fresh and lovely, and so innocent . . .'

'She is only eleven!' pleads Gita.

'She will grow,' he says, with a gleam in his eyes. 'And hormones will speed it up. You would know. Ask Parvati what she gives to her girls.'

'You are a vile man!' she says, through clenched teeth.

He grins. 'You always wanted to have your own girls, as Parvati does, so you could be a bai.'

Gita collapses on the divan, exhausted. What a wretched state to be in! She can stare down Inderlal Jha, she can pay off the bai, she can lecture on condoms, she can storm other kothas and expose the violence inside them, but she cannot do anything to protect her daughter.

She still has recourse to her own body, her own self. She may be Gita Didi now, dressed in a white saree, but she was Gulmohar before that, the most dazzling whore on GB Road. Why, she is only twenty-nine! She rises slowly from the divan, making an intense effort to look at him with longing. 'You no longer come to me,' she purrs. 'I remember the days when your hands were full of swivelling mirrors and attar bottles. Do you have other wives in your harem?'

A woman should not put on airs that do not suit her age, thinks Ramvilas.

'Have you forgotten your first love?' she coos, in a voice half affectionate and half pitiful.

She watches his face carefully for signs of lust that do not appear. Frantically, she lets her saree slip off her shoulders, unbuttons her blouse and throws her arms round him with a laugh that is both luscious and grotesque. She senses he has stiffened, begins to cry, then collects herself and chortles with delight as she swings from his shoulders. She must arouse his lust, not his pity . . . I am yours, fully yours, to be had in any way you desire!

Ramvilas watches with a mixture of bemusement and disgust. How often has he consoled himself in the folds of her flesh! Now she is smothering him with tear-stained kisses, but she is giving nothing: rather, she is trying to keep something from him. A whore does not forget her profession. She learns how to please customers as men learn how to ride bicycles. Once you know it you cannot forget it. It comes back to you instantly even if you have not used one for years. He disengages himself. 'You are not young any more,' he says ruthlessly.

Stung, she falls back on the divan.

'Your daughter is even more beautiful than you,' he says.

She snorts in contempt, vanity getting the better of her. She pulls her blouse together and wraps herself in her saree.

'A lovely girl,' he says.

'Just a girl,' she retorts. 'Not yet a woman.'

Ramvilas bends over to pick up the necklace and throws it on to the divan. 'Give this to her,' he says coldly. 'I will come again.'

He straightens his kurta, studies his spotless white pyjamas, peers quickly over the balcony into the street, then prepares to leave. 'I will talk to Inderlal tomorrow morning,' he says curtly, as he moves toward the door.

'I can reason with him myself,' says Gita. 'Send him to me. I have a lot to tell him.'

His footsteps fade down the stairs, and Gita hears him joke with the pahalvan as he leaves the kotha. She remains on the divan. She knows the rest of the script. She even knows the timeline along which it will unfold. With a sigh she picks up the necklace, studies it and makes a face. The gold polish will come off in a few days, and the pendant will not survive another fall. It is cheap, no match for the attars he once gave her. A frown clouds her brow. She stands up, turns to face the mirror that spans the wall along the divan, and studies herself. She has not done the business for years, but she is only twenty-nine. Surely she is attractive, even in these Mother Teresa clothes. True, the plumpness of her shoulders takes away from the neck – which is still firm and slender – and a fold of flesh hangs loosely at her waist, but surely there are pleasures to be had in that softness? There is some discolouration of the skin at her temples, but her eyes have lost none of their sparkle. Perhaps they have lost the tenderness of virginity . . . But can a mere girl match the finely honed skills of a mature woman?

She puts on the necklace, letting the pendant settle in her cleavage. She has neglected her appearance over the last few years. This whole NGO business was his idea, not hers! But she still has her looks. The face in the mirror has potential . . . Behind her face, to the right, a much younger one is watching her blankly. Gita turns swiftly, annoyed. 'Why are you here?'

Kiran points to the neat braids on her head. 'She has finished. She says I have beautiful hair.'

'It is too short!' scolds Gita.

'That is a beautiful necklace,' Kiran says.

Gita hastily shoves it into her blouse. 'Go back to Nasreen,' she commands. 'She will give you something to eat.'

'A morning walk is good for your health,' says Sohan Lal to Jugal Kishor. 'You must learn to walk with a straight back. Look at me, I am two years older than you!'

Jugal Kishor hobbles alongside him and chuckles self-deprecatingly. It is not sciatica that has destroyed his posture, he thinks, but the troubles he must carry on his shoulders.

They step through the mounds of cardamom in Khari Baoli, shrugging off importunate beggars who hover over the mounds like flies, and pass by Fatehpuri Masjid, where Sohan Lal notes the smashed watch shops with satisfaction. Jugal Kishor navigates through the rubble, leaning heavily on his walking-stick, feasting his eyes on the heaps of plaster and brick littered over the road. 'We should do this sort of thing every ten years,' he says, with approval.

Sohan Lal grunts. 'I do not like to see good cardamom and cloves lying spilled in the street. Has Harilalji counted the crores of spices wasted yesterday?'

'There were mistakes . . .' says Jugal Kishor, defensively.

They walk down Chandni Chowk. A short distance from Fatehpuri Masjid, their way is barred by a hillock of bricks, forcing them into a detour through Dudhiya Gali. The lane is caked with dried milk. Cauldrons and vats lie askew.

'It looks like snow,' says Jugal Kishor. 'Like a scene from a film.'

They walk across the white sheet, watching it flake on to their leather chappals. Jugal Kishor, in spite of the difficulty with which he walks, cannot suppress another chuckle. 'Rivers flowed with milk in the times of Raam,' he says. 'Here we have rivers of milk. This is Raam Raj!'

'This is Harilal Raj,' says Sohan Lal. 'Harilal could have asked the police to remove a few Bangladeshi stalls quietly. Why launch such a drive and disturb the peace?'

'It is necessary to beautify Chandni Chowk for the Moonlight Festival,' says Jugal Kishor.

'Harilal forgets he is a mere state minister,' grumbles Sohan Lal. 'This Moonlight Festival is his Apna Utsav.'

Jugal Kishor nods. He remembers Apna Utsav from when Rajiv was prime minister. He rather liked that festival, but considers it prudent not to say so. He had spent days in the Red Fort grounds with his grandchildren, watching acrobats and musicians, gymnasts and fire-eaters. It was the official IPP position – even in those days of Rajiv rule when the IPP was a small party struggling to be noticed – that the festival was a colossal waste of money, and an opportunity for corrupt ministers to enrich themselves. Rajiv Gandhi's ten crore present to himself, said IPP leaflets. Misuse of the government monopoly of television channels, said IPP officials. Pageants for our peasants, scoffed IPP leaders. But Jugal Kishor had gone because he was curious and his grandchildren loved it.

'Harilal wants to challenge Naresh Agrawal in the next Lok Sabha elections,' says Sohan Lal.

'We will defeat Naresh Agrawal,' says Jugal Kishor, dutifully.

Sohan Lal shakes his head. 'Musalmans are not fools. They will eat jalebis at the festival and sing the praises of Harilal, then vote for the candidate blessed by the imam of Jama Masjid. That Apna Utsav brought Rajiv no votes, and he was prime minister of India! What will this Moonlight Festival do for a mere state minister like Harilal?'

'There is talk in the central committee that it will help broaden our base—'

Sohan Lal holds up a hand to stop him mid-sentence. Excited, he walks faster, and Jugal Kishor struggles to keep up.

'I have heard that too many times already, and I want to hear no more! We should concentrate on people like us, people who know that you can buy cheap, sell dear and make a profit, and that there is no sin in it. This is where our country has gone wrong, beginning with Nehru. He turned his back on the hard-working people of Jan Sangh, who rose every morning to sit inside shops, serve customers, earn their keep, spend their money and keep their gods happy. He wanted songs about workers, films about scientists and freedom-fighters, not a word about the staid shopkeeper who sold soap so Nehru could take his daily bath and wipe the stink of dusty villages from his skin!'

'But Naresh Agrawal is a trader,' suggests Jugal Kishor. 'One of our own, like Harilal.'

'He is a Congress worm first, beholden to Musalmans and rick-shavalas, and *then* a trader. Who will represent us? We thought that man was Harilal, but he is bent on uprooting innocent milkmen and organising festivals, like Rajiv. What will we do next? Give tickets to Musalman candidates? What is the point of having your own party if you are going to fill it with so many Musalmans that it looks like Congress?'

Jugal Kishor lowers his head and plods on. It is not wise to contradict Sohan Lal just now. He will need the man as an ally when the battle between his sons escalates, requiring intervention by the courts and the Corporation. He must extract whatever favours he can in the next two years while Sohan Lal is still an MLA, because everyone knows Sohan Lal will not retain Matia Mahal in the next assembly election. His victory was a fluke, caused by sudden disarray in the pseudo-secular camp after Suleman switched to Ballimaran four weeks before the election. In 'ninety-eight, Matia Mahal will surely elect a Musalman, whether Suleman stands or not. Sohan Lal certainly knows this. No wonder he is against attempts to broaden the base. No amount of broadening will make him an MLA for a second time.

Dudhiya Gali takes them to another lane, from which they follow a circuitous route back into Chandni Chowk. They pass Town Hall, and Sohan Lal notes with distaste the bird-shit on the statue of Swami Shraddhanand. 'Why did they not raze this building?' he asks. 'It was built by the British – illegal encroachers too!'

Jugal Kishor dispenses an obligatory chuckle. As they approach Kucha Bansilal, he senses that Sohan Lal has begun to walk faster.

Then they come closer to the kucha and he can see why. They have cut down the peepul tree! A stump still stands, festooned with electrical wires that hang from it like roots. The signs it once supported lie scattered in a mess of branches. A hundred glass tubes are strewn across the street – the remains of the neon sign. The tree trunk is in two pieces, cutting through the remains of the Hanuman temple, whose walls appear to have been razed. The collapsible door grille lies on its side, uprooted, its tracks still visible in the dust. In the temple courtyard, where the pujari lived with the metal figurine, the floor is littered with pots, pillows, a radio and sticks of babool. Among them the metal figurine of Hanuman is upside-down, foot thrust into the air, a strange symbol visible on it.

'Who would dare destroy a temple?' asks Jugal Kishor, in hushed tones. 'To think nothing of wrenching Hanuman from his pedestal!'

Sohan Lal quakes with rage. Much as the destruction of the temple offends him, it is the shattered neon sign that sets him afire, his fury feeding on itself as he spots yet another heap of tube fragments.

'It is the tree,' says Jugal Kishor, in explanation. 'They meant to cut down the tree, but it fell on to the temple.'

Sohan Lal points to the statue of the kneeling Hanuman, still coated with vermilion, hands folded, eyes lowered in devotion, tail raised high behind his head, mute, oblivious of the dance of destruction around him. 'Why would the tree leave the statue intact? It has brought down the concrete walls, the wooden fence, the tarpaulin, the grille. Do you think it was afraid of divine retribution?'

Jugal Kishor does not reply.

'People know that Hanuman needs no permit. I know what they meant to destroy. And I know who those people are!'

With these ominous words, Sohan Lal stalks into Kucha Bansilal, followed by a frightened Jugal Kishor. His fury doubles as he walks deeper into the kucha. The lane is cluttered with rubble left by the demolition crew. He pulls up a corner of his dhoti and stuffs it into his kurta pocket, then picks his way through the islands of dirt. The stench is overpowering. He covers his nose with his right hand and inhales aniseed oil, which he had rubbed into his palms before leaving home. Briefly it displaces the stench, which returns in full force as they encounter the overflowing drains.

There is an empty space where the chai stall should have stood. The electrical junction box is still there, suddenly more visible because the stall around it is gone. Next to it the chaivala is staring silently at the hole that had been his shop. On seeing Sohan Lal he squats and begins to collect pans, stoves, planks and cans of sugar. Sohan Lal stops a short distance from him, embarrassed, guilty, afraid to approach. It is shameful enough that, even as an MLA, his assurance has counted for nothing, but it is doubly embarrassing that he wrote a letter recommending the stall for the festival. What authority can he have now over people in the kucha? Word will spread, of course, of his powerlessness, certainly to Ballimaran – does not that Musalman with yellow teeth work there? – and it will travel to Matia Mahal, where he will lose the remnants of respect he enjoys as an MLA. He had specifically asked Kartar Singh to exempt the stall, to forget about Kucha Bansilal. He does not remember seeing the neon sign on the list. Was Kartar Singh working from a different one? How dare he make such a mistake? And then there is the chaivala, bent silently over his pans . . . Should he say something in consolation? Is it not enough that the man has no son that he should be rendered penniless? Ah, Kartar Singh will pay.

Sohan Lal shuffles past Gopal, throws off his chappals at the doormat in Jamna Lal Kishori Mal, walks past the Sunmica counters and plops heavily on to the gaddi, followed by a panting Jugal Kishor who is too weak to sit down by himself. Sohan Lal relieves him of his walking-stick and helps him down. Jugal Kishor wipes his forehead with a handkerchief.

'There have been many telephone calls from angry traders demanding explanations,' Ramesh tells Sohan Lal.

'Tell them to call Harilal Gupta,' says Sohan Lal, irritably.

He turns to the alcove of Lakshmi – sitting above the offending computer – and folds his hands in silent prayer. He will have no part in this display of force. He is suspicious of cataclysmic changes – even if they are for the better – and so is Lakshmi, sitting behind glass panels in her alcove to bless gradual accumulation of wealth.

'The traders should be grateful,' says Ramesh. 'The Corporation has removed more than five hundred hawkers and pedlars, who block storefronts and hurt business for legitimate shops.'

Sohan Lal looks impatiently at him. The boy has become more vocal since he joined the committee. He does not know, of course, that almost all traders themselves encroach on public lands, and every shopfront has an extended façade that sits on Corporation property. 'The only way to please traders is to do nothing,' says Sohan Lal, with a sigh. He telephones Harilal Gupta and complains about the demolition drive. 'Everyone is angry,' he tells Harilal. 'Rickshavalas are furious because their routes have been blocked, thelavalas because their parking spots have been destroyed, and traders had already expressed their opposition . . .'

'It is necessary for the beautification of Chandni Chowk,' says Harilal. 'We must prepare for the festival.'

'I thought we were going to restrict the drive to Meena Bajar,' mutters Sohan Lal.

'That was a mistake,' says Harilal. 'I told them to spare Meena Bajar. It is a sensitive area. I will issue an apology to Musalmans about this harassment.'

Sohan Lal hangs up in disgust. The point of the festival – when the idea was first broached in the committee – was to launch the demolition drive, and the point of that was to remove illegal Bangladeshis. But now Harilal has turned his back on traders! It is this talk of broadening the base that causes people to desert their own kind.

His next phone call is to Kartar Singh. 'Kucha Bansilal was a mistake,' says Kartar Singh. 'There are so many kuchas in Chandni Chowk with confusing names – Bansilal, Bhandariya, Banwarilal, Bahadurlal, Bandhilal – that they could have mistaken this kucha for another.'

'Who will clear the streets?' demands Sohan Lal.

'The Corporation will remove rubble over the next few days,' says Kartar Singh. 'And the Hanuman temple was an accident. The tree fell on to it.'

Sohan Lal does not care about the temple. His concern is the neon sign, but he is aware of Jugal Kishor's intense interest, so he decides to express outrage in the appropriate order. 'If the temple was a mistake, Harilal will rue it. Hindus may have no spine, they may not be organised like Musalmans, but they will not stand by and watch a temple destroyed.'

'We will issue a statement saying the tree was to blame,' says Kartar Singh.

'Why was it removed?'

'It was too close to power lines,' says Kartar Singh, 'and its branches had begun to droop.'

Sohan Lal slams down the phone.

'It is just a tree,' says Jugal Kishor, soothingly. 'Those signs on it were all illegal anyway.'

Sohan Lal studies Jugal Kishor's face for sarcasm, but finds none.

'Someone will have to answer to those meddlesome environmental-ists,' he offers weakly.

'Harilalji is following the dharam of a minister,' says Jugal Kishor. 'He has five years as a minister – the first three to remove the filth of Musalmans and Bangladeshis, the last two to please them as pseudo-secularists do. We have reached the transition point. Now that he has uprooted Meena Bajar and Naresh Colony, he will apologise to Musalmans and put on the Moonlight Festival to make them forget all this. It is his dream to recreate the Shahjahanabad of Shah Jahan.'

'Will he dig up Chandni Chowk to make another canal?' asks Sohan Lal sarcastically. 'Why will Musalmans support this Moonlight Festival?'

'Why not? It is *their* culture being preserved.'

Sohan Lal sighs at such maddening logic. He shoves open his tinted-glass doors – newly installed by Ramesh – to reveal Gopal in the lane, still collecting his pans. 'I will not offer you tea today,' he says to Jugal Kishor, with ill-concealed temper.

Jugal Kishor nods and casts a glance at the chaivala. The stench of drains invades the shop through the open door. 'Spray some of your attar about,' he advises.

'I have taken the attar cabinet home,' says Sohan Lal, gloomily.

Jugal Kishor expresses surprise.

'I am afraid something will be stolen,' whispers Sohan Lal. 'One bottle of ruh chameli costs five hundred. Imagine leaving it around for the staff to see!'

Jugal Kishor nods, and Sohan Lal struggles to change the subject, because this one is painful to him. When the Sunmica counters were installed, Ramesh had had the walls lined with wooden cabinets. The attar cabinet had had to move because the new plans called for the computer to be prominently displayed. For a while, Sohan Lal performed his morning ritual at home. He set out bravely each day with a freshly soaked wad behind his ear, but all fragrance was drowned by the stench of drains as he walked through Chandni Chowk. He has since dispensed with the ritual. Why waste perfectly good honeysuckle and mahua on such transient enjoyment? Instead he rubs some natural oils into his skin. They last longer, but they do not have the same delicacy . . .

'I see you have begun to sell ready-made shirts,' says Jugal Kishor.

Sohan Lal nods defensively and wishes he could hide the shirts and trousers displayed shamelessly in glass panels at the front. It is a fad that will pass, he believes. Rolls of cloth, on the other hand, have endured for decades. Ramesh claims the margins are higher in ready-made clothes. Perhaps so, but who can guarantee stability in such a business? A shop dealing in garments must be necessarily old-fashioned, where the shopkeeper sits cross-legged on the gaddi with customers, unrolls lengths of fabric and throws them, one upon another, until the customer is dazzled by an array of colour and texture. The Sunmica counters have made this impossible. Ramesh now prefers to send cardboard boxes – full of shirts, trousers and sometimes sarees – all over Chandni Chowk. He even sells to customers who do not come to the store at all. They send in their shirt size, colour and brand, and Ramesh dispatches a cardboard box with an invoice. What kind of a business is it where the shopkeeper does not see his customer?

'Call a committee meeting in your shop,' he commands Jugal Kishor. 'We need to discuss this demolition.'

'We could have the meeting right here,' says Jugal Kishor.

Sohan Lal bristles at the suggestion. Can Jugal Kishor not see that the gaddi is the size of a pocket handkerchief? Will the members sit at Sunmica counters? And who will bring them tea now that the chaivala's stall has been destroyed?

'Unless it is difficult for you to accommodate us here,' says Jugal Kishor, quickly.

'Why should it be?' snaps Sohan Lal. 'I suggested Mangat Ram Nawal Kishor only because the last seven meetings have been held there.'

Jugal Kishor inclines his head.

'Are you not the committee general secretary?' demands Sohan Lal. 'It is your privilege to host the meetings.'

'There is no Mangat Ram Nawal Kishor any more,' says Jugal Kishor, with a sigh.

Sohan Lal knows very well what he means, but prefers to feign ignorance and commit himself to nothing. 'Have you changed the name?' he asks.

'They have drawn a wall through the shop, from front to back, and destroyed a two-hundred-year-old business.'

'Who?' persists Sohan Lal.

'Rajesh and Pavan. They have settled with each other, for now.'

'Ah,' says Sohan Lal.

'Two deep shops, each too narrow for customers, so they must stand on the ledge outside and place their order from there.'

Sohan Lal feels grateful, once again, for the gift of one son – one heir, one claimant to the throne of Jamna Lal Kishori Mal.

'Everything has been partitioned,' laments Jugal Kishor. 'The counter has been halved, the linoleum cut in two, the furniture divided to the last stool. The toilet at the back is too small to be divided, so it has been time-shared. Each brother leaves the cleaning to the other. You can imagine how dirty it is.'

Sohan Lal makes a sympathetic gesture of disgust.

'The new signs have been painted,' mourns Jugal Kishor. 'They will soon be installed side by side – Rajesh Kumar Jugal Kishor and Pavan Kumar Jugal Kishor.'

'At least they have retained your name,' soothes Sohan Lal.

'I will wince whenever I see it on those boards!' says Jugal Kishor. 'Each one will have his own shop, but where will I sit? Which of the two narrow passages belongs to me? Or is my place outside on the ledge where customers can barely stand?'

'You are still their father,' says Sohan Lal, without conviction.

'And which of my two shops shall I offer for the committee meeting?' asks Jugal Kishor.

'It can take place somewhere else,' mutters Sohan Lal. He disapproves of Jugal Kishor's indiscretion. A man should not discuss the quarrels of his sons in public.

'This demolition drive!' says Jugal Kishor. 'They tried to destroy even my shop. Pavan's side. I think Rajesh had something to do with it. I had to intercede with Commissioner Sahib. And now Pavan is furious with Rajesh.'

'Too many innocent people are being harassed,' says Sohan Lal, sympathetically.

Jugal Kishor shakes his head. 'You cannot say anything good about the young men of today. We thought they would be props in our old age. Instead, they will hasten our journey to the pyre.'

Sohan Lal shifts uncomfortably, aware that Ramesh is listening to the conversation. Here we sit like two old geezers, he thinks, with disgust. Jugal Kishor is ready to go to sleep, but I am not! I do not hobble, I do not use a walking-stick, and I want to stand in the next assembly election. I will outlive them all!

Jugal Kishor rises from the gaddi with difficulty, supported by two of Ramesh's clerks, and wearily slips on his chappals. He turns to whisper urgently to Sohan Lal: 'When a man has married off his sons and seen the faces of his grandchildren, it is time for him to disappear into the forest. I am thinking of going to Hardwar.'

He trudges off, his stick beating an uneven rhythm, his breath coming in gasps. Sohan Lal is relieved to see him go. A trip to Hardwar, short or long, will certainly be good for Jugal Kishor, and perhaps also good for the IPP committee in Chandni Chowk.

Sohan Lal's attention is drawn to Gopal, who sits in the middle of the kucha on a mountain of pans, looking forlorn. 'Take them to your kholi in Khari Baoli,' says the seth, softly. 'I will have your stall reconstructed after I get clearance from the committee.'

The chaivala looks up at Sohan Lal. There is no faith in his eyes, no trust, only a vague suspicion that wounds Sohan Lal. 'There are too many to carry on my bicycle,' he says.

Sohan Lal senses accusation in the chaivala's voice. 'It was a mistake,' he says defensively. He wishes the chaivala would wail, beat his chest, throw his pans about, bring down curses on the demolition crew. Such vulgar behaviour would make him less pathetic, less deserving of human kindness. But he stands mute, shedding no tears, making no sounds of pain, doubling the guilt in Sohan Lal's heart.

'I will have Chotu take your pans to your kholi,' he offers. 'He will stuff them into a sack and bring them to you tonight. Don't you sleep in Sushil Jain's godown in Khari Baoli?'

Gopal nods sadly.

'I will find you some work in Chandni Chowk,' promises Sohan Lal.

He knows the situation is hopeless even as he says it. Look at the man! Scratched spectacles, unbuttoned shirt and dirty dhoti! He does not have the resourcefulness of Chotu, the energy of Gauhar, or even the simple dependability of Ramesh's clerks. Could a human being be less suited for work? Could a man be more superfluous? Yet there must be something he can do to perpetuate his meaningless flicker. Perhaps he can deliver Ramesh's cardboard boxes – strapped to the back of his bicycle – to customers all over Chandni Chowk. He owns a bicycle, and can be trusted with small amounts of money.

Ramesh looks uncertain when Sohan Lal suggests it. 'I already have a man to make deliveries,' he says.

'You can add a second,' suggests Sohan Lal, 'and you need not pay him much.'

Ramesh is reluctant. 'Such an old man!' he whispers to his father, who is incensed at this.

The chaivala is merely fifty, thinks Sohan Lal. If he is old, what am I? But he does not ask this question of Ramesh. 'Old men bring the wisdom of age with them,' he says to his sceptical son. 'You cannot throw them away like old shoes.' As he says it, he wonders if he is speaking for Gopal or himself, and reminds himself, yet again, that he must set aside a good sum of money before Ramesh gets a peek at the finances of Jamna Lal Kishori Mal. He has taken over the operation of the shop, but the accounting is still in Sohan Lal's hands. Once Rukmini dies – and she does not have many years to live – there will be no one to love Sohan Lal. Jugal Kishor is right. The young men of today cannot be trusted to respect their fathers. He certainly cannot anchor the approaching moments of his dotage to Ramesh. Look at him, talking about an old man as if he were a peepul tree, to be cut down when its branches begin to droop!

Ramesh calls Gopal to the counter and inspects him indifferently. Sohan Lal feels as if he himself is being scrutinised.

'Chandni Chowk is not an ordinary constituency,' declares Harilal Gupta. 'Where else in the world will you find a street inhabited by all four religions? Gaurishankar Temple, Fatehpuri Masjid, Gurudwara Sisganj and the Baptist Church! When I campaigned, I had to fold my hands in namaste, then switch to an aadaab, then rush to say, "*Sat sri akaal*," and then . . .' Here he pauses, uncertain how a Christian might be greeted, but recovers quickly. 'Religious diversity is what makes Chandni Chowk the greatest parliamentary constituency in India.'

Harilal appears to have forgotten that he is not a Member of Parliament, merely an MLA who represents only one of the four assembly segments of Chandni Chowk. Chitra does not press the point. She has not come to split hairs but for his comments on the demolition drive, and to chance upon what is vulgarly called at her magazine a 'scoop'. He is not known to be loquacious, but on this occasion, perhaps because her reputation for widely read articles has preceded her, he is verbose. They are seated in his office in Chawri Bajar, where his family has run a flourishing paper business for five generations. Surrounded by cardboard boxes, he leans back dangerously in a reclining chair, places his hands on his heaving belly, and continues to speak. Chitra presses buttons on her tape-recorder to capture his comments.

'Four years ago, we established the Heritage Council in Chandni Chowk. People give me credit for the council, but it was Lala Surajmal who provided the inspiration. The Heritage Walk he organised was a great success. Hundreds of people walked the length of Chandni Chowk. His last words, as he lay dying at the first Heritage Council meeting, were that we should arrange a great festival to celebrate the cultural heritage of Chandni Chowk, so the Moonlight Festival is dedicated to the memory of Lala Surajmal. His dream, and mine, will now come true.'

Harilal pauses. Chitra switches off the tape-recorder, aware of two things: Harilal will not speak of the demolition drive, and he is reading from a piece of paper on the desk in front of him. She must lure him out of his office and into the lanes. When he is confronted with the rubble, he will perhaps be forced to acknowledge it.

'I would like to photograph you with people in your constituency,' she says.

'I enjoy working with them,' says Harilal, brightly.

'Should we walk through Chandni Chowk?'

Harilal groans. 'My doctor does not understand that a public servant has obligations. It is bad for my back, he says.'

'Even a short tour of the constituency?' she asks.

The word 'tour', firmly embedded in Harilal's political lexicon, strikes a chord. 'A tour!' he says. 'Yes, let us go on a tour. If you look carefully, you will also find people to photograph.'

They set off in Harilal's official Ambassador, adorned with a fluttering tricolour at the front and a flashing beacon above. The car threads its way through the Chawri Bajar paper market, then turns right and heads up Chandni Chowk in a stately fashion against the traffic. Chandni Chowk is a one-way street at this time of the day, flowing away from Red Fort. A few constables look askance at the car, intimidated by the beacon. One approaches tentatively. The driver lowers his tinted window-pane and yells: 'Transport minister!'

The constable recedes and the car continues, attracting horns and honks, disrupting the stream of rickshas and scooters. Harilal appears amused by the commotion. He turns to Chitra with a benign expression. 'All you need in Chandni Chowk is good brakes, good horn and good luck!'

She chuckles. She wishes Harilal had come alone, but he has brought his PA, who sits in the front seat with the driver and casts anxious glances at them, awaiting commands that he will spring to fulfil.

'Tell Madam about my plans for Red Fort,' Harilal orders the PA.

The PA places an arm on the back of his seat, turns round and prepares to speak. Chitra, sensing that he is waiting for her to switch on her tape-recorder, obliges.

'We will restore the eastern side of the fort,' he says earnestly. 'We will illuminate it with lights, so those who drive along Ring Road can see Red Fort as the Yamuna river must have seen it in Shah Jahan's time.'

There were no lights to aid the Yamuna's vision, Chitra thinks irreverently. But she does not interrupt.

'We will repair the fort windows and balconies,' continues the PA. 'We will fabricate new screens for them, and remove dark patches from the walls and ramparts. We will construct a landscaped park between Red Fort and Salimgarh Fort with a fence round it.'

'But people will still be able to enter the park,' adds Harilal, quickly. 'Did you know that an underground passage took the emperor directly to the Yamuna in a boat? We will clean that passage and let the public enter it. A common man will be able to enjoy what only an emperor could afford!'

'A slum has been demolished behind Red Fort,' says Chitra. 'Will the park be built on that land?'

'We will relocate those people,' says Harilal, vaguely.

'Someone suggested that it was removed because of its name,' says Chitra.

'What was its name?' Harilal asks.

'Naresh Colony.'

'Ah,' says Harilal.

A silence falls, as Harilal neither confirms nor denies her accusation. The PA wrestles to find a subject that will carry the conversation forward.

'Tell her what the park will be called,' Harilal commands.

'Dara Shikoh Park,' says the PA, with relief.

'Why?' she asks.

The PA looks toward Harilal Gupta for approval and, on receiving it, continues: 'Dara Shikoh was a scholar. He wrote, in the *Majma-ul-Bahrain* and the *Sarr-I-Asran*, that all religions teach the same fundamental truth, and the Hidden Book mentioned in the Qur'an is none other than the *Katha Upanishad*. Where will you find a Musalman scholar who has spent time with Vedantists, read the *Bhagavad Gita* and the Upanishads? He was the crown prince, and he should have become emperor instead of Aurangzeb the zealot. This park is our way of giving him what was rightfully his.'

Harilal leans forward authoritatively. 'People accuse IPP of being fundamentalist,' he says with emphasis, 'but we are the first to honour secular Musalmans who have joined the national mainstream. Dara Shikoh understood, even before IPP did, the true meaning of Hindutva: it is not a religion, it is the Indian way of life. Has the Muslim League done anything for Dara Shikoh? Have the Communist parties or Congress?'

'You still wear the uniform of the Congress Party,' says Chitra playfully.

Harilal looks smugly at his khadi kurta and pyjama. 'It is the uniform of our freedom struggle,' he says. 'My family has a long association with Congress. Gandhiji spent two nights in our Chawri Bajar house.'

'But the Gandhi cap?' she insists. 'It went out of fashion with Rajiv! Even Congress leaders no longer wear it.'

'Fashions,' repeats Harilal, without elaboration.

'Why did you leave Congress in 'seventy-five?'

'The Janata Party was a party of the people,' he replies.

'But then you left Janata for IPP. People have called you an opportunist.'

Unused to being badgered, Harilal looks impatiently at her. 'What is a party?' he snaps. 'I work for the people, not a party!' With that proud assertion, he adjusts the Gandhi cap and sinks heavily into his seat, signalling a new, uncommunicative phase. Chitra switches off the tape-recorder. She wishes he himself had spoken of the Red Fort plans so that she could attribute them to him. Now, if he chooses to deny the conversation, he will blame everything on the over-zealousness of his PA.

The car finally arrives at the eastern end of Chandni Chowk and turns right to pass Jama Masjid.

'Can we not walk here?' asks Chitra. 'I cannot take photographs sitting in the car.'

Harilal appears loath to leave the comfort of his seat. 'You can point your camera at me,' he says. 'If I lean forward, you will catch Red Fort in the background.'

'People in Matia Mahal are very unhappy with their MLA,' says Chitra. 'He did nothing to stop the demolition.'

Harilal appears interested. 'Sohan Lal is a good man,' he says. 'Perhaps we should get out here and talk to the people about him.'

He asks the driver to turn into the lanes behind Jama Masjid and stop the car. The PA helps Harilal heave his bulk out of the car.

'My Surya Namaskar is all the exercise the doctor allows me,' says Harilal, daintily. 'A pose in Hatha yoga, requiring complete control of body and mind,' he adds, misreading Chitra's lack of response.

The lanes behind Jama Masjid wear the ravaged look of a battlefield when a war has just ended. Tarpaulins lie collapsed over debris. Chairs, stools, benches, planks and utensils dot the road. Drains have overflowed – children have floated paper boats in the sewage – and armies of rag-pickers scavenge the mountains left by the demolition crew. From the ruins, a few stalls are already rising. Chitra is awestruck. She turns to Harilal, but his face says nothing. He appears to be looking straight through the rubble.

They begin to walk down the lane. Harilal's girth has expanded in the last three years. His Nehru jacket assumes a perfectly spherical shape above his legs, and the folds of his dhoti hang like curtains from his belly. He moves slowly, with difficulty, and is perhaps in need of a walking-stick. Chitra guesses that he is not yet sixty, but beads of perspiration are rolling down his temples, starting below his cap and travelling to the neck of his jacket. Two aides walk behind them, maintaining a respectful distance and adopting suitably worried expressions every time Harilal seems to be in danger of tripping. Chitra is not sure where they have appeared from. Perhaps they were following the car on foot, keeping pace as it wended its way through the traffic.

They walk past the remains of Meena Bajar, circling heaps of bangles and pyramids of broken audio cassettes. Harilal seems oblivious of the destruction. He walks with hands folded at an imaginary audience in the deserted lane and eventually stops at an array of colourful sarees hanging from a lattice frame of bamboo. 'No constituency can rival Chandni Chowk in culture,' he says.

'They destroyed three hundred shops in Meena Bajar,' retorts Chitra.

Harilal apparently notices the debris for the first time, and is annoyed. 'I told the commissioner that Meena Bajar is a sensitive area. He should not have harassed people.' He turns to the PA, who steps forward, notepad in hand, pen poised. 'Which inspector was assigned to the crew?'

'Inderlal Jha,' says the PA.

'Write a letter to the police commissioner to take action against him.' Harilal turns to Chitra. 'Whoever harasses the people shall be punished. Naresh Babu has no time for these people, and he is their MP. People approach him with petitions every day. "Naresh Babu, they are harassing me for donations!" "Naresh Babu, the DESU people have cut off my electricity!" "Naresh Babu, there are too many rickshas in Chandni Chowk!" And what do you think Naresh Babu says? He says he stands for secularism.'

His harangue complete, Harilal expresses satisfaction with the arrangements and turns to leave Meena Bajar, but a man comes running down the lane, crying. He aims to throw himself at Harilal's feet but the two aides, happy to make themselves useful, arrest his progress and hold him ten feet away from the transport minister. He is a small, weak-looking, bearded man. They search him, and his pyjama pockets reveal dozens of rusty blades.

'Who are you?' the aides ask angrily.

'They destroyed my clinic,' says Muhammad Ghayas, and breaks down again.

'Who sent you to attack Minister Sahib?' demand the aides.

'He is a poor man,' says Harilal, magnanimously. 'Let him approach.'

Muhammad Ghayas, relieved of his blades, is allowed to fall on his knees near Harilal, who remains unperturbed while Ghayas narrates his story. When he has finished, Harilal asks the PA to investigate. 'Why not take your photograph here?' he asks Chitra.

Chitra has not brought her photographer, but she has a small Nikon slung from her shoulders. She takes a picture – Harilal and Muhammad Ghayas, minister and constituent, with the domes of Jama Masjid as a backdrop.

The entourage continues. Harilal shakes his head sadly. 'It is not easy, this demolition business. The Supreme Court ordered it. I cannot ask for every stall to be erected again. I must take the traders of Chandni Chowk into my confidence. All I can do, as a representative of the people, is share their grief and fulfil their dreams through the Moonlight Festival.'

They turn a corner and come upon the remains of a red-brick building. The walls have been cleared away, furniture has been removed and kitchen utensils are scattered in the lane. Posters flutter among heaps of bricks – 'The Five Diamonds of Truth, Honesty, Discipline, Respect and Punctuality'; 'The Ideal Child'; 'The Five Habits of Good Boys and Girls'; 'Fruit and Vegetables'; a map of India.

'What is this?' asks Harilal.

'School,' says the PA. 'Children's home, funded by Suleman Mian.'

Harilal clucks his tongue in sympathy. 'Children.'

Chitra stands still, aghast. Is this all that is left? And where are the children, now that their home has been reduced to dust? They must have disappeared, no doubt, into the lanes whence they were plucked, but they are domesticated dogs who can no longer survive in the wild. Who will feed them? Who will protect them against predators? Do they still know how to steal into night shelters, avoid policemen and stake out sleeping spots on the pavement? Shalini should have made arrangements for housing them, but she could not have been fore-warned about the demolition. So, who is to blame for the end of a noble experiment? Chitra Ghosh, opportunist . . .

'Madam is not feeling well?' asks the PA, solicitously.

Chitra waves him away and shuts her eyes, fighting tears, thinking of her last visit to Sparrows two years ago for a function organised by Suleman. Shalini seemed distant, and the children were dirty and ragged. Gauhar was there too, clean-shaven, taller, looking almost like a man with a light growth of hair on his upper lip, yet with all the awkwardness of adolescence. She had found it uncomfortable to be in his presence. She did not know how, after serving his jail term, he had found his way back to Sparrows. Perhaps the seth in Kucha Bansilal had thrown him out. He must bear her some grudge for not posting his bail, but surely he understood that, after a hundred people saw him urinating in Rajghat, no court would let him go? She could tell that jail had been hard: he appeared jaded, tired and frightened. He was not the boy who had stood self-consciously when she tried to film her documentary. The onset of manhood and imprisonment had driven the innocence from his eyes, which bore the haunted look of someone who had seen terrible things and was unable to share them. Trem-bling, he whispered to her of a great bomb, a deadly mystery in

Ayodhya, so melodramatic that she had been embarrassed. She was accepting a bouquet from Shalini, about to deliver a short speech after Suleman had finished, and Gauhar had kept tugging at her and murmuring unintelligibly. Why did he insist on talking about that terrible time? The demolition of Babri Masjid, the riots that had followed, the governments that were dismissed . . . She had turned away from him, thinking she would return to Sparrows later and speak to him. But the next day had taken her to Rome for a conference on the freedom of the press, then to Berlin . . .

Now that man, her own child, is perhaps picking a pocket in Paratha Gali at this very moment. If only she could see him again . . . But here she is with the transport minister. His command could resurrect this building, and sweep back into it all her children, even Gauhar.

She turns resolutely to Harilal Gupta, but an aide brings an admonitory finger to his lips. The transport minister is seated on a chair – a Sparrows chair retrieved by an aide – and resting with his eyes shut. She waits impatiently until, fifteen minutes later, he stirs.

He knows, even before she has uttered a word, what she wants to ask, and shakes his head, contemplating the ruins. 'What can the Supreme Court do?' he asks rhetorically. 'Our own MLAs provide funds for encroachment. Most of these children would have been Bangladeshi anyway.'

The PA senses that Chitra is not convinced and adds helpfully, 'You cannot worry about every child in this city, madam. If you spend sleepless nights over the poor on Chandni Chowk pavements, you will be up all your life, counting the hours.'

This elicits a scowl from the transport minister. Chastened, the PA directs the aides to prepare for departure, and the procession continues. The lanes of Ballimaran are endless. At the best of times they are impassable because of rickshas, bicycles and carts. Now, with the ruins of the demolition drive, they are like an obstacle course. A few people recognise Harilalji and raise their hands in namaste. He responds with a grand gesture – right hand raised, gait unchecked. The presence of the aides behind him, combined with the Gandhi cap, reinforce his station in life. Even on foot he appears to be riding an Ambassador car with a flashing beacon. People who do not recognise him – and there are few – instinctively say, 'Namaste,' to him. Harilalji sails along like a ship, his enormous bulk floating steadily above the street, right hand raised in perpetual acknowledgement of his subjects, Chitra in tow.

'This is Suleman's constituency,' he says to Chitra, conspiratorially. 'See how the people love me instead of him! We have identified a hundred businesses that are older than a hundred years, thirty in Ballimaran. They will be honoured at the Moonlight Festival.'

The demolition crew has damaged a nearby sewer. The stench is unbearable. Chitra sneezes violently. Harilal casts an indulgent look at her. 'You should do Sutra Neti for ten minutes every morning. Hold one end of a silk thread. Push the other up a nostril and pull it out of your mouth, then move the string back and forth to clean the passage. It is recommended in Hatha yoga as the perfect cure for all sinus problems.'

Her interview will come to little, she thinks, if Harilalji continues to dispense medical advice or speak of the Moonlight Festival, instead of discussing the demolition drive.

'I am on a strict diet of fruit and vegetables,' offers Harilal Gupta.

The lane becomes narrower. It is lined on either side by shoe shops, raised on platforms to avoid flooding. In front of each, a concrete staircase starts at the road, spans the drain like a bridge and enters the shop. Chitra points out to Harilal that the staircases are illegal. Why are they still standing after the demolition?

'We cannot harass local businessmen,' says Harilal.

He walks quickly, hands now hanging at his sides. He does not expect to be greeted by anyone here because this is a Musalman area. Faces stare sullenly at them from inside the shops. A man sitting on a staircase looks at them. Although there is hostility in his face, the open mouth and yellow teeth give him a permanent grin beneath unfriendly eyes. Chitra recognises him. It is the factotum of Suleman, the spider who hovers over the chaivala and prevents him opening his mouth. He looks worn out. Wrinkles round his eyes have partially closed them, and his beard is sparse, clinging desperately to his bony chin. His eyes are bloodshot, and the yellow teeth are beginning to give way. The signboard on the shop – in Urdu, Hindi and English – says, 'Ghalib Shoe House.'

She wonders if she should talk to him. He will have something to say about the demolition drive and his comments will provide better copy than Harilal Gupta's. But he looks away, and they walk by. She hears him snort, but does not turn. Harilal Gupta waddles on as fast as he can, Chitra at his side, the PA behind him, the aides following at a respectful distance.

'The Musalman area will end at that corner.' He points with relief.

'Then we will go back toward Chandni Chowk and the driver will
bring the car there.' He bestows a friendly smile on Chitra. 'I have
heard a lot about you, madam. They say your articles have been
published in America. I hope you will write a long story on the
festival.'

A small group of people have assembled at the corner that denotes
the end of the Musalman area. They glare at Harilal's retinue. A
protest! thinks Chitra, with excitement.

Harilal, too, has noticed the ambush and slowed. 'My back aches,'
he grumbles. 'I should have listened to my doctor.'

'We can go past the corner and bring the car into that lane,' suggests
Chitra.

'No. Let us walk back through the Musalman area. I want to see the
people.' He turns abruptly, with a speed that belies his bulk; the PA
and the aides follow suit. Harilal walks with surprising agility,
outdistancing the protesters, forcing his aides to shuffle along. 'If,
instead of Aurangzeb, Dara Shikoh had become emperor of India, the
Musalmans of this country would not have been so backward,' he says
wistfully. 'They would have been integrated into the national mainstream. Dara was a true Indian.'

Dara is the chosen Mughal emperor, thinks Chitra. 'And Aurangzeb?' she asks playfully.

Harilalji emits a groan, as if he has been dealt a fatal blow. 'There
are fifteen crore Aurangzebs in this country,' he says. 'We want to turn
them all into Dara Shikohs.'

Ibrahim watches the minister walk by with the newspaper madam.
At one point she seemed to look at him but there was no flicker of
recognition in her eyes. He does not care. She was cool toward him
when he tried to have his picture taken with Gopal. He will not give
her the satisfaction of a greeting, and he will certainly not acknowledge the minister. Such people cannot be trusted – Bania traders and
city women with their businesses and newspapers, bent on tearing

down Musalman stalls and destroying their livelihoods. There has not been much destruction in Ballimaran – perhaps because Suleman Mian is the MLA and no one will dare cross him – but he has heard that a few silver-beaters' rooms have been torn down. The transport minister will pay! They will all pay when Suleman Mian makes it an issue.

Sharief Mirza brings out a chair to the concrete platform that spans the front of the shop, sits down, fans himself with a handkerchief and casts an accusatory glance at Ibrahim. 'That was Minister Sahib,' he says. 'And there was a madam with him. Do I pay you to sit here and gawk at people?'

'They would not have bought anything,' says Ibrahim. He rises to go inside, where it is much cooler. 'Your turn until five,' he says.

Sharief Mirza settles down to watch the street, where his task is to exhort passers-by to try on shoes. Ibrahim knows he will drift in and out of a lazy stupor all afternoon, sprawled in the chair, oblivious of missed opportunities. Sharief Mirza's family has owned Ghalib Shoe House for three generations. He is now old and worn out, with no children, and his nephew Mahmood has decided to join government service as a clerk. Ibrahim hopes to inherit part of the shop some day. Although he is not related to Sharief Mirza, he has worked at Ghalib Shoe House for thirty years. He is junior to his employer by the width of a hair, and obedient to his will only because of the vague threat of dispossession. But Mahmood has no real interest in the shoe business: it should be easy to come to an arrangement with him after Sharief Mirza's death, which, from the man's appearance, will not be too long in coming.

Ibrahim decides to take a nap in the back room amid stacks of shoes. He has been asleep for thirty minutes when he is woken by a call from outside the shop.

'Customer!' Sharief Mirza yells, then subsides into a coughing fit.

Ibrahim scampers out and collects shoeboxes left from previous customers. Sharief Mirza brings out a foot scale from the racks and grumbles about Ibrahim's laziness. Ibrahim makes a self-deprecatory gesture. Sharief Mirza forgives him with a nod and resumes his position on the chair outside, watching people, bicycles and rickshas pass through the debris in the street.

The customer is an old man, as decrepit as Sharief Mirza. He wants new shoes to replace the ones on his feet. Ibrahim chuckles. 'Did you buy these when Mirza Ghalib came to your house?'

The joke elicits a grudging guffaw from Sharief Mirza. The customer frowns, misses the joke, and shakes his head. He does not remember when, because the shoes are very old. They are so old that they have become almost an extension of his feet. He takes off the right shoe and places his foot on the scale. Ibrahim pulls it away. He takes pride in his ability to guess a shoe size at a glance. Indeed, Sharief Mirza, too, makes a great show of this when he attends to customers. He does not deign to look down, but stares at a man's face and pronounces his shoe size. He is usually wrong, but he clings to the belief that he possesses the skill, and neither he nor Ibrahim will allow a customer to use a foot scale in the presence of the other – better be wrong than lose face by not guessing.

'No need for that,' says Ibrahim loudly, so Sharief Mirza will hear. 'Size eight.'

'Seven and a half,' offers Sharief Mirza, from his chair.

The old man acquiesces and places his naked foot on the linoleum. 'This is Jaipuri,' he says, of his old shoe. 'Pure leather.'

Ibrahim suffers the customer with a patient smile. 'There is no leather in this world any more, mian. It is all rexine. Even Dilip Kumar wears rexine. And that is not a Jaipuri shoe, it is Katvar.'

'Jaipuri!' insists the old man.

Sharief Mirza rises from his chair and bends to look at the dirty old shoe. 'Malod,' he declares. 'From Patiala.'

'Katvar,' insists Ibrahim. 'From Rewari!'

Sharief Mirza storms out and resumes his position on the chair. From the walls of the shop – lined from floor to ceiling with shoeboxes – Ibrahim brings out everything he can: Jaipuri shoes, Katvar shoes, even Mojri, Pakeezah, Ghungroo and other female brands.

'There you are, mian. Take any shoe you want.'

The old man fixes his gaze on Ibrahim. 'You look weak,' he says.

Ibrahim is caught unawares. 'What is that to you?' he asks.

'I am a doctor,' says the man. 'I can bleed you. I will let the bad blood seep out. Your teeth will shine, as will your face. And your beard will grow dark and lush. I have treated thousands of people from America and England. I can show you their letters.'

'What are your fees?' asks Ibrahim suspiciously.

'It is free for you,' says Muhammad Ghayas. 'You give me the shoes, I will bleed you.'

'All right,' says Ibrahim. 'But I will have to ask Sharief Mirza.'

'I can bleed him too,' offers Ghayas.

'Where is your clinic?'

Muhammad Ghayas sighs. 'It was in Meena Bajar, but they tore it down. I will come to your kholi tonight and bring my blades.'

'They tore down four hundred shops in Meena Bajar!' says Ibrahim.

'It was a mistake,' says Ghayas, soothingly. 'Commissioner Sahib misread the Supreme Court order.'

'Who told you that?' challenges Ibrahim.

'Minister Sahib. He came by less than an hour ago to apologise.'

Ibrahim slaps the shoes down on the linoleum. 'He is the one responsible!'

Ghayas appears befuddled. 'How can that be?'

'I know,' says Ibrahim. 'Everyone knows that IPP sent a committee member, a sardarji, to make a list for the demolition. I saw him walking through Paratha Gali and Ballimaran. He came early in the morning so no one would notice him, but I was there. I followed him all the way through Meena Bajar and Jama Masjid.'

'He must have come to see where the Metro Rail will pass,' suggests Ghayas.

'He was not interested in the Metro Rail. He came to see which shops belong to Musalmans. This is what happens when you get a Delhi state and an IPP government.'

Muhammad Ghayas remains silent, confused. He has not bought a shoe in twenty years. In bigger markets in Chandni Chowk he has seen large shoe stores with glass windows. He dare not walk into them for fear of paying too much. He had hoped, in coming to Ballimaran, to find someone who would give him the shoes free in exchange for his services. He has no heart for political discourse. 'I will come to your kholi tonight, then?' he asks.

'If they tore down your clinic, why do you need new shoes?'

'I will have a stall in the festival,' says Ghayas. 'Minister Sahib told me. You cannot expect me to go to the festival in old shoes.'

'The festival will not happen until next month,' says Ibrahim.

'I need to break in the shoes.'

Ibrahim stuffs the new shoes into a bag and hands them to Ghayas. 'Fifty-five,' he says.

'But I will come to bleed you tonight!'

'You will cure people for free at the festival,' says Ibrahim, scornfully. 'You can bleed me then.'

Muhammad Ghayas pulls out his last fifty rupees, snatches the shoebox and leaves. Ibrahim throws the money into Sharief Mirza's lap and goes back inside the shop.

'Customer!' yells Sharief Mirza.

Ibrahim swears, looks up, and is horrified to see Gopal.

'Six and a half!' calls Sharief Mirza.

'Seven,' says Ibrahim, mechanically. He beckons Gopal inside, seats him on one of the rexine-backed seats, and puts his foot on a scale. 'Seven!' he declares triumphantly. Then he leans closer to Gopal and whispers, 'Why have you come here? Sharief Mirza does not like it.'

Gopal looks mournfully at Ibrahim. 'They tore down my stall.'

'They destroyed four hundred shops in Meena Bajar alone,' says Ibrahim. 'They have uprooted a dozen doctors' clinics. And you are worried about your chai stall?'

Gopal looks down guiltily, but grief overwhelms him. 'What will I do?' he asks.

'They should not have removed Meena Bajar,' says Ibrahim. 'It is a sensitive issue.'

Gopal is seized with worry that he might have missed an opportunity. 'How can I make my stall a sensitive issue?'

'Every shop in Meena Bajar is a Musalman shop,' says Ibrahim. 'That is why they were on the list.'

'Did they have permits?'

Ibrahim is shocked. 'Does a Musalman need a permit to stay in India?'

Gopal shakes his head.

'Whose city is this Dilli?' demands Ibrahim. 'Everyone comes here – Biharis, Punjabis, Bengalis, Madrasis – but whose city is it? Has it become their city just because they came here ten, twenty or thirty years ago?'

Gopal does not know the right answer.

'It belongs to *me*! I am the heritage of Dilli. No, I am the heritage of India! If they want to preserve our heritage, they should preserve me. I am the soul of Dilli!'

Gopal stares at Ibrahim blankly.

'Do not ask me how it feels to be the soul,' warns Ibrahim, then answers his own question. 'It feels terrible. But a man has to live with that responsibility.'

'But I—'

'You?' says Ibrahim. 'The soul of Dilli is Musalman.'

Gopal is disappointed. 'They said my stall has been removed for the festival, in spite of the letter I had from Sohan Lalji.'

'Suleman Mian no longer supports the festival,' says Ibrahim. 'It is another scheme to drive us out of Chandni Chowk. Even its name is English.'

From outside the shop, Sharief Mirza calls, 'Show him the Salim Shahi Joota. That shoe will outlive him.'

Ibrahim grunts assent and throws a box at Gopal.

'Will you ask Suleman Mian about my stall?' pleads Gopal.

'There will be a rally during the festival,' says Ibrahim. 'Suleman Mian has asked everyone to support it, to protest about the demolition and the festival.'

'But my stall—'

'I am talking about a rally for twelve hundred shops,' says Ibrahim. 'And you keep going on about your stall!'

Gopal rises from the rexine seat and walks to the front of the shop. Sharief Mirza, seeing his empty hands, casts a disapproving look at Ibrahim.

'He wanted leather,' says Ibrahim, after Gopal has gone.

Sharief Mirza snorts contemptuously and goes back to sleep. Ibrahim squats on the cement staircase and watches rickshas drift by. It is a lazy afternoon. He expects no customers for the next three hours. Sharief Mirza has begun to snore.

'Ibrahim Mian!'

Ibrahim looks up irritably, and his torpor is chased away by the apparition before him. He glances at Sharief Mirza – safely asleep – and gapes at Gauhar. He is taller than when Ibrahim last saw him. He looks dirty. Most of his shirt buttons are broken. His trousers are held up with string. A sack is slung over one shoulder.

'You are a dead man,' says Ibrahim, threateningly. 'You should not walk about like this!'

'They tore down the building,' says Gauhar.

Ibrahim is exasperated. Is he an MLA, that everyone should bring their grievances to him? 'I know,' he says impatiently.

This boy should have been dead three years ago, he thinks. If it was not for Suleman Mian's inexplicable weakness, the matter would have been settled. 'Let the boy be,' Suleman Mian had said. 'He is too frightened to cause trouble. Killing him will not undo the assembly election. Warn him never to go near Sohan Lal but let him live . . .' For three years, it has seemed that Suleman Mian was right, but here is the boy now, casting his offensive shadow in Ballimaran. It is not safe to have him walking around – a time-bomb waiting to explode, talking to everyone about Ayodhya. And he cannot be used for anything – not for protests, not for the rally Suleman Mian is organising at the Moonlight Festival. What use is a ghost to those who live?

'Where can I sleep?' asks Gauhar.

Does the boy take him to be his Bangladeshi father, who brought him here and cast him away like a worn shoe? Ibrahim wonders. 'Where did you sleep last night?'

Gauhar points vaguely toward a spot that may be anywhere in Delhi.

'Sleep on the pavement,' advises Ibrahim. 'All of Chandni Chowk is your home.'

'I am afraid of the police.'

Ibrahim laughs. 'That madam has softened you. You will learn to be a man again.'

Gauhar does not budge.

'Sleep inside Faquira's room,' says Ibrahim, helpfully.

'They tore it down.'

Ibrahim lays a silent curse on Harilal Gupta. 'I cannot help you.'

Gauhar narrows his eyes. 'I could go to Gopal Bhai for help,' he says threateningly.

'Gopal Bhai has left Dilli,' retorts Ibrahim.

'I saw him five minutes ago,' counters Gauhar. 'I have been watching you for two hours.'

Ibrahim is flustered. 'I will ask Suleman Mian to do something. Come back in a week.'

'I am hungry,' says Gauhar.

'What do you have in your sack?'

'Clothes.'

'Does Faquira not pay you? Go back to him. He must have set up again in another room.'

'My hand hurts.'

'Now you talk like a sahib. A seth! Faquira beats silver, Alimuddin beats silver. If their hands do not hurt, why does yours?'

Gauhar runs his tongue over his loose teeth and tells himself, again, that he will not go back to beating silver. Ibrahim sighs and draws out a five-rupee note from his kurta pocket. 'Do not come back in less than seven days,' he commands.

Sharief Mirza stirs, leans over and spits his paan into the drain with exaggerated concentration. The juices spatter Gauhar's feet. He is about to fling abuse, but Ibrahim shoos him away.

*   *   *

Gauhar clutches the five-rupee note triumphantly. It feels good to shake down Yellow Teeth. He does not need the money. He has more than three thousand rupees in the Baal Bank cash-box, stowed safely among the clothes in his sack. All he needs to do is break the lock and he will have enough to survive for months. His chief preoccupations are gnawing hunger and the whereabouts of Kiran. He finds a stall near Ghalib Shoe House and eats the best nahari he has ever had in his life – juicy, boneless mutton and thirty-six spices to add flavour to the broth . . .

He will look for Kiran in the park outside Old Delhi railway station, where he suspects many Sparrows children have made their home. His belly full, he walks contentedly through Ballimaran into Chandni Chowk, saunters past Town Hall and turns toward the railway station. The park, littered with polythene bags and paper, has long been abandoned by the Corporation. In the far corner, a grove of trees has created a canopy that looks shady and alluring. The grass there is wild and thick. Gauhar sets down his sack and throws himself on to the ground. Then he hears a sound deep inside the thicket of trees and sits up, frightened. After three years in the security of Sparrows, he is no longer master of the streets. He is accustomed to shitting in latrines. He fears men who will want to hit him, fuck him and rob him, and the cash-box hidden inside his sack makes him even more vulnerable. He gets up reluctantly, walks out of the grove and finds a jamun tree whose scattered branches offer little shade. He puts the sack under him and, using the cash-box as a pillow, sleeps.

When he wakes, the Victorian façade of the railway station is bathed in an evening glow. He is hungry again. The sounds of rickshas and cycles float into the park. He can perhaps work as a rickshavala, a coolie, a cart-puller, a rag-picker . . . He shoves the cash-box deep inside the sack, then stands up and watches the street. A boy runs into the park and disappears into the grove. Another comes, then another, until the grove holds six. They appear younger than him, between fifteen and twenty. The reason for their panic soon becomes apparent when a police jeep passes, siren blaring. The boys remain in the grove for a while, then emerge in ones and twos. They collapse on the grass and talk in worried tones. A cool breeze blows through the park, heralding a pleasant night. Gauhar approaches them slowly and stops short on hearing a cry in the dark.

'Rustam! Rustam!'

He has been spotted. Three of the largest boys hurl themselves on him. At first he easily fends them off, but then the others join in and he is pinned down. He is larger than all of them but his one hand is no match for their twelve. 'Who are you, mother-fucker?' they ask him. 'A police rustam? Did they send you to spy on us?'

Gauhar lies silently until they calm down. He is not intimidated by them. Four years ago he would have matched their vehemence with his own. His chief concern is the sack under the jamun tree. They do not yet know of it, and he will gouge out their eyes if they should cast them on it.

The boys soon realise he is not a policeman or a spy. Why would the police employ a one-handed rustam? They let him sit up, and he tells them that he saw the police jeep. They nod eagerly. The bastard police, the thullas! We have given them the slip many times! The mother-fucking thullas will never catch us, but they have captured Raja Babu and Munna!

Something about the manner of their speech catches Gauhar's attention. Their Hindi is not the Hindi of Ibrahim Mian or Gopal Bhai, or Shalini Didi or even of the children at Sparrows. It has a familiar accent, and when they talk among themselves they speak a language he understands from many years ago, from a train ride he took with his mother and father, from a home in a village very different from Chandni Chowk . . . They are speaking Bengali! It is a different Bengali from the one they speak near Dhaka, but it is Bengali all right. And he still remembers it after all these years!

He tells them his name. They tell him theirs – Johnny, Partho, Aftab, Wasif, Baba, Khoka. The names tug at his heart, lilting with the sounds of another age. 'Where are you from?' he asks Johnny.

A silence falls. The boys exchange suspicious glances.

'I am from Nadia,' says Johnny.

'Malda,' says Aftab.

Names flow comfortably – Cooch Behar, West Dinajpur, Twenty-four Parganas . . .

'You are lying,' says Gauhar.

'Where are you from?' challenges Aftab.

Gauhar pulls out the instructions, skein by skein, from a forgotten childhood. 'I am from Murshidabad.'

The boys burst out laughing.

'Fucking rustam!' says Johnny.

They advance upon Gauhar, pin him down again, and threaten to bash his head in unless he tells them the truth. 'I am from Binodpur,' he says. 'Binodpur in Bangladesh.'

They raise him quickly. Aftab embraces him.

'He is also from Binodpur,' says Johnny, in explanation.

Then they name their villages in Bangladesh, and Gauhar tells them about his journey with Bhola Dada. It is pleasing to speak Bengali, even as he stutters and gropes for words. The boys warm to him. In bits and pieces, Gauhar gathers their story. Raja Babu, their boss, has been arrested by the police along with Munna. He had broken into a house near GB Road to steal a wad of notes that he saw a trader take inside. With the money in his pocket, he was stepping out of a window when an old man came upon him. Raja Babu is no murderer. He merely swiped the old fart with a knife to frighten him. The blade barely grazed the man's cheek but he screamed and collapsed on the ground. The neighbours surrounded Raja Babu because Munna, who was posted as the lookout, had dozed off on the pavement. So now both Raja Babu and Munna are with the police. The old man is dead – not from the knife but some heart trouble – and the police are calling it murder. And they are calling Raja Babu a roshanlal, a murderer! There is no doubt Raja Babu will tell the police, after they have beaten him senseless, where the rest of the gang is to be found. This roshanlal business will be the end of them all!

The boys become increasingly mellow as they talk. 'We are pickpockets,' they say. 'We steal mangoes from stalls, but we are not roshanlals! If Raja Babu could keep his mouth shut, and if Munna was not such a lazy bastard . . .'

'Where is Raja Babu locked up?' asks Gauhar.

'GB Road police chauki.'

'Talk to the SHO,' says Gauhar. 'Maybe you can do business with him.'

'We have no money. Raja Babu was carrying everything in his pocket.'

'How much does the SHO want?'

'That bastard Inderlal Jha! He wants five thousand for Raja Babu, two thousand for Munna.'

Gauhar reflects on the situation. There are twelve hands here. Twelve Bengali hands. A one-handed man can do a lot with twelve hands. Pick six pockets, wipe six windscreens, push six carts, beat twelve balls of silver into varq, steal twenty-four mangoes . . .

'This other rustam, Munna. Is he a good boy?'

'Fuck him!' say the boys. 'Let him rot in jail.'

'But he is cheaper,' points out Gauhar. 'Raja Babu is too expensive.'

The boys look at each other. They are uncomfortable with this train of thought. Yet they sense, suddenly, that the one-handed man has power he is willing to exercise.

'Inderlal Jha starts work in two hours,' says Aftab. 'Night shift.'

'All right,' says Gauhar. 'We will go to the police station then. I am thirsty. Do you have water?'

The boys snigger. 'When we are thirsty we do not drink water,' says Johnny.

They dig deep into the grove of trees and bring out bottles of liquor and joints of hashish. Gauhar eyes them suspiciously. Mussabir Ustad taught him a lot. Then there was Bobby in Tihar Jail. But these boys make him feel inexperienced. 'What is this?'

'Bholanath!' shouts a boy, pointing to the bottle. He unscrews the cap and takes a deep swig.

'Chou En-lai!' screams the boy with the joints.

They drink and smoke for two hours. The grove resounds with shouts of 'bholanath' and 'Chou En-lai'. Outside the park, the din of rickshas and cycles is deafening.

Inderlal Jha waits for the minute hand on his wristwatch to touch twelve. He will strike at exactly three in the morning, as planned. Three constables armed with batons are sitting with him in the jeep, which is parked in a narrow alley that leads off the main street near Kotha 842. Four more jeeps sit at four other points in GB Road, packed with more than twenty constables. They are all awaiting his signal, which will be delivered on a walkie-talkie by his driver. He still has twelve minutes to occupy before the raid begins – time for a smoke. He pokes the driver in the ribs. The driver produces a bidi from his pocket and lights it for him. Inderlal pulls on it with satisfaction and watches curls of smoke waft out of his nostrils.

He spent much of the evening pacing outside the kothas in plain clothes, staking out good locations to launch the raid, ducking into alleys now and then because all of the bais recognise him. The whores came down to the street as soon as the market closed and the regular traders – sellers of water-pumps and wash-basins – went home. A few were late and picked their way self-consciously through pahalvans and customers. He watched one whore take at least seven people up the stairs over a period of three hours. She expelled each one after twenty minutes or less. The bais stood on balconies, loitering casually behind grilles but really watching business in the street, counting the customers brought upstairs by their whores. Kotha 842 was exceptionally busy this evening. All those new girls are doing brisk business, thinks Inderlal. Once, he saw Gita Didi herself on the balcony. Was she trying to send him a signal? Why would she stand for so long in plain view of the street with no whores to watch over? She does not know the exact hour of the raid, or if the raid will occur tonight – even if it will occur at all. She is a smart one, that Gita Didi. The less she knows, the better for everyone, and she knows that.

Last evening, when he received a message from her, he knew exactly why she had summoned him. The new girl had arrived two nights ago. For a regular bai, he would have called within one night to collect his fee. For Gita Didi, he had waited two. There is talk that a minister will be present at the next STREE function, so he decided to be patient. The summons from her was his reward. She is a prudent woman, he had told himself, not one to skimp on giving a poor SHO his due.

He met her in the waiting room in Kotha 842, where she sat behind a large desk with pictures of Gandhi and Nehru behind her.

'Do you know why I have sent for you?' she asked.

He was impressed by her composure. What better way to get new girls than form an NGO? He winked at her and smiled broadly. 'I understand, madam.'

She seemed to frown, but he took that in his stride and informed her of the current rates. 'Six hundred if she is under twenty, four hundred otherwise.'

Her manner changed abruptly. 'The new girl is not here for business.'

He was flabbergasted. 'What *is* she here for, then?'

Gita Didi did not answer. He put this down to a negotiating tactic. After all, Gita Didi was no virgin. She knew how to play the game.

'You are our sister,' he said effusively. 'Five hundred if over twenty, three hundred otherwise.'

She demurred again, and he realised that something was wrong. He did not know what to do. Never before had such a complicated situation presented itself. With any other bai, or a whore like Parvati, he would have resorted to threats. But this was Gita Didi, who had had her picture in English newspapers. He decided to play the victim. 'I will forgo my fee,' he said, 'but what about my head constable, my additional SHO? And ACP Sahib? And the commissioner of police? Everyone wants a cut on a new girl.'

He was not certain that the commissioner of police in Delhi would trouble himself over one whore in GB Road but thought reference to him would make his argument weightier.

'Do you know the girl is a minor?' she asked.

He was perplexed. He had often heard Gita Didi rail against Aids, which he took to be her particular cause, but never against under-age girls. It was NAARI, another NGO, that made the most noise about minors, just as AURAT harped on about Nepali girls brought into India. It required all his skill to keep the grumblings of NGOs straight in his mind. It was improper of Gita Didi to start mixing causes. 'Have you joined NAARI?' he asked.

'That does not matter,' she said sharply.

He did not want to get into all this. How the bais arranged for their whores, and what their ages were, was their business. They had their duty and he had his. 'We can do a bone-age test on the girl,' he said uncertainly, 'in about seven days' time.'

'Why should it take so long?' she demanded.

'The hospitals are busy,' he said. He had no idea if they were, but he thought it wise to lay the blame on them.

He left the kotha twenty minutes later, highly excited and full of admiration for Gita Didi, determined to plan everything for the next day. He was late in getting back to his night shift at the police station. He found the constables dozing, and a gang of seven young men anxiously awaiting his arrival. They eyed him with hostility, and followed him to his office. They stopped at the door when he walked in. He knew the type well – thieves, pickpockets, Bangladeshis, the kind he locks up daily, the type he had in his lockup at that very moment on charges of murder.

The men – or boys, because most were under twenty – pointed eagerly at him. 'He is the one,' they said. Then they pushed forward the tallest, who came into the room brazenly and shut the door from inside.

'Who gave you permission to enter?' Inderlal shouted. 'Get out or I will shoot you!'

'You have our Raja Babu,' said the man.

It became clear that these seven were friends of the two in his lockup. He had seen the tall boy before. He remembered the stump, the scrawny neck, the burning eyes, the impudent look. He was the boy who had pissed in Rajghat. Ah, so he was out of jail, taller and bolder, and consorting with these Bangladeshis! A hardened criminal, no doubt.

'Your Raja Babu is a murderer,' he said. 'Get out of here.'

With that, he stood up menacingly, baton in hand. The boy quickly raised his left hand. At first, Inderlal thought he held a weapon, but it was only a steel box.

'This is for you,' said the boy. 'If you can open it.'

Such gall, in a ragged one-handed Bangladeshi! But Inderlal seized the box and used his regulation police baton – strong cane, tipped with a steel ferrule – to break the lock. The money was in small bills of five and ten. He ordered the boy to arrange it in stacks of a hundred, then counted the stacks. The total came to 3260. He was disappointed. He reminded himself not to lock up such poor bastards in the future. It was like trying to suck blood out of a bone. 'This will buy a pickpocket if I am desperate,' he sneered, 'not a murderer.'

'Fuck Raja Babu,' the Bangladeshi said. 'I have never seen him before and I don't want to now. Give me the little boy.'

Inderlal was taken aback.

'Munna is not a murderer,' said the one-handed man. 'He was only the lookout while Raja Babu broke into the house and killed the old man. What wrong has Munna done?'

This boy knows what he is talking about, thought Inderlal. He has come here with a plan! 'All right,' he said. 'Three thousand for the little boy.'

The Bangladeshi counted and pulled out a few notes from the stack.

'Do not touch the money!' warned Inderlal. 'It is police evidence.'

'Your share is three thousand,' the boy said. 'I am taking back two hundred and sixty.'

'Who the fuck taught you all this calculation?' asked Inderlal.

The boy laughed. Inderlal put the stacks of notes into a paper bag and locked everything into his drawer. What an ugly boy! His hair lay in brown wisps on his bullet head, and his teeth glistened against his black skin. And how he stared at the money as it was transferred to the drawer! 'Carry the curse of fifty children with you,' said the boy, under his breath.

Inderlal did not know what he meant, and did not care. He went into the lockup and brought back twelve-year-old Munna. 'Here is your lookout. Take him home.'

As the boy led Munna outside, Inderlal whispered, 'Bring me ten thousand and you can have your boss.'

'Keep the boss,' said the one-handed boy, 'and fuck him every night.'

Then he smacked Munna hard across the cheek, made sure he was crying, opened the door and hurled him out into the corridor, where his six friends awaited him. Inderlal heard them cheering outside. 'Gauhar Muhammad *zindabad*!' they cried.

Inderlal spent the rest of the night dozing, and counting his three thousand. His shift ended at dawn. He slept for three hours on a bench in the corridor, then passed the day in planning the raid. It took him all afternoon to assemble four jeeps and twenty-four constables. He used the evening to scout the area. After determining where the jeeps would wait, he returned to the police station and decided to wear his uniform. A plain-clothes policeman is not impressive on television, especially during a raid. He thought of co-ordinating his plans with Gita Didi, but decided it was safer to leave her in the dark. He has warmed to the idea of STREE. An NGO, though meddlesome and bad for business, can be handy if the police know how to deal with it.

He is no longer worried about the inquiry into his conduct set up by the transport minister. He remembers telling the municipal commissioner that Meena Bajar is a sensitive area and should not be demolished, but the commissioner was adamant. So, let Harilal Gupta set up his inquiry committee. He will tell it of his warning to the commissioner. He will swear that neither he nor his constables participated in that part of the drive, and a dozen constables will back him up. After tonight even Harilal Gupta will think twice before tarnishing his record in the police force.

The driver taps Inderlal's shoulder and points to his wristwatch. It is three in the morning. GB Road is dark and silent now. The kothas – especially the Class A ones with toilets – are, no doubt, full of customers who have chosen to spend the night. Class B and C houses must have closed by now, as sinless as a school dormitory.

Inderlal nods. The driver barks an order into his walkie-talkie, and the jeep roars into life. With its siren singing stridently, it turns the corner into GB Road and screeches to a halt in front of Kotha 842. Two other jeeps cover the back of the building, while two stand at either end of the road. Constables pour out and hammer at the street door, which guards the narrow staircase that leads upstairs. 'Agrawal Pump House,' says a neon sign that blinks next to the door.

'Open the door!' screams Inderlal.

'Let us in, you mother-fucking whores!' scream the constables. 'Open your doors and let us see your fornication, your naked bodies intertwined with the sweat-stained flesh of ogres . . .' Their shouts are superfluous, because they have kicked down the door and rushed inside. The narrow staircase causes momentary confusion, because they are forced into single file.

Inside the kotha, a frantic stampede erupts. Naked men spring out of beds and rush to the back of the house, to collide with the constables running up the back stairs. *Thvakkk! Phattt!* The men are flattened against walls as policemen ram into them and squeeze by. 'Get out of the way, you mother-fucking bastards! Whoring truck drivers! Get your prick out of my face! Take that for running around naked, and take that for touching me with your diseased hands!'

Some customers try running down the front stairs, others bundle up on the floor in a foetal position. More cower in the corners of the balcony, covering flaccid penises with their hands. Six run up to the roof of the building and look over the parapet, embarrassed to look at each others' buttocks. The whores, meanwhile, set up a terrifying communal wail and run about the corridors of the old haveli, ducking into any room they can find and locking themselves in. Constables kick the doors and hammer on them with their batons. 'Open up, bitches! Open up, Sita Maiya! Open up, mothers and sisters! Open, open, open, open!' The constables cannot suppress smirks as they pound on the doors. 'Open, Hema Malini! Open, Zeenat Amman! Open, my darling Sridevi!' From behind the doors, whores sob, giggle, scream and hurl abuse at them. For a while, it seems the raid has failed. It has been contained in twenty rooms, each full of naked whores roused from their beds, courted by two constables earnestly awaiting entry. The naked men have disappeared, having made their exit when the constables' attention was diverted by the whores. These men now run down GB Road, penises bobbing, looking for corners to hide in, grabbing paper bags, sheets of polythene, cloth banners, anything, to wrap round themselves.

The only men still trapped in the building are the six on the roof, who have found sarees drying on the terrace and wrapped them round their legs. They now lean over the rails to watch the street, where a crowd has collected. There are no onlookers at this time of night: the crowd consists of newspaper and television reporters, cameramen and slogan-shouting members of a dozen NGOs. Whores from other kothas watch the scene from their balconies, staying well behind grilles to ensure they are never in full view of the cameras. Inderlal is pleased to see the reporters. He has invited them. But where did the NGOs come from? Who told them about the raid? There will be trouble between these NGOs and STREE, but there is no wishing them away now. He exhorts his constables to tear down all locked doors. He must find the under-age girls before the women's organisations get into the kotha. He knows how aggressive they can be. Meanwhile, he will reason with them and hold them off for as long as he can. He asks a constable to bring him a megaphone.

In the street below, the swarm of activists swells, and chants slogans against STREE and Gita Didi. They bear their placards angrily and demand that Gita Didi comes out to talk to them. 'NAARI – National Alliance Against Repression and Injustice'; 'PATITA – Prostitutes Against Tyranny, Intimidation, Terror and Aggression'; 'DIDI – Development Initiative for the Downtrodden of India'; 'STOP – Stop Trafficking of Prostitutes' . . . 'We do not want policemen in kothas!' scream the women. 'Stop harassing our sisters! Sex-workers are also women! Sex-workers are our sisters! Stop STREE harassing our sisters!'

Inderlal pushes the megaphone through the steel grille and points it downward. 'My sisters—'

A gale of catcalls drowns his voice.

'The police are working with you,' he says. 'We will give you a full report tomorrow.'

The women clap and jeer. He takes fright and steps back from the grille. He looks round for help, and sees Gita Didi coming down the corridor. She walks comfortably, hips swaying in perfect rhythm. She is a little too plump, but she is so fair and smooth. He wishes he were somewhere else with her, alone . . . But he must shake such thoughts from his head. For now, the raid is in danger of collapsing into a shouting match between constables and whores.

'Where are the girls?' he demands irritably. 'You said there were six.'

'You have not looked,' she says, in a honeyed tone that disarms him.

For her I will move mountains! he thinks. He points to the placards below. 'Why are they angry with me?' he asks. 'I thought they would support this.'

Gita Didi smiles. 'Do your job and let them bark,' she says softly, then turns away and stalks to the STREE office.

Inderlal follows her. A fat dark whore is sitting on the divan. She rises in agitation and grabs his hand. 'Anything you want!' she pleads. 'Two thousand! Five thousand! Call off the raid!'

He flinches. In her other hand she holds a newspaper. He sees the picture on the front page, with its caption – 'Transport Minister Harilal Gupta with Muhammad Ghayas, Traditional Healer, in Chandni Chowk'. He thinks she is trying to give him the newspaper, until he realises she is merely tearing it to shreds in her anxiety.

'Parvati!' Gita Didi commands. 'Let me talk to him.'

The fat whore lets go. Gita Didi comes toward him with a smile that unclothes him. 'This is a clean kotha,' she says mysteriously. 'There is nothing here.'

He is about to protest at her contradictory statements when she makes a gesture that stops him. She turns her eyes up, quickly, then looks at him again. Is she giving him a signal? He is befuddled. She appears annoyed. 'Bring him five thousand,' she commands the fat whore.

With a sob, the woman rushes from the room. Gita Didi points upward. 'The third floor, you fool!'

Her arm rises high, very high, pulling up her saree and revealing her blouse – which can barely contain her breasts – and Inderlal almost falters. But she is pointing upstairs!

He rushes out of the office, collects three constables and runs up to the third floor. It is much smaller. It was once the roof, to which a room was added, creating a large terrace where sarees are hung out to dry. The room has large windows, covered with fluttering curtains. Against one of the windows stands a water-cooler. Droplets coalesce on its louvred sides and roll down to the reservoir in the base – it has obviously just been turned off. He pushes the door gently. It swings open. The room is dark, but someone has forgotten to turn down the cassette-player, from which Pushpa Rani continues to pour out her heart:

'How do I describe your love when I am not overwhelmed by it?
How do I speak of your tenderness when I cannot touch your heart?
How do I mourn our separation when we have not had a tryst?
How do I complain of your cruelty when I still yearn for it?'

Inderlal holds out his hand and a constable gives him a torch. He flicks the switch and the circle of light falls on a four-poster bed where he sees, sitting close together, trembling, eyes wide, no less than six girls, holding on to each other tightly. He chortles with delight, then shuts the door so that none can bolt, approaches them, and caresses the cheeks of the first. What smooth young skin! 'What is your name?' he asks softly.

'Dimple,' she says.

'How old are you?'

'Twenty-three.'

Inderlal bursts out laughing. He has been on many raids and every whore he has unearthed in the bowels of every kotha has been twenty-three. They are twenty-three the day they are born, and they will be twenty-three when they die as shrivelled hags, if they live to be that old in these days of Aids. He should probably not touch these girls in case they are diseased. They cannot all be virgins. He should try to find out more so that he can speak knowledgeably to the television people, but there is no use talking to them: they look like frightened rabbits. What a disappointing picture they make! How much more dramatic would his entry have been had he burst in on them when they were getting fucked!

He throws his arc of light over the room and sees a desk, a dressing-table, chairs, lampstands and a coat-hanger. There is a large rug on the floor, next to the bed and, in the far corner, a wash-basin. Pictures of Govinda, Salman Khan and other film stars adorn the walls. Even a whore lives like a queen!

'Whose room is this?' he asks Dimple.

'Parvati Mummy,' she says.

He throws his light on the girls again and notices the prettiest one, sitting in the centre. She is at least half Nepali, with narrow, doe-like eyes that are almost closed in fear. He cannot resist patting her cheek. 'What is your name?'

After an interminable pause she responds, in a soft, tentative voice: 'Kiran.'

He looks deep into her eyes, then sighs and raises his finger to his lips, signalling that they should all be quiet. He walks out of the room, shuts and latches the door, then posts three constables outside it. The six half-naked men shuffle past him, sarees flapping, and disappear into the staircase. He pushes his way through the screen of sarees drying on the terrace, leans over the railing and calls to the television reporters in the street to come up. At his signal, the constables step aside from the street door and the cameramen rush to enter the building. The NGOs are held back by the constables.

Gita sees the newspeople come in, and joins them. She runs to the third floor, followed eagerly by a dozen reporters, three camera crews and ten constables. Inderlal and she wait outside the latched door until everyone has taken positions. Gita has attached a rosette to her chest. It rises and falls to the rhythm of her breathing – she is winded after her run up the staircase – and says, 'STREE,' in large red letters. Instinctively the cameramen focus on it, hypnotised by her heaving chest. Suddenly, Inderlal throws open the door and walks into the room, followed closely by Gita. The blaze of three camera floodlights blinds the girls, who sit shivering on the large four-poster bed, hugging each other. The poster of Govinda in his underwear looks down on them with a rakish grin. The cameramen circle the girls and film them from all angles. Inderlal and Gita face each camera in turn, stroking the girls' heads. Microphones are thrust toward the little faces. 'Speak! Say something! How old are you? What is your name? Are you happy to be rescued?' The girls turn this way and that, never sure which camera is aimed at them. Some giggle in embarrassment, some look as if they are about to cry. Kiran sits stone-faced, watching Gita with deadly concentration.

Gita pulls the microphones away from the girls and directs them toward herself. The cameramen follow. Soon, to Inderlal's astonishment and consternation, she is speaking directly into the cameras and everyone is listening to her. 'STREE has been watching these girls for a long time,' she says. 'They were brought four years ago from Bangladesh . . .'

'Are they broken in?' asks a reporter.

The same question is on the tip of Inderlal's tongue. He is burning with curiosity to know. Are these girls getting fucked yet? Are these whores, or are these salvageable girls? But he dare not ask.

Gita holds up an admonitory hand and the reporters are suddenly ashamed of their voyeurism. 'These are little girls,' she declares. 'They have names, mothers, fathers, sisters and brothers! They like toys, they like ice-cream, they like watching films . . . STREE does not believe in the dehumanisation of sex-workers. A police lab will conduct bone-age tests on these girls. Those found to be above eighteen will be taken to Naari Niketan, and taught sewing and knitting. Those found to be under-age will be sent back to their parents in Bangladesh and Nepal.'

'The angle is wrong!' screams a cameraman.

Gita has moved away from the four-poster bed. He cannot capture her in his frame while still showing the girls in the background. Gita is brought back hastily into the picture by skilful hands.

'How will you know who the parents are?' asks one of the reporters.

'STREE works with NGOs in Nepal to identify them,' she replies confidently.

'But who has brought them from Bangladesh and Nepal?' demands another.

Gita stares straight into the camera while her audience holds its breath. The name seems to be on her lips, but she shakes her head. 'We are all sisters in adversity,' she murmurs. 'The woman who brought these girls here is as helpless as they are. STREE does not criminalise sex-workers, even those who lure other women into the trade. STREE will work with her to rehabilitate her.'

Inderlal is irritated by this interview. Why are the reporters not interested in him? It is *his* initiative that has resulted in the rescue. The constables milling about the building are *his* men. Some are still banging on doors on the lower floors, some are manning the roof, and some are guarding the building. If it was not for the men he posted at the street door, the women of NAARI, DIDI, STOP and PATITA would have stormed the kotha and stolen Gita Didi's thunder. Even now, his constables are struggling to hold them outside the building, and he can hear them shouting slogans in the street. Perhaps he should let them in.

He walks out of the room and on to the terrace, where the swaying sarees are being greedily filmed by a cameraman. He leans over the railing. When the NGOs spot him an array of placards is raised skyward. They are all there, ravenous, bursting with passion for their causes. Why should he let this Gita Didi use him? He walks back to the room.

'For me the rescue of these girls is a personal mission,' Gita Didi is saying. 'I do not want them to suffer the fate I did.'

Inderlal grinds his teeth and storms in. 'It is time to go!' he screams at the cameras. 'This is police business.' He hustles the crowd out of the room and down the stairs. He must now arrange for the girls to be transported to Naari Niketan, where they will stay until bone-age tests can be conducted over the next few days. The constables need to escort the girls, the NGOs need to be dispersed . . . There is so much to be done, and there stands Gita Didi preening herself before the cameras!

Gita adjusts her saree, pats the rosette on her chest and walks contentedly down the stairs. She knows that the women of NAARI, DIDI, STOP and PATITA are in the street, baying for her blood. She stands at the street door and smiles disarmingly.

'These are our women,' says a woman, bearing the NAARI placard.

'We have been monitoring under-age girls for years,' says another.

'But it was I who found them.' Gita beams.

'This is harassment!'

'Don't interfere with our base!'

'I am doing what I can for my sisters,' says Gita sententiously.

The girls are brought down one at a time by the constables, seated in jeeps and driven off. Gita watches Kiran out of the corner of her eye, holding back tears. It breaks her heart to think she will live in Naari Niketan, and perhaps be sent back to Nepal in a fruitless search for her parents. Her mother can never admit to being her mother, and her father would be too happy to take her into his lecherous custody. Naari Niketan is no home, but it will keep her from the claws of her father . . .

The television cameras have lost interest in the girls. The footage of them being driven away in jeeps is less interesting than the colourful images they have captured inside the kotha. They now turn a collective eye to the placards and the NGO women. Gita speaks into the nearest microphone.

'I invite all my sisters in NAARI, PATITA, STOP and DIDI to join STREE in its endeavour. We will have a STREE stall at the Moonlight Festival. I have already spoken to Transport Minister Harilal Gupta about it.'

Then she shuts the doors of Kotha 842.

IF

Gopal stands, awestruck, in the sea swirling round a thousand food stalls. He has never seen so many samosas or so many people. Women in flowing sarees, men in silk kurtas, children in polyester shorts, sadhus in saffron, policemen in neatly pressed uniforms . . . Fat seths, thin clerks, obsequious traders, curt officials, terse guards, loquacious councillors . . . Have the beggars been issued with new aluminium bowls? What a grand mela this is – what a great festival! Lights and sounds, music, crowds and, above all, food stalls! The entire street has been decorated as if for a wedding, with arches, fluorescent lighting, oil lamps and banners. Trees are festooned with lights that vibrate to the rhythm of soft music emanating from loudspeakers, strung from every lamp-post along the length of Chandni Chowk. Far to the left, Red Fort rises majestically against the night sky, its ramparts illuminated brilliantly by lights pointed from the ground, and the national flag flutters under a red sandstone umbrella. Chandni Chowk flows straight down, like a river, from its source at Red Fort to its estuary at Fatehpuri Masjid, marked along every inch like an aircraft runway, thronged by hundreds of thousands of people. Gopal wonders why no one has illuminated the dome of Jama Masjid. It is, perhaps, a sensitive issue like the demolition of Meena Bajar.

The thought of demolition exhumes the memory of his stall, but it is fleeting because he is dressed in a creamy silk kurta that rustles round his body with the sound of prosperity. He runs his hands down his chest and belly, ironing out creases, shrinking from the men and women who jostle him. It is so smooth, so soft, so shiny. The three buttons that close the flaps over his chest have diamond studs on them. He wonders if they are real. Ah, Sohan Lalji is a wealthy seth, but he is not foolish enough to lavish real diamonds on a poor man. Then there is the saffron silk dhoti. Ramesh Babu appeared reluctant to part with it, but Sohan Lalji knew no restraint in his rush of generosity. 'Take it!' he said. 'Wear it at the festival, Gopal Bhai! It is you we are celebrating. *You* are the heritage of Chandni Chowk, the heart of Delhi, the soul of India! You did not tell me you were also a hero, that you saved the life of Sukhbir Kaur in 'eighty-four! How will it look if you stand there in a torn shirt and cotton dhoti, and if your clothes are all crumpled?'

Gopal did not know what to say. He looked at Ramesh Babu who is, after all, the master of Jamna Lal Kishori Mal. He can be inscrutable sometimes, but he is a considerate son who still defers to his father. So, when Sohan Lalji opened the glass panels and drew out kurtas and dhotis, Ramesh Babu did not object although he clearly disagreed. Sohan Lalji was not mean even with his own merchandise: Gopal Pandey is wrapped in the best silks of Agra and Banaras, not the cheap ones Sohan Lalji keeps for clerks and petty traders. Underneath his laconic manner, even Ramesh Babu is a kind-hearted man. And who can sufficiently extol the virtues of Sohan Lalji? The day after the demolition, he had Chotu collect Gopal's pans and bottles in Kucha Bansilal, put them into sacks, and deliver them to the kholi in Khari Baoli. He even interceded with Seth Sushil Jain to allow Gopal to keep his sacks there until another spot could be found for his stall. The heart of a man speaks through his deeds.

It was Sohan Lalji who had secured him work with Ramesh Babu, though it is hard, this business of delivery. If only he was slender like Ibrahim Mian, who can fly a bicycle through Chandni Chowk like an aeroplane. For Gopal, perched on the saddle with a stack of cardboard boxes digging into his back, it is terrifying to navigate through rickshas, thelas, cars and scooters. He is already fifty – too old for bicycles. He would prefer to squat comfortably in a chai stall and sprinkle crushed cardamom into boiling tea. But he must not let Ramesh Babu see his fear, or he will lose the quarter per cent commission he gets on every delivery. He has had two accidents in the last four weeks, but neither destroyed the boxes so Ramesh Babu need never know. He will not notice the bicycle's twisted mudguards. He will complain, perhaps throw him out, only if he hears of soiled shirts from customers or if boxes go missing. For now, he seems bent on breaking Gopal's back. In the last three days, his consignments have been larger. 'These are kurtas, shirts and trousers,' said Ramesh Babu, 'not bricks of silver that will weigh down your bicycle.' So Chotu loaded the bicycle with twenty boxes last week, and Gopal rode all day, weaving through traffic, balancing himself and the boxes on two wheels. It never occurred to him, in all the years of bringing milk from Dudhiya Gali to Kucha Bansilal, how difficult it is to ride a bicycle wearing a dhoti. It keeps getting tangled in the metal chain or the spokes. Perhaps it is his age.

Three days ago, when Sohan Lalji told him he was to be featured in the Moonlight Festival, Gopal went to meet Ibrahim Mian in

Ballimaran. 'It is a festival for Hindus,' said Ibrahim, angrily. 'Why should Musalmans participate?'

'But I am a Hindu,' Gopal had protested.

Ibrahim Mian appeared hurt at the claim.

Late that afternoon, Ibrahim Mian took him to a rally outside Red Fort, to protest the demolition drive. Gopal sat through the hot afternoon and watched Suleman Mian deliver his message to the people. Suleman Mian was so angry that he needed bottles of Coca-Cola to steady himself in the scorching sun. Gopal eyed the Coca-Cola as his thirst grew during the speech. He waited to hear his stall mentioned, but Suleman Mian seemed to speak of other things. 'It is all about secularism,' Ibrahim whispered into his ear. Gopal came away thirsty and disappointed, uncertain how this secularism was connected to his stall.

This morning, Ramesh Babu let him off early. 'Let Gopal Bhai prepare for the festival,' Sohan Lalji said to Ramesh Babu. So Gopal went to Dudhiya Gali to get his hair dyed. He found Ram Bibek and Banwari hard at work with a carpenter, hammering planks to make a counter. 'I have no milk to sell you,' said Banwari. 'They destroyed my stall.'

'I have not come to buy milk,' responded Gopal.

The glass panels of Banwari's ice-cream parlour were all shattered, and an errant hammer had found its way to his refrigerator. 'I will reopen in three days,' said Banwari, 'and I will never install glass panels again.'

Ram Bibek set his chair outside the shop. 'You have not come for many days,' he said to Gopal. 'Are you growing a beard in your old age?'

Gopal thought such humour was in bad taste, especially because Banwari laughed. 'It is a pity they did not kick you out of Dudhiya Gali,' he said angrily.

'They tried to kill me!' laughed Ram Bibek. 'Commissioner Sahib told the bulldozer to run me down. But this spot in Chandni Chowk will always belong to me, long after the MLAs and MPs and commissioners are all gone.'

Banwari chuckled.

'You should have seen Dudhiya Gali,' said Ram Bibek, in wonder. 'It looked like a sheet of ice!'

Banwari, whose milk was spilled to make the sheet of ice, frowned and turned to the carpenter. Gopal told Ram Bibek he had come to get his hair dyed. Ram Bibek was amused. 'There are not many trees in your orchard, Gopal Bhai. Does it matter what colour the leaves are?'

'It is a special occasion,' said Gopal, defensively.

Amid much laughter, Ram Bibek ran a dye-soaked comb through the hair that still ran down Gopal's neck, turning the strands of grey to deep black. 'I will have to dye your moustache too,' said Ram Bibek. 'That is the only fertile ground on your face.'

This caused more laughter. Gopal puckered his mouth, shut his eyes and allowed Ram Bibek to comb his moustache. When the barber was finished he gave Gopal a mirror. The jet-black moustache startled and pleased Gopal, but he was disappointed to find that his head looked much the same.

'I cannot blacken a bald head,' said Ram Bibek. 'The next time you want to look young, water the ground and grow a good harvest.'

Then Gopal suffered himself to be shaved, accompanied by more laughter. 'You will have to shave every day,' Ram Bibek said. 'Otherwise you will look like a black-and-white film – black moustache and white beard!'

Banwari and the carpenter burst into laughter. 'Like the Moonlight Festival!'

'White moon in a black sky!'

'Amitabh Bachchan!'

Gopal bristled at the insults. He demanded that the stray drops of dye be washed off his temples.

'Water is not free in Chandni Chowk,' said Ram Bibek, officiously. He pointed to the broken hand-pump, then reluctantly allowed Gopal to splash some water on his face from cauldrons sitting next to the chair.

Gopal left Ram Bibek as quickly as he could, with a cut on his throat that Ram Bibek had cauterised with a lump of alum. His face was clean, his nails were clipped, his ebony moustache was combed, and black strands of hair were flattened smoothly to the back of his head. He went to Khari Baoli, walked into Katra Badami, eyes downcast, shuffled past Sushil Jain's cubicle and quickly climbed the ladder into his kholi, grateful that no one had noticed him, and that Hameed was not around to mock his dyed hair. He changed into the silk kurta and dhoti Sohan Lalji had given him, then left Katra Badami in a hurry, shielding his face by pretending to dig something out of his eye. He walked through Chandni Chowk – which was being spruced up for the festival – in deep terror, self-conscious in his new clothes, looking down to avoid eye-contact with rickshavalas, dodging poles and tents and the electrical coils lying all around. What if Ibrahim Mian were to see him? How he would laugh to find him dressed like a peacock!

Mercifully, he met no one he knew, and he walked furtively into Lajpatrai Market, seeking out Jasjit General Store as Sohan Lalji had ordered. And who should he find in the store, seated casually behind the counter and doing no apparent business, but the sardarji himself. His first thought was that this was some trap, that he had been delivered to the sardarji so that the four lakhs could be extracted from him. But the sardarji, instead of threatening him, looked him up and down, clucked his tongue, then burst into laughter. And Gopal's mind was set at ease.

'Stand there,' said Kartar Singhji.

Gopal stood in front of a tall mirror and saw himself in his new clothes for the first time. He had to lean close and hold his head at certain angles to get a good look because his spectacles were old and scratched – he had to seek out clear sky among the clouds. He saw the warm glow of his silk kurta and the comforting yellow of his dhoti, the smooth expanse of his head and the lush black of his moustache, and was satisfied. Then he looked down – to be confronted by his old, warped chappals. Sohan Lalji had forgotten his feet!

The sardarji, also looking at Gopal's feet, made a disapproving sound. 'I would have given you new Kolhapuri chappals, but I stopped selling them a year ago.'

Gopal was crestfallen.

'No one will look at your feet,' said the sardarji, reassuringly. 'You can go now. Come to Gurudwara Sisganj at eight o'clock. You must not be late.'

Then Kartar Singhji gave him ten rupees and sent him away.

Gopal brings his wristwatch close to his face and estimates, as closely as he can, that it is now seven. It will take him thirty minutes to get to Gurudwara Sisganj through this crowd. The silk kurta is warm. He is thankful for the cool October evening. His chappals hurt the balls of his feet and remind him, again, of the flaw in his appearance, but he is now pressed against the food stalls. He watches giant kachauris, as large as footballs – bigger than his head – floating ponderously in oceans of oil. And look at those samosas, piled into a delicious pyramid on the cart to his left! He can now hear the man call out his prices. Six rupees for a plate, three for one samosa. Has there ever been a samosa so expensive, even one so plump and stuffed with potatoes, peas and onions?

Gopal clutches the ten-rupee note in his pocket. Kartar Singhji should have given him more money. But what is this? A gol gappa stall! He will have gol gappas, not samosas. 'A dozen gol gappas for ten rupees,' says the man. Ah, this is a rich man's festival. But why do these men have polythene bags on their heads and hands? Is it a new fashion? Does it add flavour? Such expensive gol gappas, served by hands encased in plastic sacks . . . but he will eat. He does not know where to turn. Should he have a kachauri, or a plate of samosas? Should he try the ice-cream with falooda, or a paapadi chaat? Or the aloo tikki, dahii gujiya, raj kachauri, chana bathura, ragraa chaat, mango juice, tamarind chutney, kadhaayi duudh, badaam pasanda . . .? He cannot eat more than one plate of anything, even if he had the money. He is getting old. There was a time when he could have wolfed down everything and still strut about Chandni Chowk. He will have a plate of samosas, after all.

In the central courtyard of Town Hall, Sohan Lal stands next to a white column and chafes at the empty chairs. There are twelve rows of them, for a total seating capacity exceeding two hundred. Combined with standing room, he had hoped to generate a crowd of five hundred for the Ramayan ballet. Where is everyone? Do they not want to watch a free show, paid for by the government? Perhaps it is because it is ballet, which, from what he has heard, is an English dance performed entirely on tiptoe. He has seen countless Raamleelas, but he has never seen the Ramayan performed on tiptoe. How will Ravan steal Sita away balanced on his toenails? And how will Raam's army of monkeys bridge the great ocean to build a bridge to Lanka? It is an abomination, yet he has been informed by the cultural organisers that an English dance is the only way to attract an audience. No one watches old-fashioned Raamleelas any more, they said. He was perhaps wrong to yield on that score, because here he stands in the unloved courtyard, watching empty chairs and bestowing ingratiating smiles on every wayward family which walks in and takes seats. His own family has not yet arrived, though he gave Sushma strict instructions to have the children ready by six. How can he herd the hordes outside into this enclosure? They are all waiting, perhaps, for the appearance by Pushpa Rani, the grand finale to the festival. No doubt they are gathered round food stalls . . . He has a craving for the sourness of tamarind. Perhaps the stalls should have been kept shut until after the opening ceremony by the prime minister. It will be embarrassing if he arrives at Town Hall to see an empty courtyard.

Yet Sohan Lal is satisfied with the arrangements. As one of the MLAs for the Chandni Chowk area, he has been largely responsible for the organisation of the festival. Suleman Mian is vehemently opposed to the idea, no one trusts the Paharganj MLA, and Harilal sits on too lofty a perch to sully his hands with actual arrangements, so it had fallen to Sohan Lal to spruce up Chandni Chowk for this evening. He does not much care for the festival, but the last few days have given him a taste for organisation. It is not such a bad idea after all. True, many shops were demolished, but most were illegal. You cannot do business in illegal establishments for ever. And even if the festival has caused all of Chandni Chowk to be shut down for a day, it will generate a great deal of business in the future.

He has had oil lamps erected along the street from Red Fort to Fatehpuri Masjid. The removal of stalls and hawkers made it easy to repair footpaths, sweep them, hammer uneven slabs into place and fill the cracks. Drains have been disinfected. Electrical cables have been neatly tethered to lamp-posts. Transformers have been boxed in with metal fences, and electrical junction boxes painted green. Arches on all kuchas have been cleaned of advertisements and posters, then white-washed. During the cleaning of Kucha Mahajani, municipal workers raised some loose concrete slabs and unearthed a small metal box. It has been claimed by Seth Jhunjhunwala as a time capsule embedded by his great-great-grandfather in the time of Bahadur Shah Zafar. Sohan Lal had it transferred to his own shop for safekeeping, until the Archaeological Survey of India can examine it. Last evening, he had Chotu break open the box. Inside it he found eight thousand rupees, silver chips bearing the imprint of Jhunjhunwala's shop, a pouch full of silver dust and, wrapped in a newspaper from twelve years ago, a dozen pieces of gold apparently taken from rings. The newspaper screamed, 'Operation Bluestar,' in large letters across its front. It was the late edition, 6 June 1984. 'Indira Orders Troops into Golden Temple,' said the headline. 'Akaal Takht Damaged. Bhindranwale Believed Dead in Assault.' There was a statement from Indira Gandhi, saying she had launched Operation Bluestar as a last resort, and a quote from Sikh organisations condemning it. Sohan Lal chuckled to himself and stowed away the box in his Lakshmi cupboard. He has still not determined what to do with it, but he has a good mind not to hand it over to the Archaeological Survey.

The prime minister will arrive with an entourage of fifty, he reflects. If the chairs are rearranged so there are gaps between them, fifty people will make a respectable audience. And if another fifty can be brought in from the crowds outside . . . It will be a grand show, no matter how selfishly people hover round the food. Town Hall is the centre of the festival. It is here that the prime minister will light a lamp to inaugurate the festival, and watch the Ramayan ballet as the first presentation of the evening. It will be followed by many concurrent performances – bhajans at Gaurishankar Temple, a sufi performance at Bhai Mati Das Chowk, chamber music in the Baptist Church, keertan near Gurudwara Sisganj . . . The cultural organisers are certainly creative when it comes to inventing superfluous events. There is a programme called 'Shahjahanabad', an exhibition called 'We The People', portraying the secular fabric of the country, a book fair at Nai Sarak, a 'Haasya Kavi Sammelan' and a qawwali at Fatehpuri Masjid, a ghazal performance called 'The Greatest Urdu Poet – Ghalib, son of Chandni Chowk', an Odissi dance outside Town Hall, a Mughal court in the grounds of Fatehpuri Masjid, kathak dancers lining the street near Paratha Gali . . . There are rides for children on caparisoned elephants, camels and horses. And then, of course, there are the food stalls. Sohan Lal wonders if he can send a servant to get him a plate of gol gappas. He should have brought Chotu here instead of letting him off for the evening.

His only regret is that Harilal Gupta has managed to represent the entire festival as his own idea, his own vision, his own creation. There is the obligatory reference to Lala Surajmal because no one can begrudge a few crumbs to a dead man – a corpse cannot pose for photographs. It is Harilal Gupta who will accompany the prime minister to the opening ceremony, stand with him when newspapers want quotes, hand the prime minister the candle with which the lamp will be lit, and smile for the photographs that will appear in tomorrow's newspapers. Sohan Lal is four years older than Harilal Gupta and has always been a faithful member of the IPP. Harilal has gone with the current that flows fastest, yet he is the transport minister of Delhi while Sohan Lal is a mere MLA. But there is time, if Sohan Lal can tame his backache and watch his blood pressure.

A squeal pierces the Town Hall courtyard. They are testing the microphones in preparation for the Raamleela. Sohan Lal decides to visit the administrative offices behind the stage. For this occasion, they have been turned into green rooms. Last-minute makeup is being applied, but everyone is somehow aware that the Raamleela will not begin on time. Sohan Lal is nudged by the man playing Hanuman. He is old, a body-builder who was once a famous wrestler. In his waning years he has taken to playing the role of Hanuman, for which he is particularly suited because of his build, and also because his upper lip has a curious swelling that gives him a simian look. 'Can I have my photo taken with the prime minister?' asks Hanuman.

Sohan Lal knows he should not harbour irreligious thoughts, but he cannot help thinking that a grown man dressed as a monkey, with a long tail held erect behind him by string tied to the shoulder, looks ludicrous. He banishes the thought, vaguely aware of divine retribution. He finds Hanuman's request distasteful, because it will require Sohan Lal to ingratiate himself with Harilalji – who controls access to the prime minister – and because Sohan Lal himself hopes to receive that honour. Before he can refuse, however, Raam himself comes running up to Sohan Lal with a more urgent problem. He cannot find his bow and arrow. There cannot be a Raamleela in which Raam does not wield a bow. This puts Sohan Lal in a foul temper. Must he now provide props for an absent-minded drama company?

A gale of noise invades the Town Hall courtyard. The prime minister has arrived! Sohan Lal must rush to the steps while the cameras are clicking. He seizes the plastic mace that rests on Hanuman's shoulders and thrusts it toward Raam. 'Take this! This shall be your bow for today!' Then he walks through the courtyard as quickly as his knees will allow him – reminded of the doctor's insistence that he lose his heaving belly – and emerges on the grand steps that lead from Town Hall into the garden outside. There is a crowd of onlookers. It is not the prime minister they watch but a grand buggy drawn by four white horses. A coachman sits high on the box as the vehicle's lone occupant steps down: Harilal Gupta! Sohan Lal grinds his teeth. What a nerve! He has arrived as if he were a Rajput prince – waving at the crowd and wearing a towering pink turban with a crisp sash that stands upright above his head! Harilal Gupta is walking youthfully at fifty-seven, scattering benevolence on his subjects, who have turned out in force to enjoy his festival.

Hanuman has followed Sohan Lal through the courtyard to the steps outside, and now implores him to arrange a mace for him. How can Hanuman appear on stage with bare hands? he demands. Sohan

Lal places a silent curse on the entire army of monkeys, then reminds himself that the curse applies only to human actors who pretend to be divine – not the Vaanar Sena itself – and snaps, 'Send someone to Kartar Singhji at Gurudwara Sisganj. He will give you something.'

Meanwhile, the buggy has departed and Harilal Gupta stands ready with a garland in his hands. Car horns and sirens blare, and there is a scuffle in the crowd, which the police try to scatter with a minor lathi charge. A few people hurl abuse, others are intimidated, and a passage opens haphazardly near the gate. The Mercedes of the lieutenant governor of Delhi slides in, bearing him with his guest, the prime minister.

Harilal Gupta lunges toward the car, garland in hand, smile in place, bending so low that he seems on the verge of falling on his face. Sohan Lal admires his suppleness: his own knees would not put up with such abuse. His inability to bow has placed him far from the Mercedes, while Harilal Gupta is within smelling distance of the prime minister. But he is gratified by the presence of the crowd, which is sure to follow the prime minister into Town Hall. It surges toward the Mercedes, held back by a cordon of policemen who strain for a glimpse of the prime minister behind the dark windows of the car. Sohan Lal looks about frantically for a garland, wondering where Harilal got his. He must push through to the Mercedes before the garlanding is complete. How careless of him not to have a garland handy! He must welcome the prime minister! He must say something, even if the prime minister is from the south and cannot speak Hindi, and represents a ridiculous party that is a mishmash of many irrelevant parties . . . Where is he from anyway? Karnataka, Tamil Nadu or Kerala? One of the other southern states? Should he greet him in English – 'How do you do?' or 'Good evening, Prime Minister Sahib'? What a sad day, when an Indian cannot greet the prime minister of India in Hindi!

Gauhar watches the Mercedes pass in a drug-induced haze. He stands unsteadily, using Aftab for support. This bholanath is strong unless you're used to it. His head spins with the two names that stand out distinctly amid the sounds around him. Bholanath and Chou En-lai, bholanath and Chou En-lai . . . What is this big white car doing in such thick crowds? Who are these fucking people jostling him, devouring plates of samosas and jalebis and aloo tikkis with juices dripping down their fat cheeks? Why won't they sit down in a neat line so that Johnny can empty their pockets? Hold me tight, Aftab, my brother from Binodpur. Keep me close, or these mother-fucking seths in their big white cars will run me over and trample me underfoot.

Gauhar turns dreamy eyes toward Aftab, who pushes ahead, cutting through the crowd like a knife through watermelon, dragging Gauhar after him. What a wonder it is to have two hands! But who the fuck is Aftab? He has only known the boy for a few weeks, and no one can vouch that he really is from Binodpur. Why is he letting Aftab lead him through the crowd? And where is the sack that should be weighing down his left shoulder? Where is his fucking cash-box? He remembers someone breaking the lock. *Bammm!* A police hammer pulverised it. That bastard Inderlal Jha. The way his eyes lit up when he saw the money! Then Gauhar remembers walking into the corridor, pulling Munna. He remembers the cheer they set up for him. 'Gauhar Muhammad *zindabad*!' They came away from the police station triumphant, victorious, carrying Gauhar on their shoulders. Aftab and Johnny and Partho and Munna and Baba and Khoka and Wasif . . . Where are all those rustams right now? They are in this very crowd, no doubt, doing business. They will all go to Inderlal's lockup if they get caught, and he no longer has the cash-box to buy them out. What wonderful gol gappas! Almost spherical, perfect, like a pair of breasts in GB Road. He must go there again and take Aftab with him. Are the whores open for business this evening? No, they have all come out into Chandni Chowk to eat gol gappas. Every woman in this crowd is probably a whore dressed up for the occasion. And what's that? Ras malai? Gulabjamun! Falooda! He must have some, but this bholanath is so much sweeter . . . Where is Kiran? Where did she go when the machines were charging at her? 'What happened to your hand?' she had asked. 'There was another beautiful girl like you,' he had told her, 'but she bit much harder . . .' How deliciously her eyelids had folded when she laughed at his joke! She must be somewhere around Jama Masjid, picking rags or begging. Could she be getting fucked? Allah! He did not get fucked until he was sixteen. That is a respectable age, when a boy or girl can handle the pricks of men. She could not be more than eleven or twelve. He cannot let her get fucked! Perhaps she is here, in this crowd? Should he look for a little Nepali girl trailing an old rich fucker who wants young flesh? But how is he to distinguish one face from another with the mist of bholanath upon him? And how is he to recognise her with juices running down every cheek, and every mouth stuffed with samosas and kachauris?

Aftab is pulling him with inexplicable urgency. Where the fuck are they going, and what is the hurry?

'Slow down,' murmurs Gauhar. 'You are hurting my hand.'

'We must get a hit soon,' says Aftab, urgently. 'At least two hits per person, or the fucking Biharis will laugh at us.'

'There will be a lot to collect after the festival,' suggests Gauhar.

Aftab laughs aloud. 'We do not pick rags! My baba brought me here from Binodpur, all the way across Bengal, Bihar and Uttar Pradesh. He wanted me to make hits – not pick rags – and to show the Bihari gangs their place.'

Gauhar does not tell Aftab that he picked rags for years before Mussabir Ustad taught him the business of fucking. Let the past bury itself. He will let Aftab, who speaks to him in that sweet Bengali of Binodpur, lead him to a hit. That, and the cloud of bholanath around him, is all he will think about. Mussabir is dead and Kiran is getting fucked somewhere, and he will allow them to fade away. If only the calluses on his hand would heal . . .

He will never go back to the silver-beating shop, even if the bulldozers have let it stand. And fuck Yellow Teeth! Five rupees was all he gave him. Five rupees, when he went all the way to Ayodhya and saw Mussabir die before his eyes. Poor Mussabir did not even receive a decent burial. Did they find his body when they removed the debris? Where did they throw his bones? There is now a Raam Lalla temple in that place, he has been told. Does Mussabir still lie under the earth, directly beneath the feet of Raam Lalla?

Gauhar gnashes his teeth. One day he will go back to that room in the haveli, run up the creaking staircase, stand on Suleman Mian's red carpet and fuck his wife, and then tell him he is a pyarelal. What is a pyarelal? Suleman Mian will ask. You are a pyarelal, he will answer, because you farm out your wife for other men to fuck!

He will do all this later, but for now he must eat. He has no money. The two hundred and sixty he saved from Inderlal were soon spent on bholanath and Chou En-lai. It is impossible to hide any money from the gang: they rifle his pockets every night, and any money they earn is put into a common pool. This business of shoving your hand into other pockets is difficult. The hand that extracts the money must pass it quickly to another waiting hand or it will be caught. Mussabir was right: a man needs two hands to push a cart, two hands to drive a ricksha, two hands to set off a bomb, two hands to pick pockets, two hands for everything except getting fucked and collecting bets on pigeon fights. No one told Mussabir Ustad that you could beat silver with one hand. Very well, he will train himself to do this new business with one hand. As soon as he has conquered bholanath he will start again. Those three years of sitting around in Didi's school and beating silver have softened him, but he can still show these rustams who is boss. They are all younger, weaker and shorter than him.

Why has Aftab brought him to the big white car with a hundred policemen around it? Does he want to spend the rest of his life in Hotel Tihar listening to Father Noronha talk about Jesus Christ? Any one of those fucking khaki-men could spot them. But Aftab is now standing right next to the car, where a fat man bends forward with a garland in his hands. A pink turban obscures much of his face but the lower half has melted into a broad grin, displaying large teeth. Then Gauhar sees Aftab's left hand move toward a pair of gigantic buttocks, where the fat man's silk kurta has ridden up to expose his monstrous silk pyjamas. His elephant thighs are about to burst through the silk tubes, so the wallet he has stuffed into his pocket forms a clear outline in bas-relief. Inviting, like a naked virgin waiting to be fucked! But how will Aftab pull out such a tightly stuffed wallet? How will he slide it up against the resistance of flesh, until its brown leather skin peeps out of the pocket?

Gauhar tugs at Aftab's hand. 'Do not try this,' he whispers. 'There are dozens of khaki-men around!' Aftab grins in scorn, then turns back to concentrate on the feast. The fat man has bent forward to open the doors of the big white car. Gauhar does not know exactly how it happens. Either the fat ox is too engrossed in peering through the dark windows of the car or Aftab's two hands deploy a magic unknown to his one, but the wallet flies from the buttocks to Aftab's left hand, then to his right hand, then to Gauhar's left hand, which shoves it deep inside his trousers.

'Run,' says Aftab. 'Meet me at Gurudwara Sisganj.'

Ramvilas walks swiftly through the crowd, berating himself for being late. He should have been at Town Hall, standing next to Harilal Gupta, when the prime minister arrived. How else is he going to make his mark in the committee? He has not been invited to the Town Hall function, and the fault is his own. He has aligned himself too closely with Sohan Lal. Everyone knows that although Sohan Lal is the chairman of the IPP committee, Harilal is the chief organiser, whose pictures will appear in tomorrow's newspapers. It was short-sighted of him not to see that in advance. Very well, he will compensate for his oversight by being within sight of Harilalji, should the prime minister need someone to run an errand.

He glances down at his neatly pressed kurta-pyjama. His hair is slicked with brilliantine and his moustache trimmed to a respectably thin line. Perhaps he should have put on a Nehru jacket: the evening is cool, and it would have imparted eminence.

He veers to the left to avoid people at the food stalls, turning in disgust from the ravenous horde. Animals! he thinks. Have they never eaten before?

After the food area he passes a few NGO stalls. The third belongs to STREE. He can see Gita in the stall with Nasreen and Manju, all three in bland white sarees that cover their entire bodies and render the stall featureless. He soldiers on. He must not let Gita see him. She is a conniving whore. He was wise not to spend nights in the kotha, or he may have found himself in trouble during the raid. Rage wells in his mind. Why did she not tell him about it beforehand? And why was Inderlal so duplicitous, after all the money he has given him over the years? He does not much mind that Parvati's girls have been taken away. It serves the whore right, for giving him the white sores. Now her girls will contaminate other men in Naari Niketan, or pollute their villages in Bangladesh. He will not miss them, and he will never touch Parvati again, but Kiran would have been convenient – a virgin just when he needed one. Ah, this virgin cure is perhaps a superstition anyway. He will get by. The sores are healing. He has managed to conceal them from his wife. He will try to stay away from the kotha for a few weeks, even months. His membership of the committee puts him under scrutiny, and he has a position to maintain. But how dare Gita treat him so? She had kept a straight face when he demanded to know why she had gone behind his back. He will deal with the bitch as soon as he has settled the quarrels between Surajmal's sons and opened his own shop. Once that is done, he will bring his wife and daughters to Delhi and send STREE back into the kotha where it belongs. For now, he must hurry to help Harilalji and see if the prime minister needs anything to eat or drink.

Gita adjusts the STREE badge on her saree when she spots Ramvilas. She quickly inspects the apparel of the other whores on her stall, then repaints the warm smile on her face, but Ramvilas passes them. She shrugs and turns back to Nasreen and Manju. They are all perfectly attired for today – no cleavage, no midriff, no navel and no upper arms. They have worn those old-hag blouses that come down to the waist to be tucked under the saree, button to the neck and have sleeves stretching to the wrists. Their hair is tied into tight buns, and their STREE badges are pinned near the collarbone, far above their heaving bosoms. She has paid only three hundred rupees for the stall – a discount because she does not plan to make a profit. This NGO rate was negotiated for her by Ramvilas, who interceded with Harilalji. She brought up the subject when he came to visit her on the morning following the raid, as part of an IPP delegation to assess the situation in Kotha 842. He was seething with anger, and she was amused at how ineffectually he controlled his temper in the presence of other IPP members. He stood behind her and muttered, 'You did not tell me about this!'

'I did not know,' she responded.

'How do you think the police found out?' he had asked, worried.

She feigned ignorance, then brought up the subject of the stall.

'I can get you a good rate,' he said sourly. Finally, when the delegation was leaving, he asked her the question she knew was uppermost in his mind: 'Where is Kiran?' She had turned a tear-stained face toward him. That must have exonerated her in his eyes, if nothing else. He gave hurried assurances about the stall and left. And he kept his word.

Things have turned out all right, she thinks, with some satisfaction. Kiran is probably in Naari Niketan. They will keep her there for months, perhaps years, then try to send her to Nepal. Hopefully, she will not fall into the hands of her uncle Jangbahadur – if he is still alive – who will surely try to sell her to someone in Delhi or Calcutta. In any case, she is safe for a few months. Parvati is hysterical now that her girls are gone: five girls taking six customers every night, each giving eight rupees for each customer to her. The police will surely question them. Who knows what trouble Parvati is in? She walks about with a forlorn look, these days. It is the look of a whore who will never be a bai. Gita can have her locked up whenever she wants, which may be a good reason to keep her around. And all those meddlesome women of DIDI, PATITA, STOP and NAARI have been put in their place. They have always treated under-age whores as their mission, yet it was STREE that uncovered the scandal and saved six lives. No one doubts now that STREE represents the whores of GB Road. Even Inderlal no longer dares to ask her for a commission.

Yes, things have turned out all right, but she is peeved that the stall is deserted. Men walk by furtively, wives and children in tow, averting their eyes. The wives are bolder. They stare curiously at Gita and her whores. A few teenagers – unencumbered by wives and mothers – stop and pick up the pamphlets STREE has spread on the counter, but they are not really interested. I do not care, thinks Gita. Cameramen have already passed her stall and filmed it. Perhaps she will be on television, and the rest will take care of itself. She turns to Nasreen and points to the deserted counter. 'We need to call out to people,' she says, 'as the food stalls do. Start announcing our programme!' she commands.

Gopal flows with the crowd on his way to Gurudwara Sisganj. A woman is shouting that this stall is for GB Road. Are these women allowed to have stalls? Now everyone will know that GB Road is right here, within walking distance. There are booklets on the counter – red and blue – and standing behind it in white sarees . . . Ganga Maiya! Are these the women themselves? Could they really be *those* women? He looks round quickly to see if anyone else has noticed, but the crowd seems indifferent. Does no one else know what these women do? They have been let out into the crowd among people with families, mothers and sisters!

A tall woman stands at the counter, reading pamphlets. There is no mistake about it: she is the madam from the newspaper, the one who used to come to ask him questions. She must not see him near this stall!

Hurriedly Gopal pushes into the crowd and tries to orient himself, in the blinding fog thrown on his spectacles by glimmering lights, toward Gurudwara Sisganj.

Chitra is taller than most men in the crowd, so she has no trouble looking over their heads and marvelling at its size. This, then, is the festival Harilal Gupta has been crowing about and Suleman has been decrying for the last four weeks. Judging by the crowds it is a success, if one overlooks the fact that people are concentrated round the samosa and gol gappa stalls and show no interest in the Raamleela inside Town Hall or the Mughal court in Fatehpuri Masjid. This is just as well. Samosas and gol gappas are part of our heritage too, perhaps a more integral part than the debaucheries of Mughal emperors or the fertile imagination of Tulsidas. And then there is this stall for STREE – Sex-workers Training, Rehabilitation and

Education Endeavour. A well-chosen name. The plump Nepali woman behind the counter stands with a smile deliberately constructed
for the occasion – a short, squat woman with large breasts and creamy
skin, possessing the kind of power that can only come to a whore
when modesty has lost all meaning and is therefore impregnable. After
a woman has been possessed in every imaginable way, what possible
harm can men do to her? She is inviolable, invincible, indestructible
. . . There is little doubt that this creamy social worker of indeterminate age is a prostitute. Which other Indian woman could stand with
such poise in a crowd of uncouth men? The politically correct word is
sex-worker, as explained by the signs in the stall. As if the work of sex
was no different from work in an office, a food stall, a cinema or a
jewellery shop. Some day she must write about this organisation. But
it is not a good time to interview the Nepali woman – not while she
stands in a blanket-like saree, protected by the armour of her STREE
badge and a lady-like smile. She must be interviewed in her natural
surroundings, at her place of work, on the assembly line of the sex-
worker factory. For now, Harilal Gupta offers richer pickings,
especially because he will be with the prime minister – a weak,
feckless prime minister who may enjoy the throne no longer than a
hundred moons, an irrelevant prime minister who is a cipher in the
uncertain march of Indian history, but a prime minister nevertheless.
Suleman, aware that she is a senior contributing editor at *India Now*,
has asked her to write something about his protest against the festival,
but she is not certain the protest is either newsworthy or relevant.

   She must push through the crowd. She will not eat the gol gappas and
samosas, or any of these other abominations – mounds of infection,
nurseries for germs, flour and tamarind mashed together by unclean
hands and unclipped nails, crawling with worms she dare not mention.
Oh, yes, they have slipped on polythene bags as a grudging concession to
the silly insistence on hygiene, but who is fooled by such gimmickry? No,
she will stay hungry and drink bottled water, which is quite possibly the
greatest convenience afforded to modern India. And she will go to Town
Hall, where the prime minister has already arrived, judging by the
slogans that extol his sacred person. But first she will watch
the ceremony at Gurudwara Sisganj, where Sikhs plan to re-enact the
martyrdom of Guru Tegh Bahadur three hundred years ago.

A stage has been erected on the marble pavement in front of
Gurudwara Sisganj. Tall floodlights bathe the stage and spill over

into the audience, which consists of Sikhs in yellow and blue turbans, silk sashes, silver shoes and sheathed kirpaans that glisten in the floodlights. The stage is a profusion of yellow and blue, the only jarring note being Kartar Singh's golden shervani. His voice is hoarse and he sweats copiously but he speaks into the microphone with passion.

'And then, my brothers, the emperor issued final orders that Guru Tegh Bahadur should be beheaded in Chandni Chowk. A large crowd gathered to see the sacrifice of this great pir. Guruji took a bath in a nearby well. He was seated on a platform under a banyan tree and Qazi Abul Wahab Borah read the fatwa. The guru requested Jalaluddin the executioner to strike the blow when he had finished reciting the Japji Sahib. The holy head flew into the lap of Bhai Jaita . . .'

Kartar Singh stops, overwhelmed. A story cannot continue unchecked through such tumultuous events. '*Vahe guruji kaa khalsa*!' he intones.

'*Vahe guruji kii fateh*!' returns the crowd fervently.

It is a significant milestone in the narrative. The assembly has listened to his plodding account for more than twenty minutes, awaiting the cathartic moment when the guru will surrender his life to the tyranny of Aurangzeb. Kartar Singh feels beads of perspiration on his forehead. He has ended his story and must move on to the next item. But where is the chaivala? He should have been on the stage by now, in time for the grand announcement that is to follow the sacrifice of Guru Tegh Bahadur. How long will the crowd continue to brandish kirpaans and celebrate the guru's martyrdom?

He turns to find an organiser from the Chandni Chowk IPP committee playing with the amplifier volume, and asks him to fetch the chaivala. 'Gopal Pandey. That is his name.'

The man is uncertain that he will find anyone in such a crowd. He is one of the few non-Sikhs on the stage and is clearly uncomfortable to be an object of scrutiny.

Kartar Singh is exasperated. 'Look for a short, plump man of fifty. Silk kurta and dhoti, worn with great care as if they do not belong to him. Bald. Old chappals. He does not know you, and would not recognise you if he did because his spectacles are scratched. Call his name loudly wherever you go, so he will hear you above the crowd. He is a little deaf. Go toward the food stalls.'

The man leaves. Kartar Singh turns back to the audience. He takes a deep breath and begins to mumble.

'The bloodthirsty emperor was not satisfied with Guruji's sacrifice, my brothers. He announced, "The headless body of the pir of Hindus lies in Chandni Chowk. Whosoever wants it may claim it!" And he imposed a heavy guard round it. Dark clouds massed over Delhi, bringing rain and storm. The guards dispersed in such weather. Lakhi Shah Banjara drove up in a cart, lifted the guru's body and hid it under bales of hay. He then dashed toward Rakabganj and set the village on fire, so the emperor's guards would think it was the entire village, not the guru's body, that was aflame. And thus the guru was cremated. The next morning Lakhi Shah had the ashes of the guru swept into two urns and buried, where Gurudwara Rakabganj Sahib now stands.'

Kartar Singh pauses to let his audience conjure Gurudwara Rakabganj in their minds, and scans the crowd for signs of Gopal or the IPP man sent to fetch him. He decides valiantly to continue. 'Bhai Jaita took Guruji's head to Anandpur Sahib and presented it to Guru Gobind Rai, who had a pyre of sandalwood prepared for the guru.'

A man touches Kartar Singh's elbow. Kartar Singh turns to him irritably. To be disturbed when telling the story of Bhai Jaita!

'They want a kirpaan,' says the man.

'Who?'

'Hanuman needs it.'

Kartar Singh is baffled.

'Sohan Lalji sent me,' explains the man.

'Ah! Hanuman from the Raamleela. But a kirpaan?'

'His mace has been taken by Raam, who has lost his bow.'

Kartar Singh angrily tears off the sword that hangs from his sash. 'Take this and be gone,' he says. The man disappears.

Chitra comes to the edge of the Sikh crowd and watches the colour palette of yellow and blue on the stage. This will make a good photograph, if it can be reproduced as the magazine centrefold. The speaker has not followed the colour code, though, and his voice is hoarse with exhaustion.

Having lost his train of thought, Kartar Singh ploughs into another story. 'Bhai Mati Das was a devout disciple of Guru Tegh Bahadur. They led him in chains to Chandni Chowk. He walked with a hero's swagger. A large crowd had gathered. The chief qazi of Aurangzeb said to him, "O brave young man, accept Islam! You will have wealth and a high position, and when you die the Prophet Muhammad will receive you among the faithful!"

' "I prefer dying to giving up my faith," replied Bhai Mati Das.'

Kartar Singh's audience stirs impatiently, confused by the chronology of events. The story of Bhai Mati Das should have come before the guru's martyrdom, not after the guru's body has been cremated and his head lies on a sandalwood pyre. But Kartar Singh continues, in a voice that trembles with emotion: ' "Do you have any last wishes?" asked the qazi.

' "Let me behold my guru in the last moments of my life," said Bhai Mati Das.

'So they stood him with his face toward the guru and tied him between two logs of wood. The saw moved to and fro, spilling his blood. He was calmly repeating the Japji Sahib when his head fell off his body . . .'

Kartar Singh notices that he is losing his audience. A murmur has emerged from the core of the crowd and travelled in all directions. They know the story already – they have heard it countless times, in every keertan and every gurudwara. Kartar Singh pauses, stuck in the moment, trapped, mute, panic-stricken. Then, as if the guru has answered his prayers, he spies Gopal standing to the left of the stage in his silk kurta. He grabs the microphone with renewed energy. 'At this spot, my brothers, at this very spot where the guru gave up his body, stands a good man who has defended a Sikh with his own life. If I have tears in my eyes, my brothers, forgive me for the memory of my wife Sukhbir Kaur, and what they did to her in 'eighty-four. I still bleed from the beatings I received, I still limp from the blows to my legs, but I do not stand here to talk about myself! I stand here to talk about the sufferings of Sukhbir Kaur. She was sitting at home reading her Sukhmani Sahib when they came for her. Who came for her, you will ask? Why should anyone want to harm Sukhbir Kaur, who harmed no one in her life? The Congress murderers, my brothers, bloodthirsty hounds!'

A roar rises from the crowd, and chairs on the stage are scraped this way and that. There are many Congress Party members on the stage. It is certainly in bad taste to stoke embers that have lain cold for twelve years. Shri Babulal, sent by Naresh Agrawal as his representative – because Naresh Agrawal himself will escort Pushpa Rani to her performance – turns to the man beside him and whispers something. Kartar Singh notices the commotion, sees the Congress Party flag on Babulal's chest, notes his khadi kurta and Gandhi cap, and is subdued. He has often used this line to great effect, but perhaps this is the wrong occasion to deploy it.

'It does not matter who they were,' he says quickly. 'They were murderers and they wanted her blood. She locked herself inside the bathroom. They beat on the door with rods, sticks and hammers. Which door can stand the fire of hate? It yielded, but there stood behind it a courageous man with a kirpaan in his hand, drawn to avenge Khalsa blood! There were many of them, but that did not matter. A man of the Khalsa – even if he is a Hindu – is the equal of an army! They saw him as you might see a great ghost, towering over their puny bodies and poised to strike against their vile hearts. And the cowards fled the punishing arm of the Khalsa. This is how Sukhbir Kaur, who had seen her son die before her very eyes – her poor Jassi! – was saved by the courage of one good man. *Bole so nihaal*! *Sat sri akaal*!'

Kartar Singh pauses for effect. He has been eloquent on the matter. He hopes the chaivala will not ruin the moment by stumbling when he comes on to the stage. 'Here is that man! The good man, the simple man who saved the life of Sukhbir Kaur from murderers!'

Pushed by a dozen hands, Gopal climbs the stairs to the stage. He ascends slowly and unsteadily and stands on the edge, looking toward Kartar Singh. He is amazed to be standing so high above Chandni Chowk. Ganga Maiya! You can see all the way to Town Hall from this height! There must be twenty lakh people in Chandni Chowk, and they are all looking straight at him! Forty lakh eyes boring right through him. He should not have worn a silk dhoti. Its folds slip round his waist. And his chappals – his uncomfortable, tattered chappals – are visible to them all. He cannot see their faces, he cannot see their eyes, but he knows they are laughing in that foggy world that surrounds the stage.

Kartar Singh watches the chaivala falter, suspended precariously on the edge of the stage, and lunges toward him, instinctively playing up the limp. What a heartrending picture he must present at this moment! Ten thousand Sikhs have seen him drag his left foot across the stage. He is trying hard to bend his knee all the way, so he can place the left foot correctly in front of the right one, but the knee will not yield. And is there not a shooting pain in the kneecap that started minutes ago? That pain never goes away. It recurs at the most inconvenient moments. But here is the chaivala. He puts an arm round Gopal and pulls him to the centre of the stage, limping alongside and using him for support, so it is not clear to the crowd who is leading whom. When they arrive at the microphone, he turns Gopal to face the audience and studies the back of his head, wishing the chaivala was more suited to the occasion – less flabby, more confident and capable of slipping into the mantle of a protector. But that was a long time ago. Even Joginder Singh, great wrestler that he was, is reduced to playing the role of Hanuman in his waning years. Why should the hero of 'eighty-four not be an unassuming, portly chaivala in 'ninety-six?

Gopal stands in the fog of his spectacles, blinded by lights and deafened by noise. There was just such a crowd when Mukesh turned into a ball of fire . . . At the very edge of the assembly, where the yellow and blue sashes run out, a tall, thin man is familiar. When the crowd roars he raises his hands and cheers wildly. The left hand holds what looks like a leather wallet, and the right hand looks like it has been sawn off. Ganga Maiya! That is the ghost of Gauhar, come back after four years! Did not Ibrahim Mian say the boy was dead, killed in connection with some trouble in Ayodhya, perhaps while trying to defend that masjid? But there is the boy, throwing up his stump, the other arm round the shoulders of another boy. Where is his beard? But that does not matter; his son has been restored to him. What a wonderful festival this is!

Gopal bends toward the microphone. If he can call Gauhar's name . . . But Kartar Singh takes it away and begins to speak.

'You do not know the full extent of Gopal Pandey's sacrifice, my brothers! He did not stop after he saved the life of Sukhbir Kaur. He has worked tirelessly since then to promote communal harmony among Hindus and Musalmans, Sikhs and Christians. When he heard about the Moonlight Festival, he decided to sacrifice his chai stall in Kucha Bansilal so the kucha could be broadened and the electrical boxes painted green. He lost his means of livelihood, my brothers, but he considers no sacrifice too great for the sake of Chandni Chowk.'

A spatter of polite applause greets this announcement. After the martyrdom of Guru Tegh Bahadur and Bhai Mati Das, and the near lynching of Sukhbir Kaur, the dismantling of a chai stall seems anti-climactic. Kartar Singh, sensing that he has their attention for just a few more minutes, launches a frontal assault: 'There are many "leaders" who claim to represent the people of Chandni Chowk, who are now shedding tears for the illegal structures that were removed, the dangerous buildings that were demolished. Who are these leaders? Have their homes been razed to the ground? Have their shops been shut down? I ask them to answer me, because Gopal Pandey lost his stall, and Gopal Pandey stands here in support of the drive, in support of this great festival, in the memory of Lala Surajmal, under the leadership of Harilalji Gupta!'

At the edge of the crowd, Ibrahim grits his teeth. 'Traitor!' he mutters. 'You are a traitor, Gopal Bhai!'

He is on his way to Town Hall to join Suleman Mian, but has stopped on seeing Gopal on the stage outside Gurudwara Sisganj. He shakes with rage at this treachery. Look how demurely the chaivala stands on that stage like a bride! A whore, all dressed up in her best finery, ready to offer herself up to anyone who will pay! And what is wrong with his moustache? Why is it all black? Does he lust after youth at his age? Has he not stood before a mirror and looked into his soul to realise that he is a poor man? He should be with Suleman Mian near Town Hall, shouting slogans against seths and Banias and the IPP thugs who demolished his stall, not displaying himself on a stage like a whore and accepting prizes from sardars. Have they given him money for this?

This ends our brotherhood and our friendship, thinks Ibrahim bitterly. Suleman Mian is right – you can trust no blood but that which flows in a Musalman's veins. A kafir is a kafir after all, with a kafir heart!

Chitra has a lump in her throat. This is the man who went on hunger strike in Rajghat to protect Babri Masjid! She has been remiss in ignoring him over the last two years, wasting her time on specious articles and sententious lament for the 'secular fabric' of India. What are those lofty subjects she deigns to comment on, seated in the eyrie of journalistic vanity? Caste equations, Hindu–Muslim violence, the Mandal Commission, Babri Masjid, the collapse of the social alliance engineered by Nehru, the dying throes of the Congress Party, the new champions of backward castes, the new leaders of Musalmans, the rise of the IPP, the drifting away of Brahmins and SCs from the Congress umbrella, the hand-wringing over 'fractured polity', the repairing of the 'Sikh psyche' . . . These are all revealed to be hollow phrases when one man – however unimpressive – stands on a stage.

She wishes he was more equal to the task. That would have blown away the cobwebs of doubt from her mind. What does the chaivala think about all this? Surely he wants to say something, with the microphone in front of him and ten thousand pairs of eyes on his face? He must say something, and say it quickly, or she will have to move on to cover the prime minister's speech at Town Hall. She will be loyal to the chaivala but only up to a point, and only in pursuit of a story.

'He is looking this way!' Gauhar exclaims.

Aftab shrugs. Gauhar turns back to cast a dreamy eye toward the stage, where the bald man holds his head at a curious angle, as if trying to peer through a narrow tunnel. This is Gopal Bhai, no doubt about it, even if Gopal Bhai did not possess such a black moustache. The sardar has repeatedly called him Gopal Pandey. How many Gopal Pandeys could there be in Chandni Chowk?

'You did not tell me you knew political people,' says Aftab suspiciously.

'He is not a minister,' protests Gauhar.

'How do you know him, then?'

Gauhar considers. He has been warned by Ibrahim Mian never to go to Gopal Bhai. No one knows what Suleman Mian is capable of. Yet here is Gopal Bhai, standing helplessly on the stage, looking like himself even with a black moustache. 'That is my father,' he says quietly.

Aftab laughs. 'You are a mother-fucking Hindu?'

'Not my Binodpur baba, you fool. He is my Chandni Chowk baba.'

Aftab nods, confused but loath to show his ignorance, aware of the possibility that every boy in Chandni Chowk has a Chandni Chowk father and does not know it. 'Let us settle the wallet,' he says.

'I thought we would share it with Johnny and Partho,' objects Gauhar.

Aftab's eyes twinkle. He snatches it from Gauhar. 'We will, after we have counted what is inside.'

Gauhar does not like this double-crossing, but relents. They spread the flaps of the wallet and peer inside. Aftab frowns, then curses, turns the wallet upside-down and shakes it violently. A single fifty-rupee note peeks out.

'What a bastard,' says Aftab. 'Such a fat elephant stuck to such a big car with such a big smile, and such empty pockets!'

Most of the thickness of the wallet, it appears, is in the padded leather flaps, not in the contents. Aftab pockets the fifty-rupee note and flings the wallet to the ground, where a dozen feet trample upon it. 'Let us go,' he says. 'We need another hit.'

'I must meet my father,' says Gauhar.

'Fuck him!' Aftab shouts. 'Do you want to make it easy for the police by standing on a stage? Why not walk into a police station and turn yourself in?'

'Fuck the police,' says Gauhar. 'I am going to talk to my father.'

He tries to push toward the stage, but Aftab grabs him from behind. Gauhar struggles to free himself. He could toss his head backward and break Aftab's nose, but decides not to pick a fight. 'All right,' he concedes. 'Let us find another hit.'

They walk beyond Gurudwara Sisganj to another area of the festival, where the stalls are filled with performers and healers entertaining a sparse audience. Gauhar points to a counter where a bearded man sits behind an arrangement of blades and bowls of water. 'I know that man. He once stole fifty rupees from me.'

'Let us get our money back,' laughs Aftab.

Muhammad Ghayas, peering through the darkness, recognises Gauhar instantly. 'You have come back!' he exclaims warmly. 'Where is your yellow friend?'

'He is dead,' says Gauhar.

Ghayas is startled. He mumbles something about the unpredictability of medicine, especially the ancient healing arts. 'All I can do is bleed you,' he says. 'Allah does the rest. Who can read His mind?'

'I have come to get my hand fixed,' says Gauhar. He lays his stump on the counter.

Ghayas stares at it doubtfully. 'This will take a lot of time.'

'I have a lot of time,' Gauhar insists.

'Who gave you a stall?' demands Aftab.

Muhammad Ghayas's eyes soften. 'Harilalji Gupta,' he says. 'He is a great leader. A secular man!'

'When will you start on my hand?' asks Gauhar.

'Come to me next week in Meena Bajar,' says Ghayas.

'Give me my fifty rupees,' says Gauhar. 'You killed Mussabir Ustad.'

'I told him not to staunch the bleeding!'

'He did not, but he died anyway.'

Muhammad Ghayas looks at the two young men. Three hands,

scrawny bodies, but young flesh full of vigour and blood. His eyes fill with fear. 'I am a poor man,' he protests.

Gauhar and Aftab exchange looks. They are bored and disappointed – not much can be squeezed out of a dried grape.

'Let us find another fat man with juicy buttocks,' says Gauhar.

They walk away from the stalls.

'Who was Mussabir?' asks Aftab.

'An ustad – the greatest ustad who ever lived.'

Gopal sighs. Gauhar has disappeared. Perhaps it was not him at all, just a thin, one-handed man. The sardarji is still talking and the army of blue and yellow Sikhs is restive. There is a plaque in the sardarji's hands, which he is obviously preparing to hand to him. Where will I hang it, thinks Gopal, now that they have taken away my stall? Will they give me money with it? Five hundred rupees? A thousand? Perhaps five thousand? The sardarji is a rich man. Look at the fat diamonds on his fingers! What price does he put on his sardarni, the one who was stuck in the window? Will he pay more if told about the man in the bathroom? But Ibrahim Mian came all the way from Ballimaran to protect me! Was that Ibrahim Mian, or someone else?

Now the sardarji has turned to Gopal, beaming. The plaque in his hands is made of dark wood, and has a glistening steel plate. He hands it over, then opens one fold of a shawl and wraps it round Gopal's shoulders. There is clapping among the sardars in the audience. A plaque of wood and a shawl, thinks Gopal, but no money.

The sardarji draws out a piece of paper from the folds of his shervani and reads from it. ' "Given to Shri Gopal Pandey. Annual Award for the Promotion of Communal Harmony and National Integration. Signed by Shri Harilal Gupta, MLA, Chandni Chowk, and Shri Sohan Lal Agrawal, MLA, Matia Mahal." '

A plaque of wood, a shawl and an announcement, but no money.

Ramvilas rushes past the food and performance stalls and heads toward Fatehpuri Masjid, where the audio people are testing microphones so the qawwali can begin. He turns toward Khari Baoli, where the police have set up a booth, and curses his luck. He had arrived in the Town Hall courtyard out of breath, disappointed by his lack of stamina, but determined to squeeze through to the prime minister – and who should he run into but Harilal Gupta, charging across the lawn like a fire engine, belly heaving, fat lips trembling in anger. He would have been happy to wait on Harilal, but not when the prime minister himself was sitting inside.

'This is a city of thieves!' thundered Harilalji.

Ramvilas expressed ready agreement, and tried to move past him but was blocked.

'Go to the police booth near Khari Baoli,' commanded Harilal. 'Lodge an FIR about a stolen wallet.'

'Did the prime minister have his pocket picked?' joked Ramvilas. 'It serves him right. One of his secular friends did it!'

'The wallet was mine,' Harilalji said, glowering.

'Do you suspect anyone?'

Harilal looked around, then whispered, so loudly that everyone turned to look, 'It is this drama company. This English Ramayan! Beggar artists!'

Ramvilas turned to go.

'It contained five thousand rupees,' announced Harilalji.

So now Ramvilas must lodge a First Information Report with the police – and bring a copy back to Harilalji – before he can get within fifty yards of the prime minister. By the time he gets back, the prime minister will probably have departed.

The police booth is a temporary wooden enclosure tucked under a neem tree. Ramvilas stalks inside, unfazed by the constables who try to stop him. The police inspector, sprawled behind a desk, regards his approach coldly. Ramvilas sighs in recognition on seeing him. 'Who gave you permission to enter?' asks Inderlal.

'A wallet has been stolen,' Ramvilas pants. 'Write down the FIR. It had five thousand rupees.'

Inderlal twists his lips, causing his thick black moustache to disappear, and opens his eyes wide in mock sympathy. 'Five thousand! We will get your money for you right away.'

'It belongs to Harilal Gupta,' says Ramvilas.

Inderlal sits up straight and opens his register, mumbling something about many wallets being stolen. He scribbles the FIR, tears off a copy, hands it to Ramvilas and sends him off with many assurances. He reprimands his two constables for letting Ramvilas into the shed without asking who he was. Then he leans back in his chair, props his feet on the desk and considers the significance of what has just happened. Details of the FIR process will be reported to Harilalji, no doubt. The lackey will not fail to spice up the brew when he pours it into Harilalji's ears. 'Police negligence,' he will say.

Perhaps he will claim that the police beat him. Harilalji is already looking for someone to blame for the Meena Bajar demolition, which is why he has named Inderlal in the inquiry that has been set up. But will not the raid on Kotha 842 count for anything? He fully expects to receive a commissioner's roll for the successful co-ordination between the police and the NGOs. And he has twenty constables to prove that he did not do anything in Meena Bajar. He will pay Harilalji a visit next week. He will go to the transport minister's bungalow and offer his services. No one can remain unmoved by a sincere offer of servitude. Meanwhile he must find this wallet thief to placate the minister. It is his lot to go burrowing after petty wallets when he could be standing guard outside Town Hall, with the chance of a glimpse of the prime minister.

Inderlal stands up, stretches, summons his two constables, and explains the circumstances of the theft, as far as he knows them. They emerge from the wooden enclosure and head for Town Hall. When they are about to turn into Chandni Chowk, they hear rustling ahead and spy a man scurrying away in the darkness. His lungi flaps wildly round his legs as he vanishes into a lane.

'Catch him!' commands Inderlal.

The two constables are confused. 'Are we not going to Town Hall to catch the wallet thief?' they ask.

He grits his teeth in exasperation. 'That is the wallet thief!' he roars.

The constables charge into the lane. Inderlal leans against a pole and waits for them to return with the man. His instinct – honed by fifteen years of service – tells him he has the culprit. He does not know why. Perhaps it is the man's seedy look, or his furtive manner, or that he chose to run. Who cares? He needs to catch the wallet thief and he has found him. That is the man – it *must* be the man! What right does anyone have to slink away into a lane without having stolen a wallet?

Sohan Lal fidgets impatiently while a woman from the Archaeological Survey of India prepares to make her presentation. The Raamleela has finished with the slaying of Ravan. Raam, standing on tiptoe, raised his mace high above his head and brought it down with full force on Ravan, forgetting that it was made of plastic. The mace burst into two with a plop, and fell at Ravan's ballet-splayed feet. Ravan trembled as if he had been hammered with pure bronze, and effected a credible collapse on the stage where, to the accompaniment of ballet music, he died gracefully. The audience clapped politely, unsure why Raam wielded a mace rather than a bow. Most put it down to an innovation associated with ballet. They have been a respectful audience, accepting with equal grace a Sita who executes pirouettes and a Hanuman who wields a kirpaan with a blade twenty inches long. And they clapped politely when Ravan stood on his toes and announced, after the Raamleela, that a presentation by the Archaeological Survey would follow.

Sohan Lal casts a furtive glance at his grandchildren. Bunty is pressed against him, asleep. Chimpu nibbles silently on his thumb and swings his feet in a gentle rhythm. Vicky is snivelling quietly in Sushma's lap. The children are exhausted. He feels a pang of guilt at having brought them to Town Hall. 'They will meet the prime minister,' he told Rukmini. He was pleased that he had secured four chairs in the central courtyard. Rukmini could not come because of her tremor, which looks less and less like weakness – as the doctor has assured him – and more and more like Parkinson's disease. Ramesh indicated that he wanted to go to Kucha Bansilal. 'The entire market is closed,' Sohan Lal had protested.

'Divali is almost upon us,' Ramesh had replied, 'and we have to take an inventory of our stock.'

Sohan Lal yielded reluctantly. He was offended that Ramesh attached so little importance to the occasion. Did he not realise that it was a privilege to meet the prime minister, and that it derived from his father's position on the IPP committee? 'Very well,' said Sohan Lal to Rukmini. 'I will take the children and Sushma.' So he has filled up his four chairs, but the children obviously do not appreciate their good fortune. Bunty, the eldest at three, was the first to fall asleep. Chimpu is awake only because of the confetti that surrounds the chairs, thrown into the audience by Raam and Lakshman in the closing sequence of the Ramayan ballet. And poor Vicky is only six months old, too young to be out anywhere. Sushma looking harried. She still hopes to meet the prime minister, who is only three rows ahead. Perhaps this will enhance Sohan Lal's prestige in his house. He feels an obligation whenever Sushma takes Rukmini to the doctor. He would have taken her himself but it is not proper, at his age, for a man to be cavorting about with his wife as if they were a young couple.

A white screen has been erected behind the stage, and a projector in the audience smartly changes the pictures on it to correspond with the presentation. The researcher from the Archaeological Survey is ready to begin. These women do not have fathers to marry them off, thinks

Sohan Lal sympathetically, so they go about digging up old buildings, studying thick books and marvelling over Musalman and English ruins. Why has she projected that insect-like scribble on to the screen? Ah, it is something written in Urdu. Why Urdu? Are we in Pakistan? Or Arabia? Is it unacceptable for Indians to project text in Hindi?

Through the corner of his eye, he can see Harilal advancing to the microphone, even as the woman spreads out her notes. This is not on the agenda! thinks Sohan Lal. But it is too late. Harilal has begun to speak, and even the prime minister appears to nod in agreement. 'Chandni Chowk is the soul of India,' declares Harilal. 'It is the home of the Hindu and the Musalman, the Sikh and the Christian. It is a symbol of religious harmony.'

Sohan Lal shuts his eyes, and wishes he could shut out the polite applause that follows without bringing his hands to his ears.

'Four weeks ago I toured Matia Mahal,' says Harilal. 'I wanted to see the sufferings of the people, caused by police harassment. I have already instituted an inquiry into that. As I turned into a lane, an old man attacked me with a knife. He wanted to kill me because the municipal commissioner had destroyed his clinic. Did I turn him over to the police? No! I asked him to display his unique healing arts at this very festival! Muhammad Ghayas has a stall near Gurudwara Sisganj. And it is people like him who have made this festival a success.'

Sohan Lal winces. Matia Mahal is his own constituency. Is Harilal trying to make a point?

Harilal leaves the microphone amid a triumphant shower of applause. The woman with the charts clears her throat and begins to speak. 'Town Hall was built in eighteen sixty-five,' she says. 'The spot on which it stands once formed part of the gardens laid by Jahanara Begum. The hall began as the Lawrence Institute of Educational and Cultural Affairs. Later, it became the municipal headquarters, and housed the European Club and library. After the British left, the statue of Queen Victoria outside Town Hall was replaced with one of Swami Shraddhanand . . .'

The audience, sparse as it was, is leaving. Sohan Lal knows where they are going. Outside Town Hall, they are crowding into a giant pavilion constructed for Pushpa Rani's appearance. Suddenly Ramvilas walks into the courtyard, panting, and sits down next to him. Sohan Lal tilts his body away from the man, angry at his presumption. He is unhappy with the seating arrangements. The first three rows are occupied by the prime minister and his aides, the aides' aides, and aides further along in the chain of command. His own chair is in the fourth row. By contrast, Harilal Gupta sits only three chairs away from the prime minister. It was Harilal who clung to the PM during the ribbon-cutting and lamp-lighting. He has used the Heritage Council well, thinks Sohan Lal. At a function held outside Red Fort this afternoon, the prime minister honoured traders who owned heritage shops, and the list was drawn from those on the Heritage Council. Jugal Kishor – walking as if the weight of the world rested on his shoulders – came up to receive his plaque with an ingratiating smile, dressed in a shervani as if he was at his own wedding. A shervani in such heat! He said something about his ancestors feeding halva to elephants, and his great-grandfather feeding halva to the Mughal emperor, and his father serving halva to Nehru. He did not mention, of course, that Mangat Ram Nawal Kishor, for which he had received the award, had ceased to exist. His back was bent into a pitiful curve, his sons were at each other's throats, yet he was in a shervani, accepting a plaque from the prime minister with a toothless smile. Vimal, on the other hand, wore nothing more than a crumpled kurta-pyjama when accepting his award on behalf of Lala Surajmal. Officially, the plaque was given to him as the proprietor of Bhagwan Das and Sons, but Ramvilas walked right up to the PM with him, supposedly to show him the way. He instructed Vimal where to stand, how to put out his hand, and how to hold out the plaque for the cameras. Vimal is an automaton, a robot, a machine controlled by Ramvilas. And when the cameras clicked on Vimal holding the plaque, Ramvilas extended a steadying hand so that it looked as if they were both holding it. This Heritage Council and this festival are an abomination. And here is Ramvilas sitting in the chair to his right, chewing paan insolently. Lala Surajmal kept the clerk in his place, but the man has run amok now that the four sons do not get on, and Vimal is his puppet – too callow, too inexperienced. The boy needs the steadying hand of an elder such as Sohan Lal.

He reprimands himself silently for neglecting his duties toward Surajmal's family. If he had taken the sons under his wing after their father's death, none of this would have come to pass. He would have held the plaque for Bhagwan Das and Sons, and the clerk would be sitting three rows behind him.

There is scattered clapping when the woman from the Archaeological Survey finishes. Sohan Lal groans on seeing the next two speakers. He has always regarded Muhammad Salauddin Qureshi as an opportunist, and is never quite comfortable with the unspoken contempt that is always present in the delicate Kashmiri face of Noor Muhammad. He turns to Ramvilas – still chewing paan – to express his discontent. 'These two are not affiliated to the Archaeological Survey of India.'

'They are affiliated to the festival,' replies Ramvilas. 'Harilalji felt it was appropriate to have Musalmans speak in Town Hall because the PM is here, and so are the newspeople.'

Sohan Lal sighs. He does not like being told of Harilalji's opinion by a clerk, and he has never approved of this pandering to Musalmans in the name of broadening the base.

Qureshi takes the microphone and, in his grating, reedy voice, briefly introduces Noor Muhammad, whom he extols as a great scholar on Mughal architecture. Then he steps aside for Noor Muhammad, who clears his throat with exaggerated care and speaks with didactic pretence in his crisp, precise voice.

'Imagine, for a moment, Chandni Chowk as Shah Jahan saw it. At one end towers the great fort, the glorious masjid and the Meena Bajar patronised by Jahanara Begum. At the other stands the mosque built by Begum Fatehpuri. Between the two, mango, banyan and jamun trees line the street, attars of rose waft along the air, princesses peep out of palanquins, military commanders gallop on milk-white horses whose tails are dyed scarlet, rajas ride on magnificent elephants with bright rings round their eyes and silver bracelets on their trunks, passing through bullock carts amid throngs of courtiers, craftsmen, acrobats, hawkers, magicians, dancers, poets, musicians, soldiers, bustling along the stately canal of Ali Mardan that flows down the centre of the street, from Red Fort to Fatehpuri Masjid, forty yards wide, lined by banyan trees, carrying in its cool waters the brilliant reflection of a full moon . . .'

As he stands beside Noor Muhammad, Qureshi feels sorry for himself. After four years in the IPP committee, he is in the habit of expressing tentative opinions on every subject, aware that he must please Musalmans as well as members of the committee. 'You will be a bridge between IPP and the Muslim community,' Lala Surajmal had told him four years ago, when inviting him to become a member. He feels more like a buffer that must take a battering from either side. He has often declaimed, in rarefied Muslim gatherings, that the way to civilise the IPP is by joining it, not shunning it. After four years during which the

IPP has been in the ascendant and he has not, he is no longer certain. Perhaps he was better off in Lucknow, among people like himself . . . His achkan collar is tight as always, and he feels he has botched the introduction. He should not have stumbled, and he should practise speaking in a deeper voice. He is grateful to be partially in the dark. A martyr must not be illuminated. A man charged with a task as difficult as his must work in the dark until it is time. When will that time come?

Noor Muhammad, swept away in the torrent of his own rhetoric, looks far out into the distance as if he can see the Chandni Chowk he is describing, and speaks reverently.

'This was the Orient as the Orientalist imagined it! This was the great trading centre of the east, where merchants from China, Arabia and Persia congregated to buy and sell precious stones, perfumes and fabulous brocades. There were havelis, shops, cafés, boudoirs, wrestling rings . . . Caged cheetahs were hawked, hooded hunting leopards were paraded, Persian cats and greyhounds were for sale!'

There is no mention of the great seths who brought commerce to Chandni Chowk, thinks Sohan Lal. As if cheetah-hawkers created the great Mughal empire! More immediate, however, is the problem of honour that has presented itself. He has not been honoured at the festival. He is an MLA from the area. He has spent countless hours getting Chandni Chowk cleaned, garbage removed, shopfronts painted, wires tethered . . . but his own shop is only thirty years old. His great-grandfather sold nothing to any Mughal emperor. No one honours cloth merchants, he thinks ruefully. Did the Mughals not wear clothes? Is it not within the realm of possibility that an ancestor of his travelled from Nawalgarh to Delhi and presented himself in Divan-i-Am, where Shah Jahan was dazzled by his silks? So, should not money be allocated for the renovation of Jamna Lal Kishori Mal, when it will certainly be handed out to these 'heritage shops'?

A second thought suddenly invades his tired mind. He turns angrily to Ramvilas. 'There was a GB Road stall.'

Ramvilas responds with a grunt, to contain the paan juices in his mouth.

Sohan Lal persists. 'Who gave permission to that . . . lady?' he demands.

Ramvilas leans over to find an empty patch of grass under his chair, collects his spittle, discharges it, then turns to Sohan Lal innocently. 'You had the list, sethji.'

'We have to be careful,' admonishes Sohan Lal. 'This is a cultural festival.'

'She paid for the stall,' Ramvilas points out.

Sohan Lal turns back to the speech and shuts his eyes. The audience is in the dark, so he will take a short nap until it is time for the prime minister to leave.

Noor Muhammad has a glazed, far-away look in his eyes. He is aware of the delicacy of his own voice. It is like well-brewed tea.

'Chandni Chowk has borne witness to great moments in history,' he declares. 'This is where Dara Shikoh was taken in chains on a dirty elephant before his brother Aurangzeb had him executed. This is where they made bonfires of British goods during the freedom struggle . . .' He falters, seized with self-pity. He does not like the Railways Department where Qureshi has found him a position. He had hoped he would not need Qureshi after that but he does, because he wants a promotion. Under Qureshi's patronage for four years, he has had little time to pursue his studies of Mughal architecture, but where can a Kashmiri go since they have destroyed Kashmir? Now he must entertain this foolish farmer from the south who calls himself prime minister. A note of sorrow weighs down his voice as he continues: 'With the coming of the English, the elephants of rajas were replaced by phaetons of English officers, drawn by Arab steeds. The canal of Ali Mardan fell into disuse, reflecting in its brackish water the rot setting into the Mughal empire. The canal, more than anything else in Delhi, symbolised the decline of Indian thought – dirty and swarming with insects.'

Noor Muhammad pauses for effect, and speaks of the canal as if it were a beloved family member: 'Ali Mardan's canal was revived, then filled up by the English. Now it lies buried under Chandni Chowk. Feet stamp on the concrete above it, rickshas honk irreverently where its waters once flowed, scooters spray soot in the air above it. The canal is no more. The moon no longer shines in Chandni Chowk, even during the Moonlight Festival . . .'

His voice drops to a whisper and he revels in his success at captivating the audience, which has fallen silent with him. A glance at the prime minister turns triumph into bitter failure, because the prime minister appears to be looking downward in deep concentration.

*   *   *

Sohan Lal is roused from his slumber by a commotion to his left. He turns in time to see Sushma run out carrying Vicky, holding him far away from her body, his legs splayed out to reveal the gobs of shit that cling to his chubby thighs. Sohan Lal is irritated. Why can she not buy those new nappies they sell nowadays, into which the child can piss and shit and not have so much as a whiff escape?

A roar invades the central courtyard of Town Hall. It comes from the stalls outside. For a horrible moment, Sohan Lal supposes something has happened to Sushma. Then he realises that she would have gone to a bathroom, if there is one in Town Hall. The ocean of people outside has just expressed its approval of something else. Is it the Mughal court or the qawwali . . . No, it is just the food stalls. A hundred stalls and he has not even drunk water! Perhaps he can leave Bunty and Chimpu in Ramvilas's care, and slip away for a few moments while this Kashmiri bore completes his lecture? Ramvilas looks at him with indecent directness as he squeezes past him. Can the man not show some delicacy? Well, he does not care a fig what Ramvilas thinks, and the prime minister is too far away to notice, unaware of his very existence. He will go and get himself a nice plate of samosas. He need not stand in a queue. All the stall owners know him. He signed their permits.

He walks out of the main courtyard. As soon as he glimpses the street he knows the applause is not for the food stalls but for Pushpa Rani. The pavilion was opened an hour ago. She may even have arrived! He wants to go in. They would have kept four seats for him in one of the front rows. There was intense haggling over those four spots, which have elevated him in Sushma's eyes. Who else can bring her so close to Pushpa Rani? Rukmini has spoken of nothing else all week, even though she could not come. He must go! To hear her sing live – he knows many of the songs by heart, and even Bunty can lisp through their lyrics – barely three metres from him! No programme on All India Radio can match that.

He turns and walks briskly back into the Town Hall courtyard. He must make a quick decision. He can wait for Sushma to complete Vicky's change, and they can all leave in a conspicuous caravan with wailing and sleeping children. Ramvilas will snigger, Harilalji will frown, Jugal Kishor will cast his eyes disdainfully on them. Even the prime minister may turn round to express disapproval. Or he can just walk out of Town Hall, make his way to the pavilion, pass through the VIP entrance and take his front-row seat. Sushma, when she finishes with Vicky, will assume he is busy with arrangements. She will not go to the pavilion by herself – they will not recognise her at the VIP entrance. When she does not find him, she will make her way to Kucha Bansilal, where Ramesh is tallying the inventory. Bunty is old enough to walk, Vicky will have fallen asleep, and Chimpu can walk with his hand in Bunty's, so they can safely make their way to their father. The children will find the performance too taxing anyway. Imagine the embarrassment if Vicky should shit or piss in the middle of Pushpa Rani's song!

He stands uncertainly for a few seconds, torn. Then he sighs and shakes his head. He will take them all to Pushpa Rani. But he must put an end to this farce of the Kashmiri man. He walks right through the courtyard, passing rows of chairs, passing Ramvilas, Harilal, the lieutenant governor and the prime minister, and stands right in front of Noor Muhammad, who stops in mid-sentence.

'Finished!' he says curtly.

Noor Muhammad remains standing, unsure.

'We are running late,' says Sohan Lal.

And then, to close the proceedings irrevocably, Sohan Lal turns grandly to the audience. 'It is now my honour to invite the honourable prime minister of India to speak to us.'

There is reverent applause, followed by expectant silence. Harilalji turns from three chairs away and looks. Ramvilas cranes his neck. Sohan Lal holds his breath. He has surprised himself by this display of boldness. Perhaps he should not have made the announcement in Hindi?

The prime minister sits in a brilliant orb of light, thrown by two lamps installed high above the columns of Town Hall. Sohan Lal had had them pointed toward the PM's chair so photographers could capture him with ease, and so that Harilal Gupta, seated three chairs away, is in relative darkness. The roar for Pushpa Rani rises anew in the street and under the bright light, the prime minister can be seen fast asleep.

A fifty-metre stretch of Chandni Chowk on either side of Town Hall has been blocked off. The only way anyone can get across is by turning into a lane and circling the area to emerge near Fatehpuri Masjid. The giant pavilion constructed in the space, large enough to hold an audience of ten thousand, is full. People stand outside it, straining their eyes toward the stage inside. The overflow stretches all the way to Red Fort. More people have gathered to hear Pushpa Rani sing than have ever gathered in the same place to hear the prime minister on 15 August, when he speaks from Red Fort. Loudspeakers have been placed on lamp-posts to the end of Chandni Chowk, so people near the Jain temple can hear Pushpa Rani as clearly as those pressed against the stage, even if they cannot see her. Her magic, of course, is in her voice, not in her face.

Pushpa Rani is too great to sing inside Town Hall. No building constructed by Shah Jahan or the British Empire is large enough to hold her, because she is the voice of every heroine on the Indian screen. There is no child who has not hummed her songs, no man or woman who will not listen, rapt, when her voice floats over Chandni Chowk. The stage is decorated with garlands shaped to form the words 'Moonlight Festival'. Pressed against it, and against the canvas walls of the pavilion, are the fortunate few who will both hear and see, who entered the pavilion while the laggards were still wiping coriander flakes off their chins. They have encroached upon all seats meant for VIPs, and no policeman is inclined to reason with them.

Pushpa Rani made her appearance a few minutes ago to thunderous applause. The organisers had her arrive in a palanquin draped with velvet curtains, and covered with sequins that shone like a thousand suns, carried on the shoulders of four bearers in saffron dhotis and red sashes. The top was shaped like the spire of a temple, and adorned with a fluttering Indian flag. When the palanquin ascended the stage, Pushpa Rani pushed aside the velvet curtains and waved to her subjects, receiving homage from ten thousand throats.

The palanquin now sits at the back, and Pushpa Rani is alone on the bare stage behind an arc of microphones, arranged to catch every sniff that may escape her melodious throat. She is a small woman clad in a modest silk saree. Standing in the centre of that vast stage, she looks vulnerable, yet unapproachable. Marigolds are strung in her braided hair. A diamond necklace glitters tastefully at her throat. After sixty years of singing for films, her voice still has the joyous lilt of a teenage girl's. The stage is so large that she appears lost on it. There are no chairs, just a small orchestra in a distant corner, respectfully awaiting its signal.

A hush falls on the crowd. Here stands Pushpa Rani, queen of melody for the last three generations. Few are old enough to remember other divas, and few believe there is any film music that has not come from Pushpa Rani. It began with her, it lives with her, it will perhaps end with her. Prime ministers have come and gone in five years, or three years, or eleven months, even thirteen days! She will stride the airwaves for ever.

A man approaches Pushpa Rani from the far corner of the stage. It is Naresh Agrawal, the Member of Parliament for Chandni Chowk. He is a fixture in Chandni Chowk, a little like Pushpa Rani is in India. Since he won his first Lok Sabha election sixteen years ago, he has been undefeated in four successive general elections, returning each time with approximately the same margin, holding together his umbrella of Muslim and Bania votes. The only exception was 'eighty-four when, following Indira Gandhi's death, he received more votes than all the other candidates combined. Age has worn him, but he remains sharp to nuances of public opinion. In a festival he strongly disapproves of – after all, it has been put together by the IPP – he has chosen not to waste his time with the prime minister in Town Hall. It is not wise for a Congress Party MP to be seen too often with a weak prime minister so heavily dependent on Congress support. Who knows how long the man will hold on to his position? Therefore, after carefully weighing all matters at hand, Naresh Agrawal has chosen to pay homage to the Queen of Hearts and Empress of the Cinema.

Nareshji stands beside the diminutive Pushpa Rani, looking tall though he is a short man. A technician runs to raise a microphone – set for Pushpa Rani's height – so Nareshji will not have to bend too far forward.

'Brothers and sisters,' he rasps into the microphone, 'I will not give a speech, because no voice can be raised in the presence of the Nightingale of India!'

The nightingale folds her hands to greet her people, and Naresh Agrawal melts away in the applause that follows. He has already been photographed with her. Ten crore people will see that photograph tomorrow.

'A rich man's festival!' mutters Ibrahim, standing in the crowd. 'What do I care for Pushpa Rani? Is she a Musalman? The real Nightingale of India is Noor Jahan, whom the Hindu Banias sent away to Pakistan. A festival for Banias, seths and English people. Why else would the gol gappa pedlars look like doctors at an operating table, with polythene bags on their heads and hands? That is not how you serve gol gappas. That is how you serve bland food in expensive hotels for weak stomachs, for English people who do not belong to Chandni Chowk, who should go back to their Chanakyapuri and Hauz Khas houses in their cars. To think that Gopal Bhai stood on that stage and let that sardarji give him a plaque! He actually thanked the sardarji for demolishing his stall!'

Hundreds of Suleman's men are scattered evenly through the crowd, angry because they have been driven away from Town Hall where they had gone to protest against the festival. They tried to stop the prime minister's Mercedes. Then they tried to picket the main gate to Town Hall, but the police threw a cordon round the area: somehow they were able to distinguish between regular people and Suleman's protesters. It is because we are all Musalmans, thinks Ibrahim, while the rest of the festival is full of Banias! These tight security arrangements have thrown Suleman's plans into disarray. The protest was sporadic and uncoordinated, and then the protesters disappeared into the pavilion, angry and frustrated but eager to listen to Pushpa Rani. This vulgar reverence for her is painful to Ibrahim. That is the problem with Musalmans, he tells himself. If a Hindu sings a qawwali or invokes the name of Allah, Musalmans are immediately converted into admirers. If a Hindu boy falls in love with a Musalman girl – which happens in every film! – they take that as a sign of brotherhood and love. Do they not see that it is always a Musalman girl who loves a Hindu boy, never a Hindu girl who loves a Musalman boy? The films know what they are saying to Musalmans – our man is fucking your woman. And if, by some mistake, the man is a Musalman, he must become a Hindu before he can fuck a Hindu woman. Why else would Yusuf Khan become Dilip Kumar? This Pushpa Rani is not even a proper Hindu. She has never married, never raised a family. Who knows anything about her morals? Yet here he is, sandwiched between Banias and clerks and rickshavalas, waiting with bated breath for her to part her lips. What will Suleman Mian's unmanly dogs do in the crowd? Will they wag their tails when that unmarried woman starts crooning? Ah! They will listen to her songs and sway to the rhythm like little children in a music class. And what of their anger at being driven out of Town Hall like dogs? A constable even kicked one in the balls, and Ibrahim heard another say something about 'katuas' and 'mullas' . . . Surely they should do something? The stones they brought with them are weighing down their pockets!

*   *   *

Pushpa Rani's saree slips from her shoulder. She raises a practised hand and wraps it over her head. Modesty restored, she takes a step forward, and appears ready to speak. The crowd screams the first lines of the song it wants to hear, the song on every lip. She speaks in a sweet, girlish voice. 'You have given me much love,' she says. 'All of India is my home. They love me in Madras, they love me in Bombay. They love me in Calcutta, and they love me in Dilli . . .'

The crowd drowns her out. Yes, yes! We love you! We love you in Dilli more than they could possibly love you in Madras! Sing us that song! Sing it for us, open your mouth and let drip those sugary words . . . Suleman is near the stage, standing anonymously in the crowd. As an MLA he is entitled to a seat in the front row, next to Harilal Gupta, Sohan Lal and their families. He can see those seats have been taken by others. They are probably wagging their tails at the prime minister. He will not, of course, take his official seat at the function. He does not want to be associated with this festival. And he does not want to be seen when the inevitable happens. This crowd is a tinderbox awaiting a spark. His men will not take the insult at Town Hall without retaliating. He knows they are seething, that their pockets are full. What they need is a signal, a starting gun that will send them off on a spontaneous sprint . . .

'An artist is beholden to admirers,' declares Pushpa Rani, 'but my throat is not what it used to be when I was younger.'

The crowd produces a collective sound of impatience. An organiser in a neat kurta-pyjama walks briskly on to the stage, conscious of being in Pushpa Rani's divine presence. He takes the microphone from her, touches the badge on his chest to set it right and speaks: 'Many of you know that Pushpa Raniji has a concert in Indraprastha Stadium tomorrow evening. She must rest her voice.'

Pushpa Rani smiles in benevolent assent. The crowd appears restive.

'There is a stall outside where you can buy tickets for the concert,' announces the organiser. 'They told me the back seats are only thirty-five rupees.'

A stunned silence falls like a blanket on the crowd. Pushpa Rani senses the disappointment of her subjects and relents: 'I will sing a few lines, because I cannot deny your love.'

The crowd heaves a sigh of relief. She clears her throat, and then those impossibly sweet notes flood the pavilion, echo through a hundred loudspeakers all over Chandni Chowk, and find their way into millions of radios, televisions and hearts.

'How do I describe your love when I am not overwhelmed by it?
How do I speak of your tenderness when I cannot touch your heart?
How do I mourn our separation when we have not had a tryst?
How do I complain of your cruelty when I still yearn for it?'

She stops. The crowd, swaying, emits a collective groan. It becomes clear, gradually, that she really does not intend to sing. There is a pause, a long pause full of foreboding. Then a single voice rises above the crowd: 'Pushpa Rani *haay haay*!'

Shocked heads turn to find the source of the curse. How can someone say such a thing about Pushpa Rani? But another voice, from another section of the audience, repeats the imprecation. A stone flies, missile-like, over their heads and lands on the stage, far away from Pushpa Rani, near the orchestra. Ah! The crowd gasps. But then another curse is screamed and a second stone finds its way to the stage, then a third, a fourth, a shower, which descends on the stage like a vengeful monsoon on a hot day. The orchestra breaks up and runs for cover behind its instruments.

We are waking up! thinks Ibrahim. We are going to destroy the Banias! He empties his pockets of stones and hurls them with all his might toward the stage. He is too far away. Many of his projectiles fall on heads in the crowd, who fling curses, pick up the stones and hurl some at the stage, some at the cannon behind them. Suleman sits quietly in the shadow of the stage, safe from bullets in the dead zone created just under the platform, and sighs in satisfaction. This is what he has been trying to tell them for hours – that it is *our* festival, built on *our* backs, organised with *our* money, made possible by the destruction of *our* livelihoods. He feels a tide of anger. Prudence counsels him to stay where he is, but prudence does not have his ear at the moment . . . He springs up, steps on to a chair and clambers on to the stage.

Naresh Agrawal's men hastily escort Pushpa Rani away.

Inside Town Hall, the prime minister continues to read his speech. Sohan Lal is drawn aside by a member of the Special Protection Group, who tells him that violence has broken out in Pushpa Rani's concert. He signals to Harilal Gupta, who signals to the lieutenant governor, who signals to the prime minister's PA, who walks up to the prime minister and whispers in his ear. The PM pauses mid-sentence, happy to be interrupted. The lieutenant governor and the Special Protection Group escort him to the Mercedes.

A posse of policemen moves toward the pavilion erected for Pushpa Rani. Inside, stones rains on to the stage. The great floodlights that had bathed it have been turned off. Suleman stands, ghost-like, at the microphone, letting stones hit him where they will, screaming so loudly that the amplifier cracks under the strain. His voice echoes through a hundred speakers strung all along Chandni Chowk, all the way to Red Fort. 'Give us back our shops!' he screams. 'Give back the stalls of tailors, chaivalas, paanvalas, naharivalas! Shut down this festival of Banias and seths and give us back the money that was taken from us! We will not let you starve us, we will burn down the festival, we will burn down Dilli, we will burn down all of Hindustan . . .'

1998

1

Trees, bungalows, signs, signals, kiosks, hoardings, footpaths, asphalt, zebra crossings . . . This could almost be a Western city, thinks Chitra, then leans back against the leather upholstery and shuts her eyes. She knows too much, has spent too much time lifting the covers to look under them to be fooled by the apparent civility of Hauz Khas and the grand flyovers of south Delhi. In any case, the car has now entered Green Park, making its transition from those who are to those who want to be. Crowded, unruly Green Park, someone's cruel joke on the science of nomenclature – it is neither green nor a park, just Green Park – bearing blithely a name that would put a more self-conscious region to shame. Scooters and three-wheelers bear down on the car like a squadron of kites, emerging from lanes no one knew existed and disappearing into crevices between buildings. She will not look at the endless eructation of commerce – clothes, refrigerators, televisions, washing-machines, scooters, mopeds, motorcycles – and the single-minded people of Delhi engaged in buying and selling even on this horribly cold, dull grey morning. She should have asked the driver to take Ring Road – a longer drive but it skirts the sinful cauldron of New Delhi.

The car climbs the flyover that spans Safdarjang airport. She rolls down the window and gasps for breath. The air is bitterly cold. A dense fog hangs over the runway, obscuring the ground and the skyline, and trapping particles of smoke belched by a million cars and buses. She knows that, far to the south-west, at the international airport, all flights have been delayed. They will land when the sun peers through the haze at noon, by which time the people of Delhi, who do not know the meaning of morning sunshine, will not be paying attention to the sun anyway. The month of January is an endless night in Delhi, with alternating shades of ash and ink.

The car descends the flyover and penetrates – like an aeroplane cutting through cloud – the stratum of smoke that hangs over the street. Chitra coughs. They now approach the great traffic intersection outside the All India Institute of Medical Sciences, where the silk routes of the city of Delhi intersect each other. Bus stops swarm with villagers who have come from across India bearing letters of introduction to their local Member of Parliament, looking for a magic cure to restore the health of their fathers and mothers, sons and daughters. They stand around the AIIMS campus, marvelling at the great capital that admits all but loves none. The car stops at the intersection and waits for a green signal. Men on scooters shut off their engines to conserve petrol and steady themselves with left feet on the ground. Three-wheelers squeeze into narrow alleys between buses and sputter impatiently. Her own car is boxed in by the green and yellow walls of Delhi Transport Corporation buses, the tyrants of Delhi roads who spit diesel smoke like a curse into the tired air of Lutyens's Delhi, polluting, polluting . . . Through an opening in the forest, she can see the giant electric billboard erected by Harilal Gupta, transport minister of Delhi. 'Keep Delhi Green!' exhorts the sign, blinking in green, blue and red letters, dancing urgently to attract the attention of those who would muddy that verdant desire.

She is aware, in her fatigued, non-seeing state, that tiny hands have been frantically wiping the windscreen of her car. She hopes they will go away after an exchange with the driver. Then, sensing imminent danger, she hastily rolls up the tinted window, but the hands cannot be ignored. They tap urgently, demanding attention. This is not work! she wants to tell the hands. Sell something that someone wants! Better still, learn to count, read and write . . . She knows they cannot see her clearly through the panes. They can see a shape, perhaps distinguish a woman behind impregnable fortifications, situated in an incomprehensibly comfortable world of limitless wealth. She can see their faces quite clearly, however, and they are disturbingly familiar. Has she seen these children before? Is that Gauhar, and is that Jolly or Sheila? But then their faces are hidden behind importunate hands – knocking on the pane, demanding their share.

She turns away guiltily, running in her mind statistics from the last issue of *India Now*, which carried a long article titled 'Lost Generation – the Street Children of Delhi'. How many did it say there were? Four lakhs? Five? She has not spoken to Shalini since the Sparrows building was torn down two years ago. Shalini has not sought her out either. She has perhaps moved on to a new cause, a new career. They must avoid each other for the rest of their lives, suspended in a relationship of mutual embarrassment, each afraid to question the other. Chitra is afraid to reveal to Shalini that she had come upon the ruins of Sparrows on a 'tour' with Harilal Gupta. Why had she not made a greater effort to seek his support? But Harilal was too wrapped up in the Moonlight Festival . . . She was loath to approach

Suleman, even though the building had been erected and expanded under his patronage. He had become far too belligerent as an MLA and she, as a senior contributing editor at *India Now*, had had to exercise discretion in her dealings with politicians. Nevertheless, she had sought an appointment with him, but a few days before it his supporters had disrupted the Moonlight Festival. When she finally met him, he launched into a harangue about the 'festival of the rich against the poor', claiming he had clambered on to the stage merely to calm the audience, and his intervention had prevented full-scale rioting. 'What about Sparrows?' she had asked.

He was baffled by the question. 'What about it?' he demanded.

'The children—'

'Children,' said Suleman, philosophically, 'are like grains of rice – once scattered, they are impossible to collect.'

Then he had walked out of the room, ending the interview.

The hands that have wiped a thousand windscreens are still there, insistent, urgent, obstinate. The faces seem to form words. She lowers the window, just a little, so she can hear them. The first one grins – dark face, crooked white teeth – and says with unaccountable shyness, 'Happy new year, madam!'

She rolls up the window again, shocked, and leans back, wondering if this is a statement of fact or a wish. Not the former, because the year has only just begun, so who can know if it will be happy? The latter, of course, but for her, not for themselves. No one, not even the bashful child who made the wish, is naïve enough to expect that this year will be a happy one for him. May this year be a happy one for you, he has said. Reverently she seconds the sentiment. The magazine leaves her little time or inclination to think about herself. She wonders, in more pensive moments, if a woman at forty-one has the right to live as she does, wedded to a magazine. Although she has been advised otherwise, she considers herself past the age when a partner could be found. She does not know, and never will, whether it was an opportunity missed or a burden avoided. Some consider her a successful woman; others have written articles about her startling career. She herself is more ambivalent, never able to put a label on the state of her mind. And what about the dark face beyond her window, who wishes her a happy new year? Insincerely, of course – he merely wants what he is owed for his gratuitous labour.

The city is building a giant system of flyovers at the All India Institute intersection. When complete, it will transmit traffic in smooth streams as a network of canals relays water. Right now, amid all the digging and cable-laying, it has made the intersection impassable. It is almost five minutes before the signal turns green, the scooters are kicked into life and three-wheelers dart forward. The hands continue to tap on her tinted windows until the car is moving too fast for them, leaving her in a sour mood. She consoles herself with the thought that she is much more effective as an editor than she could be as a lone crusader in Sparrows. A stroke of her pen can create a thousand such programmes! What was Sparrows but the vanity of an idealistic young woman?

The car glides past the sedate bungalows of Lutyens's Delhi, then circles the roundabout near India Gate. Many of the arteries that lead toward Rajpath are blocked off in preparation for Republic Day. She considers the precautions over-zealous because it is more than three weeks away, but she is aware that the word 'security' commands much reverence in VIP-conscious Delhi. India Gate is enveloped in the same grim greyness that hangs across its lawns. The traffic becomes increasingly disorderly as they approach the income-tax-office area. The driver presses the horn indiscriminately, even when there appears to be no obstruction in the road ahead. She remembers what she wrote in *Time* magazine about the single traffic rule in Delhi – good brakes, good horn and good luck! She has heard this somewhere, from some politician who is unlikely to read *Time*.

'You should not have come through ITO,' she scolds the driver. 'You could have taken Ring Road all the way to Daryaganj.'

She is being unfair to him. Even if he had taken Ring Road, he would have run into heavy traffic. She smells smoke, and remembers that the car is air-conditioned and is a Maruti Esteem, not the 800 model, which has barely enough power to churn a compressor. She asks the driver to turn on the air-conditioner. He studies her with derision in his rear-view mirror, but sets it on medium-cool. It is another amusing story for his cohorts – the madam who turns on the air-conditioner in the bitter cold of January. She pulls her shawl round her and shivers – it's better to freeze in clean air than thaw in diesel fumes.

The matter of pollution has received attention in the English press since Western environmentalists began to measure levels of carbon monoxide, nitrogen monoxide and sulphur dioxide in the Delhi air. By the standards of their urban sprawls Delhi is a toxic dump, a cloud chamber choking with smoke, with suspended particulate-matter

levels higher than their gauges can measure. *India Now* has gleefully
reported their results under screaming headlines. The denizens of
Delhi – or those who read English magazines such as *India Now* –
have finally discovered the concept of air pollution, but do not relish
having to give up their Marutis and Santros, toys they have waited
fifty years to acquire. So the axe has fallen on buses and autorickshas.
There is much talk of compressed natural gas as an alternative, cleaner
fuel for buses, although no one has any idea where such large amounts
of natural gas will come from. Meanwhile buses corral her car,
displaying hands, elbows, fluttering cloth, and belching smoke.

This will make a good cover story, thinks Chitra. Why are we
choking our city? Why are we penalising the clerks who ride in buses
when we can take ten-lakh Marutis off the roads? But this is not the
story anyone wants to read. It is also not the story she wants to write,
sitting in the air-conditioned comfort of her Maruti Esteem. The
English-reading public wants to read about Hindi-speaking politicians, their shenanigans, games, plots and counterplots, the agree-
ments they have reached, the promises they have reneged on, the
money they have stolen, the kickbacks they have received . . . That
readership, which sustains *India Now*, is obsessed with a voyeuristic
contemplation of politics while dismissing it as a rogue's occupation.
All her journalism has become a spotlight shone by the decent middle
class – people like her who speak English and pretend to live in civil
society – on the indecent 'common man', who cares not a fig for this
journalism. There is a certain comfort in doing so. Those who read it
do not understand it, and those who understand it cannot read it,
creating an occupation that is accountable to no one. She has no doubt
what the cover story will be, and the phrases that will dominate it –
fractured polity, caste-based politics, pseudo-secularists and fundamentalists, Mandal and Masjid, liberalisation and reform, communalism and secularism, the torn fabric of society . . . English tags on a
Hindi-speaking people, who will not read and do not care.

After the ITO signal turns green, the Maruti weaves through two
more lights, charges down a group of women trying to cross the street
and finally stops at the gleaming white offices of *India Now* in
Bahadur Shah Zafar Marg. Since it was founded twenty-five years
ago, the magazine has grown tremendously. At forty-one, Chitra is its
youngest chief editor. The building stands in a row of offices
displaying leading names of India's English press. The driver springs
out of the car to hold open her door. She passes into the lobby and

nods at the receptionist, behind whom the words '*India Now*' hang in large chrome letters.

'Happy new year, madam!'

Chitra mumbles something in response, crosses the lobby and steps into the lift, where the attendant gives her a military salute and repeats the maxim of the day: 'Happy new year, madam!'

We do not need a lift attendant, she thinks, as the man prepares to perform the onerous task of steering the lift to her office on the third floor. She watches him press the button, fascinated that an entire profession can be constructed out of so simple an act. Does he acquire button-pressing skills after years of practice? Is his touch more reassuring, the pressure just right? Can he press the button blindfolded, the better to handle an emergency when the lights are out? She sighs, knowing that such arguments miss the point. The man operates the lift because he exists – all things that exist must operate something.

The subject of this issue of *India Now* – the first in the new year – will be no different from that of the last few issues: the general elections due in March. When 'We the People' gave ourselves this constitution, thinks Chitra, we did not realise we would have to invoke it every fifteen months for another round of senseless balloting. Two years, three prime ministers, countless cabinet ministers, votes of confidence, withdrawals of support . . . Everyone knew the United Front was just that, a front. No one was surprised when it came undone in December, and no one expects the March election to produce a credible government. The IPP looks likely to become the largest party. No one, at least no one whom the English press will quote, wants it to win. This is true democracy, thinks Chitra, and it is hideous. Bring back the days of Gandhi patriarchy! We want Oxbridge Indians in our Parliament, expounding on the principles of socialism and modern humanism and the wonderful constructs of Panchsheel and Non-alignment, preparing to fly to heady conferences in Bandung and Beijing. The pleasures of unrepresentative politics! Who invited the common man – safely eulogised in speeches but otherwise locked away in ugly towns and uglier villages – to speak? But he has spoken. His speech is in hopeless 'regional' languages, and his sounds are cacophonous. And when this common man – who does not read journalistic prattle, has shocking notions of right and wrong, and frightful plans for the country – wields his stick at the decent middle class, where will such people go? Will they have to leave the country and seek shelter in societies that they have spent generations emulating?

Chitra passes through the anteroom to her office, nodding at her secretary. It is the second day of the year but the first working day at the magazine. She finds the task of maintaining a secretary tiresome, just as she finds it ridiculous that she should have an anteroom. It was laid down by the English, in the days when the sun shone continuously upon their empire and computers had not made word-processing a trivial task, that all important people shall have anterooms, and all anterooms shall contain secretaries. Consequently the magazine insists on her having one. As a keeper of meeting schedules the secretary is helpful, but as a human dictaphone she is hopelessly incompetent. Chitra must dictate all letters to her. If she is denied this privilege – if Chitra were to type her letters herself – the secretary will take up the matter with her protectors in the union, which also includes the lift attendant, the receptionist and all pairs of hands that operate something or other in the building. So the letters, after being dictated in maddening slow-motion, must be brought back hours later for 'proofing', at which point Chitra must point out typographical errors and other grammatical mistakes. The proofed letter must then be typed and proofed again until, presumably, the cycle of proofing and typing dissipates. The secretary exists, like the lift attendant, and all things that exist must have letters to type.

Chitra's office is large but spare. Little thought has been paid to comfort or lighting. Small windows overlook Bahadur Shah Zafar Marg. The quanta of light they admit have been largely blocked by black vinyl screens taped on the outside, installed last summer during an energy-preservation drive. It was claimed that, by blocking light and heat, they improved the efficiency of the air-conditioner – a perquisite afforded to the chief editor that takes up another window and floods the room with a drone and cool air. The furniture is Spartan and comfortless, like the room itself, but she still feels secure here, protected from the street by thick walls and vinyl screens. She keeps the air-conditioner on medium-cool, its warmest setting, which amuses her staff who cannot understand her obsession with it in the harsh Delhi winter. She has not been able to convince anyone that an air-conditioner can filter air, that it is not a mere air-cooler.

'Happy new year, madam!'

Subramanyam stands at the door, dressed in a grey shirt, tie and neatly pressed trousers. A thick cardigan covers most of his upper body, making him look middle-aged, although he is in his late thirties.

'There is nothing new about this year,' she says coldly, 'and who believes it will be a happy one?'

Subramanyam is caught off-guard. Chitra savours his discomfort. Why must he, an assistant editor, stoop to the same folly as the lift attendant? But Subramanyam seems stumped. She chuckles to reassure him, and he shuffles inside to sit facing her across her desk. After years of ascending slowly through the ranks of hacks, Subramanyam still asks for permission before entering a room, and defers uncomplainingly to Saxena, who now makes his appearance without announcement. He is younger than Subramanyam but larger in every aspect, physical and otherwise. He favours three-piece suits, which would have qualified him for sartorial splendour had they not always been crumpled.

They have come to discuss the cover story for the year's first issue of the magazine. In theory, Subramanyam presents the south Indian story and Saxena the north, on the assumption that all political news in India comes either from the northern cow belt or the Dravidian movement in the south. In reality, their viewpoints are more complicated, and they often concentrate on areas not meant to be their domain. Mrs Jain is last to come into the office, muttering something about her son, which has delayed her today. Her shawl covers her completely like a poncho – Chitra realises it is indeed a poncho. At forty-five, she provides the stern feminist balance in Chitra's editorial team, much resented by Saxena. Chitra herself does not care for Mrs Jain, but the newspaper is owned by businessmen who must pay lip-service to the trends of the times, whether they accept them or not. Chitra is grateful that neither Saxena nor Mrs Jain bothers to note the happiness that looms over the year. Instead, Saxena casts a hostile glance at the air-conditioner and opens his files.

'It is on medium-cool,' says Chitra.

That does not reassure Saxena. He pores over his files with exaggerated concentration. Subramanyam rubs his hands cheerfully, then pulls his cardigan closer about him.

' "The last rites of Naresh Agrawal," ' reads Saxena, from his notes.

'Put him on the last page,' says Chitra. 'One-page obituary.'

'He did represent Chandni Chowk for eighteen years,' says Saxena. 'We have run through two issues without acknowledging him. More than fifty thousand people were present at his cremation. MPs, ministers, even the home minister . . .'

'No more than an obituary,' she says.

Subramanyam suggests an article on the caste politics in the south, arranged under the tents of two Dravidian parties, with Congress oscillating between them.

'What about Charulata?' asks Saxena, pushing forward a newspaper photograph.

Charulata smiles scornfully in the photograph – a woman in a man's body despite her long, flowing hair, shapeless in a white salvaar-kameez, a woman whose hands, when folded together, seem to say, 'Bow to me!' rather than, 'Namaste.' A goddess come to avenge the downtrodden or a villain come to pillage them, thinks Chitra, depending on your political leanings.

'We have already written about Charulata and Ram Bhajan Yadav,' comments Subramanyam.

He is right, thinks Chitra. Much has been made of the rise of smaller, caste-based parties and their belligerent, cocky, supremely confident demagogues.

'Something non-political?' Subramanyam asks. Hs places a news article before Chitra. At its centre is a poorly reproduced black-and-white photograph. A plump woman smiles widely at the camera, holding in her right hand a large box emblazoned with the word 'Nirodh'. The caption reads, 'Gita Didi, condoms for the world!' The woman looks young, perhaps thirty, and the hands that hold the box are practised, comfortable and mature. The article is about STREE, Sex-workers Training, Rehabilitation and Education Endeavour.

Chitra chuckles. She has heard the name before, perhaps seen it somewhere. She may even have met the woman. That is the beauty of catchy acronyms. They stick in the mind and are joyfully printed by foreign magazines. This Gita Didi appears to be an ex-prostitute who runs an NGO in GB Road. She is planning safe-sex classes for her 'sex-workers', as she calls them, by distributing a dozen VCRs among GB Road brothels and showing them videos on safe sex. 'Will not the sex-workers use these VCRs to watch films and songs?' asks a reporter in the article.

'Even sex-workers need entertainment!' Gita Didi replies, with disarming innocence.

There is a list of organisations that have financed STREE, and it includes funds from the late Naresh Agrawal and discretionary funds from transport minister Harilal Gupta. In the article, Gita Didi speaks of challenges she faced when she founded STREE six years ago. 'We began by collecting five rupees from each sister in Kotha eight hundred and forty-two,' she says. 'The bai was initially co-operative, because we assured her this would bring money into the kotha, but she grew increasingly suspicious. And when I invited a government doctor to come in once a week, the bai put her foot down . . .' Gita Didi's story continues through two pages. At the end thousands of condoms are distributed and dozens of under-age girls rescued.

Yet another NGO, thinks Chitra dismissively. She has covered so many, written so much about them, then seen them fade away when the individuals who start them lose interest and move on. Each NGO sees itself as the final solution, grows until it treads on the feet of other NGOs and then, like competing businesses, they spar, split, merge, expand, are acquired or driven to bankruptcy. This Gita Didi . . . is she consequential enough to have a cover story to herself? Has her story matured sufficiently for *India Now*? A newspaper can choose its subjects indiscriminately because it must find a new headline every day. It must report a story before it can digest it or understand its full import, even if this makes it look foolish the next day. But *India Now* need not be so current. It can afford to let a story evolve before deigning to notice it, at the risk of missing the story altogether . . .

'This Gita Didi is a prostitute,' says Mrs Jain, through pursed lips.

Ah, thinks Chitra. Mrs Jain has seen a way to inject herself into the discussion.

'She wants to legalise prostitution,' continues Mrs Jain, 'as if it were a regular profession, like being a shopkeeper or a journalist.'

Chitra knows she must close the subject before Mrs Jain challenges others to express opinions. She is not worried about Subramanyam, who can be relied on to play safe, but she knows Saxena will give free rein to his tongue and a violent discussion may follow. She herself half agrees with Mrs Jain. It was she who foiled beauty contests in college, after all. But she does not hold her views with the same passion that Mrs Jain does. To her, the skewed nature of society is a natural result of the particular course taken by history, not a malicious trap laid by men for women. But she dare not let Mrs Jain glimpse that ambiguity. Moral relativism has no meaning to a woman who pins her hair into a tight bun, purses her lips at every opportunity and wears a poncho.

'Put her in the "People" section at the back,' says Chitra, with a laugh. 'See if you can get that original photograph. We do not put beauty contests on the cover so we will not put prostitutes there either.'

Everyone chuckles, even Mrs Jain. Subramanyam laughs ingratiatingly. 'We are in the Fleet Street of India. We must be careful!'

The allusion irritates Chitra. She wants to pull him aside and demand to know why the Bahadur Shah Zafar area is Fleet Street. He often compares Greater Kailash to Bond Street and Daryaganj to Savile Row, making comparisons that are neither current – who compares anything to London nowadays? – nor based on experience, because he has never left India.

Subramanyam completes laughing at his joke – Saxena has never heard of Fleet Street and therefore does not laugh, Mrs Jain laughs at nothing – and slides a rectangular newspaper clipping across the table. 'What about this chaivala?' he asks.

The clipping is small, taken from the third or fourth page of a newspaper, perhaps the 'Metro' section because the front page could hardly report such an event – the filing of nomination papers by a tea-stall owner in Chandni Chowk constituency for the general election in March. The photograph has been taken outside the returning officer's rooms in Town Hall. A thin man in a white kurta-pyjama stands in the foreground, taking up two-thirds of the frame, grinning widely. A large Sikh takes up the other third. These two flank the candidate, who appears to be squeezed between them – a short, stout, bald man, staring at the camera with an expression rendered inscrutable by opaque spectacles. The background shows a dozen men, fists raised, captured in mid-slogan, their distance from the candidate marking them as less important. The photograph is of poor quality, but there is no mistaking the identity of the candidate. She does not need to read the caption.

She flips the pages in her mind to her last encounter with Gopal Pandey. A year? Two years? Some sort of honour at the Moonlight Festival? She has not done any serious fieldwork since the whirlwind of success deposited her inside editorial offices. She remembers being disappointed with the chaivala and giving him up as sparse material. Perhaps she will have to renew the contact, in the hope that he has finally collected enough padding around himself to be good copy. The article contains a statement from a Ramvilas Sharma, who appears to be his campaign manager. 'Gopal Das decided to come into politics when his chai stall was demolished by IPP,' says Ramvilas Sharma . . . Gopal Das? Not Pandey? 'Gopal Das will protect the common man against the Hindu fundamentalists of IPP!' continues Ramvilas Sharma.

The name does not make sense, but the picture is undoubtedly that of Gopal Pandey. Ramvilas Sharma appears to be an ex-member of the

IPP, claiming to have left the party because it is dominated by religious fundamentalists. 'Many men have thrown their weight behind Gopal Das,' says he, 'including sardar Kartar Singh, a wealthy trader in Chandni Chowk who is also an ex-IPP member. Gopal Das will protect the common man against the fundamentalists! Gopal Das is the poor man's candidate! Make Gopal Das the MP for Chandni Chowk!'

There is a statement from the candidate himself. 'My election symbol is not Coca-Cola or Thums Up,' he says, 'because that is what the English people drink. My election symbol is a cup of tea, because every poor man in Chandni Chowk can afford a cup of chai every day. I have entered politics to protect the common man, to prevent more stalls like mine from being uprooted . . .'

Chitra is no longer certain this is the same man. The face is his own, the name belongs to someone else and the statements are a pot-pourri of 'secular' maxims – words currently in fashion, brazenly plagiarised, stolen from someone who stole them from someone who no longer knows what they mean. She must investigate. For now, this is a mere titbit, a piece of election trivia undeserving of mention. 'I will do some fieldwork on this,' she says.

Saxena offers to follow up on the chaivala, but she insists on keeping him to herself. Saxena next reads from a note in his files. 'There is a request from Suleman Mian, MLA for Ballimaran in the Chandni Chowk area. He wants us to print an interview with him.'

Chitra shakes her head. Suleman has become tiresome. The promise of a meteoric career has been belied. No one in the English press takes him seriously after the Moonlight Festival incident. He wants an interview, no doubt, to advertise that he is planning to stand in this general election for Chandni Chowk, where all calculations have gone awry with the death of Naresh Agrawal, the sitting MP. Suleman may yet fulfil his dream of becoming an MP, considering one of his opponents will be the chaivala!

'We will write about Suleman Mian in the next issue,' she says.

'Did we agree on Charulata?' asks Saxena.

Chitra shrugs. 'All right, but we must write more about her and less about her Dalit Samaj Party or her chances in the general election, or her ability to provide swing votes in a hung Parliament. There has been too much of that in too many articles. Find out more about her family, her background, her education . . . Is she married? Divorced?'

I am turning my magazine into a rag, thinks Chitra. She swivels in her chair – another perquisite of being chief editor, and one she treasures – and trains her eyes on the dark but transparent screen over her windows. She can see the traffic in Bahadur Shah Zafar Marg – ropes of cars, buses, three-wheelers and scooters, forming loops, knots and gnarled ends, littered with humans rushing frantically into each other, drowning in deadly fumes, shivering under a blanket of grey that seems greyer through vinyl. The roar of the street is drowned by the more meaningful drone of her air-conditioner, which is another reason to keep it on. Some day, she will start a magazine in one of the smaller cities far away from Delhi: the city is so busy being the capital of India that it no longer stands for anything Indian. It must be a magazine in Hindi – not a mere translation of what is written in an English magazine but a magazine that thinks in Hindi. Will it be possible for her mind, burnished by the most prestigious women's college in Delhi, to undo her training and think in Hindi? And when she thinks in Hindi, will all arguments be turned upside-down? Will the rights be wrong and the wrongs right? What about 'secular forces' and 'fundamentalist forces'? Can such phrases be written in Hindi? Will the very issues be different? How much of the 'fractured polity' that so concerns the English press will be visible to a Hindi mind? Will the liberal, environmentalist movement exist? Will feminism survive?

'Charulata it is,' says Subramanyam, getting up.

Chitra assents, no longer interested in the cover story. She must find out more about this chaivala candidate, whatever his name.

2:

'Whether you are Hindu or Musalman, you are poor! A poor man's friend is not a secular leader or a fundamentalist leader but another poor man . . . If you do not vote for me, brothers and sisters, vote for another poor man!'

Ramvilas's effeminate voice shuts off abruptly with a click when the cassette ends. The click wakes Gopal. He sits up on the mattress and sighs helplessly. Such a long speech, and in such difficult Hindi! Who ever thought such intricate Sanskrit-like words existed? He cannot possibly memorise the whole cassette in two days, which is the time Ramvilas Babu has given him before he must stand and deliver it in front of three hundred people. Three hundred people! Where does Ramvilas Babu find them? He is a remarkable man of infinite resources.

Gopal rewinds the cassette to listen to the speech again, determined that he will not doze off this time. He will pay attention and let it run its interminable course. Ramvilas begins his harangue – 'Brothers and sisters, I stand before you as one of your own . . .' Gopal sits uncomfortably at the edge of the mattress. His feet trail off from it and lie sideways on the linoleum floor. He has not taken off his chappals. He is not sure where to leave them, and is afraid the linoleum will become dirty if he places his feet flat on it. He tries to concentrate on the voice, aware that his constant rewinding is consuming electricity. The sardarji would disapprove if he saw this. It is a difficult task, this election business, and he would not be embroiled in it if Ramesh Babu had not changed the signboard in Kucha Bansilal.

Three weeks ago, Ramesh Babu called a man to repaint the wall facing Jamna Lal Kishori Mal. For two years, since Gopal's stall was torn down, this wall has belonged to the Corporation, and has displayed an advertisement for Sachlok Clinic, offering cures for all diseases that may prevent a man siring a son. For two years the picture of a virile man – tumescent biceps, luxuriant moustache, mountainous shoulders – has stared disapprovingly at the mannequins that stand behind glass walls, hands folded, eyes downcast with a gentle smile on their lips.

The painter summoned by Ramesh Babu slapped a coat of chartreuse green on the entire wall, obliterating the man and his moustache, working round the electrical junction box, which was painted parrot green during the Moonlight Festival and now clashes with its surroundings. Then he created, over six hours, a new advertisement on the wall, and it was not for Jamna Lal Kishori Mal – Sarees and Blouses, as Gopal had expected. It showed a girl wearing a frock, a woman in a saree, and a man in shirt and trousers. The frock was painted approximately where Gopal's head would have rested in the stall, the man stood where Gopal's benches had been laid out, and the woman – only her bust – was positioned above the junction box. The name of the new shop was written on either side of the box, running through it and bisected by it, in large white letters with black shadows under them. It was complete when Gopal returned that afternoon after making his deliveries. The painter had left, and Chotu sat in the kucha on a stool, protecting the wet paint from passers-by, touching it gingerly to see if it had dried. Small finger smudges were visible in the lower regions. 'Sushma Fancy Dresses, Importers and Exporters,' he announced brightly.

Gopal thought Ramesh Babu had opened a new shop, but he was wrong. The painter returned the next day with a wooden signboard that looked exactly like the one he had painted on the wall. He, Chotu and Gopal then climbed ladders and brought down the Jamna Lal Kishori Mal sign to replace it with the new one. Ramesh Babu stood in the kucha to admire the change with a contented look on his face. Sohan Lalji – who rarely comes to the shop – was present too. He stood on the other side of the lane, staring at the new sign. His face gave nothing away, but Gopal was saddened. The seth was a good man, he reminded himself.

Gopal has never felt the same warmth for Ramesh Babu, who has shown no concern for his age over the last two years. A man cannot ride a bicycle comfortably over the age of fifty, yet Ramesh Babu has relentlessly increased his loads, reduced his commission, and de-manded that he make more deliveries every day. He is not a con-siderate man like his father, who knew when to offer chai to his customers and when to shoo them away. The shop itself is unsuitable for a delivery-man to rest in. There is no gaddi, no floor, no corner where a man may sit and catch his breath, only the forbidding Sunmica counter, which stretches along the entire front of the shop, cutting off access to all but Ramesh Babu and his clerks. A customer may sit on the stool at the counter, but who would allow Gopal to sit there? His only recourse, on coming to the shop, is to leave with boxes for another delivery. He has often considered leaving the kucha, but what can a chaivala do after they have taken away his stall? There are the four lakhs buried deep under tins of asafoetida . . . Ah, he will not touch the snakes. There is no telling whom they will take away next. Both his sons are gone, so is it his turn to be struck dead? He is not even certain the money still exists. It has been stolen by Hameed, perhaps, or taken by Seth Sushil Jain. Besides, what could you buy now in Chandni Chowk with four lakhs? Three square feet of crawl-space under a paanvala's stall!

Even as he vowed to leave, Gopal knew he would not. He would die on his bicycle one day, hit by a car. The boxes would fly – shirts would flutter in the air, pyjamas would unfold – and he would lie splayed out in Chandni Chowk, his spectacles askew on his forehead. 'He was a good man,' Sohan Lalji would say. 'He was a slow worker,' Ramesh Babu would say. Ibrahim Mian would wipe a tear, perhaps, from his eye. Sohan Lalji would pay the Corporation five hundred rupees to have him cremated. That was how he had imagined it, until Ramesh Babu changed the signboard above the shop. Sushma Fancy Dresses was very different from Jamna Lal Kishori Mal, because the very next day Ramesh Babu accused him of stealing.

'Customers have complained,' he said. 'They do not get some deliveries. When they do, they find some kurta buttons missing, especially the ones that are gold-plated. I personally supervise the loading of your bicycle, so where do those buttons go?'

Gopal was aghast. Had he left the bicycle standing outside Paratha Gali where thieves are known to prowl? Had he looked away from the stacks on his pillion when he stopped for some chai? Could it be that, even as he wove his way slowly through rickshas, boys untied the ropes on the stacks behind him and removed boxes?

'There is no place for you in Sushma Fancy Dresses,' said Ramesh Babu.

Gopal appealed to Sohan Lalji, who stood outside the shop, chewing paan. Surely the sethji could testify to his honesty, having known him for twenty years! It was odd, in the first place, that Sohan Lalji should stand outside the shop while Ramesh Babu sat impassively behind the counter, but nothing seemed out of place once that sign had changed. And he was not surprised when Sohan Lalji turned away. He dragged his bicycle out of the kucha.

Before he had gone far, Chotu called him back. Sohan Lalji had taken pity on him. 'Take him to Sardar Kartar Singh,' the seth said to Chotu. 'Tell him Gopal is an honest man with no wife and no son, and will starve unless he gets some work.' Then Sohan Lalji put his arm round Gopal's shoulders. 'He will not turn you away. He will remember how you saved his wife in 'eighty-four.'

Gopal nearly sank to his knees. A seth resting his arm on the shoulders of a man like him! As he walked to Lajpatrai Market with Chotu, Gopal resolved to tell Sardar Kartar Singh everything he knew about that evening in 'eighty-four – the money, and the man who tore into the bathroom to kill his wife. He is not certain it was indeed Ibrahim Mian, but perhaps the sardarji could ascertain that for himself. He must still want to know the name of the villain! Gratitude had caused the sardarji to give him a plaque in front of thousands of people. Perhaps revenge would cause him to offer a job.

He entered Jasjit General Store with Chotu, and stood with his hands folded before Kartar Singh, Ibrahim's name on the tip of his tongue, but the sardarji did not ask again about the man in his house. 'I would have to be heartless to turn you away,' said Kartar Singhji.

For a week, Gopal woke up early every morning and came to Lajpatrai Market, and waited for Kartar Singhji to arrive and open the store. After the shutters had been pulled up, Kartar Singhji would go to Gurudwara Sisganj. Gopal would sit behind the counter and scan the lane, there being no other clerks in the store. Sometimes young men would come for leather belts, or fat women to buy electric mixers. The women would bring out oranges and demand that the mixer churn them to pulp in a demonstration of its power. When the mixer blades stuttered – entwined with fibres that were pulled out of the peel – the women would talk down the price and buy the mixer. Gopal never understood what type of oranges those were: their juice smelled of grease and their fibres were as strong as steel. The sardarji never seemed to mind any price. His heart had not been in the business, he told Gopal, since the death of his wife.

A week after Gopal began work at Jasjit General Store, a thin man in a spotless kurta-pyjama came to the counter. 'I have not come to buy a mixer but to work for you,' he said.

That was the first thing Gopal heard Ramvilas Babu say. The next thing Ramvilas Babu described was the election in March.

'I do not know anything about politics,' said Gopal.

'I have been talking to many people,' said Ramvilas Babu. 'They want to support a man like you. A man who has suffered, a man who is honest, a man who feels in his heart the pain of other people.'

'I like working in the store,' said Gopal.

'Kartar Singhji is about to close it down,' said Ramvilas Babu. 'It makes no profit. And you have sold many mixers for half-price to women who cheated you by damaging them with metal wires. Where will you go after the store is closed?'

'How much will this work pay?' Gopal had asked.

Ramvilas Babu had laughed. 'As much as you can count!'

The next day, a procession danced into Lajpatrai Market, with Ramvilas Babu and Kartar Singhji at its head, beating drums and chanting, 'Gopal Das *zindabad*!' They garlanded him and took him to Town Hall, where he was ushered into a room. He wondered if this

was a ploy to put him in jail and question him about the damaged
mixers, but all he had to do was sit at a desk – surrounded by a
hundred people! – and look at some papers. There were men seated
across from him, but he could not see clearly through his spectacles.
Ramvilas Babu grabbed his right hand, closed his fingers round a pen,
and had him scrawl here and there on the papers. He was astonished
at the roar that accompanied his actions. An honest man has many
supporters, even if he does not know it!

He was pleased to find an even larger crowd awaiting them when
they emerged from the room. Everyone wanted to stand next to him.
Kartar Singhji and Ramvilas Babu had to shield him on either side to
prevent his supporters trampling him under their feet. And when the
newspeople – at least three – began to take photographs, he felt like a
film star. He might have been Amitabh Bachchan himself! As the
cameras clicked, his supporters shouted slogans.

'Chandni Chowk *kaa rakhvala*, Chandni Chowk *kaa chaivala*!'

At first he was confused by them – they seemed to mention someone
other than him. Then he began to shout slogans himself. The
protector of Chandni Chowk is indeed the chaivala of Chandni
Chowk! Kartar Singhji and Ramvilas Babu told him not to join in
with the slogans, so he said no more and let them continue. On further
thought, he was disappointed that they were calling him the protector
of Chandni Chowk, when Ramvilas Babu had given him to understand that he was to protect the entire city of Delhi. Why, it was his
charter to protect all of Mother India! He decided to bring up the
matter with Ramvilas Babu the next day. A more glaring discrepancy
was of greater concern to him: they were calling him Gopal Das. Das?
A servant? Whose? He tried to nudge Ramvilas Babu, but the slogan-
shouters had no time for anyone. Ah, just a wrinkle, to be ironed out
in a day or two.

After his supporters had disbanded, Kartar Singhji brought him
back to the store in Lajpatrai Market. The sardarji removed some
Bournvita tins and swung open a wall of shelves to reveal an opening.
They peered through it together. 'This is your campaign office,' he
said.

That was when Gopal first saw the windowless room in which he
now sits – linoleum floor, a thick mattress that covers most of it,
bolsters, a bruised Godrej safe in the corner, a television, a VCR, a
cassette-player and a telephone. He was overwhelmed by the sardarji's
generosity. Far from needling him about the money – what use can

such a rich man have for four lakhs? – the sardarji had decided to become his supporter like the others. Gopal had no idea why he would need a campaign office, but he was grateful just the same. 'Do you not want me to stand behind the counter?' he had asked.

Kartar Singhji shook his head. 'You have just filed nomination papers. You are a candidate now, and you will soon be the Chandni Chowk Member of Parliament. How will it look if I have a Lok Sabha MP selling Bournvita in my store?'

Gopal found the argument perfectly sensible.

'You must spend all your time here in the campaign office,' continued the sardarji. 'Where is your kholi?'

'Katra Badami in Khari Baoli. Seth Sushil Jain's godown.'

'Bring your blanket so you can sleep here. A leader cannot sleep in a kholi.'

'What will I do in the campaign office?'

'Have you ever watched cricket?'

'I have heard of Gavaskar,' said Gopal, fearfully.

'Do not worry. I will teach you. While you sit in the campaign office waiting to become an MP you can watch cricket.'

Gopal asked the sardarji why everyone was calling him Gopal Das. Kartar Singhji advised him to ask Ramvilas Babu, who was the campaign manager. When Ramvilas Babu came the next day, bearing his speech on a cassette, he told Gopal he would look into the matter.

In the first few days, Kartar Singhji taught Gopal the rules of cricket and showed him how to operate the television, the VCR and the cassette-player. Gopal now records every match on the VCR, writes down who made how many runs, who scored quarter-centuries, half-centuries and centuries. He adds up the number of wickets taken by each bowler, the number of wickets taken in the first hour, before teatime, after lunch . . . Kartar Singhji takes away the notepad after every match, and carries the videotape home with him.

'Whether you are Hindu or Musalman, you are poor,' says the tireless voice of Ramvilas, having risen toward the end. Gopal starts and shuts the cassette-player with a groan. Ramvilas Babu's speech has run its course for the third time. His mind wandered again, and he cannot repeat a single sentence. The words tumble over one another, and he has not the slightest idea what they mean. He cannot keep rewinding for ever because he must soon switch on the television to watch the post-lunch session of today's cricket match in Calcutta, which begins in twenty minutes. Kartar Singhji will be displeased if he misses it.

The monitor mounted on the wall shows that someone is in the store. Although he has been told that his task is to watch cricket matches and memorise the speech, Gopal has been eagerly serving customers when they arrive, in the hope of proving himself indispensable to the sardarji. He gets up quickly, tiptoes over the linoleum, taking care not to let his dirty chappals touch the floor, and pushes the Bournvita shelf from behind to emerge into the store. A plump Nepali woman in a white saree stands at the counter. She appears startled to see him coalesce out of a wall. 'Where is Kartar Singhji?' she asks.

'Gurudwara Sisganj,' he says, as he sits down behind the counter and directs his gaze at a far corner of the shop. She scans the shelves of mixers and fans, and he studies her out of the corner of his eye. She is short, very round and chubby. A white saree covers most of her, but it is thin: he can detect the outline of large breasts and see smooth skin, upper arms left bare by a sleeveless blouse and an expensive-looking diamond necklace. She is of indeterminate age and character, looking both like a film heroine and the heroine's mother.

She finishes scanning the shelves and turns to Gopal, looking frankly into his eyes as if she were a man. Gopal falters under her scrutiny. How can a man, at his age, look so directly at a woman? And how can a woman – whatever her age – look into a man's eyes with such self-assurance?

'I want to buy some VCRs,' she says. Her voice is soft, girlish, and she speaks with an odd accent. He points to the VCRs arrayed in shelves along the left wall, but she shakes her head. 'I need ten of the same model.'

He is confused. Who buys ten VCRs? She seems to understand his confusion. 'I need them for my students. For all my students in all my hostels.'

He nods. He does not know what a hostel is, but the woman seems to know Kartar Singhji. Besides, he must hurry. The cricket match is about to begin and he must record every second of it. He shows her all the models, Japanese and Chinese. She already has televisions in her hostel, and she wants to know how to connect the VCRs to them. Gopal is unfamiliar with such things. He promises that the sardarji will send over a technician if she buys the VCRs. She selects an expensive model of which he has only four, pulls out a wad of hundred-rupee notes and wants to pay in full – for all ten – without bargaining. Gopal tells her to come back and settle with Kartar Singh. She throws down the wad anyway. 'Keep it,' she says. 'Kartar Singhji can count and send me the difference.'

He hides the money under the counter with trembling hands.

'I will come back for the other six,' she says.

'Where should we send the technician?' asks Gopal.

'Kartar Singhji knows.'

Then he calls a ricksha. The rickshavala loads all four VCRs into a corner of the seat. She clambers on to the ricksha without any help – such a short woman yet she climbs into the seat so confidently! – and leaves. She is almost like a man, thinks Gopal. What kind of woman can go to a shop, buy ten VCRs, pay for them, and take them to a hostel on a ricksha?

As soon as she is gone, he moves the Bournvita shelf aside and runs into the back room. He inserts a new tape into the VCR, sets it to record the cricket match, lowers the volume, and settles down to watch. The match resumes. India is batting, chasing a mammoth total of three hundred and fourteen set by Bangladesh. It is the last of three finals and the winner will win the Freedom Cup. This cricket-watching is an easy job, he thinks. He enjoys fiddling with knobs and buttons on the television. What a wonderful gadget it is! So much more slick than his oil stove, pots, pans, bottles of sugar and tea . . . The election is a minor irritant – pleasing when they shout slogans about him, tiresome when he must learn speeches – but it will be over in two months. Then he can spend the rest of his life watching cricket and selling VCRs.

He happens to look up at the closed-circuit camera, and is annoyed to find another customer in the store. The man stands patiently near the VCR shelves, wearing a safari suit, tapping lightly on the counter with his fingers. Gopal decides to run out of the room, sell the man whatever he wants, and come back before the first over is bowled in Calcutta.

The safari-suited man is large and beefy. The arms he has placed on the counter are hairy, sunburned and frightfully muscular. A Jat from Haryana, thinks Gopal.

'Kartar Singhji?' asks the man.

'Sardarji is in Gurudwara Sisganj,' replies Gopal.

'Ah! I will come back.'

The man melts away. As soon as he leaves, a worried-looking Kartar Singh hurries into the store, limping horribly with the exertion.

'There was a Nepali lady who knew you,' says Gopal. 'She bought ten VCRs!' He dutifully pulls out the wad of hundred-rupee bills. This is by far the largest sale he has seen in the store, but the sardarji appears indifferent. He is a rich man, thinks Gopal. Look at his fingers! Those stones must be worth a lakh each.

'Who was that man?' whispers Kartar Singh.

Gopal shrugs.

'What did he say?' Kartar Singh demands.

'He asked for you. I told him you were in Gurudwara Sisganj. He said he would be back.'

Kartar Singh notices the displaced Bournvita shelf. The back room is clearly visible through the opening. 'I told you never to leave that shelf open.'

Gopal stands with a guilty look on his face.

'I will watch this match myself,' says Kartar Singh, gruffly.

Gopal looks around helplessly. He has already moved his blanket and clothes to the back room, which is where he now spends his nights. Is the sardarji asking him to go back to the kholi? Is the election business finished?

'Come back in three hours,' says Kartar Singh, with a groan.

Gopal is relieved. He shuffles out of the store before the sardarji can change his mind.

Kartar Singh stalks impatiently into the back room, shuts the shelf behind him and settles down to watch the match. He senses, though he doesn't know, that this series is coloured. India won the first final and Bangladesh the second. This third final seems to be going Bangladesh's way.

The telephone rings. Kartar Singh eyes it fearfully, then picks it up with a sigh. He knows who the caller is. He has disconnected all phone lines except this one, and he has tried hard to avoid using it, but he cannot ignore this call.

'Five lakhs on India,' says the voice.

It is a command, not a request. Kartar Singh has never met the man. He sits in Bombay or London or South Africa or Dubai. Officially he is Kartar Singh's business partner, who invests Kartar Singh's money in matches whose scripts are known to him. In reality, the man in Dubai – or the don he represents – extorts Kartar Singh's money to earn returns for himself, while passing losses on to Kartar Singh, who has no stomach for this sort of thing but does not know how to get out of it. It is not easy to shake off the dons, especially when they have a clear idea of how much money he has earned during their days as punters in the same pack. A few crumbs are thrown his way, but no one would consider such large investments in uncertain matches a sound business strategy. And there is little doubt that the beefy man who called at the store is a CBI officer, investigating just the sort of phone call Kartar Singh has received.

Kartar Singh knows he is being played. India needs to make three hundred and fifteen runs to win. No one has ever chased such a total and emerged victorious. Which foolhardy punter would put his money on such an implausible outcome? 'What is the rate on India?' he asks haltingly.

There is a silence at the other end. By asking the question, Kartar Singh has challenged the man to quote a rate, to reveal who he thinks – or, rather, knows – is going to win. When the man speaks, his voice is dry and final. 'The rate is good.'

Kartar Singh sighs. He is being asked to lose five lakhs, or at least a large fraction of it, knowingly. He does not know the implications of refusal, but he does know that the dons exert power in more ways than he can imagine. It is not a good idea to run foul of them.

'Fifty thousand,' he suggests.

'Too low.'

'One lakh?'

'The rate is good.'

'One and a half lakhs.'

'I will tell Bhai,' says the voice, then hangs up.

One and a half lakhs, sighs Kartar Singh, almost certainly drained away. The collector will be at the store in less than thirty minutes to whisk away the money, which he will never see again. This is where the four lakhs of the chaivala would have been handy . . . He sits back against a bolster and flips channels aimlessly. Most are showing the cricket match. He notices the cassette-player and turns it on listlessly.

Ramvilas begins to speak: 'A poor man's friend is not a secular leader or a fundamentalist leader but another poor man . . . If you do not vote for me, brothers and sisters, vote for another poor man!'

He hurls the cassette-player into the air. It lands on the mattress, probably undamaged. The speech is irritating and stupid. Ramvilas has recorded it in his reedy, grating voice, sounding hostile even when he tries to project warmth. His accent is awkward because the language is flowery and archaic. No one understands such Hindi any more, not even Ramvilas, who pauses before difficult words, stumbling through tortuous phrases almost as if he were speaking English. None of this matters, Kartar Singh tells himself. In two months, everything will have sorted itself out.

'IPP will destroy the secular fabric of India,' says Ramvilas. 'For fifteen years I asked myself every day, "Why am I a member of this communal party?" Finally, I had to choose between my political career and communal harmony. It took courage, but I chose communal harmony. So what if it meant resigning from the committee and giving up primary membership of the party? No sacrifice is too great for the unity and integrity of India.'

Ramvilas walks so briskly that Chitra is forced into a trot to keep up with him. He is in a hurry to get somewhere. Amid the roar of scooters and cars, she pays little attention to what he says. Too many descriptions are deployed by the friends and foes of the IPP for her to pay heed. Words such as 'communal', 'secular' and 'pseudo-secular' flow in and out of political discourse like the howl of a storm that is no longer noticed as a distinct sound. She is not interested in Ramvilas anyway. She does not care why he left the IPP or what his plans are for the deliverance of his country. She has come to him to talk about Gopal. What a prosaic manager for a campaign so poetic! He is too supple, too comfortable, far too inclined to take liberties with the truth.

'I always thought his name was Gopal Pandey,' she begins.

'Das,' insists Ramvilas. 'Gopal Das!'

Chitra does not challenge him. It is a small matter. They are approaching Kucha Bansilal. She will take a detour and clear up the matter with Gopal himself. 'I am going to meet Gopal Das at his stall,' she says.

'There is no stall in Kucha Bansilal,' says Ramvilas, with relish. 'It was destroyed two years ago during IPP's demolition drive.'

'Where can I meet him, then?'

He does not answer, as if determined to hide the candidate from her. Instead, as they pass Kucha Bansilal, he slows down. 'Gopal Das is a true Dillivala – not a Punjabi who came to Delhi in 'forty-seven, not a Bengali who came in the fifties, or a Madrasi civil servant or a Bihari rickshavala, but a true Dillivala! His great-grandfather served jalebis to nawabs and their begums. His grandfather, Shyam Sundar Das, had a jalebi stall at the beginning of the century and was a Congress Party activist. Gopal's father, Manohar Lal Pandey, started a jalebi stall with Nawab Tahir Hussein Sahib, and stood ten feet from Gandhiji at his last prayer meeting in Birla House. He saw Nathuram Godse and Vishnu Karkare at close range, just before Gandhiji was shot, so he was murdered by the RSS before he could identify Karkare for the police.'

Chitra wishes she could stop and pull out her tape-recorder, but does not want to interrupt him. She vaguely remembers the story from her previous conversations with the chaivala. She will try to memorise the details that matter.

'Gopal Das himself has always been a supporter of secular causes,' continues Ramvilas. 'His son, while supporting the Mandal Commission, was murdered by IPP.'

'I thought he was protesting against the Mandal Commission?' she asks.

Ramvilas stops and looks at her irritably. 'Things are not what they seem, madam.'

Then he steps into the feisty current of Chandni Chowk traffic to cross the road, oblivious of cars that screech to a stop and rickshas that swerve to avoid him. Chitra hurries after him, collecting the abuse that was hurled at him, until their progress is arrested by a green fence that runs along the centre of the street. He strains angrily against it. 'This is what Harilal Gupta has done in four years as transport minister! What good is this fence? What good is a road if people cannot cross it?'

'It improves the flow of traffic,' she offers. 'Cars and scooters . . .'

'Only the rich drive cars and scooters,' he declares triumphantly.

'It also improves the movement of rickshas,' she suggests. 'Surely rickshavalas are not rich?'

A frown clouds his brow. 'I am not a politician, madam. I cannot argue with skill. I can only say that Harilal Gupta does not care for the common man, which is why Gopal Das is standing in this election.'

He finds a gap in the fence and rushes through it, turns into Paratha Gali and offers to buy Chitra some parathas. She shudders at the sight of the dark, grimy dungeons inside which parathas are born, and demurs. Ramvilas points to the array of pickles and presses a paratha into her hands anyway. She eats with reluctance, and with growing impatience at their foray – unnecessary in her eyes – into Paratha Gali.

'I would like to meet the candidate,' she says. 'Why are we going this way?'

'We will go to my shop Bhagwan Das and Sons,' responds Ramvilas.

'Can I ask my photographer to come there?'

'Of course! Tell them to come to Bhagwan Das and Sons, seven hundred and sixty Churi Walan, Jama Masjid.' He points to the paratha stall. 'If you buy two they will let you use the telephone.'

She thrusts five rupees into a greasy palm and telephones her photographer to give him the address. They continue until Paratha Gali leads into another lane, where they turn left toward Jama Masjid.

'Nareshji represented Chandni Chowk for eighteen years,' says Ramvilas. 'I cannot speak ill of a man who is no more, but what did he do for Chandni Chowk? True, he was a senior leader in the Congress Party, but did he clean up Chandni Chowk? Did he get us electricity and phone connections? Did he look after rickshavalas? Did he preserve temples, masjids and old havelis?'

'Harilal Gupta has promised to preserve the cultural heritage of Chandni Chowk,' Chitra points out.

'Harilalji is the IPP candidate,' sneers Ramvilas. 'He is too communal. And Suleman Mian is an independent. What can an independent MP do for Chandni Chowk?'

'He is being supported by the Communist parties.'

'The Communist parties have no base in Delhi.'

'Congress has fielded Sulochana Agrawal,' says Chitra. 'Will not the people who have always voted for Naresh Agrawal now vote for his wife?'

Ramvilas frowns. 'We are firmly against dynastic rule,' he declares. 'She is a housewife! How can she be a leader?'

'But your candidate is a chaivala,' suggests Chitra, provocatively.

'Gopal Das is a man of the people,' Ramvilas replies, with dignity. 'He is not a politician. He is not a leader. He is simply a chaivala in Chandni Chowk. Who can better understand the problems of Chandni Chowk than a man who sleeps in a kholi and owns a chai stall there?'

'You said his stall does not exist any more.'

'One or two years do not matter,' says Ramvilas. 'He has been a chaivala all his life.'

'Harilal Gupta has said he will solicit votes from GB Road,' says Chitra.

'You mean Swami Shraddhanand Marg,' says Ramvilas coldly.

'You can call GB Road by any name you like.' She shrugs.

As they walk, Ramvilas studies Chitra's face out of the corner of his eye, looking for signs of levity. Does this madam know about Gita? His association with her is now limited to public meetings and STREE conventions. As a trader, a member of the committee, almost a public figure, he must choose his associates with care. In any case, who could be interested in a fat old hag? Her plumpness, soft and delicious when she was young, is now merely another sign of advancing age. She exasperates him with her NGO talk, and he will never forgive her for cheating him out of Parvati's girls . . . But this reminds him of the sores that keep coming back. He suspects he has given them to his wife. She complains of the pain but bears it, thinking herself to be at fault. As soon as he has rented a flat in Ballimaran and brought her — with his daughters – to Delhi, he will take her to a doctor. And then he will take a vow of chastity to spare her the pain. If a weak man like Gandhi could do it at thirty-six, why can he not attempt it at forty-four? He is not aroused by his wife anyway. After his frolics in GB Road, she is like plain rice to a man who has tasted the fragrance of pulao.

'Gopal Das is a respectable man,' he says carefully. 'He will solicit the votes of all respectable people, all the poor who have honour and dignity.'

Chitra decides not to pursue the matter. She must find others who will tell her more about the candidate, perhaps the factotum of Suleman who was a fixture in the chai stall. He was eager to speak, to be photographed and interviewed. She will come back to Chandni Chowk in a week and dig him up. Traffic between her office and Chandni Chowk will be much lighter after Republic Day. 'Will Gopal Das be present at the Republic Day parade?' she asks.

'He is a common man, madam! A poor man. There is no place for a poor man at the parade. He will watch it on television.'

'He owns a television?'

'It is not his,' says Ramvilas, triumphantly. 'It belongs to Sardar Kartar Singh who, with me, has thrown his support behind Gopal Das. He has given him a campaign office, a television and a telephone. How else can a poor man fight an election?'

They are now in the Jama Masjid area. The lane has narrowed, and is lined on either side by stalls selling halal meat. Goat carcasses swing from metal wires. Slabs of beef lie on counters. The lane is an endless abattoir. Ramvilas turns away his eyes in disgust, but the stalls are impossible to deny. It is the price he has paid for four years of debilitating court battles. The final opinion of the court was issued only last Divali, and it was not as favourable to Vimal as Ramvilas had hoped. The original shop in Kucha Sugandh has gone to the three younger sons with all its antique oak furniture, itself worth lakhs of rupees. They will now spend another four years slicing it up. Vimal has withdrawn his capital from the business. If he was not such a fool, they would have received a better settlement, which would have been useful because, although the amount is substantial, rents in Chandni Chowk are no longer what they used to be. The pagari for a small shop – fifteen by fifteen feet square – can be more than fifty lakhs if the shop is at street level. After a month of scouring and haggling, all he could afford was the Jama Masjid area, which is so heavily Musalman that no one wants a shop there. He is not likely to get many new customers, but he hopes to draw from the original clientele of Lala Surajmal.

He can sense, as they walk through, that even the madam flinches, much as she tries to hide her revulsion. 'Even Musalman areas need commerce,' he says valiantly.

Chitra nods absently. She has wasted too much time ingratiating herself with the manager, when she should be speaking to the candidate.

The shop is squeezed between two notary offices in a recess in the lane. A concerted effort has been mounted to make the shopfront conspicuous. The apron of land at the front has been swept clean, the façade has been resurfaced with imitation marble, and a modern glass wall allows the casual passer-by to peer inside. A sign with raised metal letters hangs between the two notary offices, spanning the width of the shop – 'Bhagwan Das and Sons (of Lahore), Perfumers Since 1700'. Ramvilas grabs a shining chrome handle and pulls open the glass door.

'Come inside, madam.'

'Where is Gopal Das?' she insists.

'He is in the campaign office in Lajpatrai Market,' Ramvilas says.

She is annoyed. He has deceived her, but she has already asked her photographer to come here.

'Cold drink?' he offers.

It is a senseless question, considering the chill in the air. She shakes her head and steps inside with a sigh. A young man in ill-matching shirt and trousers, seated behind the steel and Sunmica counter, rises on seeing them. Ramvilas turns sharply to him. 'Madam is here, Vimal!'

Vimal throws a bashful smile at Chitra, comes round the counter and leaves the shop. Ramvilas watches his departure with a measure of parental approval. 'That is the eldest son of Lala Surajmal,' he says. 'We are partners.'

Lala Surajmal, Chitra assumes, is the old man whose picture stares down from the central wall, watching every customer with a frown that is partially hidden behind a garland of flowers. She looks around the shop. It is an assemblage of steel surfaces, chrome handles, sharp edges, shining floors and dozens of opposing mirrors that reproduce her endlessly in receding space.

'This is the most modern-looking shop in Chandni Chowk,' boasts Ramvilas. 'Our branch in Kucha Sugandh had termite-infested wooden furniture. Customers were put off by the worn look and musty smell. Here, everything is steel and glass! Seths and traders like us must also change with the times.'

Chitra nods perfunctorily.

'Bhagwan Das and Sons will soon be a landmark in Chandni Chowk, a stop for every tourist guide! It is part of our heritage, which is why so many MLAs and councillors came to the inauguration last month.'

'But the signboard says the shop is three hundred years old?'

Ramvilas is annoyed at her apparent naïveté. 'That sign is a month old,' he says patiently, 'but the business is as old as Chandni Chowk itself. Walls do not matter! What matters is the experience of three centuries that has come down to us. My great-grandfather was perfumer to Bahadur Shah Zafar. When the British stormed Red Fort during the Mutiny, Zafar sat with wads of cotton behind his ears, soaked in my great-grandfather's attars, writing poetry.'

Chitra adds up the years to determine if the story is feasible, and feels it is not.

'I have dedicated this shop to my mentor Lala Surajmal,' says Ramvilas, reverently. 'It was from him that I learned everything I know about attars. He often said to me, "Ramvilas! I want to open the purest attar shop in the world – no synthetic scents, no oils, no perfumes . . . nothing but natural attars!" And this is the realisation of

Lalaji's dreams. We grow our own flowers and prepare the attar by careful hydro-distillation in our own manufacturing units scattered all over India – attar rose from Aligarh, keora from Ganjam in Orissa, chameli and motia from Sikandarpur . . .'

Vimal staggers in with two tumblers of tea. Because both hands are full, he pushes open the glass door with his elbow. Ramvilas places one tumbler on the counter – Chitra indicates she will not drink it – and begins to sip at the other. She waits impatiently until the photographer arrives with a boy carrying lights. He looks at the mirrors and shakes his head. 'We cannot take a photograph here because those will reflect too much light,' he says.

Ramvilas suggests that they set up outside, where the façade of the shop can form the background. Chitra leads the photographer outside and he begins to erect his lights by running power cords from the shop.

Ramvilas congratulates himself on having manoeuvred the madam into the shop. She will write about this in her magazine and everyone will hear of the new Bhagwan Das and Sons behind Jama Masjid.

He was disappointed at the poor turnout during the inauguration. The entire IPP committee was present except Jugal Kishor, who had left for Hardwar. All eight councillors from Chandni Chowk came dutifully, but only two of the four MLAs bothered to show up – Sohan Lal and the member from Paharganj. Suleman spurned the invitation, as expected, and Harilal Gupta politely sent an emissary. He has recently taken to declining invitations unless other ministers are invited.

Ramvilas ascribed the sparse attendance to the political situation. Six days before the inauguration, Congress had withdrawn support from the central government. When he received the news Naresh Agrawal suffered a heart-attack and died two hours later. It would not become obvious for many more days if an election would indeed take place, but Naresh Agrawal must have known. He had just won his seat for the fifth time in 'ninety-six. He did not have the stomach for another campaign, so he chose to die. That was another reason no one from the Congress Party was at the inauguration.

Sohan Lal cut the ribbon. Ramvilas had arranged for chai and samosas, which he laid out on tables in the lane. He had wished the shop was larger, because people had to squeeze inside and compete for stools. After looking at the glass panels and crystal decanters arrayed on the counter, most were forced to spill out into the lane, where they stood shivering in the frigid evening, trying to warm themselves with chai and samosas, until Ramvilas arranged for chairs from neighbouring stalls. He had hoped no one would notice the goat carcasses swinging from metal wires, but he knew Sohan Lal had, from the way the seth's face puckered when he arrived.

He managed to seat the councillors on chairs outside, so only committee members remained inside the shop – Sohan Lal, Kartar Singh and three traders. There was much excitement and anticipation. Harilal Gupta was to be the IPP candidate for Chandni Chowk. With Naresh Agrawal out of the way, this was the first time in eighteen years that the IPP stood a real chance of winning the seat. Sohan Lal expressed some consternation that Harilal Gupta had not come when it must be obvious to him they would discuss the election. After all, it was he who was being catapulted from a mere state ministership to a seat in Parliament.

As Sohan Lal said this, Ramvilas sensed that the words stuck in his throat. He had no doubt that Sohan Lal himself wanted to be a candidate, but did not dare to reveal his intentions in the face of Harilal's obvious precedence in the committee. Also, as chairman of the committee, he could hardly push himself forward.

'Everyone thinks there will be a hung Parliament,' said Sohan Lal, 'so IPP must win every seat it can.'

'Harilalji will get the trader vote as always,' said Kartar Singh.

'That is enough to win one assembly segment, but not enough for the entire Chandni Chowk constituency. The Matia Mahal segment has too many Musalmans.'

'Musalmans will vote in a solid bloc for Suleman,' sighed Kartar Singh. 'If Communists support him, he will also get lower-caste Hindus.'

'Sikhs are returning to Congress,' said a trader.

'If only Hindus voted together, instead of scattering their votes between Congress, IPP and the Communist parties!'

'What can we do about Suleman Mian?'

The committee had fallen silent, contemplating Suleman's eventual victory. What a shame that Chandni Chowk was to be represented by a Musalman! It was on Sohan Lal's shoulders, as chairman, to devise a campaign that could contain Suleman. He folded his cap and stowed it away in his kurta pocket, very deliberately. 'I have spoken to Harilalji,' he said.

This was offensive to Ramvilas. It implied proprietary access and privileged knowledge. Did Sohan Lal consider himself the liaison between the candidate and the committee? Why had the candidate not come in person to discuss this with committee members?

'IPP is passing through a difficult phase,' said Sohan Lal formally, as if he were making a speech. 'Many decades ago, when the Congress Party faced a similar crisis, Jawaharlal Nehru devised a scheme under which party leaders would resign their positions in the government and dedicate themselves to grass-roots work. It was called the Kamraj Plan.'

Ramvilas held his breath. He knew, long before the other traders arrived at this conclusion, what Sohan Lal had in mind. He was impressed in spite of the danger that loomed.

Sohan Lal continued: 'In Chandni Chowk, IPP will launch its own Kamraj Plan, called the Lala Surajmal Scheme. I invite committee members to resign and work wholeheartedly for the victory of the party in this election.'

'But we already plan to work for the party!' protested a trader.

'There are only two strong candidates in Chandni Chowk,' said Sohan Lal. 'Harilalji and Suleman. Those who resign under the Lala Surajmal Scheme will work for a third candidate – a candidate for the poor. Every vote they solicit for this candidate will be a vote taken from Suleman.'

The committee fell silent as each member gauged the mood of the rest toward himself. It was not clear where such a candidate could come from, but Sohan Lal had already finalised everything, without bothering to consult the committee. 'It has been settled between Harilal Gupta and me,' he said.

Then he disclosed the name of the chaivala.

Ramvilas watched the faces of the committee members carefully. If there was sufficient opposition to the scheme, he was willing to express disagreement, perhaps even lead a revolt.

But Kartar Singh jumped at the idea for no obvious reason. 'The chaivala works in your shop,' he said. 'It will not look right if the IPP committee chairman employs a candidate who wants to stand against Harilal Gupta.'

Whether Kartar Singh knew it or not, thought Ramvilas, he was offering support by discussing details of the plan.

'I will ask Ramesh to throw him out,' said Sohan Lal. 'But where shall I send him?'

Kartar Singh walked the length of the shop – knocking against the knees of traders seated on stools – until he stood at the door. The walk was unnecessary, thought Ramvilas, and executed merely to demonstrate his limp. Then he turned and drew himself up. 'Send him to me. I will do this for the committee. I will be the first to resign under the Lala Surajmal Scheme.'

There was a gasp, then silence. Sohan Lal cast a withering look at everyone else, who shrank from his gaze and burrowed their faces into their stubby kurta collars.

'Kartar Singhji made many sacrifices in 'eighty-four,' declared Sohan Lal. 'He should not be asked for more. His health will not permit him to be the campaign manager for the chaivala.'

Then Sohan Lal had looked directly at Ramvilas. Even as he wilted under the attention, Ramvilas considered his options. Since Ramesh had taken over the business, Sohan Lal spent considerable energy on maintaining his weight, sugar level and blood pressure, all of which indicated that he planned to be around for a long time. It would be ten years before his health began to fail, by which time Ramvilas himself would be fifty-four. Rash as it was, this represented a possible chance to vault over the head of Sohan Lal. With the election over, and Harilalji installed as MP for Chandni Chowk, Sohan Lal's star would wane. Ramvilas could then attach himself to Harilalji, and rejoin the committee as his man. It was a risky course, but perhaps shorter than waiting for Sohan Lal to die. So he nodded.

'Kartar Singhji and Ramvilas have offered to resign,' declared Sohan Lal. 'I will convey your decision to Harilalji, and I will inform the central committee of your sacrifice.'

The councillors, who had been sitting in the cold outside, barged into the shop at that moment, blowing clouds of fog and rubbing their hands in frenzied attempts to keep warm. The urn had run out of tea, they informed Ramvilas. He had it replenished. When the inauguration ceremony ended an hour later, he sent everyone home with a cotton bud behind the ear, soaked in ruh hina.

Some day, when he has built up a base of customers, he can dispense with the brand Bhagwan Das and Sons and rename the shop Ramvilas Vimal Kumar. He has a comfortable stock of attars – stolen from the original shop – which he will mix with cheaper scents. Few can combine natural oils with synthetics as skilfully as he can, and most cannot tell the difference. As the shop expands, he will drop the second name, and then it will be Ramvilas and Sons. He has no sons, and his daughters must soon be married off, but Ramvilas and Sons sounds more distinguished than, say, Ramvilas and Company. It implies lineage and suggests continuity. It may even be the beginning of a long line, a dynasty . . .

Chitra comes back into the shop to tell Ramvilas that the photographer is ready. He steps outside, flashes a wide smile, and holds up a poster of Gopal Das. It has a picture of the candidate, with the caption 'Vote for a Poor Man, vote for Gopal Das!' running below it in Hindi. The photographer takes a few shots.

'When can I come again to speak to the candidate?' Chitra asks Ramvilas.

'I will arrange an interview,' he says vaguely, and presses a campaign pamphlet into her hands. She tells the photographer to pack up, aware that his trip, like hers, has been worthless. She will have to come back. Ramvilas, on seeing that Chitra is about to leave, runs into the shop and emerges with a small bottle in his hand, which he presents to her.

'This is attar jasmine,' he gushes. 'Made from the purest flowers!'

She looks at the bottle uncertainly, disinclined to accept anything from him, but stows it in her handbag. Ramvilas looks approvingly at her and declares, 'Gopal Das will bring back the fragrance of jasmine to India!'

Collective folly, egregious arrogance, ludicrous celebration of unworkable aircraft, faulty missiles and outdated technology, distasteful wallowing in the idiocy of Jawaharlal Nehru . . . thinks Sohan Lal, seated uncomfortably on his steel chair. Nehru must have seen such grand parades in Red Square or Tiananmen Square – where Communist leaders strove to project an image of triumph to a credulous world – and thought he would replicate the orgy in his starving nation. Like them, he pulled a shade over grinding poverty and cruel inequity. How much of his idiocy was pure incompetence, and how much a heartless manipulation of history? We will never know now, sighs Sohan Lal, but we continue to parade these old steel tubes as if they were real missiles, these outrageously plumed horsemen strutting around like peacocks, unfit for a fistfight, let alone great battles with China and Pakistan.

The chairs are placed too close together. Sohan Lal's body spills over into the one on his right, occupied by an MLA from south Delhi who belongs to the Congress Party. Both his party and his constituency make it incumbent upon him to regard Sohan Lal with disdain, so the two have had little contact in the last hour. It is cold. Sohan Lal huddles inside his thick brown coat, but no such protection is offered to his legs, which shiver uncontrollably under his dhoti. The cotton bud of attar wedged behind his earlobe is stale. Cold and crowds have served to reduce its efficacy and his nostrils are filled with unfamiliar, unpleasant odours. The MLA section of the stalls is exposed to the wind. To the right, where ministers of the government of Delhi sit on padded seats, a cloth pavilion offers some shelter. Further away still is the box for central ministers and Members of Parliament, who lounge comfortably on sofas. Beyond them is the VVIP box where the prime minister sits with the French president, the chief guest at this year's parade. Their enclosure is constructed of bulletproof glass, and electric heaters keep them warm. In front of their room, on a lower platform, stands the president of India, looking tired as he accepts the salute of an interminable procession. From his hard steel chair, Sohan Lal casts another wistful glance at the higher rows. Thirty years of public service and he still does not get a padded seat at the Republic Day parade.

'*Ghoda, ghoda, ghoda*!' screams Chimpu.

'Quiet!' admonishes Sohan Lal, although the entire assembly has burst into dutiful applause at the appearance of the sixty-first cavalry regiment. The horses are monstrously large and the riders sit officiously in ornate saddles, plumes dancing as their horses move to the rhythm of a marching band. This is a circus for children, thinks Sohan Lal, not a serious army for the defence of the country.

He regrets having brought Bunty, Chimpu and Vicky with him, although it had been his idea. 'They will watch it on television for the rest of their lives,' he had said. 'Let them see it as it really is. Let them take pride in their country once a year!' But children cannot sit through three hours of continuous grandstanding. He is not sure what prompted his offer. He has always viewed the Republic Day parade with suspicion, part Congress propaganda and part wasteful braggadocio. Perhaps he was seeking companionship during the parade, even that provided by ungrateful, intractable, excitable boys of five, four and three. He knew he would sit in the MLA section, surrounded by colleagues who were not friends, so the presence of his grandsons would provide solace. Or he has succumbed, as he often does, to the need to emphasise his position as a man with a seat in the MLA section. He is embarrassed by his own insecurity. Why does he strive to prove himself to Ramesh and Sushma as if he were perennially on notice? It must be the new sign that says Sushma Fancy Dresses. The replacement of the name Jamna Lal Kishori Mal was a watershed, even more so than the transfer of his attar cabinet out of the shop and the relegation of Lakshmi to a small recess hidden above the computer monitor. As long as the old sign hung there – bearing the names of his father and one of the uncles who advised him against leaving Bikaner – he felt the shop was his own. After thirty years, during which he had lost almost all contact with his uncles and their families, the shop still linked him to the past, leading his branch back to the trunk, and then down to the roots of his lineage in Nawalgarh. Sushma Fancy Dresses is a name devoid of genealogy. It is an alien label, chosen out of expediency, rootless and meaningless, too concise and well formed. And now it is firmly lodged above the business he built.

He does not like going to the shop any more. Ramesh is talking about removing the Lakshmi alcove from its space above the computer. 'It takes up too much space,' he complains, 'and makes the shop look old-fashioned.' What a fool the boy is! Does he not know that when the goddess of wealth leaves, she takes prosperity with her? 'We will not remove her,' Ramesh conceded. 'We will place her in a rack on the lower shelves where customers cannot see her, and someone will light one joss-stick – only one, so the odour will disperse quickly – every morning to appease her.' Ramesh cannot tolerate the gaddi either, even after it shrank to a pad in the far corner, barely large enough to hold Sohan Lal. He wants to replace it with more shelves, and thus uproot the last vestige of Sohan Lal's authority. Once that is done, he has informed his father, he will bring Sushma to sit with him in the shop – his own wife, a girl of good family, a mother of three sons.

The removal of the sign has caused it all. And that is why he must yield to vanity whenever he has the chance. The boys had to be woken up at five on a cold morning and bundled screaming into the car, which dropped them at the edge of Rajpath – even the MLA badge would not allow it beyond the first checkpoint – and they battled biting wind the rest of the way. He was grateful that the VIP enclosure was reached by separate queues and had its own security check. Those in the stalls – the 'common people' for whose presumed benefit Nehru had conjured up the magic show – must have suffered humiliating inspections through three cordons of police. They would have taken off their sweaters in the frosty morning, pulled up their shirts and allowed fat, hairy hands to run over their chests. Some would have pulled down trousers or pulled up dhotis . . . Yet there they stand, in their tens of thousands, clapping dutifully, fertile landscape for television cameras and combustible material for terrorists, who must salivate at the prospect of countless arms and legs hurled into the sky.

The crowd is smaller again this year. It has contracted as televisions have proliferated, and terrorist attacks acquired the regularity of Holi and Divali, the monsoon and the sun itself. The significance of Republic Day, so obvious to Nehru, is lost on no one. The government marks it with a parade, others with explosions and massacres. Last night, twelve hours before the parade was to start in Delhi, five armed men dragged twenty-three Hindus – nine women, ten men and four children – out of their homes in Wandhama near Srinagar, and shredded them with bullets. Then they set fire to a temple and a house, and melted into the darkness of Kashmir valley. It is a message to the government, and it has fallen on deaf ears, because the parade is progressing as planned, the president stands listlessly, the prime minister stares into nothing, and the French president nods appreciatively at the circus, displaying appropriate *joie de vivre* as befits a chief guest. The great spectacle of the Indian nation will continue, regardless of massacres and earthquakes.

The children fell asleep almost immediately after they had taken their seats in the VIP enclosure, cold winds and hard seats notwithstanding. Sohan Lal had looked benignly at them. How innocent they were, and how oblivious of the charade around them! They had slept through most of the ceremony while Sohan Lal paid attention to every excruciating detail. The presidents of India and France were welcomed, the tricolour was unfurled, the national anthem played, and a salute of twenty-one guns was followed by the presentation of gallantry awards. After the investiture ceremony, four Mi-8 helicopters carrying the national flag glided over Rajpath, causing all heads to tilt skyward. Before they had passed, three Sukhoi Su-30s appeared menacingly on the horizon. A shudder passed through the crowd. The aircraft, flying above and much faster than the helicopters, let loose a shower of petals that fluttered downward. Some were trapped by helicopter rotors and spun in violent whirlpools. People in the stalls, who had shielded their faces in expectation of bombs, heaved a sigh of relief as loudspeakers announced that the aircraft doing the 'fly-past' had mistakenly come in before their time. The helicopters fluttered away, their thunder stolen. The crowd continued to watch the rain of flowers, which had been meant for the president but was shared more equitably between him and the lesser people. This is democracy, thought Sohan Lal, or poor aim. The president brushed off a few petals that clung to his sparse hair, looking – in Sohan Lal's view – quite unlike the supreme commander of the armed forces, which he was. A few petals – sunflower – had settled on the faces of Bunty, Chimpu and Vicky. Sohan Lal had not removed them.

The next hour was a mind-numbing parade of khaki-clad regiments and contingents of paramilitary and auxiliary forces, which melted into one another and became a mass of grey-green, until the NCC group lost its marching rhythm, stopped and regrouped by on-the-spot marching. The president, who stood on a platform to take the salute, lost his balance and stumbled, causing a flurry of activity in his security detail. For a moment, Sohan Lal wondered if he had been shot, until he remembered that he – like the prime minister and the French president seated behind him – was protected by a sheet of bulletproof glass. The men of the Special Protection Group standing behind him broke his fall, repositioned him centrally on the platform, reattached his right hand – palm down – to his temple, and directed the NCC contingent to continue. A short announcement was made to request the public to take their seats again.

The trick riders of the Border Security Force were the ones who woke the children. They flowed down Rajpath on motorcycles, preceded by the sputtering of twenty engines, balanced on the seats in unlikely formations, connected by human ladders, chains and pyramids. Once awake, the children sat spellbound, watching mock-ups of great missiles glide by on trucks. Nehru's gift to the nation, thought Sohan Lal sourly – grand parades and the shells of missiles.

It has now been three hours. The children are tired and hungry. An occasional horse stirs them out of their lethargy, but the experiment has been a failure. It is time for pavilions and floats to drive by, one for each state, and one for each government department. A pavilion for

Rajasthan, a pavilion for the army, a pavilion for Bihar . . . The Bihar pavilion shows a coal mine in Jharia, with smiling miners standing at the shafts and holding up black gold. There are two worlds, thinks Sohan Lal, one in Bihar and one on the float. The one is inhuman in its penury and brutality, the other is sanitised by the insensitivity of Indian officialese. The one is mean in every detailed fibre, the other has no detail at all because it is made of crude cardboard. It is an exhibit fit for children, naïve enough for their minds, painted in sufficiently broad strokes for their comprehension.

Inside his bulletproof bubble, the president stares through the Bihar tableau with an inscrutable smile. The prime minister, behind him, is engaged in delivering a lengthy soliloquy to the French president. Sohan Lal is certain that he is not discussing the parade. He is discoursing, perhaps, on the leftist revolution in India, employing Marxist phrases he learned at college. He is a soft, effeminate man, thinks Sohan Lal, meant to while away time in dimly lit rooms at the India International Centre, engaged in endless circumlocutions about Fabian socialism, causing no harm, making no difference, stepping on no one's toes. Even now, thrust into the prime minister's position by accident, he appears uncertain of his power and is reluctant to exercise it. He is neither gentry nor upstart, lacking Gandhi pedigree to be the one and the bluster of grass-roots politicians to be the other. The accident of history that made him prime minister will be rectified in two months, thinks Sohan Lal. He is officially a 'caretaker' prime minister now, and no one expects him to remain even that after the election. The ludicrous coalition he heads will disintegrate. Why, he will be fortunate to retain his seat in Parliament. Sohan Lal shakes his head, marvelling that there are still people who expect this prime minister to return to power.

Two months ago, after Congress withdrew support from the government, news of Naresh Agrawal's heart-attack spread rapidly. The next morning, Sohan Lal had the driver take him to Harilal Gupta's offices. As transport minister in the state government of Delhi, Harilal has his own office suite in the assembly complex. He was in celebratory mood. 'We must express heartfelt condolences,' he had warned. 'Congress will use this to generate sympathy. Remember the Indira wave? We must be careful, very careful.'

They walked out on to the lawn behind Harilal's office. It was almost noon. A late November sun shone pleasantly, having chased away the fog that had hung all morning.

'We must attend the cremation,' said Harilal. 'In fact, I will carry Naresh Agrawal myself! I will lend him my shoulder, for his eighteen years of service to Chandni Chowk.'

'They are not going to Shantivan or Rajghat,' reminded Sohan Lal. 'They will travel a few kilometres outside the city.'

'I did not mean to actually carry him!' admonished Harilal playfully. 'I just meant to place my shoulder under him for a short while.'

Sohan Lal chuckled, embarrassed at having made the ridiculous assumption that Harilal, transport minister, would suffer himself to be burdened with a dead body. He had suddenly felt sorry for himself. Here he was, walking on Harilal's lawn, listening to Harilal's opinions, keeping one step behind him to indicate that he could choose the direction of their walk. The garden was an assertion of Harilal's power. Sohan Lal had no interest in flowers aside from the attars they yielded, but he could tell that the lawn was well tended. The grass was lush and flowers grew in abundance. Who could look out on such a profusion of red and yellow in Delhi unless he was an industrialist or a minister, or a dead Gandhi with his own necropolis along the Yamuna river?

Harilal noticed him gazing at the flowers and added his commentary: 'These are bougainvillaeas. November is not the season for them, but I insist on having them all year round.' He pointed to the red-brick wall surrounding the garden. 'I had that raised and topped with barbed wire. There was a breach of security three years ago when someone jumped over it to steal my flowers.'

My flowers, thought Sohan Lal. What a wonderful ring those words had! My flowers, my garden, my office, my people, my city, my country . . .

'Suleman is my main concern,' said Harilal suddenly.

Sohan Lal had stopped and re-oriented his mind. It irritated him that Harilal assumed himself to be the IPP candidate for Chandni Chowk before the committee had met or discussed it, and even before the election was announced. 'We do not know if there will be an election.'

'There will,' declared Harilal. 'Nareshji made that assumption, and he could not be wrong. Why else would he take the news so hard?'

'Suleman will stand as an independent,' said Sohan Lal. 'We do not yet know whom Congress will choose to replace Naresh Agrawal.'

'Nareshji does not have a son,' Harilal pointed out.

Sohan Lal nodded, having often consoled himself with this when comparing his fortunes with Naresh Agrawal. 'Two daughters, but no son.'

'Then his wife will be the Congress candidate,' said Harilal.

'A housewife!' Sohan Lal scoffed.

'She will not split the Musalman vote. That will go in a solid bloc to Suleman. Lower castes are with him too – rickshavalas, chaivalas, thelavalas, hawkers . . . Congress stands no chance, even if they do convince Nareshji's wife to stand. Suleman will take OBCs, SCs and Musalmans, and that is enough to win in Chandni Chowk if there is no split.'

Harilal stopped abruptly, throwing Sohan Lal off-balance in his attempt not to overshoot. 'We need a secular candidate.'

Harilal was not a loquacious man. He always chose his words carefully. Sohan Lal wondered what could be on his mind, and when it had been made up. 'A Musalman?' he asked.

'No, a Hindu who appeals to Musalmans.'

'How can a Hindu appeal to Musalmans?' enquired Sohan Lal.

'Because he has Musalman friends, because he is poor, because he has a secular image that will tug at the heartstrings of leftists and Communists. Such a man can split lower-caste Hindus and Musalmans with Suleman. Not a single trader will vote for such a man or for Suleman. Those votes will come in a bloc to IPP.'

It dawned on Sohan Lal that Harilal already knew exactly the type of man he wanted. 'A man with nothing to distinguish him from another human being,' said Harilal. 'A man who looks like every rickshavala, every coolie, every tailor and every hawker in Chandni Chowk. A man so devoid of distinguishing traits that he is often mistaken for someone else. A man whose name no one can remember, whose voice no one can recall, whose face no one can bring to mind. A man who makes no marks in the sand, leaves no imprint on the parchment of life. A man without family, ambition, plans, preoccupations, history or future.'

Sohan Lal's heart beat fast. He had spoken to Kartar Singh before coming to meet Harilal Gupta, and the sardar had put forward a name. At the time, he had thought the idea foolish . . . 'Who would vote for such a man?' Sohan Lal asked.

'Who would not?' countered Harilal Gupta. 'He is a man everyone identifies with but no one wants to become, a man who is poor, docile and gullible, incapable of guile or aggression. A common man. A simple man. A man as harmless as a fly, a man of the people . . . Can you get me such a man?'

'I have known him for twenty-five years,' said Sohan Lal.

The next day, Sohan Lal, Harilal and the entire IPP committee accompanied the procession that took Naresh Agrawal to his cremation. The Congress Party bade him farewell with much noise. A request was made that he be given a small plot along the Yamuna, sandwiched between Gandhi in Rajghat and Nehru in Shantivan. For all his staying power, however, he had been a mere MP. That stretch of the necropolis is reserved for the greater ghosts of prime ministers and their families, so the request was denied. The procession began in Chandni Chowk, where it stretched from Red Fort to Fatehpuri Masjid, and wound its way along the Yamuna to the outskirts of Delhi, where more than a hundred thousand people – so claimed the Congress Party – watched his cremation at a funeral Shah Jahan would have envied.

Over the next three days, Sohan Lal and Harilal Gupta devised the outlines of the Lala Surajmal Scheme. A week later, Kartar Singh and Ramvilas resigned from the committee and gave up their membership of the IPP, eliciting gloating commentary from Congress and the Communists. Two days later Ramesh threw Gopal out of Sushma Fancy Dresses and a week after that the secular candidate filed his nomination papers as an independent, and was allotted his election symbol – a cup of tea.

Sohan Lal does not know, and does not much care, why Kartar Singh supported the Lala Surajmal Scheme with such enthusiasm when some resistance would have been natural. He has a better understanding of Ramvilas's motives. After the election, Ramvilas expects a quick rehabilitation. He has probably imagined a welcome ceremony – the wayward son coming back into the family – and an enhanced position in the committee. He does not know that the vacancies created by their two resignations, and the one created by Jugal Kishor's, will all be filled before the election, making re-entry difficult. Harilal shall become MP and Sohan Lal shall be re-elected MLA in the assembly elections that follow later this year, because he will allot himself Harilal's assembly segment of Chandni Chowk, which has never voted against the IPP. And if something should happen to Harilal – death is the only retirement for politicians – there will be a natural candidate to take over the Lok Sabha seat for Chandni Chowk.

'*Haathi*! *Haathi*!' screams Vicky.

Sohan Lal's reverie is shattered. The tableaux of states have completed their monotonous crawl. Vicky's attention has been captured by rows of caparisoned elephants who saunter down Rajpath, bearing monstrous howdahs, inside which sit dozens of children who have received this year's bravery awards. They wave at the crowd as at a throng of adoring subjects. Vicky – who has just learned to identify animals, to Sushma's delight – is beside himself at the sight of so many elephants passing so close to him. Sohan Lal feels a tug of enthusiasm. How wonderful it is to have his grandsons with him! If only Ramesh and Sushma had been more particular about their names – true, they all have a 'school name' which is written in the register, but no one will call them anything other than Bunty, Chimpu and Vicky, which sound like names for dogs. They are healthy boys, inheritors of a great business, custodians of the family name, guardians of its legacy and wealth: they should have had weighty names, like Jamna Lal, Kishori Mal, Sohan Lal . . . Such names imply ancestry and sit comfortably on men of consequence, even if they are long, out of fashion, and too closely associated with old men in dhotis. If a boy is named Chimpu, how does he know what kind of man he must grow into?

The president is now seated on a chair, because the caparisoned elephants are not part of the armed-forces parade. He, too, will be replaced as soon as his term is over, thinks Sohan Lal. This is the first time, in fifty years of sham elections, that a central government of the IPP appears possible in Delhi. No one thinks that it will get a majority in the Lok Sabha, but it will seek allies – fickle allies, unstable coalitions – and make unsavoury compromises. It will court every vote assiduously and fight each seat with determination. This is also the first time it appears possible that the IPP will win Chandni Chowk. But then there is Suleman.

Sohan Lal looks to his left and watches Suleman, seated six chairs away from him, beyond Vicky. How old is this man? Barely over forty, and can pass as younger if you go by the firm skin and angular jaw. He is a mere MLA like himself. He sits on the same hard steel chair, as far removed as him from the prime minister and the French president. Yet he is on the edge of it, ever ready to leap up and bound forward. His clothes are neatly pressed, his hair is oiled and pasted slickly to his head, his pencil moustache is combed. He certainly dyes his hair. But these, of course, are not the attributes that strike those who meet Suleman because his face is constructed round his eyes – which never falter, never turn away, but bore through everything with unseemly arrogance. If Harilal Gupta does not win for Chandni Chowk, this will be the man responsible.

The elephants have passed, and the parade is drawing to a close. The children are slumped in their chairs. The president's entourage is preparing to whisk him away with his guests. Four white Ambassadors roll down Rajpath, shepherding a black Mercedes. The president, looking tired, is helped into it. The French president follows him politely, and the cavalcade moves down Rajpath in a blare of sirens, headed for Rashtrapati Bhavan. Security men scurry to prepare for the departure of the next VVIP, the prime minister.

Sohan Lal shakes his grandsons awake. If they remember this 26 January, they will perhaps recall only the elephants, not the president, the prime minister nor even Suleman. That is just as well, because elephants will walk down Rajpath long after the three are gone.

A small stampede has begun in the common areas, where the police have been over-zealous in herding the public out of the bamboo enclosures erected for the parade. The crowd has waited more than twenty minutes for the departure of the VVIPs. Now that the prime minister seems to be stepping into a car, they have made a frantic movement toward the gates, where policemen have forced them to walk single file. This has resulted in a ripple travelling backward into the bamboo corrals, where a wide river had suddenly confronted a narrow gorge. The stampede is minor: a few people may sustain scratches, but little more. Sohan Lal walks down the rows of VIP chairs carefully, holding Bunty's hand, having ensured that Bunty holds Chimpu and Chimpu holds Vicky.

Kartar Singh pays off the taxi and limps into the airport terminal. He keeps his head down and walks with a briefcase pressed to his side, hoping no one will pay too much attention. Only ticketed passengers are allowed into the terminal. He shows his and shuffles past. The airport is busy so early in the morning, and the line at his counter is long. Normally, he would have tried to cut through, pretending some emergency for his child, mother or wife. Today, he does not dare to draw attention to himself and joins the queue, behind a woman and her three children, and frets that he will miss his flight.

Any one of these policemen who stalk the terminal with walkie-talkies might be a CBI officer armed with his name and photograph. The woman in front of him might be an undercover agent. It is far-fetched – that a harried mother of three is quietly scanning the crowd for his face – but is that not what undercover policing is all about? Will she now try to strike up a conversation? What should he give as his name? It should be appropriate to his age – Mohinder Singh, Joginder Singh, Bhupinder Singh – and he must tell her he never married, to avoid giving names for his wife and children. He must be casual, cheerful, nonchalant, like a man who travels often. He can handle her all right, but what if the man in front of her joins the conversation? He will surely ask what Kartar Singh does for a living. He cannot possibly mention Jasjit General Store when they are watching it day and night.

He should have extricated himself from this business when he could, two years ago, when Sukhbir had just died and the dons had not warmed to his so-called 'touch'. Now he is known as the man whom victory follows even in the riskiest bets. It is he who wins or loses a match, not the players or umpires. He can steer it simply by placing a bet. After India won the third final and lifted the Freedom Cup in Calcutta, Bhai himself had telephoned. He was ecstatic. His voice boomed triumphantly from Dubai, or wherever he was. 'You have the touch, sardarji! No team has ever made three hundred and sixteen before. It was *your* money that steered the game!'

Kartar Singh had mumbled something about his one and a half lakhs.

'I will look into that,' said Bhai noncommittally. 'But you are a patriotic man. You bet on India even when everyone thought it would lose! I will call again when I need you to bail out India.'

Bhai had hung up, firming up Kartar Singh's position as an unwilling financier on bets the don deems risky, bets that Kartar Singh neither understands nor controls, and often does not know about. They are complex, and the odds are calculated from derivatives of scores rather than the scores themselves. 'You have the touch!' the don's men say. But when they sit down and calculate his winnings, they always find derivatives that are too large or too small, and money flows back in driblets, or not at all. He has tried to keep up with the numbers by watching each match carefully, but his heart is not in the game. He is increasingly isolated in Vasant Vihar. 'It will be our prison,' Sukhbir had said. How right she was!

He assigned the task of collecting statistics to Salim, but he was absent-minded and clumsy, dozing off in the middle of matches and missing important runs. And that was when Kartar Singh became aware of beefy, safari-suited men lounging around Lajpatrai Market, walking into the store to enquire about leather belts or mixers, asking where the owner was, never buying anything. It was the CBI, no doubt. Was Salim colluding with them? The ungrateful bastard! A young man is no different from a whore – he will go with whoever pays him most. Bishan, whom he had raised almost as his own son and treated much like Jasjit, was not above treachery. What faith could he have in Salim, a Musalman from some Bangladeshi school run by a madam, a man with treachery in his very blood?

Sohan Lal had come to see him the morning after Naresh Agrawal's death, and Kartar Singh suggested that he loan him the chaivala for a few months. Perhaps the man could be taught to maintain statistics for cricket matches. Although he did not say this to Sohan Lal, Kartar Singh had also hoped the chaivala could be induced to talk about those four lakhs. If he had them, they would be in his kholi because his stall had been searched thoroughly before it was demolished. True, he showed no signs of possessing the money, and four lakhs was not a large sum, but a man must not leave loose ends when tying the knot of his life. Once that business was settled, Kartar Singh would have cleared his debt to Sohan Lal. Then he would forget about the dons, the CBI, the politics of the IPP committee, and go to Canada.

The next day, he threw out Salim and the accountants. The store was not earning much anyway. Why keep them around as the eyes and ears of the CBI? They were shocked, all of them, the turncoats! With the chaivala installed in the store, keeping the cricket records, Kartar Singh thought the danger had passed. But then the safari-suit visits, which had stopped when Salim left, resumed. And now he knows they have always been in pursuit, though they were momentarily thrown off the scent.

It is shameless how Sohan Lal has been going around touting the chaivala's candidacy as his own idea. Let him have that pleasure. Let him have his Lala Surajmal Scheme. No one is fooled by such tricks, though it was pleasing to see Ramvilas squirm and fidget when he was forced to resign. Serves him right. How dare that clerk presume to call himself a seth just because he has managed to swindle poor Vimal? If Lala Surajmal had kicked him out before he died, the business would not have left the family.

Sohan Lal has his eye on the parliamentary seat in Chandni Chowk, which might fall to him after Harilal Gupta. It is a futile ambition. Sohan Lal is a few years older than Harilal Gupta, who is not yet sixty. Harilal's waist may have expanded uncontrollably, but who heard of a man giving up a seat because of poor health? Harilal will live long, if only to fill the Chandni Chowk seat. Sohan Lal is fortunate, however, that Jugal Kishor has dropped out. He left for Hardwar without even bothering to resign from the committee a full month before Sohan Lal had hatched the Lala Surajmal Scheme. The doctor said it was sciatica, but everyone knew Jugal Kishor's two sons had broken his heart with the wall they erected right through Mangat Ram Nawal Kishor. He was given a warm send-off by the IPP committee. Everyone was gracious and Sohan Lal was especially generous with his compliments. 'I have reached the age when a man must take sanyaas,' said Jugal Kishor at the ceremony, forgetting that, at sixty-one, he was two years younger than Sohan Lal. 'He must renounce worldly possessions and go into the forest,' he declared. That was dramatic, because in fact he was going to live with his wife in a flat in Hardwar, which he had built over the last two years with money he had kept from his sons. 'The next news you have of me,' declared Jugal Kishor, 'will be of my death.' There were sincere protests at this train of thought. 'Everyone can afford to be generous to a dead man,' said Jugal Kishor. The committee members had chuckled uncomfortably. 'So a man must enjoy death while still alive,' Jugal Kishor said philosophically, 'because his fellow humans will then love him truly.' They had clapped loudly to drown these words. 'The *Bhagavad Gita* counsels that all those of advanced age should consider this living death,' Jugal Kishor had said at the end and looked hard at Sohan Lal, who pretended not to notice.

He himself is not old enough to go to Hardwar, thinks Kartar Singh. And he does not have a wife, as Jugal Kishor does, to share his last moments. Very well, he will go to Bangalore, and then Ootacamund in the south. He will live simply, alone and unnoticed among unfamiliar people in an unfamiliar place. They are watching the store, no doubt. It is good to have the chaivala there. He knows nothing so he will tell them nothing. They are watching the house in Vasant Vihar too, but they will find no paper records there. In a few months, after the cricket-betting scandal has dissipated, he will come back to Delhi to sell the store and the house in Vasant Vihar. And then, for his own sanyaas, he will go to Canada.

The line is moving so slowly that he will surely miss his flight. He approaches a uniformed man, who tells him the flight to Bangalore has been delayed to allow for late passengers. Ah, he thinks gratefully, they are waiting for him.

The official takes him to a second queue to speed him through, and he suddenly finds himself at the counter. He fumbles with his ticket. Why does the girl scan it so carefully? Does she see something odd in it? It is a standard ticket, economy class. She asks if he is checking in any baggage. He says no. She looks up quizzically. 'You are travelling all the way to Bangalore without baggage?' she asks. He realises he has been foolish – who goes so far with only a briefcase? She will remember him. 'I am going on a business trip!' he says desperately. 'I will be back soon.'

'This is a one-way ticket,' she points out.

Kartar Singh is furious. Does she bear him a grudge that she is bent on proving him wrong? 'I do not know my return date yet,' he sputters. He knows the two answers do not fit. If he does not know his return date, why is he travelling with only a briefcase? The woman asks him to place it on the scale. He hopes she has decided he is disoriented, and no more.

'Twenty-five kilograms,' she says accusingly. 'What is inside the briefcase?'

Kartar Singh feels beads of sweat on his forehead. The briefcase is half filled with cash. Two lakhs. He wishes he had chosen larger bills. 'Books and ledgers,' he says. 'I can pay for the extra weight.'

'We cannot allow this as hand-baggage. You must check it in.'

Kartar Singh stands at the counter and slumps, trapped. 'Check it in,' he says, with a sigh.

'Unlock it,' she insists.

He asks why.

'Standard procedure for checked-in baggage,' she says. 'If they suspect it contains a bomb or narcotics, they will search it. If they cannot open it, they will break the lock.'

He unlocks it. She weighs it again – as if the unlocking has made it heavier! – then slaps it violently on the conveyor-belt behind her. He watches it flow down the channel and disappear into the wall as he delivers a silent prayer that he will see it again. The briefcase is half full because he had hoped to fill it with money recovered from the chaivala. He had had Bobby ransack the kholi in Khari Baoli last night. Bobby said he scattered every heap of clothes, looked inside every box, ran his knife through every sack of turmeric and black pepper, but found nothing. Perhaps he was lying. Although he has been reliable in the past with much more dangerous assignments, there is a reason that no one trusts a man with a hare-lip. Once the upper teeth are exposed, part of his humanity dissolves away. Also, four lakhs is a large amount for Bobby, enough to turn his head. Perhaps he should have asked the chaivala directly. The man is sitting in the store at this very moment, idling away his time, memorising flowery speeches. What use could he have for the money? Why could he not have revealed where it was and saved him the business with Bobby? In any case, he has now asked Ramvilas to look into it. Perhaps the clerk can uncover what the rabbit could not.

Kartar Singh moves toward the departure gate, clutching his boarding pass. Three men in safari suits are watching him from three different points. He senses them instantly, although they stand far apart and do not communicate with each other. Is this the end, then? It is just as well Bobby did not find those four lakhs. When they open the briefcase, they will find two lakhs, not six.

He takes larger strides toward the gate. He feels he will be safe once he passes through it. Surely they will not follow him into the aircraft? No one will find it suspicious if a man runs through the concourse, thinking he is late for his flight. He tries to break into a trot, but his knee hurts. He looks down at his left leg, and is shocked to see that he is limping horribly. What is going on? Has his knee gone bad again? If only they could see him now, those who snigger that he limps when it is convenient! Or is this cruel punishment for the times when he has played up his disability?

The men are moving toward him! They are converging on the departure gate. Their pace is timed to coincide with his arrival there. He must run faster! Should he turn away? They are taking larger strides! One is almost at the gate. He has passed it and continues beyond. The second loiters and the third has changed course and is now heading toward the check-in counters.

Kartar Singh reaches the gate, flashes his boarding pass, and limps through, unchallenged. '*Sachche Padshah*, you have given me another chance!' he whispers, as he enters the vestibule that will lead him to the aircraft.

Another pyarelal, thinks Gauhar.

The man is thin and sinewy, wasted from exertion. His wife is eight months pregnant. Her belly overflows the saree. She stands in expressionless neutrality, neither happy nor sad at the turn of events. The baby is from one of her customers. Her husband stands apologetically before Gauhar, pointing an accusing finger at the protrusion. 'I beat her soundly when she began to vomit and told me about this!' he says. 'I asked the bitch to take every precaution, but who can trust a woman? I asked her to stuff sugar into her mouth and take long walks in the evening, I asked her to eat two kilograms of datura every day, I even shoved it down her throat, but who can undo what has happened? I took such good care to bring her the best men – always making sure they carried no disease – and she repays me by breeding brats! There is nothing to be done but get a midwife. She will clean her out, rid her of this curse.'

'Get her one, then,' says Gauhar. 'Why have you brought her to me?'

'She will not let me clean out the baby,' protests the man. 'For a month she has begged and screamed. She wants to keep the baby, although she cannot feed another mouth. I told her to get the father to pay! But she has no idea who the father is.'

'He brings me seven men every night,' adds the woman. 'Any one of them could be the sinner.'

'I told her we had no choice but to call a midwife,' says the man. 'Then she fell at my feet.'

As her husband narrates the story, the woman falls at his feet again, in a re-enactment that Gauhar watches with impatience.

'Let me keep this one for my later years, a prop to love me in my old age . . .'

The man laughs and winks at Gauhar. 'If it is a boy, he will be a pimp. If it is a girl, she will be a whore like you.'

The woman continues to snivel, her head crushed against her husband's quivering thighs.

He sighs. 'Even a stone erodes when the wind is persistent,' he declares philosophically. 'So have I. She will have her baby in a month from now.'

Gauhar nods. He understands now.

'What will I eat until her belly is flat again?' asks the man, rhetorically. 'And where will I throw the thing that comes out?' He shakes the woman off his legs and takes a step closer to Gauhar. 'I have thought of getting rid of her!' he whispers. 'I can go to GB Road and find myself a good Nepali girl. But I am a God-fearing man and a man must stick by his wife . . .'

Gauhar sighs. This is a common predicament for a pyarelal. When a man pimps for his wife, pregnancy is doubly inconvenient.

'Today is Eid,' says Gauhar. 'You should spare her.'

The man is overwhelmed by the magnitude of his own sacrifice. He casts a glance of annoyance at his wife, defeated by the impertinence that has put him in such a difficult situation, then looks expectantly at Gauhar.

'Twenty-five per cent,' Gauhar offers. 'Five rounds every day for one week. At the end of the week I will give you twenty-five per cent.'

The man is aghast, or pretends to be. 'Raja Babu! How will I live on twenty-five per cent? She will do all the work. Why should she get only twenty-five per cent?'

Gauhar lets his eyes rest on the woman, who wilts before his gaze. Then he directs a sneer at the man. 'She will do all the work? Take her away, then. She can do it by herself and you can keep a hundred per cent. And you can also protect her when the police come.'

He signals to Munna, who begins to lead the pair out of the room.

'Raja Babu!' The man's tone indicates an acceptance of terms. 'Can I have an advance?' he asks pitifully.

Gauhar nods. Munna hands over twenty rupees to the man, who presses the note gratefully to his forehead, then retreats from the room.

'Pyarelal!' mutters Gauhar. 'Pimp!'

He does not bother to look at the wife as he abuses her husband. She betrays no response. Now he studies her. She is slight. Her blouse is wrapped tightly round narrow shoulders. Every part of her body except the protruding belly is covered by a yellow saree, which is also wrapped round her head, making her seem oddly respectable. With a chuckle, Gauhar pulls the saree from her head, exposing jet-black hair in a tight braid. He tugs again to expose the blouse, and is disappointed to see small breasts. This will have to do.

'Bholanath!' he screams.

Munna comes into the room with a reefer of ganja. Gauhar takes a long puff, offers some to the woman, then flops down on an old sofa in the corner. He asks the woman to sit beside him, using a bottle of bootleg whisky to lure her to the sofa. Then he dismisses Munna. 'Allow no one into the den,' he orders, as Munna leaves.

He knows he can trust Munna, who is fiercely loyal to him – much more so than the others, who are out working the streets of Chandni Chowk, Shahdara and Naya Bajar, picking pockets, stealing stereo systems, grabbing bags of cash, selling liquor and hashish. They are supposed to give him fifty per cent of all their earnings every evening, but he knows they never do. It is unrealistic to expect complete honesty in thieves. He is afraid they will rebel if he pushes too hard for his share. He has noticed sullen looks, especially on the faces of Johnny and Partho, who are about to turn twenty. At that age, a pickpocket graduates to more rewarding work, and it is no longer cost-effective to have him in the gang. That is the age when an honest pickpocket turns into a rustam. He is not worried about Aftab. Although Aftab is the eldest – second only to Gauhar in seniority – the bond of Binodpur ties them together, and he has often hinted that Aftab is his deputy and second-in-command without explicitly anointing him. He needs to weed out Johnny and Partho over the next year without inciting an uprising. He does not want to go the way of the previous Raja Babu, rotting in Inderlal's jail.

That Inderlal was a reasonable man – full of bluster at first, but calm and calculating once he realised that Gauhar meant business and would not be cowed. Gauhar had recognised him on entering his office. This was the same rustam who had questioned him after the Rajghat pissing, and had taken him to court in a police jeep. Then he had been a two-bit policeman. Now he appeared to be a big man. His moustache was thicker, his uniform spiffier, and his swagger that of a full inspector. Gauhar knew the type. He had seen hundreds in Tihar, and Bobby had taught him not to be intimidated by them.

Buying out Munna rather than Raja Babu was, thinks Gauhar, the wisest decision of his life.

'What about Raja Babu?' Partho had asked, when Gauhar stepped out with a crying Munna.

'I will have him released tomorrow,' said Gauhar. 'That will give you one full day to hide, because when he comes out he wants to kill Munna and the rest of you. He thinks you set him up.'

Aftab raised a hand and shouted, 'Gauhar Muhammad *zindabad*!' Munna forgot his wailing and repeated it. The rest joined in. They carried him back to the park on their shoulders, and they never asked about Raja Babu again.

There was a great celebration in the park that night, long after all trains had left Old Delhi railway station, taxis had disappeared, rickshavalas had gone to sleep and coolies were snoring. He remembers little of the next few weeks except that he was in a perpetual daze of bholanath and Chou En-lai. They took him all over Chandni Chowk, into crowds, buses, cinema halls, bus stops, circuses . . . They stole everywhere, tore and cut, nicked and slit. Their hands were so nimble, their spirits so high, their hearts so bold. He remembers being led by his hand, the stump flailing drunkenly in the air, through that great festival when he thinks he saw Gopal Bhai. Ah, to be always swimming in a sea of bholanath, watching money flutter in the wind all around you! What can a man not do with one hand?

It took him a month to get used to the liquor and ganja, and to anoint himself Raja Babu. The boys do not have the hidden cash-box that he has, and they do not have Inderlal's ear. He never told them how much he paid Inderlal, or whether he had paid anything at all. They imagined wild and fantastic sums and he encouraged such speculation, with the belief that he had more money stowed away. Life is easy as Raja Babu. He need not pick pockets any more. He was not much good at it anyway. It is an occupation for two hands attached to the same pair of shoulders. Ah, he would much rather be a Raja Babu. Fifty per cent of everything is not a bad rate in return for police protection, even if it works out to twenty or thirty per cent.

He likes the boys. They remind him of friends he had in Binodpur, before his parents followed Bhola Dada across the Ichchamati river to Bongaon, and then to the endless chain of trains and buses until they vanished behind Red Fort. 'This is the river Ichchamati,' Bhola Dada had said. 'It grants every wish.' It has indeed granted Gauhar's wishes, sort of. He speaks Bengali with Partho, Johnny and Aftab, just as he spoke it in Binodpur. Johnny and Partho have an odd accent, but he feels he has returned home, somehow, when he talks to them. They all know he is from Binodpur, and he makes a great show of being Bangladeshi, because they would not accept anyone else as Raja Babu.

It is convenient that they are all younger and weaker than him. Even with his one hand, he could wrestle any of them to the ground. If two or three were to attack him together, however . . . But Aftab will never turn against him, and Munna keeps watch over him. He sits at his feet as a dog sits next to his master, springing to fulfil every wish. If Johnny and Partho try to storm the house, Munna will be his prop, holding it up.

The woman has begun to relax under the influence of Chou En-lai. He pulls her closer and examines her face carefully. She is not beautiful but she has the ripe feel of a woman in bloom. Ah, no. He will save that for GB Road. This is business, not to be mixed with pleasure. He gives her another bottle of whisky. She holds it casually. A giggle trips from her mouth, which hangs open.

'What is your name?' asks Gauhar playfully.

'Ruby,' she says, and giggles again.

It is not her name, Gauhar knows. It is the trade name she uses with her customers, which is fine with him. He will call her Ruby. He takes the bottle from her. She does not want to let go but he is much stronger.

'*Bijness!*' he admonishes. A whore must never forget that she has been contracted for business, not pleasure. He pulls her up from the sofa and rearranges her saree so it covers her bosom. It will not do to have her look like a whore among respectable clients. 'Come.'

He pulls her outside the room. Munna stands up at their approach. With a nod at him – he will remain on guard until the others return from their rounds – Gauhar sets out with Ruby. They walk through lanes that connect Shahdara to the Red Fort area and stake out the intersection where Chandni Chowk meets Netaji Subhas Road. It is the busiest junction near Red Fort. Thousands of scooters, rickshas, cars and buses pass through it at this hour. The light turns red. Scooters slam on their brakes reluctantly, buses screech and grind to a halt, three-wheelers teeter dangerously, then lodge themselves into some crevice among the cars, all raring to go as soon as the light turns green. Two hundred engines idle in unison, belching black smoke and sending a thunderous roar into the sky.

Gauhar advances with Ruby into the stalled maze. He has only a few moments to select his client. Marutis, Mercedes, cars with dark windows, three-wheelers, rickshas, scooters . . . The car must not be too rich or too modern, yet not quite middle class. The middle class is full of stingy bastards. A family is better than a single man. A small family, perhaps, like the man balancing himself on his scooter, revving up his accelerator with practised impatience. His wife wears a cotton saree with a pleasant print, not too expensive but not cheap. She is a little plump, and in her arms is a child of no more than three months.

'*Maayi baap!*' Gauhar calls to them, throwing out the right hand with its stump and pointing to Ruby's swollen belly. 'Mother! Father!'

Ruby sets up a terrifying wail that begins with a high-pitched scream and descends to a low, guttural snivelling. Her hands flail, tearing at her hair, then descending over her breasts and coming to rest on her belly. 'My wife is in pain, *maayi baap!*' says Gauhar to the man, casting woeful glances at the wife seated behind him. 'Nine months already, and who will feed the extra mouth? Take her to the hospital, *maayi baap*! Her water has broken. Take her to a doctor, if you have compassion in your heart! Take her to someone who can care, someone who will deliver the baby, or she will plop it right in your lap, right here in the traffic in front of your scooter! Hurry! Can you not see her water has broken? This is not a matter that can be discussed! This is the very basis of all that defines motherhood! Will you let her die on the street, madam, right before your very eyes? There is a child in her belly, three months younger than your own. Think of the child as yours, think of the cry of a woman in pain. Reach deep down into your heart, you mother-fucking bastards sitting comfortably on your scooter, and find the nugget of pain that will stick in your throat . . . Ah, you do not have space on your scooter? You are going to visit your sister and you cannot pause to help us? No matter. Can you give us the fare for the taxi we will take? Do not trouble yourself, just give us a little money and we will take a fucking bus to the hospital – but hurry! Can you not see her water has broken? Can you not understand the urgency of the situation? Can you not fucking *understand* that she is giving birth *right here?*'

The man is unsure. His instinct tells him something is wrong. Perhaps a pillow is hidden under the saree. But he can see the bare skin of the swollen belly. He feels cheated, he knows he is being taken advantage of, but he cannot appear heartless in front of his wife. And the naked, swollen, offending belly will not go away. The light has turned green. Scooters and cars are scrambling to be the first out of the intersection. The roar of engines rises. The man thrusts a ten-rupee note into Gauhar's hands, then twists the accelerator on his scooter handle and speeds off. Ten rupees? Ten rupees will not pay for a minute of a doctor's time, you bastard! He will deliver the baby and leave the woman open on the table, unstitched, bleeding, doomed because ten rupees cover the extrication of the beast from its sinful pouch, not the stitching of the pouch. Go, you bastard with the scooter! May your baby be hurled into the air the next time you brake and shatter its little skull on the asphalt.

Gauhar walks angrily through moving cars and steps on to the footpath, dragging Ruby behind him. She lacks the instinct for the job. With other women he has collected twenty-five, even forty rupees, and not all were as visibly pregnant. With a belly ripe as a pomegranate, she is unable to arouse sympathy. What a rustam that husband of hers is! He assured Gauhar his wife was a natural thief, a chest-beater who could melt hearts of stone, a shameless bitch who would stop at nothing to shake down fat women for their money. And here she is, contented with one wail, a wail that barely moved Gauhar's own heart. She is too used to being a whore. A whore need do nothing because she already has what the customer wants. This job relies on compassion, not lust, and compassion is much more difficult to arouse. It must be wrung out of a man like the last drops from an already-dry towel. He must talk to the husband – twenty-five per cent is more than he deserves for such merchandise.

'I want to go home,' says Ruby.

'Shut up!'

They must shake down at least two more customers before ending the round and returning to the room, where her pyarelal husband is sure to be waiting to receive his share. The next wave of traffic contains fewer cars and scooters, and there is no opportunity to approach any. The road appears to be partially blocked off, and the intersection fills with onlookers, who have collected to watch an approaching wedding party with a brass band, clarinets, tubas and drums. The traffic has been held up for them. Now I must wait for these bastards to clear the area, thinks Gauhar. They will stop and dance, of course. Which wedding party passes up the chance to dance at an intersection? And who in a wedding party cares about a whore with a swollen belly?

The procession has marched up Chandni Chowk. On entering the intersection, it loses momentum. The front guard is uncertain of the route. Not knowing whether to turn left or right, or to march straight toward Red Fort, people stand around and shout slogans. Gauhar realises that it is not a wedding party. There is no horse, no umbrella, no fly-whisk fanning the groom. Very well, he must do business wherever he can. He approaches a man and thrusts Ruby forward. '*Maayi baap*! My wife is in pain, *maayi baap*! Her water has broken . . .' But the man pushes her aside, throws up his hands and continues to chant slogans.

'Gopal Das *zindabad*!'

'Vote for Gopal Das!'

'Vote for the chai cup!'

There is a groom after all, thinks Gauhar, but he is asking for votes instead of a wife. Fuck this Gopal Das! May he lose whatever he is fighting for! What right has he to come charging through Chandni Chowk when Gauhar is doing business? No money can be made out of the beggars who shout slogans in processions. The going rate is lunch and forty-five rupees for a day. How can a man who earns forty-five rupees spare anything for a pregnant whore, even if she were bleeding right into his lap?

The men are shouting with increasing fervour. Gauhar knows why. Their passion rises when a man in white kurta-pyjama approaches them, and wanes when he moves to some other part of the crowd. No doubt he is counting the slogans and keeping tabs on volume. He seems to be directing them toward Daryaganj. Gauhar saw him years ago in Kucha Bansilal, seated on the edge of Seth Sohan Lal's mattress, writing furiously. He is some kind of clerk – natty, smooth and unreliable. A man with clean clothes and slicked-down hair cannot be trusted. He speaks insistently with someone on his left, pushing him to the right against his will. So there is a groom after all! He is short and bald, waddles more than he walks, has no horse under him or umbrella over his head. Much of his face is hidden behind the thick garlands that ring his neck. He walks with hands folded in front of him, with a communal namaste toward people he cannot see because of the garlands. A large board rises behind his head, held by a boy, who raises it higher with each slogan. It displays a cup of tea and a slogan in Hindi – 'Vote for Gopal Das! Independent.' The bald man moves slowly, carefully, as if the road is sprinkled with nails.

The kurta-pyjama man manoeuvres the groom into a central position and holds up his hands, silencing the slogan-shouters. The groom is about to make a speech. The kurta-pyjama man pushes aside the top two garlands, revealing most of the groom's face – foggy spectacles, grey moustache, parched lips. Gauhar gasps.

'Brothers and sisters,' murmurs Gopal.

'Louder!' commands Ramvilas.

'Brothers and sisters!' Gopal exclaims. 'Today is Eid-ul-Fitr! Today is also the day Mahatma Gandhi was felled by the fires of hate . . .'

Gauhar watches, wide-eyed at the improbability of what he sees before him. He remembers a clean, radiant Gopal Bhai who stood wearing an expensive kurta on a stage, letting a fat sardarji throw his arms round him . . . Has Gopal Bhai's health deteriorated so much in two years? And why do they keep calling him Gopal Das? Gauhar cannot control himself. He lets go of Ruby's hand and rushes forward, coming to a sudden stop in front of Gopal. The garlands have ridden up his face again. A few strands of grey are sprinkled round his ears. He looks worn out, weatherbeaten, but it is Gopal Bhai all right, the same man, the same chaivala, trying to recognise him through scratches in his spectacles. Gauhar holds up his right hand and brings the stump close to Gopal's face. 'Gopal Bhai!' he shouts.

'Gauhar?' asks Gopal.

'You cannot stop!' scolds Ramvilas.

'You are so tall,' wonders Gopal. 'Where is your beard?'

'I have been a Hindu for six years.'

'I thought you were dead,' says Gopal.

'Not dead! Just a Hindu.'

'Where have you been?'

'Never ask me that again,' says Gauhar, mysteriously.

Ramvilas eyes Gauhar with suspicion and turns to Gopal. 'Who is this man?'

'My son,' says Gopal.

'Your son was killed by anti-Mandal IPP people!' Ramvilas retorts angrily. At a signal from him, a man grabs Gauhar's arm and pulls him aside.

'Let me go, mother-fucker!' he screams.

'Start walking toward Daryaganj,' Ramvilas tells Gopal.

'I must speak to my son,' Gopal insists.

'Your son . . .'

'I have not seen him for six years!'

'Talk to him after your rally today.'

'My legs hurt,' complains Gopal. 'Can we not get a taxi, Ramvilas Babu?'

'Who will see you in a taxi?' sneers Ramvilas. 'This is a campaign, not a picnic! We have to cover Daryaganj, then Ballimaran, then Jhandewalan . . .'

'A ricksha!' pleads Gopal. 'People can see me in a ricksha. I can stand in it and fold my hands. I have seen Suleman Mian campaign from a jeep. And Harilalji waves from an Ambassador car. No one walks the entire length of Chandni Chowk!'

'You are the poor man's candidate,' says Ramvilas curtly. 'You must behave like the poor.'

Gopal hangs his head.

'And where will we get money for rickshas and taxis?' adds Ramvilas. 'A campaign costs a lot. At least one crore.'

Gopal sighs and turns to his right. He wishes he could have a frame jutting like a cantilever from his waist on which to rest his folded hands. He will now have to walk all the way to Daryaganj. And when will they let him speak to his son?

'A few lakhs are enough to start a campaign,' says Ramvilas. 'Two lakhs, three, four . . . You would not have three or four lakhs, would you?'

On hearing this Gopal stumbles. It is impossible! Ramvilas Babu could not be referring to *that* money! Who knows if those four lakhs still exist? Might they not have withered away, rotted or died a slow death for lack of air? Does money suffocate?

Gauhar feels a fire rising within him. This is Gopal Bhai, the baba he never had, the only man in Chandni Chowk who is not a pyarelal or a rustam. His father is restored to him in spite of every obstacle put in his way by Yellow Teeth and Suleman Mian! What is four lakhs? Aftab, Munna, Johnny and Partho can collect that in a few weeks, if they concentrate on gold chains and diamond rings and do not bother with wristwatches . . . And why should the money not be given to Gopal Bhai, his baba? With a sudden burst of energy, he shakes off Ramvilas's man and catches up with Gopal. 'I can arrange for money,' he says eagerly.

Ramvilas is irritated at his presumption. 'I told you to go away!'

'He is my son,' insists Gopal once more.

Ramvilas snorts angrily. The chaivala must be losing his mind with age. Did he not see the ball of flames that swallowed his son? Ramvilas remembers very well – a callow, scrawny boy in a shocking yellow shirt and mud-coloured trousers, with a chest so bony that his collarbones could be seen clearly through the shirt. 'There will be a man standing behind you with a blanket,' Ramvilas had told him. 'It will put out the flames immediately. We will take you to the best hospital, give you the best doctors. You shall be famous, leaders will visit you, even the PM might come to the hospital . . .' But that is an old story.

'What is your name?' Ramvilas asks.

'Gauhar Muhammad.'

'Today is Eid,' says Ramvilas. 'What are you doing here?'

Gauhar laughs. 'I am a Hindu.'

Ramvilas digs deep into the recesses of his mind. Does he know the man from somewhere? A Musalman man with one hand . . . 'Have you worked in election rallies?'

Gauhar laughs, raises his right stump and screams, 'Gopal Das *zindabad*!'

Ramvilas snatches the placard from the boy behind Gopal and hands it to Gauhar. 'Take this! You must hold it upright.'

'About the money—' begins Gauhar.

'Come and talk to me later in the evening.'

Ramvilas eyes the onlookers, who are dispersing. The rally is a flop. They have attracted little attention. Instead, they have been hounded by traffic police, chased by buses, run down by scooters, and he must pay out a thousand rupees to the slogan-shouters when they finish in Daryaganj, with the exception of the one-handed Musalman, who seems to be working for free. It is not clear how he could be the son of the chaivala, but that does not matter. He is a Musalman, which cannot harm a secular candidate. The chaivala has turned out to be a disappointment. He has no fire in his belly, no stomach for a fight, no desire to raise his voice and be heard. It is laughable to believe he will draw Musalman and poor votes away from Suleman, no matter how many one-handed Musalmans he counts as his sons. Perhaps the whole idea is doomed. A secular candidate cannot be launched without active help from the IPP, and the IPP washed its hands of Ramvilas as soon as he resigned. Sohan Lal knew what he was doing! And Kartar Singh is running scared of the CBI, unable to help. No one has seen him for two days.

Ruby runs out of the crowd and clutches Gauhar's hand. He shakes her off. 'Go back to your pyarelal,' he scolds her.

'What about my commission?'

'Tell your pyarelal to come tomorrow. I will settle your account. You are a good-for-nothing whore.'

Ruby slinks away, snivelling. Gauhar holds up the placard and prepares to march. There is dread in his heart. He knows he is breaking a rule that has stood for six years, enforced by vague threats from Ibrahim Mian, and the ghost of Suleman Mian behind him. He must never talk to Gopal Bhai, never set foot in Kucha Bansilal, never speak to Sohan Lalji . . . But this is his father, and who can keep a man from his father? If Ibrahim Mian threatens him again, he will kick in those yellow teeth. He raises the placard high. 'Gopal Das *zindabad*!'

'My son has come back to me,' says Gopal, warmly.

'Start walking!' commands Ramvilas. 'There are many poor votes in Matia Mahal.'

The Musalman man's enthusiasm infects Ramvilas. He has come this far, swimming against the tides generated by Surajmal, Sohan Lal and Kartar Singh. He will not step back now. He will bring to bear all his energy and creativity. The chaivala must gain attention if Harilal Gupta is to win. Who are his allies? Not Harilal Gupta. Not Sohan Lal. Not Kartar Singh. No traders, no seths, no businessmen, no IPP committee members. The newspaper madam, if he can manipulate her. The rickshavala union, if he can bring them round. The tailor union, if he can pay them enough. Muhammad Salauddin Qureshi, who can be lured from the IPP with no more than a generous meal. Noor Muhammad, who will follow Qureshi out like a dutiful dog. And Gita, his Gulmohar, if he still has something to offer her.

'Gopal Das *zindabad*!' screams Gauhar.

The Naari Niketan building sits at the far end of GB Road, tucked away in a narrow lane full of paan stalls and water-pump shops. It is an old one-storeyed structure to which another floor has been hastily added, to keep up with the influx of newly rescued girls from GB Road. A new one arrives every few days. Some are pregnant, some have children, and most are Nepali or Bangladeshi. In the last two years, because of the proliferation of NGOs that make this their cause, Naari Niketan has been overwhelmed with inmates, but has no resources to dispatch the girls elsewhere. Social-welfare authorities have therefore decreed that it is reserved for under-age girls, leaving 'adult victims' to fend for themselves.

Ramvilas walks through the front office into a narrow corridor, which opens into a hall. The walls are lined with bunk beds, three high, giving the entire building the appearance of a three-tier train compartment. A cluster of women hold pads, pamphlets and pencils, with Gita Didi in the centre. Ramvilas advances toward them, passing bewildered girls who sit up in their bunks, jump out and follow him. He recognises Manju and Nasreen, while Gita herself is interrogating a trio of girls who giggle with each answer.

She wraps her saree round her shoulders, notices Ramvilas and frowns. Then she turns back to the girls. Manju and Nasreen scribble furiously. Gita's appearance gives Ramvilas pause. Her hair is pulled back harshly from her face, tied into a bun and stuffed into a net. This, with black-rimmed spectacles – he has not seen those before – and her stern manner make her look like a school-teacher. He is disappointed. He waits. After a few minutes, she dispatches Manju and Nasreen. Ramvilas steps into the space created by their departure.

'Why have you come here?' she asks stiffly. 'I thought you were a seth now, too respectable to be seen with me.'

He smiles. 'Only a seth, not a committee member. Who said seths were honourable? Besides, you are now famous.'

He unfolds a copy of *India Now*. She turns away dismissively, but he does not miss the glint of triumph in her eyes. He opens the magazine to the 'People' section on the last page, where she is pictured holding up a box of condoms labelled 'Nirodh' and smiling at the camera. 'Gita Didi,' gushes the caption, 'condoms for the world!'

Ramvilas studies the picture, then Gita's face. Both tell a story of decline. Her skin – what little of it is not wrapped inside the white saree – is blotchy, her eyes are surrounded by pathways, her cheeks sag, and there are even a few strands of grey in the tightly combed hair above her ears. She has metamorphosed into a matron at thirty-one. The juicy lower lip, still juicy, no longer droops suggestively but snaps shut when she is silent. It is his own doing. He has turned a talented whore into a nun.

'They should not have put Charulata on the cover,' says Gita, with a touch of petulance.

Ah! Vanity still lurks under the NGO armour, thinks Ramvilas.

He turns the magazine over and studies the cover. A much-garlanded Charulata stands behind a microphone, left hand thrust high into the air, addressing a crowd that looks like the entire population of India.

'Look at her!' says Gita. 'Fat, ugly, shapeless, almost like a man.'

Almost like a man, muses Ramvilas, but she may decide who will be the next prime minister.

Gita holds her head up defiantly and turns back to the girls. 'I have my work to do,' she declares.

'Why is STREE in Naari Niketan?' he challenges. 'These girls have already been saved.'

'We are here to ensure that our money is spent properly,' she says.

He shrugs. The girls, who have been watching them curiously, now clamour for the magazine. Ramvilas lowers it and lets them see Gita's picture. They compare it to her face, then laugh and cheer. Word travels down the compartment that the schoolmarm who has been needling them with irrelevant questions is really a film star. Ramvilas realises his mistake. 'We cannot talk here,' he says.

'What have we to talk about?' she retorts.

'Did you visit my candidate?'

'Yes. He cannot win.' She turns swiftly and walks out of the room, trailing a pack of girls. Ramvilas follows. 'He is useless,' she says. 'I stood at the counter and took a good look. He was too bashful to let his eyes meet mine. Such a man cannot win.'

'We don't want him to,' says Ramvilas, and regrets having said so much. 'But he will win with your support,' he says quickly.

She walks into a room lined with sewing-machines. The clatter stops as soon as she enters. Word of her celebrity has preceded her. She asks the girls to resume sewing. They reluctantly swing their feet on to the pedals, but continue to watch her. Manju and Nasreen walk by each row of sewing-machines, bending over to study the girls' work.

'You must help him launch his campaign,' says Ramvilas.

'Why does he want to become an MP?' asks Gita.

'He is penniless, has no home, no shop – what else can he be? You have to help him.'

'I have no money either.'

He knows she is lying, and marvels at the confidence in her eyes. 'Does STREE not get money from Harilal Gupta's discretionary fund?'

'It is a drop in the ocean.' She snorts. 'I distribute ten thousand condoms every day, I co-ordinate two hundred doctor visits every week, I organise sex clinics and workshops every month. I tour rehabilitation centres, Naari Niketans, police stations . . .' She stops, overwhelmed by the number of her activities.

'Of course,' he says quickly. 'I know STREE has been doing a lot of good work—'

'But you do not know!' she retorts. 'There are more than ninety kothas in GB Road, more than three thousand sex-workers, and each has six customers every night. If I distribute ten thousand condoms every day, and half are used, can you calculate how many women serve their clients without condoms? Can you estimate the impact on the spread of Aids? Can you tell me how I can distribute the fifty boxes I need every day if I do not have the money to buy them?'

He is irritated. He is asking her to return a favour – did he not come to her aid when she needed Kiran pulled out of that school? – and she has slapped him with a demand for money! 'You do not need more funds,' he says firmly.

'It takes a lot of money to keep whores alive and functional inside GB Road,' she hisses. 'The government inspector wants a cut before he hands out free condoms – ten rupees per packet – and before he issues a disease-free certificate. Do you know how much it costs to arrange hospital visits, police protection, classes about STDs, films and videos—'

'Films?'

'Yes, whores like to watch films,' she says challengingly.

Ramvilas sighs. She has left out the largest item from her list but he will not press the point, for now. He knows exactly how much she gets from Harilal Gupta's discretionary funds every month. It was he who engineered the allocation three years ago. He has not kept good accounts or asked her to provide any, but he suspects that the total amount given to STREE has run into many lakhs. The new posters and placards in the STREE office cannot account for it all, but he will save that weapon for now. He must distract her from this self-righteous tirade. He indicates the girls at the sewing-machines with a sweep of his arm. 'Where do they go from here?'

Gita smiles. 'We try to find them employment outside GB Road.'

'Does it work?'

'No. Sewing and knitting are not skills that can get them jobs. Every woman is supposed to know them, but no one can make a living with them.'

'When do the girls leave?'

'At twenty-one,' she says, with a sigh. 'I do not know where they go.' She walks out of the sewing room into an unkempt courtyard. He follows her.

'You do not have to make a donation,' he says. 'I just want STREE to offer him public support.'

Gita laughs. 'STREE will support any candidate who fights for the rights of women.'

'He has never been to GB Road. Is that not good enough?'

She fumbles in her handbag and brings out a sheaf of papers.

'I did not realise you already had a list of demands,' says Ramvilas.

'This is the ITP Act from 'eighty-six,' she says. 'Immoral Traffic Prevention Act.'

He frowns, even as he wonders how she picked up sufficient English for the words to roll so easily off her tongue.

'Whoring is illegal in India,' she says. 'Did you know you were breaking the law all those years?'

He is embarrassed at this reminder. He has not visited GB Road – as a customer – for two years. Even in his position, it is not difficult to lose himself inside a kotha without public knowledge. The STREE office is an oasis in the desert of sin, where prominent politicians make campaign stops and allow themselves to be photo-graphed with whores. It is a shrine, a place of pilgrimage, an island of truth and dignity in the dark, swirling waves of GB Road. A respectable trader might drop by to make a charitable donation or to inform himself of the latest initiatives to empower women. Once inside Kotha 842, it is possible that the visitor might find his way to rooms on the upper floors, four-poster beds . . . But Ramvilas has resisted the urge. The white sores have aided his resolution. Besides, a man with two daughters must exercise restraint. The older one is already eighteen. He will start looking for suitable boys as soon as this Lok Sabha election is over. Once Harilalji is installed as MP, there are no limits to the influence he may wield. A man so intimately associated with a Member of Parliament should be able to find good husbands for his daughters, even if the dowry is less than substantial. And when he has disposed of them, he will consider a turn to the spiritual world, unless Harilalji finds more worldly matters that require his attention.

'We want prostitution legalised,' says Gita, 'which will make it easier for you to come to GB Road.' She smiles.

'I do not plan to do so,' he says coldly.

'We want to be called sex-workers. There are twenty lakhs of us in India. We want clinics for venereal diseases, insurance, vacations – everything a school-teacher gets.'

'You speak like a politician,' grumbles Ramvilas.

'You are asking me to support a politician,' she returns.

'But he is not a politician,' Ramvilas protests. 'He is a man of the people!'

'Whores do not vote for men. They fuck them.'

Ramvilas is taken aback. 'I cannot do much,' he hedges. 'I am not even a member of the committee! Why do you not ask Harilal Gupta?'

Gita stiffens. 'Have you seen the board at the entrance of GB Road? It was installed by Harilal Gupta.'

Ramvilas cannot suppress a laugh. He saw it fifteen minutes ago, as he walked into GB Road. It is a giant hoarding with a plain white background and 'He who comes to GB Road is an ass' splashed across it.

'Who is it for?' asks Gita. 'Those who come for whores come at night. They cannot read it in darkness. Those who come during the day only want water-pumps and wash-basins.'

Ramvilas sighs. She has erected a façade of formality between them. No one is within earshot in the courtyard, but she keeps up the pretence. He considers shaking the saree loose from her shoulders, but is afraid he will be rebuffed. His Gulmohar, if she still lives, is buried too deep inside the NGO chairperson.

'Gopal Das will support all your demands,' he says wanly. 'You must come to our campaign office in Lajpatrai Market, with as many whores as you can, for a support rally.'

'Why does he need the support of whores?' she asks.

Ramvilas chuckles. 'A whore is worth a thousand nuns! Starvation interests no one, poverty is boring, communalism is out of fashion and secularism is losing its flavour. That leaves rape, incest and prostitution. Who can turn away from the spice of life? Who will fail to notice a candidate supported by whores?'

Gita smiles in spite of the insult. He does not want to tell her that she brings additional publicity because of the *India Now* article. It is not a good idea to raise her in her own estimation.

'All right,' she says. 'Come to the STREE office tomorrow.'

'I cannot go there,' he says firmly.

'GB Road is the haunt of truck drivers, students, rickshavalas and thieves. You cannot expect to find respectable Chandni Chowk traders there?'

'We can discuss all the details here,' he insists.

'You have still not told me what I get in return,' she says.

'Gopal Das will support your causes.'

'That means nothing. He is only a candidate, not an MP. What will you do for me?'

Ramvilas allows himself a short pause. 'I will tell no one about Kiran.'

She does not react, and he admires her equanimity, even as he wishes he had not helped her acquire it. 'I have no idea where Kiran is,' she says, in a level voice.

'She is certainly not in Naari Niketan.' He shrugs. 'She is under twenty, so if she is not here, could she have been sent to Kathmandu? There is no record of that. Where could she be, then? Sitting in some kotha in GB Road, under the protective gaze of a bai, who has promised not to put her to work? Could the bai be receiving a grant every month in return for forgoing her fee? And what a fee that would be! The girl is thirteen, perhaps a virgin, and beautiful. Who would give the bai such a generous grant? Could it be STREE, lavishly supported by the discretionary funds of Harilal Gupta, MLA for Chandni Chowk and transport minister in the Delhi government?'

'Naari Niketan is no place for a young girl,' whispers Gita. 'Even if she is not raped, she will be thrown out at twenty-one.'

And in Kathmandu, she thinks bitterly, her uncle Jangbahadur waits with another Bikram, leering at a girl who is seventeen, holding her face in his hands, letting her see the dark lines in his gums. 'You will break many hearts with your almond eyes,' he says heavily. Bikram runs his thumb over the parting in her hair, depositing a line of imaginary vermilion. 'Now we are married,' he says. 'This is where all our husbands live,' says a giggling Nasreen. 'This is attar chameli,' says a slight man in a neat kurta-pyjama, 'mixed with a few drops of attar bela . . .' What if she had never left Sindhupalchowk district, never come to sinful Kathmandu, never seen Jangbahadur or Bikram or Ramvilas or the bai? Can she undo the last fourteen years, cling to her father and beg him to let her stay at home? 'Do not send me away to Kathmandu. You do not know what dangers lurk there . . .' Why was *she* chosen to suffer this fate? If only she could shut her eyes and let a gust of wind take her back to Sindhupalchowk district! And then there is Kiran.

'Do not look so sad,' says Ramvilas. 'Kiran will remain where she is.'

Gita sighs deeply. 'When do you want this rally?'

'Tomorrow.'

'I need more time than that.'

'In three days,' he says. 'Bring a few hundred whores. Push your Musalman whores forward.'

'I thought secularism was losing its flavour?'

'A little cardamom, no matter how old, never takes anything from a cup of tea.'

'All right. I will send you a speech for him.'

'You cannot write his speeches!'

'I can, if I am listening to them,' she says.

'In three days,' he repeats. 'At eleven in the morning, not a minute later!'

Nasreen comes into the courtyard to tell Gita the classroom is ready.

'It is time for your speech to the girls,' says Ramvilas, brightly. He hands Nasreen the copy of *India Now*. 'Show this to them,' he tells her. 'Gita Didi is too modest!'

They walk back into the sewing room. Ramvilas heads for the corridor lined with bunk beds.

'Ramvilas Babu!' calls Gita. He stops. 'You have not told me who this man is. This Gopal Das. Where did you find him?'

Ramvilas chuckles. 'Think of him as Mahatma Gandhi. People do not notice him until he is straddling them.'

He wonders irrelevantly if a Nepali whore – even a whore turned Didi – has heard of Gandhi, then walks briskly through the front office, pushes aside the curtain and leaves the building. He is suddenly blinded by the sun in GB Road. Standing before him is Inderlal Jha, SHO. Ramvilas ignores him, rebuffing his attempt at a familiar greeting. He has little doubt that Inderlal makes a note of all visitors, information he can trade in the future. But Ramvilas arrived in the middle of a visit by STREE so he is secure, and he will not allow the SHO to put him at a disadvantage by acknowledging his presence. He looks straight ahead, and walks past commodes and wash-basins stacked on the road. This is a market, not a whorehouse, and he has as much right as anyone else to walk through it without being accosted by the likes of Inderlal.

A golden bow and arrow, constructed of light, durable plastic, sit in the blubbery, cushioned palms of Harilal Gupta. A quiver of polyvinyl chloride swings behind his shoulder, and on his head nestles a crown of cardboard, covered with golden wrapping-paper and studded with imitation pearls. Pendants of tin oscillate gently from his earlobes, while necklaces and beads slide down his chest and ride above his belly.

'We must slow down, Harilalji,' implores Sohan Lal. He is exhausted by the morning's campaigning. Now, as they struggle to attract an audience in the lazy afternoon, he wonders at the other man's boundless energy, then remembers that Harilal is ferried from stop to stop in an Ambassador, whose flashing beacon clears the way. The car has just left after depositing him at this corner, and men have been dispatched to alert traders to his presence.

Kinari Bajar has dressed itself up for Harilal Gupta's visit. Most shops display the saffron flag of the IPP. Storefronts have been washed, walls painted and signboards scrubbed clean – Vinod Trading Company, Nathuram Garments, Manoj Saree House, Baburam Harichand . . . The shops stretch in an endless line of glass façades, behind which stand mannequins in bright red gha-gharas, their pale skin dazzling in the afternoon sun, their hands folded as if to greet Harilal, who has descended on the market dressed as Raam.

A ricksha travels with Harilal's entourage, carrying a loudspeaker which now switches abruptly from a Hindi film song to chants from the *Bhagavad Gita*. '*Yadaa yadaa hi dharmasya . . .*'

Traders arrive at the corner in ones and twos, herded from their shops, brought by the promise of spectacle, speeches and hot cups of chai. Harilal watches them approvingly, uses the arrow to scratch his back discreetly, replaces it in the quiver, then turns a cheerful face to Sohan Lal. 'Campaigning is not for the weak, Sohan Lal.'

Sohan Lal suppresses a retort. Harilal watches the loudspeaker drift into another lane, calling the faithful from beyond the perimeter of Kinari Bajar, then bestows another nugget, in English, on him. 'No pain, no gain!'

'We must begin,' says Sohan Lal. 'The crowd is large enough.'

'Why have they taken the loudspeaker away?' asks Harilal, irritably.

A man is sent to bring back the errant ricksha. The speech cannot begin without invocations from the *Bhagavad Gita*, for which the lungs of the loudspeaker are necessary.

'Find me a platform,' commands Harilal.

A dozen men leap from the crowd and usher him into a shop foyer, from which he will address the rally. Sohan Lal is annoyed. As chairman of the IPP committee in Chandni Chowk, and therefore of Harilal's election committee, the honour of choosing the plank, chair or table from which Harilal will speak falls to him. It is not a trivial matter. The shop that forms the backdrop will appear in dozens of newspapers, and the owner can be expected to make a generous contribution to the committee.

Sohan Lal looks about hurriedly and spies the small, understated sign above Baburam Harichand. He knows the seth. He has bought gha-gharas from him for both his daughters' weddings, as well as jewellery, garlands and a thousand knick-knacks worth more than twelve lakhs, even in those days. He grabs Harilal's free hand – the other holds the bow – and pulls him authoritatively toward Baburam Harichand and the low concrete platform that rises in front of the glass façade.

Seven people, of whom three help and four hinder, assist Harilal in climbing the two steps to the platform. It takes him a few seconds to catch his breath, regain his composure, and realign the quiver on his back. He counts approximately a hundred people in the audience – not as many as he had hoped, but a respectable number for a sleepy afternoon almost forty days before the election. The ricksha with the loudspeaker has been retrieved, and wheeled round to face the crowd. The man sitting in it is waiting for his cue, microphone in hand. Harilal blesses the seth who owns Baburam Harichand – the man has come forward rapturously with folded hands – and raises his bow high in the air.

The traders fall silent in anticipation. Harilal extracts an arrow from the quiver, mounts it on the bow, pulls the string and lets go. It sails into the air, then plunges into the crowd, who scramble for the prize. A cry of '*Jai Shri* Raam!' goes up, and the loudspeaker inserts itself into the mêlée with hurriedly chanted lines from the *Bhagavad Gita*, in no particular order. *Whenever there is a decline of dharam, O Arjun, I shall manifest myself to strike down sinful ways. For the true yogi sleeps when the others wake and wakes when the others sleep . . .*

Harilal Gupta stands with his hands folded, Raam, Krishna and Arjun rolled into one. It does not matter which incarnation he represents because he is the embodiment of dharam. He wears a silk dhoti. He stands in wooden sandals, whose clackety-clack sounds echo when he acknowledges those to his left and right. He has passed under bunting and arches decorated with the bow and arrow symbol of the IPP, and is wearing a beatific smile, come to cleanse Chandni Chowk of its sinful ways, making good the promise Krishna made to Arjun in the *Bhagavad Gita*.

'Protect us, Harilal!' roars the loudspeaker. 'Protect us in this Kaliyug! Slay every demon, whether he be Ravan, Kumbhakaran, Meghanaad, Mahishaasur . . . It is you who must scatter the sinful cloud that blankets the great land of Bharat and blow it away!'

The traders, encouraged by men hired for the purpose, cry '*Jai Shri Raam!*' again, ignoring the confusing assortment of villainous names that issue from the loudspeaker. What does it matter? They are all evil, and here stands Harilal, all eighty-five kilograms of him, ready to deliver them from these demons.

Harilal hands his bow to an organiser and raises his hands to calm the crowd. 'My brothers and sisters,' he says.

Sohan Lal, just below the platform, notes that there are no women in the crowd. But Harilal is reciting from a script, perfected after fifteen renditions this morning.

'They say that IPP is communal,' Harilal goes on. 'Let me ask you, in his eighteen years as your MP, did Nareshji ever sanction any money for the restoration of a Musalman haveli?'

The traders answer: a resounding 'No'.

'Many of you have seen the work that has begun in the Red Fort grounds, for the building of a great Dara Shikoh Park. Why am I spending money to celebrate a Musalman, you will ask? Because I am celebrating a Musalman who joined the national mainstream before there was a nation! I am celebrating a secular Musalman, a liberal Musalman, a Musalman who understood that Hindutva is not a religion, but the very core of the Indian nation!'

Sohan Lal wonders if the afternoon has taken its toll on Harilal. This is Kinari Bajar, hive of God-fearing traders who form the bedrock of IPP support. What do they care about the Dara Shikoh Park, or Dara Shikoh, or any other lecherous, incestuous Mughal? He himself considers the crumbling monuments wasteful. He has little patience with those who speak nostalgically of Delhi's cultural heritage, as if they lived in those times and are comforted by the presence of decrepit, decaying buildings. The octagonal area covered by Red Fort could house a gigantic market for electronic goods. Lajpatrai Market could be moved into the fort grounds. The walls could be demolished, the gates could be widened . . .

The morning has been hard on Sohan Lal. His back has ached since he stopped taking his morning walks. The campaign requires frenzied preparation for every stop. Shopkeepers must be informed, stores cleaned, placards painted, buntings hung and men hired to shout slogans. This involves hours on the telephone and no exercise. With Ramvilas gone from the committee, many clerical tasks that could have been delegated to him now fall on Sohan Lal's drooping shoulders.

Harilal, master of public speech, senses he has lost the sympathy of the audience. He pauses suddenly, in mid-sentence, and buries the remains of Dara Shikoh Park: 'This is Kinari Bajar, where every bride dreams of coming before her wedding. More weddings are planned here than in Hindi films!'

This elicits laughter from the traders.

'So why is it that every trader in Kinari Bajar complains about business? Who is cutting into your margins? Who brings cheap garments into the market and undercuts your prices? Who allows Chinese goods to destroy our trade? There is a simple answer, my brothers. It is the Indo-Nepal bilateral treaty. You may not have heard of it, but it takes two hundred rupees from your pocket every day.'

Sohan Lal heaves a sigh of relief.

'The Congress Party is a friend of Nepal,' declares Harilal. 'It is more interested in Nepali shops in Kathmandu than Indian shops in Kinari Bajar. "Nepal is a landlocked country," said the Congress Party in Parliament, "so we will let Nepal import goods through Indian ports." Why is this bad for the traders of Kinari Bajar? Because these goods, while passing through the land corridor in India, are dumped into the Indian market. Somewhere in Bihar and UP, they stamp Indian labels on yarn and fabric imported from China. So you have counterfeit Reliance, Indo Rama and Century Enka. You have fake Duracells, fake Reeboks, fake Nikes, fake Rolexes, fake teri-cotton, fake polyester, fake cotton towels, fake silk kurtas, fake ghagharas . . . Chandni Chowk has become China Chowk!'

The traders clap. A few shout angry slogans against the Congress Party. Tell those bastards to go to Beijing if they like China so much!

'How can an honest trader in Kinari Bajar compete at selling pencils against a large industrial house in China?'

'He cannot!' yells the crowd.

'The first thing I will do when elected your MP, my brothers, is have this treaty abolished.'

Sohan Lal nods. Naresh Agrawal made the same promise during the last few elections, but no one remembers Naresh Agrawal now.

Harilal raises a hand to silence the crowd. A shadow falls over his face. The crowd, in harmony with him, finds sorrow in its own heart, aware of bad tidings before they are shared.

'Naresh Babu was my senior,' Harilal rasps, in a tragic voice, 'in age, in public service, in wisdom.'

The traders nod sympathetically.

'But Naresh Babu was part of the Congress Party, and bound by party discipline. It is a party of appeasers and pseudo-secularists, a party that aims to feed our neighbours before it puts food into our mouths. More than twenty-five thousand Bangladeshis cross the border into India every day, and the Congress Party looks the other way. They come into Bengal, then move west to Delhi and Bombay until it is impossible to ferret them out. Who knows how many of you, standing right here, are Bangladeshis?'

There is an uncomfortable moment. Traders cast sidelong glances at each other.

'Two years ago I had Naresh Colony demolished. I uprooted the stalls of these Bangladeshis. I tried to send them back to Bangladesh. English newspapers say – if you care to read them – that those people are poor, not illegal. When was it a crime to be poor? Those English reporters – all unmarried women – should be sent to Pakistan and Bangladesh, where they belong. Their hearts beat not for the poor children of India, or the poor Harijans being converted to Islam and Christianity. Their hearts beat for illegal Musalmans!'

Sohan Lal is suddenly alert. Why has Harilal ventured so far? The demolition drive was not popular with traders, many of whom lost their stalls. And everyone knows that Naresh Colony has sprung up again behind Red Fort. Kinari Bajar was relatively unharmed by the drive . . . Harilal should move on quickly to another subject!

Harilal sighs. 'And now let us talk about the Musalman candidate.'

At the far edge of the crowd, Ramvilas chuckles. He has been with the procession for two hours, awaiting this moment. He has made eye-contact with Sohan Lal a few times, and once he even crossed Harilal Gupta's path with folded hands. He cannot be seen here openly. He is here to collect information and see how the talk of a 'Musalman candidate' goes down. He will receive instructions after the crowd has dispersed.

'Suleman Mian *murdabad*!' shouts someone in the crowd.

Harilal Gupta frowns and casts an admonitory glance toward the heckler. 'Suleman? I am talking about this chaivala, this man who calls himself the candidate of Musalmans and poor people. What is his name?' In an elaborate pantomime, he lends an ear to Sohan Lal, standing a few feet below him, listens carefully, then straightens up. 'His name, I am told, is Gopal Das.'

The traders laugh, convinced that Gopal Das is a ridiculous name, like Chappal Ram or Nanga Mal or Garib Das. Harilal Gupta rolls the name on his tongue, savouring its obvious ineligibility. 'Gopal Das! This Gopal Das has come to represent Musalmans in Chandni Chowk. He has no agenda, no plan, no record of public service, but it seems that Musalmans still want to vote for him. And now he also wants backward-caste Hindus to consider him their leader!'

The traders erupt in scornful laughter.

'Let them have their Musalman candidate, my brothers. I will not work to divide people!'

Ramvilas claps happily. The labels are important. The Musalman candidate versus the IPP candidate . . . 'Musalman candidate' is the term that will leave Suleman rootless. He must somehow insert it into the articles they are going to write about Gopal. 'The sex-workers of GB Road have come out in support of the Musalman candidate . . . the common man's candidate, the candidate for those left behind . . .' But the English press is ineffective. Those who read it do not vote, and those who vote cannot read it. He must get it into Hindi and Urdu newspapers.

On the platform, Harilal has finished his speech with a flourish, leading the traders into a crescendo of '*Jai Shri* Raam!' Ramvilas watches him with a mixture of derision and admiration. He is fat and slow but manages not to look ridiculous even while standing in front of three pale mannequins, surrounded by laces, tassels and sequins.

A garland of currency notes – fake, thinks Ramvilas – is thrown round Harilal's head, and he is heaved off the platform by seven pairs of hands. He sails down the lane with a growing entourage, to the clickety-clack of his wooden sandals, carrying his enormous girth like a well-captained ship through balmy waters.

The next stop is the Shiv temple in Kinari Bajar, which somehow escaped the bulldozers two years ago. It is small, no more than six feet across, and open to the elements. Bricks have been hastily slapped together with mortar round the trunk of a banyan tree. A phallus of black soapstone is driven like a stake into the ground. Narrow planks – the remains of a wooden bench – have been hammered into the wall around it to form shelves for other gods. A transverse branch of the tree bears a wooden board, announcing that the Kinari Bajar Traders Association maintains the temple.

Harilal approaches with folded hands. A pujari appears, arranged by Sohan Lal, and puts a tilak on his spongy forehead. There is no platform, so the audience is pushed up against the candidate. The loudspeaker has been unable to squeeze into the temple area, so Harilal begins without it: 'I am here to make a pledge,' he declares. 'Let Shiv be my witness that I will drag our Hindu society out of its moral abyss. I refer, my brothers, to GB Road, that cauldron of sin in Chandni Chowk. English newspapers say that those women – if you can call them women – are our sisters, that they should be honoured, not reviled. I will tell you what I have done, my brothers. I have installed a board in GB Road, so everyone who comes at night may see it – "He who comes to GB Road is an ass!"'

There is laughter. Harilal Gupta holds up a hand to quell the levity, and continues: 'Indian society has accorded a place of honour to the woman. The West tells us to treat the woman as an equal. "You are backward," we say to the West. "We do not treat the woman as an equal, we treat her as our superior! We raise her to be a goddess! We worship her as Lakshmi and Durga and Saraswati!"'

This goes down well. The traders are gratified. Then Harilal raises a cry of anguish: 'How is it that our sisters, whom we raise to be goddesses, end up in GB Road? Ah! It is not our sisters, it is Bangladeshis! Forty per cent of the prostitutes in GB Road are from Bangladesh. Not only does the Congress Party encourage illegal criminals, it encourages the corruption of Hindu society!'

Someone in the crowd suggests that at least half of the prostitutes are Hindus from Nepal. The organisers turn hostile faces toward him. Harilal is annoyed. He does not like this format for his meetings, where anyone can chip in. He prefers platforms and rallies, where he can dominate the proceedings with a microphone. 'The girls from

Nepal are trapped into becoming prostitutes,' he says irritably. 'They come here looking for work, not to soil their honour. It is Bangladeshis who have prostitution in their blood.'

Sohan Lal hurries to the edge of the crowd and signals to the loudspeaker man, who has parked his ricksha behind the temple. The man cranks his turntable and the loudspeaker chants lines from the *Bhagavad Gita*, declaring the end of the meeting.

Whenever there is a decline of dharam, O Arjun, I shall manifest myself to strike down sinful ways. For the true yogi sleeps when the others wake and wakes when the others sleep. You have the right to your duty, Arjun, not to the fruits that accrue . . .

'India is a jungle,' says Ramvilas to Gopal. 'At its centre, on a large mound called Raisina Hill, lives an elephant called the president. He moves slowly and lives long. He can crush anything, but most animals are too quick to be trapped under his feet. He bothers no one, no one bothers him.'

'I have seen the president on television,' says Gopal.

'The prime minister is a lion, king of the jungle, surrounded by tigers, who are his ministers.'

'What am I?'

'You will be a wolf, an MP. Sohan Lal, Harilal Gupta and Suleman are MLAs – a fox, a jackal and a hyena – aggressive but cowardly. They prostrate themselves before the bear, their chief minister, who sleeps much and says little.'

'What is Kartar Singhji?'

'He was once a councillor. Councillors are monkeys. They swing from branches and chatter through the night. The jungle is rich in animals – mayors, state ministers, corporators – but none matters to a wolf.'

'What do all these animals eat?' asks Gopal.

'The jungle is crawling with crows, pigeons, cats, dogs, rats, snakes and scorpions – shopkeepers, clerks, rickshavalas, chaivalas. There is sufficient food for everyone. Have you not seen how fat Harilal Gupta is?'

'What is Gauhar?'

'Your Musalman boy? He is a cockroach, surrounded by spiders, flies, bugs and beetles.'

'Ibrahim Mian?'

'A mosquito, buzzing constantly against the ear. Do you understand now?'

Gopal chuckles. 'There are too many animals!'

'You do not need to learn about all of them. Just remember to cower before the lion and the tiger. Glare at the jackals, hyenas and foxes. Eat the snakes and scorpions. And crush the insects.'

Gopal nods gravely, his education complete. They are seated on the mattress in Jasjit General Store, with stacks of posters in a corner. The television and VCR have been pushed to one side. A cassette-player lies in Gopal's lap.

'Now let me hear the speech I gave you last evening,' says Ramvilas.

Gopal sighs and switches on the cassette-player. 'Such long words!' he protests.

'Turn that off,' Ramvilas commands. 'You must deliver it in an hour. Do you think you can have the tape playing while you speak?'

'You could stand behind me and help when I forget the words,' suggests Gopal.

Ramvilas adopts a tone of outrage. 'Campaigning is hard work, Gopal Bhai! It involves blood and sweat. It is not a cricket match. Start speaking. I will help you as you go along, but you are on your own once you step out of this room.'

Gopal rises from the mattress with difficulty. His joints have fused from hours of sitting. For twenty years, until they took his stall away, he sat in his stall with one knee on the ground and the other raised in the air. That was all the space he could afford. Now, at Ramvilas's insistence, he sits cross-legged with both knees splayed. 'That is how they sit in political meetings,' says Ramvilas, 'and you cannot look like a chaivala among them.' It is one of the many ordeals he must suffer in this difficult campaign.

He polishes his spectacles and puts them on again, with no apparent improvement in his vision. Ramvilas Babu looks intently at him, striking dread into his heart. How does the speech begin? If he can get past the opening sentence, the lines will flow like water gurgling down a drain. 'My sisters . . .' he begins tentatively.

Ramvilas nods. Encouraged, Gopal raises his voice and adds a tremor of passion: 'My sisters, Gopal Pandey stands before you today . . .'

'Das! How often must I remind you? Gopal Das.'

'But my father was Manohar Lal Pandey—'

'It does not matter,' says Ramvilas, curtly. 'You are Gopal Das.'

'You said you would explain.'

Ramvilas grits his teeth. 'Do you know who Rajiv Gandhi was?'

'He was the PM.'

'Exactly! He was the PM. Would it matter if he was Rajiv Gupta, Rajiv Arora, Rajiv Sharma or Rajiv Subramanyam? He was the PM, and that was all that mattered.'

The point is not immediately obvious to Gopal. 'Everyone knows me as Gopal Pandey.'

Ramvilas makes a contemptuous sound. 'Who is "everyone"? How many newspapers have written about you? Have you appeared on television? How many people have ever heard of you? Or are you talking about your yellow-toothed Musalman? Your one-handed son?'

'All right,' says a crestfallen Gopal. 'My sisters, Gopal Das stands before you today . . .'

Ramvilas wipes his forehead with a handkerchief. A windowless room can be so clammy, even in January. When Sohan Lal had sprung the Lala Surajmal Scheme on him, he had said little about the candidate. 'A simple man,' said Sohan Lal, 'a chaivala, a lump of clay you can mould as you wish.' He did not say that the candidate was half blind, a half-wit and a Brahmin. The Pandey name is suicidal. Who will vote for a Hindu Brahmin in a constituency full of Musalmans, SCs and OBCs? There probably exists no MP with that name, unless he has successfully lived down his ancestry. 'Das' is a safer tag, a name designed especially for political candidates. A 'Das' is a servant – of God, society, the city, the country, the system and the people. No one knows where a man named Das has come from. He could be from anywhere in northern India – Bengal, Bihar, Uttar Pradesh, Rajasthan, Maharashtra or Gujarat. He belongs to no particular city or community so he belongs everywhere. Even his caste is indeterminate – a Bania or a Kayastha, sometimes a Khatri, perhaps even an SC or OBC, but certainly not a Brahmin. A servant of the people is never a Brahmin.

'A vote for Gopal Das is a vote for the people!' Gopal concludes with a flourish, warmed by the flow of words, beginning to believe what he is saying even if he does not understand it. He stands triumphantly, beaming down at Ramvilas, expecting applause.

'Very good,' Ramvilas allows grudgingly. 'Sit down. You should not remain standing after you have finished. Never forget to say "*Jai Hind*" at the end of a speech.'

'Ganga *Maiya*,' says Gopal, with a deep breath.

'Never say that!' Ramvilas pounces. 'Only a Hindu calls the Ganga mother. And never use Raam or Krishna in a speech.'

'But your name has Raam in it, Ramvilas Babu.'

Ramvilas laughs. 'I have a communal name! You can call me Ghalib.'

'Who is Ghalib?'

'You don't need to know.'

Gopal sinks back to the mattress, and decides that this a convenient time to lodge a request. 'I would like to spend nights in the kholi in Khari Baoli.'

Ramvilas raises a suspicious eyebrow. 'Why? Is this room not comfortable?'

'I told Seth Sushil Jain I would keep watch over his stock. I have done so for twenty years.'

Ramvilas laughs. 'You are a wolf now! Why must you keep promises made to snakes and scorpions? How will it look if a Lok Sabha candidate is found guarding sacks of turmeric?'

Gopal shrugs unhappily. This room is too large for one man. The mattress stretches infinitely over the linoleum. At first, he was pleased by how soft it was. He lay spreadeagled on it, arms and legs stretched out as far as possible, and marvelled that he still touched no walls. To have a television at your disposal, day after day! But the absence of sacks has left him defenceless. The smell of turmeric mixed with asafoetida has lulled him to sleep for years. In this room, his nights are sleepless, robbed of all fragrance but that of detergent. He does not understand why there are a dozen telephone lines – all disconnected – or why there is a safe that looks as if it has received a frenzied beating.

'I could stay in the room all day and go to the kholi at night,' offers Gopal.

Ramvilas shakes his head, wondering what is on the chaivala's mind. He has not forgotten what Bobby told him last week. The man might have exaggerated – he has never been reliable with information

– but he could not have concocted the whole story. Sardar Kartar Singh is a thorough man, to try to clean up before he ran away!

'Seth Sushil Jain has thrown you out of the kholi,' says Ramvilas. Gopal sighs.

'You must not go to Khari Baoli again.'

'Where will I shit?' demands Gopal.

'Not behind the old post office,' says Ramvilas. 'There is a new Sulabh Shauchalay outside Lajpatrai Market.'

'They charge two rupees!'

'I will pay for you to go there. You are a candidate now. It will not look good if you are found shitting next to a hand-pump.'

Gopal remains silent, quiescent.

'You must stop dyeing your moustache,' continues Ramvilas.

Gopal looks hurt. He first had his moustache dyed two years ago, when Sardar Kartar Singh had him stand on a stage and accept the plaque for protecting Sukhbir Kaur. Ram Bibek is careless with the strands of hair that sprout from his ears, so they remain grey. He does not mind this. He believes the moustache defines his face. He had looked magnificent in the newspapers, with the jet-black moustache and the silk kurta, accepting the plaque from Sardar Kartar Singh. 'Could you get me a silk kurta?' he asks. 'And a silk dhoti?'

Ramvilas snorts. 'You are a poor man's candidate!'

'You want me to wear torn clothes?' asks Gopal, offended.

Ramvilas smiles. 'I do not want you to change anything but your name. Everything else should remain as it is.'

'Could I have new spectacles?'

'Why? What is there to see?'

'I would like my ears cleaned before the newspeople come,' says Gopal. 'Can you get me an ear-cleaner?'

The matter appears trivial to Ramvilas. 'I will find someone,' he promises. 'Now, I want you to memorise these names. Chandni Chowk Lok Sabha constituency has four assembly segments – Ballimaran, Chandni Chowk, Paharganj and Matia Mahal. Matia Mahal is where you must campaign most because it has a Musalman majority.'

'Musalmans will vote for Suleman Mian,' says Gopal.

'Never say that again!' scolds Ramvilas. 'You are the natural inheritor of Musalman votes.'

'But Suleman Mian—'

'Does Suleman Mian ride a bicycle?'

'No.'

'Does Suleman Mian wear a cotton dhoti?'

'No.'

'Does Suleman Mian live in a kholi in Khari Baoli?'

'But—'

'Did Suleman Mian risk his life to protect Kartar Singhji's wife?'

'But, babu—'

'You are a man of the people. Hindu and Musalman, OBC and SC, they will all vote for you.'

'But Suleman Mian—'

'Is a pseudo-secularist.'

Gopal blinks, absorbing the term.

'Remember this! Suleman Mian, pseudo-secularist.'

'Sohan Lalji?'

'Fundamentalist.'

'Nareshji Agrawal?'

'His wife. Status-quoist.'

'Could you put these in the tape-recorder for me?'

'You must memorise them now, before you step outside the room. Remember, communal fundamentalists brought down Babri Masjid, pseudo-secularists appeased Musalmans, upper-caste Manuvadis protested against the Mandal Commission—'

'Mukesh!' remembers Gopal.

'Memory can play tricks with the mind,' Ramvilas warns. 'How do you know it was your son in that ball of fire?'

'I know, babu! I saw him!'

'But how do you know he was not supporting the Mandal Commission? Did you hear him shout any slogans?'

'He was quiet—'

'He was protesting in support of the Mandal Commission,' declares Ramvilas.

'You cannot tell who is protesting against what in a large crowd.'

'And how do you know they did not murder him?' demands Ramvilas. 'Have you ever known anyone who wants to set fire to himself? Your son stood there to support OBCs – a good boy who wanted fair treatment for the less fortunate sections of society. He stood there to express himself freely as anyone can in our society. But upper-caste lumpen elements – yes, they were lumpen elements! – surprised him by throwing a burning rag on his body. They were upper-caste criminals trying to incite violence.'

Gopal hugs himself closely, cowering at the thought of the people who took his son from him. Of course! They must have thrown a rag at him. It was difficult to see clearly in the crowd. Who would notice a rag? And who would hear Mukesh's cries once the fire had enveloped him?

'People sympathise with you,' says Ramvilas, quietly. 'You must let them know – rickshavalas, thelavalas, paanvalas, men who bear sacks, lift baskets, beat stones, fire furnaces, fold sarees, stand on street corners to bring customers to their seths . . . They are your friends, your brothers and sisters. Ask them to vote for you, and never forget to tell them about the upper-caste atrocities on your son.'

'Ganga *Maiya*!' gasps Gopal. 'How will I step out into the street among such vile people?'

'Who was that one-handed man at your rally last week?' asks Ramvilas.

'Gauhar, my other son—'

'That is a Musalman name.'

'He slept in my box for two years until he disappeared.'

'Disappeared?'

'I don't know. He said he was going to Ayodhya.'

'Ah! He must have gone there to protect Babri Masjid. Keep him close to you. Have him stand with you wherever you go.'

'But he has his own business now.'

'What business can be more important than supporting his father? Don't you need a family member with you in the campaign?'

'I will ask him.'

'Why does he call himself a Hindu?' asks Ramvilas.

Gopal shrugs. 'He is a Musalman.'

'And that man with yellow teeth?'

'Ibrahim.'

'Ask him to join you.'

'He supports Suleman Mian,' says Gopal, wistfully.

'What can Suleman Mian give him that you cannot?'

'He is a Musalman,' says Gopal.

'Who is Suleman Mian to claim all Musalman votes just because he is a Musalman? Does he keep roza? Does he answer the azan? Does he do proper vajoo before every meal? How do we know he is a proper Musalman? You are a God-fearing Hindu, and a God-fearing Hindu is a better friend of God-fearing Musalmans than a Musalman given to kufr.'

Gopal nods absent-mindedly, half of his mind on Ramvilas's words, the other half on sounds outside the store, in Lajpatrai Market, that are getting louder. 'Gopal Das *zindabad*! Gopal Das *zindabad*! Gopal Das *zindabad* . . .'

'Women!' gasps Gopal. 'Why have they come here?'

Ramvilas smiles. 'To express their support.'

'You will protect me,' Gopal pleads in desperation, 'won't you, babu?'

'You are in no danger. They are from GB Road.'

'I have never been to GB Road!'

'That is why they are here. They think of you as their brother.'

'But I do not know them!'

Ramvilas stands up. 'They know you. Stay here. I will see what they want.'

'Wait!' says Gopal. 'What about the ear-cleaner? What if there are newspeople with the women?'

'We will ask them to cut your ears out of their pictures,' says Ramvilas.

He runs his hands over his kurta to smooth it, slicks down his oily hair, adjusts the diamond stud on his collar, pushes open the Bournvita shelf from behind and steps outside, closing the shelf after him. He is back in a moment. 'Come outside, Gopal Bhai! They want to express their support.'

'Perhaps you could meet them and accept it.'

'Who am I to accept their support? You are the candidate. Stand up! No, do not slouch! Stand up straight. And remember, you must defeat those upper-caste criminals . . .'

Ramvilas pushes the shelf aside, and a chorus of voices assaults Gopal. 'Gopal Das *zindabad*!'

Female voices! Hundreds of female voices, shrill voices, desperate voices, voices gasping for breath!

'Raise your hands,' whispers Ramvilas.

Gopal folds his hands in a namaste and holds them up.

'Higher.'

The voices become shriller as his hands rise, folded, high above his head. He watches the sea of heaving bosoms before him. Ganga Maiya! The women are dressed in red and yellow sarees wrapped carelessly round their shoulders, revealing chests and arms and midriffs, colourful blouses with sequined sleeves, hair tied in ribbons and braids, large red bindis, lips red with paan and lipstick . . . These are women with the presence of men, women who are unaware of modesty, who hold placards and shout slogans, and raise their arms high to reveal their armpits! Each placard has a cup of tea painted in one corner and a familiar face in its centre – that of an old man, balding, greying, with thick foggy spectacles. That is *his* face! Where did they get his picture? And why is his moustache grey in those pictures, when he is certain he had it dyed a few days ago? For a brief moment, he entertains the thought that these are hijras – he is being applauded by an army of eunuchs! But, no, their voices are too shrill, their chests are too full, and they are too feminine in spite of their aggression.

'Gopal Das *zindabad*!' scream the women.

Ramvilas surveys the crowd approvingly. There are at least three hundred whores in the rally. Gita is resourceful. It is not easy to assemble so many at such short notice, and to give a placard to every third whore. Gopal's election symbol – a cup of tea – is on every one, with his face and a slogan in large red letters. Ramvilas chuckles. There is no shortage of war cries in the world of STREE – 'Sex-workers Training, Rehabilitation and Education Endeavour'; 'Aids Is Our Collective Responsibility'; 'Fifteen Under-age Women Rescued'; 'Thirty-three Former Sex-workers in Naari Niketan'; 'Three Sex-workers Sent Back to Nepal'; 'Gopal Das Will Empower Women'; 'Vote for Gopal Das'; 'A Vote for Gopal Is a Vote for a Woman'; 'Chandni Chowk Needs Gopal Das'; 'Our MP Must Be One of Us'; 'Gopal Das, Independent'; 'STREE supports Gopal Das'; 'Vote for the Cup of Tea'; 'STREE for Sex-workers, Sex-workers for Gopal Das . . .'

Gita Didi stands at the front in a modest cotton saree with a large red badge that says, 'STREE,' flanked by Manju and Nasreen in white salvaar-kameez. Nasreen carries a poster that shows a sick woman sprawled on a bed. 'Your husband gave her Aids,' says the caption. The whores cheer lustily, glad to be out in Chandni Chowk. Aside from short trips to stores in GB Road, where they buy clothes and jewellery, and a few visits to whores in other kothas, most rarely leave the GB Road area. Today they walked up the entire length of Chandni Chowk, swinging their hips and allowing their sarees to fall round their bodies, giggling at the dread they struck in timorous shopkeeper hearts, letting rickshas and scooters gawk at them. They are aware that wherever they go a crowd forms, every member of it embarrassed to be looking yet unable to tear away his eyes. It is a wonderful idea, this procession in Chandni Chowk, and they bestow their gratitude on the man who caused it. The great Gopal Das! Gopal Das *zindabad*!

Jasjit General Store sits on an elevated platform, so Ramvilas and Gopal stand on a natural stage, but a much larger crowd has now collected around the whores, to whom Gopal is invisible.

'Stand on the counter,' commands Ramvilas.

'What if it breaks under me?' asks a horrified Gopal.

'Kartar Singh will build a new one.'

Ramvilas places a stool next to the counter.

Gopal slips off his chappals. Ramvilas places his hands under the chaivala's armpits and pushes upward. Gopal raises his dhoti, heaves himself up with a groan and places one foot gingerly on the counter. Then he pushes down on Ramvilas's shoulder and straightens. A cry goes up among the whores. At the same time, his spectacles come clattering down to the floor. 'I cannot see!'

Ramvilas picks them up. 'You do not need to see,' he says quietly. 'Begin your speech.'

Gopal stares at the swirl before him. There are moving shapes of red, yellow and black. Far in the distance he can distinguish white and grey forms, perhaps men's kurtas and dhotis. The placards are blobs of white and red that dance before his eyes. But he must speak, he must retrieve the tortuous sentences he has memorised over the last two days . . .

'My sisters!'

The sisters trill their approval.

'My sisters! Gopal Das stands before you today as one of your own. I am not a rich man. I am not a great man. I am not a man of good family . . .'

The whores clap.

'They have declared your work to be illegal,' says Gopal. 'But who deserves punishment? The sex-worker or the customer? Or the bai, the pahalvan, the kotha owner? In being raped, my sisters, you protect forty crore women from being raped. By possessing you, the Indian man possesses the forty crore women of India. By giving your honour, you protect the honour of the Indian woman. You preserve the social fabric of India. We should honour you instead of reviling you. We should place you on a pedestal.'

Gopal stops. The rest of the speech is a blur in his mind. He looks down at Ramvilas nervously and finds no sympathy there. The whores, who had been getting ready to applaud, are confused by the sudden pause. Gopal is seized with panic. He begins again: 'They have declared your work to be illegal . . .'

Ramvilas scans the crowd. Three television cameramen have appeared at the far end. He motions to them to advance, and they wade through the crowd like boats cutting through waves. Whores scatter, men are pushed aside, until the crews – eyes and ears intent on the speaker – stand outside the store, just below the platform. This should provide a good angle for Gopal, thinks Ramvilas. He must not allow the cameras to clamber into the store, because that will bring Gopal lower on the horizon.

'A vote for Gopal Das is a vote for the people! *Jai Hind*!'

Ramvilas starts. The speech was supposed to be eight minutes long, but Gopal has wrapped it up in two. He glances at Gita Didi, whose brow is furrowed. There are many promises in that speech – promises made to STREE, to sex-workers in GB Road – that Gopal has skipped. Ramvilas makes eye-contact with Gita, explaining silently that he will set things right. It is a small matter – what is the value of the spoken word? It is forgotten as soon as it is uttered. There will be a written statement. She seems to understand because she begins to clap. The whores join in with such force that Gopal is almost knocked off his feet.

During the applause, Gita Didi commandeers a television crew. Microphones are pointed at her, and she speaks haltingly of her mission. Her Hindi is still sketchy, notes Ramvilas. She mixes it with Nepali words, and her syntax is often awkward, but she is glib in a childlike way. 'Sex-workers are like other workers,' she says. 'We are like clerks, rickshavalas, peanut-sellers, cobblers and porters. We want rights just as they do. And we want the respect that any other profession gets. Gopal Das has promised us a life of respect. Gopal Das will provide us with full legalisation, will recognise us as a union, will grant us full rights . . .'

Ramvilas watches with a mixture of amusement and admiration. Are those the words he has put into her head? They seem so much more substantial in broken Hindi.

'Here is Nasreen,' says Gita Didi. 'And here is Zubaida! Zeenat! Salma! Parveen! They are sex-workers, and they are Musalmans. Who can be more downtrodden in this society? And we are united in our support for Gopal Dasji.'

Ramvilas notes that the cameras feed hungrily on the tableau of

Musalman whores. Gita Didi slips a hand into her bodice and pulls out a golden purse, decorated with a monogram in large letters – STREE. 'The sex-workers in GB Road have dreamed of such a candidate for years,' she informs the microphones. 'We will not let him fall short against rich upper-caste candidates. This purse contains thirty-six thousand, seven hundred and fifty-two rupees! What is special about that amount? It is the sum of everything earned by every sex-worker in GB Road last night, after paying bais, owners, pahal-vans and the police. We work for the bais and the police every night, but last night we worked for Gopal Das. Every man who sinned against womanhood last night did it for Gopal Das! These thirty-six thousand, seven hundred and fifty-two rupees are the contribution of STREE to the mission of Gopal Das.'

Gopal cannot see the purse clearly in the fog before his eyes, but he gasps at the amount. Thirty-six thousand rupees! He sees the shining golden blob sail through the air, borne on a cushion of hands, until it enters the shop and disappears into a pair of hands close to him.

'Ramvilas Babu! Can you give me the purse?' he asks.

Ramvilas lets Gopal grasp it. 'Hold it high above your head,' he commands.

Gopal raises it.

'Gopal Das *zindabad*!' cries Gita Didi.

The whores return the cry.

'You are very popular today,' says Ramvilas. 'Your campaign is now on track, Gopal Bhai!'

Gopal clutches the purse, squeezing it hard to prevent the money falling out. Thirty-six thousand rupees! How can such immeasurable treasure be contained in so small a purse? Perhaps it is in hundred-rupee notes. You cannot choose smaller ones when you make such a large donation. How many hundred-rupee notes are required to make up thirty-six thousand? A hundred? Five hundred? A thousand?

The crowd has taken up the chant begun by Gita Didi. 'Gopal Das *zindabad*!'

'Babu . . .' Gopal begins.

'Do not say anything now!' says Ramvilas, sharply. 'Just keep holding the purse high in the air.'

Gopal looks at the red and yellow waves before him, crashing against each other, swaying in unison, then breaking up.

'Have you ever been to Dilli?' whispers Ramvilas.

'We are in Dilli,' says Gopal.

'Not *this* Dilli.' Ramvilas snorts. 'The *real* Dilli! The one where real Dillivalas live and rule. The one with wide roads, large gardens, lovely flowers, red-brick bungalows . . .'

'I have seen India Gate,' says Gopal.

More than twenty years ago, with a young, docile Mukesh at his side, Gopal had taken bus number 502 to Mehrauli. It wound its way through the boulevards of New Delhi, affording him glimpses of the Supreme Court, India Gate, Rashtrapati Bhavan. He saw them all through the large windows of a bus and pointed them out to his son, who would have been twenty-nine today. Twenty-nine! Married – a father, perhaps.

'One visit does not count,' says Ramvilas dismissively. 'And you must have gone in a bus. You need to sit in the back of a car and watch the gardens glide by silently, in the dull glow of tinted glass. That is when you will have seen Dilli.'

Gopal is not sure he understands the distinction. His hands are beginning to hurt, and the crowd shows no sign of dispersing. 'May I lower the purse now?'

'Hold it up, Gopal Bhai, hold it up! You will soon see Dilli, and you will see it through the tinted windows of a car.'

'*Gar Firdaus bar roo-e-zameen ast*
Hameen ast-o hameen ast-o hameen ast . . .'

Suleman recites monotonously, recalling verses from memory, pulling them out painstakingly and slapping words, one upon another, to form tired couplets. He does not speak Persian and he has no gift for correct pronunciation, but he does not care. He quickly translates into Hindi.

'*If there is Paradise on earth*
It is this, it is this, it is this . . .'

'Those are the words written on Divan-i-Khas in Red Fort, my brothers,' he declares. 'Let me ask you now. Which one of you thinks Chandni Chowk is a place of bliss? Which one of you sitting here, without a job, without clothes, without food, thinks he is in Paradise?'

He scans the audience, daring someone to answer in the affirmative.

'Did the poet Khusro lie? Was he making false claims?'

There is a reverent shaking of heads. The poet did not lie, a poet cannot lie . . .

'They have taken our Paradise and turned it into our prison,' Suleman announces.

There is scattered clapping. Noor Muhammad, standing a few feet to Suleman's left, recedes into the background, aware of the shaft of light that glances past his straight, angular, aristocratic nose, and lowers his eyes in embarrassment. No place can be Paradise when proclaimed as such in cacophonous accents. He cannot bear to hear the language of Omar Khayyám spoken thus. This Suleman Mian lets Persian drip like Urdu, the language of the market, or barks it like Hindi, the language of Banias. It is not a sledgehammer tongue, to be slapped on a counter like the carcass of a goat! It is not to be employed in issuing commands, but for the description of a perfect sunset. Who gave licence to this uncouth man to defile Khusro? His ancestors come not from Persia but from the horrible east – somewhere in Bihar and Bengal – if you look at his swarthy complexion, weak nose, ill-defined chin, cruel upper lip and pencil moustache.

'There is a reason I stand here in Gali Qasim Jan,' declares Suleman. 'I could have held a meeting anywhere in Chandni Chowk because all of it is my home, but I choose to meet you in this haveli in Gali Qasim Jan. It is too small for so great a gathering – but every brick in its walls has a story to tell. And I want you to hear that story today.'

Suleman pauses for effect. It was Noor Muhammad's idea that he hold a meeting in the old home of Ghalib. He thought it would remind Musalmans that they shared a history. Once made, the suggestion took wing, even after Noor Muhammad discovered, to his horror, that Suleman neither enjoyed nor cared much for Ghalib, having grown up on Hindi film songs, thinking the cinema lyricists to be great poets.

The gathering is not large. There are only fifty people in the courtyard, and a few more in the lane outside who came to the mosque at the corner but strayed toward the haveli out of curiosity.

The setting is prosaic. The entrance is guarded by a pharmacy on the left and a general store on the right, leading to a small courtyard with an open staircase that rises to a second floor, where a telephone booth is plastered with STD/ISD rates. The rest of the upper floor is no longer accessible. There is no electricity in the decrepit structure so Suleman has arranged for oil lamps, which hang from nails hammered into the walls. Each nail is a stake driven into the heart of Noor Muhammad, as are the banners announcing Suleman's candidacy, and the ubiquitous pictures of his election symbol – the bicycle – which have been carelessly strung round the courtyard. Why must they damage the monument to hold this meeting? It is not as if Ghalib himself will vote for Suleman!

'The story of Mirza Ghalib cannot be told without the story of wine,' announces Suleman. 'And I will tell you a tale by the poet Hali.'

Suleman makes eye-contact with Noor, the tutor for the story. Noor looks away.

Suleman begins: 'Ghalib composed his verses where I now stand, heady with wine, working in his head late into the night. Whenever he completed a verse, he would tie a knot in his sash. In the morning, awakened from his stupor, he would look at the knots and recall his verses so he could write them down . . .'

An appreciative murmur runs through the gathering. Ibrahim, sitting in the front row as a member of the audience, sets up a loud 'Shaabaash!' which he hopes will be echoed by others, but the crowd does not respond. This is not good, thinks Ibrahim. This haveli event was foisted on Suleman Mian by the stuffy fop from Kashmir. How can fifty people create noise sufficient for a public meeting? Rallies require crowds, and crowds require hired hands, not lovers of archaic poetry. How many of these people have been paid? And why should they clap if they have not?

'I cannot remember all the great names in Ballimaran's history,' continues Suleman. 'The nawab of Loharu – whose haveli this was before it came to Ghalib – the poet Hali, Hakim Ajmal Khan, Hasrat Mohani . . . Have you heard the ghazal "Chupke Chupke" sung by Ghulam Ali? It was Hasrat Mohani from Ballimaran who wrote it.'

This revelation stirs some interest. A few people hum the first lines of the ghazal, then fall silent. Suleman draws a silk handkerchief from his shervani and passes it over his face. He is used to declaiming to boisterous crowds about Babri Masjid, police brutality and the Mandal Commission. This speech on poetry, pressed on him by Noor

Muhammad, leaves him cold and clearly has no effect on his audience. He must begin the phase of lamentation. 'This is a great city, this Dilli, my brothers. The Banias have ruined the city of Zauq, Zafar, Dagh and Mir. Do you remember what Dagh Dehlavi wrote of this Dilli?

> *'Beggars and rich, old and young, all are in tears,*
> *A world cries for the Delhi that is no more . . .'*

At this Ibrahim claps wildly. People behind him join in, and Suleman basks in the applause.

'Why is this haveli in such a condition?' demands Suleman. 'Do you think a Bania will restore it? Will a Bania bring back the days of Ghalib and Mir? Or do you think it will be dogs like Muhammad Salauddin Qureshi?'

The mention of Qureshi brings forth a scornful laugh.

'We understand the mind of IPP. It is the enemy of Musalmans and secularism in this country. But we do not understand turncoats like Qureshi who, being Musalmans, join IPP in the hope of getting Rajya Sabha seats.'

Noor Muhammad recedes further into the shadows of Ghalib's haveli. He broke off contact with Qureshi a year ago, when it became clear that Qureshi had no plan to pull him out of Railways and find him something in the Public Works Department.

'You have had a Bania MP for eighteen years,' says Suleman. 'It is time to elect one of your own, to bring true the dreams of Dagh Dehlavi for our Dilli.

> *'Allah! Again inhabited and prosperous, let us see it,*
> *Allah! As the fulfilment of our desires, let us see it . . .'*

'You will live in Shahjahanabad again, my brothers!'

Suleman holds up a hand to silence the crowd, even though it has already fallen silent.

'IPP tells us that we are traitors, that we love Pakistan. Does it know that it was *our* blood that was spilled during British times, when Hindus were collaborating with the English, becoming clerks and ministers in their government? Do not believe what I tell you! Hear it from the English themselves. Hear it from Sheikh Noor Muhammad, a great scholar of Mughal architecture, who left IPP after years of trying to secularise it.'

Suleman turns triumphantly to Noor, like a pupil who has just finished a difficult rendition and expects approval. Noor cringes. When he had proposed the idea, he had imagined a sedate, scholarly gathering. He had not known of the telephone booth at the end of the staircase, which has refused to shut down for the meeting. He pulls out a letter from his kurta pocket with an air of deep resignation. When he stumbled upon it in his research, he had tasted the ecstasy of illumination. It laid to rest many niggling doubts. It was sent by the British prime minister Lord Palmerston to Lord Canning, viceroy of India, immediately after the Mutiny of 1857. It is unlikely that anyone in the crowd understands English, but he reads the letter anyway in a sonorous voice: 'Every civil building connected with Mahommedan tradition should be levelled to the ground without regard to antiquarian veneration or artistic pre-dilection . . .' This, to Noor, is vindication of his belief that British rule was especially harsh on the Persian, Arabic and Turkish tradition to which he belongs because it was more assertive of its freedom than the Indian one. But he senses, as he reads the first line, that the crowd is indifferent. He pauses, feeling sorry for himself.

'Translate it into Hindi,' says Suleman.

Noor clears his throat. Suleman, suddenly impatient, pushes him aside.

'Did you hear that letter?' he ask rhetorically. 'Does this not show what Musalmans sacrificed for this country? And what have we received in return for our sacrifice? The fundamentalist IPP, which calls us traitors!'

The audience nods. The letter is suddenly clear, its meaning far more cogent than what could be conveyed by mere words. Noor takes a step outside the haveli, wishing he could be swallowed by the shadows of Gali Qasim Jan. Suleman begins to recite another poem, falters, decides to abandon the script and launches into a passionate tirade that follows a second script, this one written by Ibrahim.

'Leave aside poets and artists! Ballimaran is the street of silver-beaters. Have you heard the *thukk, thukk, thukk* that echoes late into the night? It is the song of the silver-beater, my brothers! Do you know how unrewarding his task is? Yet how wonderful the varq he rolls out! Tasteless in itself, it gives flavour to gulabjamuns, barfis and mangoes. Hindus bite daily into these foils of silver squeezed from the blood of a Musalman. Is there a silver-beater among you?'

Ibrahim violently nudges two men on his left, and they rise to their feet.

'I see two men who spend their lives tickling the tastebuds of rich Marwari seths!' cries Suleman.

He beckons Faquira and Alimuddin with an expansive, benevolent gesture. They advance uncertainly. They have come directly from their shop – reconstructed after the demolition drive two years ago – goaded and accompanied by Ibrahim, who insisted that they did not change into clean kurtas and pyjamas.

'Look at their hands!' cries Suleman.

Embarrassed, Faquira and Alimuddin hide them hastily behind their backs, but Suleman grabs Faquira and holds up his right hand, letting everyone see the calluses. 'These hands bear the mark of service. The inscription on this man's grave will read, "Let only the humble grass grow upon my grave, for grass is the best covering for the poor."'

Noor, standing outside the haveli now, winces. That line is his gift to Suleman. Jahanara, gentle princess, forgive this desecration of your memory . . .

'Your leaders do not see the calluses on Faquira's hands,' laments Suleman. 'And now they are talking of removing the haj subsidy.'

The audience gasps.

'Chandni Chowk has four assembly segments,' explains Suleman. 'IPP won three in 'ninety-three. But if you break up those four segments into their eight wards, IPP had a lead in only four. So how did it win three segments? Because of a vote division among Musalmans, and a fortuitous division of those winning wards among different assembly segments. That is why Sohan Lal Agrawal is an MLA, and that is why Harilal Gupta is an MLA. We must not let that happen again. Musalmans must not allow their votes to be divided. There is only one MP for Chandni Chowk, and we want him to be a Musalman!'

Noor turns away from the haveli. A group of ragged men is striding down the lane, putting up posters on walls. They are young – in trousers, jeans and T-shirts – led by a tall, thin, excessively dark man with dirty hair. He points here and there, ordering them about, scratching his head with one arm that ends in a stump. They carry stacks of posters and four buckets of a paste, which they apply directly with their hands before slapping up the posters. They pass the haveli and plaster it indiscriminately, treating the home of Ghalib no differently from the pharmacy to its left. Noor is horrified to see a bald man in foggy spectacles smiling shamelessly from the walls of

Ghalib's haveli. 'Get away from here, you thieves!' he screams at the men. 'This is a national monument! You cannot stick posters on it!'

The one-handed man approaches Noor threateningly. They are both tall and thin, one erect and aristocratic, the other lanky and beggarly.

'What is a national monument?' asks the man.

Noor is horrified. The effrontery! The sheer gall of a cripple – a man from Bihar or Bengal or one of those cesspools of disease – to flaunt his ignorance with such pluck! 'This is the haveli of Asadullah Khan Ghalib,' he declares, with dignity.

'Fuck Ghalib,' says the man.

The men stick up more posters. Noor wrings his hands, stamps his feet, then rushes into the haveli to seek help. Suleman Mian has the meeting in his thrall. He holds Faquira and Alimuddin in his arms, one on each side, crushing them to his slender frame.

'These men have beaten silver for thirty years. Their arms ache, their teeth chatter. They tell tales of Hatim Tai and Alif Laila to pass the time as they beat yet another pellet into a silver leaf . . . These are the men I represent. These are the men whose votes I seek. Who will protect them? A Bania MP?'

The crowd titters.

'And these are the men whose shops were destroyed by Harilal Gupta.'

The crowd falls silent. Suleman has timed the revelation well.

'There were bulldozers, my brothers! There were Hindu policemen with guns, inspectors in jeeps, with sirens and loudspeakers. They pulled Faquira and Alimuddin out of their shop and flung them into the street. They threw away hammers, pestles and mats, and they stole stacks of varq from the shop. Why do you think they did this? "Illegal construction," they said. Do you think a room where a man earns his livelihood can be illegal? What will they call illegal next? This haveli of Mirza Ghalib? Will they destroy his poetry because it was written in an illegal haveli?'

Faquira and Alimuddin cast confused glances at the crowd. Almost everyone is their neighbour. Most people in the crowd know that they crawled back into their shop the very next day and restocked it with silver. Business has continued since the demolition drive. It has been two years now. No one really remembers the drive any more . . .

'Six years ago they tore down Babri Masjid,' continues Suleman.

'Two years ago they tore down your shops. Tomorrow they will come into your homes. And what will they destroy after that? Jama Masjid?'

There is stunned silence. The thought is revolting. It is even somewhat scandalous that a Musalman should say this. Suleman draws himself up for a final appeal. 'I do not want your vote if you do not love me as your brother. But if you love me as a Musalman, if you want to be rid of Banias from IPP and Congress, you have only one man to vote for, only one symbol to think of. Vote for the bicycle, my brothers! Vote for the bicycle!'

'Suleman Mian *zindabad*!' cries Ibrahim, springing up.

Faquira and Alimuddin, relieved that attention has shifted from them, take up the chant. Outside the haveli, Gauhar pauses, runs his hand over the last poster of Gopal to smooth out the wrinkles, and peeks inside to identify the source of the commotion.

'Suleman Mian *zindabad*!' says the crowd.

Gauhar gasps in fear, horror, anger. It has been six years since he stood so close to Suleman Mian. This is the man who sent him to Ayodhya, who still owes him ten thousand rupees, who declared him dead and forbade him to meet Gopal Bhai . . . Gauhar is aware of the presence of his friends. Seven strong boys – Johnny, Partho, Aftab, Munna, Wasif, Baba, Khoka – each ready to get into a scrape, pick a fight for him. They have many thefts, robberies, knifings, fistfights under their belts. Who is this puny little man called Suleman Mian? And standing beside him is that toothless dog who once had yellow teeth, who threatened him with his life! 'Five hundred rupees if you go to Suleman Mian's meeting,' Ramvilas Babu has told him. Five hundred rupees for slogans, a thousand for a fight . . . And here is that bastard Suleman Mian, who still owes him ten thousand!

'Suleman Mian *murdabad*!' yells Gauhar.

At first, no one notices. Gauhar's '*murdabad*' mixes with the '*zindabad*' of others. Gradually, the crowd becomes aware of a dissenting voice, looks round, locates the source outside the haveli, and falls silent in confusion. A lone voice continues to scream: 'Suleman Mian *murdabad*!'

Suleman frowns and looks outside the courtyard. He recognises Gauhar instantly. 'What is that boy doing here?' he hisses to Ibrahim.

'He ran away from Faquira two years ago,' stammers Ibrahim.

'Why did you not tell me?'

Ibrahim advances upon Gauhar threateningly. Even as he does so, he notices that Gauhar is taller, stubborn and resentful, and a wall of other boys stands menacingly behind him. Ibrahim loses his confidence. 'Get out,' he stammers.

Gauhar stands firm. He is much stronger than Toothless Beard. And at his side stand seven more strong men. 'Gopal Das *zindabad*!' they scream in unison.

'Gopal Das!' yells Aftab. 'Musalman candidate!'

Then the seven beat their buckets – now empty of glue – with their hands, block the entrance to the haveli, and set up a scandalous chant. 'Suleman is a bastard, Suleman is a thief, Suleman is a bastard, Suleman is a thief . . .'

Suleman stands stone-faced. From the scanty beards and accents of the boys, he knows they are all Bangladeshi Musalmans. This meeting has gone wrong. To have eight Musalmans stand in front of fifty others and call him a thief, refer to someone else as a Musalman candidate . . . 'Let us go!' he mutters to Ibrahim. 'And tell me about this Gopal Das.'

Gauhar and his friends follow Suleman all the way to the Ambassador. 'Suleman is a bastard, Suleman is a thief . . .' Gauhar screams, with all the passion in his heart. This is the bastard who took away Mussabir. This is the bastard who stole my money!

The Ambassador speeds away. Gauhar spits after it. Sheikh Noor Muhammad stands outside the haveli and shakes his head. The eight men will not stop shouting slogans even now that Suleman has left. A man is on a long-distance call in the telephone booth upstairs, quoting grocery prices in Chandni Chowk as if the power of his lungs must ferry his voice to the other city, and the telephone is merely a prop. His voice mingles with the slogans of the eight men. Each defiles the haveli of Ghalib, thinks Noor Muhammad.

'Jaggery ten, atta thirty-two, maida sixty, suji two per quintal, sakoti, bulandshahar and biznor forty each, Gopal Das *zindabad*! Douralla, modi, simbhauli twenty per kilo, Gopal Das *zindabad*! Agota, urad, moong, Gopal Das *zindabad*! Masoor, lobia, chitra, soybean oil, coconut oil, Gopal Das *zindabad*!'

IF

'Our poor sisters earn twenty-five rupees in a night, having given their bodies to six truck drivers, six husbands who cheat their wives . . . What kind of a society has the Congress Party created for us? And IPP wants nothing more than a Raam temple in Ayodhya. Is the Raam temple more important than the honour of one sister in GB Road?'

Gopal keeps pace with the cassette-player, matching Ramvilas's reedy voice with his own. He has played the tape countless times. He likes such speeches. They are short and easy to memorise. When he falters he can supply the words all by himself, drawing on lines from films he has seen. The other speeches – about the poor man's candidate – are more complicated. He dreads them, and requires the assistance of Ramvilas Babu when he delivers them. He looks forward to the end of this election whirlpool in thirty-three days. As soon as all the speeches are delivered and all the votes cast, he will go back to the kholi in Khari Baoli.

He stretches out on the mattress, tired. It is late in the evening. The shops in Lajpatrai Market have lowered their shutters. The only living things to be found in the lanes are dogs, beggars, thieves and policemen. He must rise and draw the doors of Jasjit General Store. Kartar Singhji has gone to Simla for a holiday, Ramvilas Babu told him, so it is his responsibility to lock up at night. He glances up at the monitor on the wall and is surprised to see a man in the store, looking straight at the closed-circuit camera mounted behind the counter. The man calls for Gopal – how does he know his name? – then settles on a stool. His face is in shadow, but the wispy beard is familiar. Even in the blue haze that the camera imparts to everything, it is clear that there is something wrong with his teeth. It is Ibrahim Mian!

Gopal pushes aside the Bournvita shelf and rushes into the store, then stops short behind the counter, shaken by the other man's appearance. This is not Ibrahim Mian: it is his ghost.

'There you are,' says Ibrahim, softly. 'I thought I was in the wrong store.'

Ibrahim looks much older than Gopal remembers. His teeth are gone, except for two fangs that protrude monstrously over his lower lip, decayed into translucency, like solidified beads of lime juice. His beard is much denuded – the hairs that remain hang in disconsolate strands.

'You have not come to me for two years,' Gopal accuses him.

'You have no tea to offer me!' retorts Ibrahim.

Gopal shrugs. Ibrahim stopped coming to Kucha Bansilal after they tore down his stall. Ramesh Babu would not have allowed him into Jamna Lal Kishori Mal anyway.

'You are not a chaivala any more,' accuses Ibrahim.

'But I still have my stall!' says Gopal.

He runs back into the room. A few days after he was brought to Lajpatrai Market, Kartar Singh had all his clothes transferred from the kholi. They are bundled in a corner, surrounded by utensils, soap, a pocket mirror and a comb. Behind this heap sits a large sack, upright, full of pots, pans and bottles from the stall. Gopal rummages through it and pulls out tins of sugar and tea, a strainer, a few cardamom pods and a box of milk powder. At the bottom of the sack, wedged between china cups, he finds Ibrahim's glass tumbler.

He has no kerosene for the stove, but Jasjit General Store is brimming with electric kettles, arranged behind glass shelves like troops in neat formations. He snatches one and puts water to boil. Five minutes later, he triumphantly slaps Ibrahim's glass tumbler on the counter, sloshing with tea. Ibrahim grins, and Gopal notes the toothless black gums.

'This is how I remember you!' says Ibrahim.

The words, and Ibrahim's appearance, sadden Gopal. He watches Ibrahim slurp the tea, and lays the cornucopia of Jasjit General Store at his feet: 'Do you want some Bournvita? Horlicks? Some hot cocoa?'

Ibrahim shakes his head. Gopal spreads his arms in an expansive gesture that sweeps the gleaming shelves on either side into his arms. 'My stall has grown, Ibrahim Mian! What would you like to buy?'

Ibrahim drains his tumbler and sets it down on the counter. 'I have not come to buy anything,' he says.

Gopal looks at him uncomfortably. It had not occurred to him, until now, that there was a purpose to Ibrahim's visit.

'They told me that you had repented for your behaviour,' says Ibrahim. 'I have tried for two years to forgive you. No matter how great a brother's crime, it is always forgiven. I have tried, Gopal Bhai, and I almost succeeded! So when they told me you had repented, I could not stop myself. I forgive you! I forgive you!'

Gopal concentrates hard on those words, wheezing, causing his spectacles to fog up. 'Forgive what, Ibrahim Mian?'

Ibrahim looks hurt. 'Have you forgotten? Do you not remember what you did to me, Gopal Bhai?'

Gopal remains silent.

Ibrahim sighs. 'It is natural you have forgotten. You don't want to be reminded of the painful past. Can you imagine the pain I felt when I saw you standing on that stage in a silk kurta and silk dhoti with your moustache blackened like shoe polish?'

'My moustache is not dyed now,' says Gopal, mournfully.

'Ah!' Ibrahim is triumphant. 'You look like a poor man now, as you should. Your head is as bald as a riverbed, your face is unshaven, your shirt has buttons missing, your dhoti is crumpled and dirty . . . I have no complaints now, because this is how I remember you! But what happened to you at that festival?'

'Which festival?'

'The one the Hindus celebrated in Chandni Chowk after they destroyed our shops. The one with the English name.'

'Ah, that was a long time ago.'

'Two years is a long time to you!' says a hurt Ibrahim. 'For two years I have struggled to find forgiveness in my heart. Can you imagine how difficult it has been? There you were, in a silk kurta and silk dhoti, accepting prizes from the same people who had destroyed your stall! There were diamond studs on your kurta!'

'Those were not diamonds.'

'And your moustache was black as coal!' says Ibrahim, bitterly. 'It was as if Gopal Bhai, my brother from Kucha Bansilal, had forgotten himself and thought he was a young man. I asked myself if you were a traitor. "A kafir cannot be trusted," says Suleman Mian, "because the blood that flows in his heart will never change." I thought, for a moment, that Suleman Mian was right. Gopal Bhai should be with Suleman Mian near Town Hall, I told myself, shouting slogans against seths and Banias and IPP thugs who have demolished his stall, not preening himself on a stage like a whore and accepting prizes from sardars.'

'They gave me no prize,' protests Gopal.

'They have given him money for this, I told myself, and he is too hungry to spurn their offer. That is what I told myself.'

'They gave me no money.'

'"We will help our Gopal Bhai," Suleman Mian said to me. "We will get his shop back. We will launch a movement against these rich seths, we will sit on a dharna, we will go on hunger strikes, we will not sleep until they give Gopal Bhai his stall back." This is what Suleman Mian said to me before we came to Chandni Chowk. And then we saw you standing on a stage in a silk kurta, thanking the sardarji for clearing away your stall, feeding the snake that bit you!'

'They took back the silk kurta.'

'I have forgiven you. Suleman Mian was furious, but I begged him to be kind to you. "Gopal Bhai has a heart of gold," I said. "He stands on a stage with IPP people but his heart is with us." Suleman Mian would not believe me, but I was firm with him.'

'You are a true friend, Ibrahim Mian.'

'Friend? No, I am your brother.'

Gopal is relieved and overwhelmed. 'Have you come to buy something? Just take it for free. I will talk to sardarji and he will understand.'

Ibrahim sighs. 'I do not want to buy anything, Gopal Bhai. I am satisfied now that you see your mistake. A man makes mistakes and his brother forgives him.'

'You are a good brother.'

Ibrahim gets up. 'All right! Let us go to Suleman Mian.'

Gopal is startled. 'Why?'

'To admit your mistake to him. Then you can declare your support for him.'

Gopal fidgets. This is Ibrahim Mian, he tells himself. Ibrahim, only Ibrahim with his falling teeth . . . But Suleman is another matter. How will he face those fiery eyes? Will he not tremble and fall to the ground? 'I will come tomorrow,' he says uncertainly, 'with Ramvilas Babu.'

Ibrahim snorts. 'Why have you got yourself mixed up with IPP seths?'

'He is not with IPP any more.'

'You must come now,' insists Ibrahim.

Gopal does not move.

Ibrahim sighs and sits down at the counter again. 'It breaks my heart to see you waste your life in this election business. Why do you want to go walking through lanes and fold your hands before strangers? Why do you want to make speeches? This election business is for leaders, people like Suleman Mian. And for thieves like Harilal Gupta.'

'Suleman Mian is a great leader,' says Gopal, eagerly.

' "Gopal Bhai is a good man," Suleman Mian tells me. "He should come and join me in my fight if he wants to do public service. Why does he want to fight alone? It is a difficult fight!" '

'Very difficult . . .'

' "If he works with me," Suleman Mian said, "he will get to travel in my Ambassador. He will sit behind me when I become MP. He will walk with me when I visit Chandni Chowk. He will look after my constituency. And he will get his chai stall back." '

Gopal sighs. He has thought of the chai stall many times.

'And do not forget Mukesh,' says Ibrahim, quietly.

'They murdered him!' says Gopal. 'The upper-caste criminals!'

'Will you let his sacrifice go in vain? We must fight for Mukesh, you and I, and Suleman Mian will lead us. You are causing polarisation, Gopal Bhai. It is not good for the unity and integrity of the country. You must stop this election business and work with Suleman Mian for the sake of the country. For Mother India!'

'But Ramvilas Babu—'

'He is a snake!' hisses Ibrahim. 'He is a clerk, a thief who stole money to start his own shop. You and I have been brothers for twenty years. Why would you want to work with someone else? Come to Suleman Mian's office tomorrow, behind Jama Masjid.'

'I will have to wait until Sardar Kartar Singh returns from Simla. He has left me in charge of the store.'

'You saved that man's wife from falling through a window, and what did he give you in return?'

That moment flashes clearly in Gopal's mind. Suddenly, the store appears crowded with people lining the shelves, filling the counter, overflowing into the lane. Every face is turned to him, waiting expectantly for the great revelation he dare not make.

'It was you, Ibrahim Mian!' he whispers.

Ibrahim's eyes are cold. 'Your mind is failing with age.'

'What were you doing in sardarji's house?'

'You talk like an old man,' says Ibrahim. 'What house?'

Gopal pauses, suddenly confused. The picture of that moment is fresh in his mind – a fat woman flailing in the window, a commode next to him, ominous sounds in the hall outside . . . But the man who stands in the door gradually loses his form, becoming an indistinct blob. 'It has been a long time . . .'

'It is not your fault,' says Ibrahim, reassuringly. 'This election business has exhausted you. You can rejoin the national mainstream.'

'What is the national mainstream?'

'Suleman Mian,' replies Ibrahim. 'But you need not worry about that.' He stands up. 'It is getting late. I will expect you in Suleman Mian's office tomorrow morning at eleven.'

Gopal, behind the counter, watches Ibrahim sullenly. 'I will come with Gauhar,' he says.

Ibrahim fixes Gopal with a glassy stare. The lower lip hangs loose, revealing the dead gums. 'Who is that?'

'Gauhar Muhammad,' says Gopal, stubbornly. 'Why did you tell me he was dead?'

'He is dead,' repeats Ibrahim.

'He has come back. He came to my rally. He has a gang of his own – many strong boys who will do anything for me. My son has come back to me!'

Ibrahim frowns. 'You should not associate with that man.'

'Why not? He is my son.'

'You last saw him six years ago. Did you ask him where he was all those years? What has he been up to? How has he earned a living? And why has he come back now?'

Suddenly Gopal is worried. In his joy at seeing Gauhar, such questions had not occurred to him.

'Is he in the store now?' asks Ibrahim fearfully.

'I do not know where he sleeps, but he will come here in the morning.'

Ibrahim is relieved. 'Come behind Jama Masjid alone,' he commands. 'Suleman Mian does not want to see ghosts.'

'I will come with Ramvilas Babu,' insists Gopal.

Ibrahim mutters something, then sits down again. 'Do you know Muhammad Salauddin Qureshi?' he asks.

'A Musalman?'

'A dog,' says Ibrahim. 'A turncoat who associated with IPP. Suleman Mian often said to him, "You are a Musalman, why not work for the secular community?" But he insisted on being with the communal IPP, where they speak of Hindutva and the Raam temple.'

'Is Qureshi Sahib with Suleman Mian now?' asks Gopal.

Ibrahim shakes his head. 'Yesterday, Qureshi was returning to his house. He took a bus from ISBT. Three men got off with him in Bahadurgarh. When he did not come home at night, his wife thought he was busy in Chandni Chowk with election work. This morning, his body was found outside Red Fort, sprawled in the moat.'

'He must have fallen asleep there,' suggests Gopal.

Ibrahim looks scornfully at him. 'Only his body was in the moat. His head was delivered to his house in Bahadurgarh.'

Gopal stares at Ibrahim in horror. This is Ibrahim Mian, who drinks his tea from the Musalman tumbler: why does he appear to metamorphose into a wolf under the dim lights of the store? Are those fangs getting longer? Why do the eyes glint so viciously? 'Who sent those men?' whispers Gopal.

'How should I know? Anything can happen in an election. Suleman Mian has connections with all types of people. Some are good and some are bad. How will I forgive myself if something should happen to you?'

Gopal sits very still, watching Ibrahim study a leather belt behind a glass panel. Ibrahim pushes aside the panel, unhooks the belt from its moorings on the shelf, and holds it up. 'How much is this?'

'Take it!' pleads Gopal. 'It is yours.'

Ibrahim rolls up the belt and walks out of the store. Gopal lowers the shutter with trembling hands.

12.

Ramvilas holds up a hand to silence the crowd, turns and rushes into the store. He nearly slams into the Bournvita shelf, swings it open and barges into the back room, where he is shocked to find Gopal seated on the mattress, cross-legged, dishevelled, eyes shut, head on his chest.

'It is already eleven!' protests Ramvilas. 'I asked you to be up by eight.'

'I have not slept all night,' whispers Gopal.

Ramvilas is exasperated. 'The Chandni Chowk Ricksha-Pullers Union has come to declare its support for you. They have brought a large donation. There are hundreds of rickshavalas outside, chanting slogans. Every shop in Lajpatrai Market has shut down to watch the spectacle. Do you think they care how you spent the night?'

Gopal sighs. Ramvilas suppresses the urge to kick the chaivala into action.

'What could worry a candidate like you?' he says softly. 'You are gathering support by the day!'

'I cannot go outside in this state,' says Gopal.

Ramvilas chuckles. 'You are the common man's candidate. It is right that you should look like a common man.'

Gopal shakes his head. 'I opened the purse last night,' he says.

Ramvilas frowns.

'The purse those ladies from GB Road handed to me,' explains Gopal.

'What about it?'

'It was empty.'

Ramvilas shrugs. 'Why should it contain anything?'

'They said it had thirty-six thousand rupees in it.'

When he had first held it, Gopal had wondered how such a small purse could contain so much money. Even allowing for hundred-rupee notes, it had felt too light, and it had flattened under the pressure of his hand. It should have bulged a little, offered some resistance. Gopal had wanted to ask Ramvilas Babu about it, but the ladies stood in front of him, holding placards and chanting slogans, and there were newspeople with their cameras. It seemed impertinent and irrelevant to bring up the matter, especially when Ramvilas Babu was so certain of the money.

'Ah, yes,' says Ramvilas. 'They did mention thirty-six thousand rupees.' His tone indicates that all is explained.

'That Gita Didi cheated me,' Gopal says. 'I should never have trusted a lady who—' He stops, unable to bring himself to declare her profession.

Ramvilas shakes his head in resignation. 'I have told you many times that such matters should be left to me. How do you know the purse was empty?'

'I held it in my own hands!'

'Yes, but how do you know it was empty? Suppose it had thirty-six thousand rupees inside it. What would you have done with the money? Used it for the campaign, printed posters, hired crowds, rented rickshas, loudspeakers and mikes, paid for rallies and flags and banners. And why would you do all this? To get votes! To tell people you are the poor man's candidate. That is exactly what the purse did for you. Three thousand ladies from GB Road have declared their support for you, with ten thousand people watching. Five lakhs have read about it in newspapers, and fifty lakhs have seen it on television.

Who knows how many votes you have already received by spending those thirty-six thousand rupees?'

'But the money—'

'The money was there, Gopal Bhai! It was there but you spent it, so the purse was empty.'

Gopal sits in great confusion.

'This is how campaign contributions are made,' Ramvilas reassures him.

'I thought I could buy a silk kurta with the money.'

'There is no time to buy kurtas,' scoffs Ramvilas. 'Five hundred rickshavalas are standing outside, chanting your name. You cannot turn them away!'

'But my dhoti—'

'They will not look at your dhoti, and they will not look at your ears. Have I not promised to find you an ear-cleaner? You will have clean ears in three days. Go to the rickshavalas now, and give them the ricksha speech.'

'I do not remember it.'

'I told you to listen to the tapes regularly!' Ramvilas scolds. 'All right, stand next to me and smile at them. I will speak for you.'

Before Gopal can respond, Ramvilas flings open the Bournvita shelf. A roar from hundreds of rickshavalas assails the store, accompanied by blasts from ricksha horns. 'Look at them, Gopal Bhai! They have all come for you!'

'I will stay behind the counter,' says Gopal, panicking. 'If I stand up on it, they will see my dirty dhoti!'

'Which is why you must stand up on it,' says Ramvilas.

He uses a stool to push Gopal up on to the counter. The rickshavalas cheer on seeing Gopal, who folds his hands in front of him, then raises them high into the air.

'Speak!' whispers Ramvilas.

'I told you I do not remember the speech.'

The cheering subsides into an expectant murmur.

'Brothers!' shouts Ramvilas, at the top of his voice, which becomes shriller as it rises. 'Gopal Das does not pull a ricksha because he is too weak. He does not push a cart because he is too old. He does not make paan because he does not know how to. He does not do *anything*, all day or all night, and he will not do anything when he becomes your MP, because *he is already one of you*! Vote for Gopal Das! Vote for the cup of chai!'

It is almost noon. The sun has come up and dappled the light sheet of fog that hangs over Lajpatrai Market. There are more than five hundred rickshavalas in the crowd. In the centre, representatives of their union wear important-looking badges and clean kurta-pyjamas. Around them, lower-level functionaries bear placards: 'Chandni Chowk Ricksha-Pullers Union'; 'All India Ricksha-Pullers Union, Chandni Chowk branch'. Further away from the centre are ricksha-valas who have been pulled away from their shifts. They wear kurtas and lungis, and have come for a while before going back to work. At the perimeter of the crowd are hundreds of rickshas, which belong to rickshavalas who have stopped out of curiosity, who are not active in the union. They sit on their rickshas and press their horns whenever the crowd claps.

'Gopal Bhai will not speak to you,' declares Ramvilas. 'You have heard many speeches, you have received many promises from people like Sulochana Agrawal, Harilal Gupta and even that man who, although a Musalman, does not live like one!'

There is a buzz in the crowd as Suleman's name flits from one mouth to another.

'Gopal Das will not make any promises. What can he possibly do for you? Can you not see the state in which he lives? Can you not see that this man is *incapable of doing anything*? Such a man makes no promises because he does not want to lie to you. If he was the MP for Chandni Chowk, he might fix a minimum fare of five rupees for every ricksha. He might say, "Once you step into a ricksha you must give the poor man at least five rupees!" It does not matter that you have travelled merely from Red Fort to the Jain temple, you have used a poor man's ricksha, caused him to sweat, denied him the opportunity of a greater fare so you must give him five rupees. Gopal Das might say, "Why do you charge interest on a loan given to a rickshavala? Why not let the poor man buy a ricksha without a crushing burden over his head? Should not this loan be interest-free, considering the poor man charges only five rupees?" He might say all these things but he will not, because he is not your MP.'

This complicated reasoning creates bewilderment among the rick-shavalas.

'Some others may tell you, "We were poor once, we understand your pain." But you should ask them, "Are you poor *now*? Can you understand our pain *now*? If you were poor once, we gave you our votes then. Why should we vote for you now? Gopal Das, my brothers, was not only poor *once*, he is poor *now*! He was poor the day he was born, he was poor through his short youth, he is poor in his old age, and he will die a poor man! He will *always* be poor!'

This elicits cries of sympathy from the rickshavalas. The union representatives begin to make their way through the crowd.

'I can see Taslimuddin Mian coming toward me!' screams Ramvilas.

Taslimuddin Mian – in a neat kurta-pyjama and a Nehru jacket of khadi – pushes through the crowd and climbs into Jasjit General Store. He turns to face his union members and withdraws a sleek white envelope from his pocket.

'Fifty-five thousand rupees!' screams Ramvilas. 'One day's wages from every rickshavala in Chandni Chowk!'

Gopal takes the envelope with trembling hands and holds it high in the air. As the crowd cheers he casts a glance at Taslimuddin. Gopal's legs quiver in fear. He has seen this man before, standing behind Suleman Mian at rallies. And now he has pulled Ramvilas Babu aside to whisper something into his ear! What could they be talking about, and why does Ramvilas Babu nod every time the word 'Suleman' escapes the lips of that man? This must be the man Ibrahim warned him about last evening, the man who severed Qureshi Sahib's head from his body! They have come to do the same to him! And Ramvilas Babu nods when told of the plot!

The noise from the crowd dies down until Gopal can hear nothing but the furious beating of his heart. They know, they all know, that he is going to die! They are putting together a plan to kill him even as he stands defenceless on the counter!

'Help me get down!' he pleads.

Ramvilas breaks off his conversation with Taslimuddin and turns to him irritably. 'Stay a little longer,' he commands. 'Let them see the envelope.'

'They will kill me!' Gopal whispers urgently.

Ramvilas frowns. 'Who will?'

'I want to go back to my kholi,' pleads Gopal. 'I do not want to be in this election. Ibrahim Mian said I should withdraw—'

Ramvilas looks angrily at Gopal, puts a foot on the stool and pulls him off the counter. 'Is Ibrahim the yellow-toothed friend of yours?'

'His teeth are all gone now.'

'When did you meet him?'

'He was here last evening.'

Ramvilas curses under his breath, then looks at the restive crowd of rickshavalas. 'Come with me.'

He takes Gopal by the hand and storms out of the store. Taslimuddin scampers to follow them, but is held back by union members who demand his attention. The crowd watches in consternation as the focus of its energy is removed.

'Gopal Das must go to meet the Chandni Chowk Taxi-Drivers Union,' announces Ramvilas, by way of explanation.

The crowd falls back, unconvinced. Ramvilas tears through it, dragging Gopal, who raises his dhoti with one hand so he will not trip over it. The other hand still holds the envelope said to contain fifty-five thousand rupees. 'Where are you taking me?' he asks breathlessly.

Ramvilas does not reply. He pushes through rickshas and scooters in Chandni Chowk, carrying a small crowd of rickshavalas in his wake. They think they are part of a procession that has set off from the rally. 'Gopal Das *zindabad*!' they shout, looking round to see why Taslimuddin has not joined the procession.

Taslimuddin, meanwhile, stands near the counter in Jasjit General Store, annoyed. What kind of rally is this? There was supposed to be an elaborate ceremony around the donation. Unless he can announce the fifty-five thousand rupees to the whole world, how will he show it as an expense in his books? Ramvilas Babu had promised him a long speech, an embrace from the candidate and a position in the Chandni Chowk Heritage Council. You cannot trust politicians. He should have held on to the envelope until after his speech.

Ramvilas turns into Paratha Gali, Gopal stumbling after him. The rickshavalas have fallen back. No one notices them as they find their way through stalls of parathas and pickle. The smells are pleasant. Gopal wonders if they are going to stop and eat something. Perhaps a methi paratha wrapped round a slice of mango pickle . . . But Ramvilas pushes through Paratha Gali and turns toward the lanes that lead to Jama Masjid.

'Where are we going, babu?'

The lanes behind Jama Masjid are choked with stalls that have come up since the demolition drive. Musalmans! thinks Gopal. So many Musalmans, who turn to stare at them! The two of them are noticeably Hindu – Ramvilas in a kurta-pyjama, Gopal in a kurta and a dhoti that barely comes to his knees. It is not safe to walk among so many Musalmans . . . bearded men in shervanis huddling outside chai stalls, women in burqas flitting between bangle shops, a large man draped in a shawl, surrounded by a cloud of smoke from his bidi, schoolgirls in uniform walking in the middle of the lane, oblivious of rickshas and scooters . . . Too many Musalmans! They pass the fish market, stalls selling biryani, haleem, halva, rose-water, attar, pakoras, jalebis, roasted chicken kababs, dates, vermicelli . . . A man stirs a mass of sweet rabari in a cauldron. A boy kneads dough outside a stall. Another pours hot milk into a large vat, where it turns frothy. He is going to make more jalebis, thinks Gopal, to add to those already bobbing up and down in his cauldron. Such large ones, each the size of a plate!

'Can we eat something?' Gopal asks.

Ramvilas continues to walk briskly, and Gopal hurries after him. What is this white line that travels along the drain? Ah, Gopal heard about this when the Corporation tried it in Kucha Bansilal. It is pesticide that the Corporation sprays every week all over Chandni Chowk, except in Kucha Bansilal where Sohan Lalji refused them permission for fear the smell would turn customers away. And here is a policeman, a Jat from Haryana who stands around with nothing to do. A Hindu! A Hindu in this forest of Musalmans! They should eat now.

Then Gopal sees an ear-cleaner, squatting next to the drain on a sack, his needles and pluckers spread out before him. 'You have brought me this far to have my ears cleaned?' he asks breathlessly.

But they run past the ear-cleaner, and a man selling red turbans whom Ramvilas Babu pushes away impatiently. They enter a lane and walk along the Jama Masjid wall, stepping over pots and pans and children, then turn the corner. They are at the steps that lead up to the masjid courtyard.

'I am not a Musalman, babu,' says Gopal.

Ramvilas chuckles, pulling Gopal behind him as he runs up the great staircase. 'You do not have to be. This is a democracy of Hindus, not the empire of Shah Jahan. Anyone can go inside Jama Masjid.'

Gopal huffs and puffs behind Ramvilas, trying to slow down the nimbler man.

'Besides,' says Ramvilas, 'you have not come here to talk to Allah.'

At the top of the staircase, they remove their chappals and receive tokens for them. A man points to Gopal's dhoti, which has ridden up to reveal his knees. 'You need a lungi to cover your legs and a topi to cover your head,' he rules.

'Who says so?' demands Ramvilas.

The man raises an index finger skyward, indicating that the command has come from Allah himself. His companion, standing in the shadow of the towering door with yards of lungis slung over his shoulder, accosts them.

'Lungi and topi for twenty,' he says.

'Do we look like foreign tourists?' Ramvilas demands, and points to Gopal. 'Can you not see how poor this man is before quoting such rates?'

The man acquiesces. 'Five rupees for each of you, sahib.'

'But I do not want a lungi!' says Ramvilas, pointing to his full-length pyjamas.

'All right,' says the man, crestfallen. 'Eight rupees for two topis and one lungi.'

'Do you not see the topi on my head?' challenges Ramvilas, straightening his Gandhi cap.

'That is a Hindu topi,' says the man.

'You do not know who you are speaking to,' says Ramvilas, imperiously. 'Calling this cap a Hindu topi could get you into jail for communal comments! Do you want to incite a communal riot?'

The man backs down in fear. He is used to white women in shorts who gladly hand him fifty rupees.

'Five rupees for a topi and a lungi, for the old man in the dhoti,' he offers.

'All right,' says Ramvilas.

The man hastily wraps a lungi round Gopal's dhoti, ensuring that it covers his legs to his ankles, and presses a topi on his head.

'Now I look like I am wearing a saree!' protests Gopal.

'Come.'

'They will steal my chappals!' says Gopal.

Ramvilas laughs. 'Musalmans say they have the Prophet's chappals inside Jama Masjid. Perhaps we can borrow those.'

The lungi man frowns at Ramvilas, confused and impressed by this powerful personage who knows so much about Jama Masjid.

'And while we borrow the chappals, we can also take a look at the Prophet's hair, which lies next to it. No one votes for a bald candidate.'

'People will overhear you!' says a shocked Gopal.

'You are walking through Shahi Darvaza, Gopal Bhai. This entrance was reserved for the emperor. Now it opens to all on Fridays . . . Do you sense the distance you have travelled in three hundred years? We have raised you to the status of Shah Jahan.'

Ramvilas pulls at Taslimuddin's envelope – which Gopal has been carrying – and stuffs it into his kurta pocket. Gopal consoles himself that money, like bare legs and heads, is forbidden inside Jama Masjid.

The Friday namaaz has finished. Those who have not left have decided to sleep in the courtyard, in the shade of Shahi Darvaza. The two step into the courtyard and pick their way through sleeping forms, walking across its rectangular grid of white lines. The stone floor feels cool to their bare feet until they reach the middle of the courtyard, which the sun has burned into a hot plate, so even on a cool February day they suddenly step on embers.

'It is hot!'

'The approach to Makka Sharief is perilous,' says Ramvilas, poetically.

A man emerges from one of the many recesses in the masjid wall and charges toward them. 'I will show you the Prophet's hair,' he says. 'I will show you His footprints on stone, a chapter of the Qur'an from the original Holy Book. I will show you His very own chappals . . .'

'Gopal Bhai needs chappals!' says Ramvilas, playfully.

'I will decipher for you the eleven inscriptions in the courtyard . . .'

'We do not have the time for inscriptions!' he scolds the man. 'Do I look like a white man to you?'

The man melts into the shade. Gopal points to the qibla wall. 'Should we not go that way?'

'That way lies Makka Sharief,' chuckles Ramvilas. 'But you have not come here to pray. Twenty-five thousand of the faithful have already implored Allah this morning.'

'Why else have we come to the masjid?'

'You are a secular candidate. It is your business to come to mosques.'

They pass the central water tank in the courtyard, now deserted after the Friday namaaz, lined with pigeons.

'Can I wash myself?' asks Gopal.

Ramvilas shakes his head. They skirt the tank and raise a cloud of pigeons, then head toward the south-western corner of the compound, where Ramvilas pulls Gopal into the southern minaret. 'Let us go closer to Him.'

'I cannot climb so many steps!' says Gopal.

Ramvilas climbs. Gopal struggles after him, stumbling in the lungi, steadying the cap that wants to slip off his head at every step, unable to see clearly in the darkness into which they have plunged. They emerge from the stairwell into sudden light at the top of the minaret. Ramvilas steadies him. 'Take a look.'

Gopal is exhausted, sweating, breathing heavily with an intensity that almost makes his heart burst. The cap sits crushed on his head, its shape defeated by perspiration, its perch threatened by a ferocious breeze. The lungi clings stubbornly to his shanks. The sun – belying its February incarnation – shoots its arrows mercilessly on him.

'Here you are,' says Ramvilas calmly. 'One hundred and twenty feet above the ground. This is the Masjid-i-Jahan Numa, the masjid with a view of the whole wide world! Look to your right! Far below you is Shahi Darvaza. Do you see the rickshas crawling under its great staircase, looking like ants scrounging for food? Under those rickshas is a ribbon of asphalt. Raise your eyes beyond the asphalt to see the great Red Fort. Can you imagine the emperor leaving the fort in his palanquin, attended by a hundred bearers, and arriving at Shahi Darvaza to enter the masjid? Now look to the north. See the sandstone walls, above which sit the magnificent domes of Jama Masjid – white marble inlaid with black, wrung over six years out of the blood and sweat of ten thousand Hindus. Raise your eyes beyond the domes, and laid out before you is the great city of Shahjahanabad.'

'I cannot see,' complains Gopal, trying to find clear windows in his scratched spectacles.

'Why do you need these?' asks Ramvilas. He snatches away the spectacles. 'Look at the forest, not the trees!'

Gopal flails his arms to retrieve his spectacles, but Ramvilas will not return them. Gopal sighs, presses the cap on to his head, and tries to concentrate on the scene before him: the sea of Chandni Chowk in a great fog. It is noon. The sun hangs overhead, beating down on every building, every lane, every moving figure in the vast maze. A dull haze drains Chandni Chowk of all colour except shades of grey. Little white buildings cast shadows on their neighbours, creating a chiar-oscuro pattern that stretches from Jama Masjid to the horizon, where it melts imperceptibly into a grey sky. Inside this ocean of grey move countless rickshas, cars and scooters, plodding along ribbon-like lanes. The city lives and breathes a hundred sounds that coalesce into a deep hum, like the rumble of a hundred electric generators in the basement of a tall building.

'Do you see Chandni Chowk, Gopal Das?' asks Ramvilas, with rhetorical flair. 'Do not look for buildings or people, lanes or stalls. Tell me if you can see Chandni Chowk in its entirety. Ah, you do not

see clearly without your spectacles, but can you *hear* Chandni Chowk?
Listen closely, above the horns of rickshas, the sputter of scooters, the
hum of motors, and you will listen to them crying out for you.
Rickshavalas, beggars, fruit-sellers, flower-boys, paanvalas, chaivalas,
whores, rag-pickers! Scheduled Castes, Scheduled Tribes, Other Backward Classes, Musalmans! Tailors, barbers, masseurs, dyers! They
are crying out for you, Gopal Bhai. You have come through Shahi
Darvaza. You will go out through it and you will see them standing
beneath the stairs, awaiting your return!'

Gopal gasps. So, this is why Ramvilas Babu has brought him to
Jama Masjid! To show him his city. It is *his* city, his dominion, his
kingdom!

'You are Shah Jahan! No, you are more than Shah Jahan because
you are not a Musalman. You are Arjun, watching armies arrayed
against you in the battle of Mahabharat. Will you now lay down
your arms because a few whores gave you a purse full of air? Will
you be disheartened by rickshavalas who gave you an empty envelope? Will you be stopped by the threats of a doddering, yellow-
toothed fool or the menace of an uncouth snake with a pencil
moustache? Who are these people to stop you in your great task,
when you are Arjun?'

Gopal stands, open-mouthed. In the flurry of lines, the one he
remembers is about the empty envelope from Taslimuddin.

'Do you see the flecks of white and black in the ocean before you?
They are your people, standing with eyes turned skyward, awaiting
your decision! And if you do not choose to fight for them, who will
raise them from their filth? Where will the whores, rickshavalas and
beggars go?'

Gopal watches breathlessly. The panorama before him is suddenly
clear, as if the haze has lifted and his eyes have sprouted spectacles of
their own. The weight of the revelation bears down on him, yet
determination straightens his spine. I am Arjun, he thinks, his heart
hammering with the urgency of the great moment, mixing metaphors
in a scramble of imagery. *Baa Adab! Baa Mulaahizaah, hoshiyaar!*
Abul Muzaffar Shahabuddin Mohammad, Sahib-i-Qiran Sani . . . I
am Shah Jahan, I am Arjun, I am Krishna. I am Time!

Standing next to Gopal, Ramvilas studies his face carefully. Chandni Chowk appears to stand still, even as its parts move frantically. Red
Fort casts an ominous shadow on its ramparts.

'You are standing on the cusp of a great moment,' says Ramvilas, quietly, 'and all you talk of is money – a little money that some whores and rickshavalas did not give. Three lakhs or four is all you need to start everything, and crores will pour into the vessel.'

'Four lakhs?' asks Gopal, dreamily.

'Of course, you are only a poor chaivala,' says Ramvilas, carelessly. 'Where would you find four lakhs?'

'I will give you four lakhs!' exclaims Gopal.

Ramvilas watches him intently.

'Arrange for five men,' says Gopal. 'We have to dig up four lakhs tonight.'

Ramvilas nods. 'Five men. All right. Let us go now.'

Gopal cannot tear himself away from the scene before him. He is part of it, and it is so inextricably a part of him that leaving the minaret will be like pulling out his innards. 'Can we stay here for a while?'

'It is past noon,' says Ramvilas, 'and you are a Hindu. The masjid is closed to non-believers every afternoon.'

That night, five men break into Katra Badami in Khari Baoli. They tiptoe in – followed by a man in a neatly pressed kurta-pyjama – to avoid waking up the dozens asleep in ground-floor cubicles. They have a key to the stairwell. They climb three storeys in silence, feeling their way along walls, navigating by the smells of pepper, cardamom and cloves, in sacks stacked from floor to ceiling on every storey. On the third floor they stealthily climb a ladder, one by one, to enter a false ceiling where the smell of turmeric is unbearably strong. Inside the kholi, they move fifty sacks of Sushil Jain's turmeric – each sack requiring two men to lift it – to create a passage between the sacks and a wooden partition. They crawl to a door in the partition wall, and bring out their tools. The lock is easily broken with one blow of a hammer. It is already thin in its clasp, where someone has filed a groove.

The partition creates a small room within the kholi. Inside it, the men move a wall of asafoetida tins to expose three steel trunks, lined up along the wall, next to ventilators covered with curtains. Ramvilas pushes aside a curtain to look down into the darkness of the katra. Nothing stirs. Then he turns to a man and nods. The man grins. His upper lip – slit into two like a rabbit's – parts and his teeth shine even in the dark.

They break the locks on all three trunks in one swift motion – three hands on three locks. Ramvilas hands a fifty-rupee note to each man, and they file silently out of the double ceiling, climb down the ladder and disappear into the darkness of the katra. After the men have been gone for five minutes, he opens the trunks and empties them, stacking red buckram-covered binders on the floor. At the bottom, belts of white cloth lie coiled like snakes. Look for four, Kartar Singh has told him. He pulls them out and squeezes them to ensure they are full. As he replaces the binders, he opens one and studies its yellow leaves, smeared with vermilion swastikas drawn by the wavering hand of an accountant, and bursts into silent laughter. The reason for the steel trunks, the asafoetida tins and the wooden partition, so carefully hidden behind turmeric sacks, is suddenly clear to him. These are the account books Sushil Jain has hidden from income-tax inspectors. The asafoetida is a perfect cover. In such high concentrations, it smells like shit. Even the income-tax department does not want to wade through shit to unlock the secrets of Sushil Jain's business.

He stacks the binders back in the trunks. Then he pauses, considers, and selects two that he will take with him. It is never a bad idea to insure against the future. Who knows how important Sushil Jain may become some day?

He shuts all three trunks, stands up and stuffs the two binders into the waistband of his pyjama, then shakes the cloth belts to dislodge the asafoetida grains clinging to them. Then he lifts his kurta and ties all four belts, one by one, round his body, starting at the chest and working down to the waist. The buckles are set very wide, as if they were meant to go round a fat man. Even the last hole – meant for the narrowest waist – leaves the belts somewhat loose round Ramvilas's slender frame. He chuckles, aware that the belts rode on Sohan Lal's heaving belly before they entered Kartar Singh's store.

Then he steps out, pulls the partition door shut, and climbs down the ladder. He goes out of Katra Badami into the moonlit streets of Khari Baoli, passing men asleep on carts, walking stiffly because of the armour round his body.

13

'I have supported you for fourteen years,' says Suleman. 'Do you not remember the day you first came to me, after being turned down by every councillor, and I promised you money and a building? You said – I remember your words! – that I was an idealistic young man, that I was to be the hope of impoverished children in Chandni Chowk. Why do you not write about me, madam?' He chooses his words carefully, balancing accusation with entreaty.

His voice is strained, thinks Chitra, and his patience is wearing thin, but he knows he must hiss, not growl. He discharges his duty with barely concealed rancour, making a plea for help under layers of bravado.

'You write about this chaivala. Who is he, this fat, bald fool who does not even know his own name? Why do you waste time on him when you can write about real candidates?'

Suleman sits on the edge of a sofa, his tension extending to its armrests, which he clutches with particular vehemence. He is dressed in a silk kurta-pyjama and a Nehru jacket. Age is telling on him, she thinks. Age, or the strain of a lifetime's campaigning. The eyes are still sharp and predatory, but there is exhaustion in them too, which she has not seen before. Creases form round them every time he concentrates, and they have lost the knack of homing in on an object and staying there, unblinking and immobile. As soon as they have come to rest on her face, they dart away, flit here and there. This is a mark of uncertainty, foreign in Suleman. The moustache is still thin, still neatly combed. The hair is still black, though he must dye it to keep it so. He is almost forty-two now. In the geriatric ward of Chandni Chowk politics that makes him a teenager, but his body is not conscious of the distinction. It will fail him sooner than his mind.

She does not remember the Nehru jacket – when did he start dressing like a Congressman? He has spent his entire life fighting the Congress Party for the Muslim vote. Has he adopted the Nehru jacket as a prop in his political theatre? When she next sees him, perhaps his head will be adorned with a Gandhi cap. He bites his nails. She is not sure where his anxiety springs from – the political battlefield or simply a craving for a cigarette? It amuses her to think he is not smoking out of deference to her. There are three glass tumblers on a side-table within easy reach. He seems to drink from one every few minutes, needing constant replenishment as an ineffectual substitute for nicotine. The compromises a great Mughal emperor must make in these modern times! Imagine Shah Jahan asking his beloved queen, Arjumand Bano Begum, if she really wanted the fourteenth child that would end her life!

'I could not believe my eyes when I saw this,' says Suleman, brandishing a newspaper. 'You call him a "secular candidate"! A poor man who will represent the poor! How can you be so naïve as to believe that? If he is the secular candidate, who is Suleman Mian?'

The use of the third person to refer to oneself is the last refuge of arrogance, thinks Chitra. What does Suleman see when he looks into the mirror? His attempts to raise himself above his origins have been only half successful. No one will be impressed by the approach to this haveli, inside which he has built the nerve centre of his campaign. The lane is narrow, with tall, crumbling havelis on either side, and open drains that have long overwhelmed the pesticide sprayed by the Corporation. Children play cricket with stumps made of bricks. They have no windows to break. Some day they will drive a ball into a sagging wall and bring a tired mountain of plaster, concrete and rubble down on themselves. The staircase inside this haveli – does it belong to Suleman, or has he merely commandeered it? – will crash down one night, unable to carry its own weight, emblematic of the declining Mughal empire that built it, burdened with fawning emirs, decadent courts, senile emperors feasting on biryani and infatuated with young boys. Powter pigeons have made their nests in recesses in the ceiling, and the entire ground floor is carpeted with bird-shit. Every step you take inside the haveli, every swift movement, sets the cavern aflutter.

To come to this haveli, she had to walk by Sparrows, or the remains of the building that was Sparrows. It is a lively lane, reminiscent of the esoteric Orient to a tourist but a symbol of crushing poverty to her – ear-cleaners, pigeon stalls, chess-players, masseurs, acrobats, computer astrologers, aphrodisiac-sellers, wrestling rings, roadside dentists, vendors of 'corrective' amethysts and bhishtis carrying water in goatskins. What was the water for? she wondered, as she passed them. Did someone drink it, or was it part of the monstrous theatre of Chandni Chowk, performed daily for someone's visual titillation? This is where Suleman Mian lives, she told herself, or pretends to live. This is certainly where he grew up. Was the poison in his manner a natural consequence of the brutality in this lane?

As she passed the ruins of Sparrows a boy came up to her, pointed to her camera and asked her to take his photograph. He stood in the wreckage. The demolition of the building has created a vast open space in the narrow lane. Jama Masjid rises majestically in the background, suddenly visible. The angle in the photograph was unusual. She was looking at the masjid from behind, yet the picture was beautiful. The boy knew it. He had probably fought others for rights to that spot, because after she took the photograph he followed her around, insisting on being paid. It is a neat trick that perhaps works well on white tourists. The boy knew somehow, without being able to articulate it, that the picture would make a gratifying addition to a photo album – 'Poor boy behind Jama Masjid, Chandni Chowk, Delhi, India'.

She paid him five rupees and turned into Suleman's narrow lane, wondering why a rising political star should choose this spot in the constellation. Having risen from the stench behind Jama Masjid, she told herself, the man cannot get away. Then she climbed up the tottering staircase and was admitted into the colourful kingdom of Suleman Mian.

'Please!' he had protested, when Chitra, seeing the blood-red carpet, made a motion to unstrap her sandals. So she had stepped on to the carpet in them, with all the filth of Suleman's lane sticking to them.

Now, sitting uncomfortably on the sofa, she realises that his effort to leave behind his squalid childhood, even as he tries to identify with his people, has led to contradictions in his style, utterances and political persona. The grey haveli makes a statement: it makes him one with the children playing cricket, the paan stall, the bearded jalebi-maker, the bangle-seller and the perfumer. The room inside the haveli, where he has held court throughout his reign, makes a different statement, addressed not to the children outside but to the underlings who stand behind him, and perhaps also to himself. So, while the haveli provides an appropriate façade to his political farce, his own room covers the expanse of his vulgar imagination. The one is humble, the other arrogant, and this explains the appearance of the room.

In the far corners stand two excessively ornate brass lamps whose polish, she observes, has long faded. Their light is almost entirely diffused by curiously large shades. They appear to have no functional value because the room is illuminated by a naked bulb that hangs from the ceiling. That the room needs to be lit even on a bright afternoon can be blamed on three cupboards, each standing inside a window and blocking it. The walls have been painted cream, perhaps to contrast with the peeling grey of the haveli. The sofa on which Suleman sits has shocking maroon upholstery. Hers, which is smaller and to his left, is covered with similar fabric. The sofas face a highly polished coffee-table, perhaps the most expensive item in the room, and everything sits on the carpet that extends almost to the door, because the stone floor is cold in winter. The carpet is offensively red, vulgar in its resemblance to blood. The only free window is covered with a thin, translucent curtain of shining material, the kind used for royal costumes in cheap theatrical productions. It keeps out neither light nor the stench of drains in the lane below. Suleman Mian's consti-tuency invades his inner sanctum. He does not see, perhaps, the incongruity of his position – that he, the man who would be king of Chandni Chowk, must cover his eyes every day while leaving this garish room, to avoid seeing the ocean of squalor surrounding his *faux* court.

When a famished beggar feasts, she thinks, he rises with indiges-tion. Is this room a failed attempt to recreate Shah Jahan's Divan-i-Khas? Suleman's idea of forbidding luxury? This is how art directors design their sets for song-and-dance sequences in films. Or it is where the villain sits – stroking a cat – to utter bombastic lines before the hero charges in and scuppers his grandiloquent schemes. There is no cat at Suleman's side, but there are two associates, if they can be called that. One is the toothless, bearded man she has seen with him for years, whose mouth is permanently fused in a grin even when his forehead sports a frown. The other is a neat, prim man with aquiline features, who looks at her in mute appeal that he should not be considered part of this setting.

'You know I am going to win, madam,' says Suleman, newspaper now curled in his hand. He takes an anxious sip of water.

He is putting on a show, she thinks, not so much for her as for his associates, who watch him carefully. He cannot betray signs of nervousness. He is the aggressive scrapper to whom they have hitched their wagons, and he must continue to run at breakneck speed. He has held them in his thrall for more than a decade. He cannot snap his fingers and break the spell now.

'But it does not matter whether I win or lose,' he continues belligerently. 'I supported you when you had no one to turn to. Do I not deserve your gratitude? Who gave you money for that – that Sparrows when you needed it? Who gave you the building?'

He says 'Sparrows' with great effort. In his years of pacing the corridors of power he has not cared to pick up any English.

'The building was torn down,' says Chitra. 'It was illegal.'

It is an unkind remark. Surely she cannot fling the law at him having used the building for so many years. Why, he is the man who set her on the path that has led her here! But she cannot resist the dig. Something about his manner invites offense.

'So now you are worried that it was illegal! You sit on that sofa, calling yourself a big English journalist, and you do not accept that this has happened because of Suleman Mian.'

Prod an arrogant man and he always becomes churlish, she thinks. Yet as she considers a response, his face relaxes, even if his eyes do not. He has decided to be charming, because he turns to the toothless factotum on his left and, in a manner that is markedly different from the respectful tone he reserves for her, barks, 'Chai!'

The man leaves the room before she can decline the offer.

'I will be an MP soon,' he assures her.

The remaining associate gives an almost imperceptible nod.

'I will keep a special place for you in the press box,' purrs Suleman. 'Every Parliament meeting, every bill, every motion . . . you will know about them all! Why would I want to have anything to do with others when you are the one who supports me in this election?'

He is not a successful charmer, she decides. No matter how many smiles he paints on his face, his eyes remain pinpoints of fire.

'I do not support Gopal Das,' she says. 'I merely write about him because he is a symbol.'

'A symbol?'

She wants to say, 'A symbol of truth and democracy, a symbol of all that was promised when we, the people, gave to ourselves this intolerably lengthy Constitution . . .' But the words do not come. She is embarrassed to utter them. Even if he does not burst out laughing, she knows he will scoff at her, and force her to doubt herself.

'Symbols can be powerful in this country,' he warns. 'Have you seen the children who received bravery awards on Republic Day? This is the India of Nehru, where bravery is conferred by an Act of Parliament. Who can doubt the power of a symbol?'

She sighs. He knows all about symbols, of course. They are the merchandise he has hawked for a decade.

He leans toward her with sudden intensity. 'Let me tell you a story.

When the English king came to India at the beginning of this century, they built the Gateway of India for him in Bombay. But who cared for a stone gate that meant nothing to anyone? So, when the king came to Delhi, he appeared on the ramparts of Red Fort with his queen, wearing the glittering crown and colourful robes of a Mughal emperor, waving to a cheering crowd of five lakhs. Why do you think George did that? He wanted to leave no room for doubt that he was the inheritor of Shah Jahan's throne. He was the symbol of monarchy in Hindustan, and that was lost on no one.'

Chitra nods, aware that the Kashmiri man standing behind Suleman – what else could he be with those sharp features? – has listened to the story with great interest.

'So you must not treat symbols lightly,' says Suleman. 'Why do I wear a kurta? Why do I say "Namaste" when we meet? Why is my election symbol a bicycle? Why did the Musalman Nasim become the Hindu Madhubala before she became a star? Symbols are all some people have to eat and drink. You must not call the chaivala the poor man's candidate. You must not speak of his association with Musalmans!'

'But I do not,' she says.

Suleman produces the newspaper again and unfolds it to display her article. 'I do not read English,' he says, 'but my friends say you have praised the chaivala. Is that not called support? You talk of his adopted Musalman son – a one-handed boy from Bangladesh who calls him father. Is that something you should write about? It is a political stunt, but you make it sound like a Hindi film, where Musalmans and Hindus celebrate Divali together.'

She savours his agony and decides to twist the knife. 'You have often told me your voters do not read English magazines.'

An expression of pain passes over his face. 'Everyone copies English magazines, these days. Hindi and Urdu newspapers reproduce what *you* print! They have no minds of their own. Is there nothing called gratitude in this world? Can you not say kind words for the man who has promoted you?'

He casts a glance – a mere flick of the head – at the man standing beside him, who now takes a step forward to be introduced. 'This is Sheikh Noor Muhammad,' says Suleman, 'a great scholar of Mughal architecture. He has offered me his support in this campaign.'

Chitra nods.

Suleman looks at her pointedly. 'All educated Musalmans in the community are beginning to offer me support. Qureshi Sahib telephoned me four days ago, saying he was tired of the communal ways of IPP. He had planned to meet me outside Jama Masjid the morning he was killed.'

Chitra shivers. The room has suddenly become cold. The murder of Muhammad Salauddin Qureshi is still on the front pages. She has a good idea who may have been behind it, but she dare not suggest it even to herself.

'The IPP committee did not like Qureshi Sahib's decision,' says Suleman. 'You can see how they repaid him.'

Chitra feels tired. She is well past the age when she should sit in hostile rooms and fend off the recriminations of self-important men. Her body has cheated her in unexpected ways, so she has given up trying to appear youthful. Soon, she will acquire the matronly solidity of a woman who has never known the meaning of youth. What will be her reward for lifelong maidenhood? Will it be the ascent of this upstart to Parliament? Or an unlikely triumph for the chaivala? There is something not quite right about the candidacy of Gopal Das. Much is wrong with that manager of his. The most plausible outcome is an easy victory for Harilal Gupta, once Suleman and the chaivala have split each other's vote. Could it be, however, that Gopal Das, with his flaws, is the antidote to the malaise called Suleman? Could she half shut her eyes and ignore the inconvenient footnotes to the story of Gopal Das? She will write a sweeping article on Gopal Das! 'A Man of the People'! And that article will bury the stink of Suleman Mian, with his associates, his haveli and the sheer effrontery of maroon sofas on a blood-red carpet.

'Will you not help me?' asks Suleman, with his eyes closed in surrender.

After Shah Jahan had disposed of Arjumand Bano Begum, Chitra reminds herself, he built Taj Mahal for her. Suleman is no Shah Jahan. He must seek permission, swallow his arrogance, debase himself. But what poison lies behind those honeyed words? When they fail, will he direct his sting at her?

The toothless man brings two cups of tea on a steel tray. As Suleman drinks tea, Chitra studies his face, which is easier to do with the burning eyes out of commission. It is like watching the sun through tinted glass. His mouth curls down under the moustache in a childlike, vulnerable manner. She has never noticed it before. He looks harmless, almost innocent, like a man who will be pained by her article but unable to do anything about it. She is not fooled, of course. She knows the eyes will open soon, and decipher the resolution in her face. She is suddenly afraid of his humiliation.

14

A Man of the People
Chitra Ghosh, Chief Editor, *India Now*
1 March 1998

Who is Gopal Das?

Another election is upon us – another campaign, another set of symbols, slogans, promises and scandals, but the same candidates in Gandhian garb, wrinkled and worthy, hands folded, smiles pasted, promising another five years of stasis while delivering two or three. The Chandni Chowk Lok Sabha constituency, which would have safely voted for its sitting Congress MP, Naresh Agrawal, is faced with a riddle. Naresh Agrawal has passed away, and it must choose between Sulochana Agrawal, his widow and the new Congress candidate, Harilal Gupta, transport minister in the state government and the IPP candidate, and Suleman Mian, a local politician who had stood as an independent but is supported by the Communist parties. No one in Chandni Chowk gives much thought to these three, because everyone is talking about Gopal Das, independent. So who is Gopal Das?

Let us begin with a physical description. Gopal Das stands five feet two inches tall. He wears a checked shirt – usually with missing buttons – a dirty dhoti that is pulled up to his knees, and kolhapuri chappals that are worn, frayed but functional. He is bald in a dignified way. He does not dye his drooping moustache, or the tufts of hair that sprout from his ears. His spectacles are old and scratched, and perhaps not powerful enough for his failing eyesight, so he must constantly peer through windows in his glasses, trying to bring objects into focus. He sports a belly – which man does not unless he is an athlete? – and the folds of skin under his chin tremble like the dewlap of a cow every time he opens his mouth, which is infrequently. He is your father and your brother, though you wish he was neither. He is the man you do not want to become but find yourself becoming again and again. Gopal Das is Everyman. In a crowded Chandni Chowk afternoon, no one would notice his stubby frame, and that is his greatest asset – nothing distinguishes him from the people he seeks to represent. His appearance is merely a consequence, not the cause of his self. Which is why he seeks to become a Member of Parliament. What else is representative democracy? Who could be more representative than Gopal Das?

When Gopal Das first began campaigning, he was told that he was not a Dillivala. Some suggested he was a carpetbagger from Bihar, others that he was a Bhaiya from Uttar Pradesh. We can ask ourselves, in turn, what is a Dillivala? In a city where everyone is an immigrant, who are the native sons? Politicians who infest the city? Punjabis who came during Partition? Tamil Brahmins who came in the last thirty years, or Biharis who came in the last twenty? The answer, of course, is that Delhi belongs to no one, so it belongs to everyone. Gopal Das spent much of his life in a kholi in Khari Baoli, behind sacks of turmeric where it is always dark, no matter what the time of day. It is well known in Khari Baoli that the workers who cart sacks of pepper, nutmeg and cinnamon sneeze violently every time their nostrils encounter the cloying smell, even as the seths whose cubicles line the lanes sit placidly, unaware of the smells. You can tell who lives in Khari Baoli, and how long he has lived there, by how often he sneezes. Gopal Das has been raised by sacks of turmeric and tins of asafoetida, and has never sneezed. He is a citizen of Khari Baoli, a Dillivala whose family has known no other home.

What do we know about Gopal Das? Is it possible to trace the ancestry of a man who says so little about himself? More than two hundred years ago, after the British had won at Plassey and Buxar, Parshuram Das made his way westward from the plains of Bihar and arrived in the great city of Shahjahanabad. There, along the moonlit canal that flowed from Red Fort to Fatehpuri Masjid, he set up a stall where he fried jalebis in cauldrons that sat on a bed of coals. He kept his own buffaloes, not trusting the milkman, and relied solely on khand – unrefined sugar – instead of using chaashni, the sugar solution everyone else used, because khand gave his jalebis a sweeter flavour.

Parshuram was not an ambitious businessman. His jalebi business shrank through the generations, never growing beyond a small stall that sat five hundred yards from the Lahore Gate of Red Fort. After the Mutiny, the British destroyed the market between Red Fort and Chandni Chowk, rendering thousands – such as Parshuram's great-grandson Ram Bharose Das, who both lived and worked inside the jalebi stall – homeless. Ram Bharose's son forsook jalebis and set up a tea stall in Paratha Gali. That stall served the family for three generations until it was uprooted by another set of masters – the Indian government in 'forty-seven, which cleared lanes in Chandni Chowk to make way for refugees from Punjab who had fled the Partition riots.

Shyam Sundar Das, Gopal Das's grandfather, was not particularly troubled by the demolition of his stall in Paratha Gali, because he was already wedded to the freedom movement as a Congress Party activist. He received the news silently in jail, serving a sentence for his participation in the Quit India movement. He was released soon after Independence, and was present in the prayer meeting at Birla House when Gandhiji was shot. He was murdered by the RSS when they discovered he had seen the killer Nathuram Godse and his associates, and would be able to identify them.

Gopal Das's father, Manohar Das, moved the chai stall to the newer Kucha Bansilal, setting it under an electrical junction box, under which Gopal Das spent much of his childhood and youth, taking over the stall on his father's death. Gopal Das is not a great businessman. He lacks the acumen – some would say cunning – required for the expansion of a shop. In the riots of 'eighty-four, he rescued Bibi Sukhbir Kaur, wife of IPP leader Sardar Kartar Singh, from rioters armed with knives and rods. Gopal's only son, Mukesh, was killed during the Mandal Commission riots. A few years ago, Gopal Das adopted a poor, invalid Muslim boy as his son. In subsequent years he has struck up friendships with Muslim workers, staged dharnas in Rajghat – for which he nearly went to prison – and participated in rallies against demolition drives and police brutality. Two years ago, the state government of Delhi honoured him in a ceremony outside Gurudwara Sisganj for the courage he showed in protecting Bibi Sukhbir Kaur. Ironically, shortly before that honour, Gopal Das met the fate suffered by his ancestors: a callous IPP administration, led by Delhi transport minister Harilal Gupta – who is now fighting for the same parliamentary seat as Gopal Das – demolished his stall. Since then, Gopal Das has worked at odd jobs, carting boxes on his bicycle and, lately, serving as shop-clerk in Sardar Kartar Singh's general store.

Before we leave the astonishing two-hundred-year-long journey of Gopal Das, we should note the obvious. No less than three times have the reigning powers – the British, the government of India and the Municipal Corporation of Delhi – uprooted his stall. On all three occasions, he has responded by turning the other cheek. 'An eye for an eye makes the whole world blind,' said Mahatma Gandhi. He would have recognised Gopal Das, had he met him, as the one-eyed man who would not gouge back.

It is not enough to say that Gopal Das is a true Dillivala. We must also investigate his positions on issues that matter to the people of Delhi. What does Gopal Das stand for? Does he hold that a mosque should be rebuilt on the site of Babri Masjid? What does he think of the Mandal Commission? Does he support the Women's Bill? Does he believe India should develop nuclear weapons? Will he support the Congress Party if elected? Will he support the IPP? What are his views on coalition governments at the centre? Does he think the Non-aligned Movement matters any more? A first answer, an easy answer, is that Gopal Das says precious little. That is also a frivolous answer, an arrogant answer, an answer that reduces to the confines of an election plank the entire philosophy of a candidate. Gopal Das may not say much, but he listens, and his laconic nature enhances his ability to listen. His foggy spectacles do not allow him to study the fine lines in a picture. It is, perhaps, this inability to see detail that allows him to embody – we cannot say articulate, because he rarely speaks – the real issues in our society. So what does Gopal Das stand for? To answer the question – because the candidate will not answer it himself – let us take an analogy from the *Bhagavad Gita*. When asked, 'What is the Soul?' Krishna can answer only in negatives. It is not this, not that, not that either . . . The same can be said for Gopal Das and his policies. 'He does not stand for the minority appeasement policies of the Congress Party,' says Ramvilas Sharma, his campaign manager. But he does not care for the strident Hindutva of the IPP either, or the Marxist foofaraw of the Communist parties. Gopal Das is not bound by ideology or imprisoned by the agenda of any party. The solitary plank in his campaign platform is that he is a poor man's candidate, a secular candidate, a human being with nothing to recommend him but his humanity. Finally, of course, it must be understood that a man like Gopal Das – a candidate who is less a candidate than an expression of the people – need never stand for anything.

Ah, but he must stand for *something*! The question remains, not least because there are those who would like to see Gopal Das sink into the netherworld under the weight of this question, as did the generous king Bali under the foot of Vishnu. We can rely on Ramvilas Sharma to provide some clues. Mr Sharma was a member of the Chandni Chowk IPP committee who resigned in disgust at the IPP's Hindu fundamentalism. 'As a proprietor of Bhagwan Das and Sons (of Lahore),' he told *India Now*, 'I deal in exquisite attars and perfumes. How could I continue to hold my nose and ignore the stink of IPP policies?' Gopal Das plans to fix minimum fares for rickshas in Chandni Chowk, according to Mr Sharma. He intends to bring a bill to give prostitution the status of a cottage industry, thus regulating it rather than criminalising it, and making sex-workers eligible for loans, tax rebates and incentive schemes for the expansion of their business. He wants to create a union of rag-pickers, designating areas of operation for each group . . . There is much Gopal Das wants to do, according to Mr Ramvilas, and his guiding philosophy is his complete identification with the poor and dispossessed.

One might categorise the candidacy of Gopal Das with the dozen others in every constituency in India, which garner a few hundred votes, forfeit their deposits, and are never heard of again. We must not presume and we must not generalise, because of the growing list of Gopal Das supporters. The first organisation to throw its weight behind Gopal Das was STREE, Sex-workers Training, Rehabilitation and Education Endeavour, an NGO in the GB Road area of Chandni Chowk. Gita Didi, the convener of STREE, told *India Now* that Gopal Das has promised a repeal of the Immoral Traffic Prevention Act of 1986. 'By declaring prostitution to be illegal, ITPA merely provides an excuse for the harassment of sex-workers,' says Gita Didi. Last month, STREE donated more than thirty-six thousand rupees to the campaign of Gopal Das. 'The sum represents one night's earnings by every sex-worker in GB Road,' says Gita Didi, 'after deducting the exorbitant fees of the bais, the pahalvans and the police.'

(Inderlal Jha, SHO of GB Road police station, expressed surprise at Gita Didi's claim. He told *India Now*, 'Our duty is to weed out under-age girls and provide the sex-workers with protection from violent customers, not to extort money.' He has called Gita Didi's charges baseless and politically motivated.)

The Chandni Chowk Ricksha-Pullers Union has given fifty-five thousand rupees to the campaign of Gopal Das. The All India

Ricksha-Pullers Union has donated twenty-six thousand, the Chawri Bajar Tailor Union thirty-two thousand, the Nai Sarak Booksellers Association sixty thousand, and the New Delhi Rag-Pickers Union five thousand. When he visited Kinari Bajar, the Kinari Bajar Traders Association threw a garland of currency notes – worth more than ten thousand rupees, according to a member – round his neck.

This brings us to a very significant question. Why is Gopal Das fighting this election? Why does a man who is representative of his people actually want to represent them? What inspired Gopal Das to jump into this fight? Was it the riots of 'eighty-four, when he saw innocent Sikhs hacked to death? Was it the cigarette butts of the IPP that charred his son? Was it the police brutality that locked up his adopted son? Was it exasperation at the failed dharnas and processions that nearly took him to jail? Was it the demolition of his tea stall? Or was it the broad, indefinable discontent that is lodged in the heart of every person who lives in Chandni Chowk?

Whatever its inspiration, Gopal Das's campaign continues to flower. The seed was sown by four lakhs provided to Mr Ramvilas Sharma by an anonymous donor. It is a small amount, a mere drop in the ocean that must be filled to float the ship of a Lok Sabha campaign. But Gopal Das – a man who has served countless cups of tea in his life – knows the art of making mishri. Just as a sugar crystal, when suspended in sugar solution, collects crystals around it, his four lakhs have become the core of a growing campaign fund that is now measured in crores. We have already mentioned the organisations who have contributed to the campaign. Less known, and less visible, are the smaller contributions by citizens of Chandni Chowk. Without making grandiose speeches, extravagant promises or television appearances, Gopal Das has become the chosen one of the poor in Chandni Chowk, carrying forth their dreams and aspirations, their only hope of deliverance from the cycle of poverty and repression. The streets of Chandni Chowk ring with the song of Gopal Das. Beggars and cripples beg in his name. Paratha Gali adds a special coat of ghee to its parathas, and the extra rupee goes to his campaign. Rag-pickers clean windscreens and ask for money to elect Gopal Das. Silver-beaters chant his name when beating silver. Peanut-sellers have a Gopal Das Special, mullas in mosques talk of Gopal Das during namaaz, pandits in temples sing his name after the aarti. In the lanes behind Jama Masjid, poor nahari-sellers garland him with currency notes, stitched together with a day's earnings. Even pickpockets have stepped up their activities in the Chandni Chowk area, and the money is funnelled into the Gopal Das campaign by indirect channels. Every poor man in the streets of Chandni Chowk seems to say, every morning, 'Today I earn for Gopal Das!'

Muhammad Ghayas is a decrepit old man who begs at a corner near Fatehpuri Masjid. On a Friday, when the masjid is crowded, he can earn up to twenty rupees. He will vote for Gopal Das, he says, if they let him vote. They uprooted his clinic in Meena Bajar two years ago. He performed in the Moonlight Festival, and was promised a new clinic by Harilal Gupta, transport minister, but they gave him twenty rupees and threw him out of his makeshift stall at the festival. He will vote for Gopal Das, and he will vote with a vengeance.

The man who cleaned Gopal Das's ears last week received in payment the promise of a permanent stall. He will vote for Gopal Das too. Gopal Dasji will be the MP with the cleanest ears, he claims, so he can listen to the sufferings of the people!

The establishment has not been blind to the gathering storm. It has watched with growing concern this evolution of a man of the people. Retribution has been swift and violent. Six days ago, the chief election commissioner dispatched an officer to determine if Gopal Das had exceeded his campaign expenditure limits. The donations from STREE and rickshavala unions, it is alleged, violate the limits set by the commission. The candidates of the Congress, IPP and Communist parties have launched a smear campaign against him, making unsubstantiated allegations about his past. A team of CBI and Delhi police inspectors descended on his campaign office last week in Lajpatrai Market. The raid was conducted, ostensibly, to unearth evidence in the mushrooming cricket-betting scandal. The office is in a store that belongs to Sardar Kartar Singh who was, until he resigned to join Gopal Das, a member of the IPP Chandni Chowk committee. By shutting down the office, the IPP accomplishes two goals: it punishes Kartar Singh for disloyalty, and obstructs Gopal Das in his campaign. A thorough search of the premises revealed no evidence of cricket betting. An old safe was broken open – even the CBI must keep up appearances – to reveal posters and campaign literature. Sardar Kartar Singh employs no clerks or accountants who could be questioned, and he himself is believed to be in Simla. The only witness to 'illegal betting activity' was Gopal Das, who barely understands cricket. Mr Ramvilas Sharma called the raid an IPP plot to thwart Gopal Das's campaign, and has filed a case in the Supreme Court under the Representation of Peoples Act. 'We all know where cricket-betting dons sit,' said Mr Sharma. 'They sit in Dubai, London and South Africa! And we all know where the money comes from – Khari Baoli, Kinari Bajar, Nai Sarak. So why must the police raid the campaign office of a chaivala who is trying to sustain a campaign? Secularism is now a crime!'

The word 'Das', as we all know, means 'servant'. Gopal Das, servant of the people, political *flâneur*, common man *extraordinaire*, is in every sense a man of the people. He is India, struggling to express herself, collecting support with every step he takes through the circuitous lanes of Chandni Chowk. His election symbol, a cup of tea, finds itself painted on more and more banners every day, a beacon of hope to millions of people, an embodiment of every man's anger. He is poor, useless and of no consequence, therefore he is a man of the people. Every generation produces one man, just one man, who marshals the discontent of the dispossessed and directs it, not at an institution or a person, but at the injustice, oppression, poverty and inequity of society. This generation has chosen its man, and he walks under the banner of a cup of tea. And what better constituency to try this great experiment in democracy than Chandni Chowk, which has stirred itself countless times against repression and injustice? It was here that Tegh Bahadur challenged Aurangzeb, Indian soldiers defied the British to install a Mughal emperor in Red Fort, and patriots welcomed Lord Hardinge to his new capital with a bomb. A hundred years ago, the trumpeting of elephants mixed with the sounds of cartwheels and itinerant musicians serenading Mother India. Fifty years ago, the patriotic strains of 'Vande Maataram' rang through Chandni Chowk. Today, the campaign procession of Gopal Das winds its way from Fatehpuri Masjid to Red Fort.

This is not a story about a chaivala. This is not the story of Chandni Chowk, or the election, or the shape of the next government. This is the story of India. In two weeks, the citizens of India will vote, and voters in one constituency will alter the course of the nation. Gopal Das has brought back the fragrance of jasmine to India, and what a wondrous fragrance it is!

15

Babulal tests the microphones – 'One two three, one two three' –
climbs down from the stage, and walks to the Ambassador car waiting
beyond the crowd. He knocks on the driver's window and, when it is
lowered, whispers into the driver's ear: 'Tell Madam the stage is
ready.'

The driver nods and rolls up the window. His manner indicates that
his passenger is not yet ready, and more time will elapse before she
emerges to address the gathering. Babulal sighs and loiters.

The crowd is small, consisting chiefly of coolies and cobblers
rounded up by the station-master. The Victorian spires provide an
ominous, dull-red backdrop to the meeting. It is a busy afternoon,
punctuated by the clattering, hissing and wheezing of trains, rent by
shrill whistles and the strident trumpeting of diesel locomotives. The
coolies fret over missed opportunities, eyeing the deluge of passengers
loaded with suitcases, bedrolls and fruit-baskets, and look anxiously
toward the stage, wondering when the meeting will begin so it can end
before all the bedrolls have been spirited away by other hands.

Babulal will never say this aloud, but the election is not the same
without Naresh Babu. He learned the art of managing campaigns
under Nareshji – and what wonderful campaigns they mounted! Five
consecutive Lok Sabha elections over sixteen years, and five consecutive victories. It was well known, when all the rhetoric had been
exhausted, that Naresh Agrawal's umbrella coalition of traders,
Muslims and lower castes was invincible in Chandni Chowk. On
hearing of Nareshji's heart-attack, he had rushed to Pandara Road –
where Nareshji lived in the verdant line of bungalows reserved for
MPs – but Nareshji's heart had stopped beating long before he entered
the front door.

Babulal was of the opinion that one of the two daughters should be
asked to stand for Chandni Chowk. Had not Indira succeeded Nehru,
after a suitable gap of two years? Everyone knows that a man must be
succeeded by his son and, if he does not have a son, by his daughter.
His wife is called upon to enter public service only if his children are
too young, and then only to fill the gap until they are of age. There is
irrefutable logic behind this order of succession. A son or a daughter
can claim the vigour of youth. They symbolise a natural transfer of

power to the next generation. A wife is merely a surrogate who will not last much longer than her husband. Did not Rajiv succeed Indira? And is not everyone waiting for Rajiv's children to succeed him? A democracy demands succession through children. A wife, or a husband as in the case of Indira, is merely an inconvenient diversion, a branch that has already sprouted its fruit, an appendage that leads nowhere.

He was overruled. Sulochanaji expressed a keen interest in standing for Nareshji's seat, sealing the chances of her own daughters. He is a loyal soldier. He has worked for Nareshji all his life. He will not desert the family. But where will the family be if Chandni Chowk – for sixteen years a fiefdom – slips out of its hands? Traders will go back where they naturally belong – to the IPP. But to think that Suleman, this upstart, has laid claim to the Musalman vote! And this ridiculous chaivala, calling himself the poor man's candidate as if Naresh Agrawal had never existed! Ah, this is all rain and thunder. When they go to vote, they will all come round. Everyone knows that Congress will complete what Naresh Agrawal began.

The car door is pulled open, and Sulochana Agrawal emerges to a shower of applause. She holds her hands high, folded together. She is a slight, unassuming woman, dressed in a plain saree secured to her shoulders with many pins. A corner of it covers her head, where it is secured to her hair, which is in a tight bun. Her eyes are hidden behind sunglasses, and she wears no jewellery. Her campaign dress was carefully selected by Babulal, to heighten her resemblance to Indira Gandhi.

A flurry ensues among the organisers, all dressed in white kurta-pyjamas with saffron, white and green rosettes on their chests, the colours of the Congress Party. Babulal leads Sulochana to the elevated stage, which stands in the centre of the railway-station car park. She ascends a wooden staircase, approaches the microphone and stands with hands folded, displaying the vulnerability of fresh widowhood.

Babulal introduces her. As the most senior Congress activist in Chandni Chowk, he has the privilege of calling her 'Sulochanaji' while others must restrict themselves to 'madam'. Then he recedes into the background.

'Three lakhs followed Nareshji on his last journey to the Yamuna,' Sulochana Agrawal begins, in a soft, patient voice. 'I ask those three lakhs to vote for me.'

An exaggeration, thinks Babulal. But who among these people can understand a number so large?

'Many people wanted Nareshji to retire,' she says. 'They wanted him to take sanyaas, to go to Hardwar as a man should in his waning years. But Nareshji said, "How can I take sanyaas when there is so much work to be done? I will die fighting for Chandni Chowk." And he did! He sacrificed his life for Chandni Chowk. If you loved him, help me fulfil his dreams.'

This brings a few raindrops of applause. Babulal shuts his eyes and pretends to concentrate. Ah, the magic of a campaign! If only the speaker had been his constant friend, his guide, his companion!

Sohan Lal climbs painfully up the wide staircase in the railway station, noting the paan stains on the walls, and limps into a passage that runs the length of the building. He leans heavily on his stick. In his other hand he clutches a rolled-up magazine. To his right there are offices – station-master, assistant station-master, line supervisor, control room – and to his left a balcony that looks out over the car park at the front, where Sulochana Agrawal is in the middle of a monotonous speech. His knee hurts and he decides to stop for a moment. He stands at the balcony and watches the gaggle of coolies with mild derision. She stands no chance. A woman needs more than widowhood to claim her husband's legacy. A son, on the other hand, can step effortlessly into his father's place at the counter. There is no denying the obvious truth: after all his victories, Naresh Agrawal has been defeated by his inability to produce a son. And that tall, wiry man who stands at the back, the one wearing a Gandhi cap, must be Babulal, now old and haggard like his dead master.

He notices a cake of bird-shit on the outer ledge of the balcony. In the driveway below, sweepers with long brooms are at work, collecting garbage into heaps, which will be scattered again as soon as the wind picks up. The pain in his knee has subsided. He turns and walks down the corridor to another set of offices that overlook the car park. He knows the supervisors, and has requisitioned a room for a few hours. He limps in and notes sourly that Ramvilas does not stand up to greet him.

Ramvilas is seated in a large easy chair, the type ubiquitous in railway-station waiting rooms – a wooden frame strung with plastic mesh – and is engaged in looking out of the window. He has taken care to place another easy chair to his right. When he hears Sohan Lal approach, he turns, smiles and delivers a mild reproof: 'It is not polite to call a man, then keep him waiting, sethji.'

Not an iota of concern for my knee or my backache, thinks Sohan Lal, darkly. When a clerk becomes a trader, he forgets himself faster than night forgets day.

Sohan Lal approaches the second chair and sits down with difficulty, letting his stick drop to the floor beside him. He notices that the chairs have been placed strategically: they afford a clear view of Sulochana Agrawal's ragged audience.

Ramvilas pulls out a small vial from his kurta pocket and places it in Sohan Lal's lap. 'Three drops of champa mixed with a pinch of harshringar,' he says. 'Not many people can appreciate it.'

The compliment softens Sohan Lal, but he is not mollified. 'I have heard Bhagwan Das and Sons is not doing well,' he says.

'The location is not ideal, and Vimal is lazy. He should be sitting at the counter right now, but he is probably at home, eating parathas, or in a cinema watching Madhuri Dixit shake her hips.'

Sohan Lal makes a sympathetic sound.

'Lalaji knew his sons had no knowledge of attars,' continues Ramvilas. 'Whenever one priced an attar wrongly he would draw me aside and say, "Ramvilas, I know I can trust you to take good care of them when I am gone. Someone needs to keep the business alive. They are my sons by birth but you are the true inheritor of my art." It is a great business he built, and Bhagwan Das and Sons will carry on the tradition.'

'I have heard that the division was unfavourable to Vimal,' persists Sohan Lal. He knows he has struck a blow when he sees Ramvilas clench his lips.

'Everything that was valuable came to us,' insists Ramvilas softly. 'We got the electronic balances, the vials of pure attar, the crystal decanters and ivory boxes.'

'But the furniture stayed at the original shop in Kucha Sugandh.'

'It is mouldy, decaying.'

'What about the workers?'

'I will train new ones,' says Ramvilas. He leans eagerly toward Sohan Lal. 'I know what you are thinking! The capital is all Vimal's, and he is a partner in the business. But where does it say that the walls belong to him? Is his name written on the attar bottles, or the steel counters, or the cash-box? He who controls the cash-box controls the business . . .'

He stops. In his eagerness to make his point, he has been indiscreet, and Sohan Lal acknowledges this with a cruel smile. Ramvilas rushes to fill the void. 'Have I told you about incense sticks? They are cheap to manufacture, and there is great demand these days. I have realised that the attar trade is not profitable in itself, but add some attar to incense sticks and people will pay much more. And I've just begun to sell soaps that are free of animal fat. More than twenty fragrances! Musk, patchouli, khus, raatraani, jasmine, sandal, rose . . .'

'I did not call you here to talk about soap,' says Sohan Lal.

Ramvilas stops.

'Or to make a campaign contribution to your candidate.'

Ramvilas chuckles. 'I am glad you say that, because we cannot accept any more money. Have you not heard? The chief election commissioner is auditing our expenses, saying we may have exceeded expenditure limits.'

Sohan Lal notes with disgust that Ramvilas actually winked when saying this. A clerk presumes conspiratorial intimacy with him!

'Campaign donations are useful,' says Ramvilas, philosophically. 'Taslimuddin can show expenses of fifty-five thousand, Gopal Das can get publicity worth that much. And the money, why should anyone see it?'

Sohan Lal knows, of course, that the long list of contributions is a sham, enabling the contributors to squirrel away money for themselves. He also knows that Ramvilas knows he knows. Everyone knows. But he disapproves of braggadocio. A magician must profess wonder at his magic, not denigrate it as mere sleight-of-hand. It also irritates him that Ramvilas refuses to bring up the obvious reason he has been summoned. Very well, he will bring it up himself.

'There was a committee meeting yesterday,' he says ominously.

'Ah,' says Ramvilas casually. 'An IPP committee meeting?'

Sohan Lal ignores the implied distance between Ramvilas and the IPP. 'Everyone was of the opinion that you have done very good work. It is commendable, the way you have managed this chaivala's campaign. There will certainly be a great dent in Suleman's Musalman and lower-caste vote.'

Ramvilas nods and smiles, acknowledging the praise as his due.

'Even Harilalji is impressed.'

Ramvilas continues to smile blandly, taking care that the smile becomes no wider at the mention of Harilal Gupta.

'But this, this—' Sohan Lal reaches over and slaps the magazine on to Ramvilas's lap. Ramvilas picks up the copy of *India Now* and smoothes its creased cover, pretending to see it for the first time. 'Who is Gopal Das?' asks the cover, in a banner that runs across the top, diagonally, and obscures the *w* in *India Now*. The picture is that of Gopal Das, independent candidate for Lok Sabha for the Chandni Chowk parliamentary constituency, standing with hands folded in a street, surrounded by rickshavalas and rag-pickers. Garlands are heaped on his chest, stopping just below the neck where folds of skin hang over the flowers. The mouth is twisted into a wide smile, but the camera has not penetrated the spectacles, so the eyes are hidden behind two rectangles of fog. If the context was unclear, the smile could be mistaken for a gasp, a cry or a howl of fear, but it can be inferred – if not seen – that this is a happy Gopal Das, candidate for Chandni Chowk. At his side, a little behind him, a clean Ramvilas beams at the camera, definitely aware of his slicked-down black hair. On the candidate's other side, deep in the background and out of focus, the camera has captured half of Gauhar Muhammad, dark, dishevelled and identifiable by his stump, raised in mid-slogan. The question asked in the slanted banner at the top, 'Who is Gopal Das?', is answered by another question that runs across the bottom of the picture, left to right, 'A Man of the People?'

'This is beyond the limit!' fumes Sohan Lal. 'Have you any idea how much damage this could cause to Harilalji?'

'It is only an English magazine,' says Ramvilas, dismissively.

'It has been reprinted in every newspaper, every magazine, English, Hindi and Urdu! What kind of effect do you think this will have in Chandni Chowk? I had the Hindi edition delivered to Kucha Bansilal, and I found everyone talking about it, even traders! Do you know what she has called him? Ah, of course you do, because you put the words into her head. A man of the people! The embodiment of the common man!'

'That was the intention of this campaign,' says Ramvilas, coolly. 'Was it not you who suggested a common man's candidate to Harilalji?'

'Yes, but not a man whose face appears on magazine covers! And why are you in this photo right next to him?'

Ramvilas gazes at Sohan Lal with innocent eyes. 'I am his campaign manager.'

Sohan Lal grits his teeth. The obvious pleasure that Ramvilas derives from his presence in that picture doubles the severity of his offence. A clerk – a mere *clerk*! It is clear that this man has forgotten his antecedents. Does he not know that it takes generations of prosperity to pull yourself out of the middle class?

'This chaivala's family history,' demands Sohan Lal. 'Where did she get that?'

'She has done a good deal of research,' suggests Ramvilas.

' "Gopal Das has brought back the fragrance of jasmine to India"!' sneers Sohan Lal.

Ramvilas thinks of the five-rupee bottle of synthetic perfume he handed to Chitra, telling her it was a vial of jasmine. 'She plagiarised that line from me,' he says gleefully.

Sohan Lal knows that this is not the time to lose his temper but is unable to compose an expression that will not convey his feelings. In a frenetic desire to keep himself busy, he leans over, picks up his walking-stick and lays it diagonally on his lap, taking care not to disturb the vial of attar balanced on his left thigh. He fans himself with his cap, looks vacantly out of the window and clucks at Sulochana Agrawal, still trudging through her speech. Then he lays the cap on his right thigh – where it collapses into a flat rectangle – and carefully constructs a neutral expression. 'Tomorrow is the last day for with-drawal. Go to the returning officer's rooms early in the morning, just to be safe.'

Ramvilas does not respond. Sohan Lal continues to watch Sulo-chana Agrawal as he waits for his answer, then turns impatiently. 'Is it settled, then?'

'The returning officer's rooms?' asks Ramvilas.

'To withdraw the chaivala's name,' says Sohan Lal, through gritted teeth.

Ramvilas looks out of the window, and Sohan Lal realises that something is horribly wrong. 'This has gone far enough!' he says furiously. 'You will announce the chaivala's withdrawal tomorrow!'

'Gopal Das will fight this election,' says Ramvilas, softly.

'You cannot be serious! You know the man is a joke. Surely you do not think people will vote for him? He will lose his deposit!'

Ramvilas does not reply.

'And where will you be after that?' says Sohan Lal. 'You are a very good worker. Do not make a big mistake and destroy your career.'

Ramvilas says nothing.

'Do not be a fool, Ramvilas! It is one thing to get stories in magazines, and a few lakhs from unions and prostitutes. It is quite another to fight an election. You have been in politics for fifteen years, how can you be so naïve? The committee-secretary position is open. I need someone young and energetic to take up that responsibility. After Harilalji wins the election . . .'

Ramvilas arches his eyebrows, and Sohan Lal gasps at the look on his face. He is questioning that Harilal will win! Sohan Lal leans to his left with raised forefinger, trembling, unable to control his anger now. 'You are a fool!' His voice rises. 'You will fade into darkness in two weeks, and you will come grovelling to me for membership of the committee!'

'Which committee? I resigned from the IPP under the Lala Surajmal Scheme,' says Ramvilas.

Sohan Lal makes a violent attempt to rise, sending the attar bottle flying out of his lap. It crashes to the floor, spraying glass shards at his feet and releasing its potent perfume into the air like an invisible mushroom cloud. Sohan Lal sits back with a sigh, afraid to move his feet in the minefield of glass. Ramvilas summons a sweeper. They sit silently, immobile, lifting their feet gingerly as the broom sweeps away glass crystals.

'I have been trying to telephone Kartar Singh for two days. Where is he?' Sohan Lal asks, after the sweeper has gone.

'Out of town,' says Ramvilas.

Sohan Lal hopes to deflate Ramvilas's self-assurance by reminding him that he and Kartar Singh were meant to manage the chaivala's campaign jointly. If he can make Kartar Singh see reason, Ramvilas will be left with no choice. But first he must find Kartar Singh.

'Where has he gone?'

'I do not know,' Ramvilas says. 'He left before the CBI raid on his store.'

'Did they find anything?'

'No,' says Ramvilas. 'But sardarji has handed over the campaign to me.'

Sohan Lal knows the CBI has launched a national manhunt for Kartar Singh. He has even heard, though he does not believe, that Kartar Singh may have fled to Canada under a false passport. If only he could be located in the next two days! Kartar Singh's absence leaves Ramvilas in charge of the chaivala. Very well. The clerk leaves him no choice. He will now have to fulfil an unpleasant duty. 'The chaivala is a flawed candidate,' he says.

Ramvilas smiles. 'The better to represent a flawed constituency! His imperfections endear him to the people.'

'Not if they find out he is in league with IPP,' says Sohan Lal, savouring the confusion on Ramvilas's face. 'Could it be, perhaps, that the poor man's candidate is really a Hindu fundamentalist? What does he think of Babri Masjid?'

'Gopal Das is a secular man,' says Ramvilas. 'He denounces the IPP hoodlums who destroyed Babri Masjid.'

'Is that why he sent his son to Ayodhya to bring down the masjid?'

'His son was killed two years before that,' says Ramvilas.

'Not *that* son!' retorts Sohan Lal. 'The son he adopted, the Musalman boy.'

'What of him?'

'He was inside Babri Masjid when it came down.'

Ramvilas laughs incredulously. 'This is too far-fetched for anyone! Is that the best IPP can come up with?'

'It can be proven,' says Sohan Lal.

Ramvilas pauses, his mind a whirl of possibilities. He does not know much about the one-handed Musalman. The boy is shadowy. He sometimes calls himself a Hindu, and his relationship with the chaivala is suspect. Very well, he will have a conversation with the boy. Whatever the truth behind this, it must be forgotten.

'The police will question the boy,' says Sohan Lal. 'They have ways of reinvigorating the mind to bring back lost memories.'

'The boy remembers nothing,' says Ramvilas.

'There is a barber who does,' says Sohan Lal.

Ramvilas is silent, caught off-guard, exasperated to be in the dark over such an important detail.

'A barber named Ram Bibek remembers a boy on the fourth of December, nineteen ninety-two, two days before the structure was destroyed in Ayodhya. He remembers because the boy had one hand. His right wrist was a stump. "I do not shave Musalmans," Ram Bibek said to the boy. "I will be a Hindu when you are done," said the boy. He said his name was Chotu, but Ram Bibek knew he was lying because he was clearly a Musalman. He asked the boy who his father was, and the boy said, "Gopal Pandey."'

'No one will believe a barber,' says Ramvilas, with affected bravado.

'A thousand people saw a one-handed man in Ayodhya,' says Sohan Lal.

When he had first seen Gauhar in the picture with Gopal, standing indistinctly behind the chaivala, Sohan Lal assumed it was someone else, because the boy had died in Ayodhya. Then he had made enquiries that left no doubt in his mind. Here was the boy again, a bomb that could destroy Suleman. But Suleman paid his dues in the assembly election of 'ninety-three. Now it is more important to pit the boy against this chaivala who has the effrontery to take himself seriously.

Ramvilas is at a loss.

'Gopal Das is a closet fundamentalist!' says Sohan Lal, with relish. 'The barber will be in the news next week, six days before the election.'

Ramvilas stands up and looks out of the window.

'I will be at the returning officer's rooms tomorrow morning,' says Sohan Lal. 'I will wait for you to come. Gopal Das can make a statement when he announces his withdrawal, throwing his support behind Harilal Gupta.'

'They should have chosen the daughter,' says Ramvilas. 'The wife is no good.'

Sulochana Agrawal's tired speech has ended, and she is being escorted to the Ambassador by Babulal. The coolies stream out of the car park, ready to attack the railway platforms where mountains of bedrolls have accumulated.

Ramvilas turns from the window and leaves the room swiftly.

Sohan Lal collects his stick, makes an attempt to heave himself up, fails, and is reminded of the doctor's constant admonition to lose some weight. He will wait until he has caught his breath. The conversation has drained him. He gazes at the magazine lying on the floor where Ramvilas left it. *India Now*: 'Who is Gopal Das?' He sighs, horrified by the vulgarity of his own words to Ramvilas. He likes the cut and thrust of committee meetings. He likes feints, jabs and throws. He does not like naked aggression. A seth does not threaten, he merely suggests. Is it wise to bring the ghost of this one-handed boy back into the world? True, the boy is irresponsible, on top of being a Bangladeshi and a Musalman. It could even be said that he has brought this upon himself by coming back to life. But surely poverty and a single hand is punishment enough. God has already taken His revenge. It is not right that humans should persist where He has finished. Ah, Ramvilas is too prudent to do anything rash to the boy. Soon the chaivala will withdraw, the boy will fade back into the shadows of Chandni Chowk, and no one will remember that a seth had threatened a clerk. Sometimes, a man must knowingly exercise bad taste.

Ramvilas leaves the railway station in a hurry, flags down a ricksha and goes to Lajpatrai Market. Although he has come to meet Gopal, he is irritated to find him asleep in the back room.

'Why are you not out campaigning? Did I not ask you to walk through Chawri Bajar today? That is the core of Harilal's support.'

Gopal shrugs.

'Where is your Musalman son?' asks Ramvilas.

'He is out sticking up posters,' says Gopal.

'Will he come back here?'

'In the evening.'

'Send him away for two weeks,' says Ramvilas.

'Where can I send him?'

'Anywhere. Bombay. Madras. Calcutta. Give him money for a train ticket.'

'He will not listen to me!' protests Gopal.

'Are you not his father?' asks Ramvilas.

Gopal shrugs. 'What has he done wrong?' he asks.

'Go to Chawri Bajar now,' commands Ramvilas. 'And I do not want to see the boy when I come here tomorrow.'

16:

Gopal Das smiles down at scooters in GB Road from a hundred posters, strung along ropes that criss-cross the street. He beams up at them from commodes, wash-basins and urinals that lie heaped outside every shop. Shopkeepers have resigned themselves to this indiscriminate postering. Posters spring up on anything that cannot move. 'Take this wash-basin!' they say to their customers. 'The first time you wash your hands, the poster will come off and you will no longer have to spit over a bald head that looks up at you through milky spectacles . . .' Three days ago, a dozen stray cows were found sauntering down GB Road with Gopal Das posters pasted to their rumps.

At the entrance to GB Road a stall is strung with loudspeakers, which hurl Pushpa Rani's ageless voice at scooters and rickshas, and the kothas beyond. It is the same song on a perpetually repeating loop.

> *'Should I lay flower petals in your path?*
> *Should I stand outside your house all night?*
> *Should I serenade you every morning?*
> *What should I do that will not devalue my love?'*

It is really a man's song, but Pushpa Rani, having sung every song her music directors could think of over sixty years, has taken to rerecording old gems previously sung by male compatriots who are long dead. From time to time, when Gauhar has caught his breath and recharged his lungs with oxygen, he cuts off Pushpa Rani to deliver a torrent of slogans through the loudspeaker. He sits in the stall, holds the microphone in his good hand and raises his stump with every cry. 'Vote for Gopal Das! Vote for the man who will give *you* a seat in Parliament! A vote for Gopal Das is a vote for yourself! Vote, vote, vote, vote, vote, vote . . .' And then his voice dies to a whisper, and Pushpa Rani resumes her love-making, until Gauhar can marshal his forces again.

The stall is a little wooden structure plastered with posters. A counter runs across the front displaying campaign literature, behind which there is a bench. Sound-amplification equipment is tied down in one corner. Banners and placards lie in a pile in another, to be used in rallies that start from the counter, run up and down Chandni Chowk and return three times a day. Gauhar mans the stall, monitors the placards, and sustains a constant battle cry on the loudspeakers. He mixes Bengali and Hindi in his slogans, but no one cares. The amplifier is unable to keep up with his voice, so the slogans are too garbled for anyone to understand, except for the word 'vote' and the name 'Gopal Das'.

Vote, vote, vote, vote, vote, vote . . . mouths Gauhar. He is breathless with excitement. He has done nothing in the last two weeks but sit in the stall and walk in rallies with Gopal Bhai. The days are busy and the nights are long. He has worked tirelessly and, always, at his side is a bottle of Chou En-lai and a joint of bholanath . . . Never before has he felt such a deep debt of gratitude or such warmth as he now harbours for Gopal Bhai. Anything for Gopal Bhai! A campaign, a thousand rupees, an all-night vigil, a crowd . . . He has commandeered the services of the entire gang for the purpose. Gopal Bhai must win, whatever that means in the wider world. Equally important, that bastard Suleman Mian must fall flat on his face. There is nothing a one-handed man cannot do if he makes up his mind to it, and Toothless Beard shall see for himself the power of a Bengali gang. Vote, vote, vote, vote . . .

'Raja Babu!' calls Munna.

He appears from nowhere, slinks up to the counter, throws a wallet at Gauhar and vanishes into GB Road, melting into the crowd as quickly as he had emerged from it. Gauhar spirits it away from the counter, flips it open and draws out three hundred rupees, all with the one hand he has trained over two years. The money goes into his pocket, the wallet into the heap of placards. His pockets are now bulging with cash – two thousand eight hundred rupees to be spent on the campaign. He expects Aftab, Partho and Johnny soon, and they never bring in less than five hundred rupees in a day. After he has given them their commission, he can still hand over two thousand to Ramvilas Babu. He wishes he could give the money directly to Gopal Bhai, or use it himself to hire people, print placards and rent rickshas. There is something not quite right about this Ramvilas Babu. He is too oily, too clean-shaven, and his kurta has no creases. Every evening, when Gauhar walks into Bhagwan Das and Sons behind Jama Masjid and hands over the money, he is disturbed by the look on Oily's face. It is a look he understands. He has seen it on a hundred rustams and pyarelals. Oily snatches the money a little too quickly. His grip on the notes is too strong, the pressure in his knuckles too great. Last night Oily was annoyed when Gauhar walked into the steel and glass shop empty-handed.

'We collected nothing today,' said Gauhar.

'Has Gopal spoken to you?' asked Oily.

Gauhar shook his head.

'You must go to Calcutta,' said Oily.

Gauhar was instantly suspicious. He had heard of a government programme – Operation Pushback – to return Bangladeshis to Dhaka. Was this a trick to get him out of the country? 'I will go nowhere until Gopal Das has won,' he said.

Oily pulled out a stack of hundred-rupee notes, peeled off three and threw them on to the counter. 'Go to Calcutta,' he said. 'I do not want to see you again.'

Oily had a nerve! To throw at him three hundred rupees – almost certainly earned by Gauhar's own gang – as if he were a beggar!

'The Bangladeshi government will not take me back,' Gauhar sneered. 'Have you not heard what happened to the first batch who were sent over the border?'

Oily looked confused. Gauhar snatched up the money. 'I will print more posters for Gopal Bhai with this,' he said grandly. Then he stalked out of the shop, letting the glass doors bang. He did not care if he shattered a pane or two.

He is glad he did not yield to Oily last night. He fills his lungs, snatches the microphone and bellows at the top of his voice, cutting off Pushpa Rani with a vengeance. 'Vote, vote, vote, vote, vote, vote . . .' The word comes out violently, each time delivering a blow to the well-oiled head of Ramvilas. Fuck this Ramvilas! He will tear off that neat kurta-pyjama and parade him naked in GB Road if the bastard dares to come near the stall!

To Gauhar's left, a sudden cry goes up.

'Gopal Das *murdabad*!'

It is a jarring note in the harmony of GB Road. Gauhar leans over the counter to discover that a procession of women is marching toward the stall. A large banner travels with them – IOW: Indian Organisation of Women. The women are city types, like Chitra Didi, wearing dark glasses and lipstick. Who the fuck are they, he wonders, and what could they possibly have against Gopal Bhai? He climbs over the counter and jumps into the road. If the women come any closer, he will attack the bitches!

On seeing Gauhar's belligerent stance, the procession falters and stops a short distance from the stall. A woman walks up, turns to face the others, and speaks in an angry voice. 'Gopal Das has said he will legalise prostitution!' she screams. 'Who is Gopal Das to legalise prostitution? Is it a job like knitting or sewing or working in an office? Does he know what it is like to be a prostitute? How dare he call them sex-workers, as if what they do is just another line of work? These women are not sex-workers, they are prostitutes, and prostitution is not a profession! Work is associated with dignity and pride. How can selling your body be a profession? No woman on earth wants to do it. She does it out of helplessness, or she is forced into it. Legalise prostitution? No! We want to *end* prostitution, we want to *eradicate* it, we want to *criminalise* it, we want to *cure* our society of it. We do not want to *legalise* it!'

Ah, thinks Gauhar. These are just whores from GB Road dressed up as city women, pretending to be modern. They have no customers in daylight so they protest. As soon as night falls, they will go back to their business.

He jumps back into the stall, turns up the volume of Pushpa Rani's song until the loudspeaker chokes, then sets up a deafening chant that drowns the unamplified voices of the women. 'Vote, vote, vote, vote, vote, vote . . .'

After twenty minutes the IOW representatives disperse, defeated. Gauhar flings abuse at them, then settles down to take a nap behind the counter.

'Gauhar!'

He shakes himself awake with a curse. He does not know how long he has slept, and how many deliveries he has missed, in case Partho, Johnny or Aftab turned up. An old man stands at the counter – dirty kurta, scattered clumps of hair, eyes weighed down by bags of skin, hollow cheeks that have collapsed into his face. A perfect set of teeth is fitted tightly inside the mouth, and looks as though it has been inserted surgically. It is exposed through a cleavage in the upper lip. There is no doubt who this is, though he has decayed much in the six years since Gauhar has seen him. There is also no doubt why he has come here, so the first thing Gauhar offers is an excuse.

'I will return your Gandhi,' he says. 'I was taken away before I could do the job.'

Bobby smiles, and his upper lip falls away. It has withered to nothing. The smile is grotesque. The teeth are fake, thinks Gauhar, reminded of the many old men whose dentures had fallen out when they tried to chase him after he had swiped their purses, watches, chains, everything but their teeth. Old men were made to be robbed, and Bobby looks vulnerable, weighed down by a large cloth bag that swings from his shoulder. 'Keep the Gandhi,' he says.

His voice is hoarse, almost a whisper, and Gauhar is suddenly afraid. Bobby, with eyes like marbles suspended inside those horrible bags, no longer looks vulnerable. This is Bobby, after all, master of Tihar Jail, arranger of men, purveyor of tobacco, sergeant of guards. His eyes are not out of focus, as old eyes should be.

'I thought you were in jail,' says Gauhar.

Bobby sighs. 'I need to stay outside for a few months,' he says cryptically, and his manner indicates that he goes in and out of Tihar as he wants.

'I can give back the Gandhi with five per cent interest,' Gauhar offers again.

Bobby shakes his head.

'Why have you come, then?' asks Gauhar.

Bobby smiles his horrible smile, and flicks his head in the direction of GB Road. For a moment Gauhar is puzzled, then bursts out laughing. He is no longer intimidated. The bastard has come to get himself a whore! 'You are too old for that!' Gauhar chides him.

Bobby leans forward with a leer. 'It is more fun when you are old! You will see.'

Gauhar slaps him on the shoulder – almost dislocating it – and points to a hoarding that stands next to the stall. Bobby looks at it blankly. Gauhar reads aloud the black letters that run across the white background: 'He who comes to GB Road is an ass.'

Bobby laughs, and they admire the board together. Someone has sketched an ass on it – head, hoofs, body and tail scratched out from the white paint, leaving lines of steel-grey tin shining beneath. There are many other scrawls – a penis with testicles, a triangle meant to represent the vagina, a whole copse of penises in varying stages of tumescence.

'I must go now,' says Bobby, with a twinkle in his eye. 'Give me some placards.'

'Are you going to show them to whores?' laughs Gauhar.

'We want everyone to vote for Gopal Das,' says Bobby.

'All right,' says Gauhar.

He throws three placards on to the counter. Bobby picks them up and turns to go. Gauhar considers his unsteady frame, weighed down by the placards. 'Bring them back as soon as you are finished,' he says. 'How will you carry them with that large jhola on your shoulders?'

Bobby shrugs helplessly. Gauhar considers. It is a good idea to keep something as a sort of deposit, so Bobby will return the placards. This is Bobby, after all, who smuggles wires and matchsticks in the soles of shoes. Who knows what he will do with the placards? He could sell them for the wood and cardboard. The jhola will surely bring him back.

'Leave your jhola here,' he suggests.

Bobby extricates himself from the bag with difficulty and places it on the counter. Gauhar flings it on to the heap of placards.

'Show the bitch that you are still a young ass!' exhorts Gauhar. 'But be careful! Do not bite her with those teeth!'

Bobby grins. The teeth stare shamelessly through the portcullis of his upper lip. He turns slowly, raises the placard and walks away.

Gauhar shrugs. Old men are useless. They cannot shout slogans, cannot hold a placard high, cannot stand for long in the cold. In any case, Bobby will throw aside all placards when he sees young flesh. The campaign needs younger boys, like those in his gang, but he cannot waste them on placards and banners.

'A babu in Paratha Gali!' shouts Partho, coming up to the counter and splaying his hand on it, palm down. A small velvet purse is trapped under it, its mouth closed by a drawstring. Gauhar loosens the string and gasps. Three gold coins glint at him. He holds them between thumb and forefinger, dazzled. Small coins, each worth seven thousand rupees, worth more than the head of the queen that sullies them.

'Fucking rustam!' says Gauhar, full of admiration despite himself.

Partho lets out a boisterous cackle in acceptance of the compliment. Then, seeing passers-by stare at him, he raises his fist in the air and shouts, 'Gopal Das *zindabad*!'

'Vote, vote, vote, vote, vote, vote . . .' shouts Gauhar, into the microphone, his voice floating on wings of joy. From where he stands at the counter, he can see the grilles of the first kotha in GB Road, behind which whores have begun to appear as the afternoon wanes. Bobby is there somewhere, fucking. At sunset the shops will put away their commodes and wash-basins, the shopkeepers will go home to their fat wives, and the whores will come down to the street. And then Gauhar will close the counter . . . Three gold coins, twenty-one thousand rupees, to be kept away from that sly Ramvilas Babu, to be used for bholanath, Chou En-lai and cigarettes, and those smooth limbs behind the grilles, so willing, so supple! But he cannot keep the purse in the stall. Too many people enter and leave, take placards, put them away, and Ramvilas Babu is always around, scrutinising, ferreting out secrets. He throws the purse back at Partho. 'Meet me in the railway park at midnight,' he says.

Partho nods and slips it into his shirt pocket.

'No more business for you today,' says Gauhar. 'Keep it in a safe place.'

But Partho is already gone. Gauhar laughs. The boy is good, very good. But it is these good boys who turn out to be snakes. Something changes in a boy when he turns into a man. The boy is a faithful dog, the man a disgruntled hound. Partho has his eye set on becoming Raja Babu some day. This is a difficult business. If Gopal

Bhai wins this election, Gauhar will ask him to find him a job, but not as a silver-beater or a tout for a seth. Those are filthy jobs, little better than getting fucked by old men or taking bets in pigeon fights. He will ask to be a clerk in a railway reservations office. That is a secure, comfortable job, he has learned. He will have to do little for the rest of his life, and he will rise to be head clerk when he is sixty. Once Gopal Bhai makes him a clerk, he can marry. Whatever happened to the Nepali girl in Didi's school? She was pretty, but there are many other girls like her. Why, there are so many beautiful whores right here in GB Road! But he cannot marry a whore. No, a good girl, a God-fearing girl who will be faithful to him. A good Musalman girl.

The afternoon has spent itself. Evening will be cold, and night will be bitter. Gauhar draws a thick blanket round himself. The shops will close in an hour. There is a large crowd in the street at this time, when early clients of kothas mix with late purchasers of commodes. Leaning over the counter, hugging the blanket, he tries to guess who has come on what business – buying commodes or flesh – when he sees Inderlal Jha step out of a police jeep a short distance from the stall.

'*Salaam*, sir!' he calls, in mock salute.

He has avoided Inderlal for two years, trying not to cross paths with him. Inderlal does not much mind the gang as long as they stay away from GB Road, but he is an unpredictable snake, and that belly of his knows no depth: his appetite is limitless. Who knows what demands he may make, knowing as much as he does about the gang? He recognises Munna and Gauhar, and perhaps had a good look at the other members when they went to the police station two years ago. A snake has a tenacious memory, they say. It never forgets a face that has once registered in its mind's eye.

Inderlal walks to the stall and raps the counter with his baton.

'Permit?'

Gauhar nods, pulls out a piece of paper from his trousers, unfolds it and lays it flat on the counter, not letting go of it while Inderlal studies it. The forgery was prepared for Gauhar in Khari Baoli and cost him ten rupees. Inderlal, who has never seen a permit in his life, grudgingly approves it with two knocks of his baton. Gauhar's promptness has unnerved him. He has been demanding permits for fifteen years, always with the intention of getting a little something for himself. He did not know, until now, that permits existed. He feels humbled by the experience. Yet this is the thief who barged into his police chauki and asked that his friends be released. He cannot allow a one-handed freak to get the better of him.

He points threateningly at the heap of placards and the audio equipment. 'What is that?'

'Election material,' says Gauhar, brightly. 'Gopal Das *zindabad*!'

Inderlal is unmoved by the slogan. With a flick of his baton, he motions two constables into the stall. They push aside the hinged door and pace roughly behind the counter, turning up placards, kicking banners, twisting knobs on the amplifier.

'What are you looking for?' demands Gauhar. 'You will damage the placards!'

'Where have you hidden the ganja?' demands Inderlal.

Gauhar laughs. 'I don't keep reefers in the stall.'

The constables unearth Bobby's jhola from the heap of placards. 'Ganja!' declares Inderlal triumphantly.

'It is not mine,' protests Gauhar.

Inderlal loosens the string that seals the mouth of the bag. His fingers close round a metal box wrapped in red and blue wires, studded with electrical contact-points. He pulls it out of the bag and brings it close to his face. A ticking sound emanates from it, growing louder as the box travels toward his ear.

'What is it?' Gauhar asks curiously.

Inderlal does not reply. He hurls the box back into the stall and runs frantically. The constables follow him out.

'Where are you going?' demands Gauhar. 'Sister-fucking bastards—'

The counter slaps Gauhar in the face, lifts him off his feet and hurls him against the tarpaulin ceiling. He is raised high into the air, vaguely aware that he can see far out into GB Road, where the crowd of shoppers, pimps and whoring men has turned to look at him. Everyone is staring at me, he thinks. Everyone wants to vote for Gopal Das! But now they seem to be rising higher. I can no longer see over their heads. I must look up to see the tops of buildings . . . The last thing he sees, before he hits the ground and his skull shatters, is three whores in the balcony of a kotha, leaning so far over to watch him that their breasts swing outside their low-cut blouses.

✻   ✻   ✻

Inderlal rises to his feet a few seconds after the explosion has died away and looks through the shredded canvas top of his police jeep. It was fortunate that he left it parked some distance away. Pieces of metal and wood have slammed into the windscreen and shattered it, bathing him in shards of glass but causing no apparent harm. One of his constables crouches beside him. The other is either dead or has run to safety. Inderlal walks gingerly toward the spot where the stall stood. Two wooden posts have survived the blast. They lie on their sides with pieces of tarpaulin still connecting them. A knee-deep crater has been excavated in the road. Next to it, one side of a building has been extensively damaged, exposing wash-basins inside a store, and a bed in the kotha on the upper floor. All of the window-panes in this building, which was closest to the stall, have shattered. To the left of the stall, the remains of a hoarding lie in gnarled strips of tin, declaring in large black letters, 'He who comes to GB Road is an ass.' The street is littered with debris. A scooter is on its side, rear wheel still spinning, the rider lying in a pool of blood.

A powerful bomb, thinks Inderlal, but without shrapnel, or there would have been many more dead. And certainly without RDX. This is a locally made device. A battery, some wires and a timer have survived the blast. It will take the forensic people a few hours to determine the composition of the bomb. Meanwhile he must estimate the damage. The scooter rider is moving, which means he is shocked and injured but not dead. The constables are tiptoeing toward the crater. Next to it there is a heap of rubble and a mangled corpse. One arm is splayed in the street, fist clenched. The other is raised to cover the face, ending in a stump as if the wrist has been blown off. An old gramophone sits in the remains of the stall. The explosion has swirled round it but left it untouched, as if it were sacred space. Inside that oasis, Pushpa Rani sings bravely:

> '*Should I lay flower petals in your path?*
> *Should I stand outside your house all night?*
> *Should I serenade you every morning?*
> *What should I do that will not devalue my love?*'

17

The bus leaves Ring Road and turns away from the Yamuna river, flowing with a stream of rickshas and scooters that will take it toward Chandni Chowk along the sandstone walls of Red Fort. Ramvilas sits at the front, in a little seat just behind the driver so that he will not have to talk to the passengers. He finds their high spirits annoying. They behave as if they are going to a community picnic, instead of to cast their votes. At one point, when the bus rolled out of Naresh Colony, they had even broken into song – an unintelligible chant, perhaps in Bengali, from some forgotten corner of Bangladesh. For almost five minutes he sat mute, trying to bury his head in his kurta collar, buffeted by fifty-five shrieking female throats. Finally, he turned and told them they would be arrested unless they kept quiet. The singing died away slowly, like a motorcycle engine sputtering to a standstill, and the silence has endured, but he senses hostility among the passengers. Ah, he will sweeten it with money.

The bus is stuck in traffic. He taps the driver's shoulder to impart to him a sense of urgency. It is already eleven. The sun, which made itself known only an hour ago, has climbed high in the sky, and this is his first sortie. The delay was caused by the sun. The women did not want to leave their homes – even homes made of blue tarpaulin and Dalda tins – until they felt its warmth on their cheeks. He had not counted on such grey weather. It is already two days after Holi, and everyone knows that Delhi becomes warm – suddenly and viciously – after Holi. The day before, people shiver in blankets and sit around fires. The day after, they dust their ceiling fans. He arrived at Naresh Colony at eight in the morning, but he knew he had miscalculated as soon as he stepped off the bus and saw the clouds formed by his breath.

He was disappointed to find that the men were away, pulling carts in Chandni Chowk. Election day is a national holiday. All offices – government and private – are closed, but Naresh Colony is a country in itself, a nation of war widows whose husbands will return from their campaigns, if they return, at sunset. 'What work will they find today?' he had asked the women. They shrugged. If the men do not work today, they do not eat tomorrow. They must utilise every waking moment to compensate for the wasteful hours of sleep. The women will have to do, said Ramvilas to himself.

He had no trouble in enlisting their support. The denizens of Naresh Colony remember the demolition drive of 'ninety-six very well. In the two years since, they have recovered their pots, tins and sheds to resettle their land, but they know Harilal Gupta is still transport minister in the state government, and they dread the possibility that he may become a Member of Parliament. They have seen bulldozers before, and do not want to see them again. And then he told them about the Dara Shikoh Park that was to go along the east wall of Red Fort. 'They will bury your Naresh Colony under it,' he said. 'Madams from the city will walk about in the park in expensive sarees, and you will lie under the sod, trampled underfoot.'

'We do not know who this Dara Shikoh is,' said the women.

'You do not need to,' said Ramvilas, 'because he will soon be sitting inside your home.'

They still have a corner in their heart for Naresh Agrawal – their patron of long standing – but his image took a beating when he failed to protect them in 'ninety-six. Even more damaging to his reputation has been his decision to die without making provision for them. He had long promised them brick-and-mortar homes. Although they will not openly say so – you cannot speak ill of a departed soul – they are seething with anger at his inconvenient departure. He has tricked them, caught them unawares by leaving in such unseemly haste. 'Nareshji has left us fatherless,' say the women – with a tear in one eye and a hint of revenge in the other, 'and Sulochanaji has never once visited us!'

After the women agreed to come, he had to stand for almost two hours amid the bricolage of their shelters, waiting for the sun to break through clouds. And then it was a race to pack them into the bus while keeping their children outside it. After all the talking, waiting and singing, he has finally managed to bring his fifty-five votes to Chandni Chowk. They have reposed their trust in Gopal Das, who will build a grand perimeter wall round Naresh Colony, and raise a building that will rise higher than Shah Jahan's crumbling fort. Once it is complete, Ramvilas has assured them, you will be able to look *down* into the Red Fort compound and see Divan-i-Khas from *above*.

It is a pity the fifty-five husbands are missing, but the women will suffice if he can convince the election officer in the booth that their names are on voter lists. He has stationed his best men at this booth, skilled in the art of election-officer engagement. Election officers can be pliable and co-operative, reflects Ramvilas, charged as they are with safeguarding that most inalienable of rights that we, the people, have conferred on ourselves . . . The bus completes its circuit of the Red Fort perimeter and approaches the junction with Chandni Chowk. He asks the driver to stop. The voter booth is half a kilometre away but there are policemen around it, and if they see the bus there will be trouble. There are some silly restrictions on bringing voters to booths.

'You must get off here,' he tells his passengers. 'You have to walk the rest of the way.'

There is some grumbling, which he quenches with ten-rupee notes, one placed on each open palm. 'Do not forget the Dara Shikoh Park!' he warns. 'Put your stamp on the cup of tea!'

The women let out a collective guffaw and file out of the bus with renewed determination, ten rupees folded and knotted tightly in fifty-five saree corners.

'Remember the cup of tea!' he calls.

When the procession has turned the corner, he instructs the driver to take Ring Road toward Shahdara, from where he can loop back to reach the other two slums in the Red Fort area. There are too many empty spaces, he thinks. These open fields should have been chock full of slums, people, voters . . .

The last few days have been difficult for him. His run of ill luck began with the purse robbery in Paratha Gali. He had brought away three gold coins from Bhagwan Das and Sons, thinking he would put them in his safe-deposit box at the bank. Vimal does not notice the gradual depletion of these coins. He does not know how many there were and is too distracted to take an inventory. Lala Surajmal kept them in the shop rather than at home because he had no faith in his sons. He was right not to place his trust in them when he was alive, Ramvilas thinks, considering how careless they are with his wealth after his death. But Ramvilas, the inheritor of Lalaji's legacy, takes care of the bequest. Surely Vimal will not mind if the coins are transferred to the bank, where they are much safer. With the coins sitting silently, cheek to cheek, inside his kurta pocket, Ramvilas had stopped to eat in Paratha Gali when a dirty beggar approached him. He was no more than twenty. 'You look like a healthy man,' he had scolded the boy. 'Get yourself some work!' The boy had grinned and run away, perhaps ashamed. Ramvilas had felt a sense of satisfaction.

All such boys needed was a fatherly reprimand, he told himself. It was not wise to pamper them by giving them money, when a well-meant admonition could set them on the right path. Thus warmed by his good deed, he had rewarded himself with an extra paratha. Only on reaching the bank, when he slipped his hand into his kurta pocket to draw out the purse, had he discovered the theft.

The bus swerves. Ramvilas gnashes his teeth. If he ever sees that boy again . . . The last few days of the campaign have been rough. There are stories, even in Hindi newspapers, that point accusing fingers at Gopal. What is Gopal Das going to do about the Mandal Commission? Will he agitate against it, as his son did? This reference to Mukesh is undoubtedly the handiwork of Sohan Lal. Who else remembers that misguided boy? The seth has been vicious in his disinformation campaign, attacking Gopal's ancestry, his dead wife and his chai stall. 'Gopal Das is a thief,' say the newspapers. 'He was thrown out of Jamna Lal Kishori Mal, a garment shop in Kucha Bansilal, when the proprietor discovered he had stolen three boxes of silk kurtas. Gopal Das always had a fascination for silk kurtas. And where is that Musalman boy,' ask the newspapers, 'whom Gopal Das pretends to have adopted? Where is he now, and where was he six years ago when Hindu fundamentalists shamed India by tearing down Babri Masjid in Ayodhya?'

This last titbit had given Ramvilas pause. He should have paid more attention to the one-handed Musalman, as a prudent man would to any Musalman at all. Who was that man and what did he know? How does Sohan Lal know so much about him? There are too many stories, too many secrets . . . It is a relief the boy is dead. These news reports do not worry him too much. It is routine to release such information a few days before an election. Suleman is said to have six wives in different parts of the city, Harilal Gupta is alleged to have a stash of seven crores. Where is the man who has no patch on his clothes? Some of the controversy may even have helped Gopal Das: people are suspicious of saints. No, these stories do not worry him. Few care to read them, and the women of Naresh Colony do not read at all. Equally irrelevant is the ruckus raised by the Indian Organisation of Women, a group of city women who have made it their task to raise Indian women to the level of shamelessness acquired by women of the West. 'We want to wear trousers and shorts,' they say. 'We want to sleep with many men. We want to have relations with men before we are married, and we want to choose our husbands by ourselves. We want to work in offices, and we want to be managers!' He has no patience with such women. They should go and live in America, where their type is tolerated, but they insist on imposing themselves on the virtuous women of India, and now they have found a target in Gopal Das.

Ramvilas chuckles. They should meet Gita or Parvati, Manju or Nasreen. What do they know about selling bodies? And why must they interfere with Gopal Das? 'Let us not talk of victims and rescuers,' say these prudish women in their college seminars. 'Let us talk of the customers. They are the ones who should be punished!' Do that, thinks Ramvilas, and you will have to castrate every man on earth. He has assured these women that Gopal Das will talk to the customers. He will round up pimps and bais and pahalvans and, yes, he will bring about 'systemic changes' rather than provide 'window-dressing'. Ramvilas has reasoned with them in their own vocabulary, hoping to head off their disruption in the days before the election, to no avail. Every day for the last week the women have held rallies and protests, standing outside Kartar Singh's store and shouting slogans, frightening poor Gopal Das whom they deride as debauched and lecherous. 'Gopal Das is a womaniser,' say the IOW women in salvaar-kameez and thick spectacles. 'Gopal Das visits prostitutes, Gopal Das objectifies women . . .' Where do these women learn such words? Is there a book somewhere – a *Bhagavad Gita* of city women – that was written by someone in America and slipped under their pillows?

The Holi rally was a mistake, he now admits to himself. It merely provided fresh ammunition to the IOW women. In his fifteen years in politics, Ramvilas has never been guilty of poor judgement. His actions have always been prudent, aimed at improving his position inside or outside the IPP committee. Yet the Holi rally was his idea, a lapse brought on by the constant pummelling in newspapers and magazines. He had thought, in suggesting it to Gita, that it would generate goodwill for both STREE and Gopal Das. How heartwarming to see the whores in GB Road scatter the pink powder of gulaal into the air, celebrating the eternal love of Krishna and Radha! How touching to see them smear one another's cheeks with the colours of Holi, then march along their gloomy street in a riot of colour to turn a temple of flesh into a house of saturnalia! And to have the people's candidate join them in this celebration! Gopal Das, after all, is the man who will embrace the poor and the dispossessed. Which shop-keeper, rickshavala or even seth in Chandni Chowk would argue against that?

The concept was more robust than its execution. When the whores of GB Road were given gulaal and buckets of blood-red paint, they went berserk. They ran into their kothas and doused customers, threw water-balloons from balconies into the stores below, attacked bais, pimps and pahalvans with water pistols, danced naked on rooftops, and turned the entire street into a blood-red river. Gopal Das was there, all right, carried along with the current of whores, borne on their bare shoulders, seated amid flowing red hair and bouncing breasts painted pink and blue. Ramvilas had put up a good front when the television people arrived. 'Gopal Das has given sex-workers the respect they deserve!' he declared, himself covered in a coat of green and black. That comment was scooped up and hurled back at him by the IOW women the next day. 'What kind of respect is this?' demanded the IOW. 'The red colours of Holi represent the flow of menstrual blood,' said the IOW. 'What kind of message is Gopal Das sending with his licentious behaviour? What kind of society lets prostitutes play Holi, as if they were normal citizens like blacksmiths and cobblers, porters and clerks? Is the love of Radha and Krishna – unblemished on its platonic perch – no different from the flesh trade inside sordid kothas?'

Ramvilas lays a silent curse on the Indian Organisation of Women. Sexless shrews! May you remain unmarried for eternity! Where do these women pick up theories about menstrual blood? They are all virgins, no doubt, even the married ones. But the Holi rally was certainly a mistake. It has now been two days, and he still smarts from bruises the whores inflicted on him when they slapped paint-smeared palms on his buttocks. His face bears traces of green, black and maroon. The colours have not gone down well with Musalman voters. There have been grumblings about the Hindu candidate going back to his ilk. Two months of careful identification with Musalmans has been compromised. What will happen to Gopal Das if Musalmans go back to Suleman Mian?

A few thousand Musalman votes lost, no doubt about it. The city women, by themselves, do no more than make noise in English newspapers. Of greater concern is the chief election commissioner's letter, brought by an officer from the Election Commission. 'An audit has revealed disturbing violations,' said the officer. 'Gopal Das has exceeded the expenditure limits for a Lok Sabha seat.'

'But we have been very careful!' Ramvilas had protested.

'Yes,' said the officer sarcastically, 'but we were even more so. We recorded your rallies on video cameras. We have added up the exact

number of rallyists you have paid, rickshas you have rented, microphones you have bought, posters and banners you have printed . . .
and we have added up all the expenditure you must certainly have
incurred. With each union giving you more than fifty thousand, it has
rapidly increased!'

'But we received no donations,' said Ramvilas, in a moment of
indiscretion.

The officer took that in his stride. 'Ah, you received no donations,'
he laughed, 'just envelopes stuffed with money!' Then he left, indicating he would be back, and strongly hinting that there must be
something for him the next time he came.

It is too late to disown those donations, even if that madam had not
made a careful list of them in her article. He has given Gita a receipt
for thirty-six thousand, Taslimuddin a receipt for fifty-five thousand
. . . STREE is certainly poorer by thirty-six thousand, against that
receipt. The money is probably at Gita's throat, in the form of a
diamond choker he noticed two days ago.

'Shahdara,' announces the driver.

Ramvilas brings out a handkerchief and wipes his forehead: it is
humid inside the bus. Then he shakes off the shadows that surround
him. Let the Election Commission stew and let the city women vent
their outrage. He will keep his eyes focused on the dispossessed of
Shahdara, who must be brought to the nearest booth where willing
election officers await them with voter lists. He will do his duty, and
the rest of the world can carry on as it pleases. Isn't that what Krishna
told Arjun in the *Bhagavad Gita*?

'Stop here and wait for me,' he tells the driver. 'I will be back with
people.'

Sohan Lal stands near the Jain temple and watches more than fifty
women file past him on their way to a voting booth. They are ragged,
perhaps from one of the slums near Shahdara. He wonders if he
should intercept them, but consoles himself that they could be
Harilal's voters, brought by IPP activists. He will let them be. The
pains have returned, in his back and his swollen legs. 'Too much
standing around,' says the doctor. He is sixty-three. He should be
sitting on a comfortable gaddi, ensconced among bolsters, watching
his son give orders to his staff and his grandsons play Ludo . . . Why is
a man in his position scrutinising poor women in tattered sarees,
trying to determine whose voters they are?

He is pleased with the turnout. Most appear to be IPP voters, which means Harilal's managers are doing their job. The atmosphere is festive in most booths along Chandni Chowk, where Harilal's support is greatest. Sohan Lal decides to walk up and down the street. It will do him good. He will not venture into the lanes behind Jama Masjid, where he will encounter hostile glances. He ambles along, leaning heavily on his cane. The colours of Holi still cover the road in red and pink blotches. It was a boisterous Holi in Chandni Chowk, he has heard from his staff, including an outrageous celebration in GB Road. He had stayed at home and watched his grandsons play Holi. The memory warms his heart. How gratifying to see Vicky – not quite two – stagger on to the balcony with a water pistol! It looked gigantic in his little hands. It was too heavy for him. He lifted it with difficulty, balanced it on the steel rail that runs round the balcony, tipped it over as much as he could and pressed the trigger, squirting a stream of red, screaming, 'Holi *hai*!' at the top of his voice. The jet fell harmlessly into the street but Vicky did not care. He had seen his brothers do it and he was happy to have repeated the trick, laughing even when the gun, tipped too far over the railing, slipped out of his little hands and plunged on to the road.

It would be so much more pleasant, thinks Sohan Lal, if he could spend the rest of his years watching Vicky play Holi, burst fire-crackers during Divali, go to school, grow up to be a young man, get married, have children of his own . . . But then there is Harilal Gupta and the election. There is Suleman to be disposed of, and there is that snake Ramvilas.

A large advertisement was published yesterday in all the English newspapers of Delhi, exhorting Sikhs to vote for the chaivala. It included a testament from Kartar Singh. 'If it was not for Gopal Das my dead wife would have remained stuck in a window . . .' Sohan Lal grimaces. He had thought Kartar Singh was on the run from the CBI. Is he so confident of himself that he can place advertisements in newspapers? Has he, like Ramvilas, decided to burn his bridges with the IPP? Or was Ramvilas placing spurious advertisements in Kartar Singh's name?

He must have a talk with the sardar after the election, assuming he can locate him. Ramvilas is an arrogant fool who will soon find his place, but the sardar can be brought back to earth gently. English newspapers generate more noise than votes. Indeed, Sohan Lal has even seen a piece in a foreign magazine, brought into Kucha Bansilal by an IPP worker, extolling the rise of the common man. It is headed 'The Man Who Would Be King', and explains – for the erudition of its foreign readers – that 'Das' means 'servant', then raves about a 'great experiment in democracy'. So much fuss over a chaivala!

Such matters move in waves, muses Sohan Lal. This one will subside immediately after the election, when the chaivala's campaign has been buried. No matter what the English newspapers say, the Hindi ones are full of questions about his candidacy. Has he raised a Musalman boy, ask the newspapers, or a dog that urinated in Rajghat and defiled the last repose of the Father of the Nation? The thought of the Musalman boy causes him a stab of pain. Of course, Ramvilas could not have had anything to do with that. He is a clerk, given to conniving and back-biting, not violence. On the other hand, Suleman is just the type to do such a thing. He certainly had a lot to lose from the one-handed boy's rebirth. Well, Suleman did not find out about the boy from him, so his conscience is clear. If the boy chose to advertise his existence, no one can be blamed. One Musalman has been killed by another, that is all.

Babulal awaits his turn at a polling booth in Khari Baoli, where his family has lived for generations. He will vote on the 'hand' symbol of the Congress Party, of course, knowing it is futile. He has maintained a cheerful face throughout the campaign, even telling his workers that Nareshji had been promised a ministerial berth, should Congress form the next government. That berth would now devolve to Sulochanaji, if she should become MP for Chandni Chowk. Sheer bravado, he knows. When all the votes have been cast and counted, and all the rigging and booth-capturing has been allowed for, there is little doubt that Harilal will emerge victorious. Sulochanaji can console herself that she would not have become a minister anyway, because no one seriously believes that Congress will get a majority. A hung Parliament is most likely, and none of the small, caste-based parties is likely to support Congress. Another election, another pot-pourri government, another faceless prime minister thrown up by the permutation of numbers, another two years of excruciating instability. Where are the Gandhis and Nehrus who ruled for decades without rebellion, who strode the Indian nation like Mughal emperors and who *looked* like prime ministers?

He has never voted before. What sense can there be in stamping a piece of paper, knowing very well that the actual count will be determined by others? And what difference can his solitary vote make? He looks around and sees clerks, rickshavalas, day labourers . . . He is confirmed in his belief that only riff-raff vote. Respectable people sit at home and watch the results on television.

The queue finally enters the old post-office building, which has been converted into a polling booth. The entire area stinks of shit, weevil-ridden turmeric and rotting pulses that have been collecting in the post office for years. It was cleaned only half-heartedly for election day. He recalls how, under Rajiv Gandhi's Sulabh Shauchalay Scheme, a row of latrines was built in the lane for the labourers in Khari Baoli who arrive daily in droves from villages in Bihar and Uttar Pradesh. They were used a few times and abandoned in favour of the grassy embankment beyond the ceramic walls. There is some affinity be-tween villagers and grass, thinks Babulal. They shit better on it. When they squat on a clean ceramic floor and look down, their own reflection frightens them and hardens the shit in their rectums. So now the voters of Khari Baoli, booth number sixty-three, must hold their noses when they vote for their MP.

After twenty minutes, Babulal finds himself at the head of the line, standing at the desk of an election officer. 'Babulal Goel,' he announces himself.

A dozen men scan his face. One is a Congress worker, deputed to weed out imposters. Babulal watches the election official search the voter list. He picks up a page marked G and runs his finger down the names – Babita Goel, Babloo Goel, Babulal Goel . . .

'Babulal Goel has already voted,' he says.

'Babulal Goel of Khari Baoli! Are you sure?'

The official shrugs.

'It was a false vote!' fumes Babulal.

The official shrugs again, impatiently. Voters do not come with their names written on their foreheads. Observers of Congress, the IPP, the Communist parties and the independents are arrayed behind him, consuming tea and irritating him with their banter. If they do not challenge the identity of a voter, what can he do? Is he supposed to know every beggar in this dirty, crowded constituency?

Babulal gnashes his teeth and turns to the Congress observer. 'Have you been asleep?' he demands. 'Do you not recognise me? What were you doing when my vote was cast?'

The man, who is really a boy, makes a helpless gesture. He knows most people from his katra in Khari Baoli, but he does not recognise

Babulal Goel as the campaign manager for Sulochanaji. He cannot possibly challenge every old geezer who comes in calling himself Babulal or Baburam. It is such a common name! And he is tired of sitting in this dark building, which stinks as if a thousand rickshavalas had farted in unison.

'I will be back!' shouts Babulal, leaving the booth in a huff.

In the Jama Masjid area, a school has been converted into an election booth for the day, located near the ruins of Sparrows. A short distance away from it, Chitra sits on a chair that her driver has miraculously produced and watches the men outside the booth, dressed in long kurtas and churidaar-pyjamas, stroking their beards, staring at voters as they approach. Everyone knows they are Suleman's men, and everyone knows the message their stern faces deliver. This is Suleman's area, and whoever dares enter the booth has but one symbol on which the circular stamp must be applied – the bicycle of the poor man, symbol of both his poverty and self-reliance.

She has witnessed many elections, and she would have to be exceptionally naïve to be shocked at what she sees. She is aware of the intricate web of relationships, favours, obligations and loyalties that culminate in the journey of a voter to a booth. Even as she arrived in Chandni Chowk, her car had to circumambulate a 'shrine' in the middle of the road, hastily erected to propitiate some voting bloc. In a matter of months, the temple – or the mosque or the memorial or whatever it is – will claim this land for its own and expand. One day, the entire city of Delhi will be squatterdom, overrun with temples, stalls, baskets, paan and chai boxes. Every morning the city will rise at dawn, brush its teeth with sticks of babool and bathe under hand-pumps. Then everyone will resume their positions behind boxes and stalls, watched over by the benevolent leaders who collected their votes.

Suleman's men are nervous, which shows in their increased aggression. She is amused to think she is at least partly responsible for this through her championing of the chaivala. Perhaps she should have been more scrupulous in her writing. She has looked the other way, now and then, and glossed over details. She has not considered every angle, as journalistic etiquette requires. She has not carried quotes from dissenters. She has abandoned balance, but can one be balanced when covering a story of such significance? When the whole is so grand, do the parts count?

Her greatest omission, of course, is the story of Mukesh Pandey, the son of Gopal Das. It was his 'self-immolation', in the political vocabulary of those days, that had brought Gopal to her attention. But the son set himself on fire – or was set on fire – to protest against the same Mandal Commission that the father now supports, or is said to support. The story of Mukesh Pandey does not fit with the rest. Mukesh was merely the child born to Gopal's wife, who died in childbirth and left the son as a memento and a burden. Should the wife have been part of the story? Chitra does not remember her name. In any case, the son who matters is Gauhar Muhammad. Gopal Das, the people's candidate, will raise all one-handed Musalman boys from oblivion and give them a home, a family, a reason to look forward to adulthood. The details are irrelevant, because Gopal Das is not defined by the people who crossed his path in the past but by those who fit harmoniously into his present incarnation. How true can his past be if it does not explain his present? Did he ever have a wife, or a son named Mukesh? The demands of truth are more subtle than the mere enumeration of facts. Which is why Gopal Pandey is named Gopal Das, and has a Musalman son named Gauhar Muhammad.

Gauhar is dead, of course. Suleman may be responsible, or the IPP, or Congress, or any of a dozen groups who hate Gopal in this city where everyone hates everyone else. She read an account of the explosion and was moved almost to tears. Gauhar was her last link to Sparrows, the only child born of that great experiment who had achieved adulthood. The others have melted back into the shadows of Chandni Chowk. They are perhaps picking rags, stealing fruit, being sodomised or languishing in jail. Gauhar was her only alumnus . . . and Sparrows is dead now, its last trace blown apart by a bomb.

A shout from the booth distracts her. One of the men with beards has raised a rifle – where did he get it? – and pointed it at a group of women. They cower, and the crowd screams for help. 'Go away,' say Suleman's men. 'Go home! Suleman Mian is coming to vote! You cannot hold him up!'

Chitra berates herself for not having brought a camera. This would have been a picturesque front-page embellishment. A dozen women in salvaar-kameez – poor Musalman women whose eyes are wide with fear – shrinking from three men in long kurtas and churidaar-pyjamas and a rifle pointed at the heart, ready to fire. The women carry little posters, covered with illegible scrawls in Urdu surrounding a crude sketch of a cup of tea.

'Suleman Mian *zindabad*!' shout the men. They fix their eyes on the women as they chant. The women retreat, but their path is blocked: wailing sirens herald three Ambassador cars, navigating carefully along the narrow lane. The vehicles stop. A dozen men in khaki pour out and take up positions, guns at the ready. Suleman emerges as a small, solitary figure from the central car, his hands joined in a namaste. The men with rifles burst into raucous applause. 'Suleman will win, Suleman will win, Allah! Suleman will win or we will burn down Chandni Chowk! There shall be one Chandni Chowk ruled by Suleman or there shall be no Chandni Chowk! Suleman will win, Suleman will win, Suleman will win . . .'

The cars continue to disgorge people in kurtas and churidaar-pyjamas, like a circus-clown act. Chitra watches from her vantage-point, aware that she is no longer in Suleman's favour, that any request for an interview will be rebuffed. He enters the polling booth at the head of a procession, accompanied by gunfire. The men bar all entry into the booth, or even into the lane, while he is inside. When he emerges – a law-abiding citizen who has exercised his constitutional right – he is garlanded and escorted back to his car. The security men get in and the cars back out of the lane, like a reel of film running in reverse. Gunfire and slogans announce his departure: 'Suleman will win, Allah! Suleman will win, Allah! Suleman will win or we will burn down Chandni Chowk! Suleman will win, Suleman will win, Suleman will win . . .'

Manju walks briskly into GB Road and makes her way to Kotha 842. As she approaches, she looks around quickly to ensure she is not being followed, then steps inside the door and runs up the staircase. Seven powerful electric bulbs – recently installed – flood the passage with light, illuminating boxes of condoms and the signboard announcing STREE. She pushes aside the curtain, runs into the room and collapses in a chair, exhausted. Gita Didi, at her desk, regards her with surprise and concern. 'Why are you back so soon?' she asks.

'They are guarding all booths,' says Manju. 'It is impossible.'

Gita peers over her black-rimmed spectacles. 'How did they know who you are?'

Manju sighs. 'Inderlal Jha. His constables are everywhere, in plain clothes. They recognise every sex-worker in GB Road.'

That bastard! thinks Gita. To spy on her girls after she has paid him thousands of rupees over the years! No doubt he has received more from the IPP or Suleman, or whoever has employed him to point out her girls.

Manju holds up an index finger to show the blue splotch inked on it inside the polling booth. 'I voted under my own name,' she says, 'but when I tried to go back in, Inderlal's man was there, scrutinising every face. He began to laugh when he saw me. 'You are not Shalini Jain,' he said, 'you are a whore!' I wanted to slap him, but there were many policemen around. I covered my face and ran. I cannot go back!'

Gita purses her lips. She is tired. She has been up since early morning, poring over voter lists, dispatching her whores to cast votes for Gopal Das using other people's names. She had counted on the anonymity that accompanies a whore in the bright glare of day. True, the respectable citizens of Chandni Chowk have frequently sprayed their seed in cubicles and kothas, but who remembers a whore's face, seen once in the dim glow of night? And who would like to exhume such memories, which the mind buries as quickly as it can? It is safe to assume a man will not recognise, by day, a whore he has ravished at night. But a policeman is not bound by the rules of civil society. By social decree, he is outside the pale of decency. It is his business to consort with thieves, pickpockets and whores, and his living depends on how well he knows them. The commission of Inderlal's men is tied to faces in GB Road, so they have memorised every line on every brow. They can tell Manju the whore from Shalini Jain, wife of a trader in Khari Baoli, merely from the way she bats her eyelids.

'Where is Inderlal now?' asks Gita.

'In the police station, monitoring the election. His men are every-where, and he will reward the one who identifies the most sex-workers. You should go and talk to him.'

'Nasreen!' calls Gita.

Nasreen peers through the curtain.

'How many burqas do we have in the kotha?'

'We have twelve Musalman girls,' says Nasreen, 'so twelve burqas . . .'

'Bring them to me.' She leans back in her chair and thinks of the Holi they played two days ago. It was the most boisterous ever played in GB Road. Whores pulled one another's hair, threw paint down blouses and cleavage, pulled off sarees and shut down the GB Road market until shopkeepers called the police. Gita paid for the paint and water pistols from STREE funds. What a scene it was! Krishna and

Radha would have been ashamed of their timorous love, had they seen the full-throated lust of whores. The thought of Holi sends new warmth into her heart. She sits up straight at her desk, adjusts her bun and straightens her white saree. She feels like a general preparing for a battle. Everywhere she looks the enemy is arrayed against her – Suleman, Inderlal, Harilal, even Ramvilas . . . She is resolved to win the battle for the one man who has never threatened her, the one male whose masculinity casts no pall on a woman's honour, the one man who can play Holi with a hundred whores in platonic abandon.

Nasreen pushes aside the curtain and comes in, six burqas hanging on each arm. She is followed by dozens of whores, who crowd round Gita's desk, awaiting orders. She stands up and faces them, intensely aware of the picture she presents. She knows there are bags under her eyes. The white saree she once wore to protect her modesty now hides the imperfections of her skin. She knows her flesh will sag with each passing year, but it does not matter now. She is Gita Didi of STREE, social worker and political activist, a disembodied spirit whose femininity is inessential, who is immune to senescence and death.

She picks up the voter lists and studies them carefully. 'You are Khalida Begum.' She points to Manju. 'Kholi thirty-two by six, Meena Bajar, Jama Masjid.'

Manju gasps. 'You want me to become a Musalman!'

'You are Abida Bibi,' says Gita to another whore. They giggle. Gita runs through a list of twelve names – one for each burqa. 'You are Shamim, you are Fareeda, you are Salma, you are Parveen, Noor, Shirin, Zeenat, Jamila, Zareena, Shamshad . . . We are all Musalmans today. Allah will protect our modesty, and Gopal Das our honour. Go and vote for the cup of tea!'

She motions to Nasreen, who takes every woman's index finger and dips it carefully into a dish of oil, erasing the blue mark that indicates they have already voted. Gita points to a stack of placards lying in the corner, each bearing the picture of a bicycle. 'Take these! No one will molest you.'

They giggle again and slip on their burqas. Gita notes, with concern, that their bodies still bear the red, green and pink splotches of Holi bacchanalia. 'You must be careful not to expose your arms,' she warns. 'Inderlal's men will suspect something if they see Musal-mans who have played Holi. Go now, vote for the cup of tea and come back quickly. You have much work to do today!'

She waves off her women and studies a chart on her desk, preparing to commandeer burqas – and the bodies that will wear them – from other kothas. She does not know much about this Gopal Das, but somehow, in a world where nothing is as it seems, she knows he hides no secrets. 'There are only three thousand of you but I have to arrange for many lakhs,' Ramvilas had scoffed, when she told him that GB Road would vote for the chaivala. She sits back with a smile – today, every woman in Chandni Chowk will find herself turned into a whore.

Twelve women emerge from Kotha 842, clad in black burqas from head to toe, each brandishing a placard. 'Suleman Mian *zindabad*!' chant the burqa-women, as they make their way to a polling booth.

Chitra rises from the chair in which she has sat all day, fifty feet from the booth behind Jama Masjid. She must return to her office and write her story. The election has turned sleepy. It is late afternoon and the booths are about to close. The threat of violence that reared its head this morning has receded. Suleman's men sit on stools around the booth, guns laid across their laps, sipping tea and chatting, keeping a careless eye on the voters, most of whom appear to be Suleman supporters. There has been a steady increase in the number of women as the afternoon progressed. They arrive in droves, wearing black burqas, carrying placards with the bicycle symbol painted on them.

The room behind Jasjit General Store is windowless so it is dull even at noon, when the sun shoots a few arrows through cracks in the Bournvita shelf. Now, as evening approaches, it is dark, lit by the blue glow of the television screen, which is showing the final hour of voting. Gopal sits in the dark, his back to the television. He has not switched on the fluorescent tube on the ceiling. The words of the announcer roll into each other. He does not want to see, he does not want to hear, he wants to cry . . .

He had cried when he first heard the news from this very television, reported within twenty minutes of the incident. What a ruthless messenger it is, relaying with cold composure such horrible news. There was the face of the moustachioed SHO from GB Road, smirking at the camera as if the explosion was a great personal achievement. There was only one death, he said repeatedly, because of the quick response by GB Road police. He spoke with great pride, as if the bomb blast had been a particularly successful operation. Newspapers dismissed it, saying it had a 'low death toll'. A low toll, but it had claimed his son! If one person had to die, why could it not have been that smug SHO? A vile thought, despicable thought, but he cannot wish it away.

He had not wanted to play Holi. How could he, after they had blown to shreds his only remaining son? Both sons taken before they were twenty-five, and Ramvilas Babu wanted him to play Holi with those ladies in GB Road! 'It is good for the campaign,' he had said.

'What campaign?' Gopal had asked him. He did not want to win any election. He wanted to go back to his kholi in Khari Baoli, crawl under his old blanket and go to sleep. But he had been cajoled into that Holi, and what an outrage it had been! Some of those ladies were half naked! Everything was visible through their drenched sarees and skimpy blouses! The outline of their bodies, the trembling of their thighs, the frolic of their breasts! He was horrified, but secretly pleased when they lifted him on to their shoulders and carried him. He does not want to know what he touched but he can guess. Something moved inside his heart. There was infinite sin but a comforting compliance in their bodies. The way their soft flesh had yielded under him! He must protect himself against such ladies. It was not his idea, that vulgar celebration.

In the evening, Ramvilas Babu told him he must wash the Holi stains off his face and neck. 'They will hurt your image with Musalmans,' he said.

'Why did you ask me to play Holi, then?' he had demanded. The stains are still there, of course. Who can scrub away the colours of Holi in two days? They are like wounds of war. They will heal slowly.

Today has been a sad day. He is afraid to leave the store. Early in the morning, Ramvilas Babu had taken him to a booth to vote. There were many people from the newspapers, and they had many questions for him, but Ramvilas Babu waved them away. Gopal had never voted before, and was disappointed to find that the booth consisted of a desk and a few stalls in one corner of a sales-tax office. A babu from the government showed him how to stamp the ballot paper, laughing when the stamp found its way to the cup of tea. 'You are not supposed to make your vote public,' he admonished Gopal playfully, as he daubed his index finger with a blue pen. When Gopal emerged from the building, Ramvilas Babu asked him to hold up his hand so that the newspeople could photograph the inkstain on his finger. 'Gopal Das has voted,' declared Ramvilas Babu, 'and Gopal Das will win!'

Someone threw a garland round Gopal's neck. He could tell, now that he has borne the weight of so many garlands, that this was made of fake currency notes. He tried to take it off but Ramvilas Babu bade him keep it on. 'It makes you look like a leader,' he said. Gopal came back to Jasjit General Store, and has sat in the back room all day, drained of the desire to eat, drink or urinate. Mukesh is dead and Gauhar is dead . . .

He looks around the room. The mattress is wrecked. Its sheets have not been washed for weeks. His clothes lie everywhere, some in sacks and jholas. Ramvilas Babu said he should not wash them. The sack containing his pots, tins of sugar, tea, cardamom and milk powder sits in a corner. He will go back to the kholi tonight. He has heard of the robbery that took place there last month. Hameed has told him about it, and also that Seth Sushil Jain regrets having lost Gopal. 'As long as you slept in the kholi,' said Hameed, 'there was no robbery.' Hameed can help him transport his clothes and sacks to the kholi tonight. He will speak to Seth Sushil Jain tomorrow.

Ramvilas pushes open the Bournvita shelf from the outside and admits a wide beam of light into the room. 'You are sitting in the dark,' he observes.

Gopal does not respond. The television continues to talk.

'The booths are about to close,' says Ramvilas. 'Everything is in the ballot box now.'

Gopal rolls up his old blanket and collects a kurta from the heap lying in the corner. His bicycle stands outside the store, chained to a pole. He will wedge the blanket into the cage above the rear wheel.

'What are you doing?' asks Ramvilas.

'I am going back to my kholi.'

It is past midnight. Khari Baoli is deserted. Traders have shut their shops and gone home. Carts line the edge of the street, resting on their handlebars, piled high with sacks of suji, jaggery, bijnor and sakoti that will be unloaded tomorrow and stacked inside rooms, godowns and cubicles in every katra. The street that never stops talking is unnaturally calm, sunk in deep slumber after an exhausting day. The asphalt on the road is bathed in the dull red of Holi, which is already yielding to the colours of turmeric, visible where an occasional lantern pierces the darkness.

Chitra stops next to a cart and taps its handlebars. A man sleeps above the mountain of sacks, wrapped from head to toe in a jute blanket. Although she could reach up and shake him, she prefers this vicarious contact. The man turns on to his side and peers over his blanket, reluctant to expose more of his body to the freezing night air.

'Where is Sushil Jain's shop?' she asks.

He does not reply, either because he does not know or because he does not care to tax his groggy mind at this hour. He slides back under the blanket.

Chitra goes to the next cart, then the one beyond it, until she realises that Sushil Jain must be a common name in Khari Baoli, carried by hundreds of traders. She begins to enquire about Katra Badami, and is directed to a dark haveli. She stands outside it and composes herself, running through the endless newspaper accounts that have combined to form a montage – rigging and booth-capturing in Chandni Chowk, minor incidents of violence, relatively peaceful election, allegations of voter intimidation in the Jama Masjid area, sixty-five per cent voter turnout, large turnout by minority women, rickshavalas, day-labourers and slum-dwellers . . . They will analyse it endlessly on television for the next two months, by community, caste and class, they will hold forth on voter disenchantment and pontificate on the anti-incumbency factor, but what do these analyses matter now?

She walks into Katra Badami, passing under a narrow arch painted with an advertisement that promises instant sexual vigour, no matter how stubborn your impotence. It is partially obscured by other posters promoting massages and a phone service. The passage inside the katra has been narrowed by walls of sacks on either side, which yield to tins of castor and mustard oil. The katra is alive, even at this time of night. Slowly her eyes make out men sitting over lanterns, playing cards. She stops and reconsiders. By day the katra is a centre of commerce too busy to catch its breath, but by night it is a dormitory for clerks who work in its rows of cubicles. The men are wearing lungis and dhotis but are naked above the waist. No woman comes into the katra at night. She will perhaps outrage their modesty by going up to them and asking about Gopal Das. So she slinks past quietly and walks deeper into the katra. The passage becomes narrower. There are shops

packed atop each other, behind, beneath and between . . . She knows
how this happens. Like cleaving cells, the cubicles divide again and
again to accommodate each succeeding generation as a family business
is partitioned repeatedly, each share smaller than the last. Paan stalls
are tucked away under concrete platforms, jalebi shops on the slab of
concrete overhanging a drain, spice markets with double and triple
ceilings that leave no more than crawling room between them, packed
with sacks, bags and tins of asafoetida, cloves, cardamom and saffron.
A thousand smells assault her, mixing with the common odour of red
pepper and turmeric.

In one cubicle she stumbles on a dozen men unloading sacks from a
handcart, large white handkerchiefs over their faces – to protect their
noses from the spice, she guesses. 'Where is Sushil Jain's godown?' she
asks. One points upward. At first she thinks it is a joke. Sushil Jain's
godown is up there in the heavens, nestling in the hills of Swargalok
where gods keep watch over it! But no, he is merely saying it is on the
upper floor. 'Where are the stairs?' she asks. The man mumbles
something, which is lost in the folds of his handkerchief. Then he
points to the left, toward the men playing cards, where the katra is
somewhat more spacious. Does he mean the staircase is that way, or
does he mean she should ask the men?

'Do you know where Gopal Das lives?' she persists.

The man does not know. His eyes – the only part of his face she can
see above the handkerchief – narrow in annoyance and he goes back to
work.

She finds her way back to the card-players, wondering why no one
knows about Gopal Das. Are these not the people who have voted
for him? Or have they voted for the cup of tea without bothering
about the man behind the symbol? Or Gopal Das is a common
name, a name that could belong to a thousand people in Chandni
Chowk, and this Gopal Das has not lived in the katra for three
months. Or, and this is perhaps the reason, the election is no longer
on anyone's mind now that a full day has passed. After all the
speeches about the will of the people have been made, the people
merely want to go on with their lives. They have discharged their
tiresome duty, and they do not want to be reminded of it. A high
turnout, say the newspapers. The Chandni Chowk parliamentary
constituency has set a record in the number of minority women
voters. It is a heartwarming trend, the chief election commissioner
has declared . . . Well, it does not matter now.

As she approaches the card-players she notices a staircase tucked away in a narrow recess adjacent to their cubicle. She cannot enter the stairwell without being noticed by them.

'Namaste!' she calls out loudly.

Her voice rings through the katra, causing a momentary flutter among pigeons in the upper cubicles. The men stop their game and peer into the darkness. Then they see her step forward and stare at her uncomfortably. She is familiar with this reaction. Although she is dressed in a saree and her hair is plaited in braids, they can tell instantly that she is a city woman from her gait, poise and height. And they can hear the command in her voice. No housewife speaks to men with such confidence. She is instantly a 'madam' to them, and they do not know how to react to madams. So they stare and scowl without being aware of it, and she runs past them to the staircase. She senses, even if she does not hear, their collective sigh of relief, combined with their obvious astonishment that a woman such as she is climbing the staircase in Katra Badami so late at night.

The stairs are dark. She comes to the first landing and stops. She is in a large hall piled from floor to ceiling with sacks. 'Gopal Bhai!' she calls softly. She continues to the second floor, also full of sacks, then the third. The smell of turmeric, mild at first but strong now, is choking her. She is wading through an ocean of turmeric, hundreds of quintals of it, which makes it difficult to breathe. She sneezes and leans against a wall of sacks. In a few moments the smell dulls her senses, and her nose settles into a new equilibrium. She notices that the third-floor ceiling is very low. It has been added later to create an additional floor in the same vertical space. A rectangular hole has been cut into it and a ladder is placed against the opening. She climbs it.

The double ceiling encloses a vertical space of five feet. Ventilators on the third floor serve as its windows and are shielded with incongruous cloth curtains, which sway gently in the breeze. The thin fabric admits moonlight, which gives the ventilators a dull blue glow, exposing mounds of overflowing sacks. She wonders why Sushil Jain would want to beautify a godown with curtains. A wooden partition that once stood along the length of the space has been largely torn down, the pieces scattered across the floor. She crawls toward the far corner, past dunes of mustard, sesame and cottonseed, pistachios, apricots, figs and walnuts. The smell of turmeric assaults her again and she sneezes uncontrollably.

When she has recovered, the outlines of turmeric sacks come into
focus in the far right corner. He is sleeping on one under a blanket.
    'Gopal Bhai!'
    The blanket stirs. 'Gauhar?'
    He sits up with the blanket wrapped round him. She remains on all
fours, trembling at the impossibility of it all, preparing to tell him,
looking into the frightened eyes of the new Member of Parliament for
Chandni Chowk.

Look how far the crowd stretches! says Gopal to himself, as he sits on
the shoulders of a large man who is being buffeted from all sides by
waves of people. There are a thousand men here, or lakhs, or crores,
and everyone wants to be close to the shoulders on which he rides. To
his left looms Red Fort, silhouetted against the sky, and to his right,
through the haze of Holi colours, he can see Fatehpuri Masjid. All of
Chandni Chowk lies before me, and it is a river of men that celebrates
me. Their cries are unintelligible, their dances have no rhythm, but
they sing and dance for him as they blanket the street with red and
green powder. 'We will play Holi today,' they sing, 'we will play Holi
tomorrow, we will play Holi all year, we will play Holi for five years!'
A band of tea-stall owners has overrun the balcony of a katra. They
lean far out over the railings, banging cups and saucers in a paean to
their new MP. Gopal watches them, fascinated. That is expensive
china! He gasps when a saucer shatters and the pieces fall into the
crowd.
    Who are these people? Most do not look like chaivalas or rick-
shavalas, yet they dance as if intoxicated, grab his knees, try to hold
his hand, and struggle with the man under him for possession of his
body. Hands pull him off the shoulders and deposit him on others,
carry him onward – floating above their heads – until someone sets
him on the ground, and the crowd closes in on him. He can no longer
see Red Fort or Fatehpuri Masjid, but he can hear the slogans. 'Gopal
Das *zindabad*!' They are pressed against him and scream at the top of

their voices. Tall, thin, dark men in torn shirts and trousers . . . And
that one, raising his fist in the air? Is that Gauhar? Gauhar! But the
man does not respond. Ah, he has now raised both hands. But so many
wear muddy trousers and yellow shirts that any could be Mukesh. 'It
is a miracle,' shouts someone, 'a miracle of democracy!' A miracle,
thinks Gopal, inside the walls of bodies closing around him, that
Mukesh has come back to him! If so much can happen that was not
foreseen, perhaps a small extension is possible? Mukesh is definitely
here, if only to see the crowds that have come to celebrate him.

What would Manohar Lal Pandey make of this? wonders Gopal.
Would his eyes well with tears? It has been twenty-four years since
Manohar Lal died – he still does not know why – and Gopal travelled
to Sasaria to bring Mukesh to Delhi. 'You are going to leave me
alone!' his freshly widowed mother said, as six-year-old Mukesh clung
to her. But he brought Mukesh to Khari Baoli anyway, hoping to fill
with the son the emptiness left by the father. If only Manohar Lal
Pandey – or Manohar Das, as they would now call him – had lived to
see his son become MP for Chandni Chowk! And what of Sushila? It
has been a long time since he thought of her, since the eye of his mind
dwelt on her face. Twenty years, perhaps more. He did not see her die.
When he reached Sasaria, Mukesh was alive and she was dead. He
barely knew her. She has melted away from his consciousness – a
phantom wife who might never have existed. His mother had wanted
him to remarry, especially when he brought Mukesh to Delhi. 'How
can a man raise a son without a mother?' she had asked. He never said
no, but he went to Sasaria so infrequently after Sushila's death that the
opportunity never arose. He was comfortable in Khari Baoli, in spite
of Sushil Jain's temper and Hameed's needling. And he was comfortable in his chai stall. He never took Mukesh back to Sasaria, so the
boy grew up without a mother. A good idea, perhaps. It would have
broken her heart to see those upper-caste criminals burn him alive. But
if Mukesh had lived to see this moment . . . There they are, Mukesh
and Gauhar, standing in the throng before him, shouting slogans,
pushing away the men who now rush at him. He can see them
distinctly in the foggy cloud before him. Now he is on shoulders
again, and people are climbing on top of one another for a better look
at him, crowding rooftops, filling windows and balconies, extending
all the way into the sky. They are serenading him from the clouds.

'MP Gopal Das *zindabad*!'

A sudden arpeggio bursts through the crowd. Rickshavalas are squeezing their horns. A procession of whores, who have run down Chandni Chowk in colourful clothes, joins in, throwing fistfuls of gulaal into the air and singing bawdy songs. Through windows in his spectacles, Gopal catches glimpses of sarees tied low on waists to reveal deep navels, and blouses wrapped tightly round thick arms and chests, and turns away. Why have these ladies come again? Why do they leave so much of their breasts exposed? It is not proper for him to be looking at them, now that he is a Member of Parliament, but they have surrounded him. They dance round him and their bodies are near-naked no matter where he turns . . . Ah! Between the throbbing shoulders and shaking hips he can see the English madam, dressed modestly in a salvaar-kameez. He will look at her, he will try to go toward her to thank her for writing those stories about him. But how can he go to her when he is riding on the shoulders of someone else? And why does the madam look so dreamily at the crowd? Are those tears in her eyes? Ganga Maiya! Has he done something horrible that a good woman who speaks English and works in an office with men is crying in a crowd?

'Gopal Bhai! Gopal Bhai!'

Gopal peers through the swinging bodies of whores. It is Ibrahim Mian, wading through the crowd with fiery determination. A torn kurta flaps round his skeletal frame. He grabs Gopal's hand, his eyes streaming with tears. 'Gopal Bhai!' he repeats, in a hoarse, uncertain voice.

Unable to say more, he reaches up, pulls Gopal's face down and cups it in trembling hands, tears rolling down his cheeks to settle in his beard. 'I knew, I knew!' he stammers.

'Ibrahim Mian—'

'Do not say a word!' scolds Ibrahim. 'I always knew you would win. I asked Suleman to step aside many times and let you consolidate the anti-IPP votes. That Suleman, he is not a man of the people like you. He goes around in an expensive Ambassador car. He is a rich man, interested only in rich Musalmans. Have you seen his haveli behind Jama Masjid? Carpets as thick as mattresses!' He clutches Gopal in an embrace. 'I said to Suleman, "Gopal Bhai is my brother! Why do you want to stand in his way?" But he would not listen to the wise words of an old man. Who is this Suleman Mian? A boy born yesterday! A rash child! What does he know about the ways of the world? It is people like you and me, Gopal Bhai, who understand how things work. Our grey hair speaks of wisdom.'

There is no substitute for true friendship, thinks Gopal. Look how his friends have come back to him, in spite of all that has happened!

'You are my brother,' continues Ibrahim. 'My own family! I always knew Suleman was a thief. One shop, just one little kholi in Balli-maran was what I wanted from him. A kholi of my own where I could sell rexine shoes. Was it too much to ask after so many years of service?'

'Not too much, Ibrahim Mian, not too much.'

'Go on, say it!' implores Ibrahim. 'Declare to all these people that you will build me a kholi in Ballimaran!'

'Right now?'

'Yes, right now! We are brothers, you and I! Brothers from Bihar!'

'But your great-grandfather was a silver-beater in Ballimaran,' says Gopal.

'What silver-beater? My great-grandfather never left his village in Bihar. Neither did my grandfather, nor my father. I came to Balli-maran twenty-five years ago. I am a Bihari like you!'

'All right,' says Gopal, uncertainly. 'I will discuss your kholi with Ramvilas Babu.'

'Why should you discuss it with anyone?' demands Ibrahim, in a huff. 'Declare it now!'

'I cannot declare anything now,' pleads Gopal. 'There are too many people here. That madam is looking straight at me!'

'Ah! There will be many madams. Come with me.'

'Where? Thousands of people are blocking my way.'

'You are an MP now, Gopal Bhai. You can go where you want!'

Ibrahim supervises Gopal's descent from the shoulders that bear him, then grabs his hand and pulls him through the wall of whores and rickshavalas, scolding them for standing in the way, scattering them as a battle tank would scatter infantry.

'Make way for MP Sahib!' he screams. 'Get away, whore! Who is this rickshavala, interfering with important business? Do you want the police to arrest you?'

'You are taking me to Kucha Bansilal!' says a panicked Gopal. I cannot go back there to face Ramesh Babu! he thinks. Who knows, the police may be waiting for me? Where will I get the missing kurta buttons – all gold-plated! – that he says I stole? 'Not to Kucha Bansilal!' he pleads.

'Why does that frighten you?' laughs Ibrahim. 'Do you not see how everyone moves out of your way?'

He tears through the crowd, an important man by the side of an important leader, grand and impressive in spite of his wispy frame and the torn kurta that hangs woefully from his thin shoulders.

This is where the Hanuman temple used to be, says Gopal to himself, before the peepul tree crushed it. And this is where Sohan Lalji had his electric signboard. And this is the kucha, not too different, perhaps a little wider, but full of so many people he can barely walk. But why is Ibrahim so insistent on going into the kucha? What can be gained by picking a fight with Ramesh Babu? This is a joyous occasion, a moment of forgiveness and celebration. Why rake up old issues? Does it matter that he does not remember stealing those gold-plated buttons? He may have misplaced them or pulled them out of kurtas absently. He did have a tendency to handle them roughly. He has become more and more forgetful with age. Why blame a young man like Ramesh Babu for his own failings?

'Here we are!' says Ibrahim, shooing away the crowd that has collected around them.

Gopal stands speechless, staring at his old chai stall, sitting exactly where it always had under the electrical junction box, looking as it had fifteen years ago, before he began to expand it with benches and stools. The wall behind the box is chartreuse green, painted with a girl wearing a frock, a woman in a saree and a man in a shirt and trousers, while the box is a bright parrot green. They have cemented the drain underneath and laid planks to cover it. And seated on the planks is a wooden chest – his chai stall! – four feet high and seven feet long. Inside it he can see cups, plates, tins of sugar, tea and cardamom, his old oil stove and a pail of milk. Ibrahim swings open the junction box to reveal his Musalman tumbler lying in one corner, below an array of switches and wires collected into neat sleeves. 'Even the prime minister cannot kick you out of here now,' declares Ibrahim.

The crowd sends up a loud cheer. Standing across the lane, under the new wooden sign in his shop, Ramesh Babu is gazing benignly at Gopal. And next to him is Seth Sohan Lal himself, perched precariously on a stool with his legs crossed.

'I had your pots and pans brought from Sardar Kartar Singh's store,' says Ibrahim, triumphantly.

But Gopal keeps looking at Sohan Lal, who wears on his old face an expression of kindness. Has he been forgiven? Are the gold-plated buttons no longer in contention?

'Why do you keep looking at sethji like that?' scolds Ibrahim. 'He is from your constituency. Go and talk to him.'

Gopal approaches the white mannequins of Sushma Fancy Dresses, who continue to look at him blandly. He folds his hands before Sohan Lal, who makes an unsuccessful effort to get off the stool. 'You will forgive me, Gopal Babu, if I keep sitting! These knees are old . . .'

Gopal gasps. The seth has just called him Gopal Babu!

'Ask him, sethji,' says Ibrahim, playfully, toothless black gums glinting.

'Chai!' orders Sohan Lal, with a theatrical flourish.

Gopal rushes back to his stall and squats under the junction box. There is sympathetic laughter in the crowd.

'You are a humble man, Gopal Bhai!' screams Ibrahim.

The crowd expresses agreement.

'Why would you make chai now? You will sit in Parliament with other MPs, and the prime minister will come to ask for your vote.'

'No one will demolish your stall,' says Sohan Lal. 'We will guard it with our lives. It is part of our national heritage. You should come and visit it often, Gopal Babu. I will have it swept every morning. We have always been neighbours, we have greeted each other every morning. Now I can take my problems directly to my MP by shouting across the lane!'

The crowd laughs.

'This is not your victory alone,' continues Sohan Lal. 'This is a victory for Kucha Bansilal!'

'Gopal Das *zindabad*!' declares Ibrahim, and the crowd responds.

Sohan Lalji is a good man, thinks Gopal. It was his son who brought up the matter of gold buttons and treats his father no better than he treated me. The poor man must watch his son fritter away the goodwill he has generated over the years. Men of our generation have character. They are not swayed by pride and wealth. Look how humbly he speaks to me, perched on a stool, although he is a great seth who earns crores every month! There is even a chance that he will give me that silk kurta – the one Ramesh Babu took away in 'ninety-six. For now I must remain silent because they are shouting slogans and Ibrahim Mian is shouting loudest . . . Who is that man, though? He has a notepad in his hand, a bag slung over his shoulder and he is looking directly at me. He does not shout slogans. Instead he is asking the same question, again and again: 'Whom do you support, Mr Gopal Das?'

He is a small man but he is very insistent. Then Gopal notices that there are other men and women around him, with microphones, notepads and tape-recorders. He sighs in pain. What do these newspaper people want now? Has he not won? Must he still have an opinion on Babri Masjid, the Mandal Commission and the legalisation of prostitution? A man should be able to rest and think about nothing after he has become a Member of Parliament. He has nothing to say. What can there be to talk about now? Ramvilas Babu has given him no speech for the occasion. Where is Ramvilas Babu?

'Gopalji will work for the minority community!' shouts Ibrahim, over the crowd.

Gopal is aware that the crowd has fallen silent in deference to the newspaper people, whose questions now arrive in a fusillade. Whom will you support, Mr Gopal Das? Are you aware that we have a hung Parliament? If a coalition government is formed, where do you stand? Has Congress approached you for support? Has the IPP approached you?

Ibrahim pulls down the lid of the stall, turning it back into a box. Then he marshals the men standing around him to pull it from under the junction box, and helps Gopal climb on to it so he can address the crowd.

'Brothers and sisters,' says Gopal, uncertainly, 'whether you are Hindu or Musalman, you are poor. A poor man's friend is not a secular leader or a fundamentalist leader but another poor man . . . If you do not vote for me, brothers and sisters, vote for another poor man!'

'Talk about the minority community!' hisses Ibrahim.

Gopal falters, searching in his mind for speeches, past and present. 'My sisters, Gopal Das stands before you today . . .'

'The minority community!' shouts Ibrahim.

A frightened Gopal loses his composure and ends mechanically: 'A vote for Gopal Das is a vote for the people!'

There is sudden silence, then raucous laughter. Gopal wants the box to swallow him as it once swallowed Sardar Kartar Singh. 'I will support the rickshavalas!' he screams above the crowd. 'I will support the ladies of GB Road—'

Then he feels a hand pressing his knee urgently. It is Ramvilas Babu, standing next to the box.

'Let Gopal Bhai speak,' says Ibrahim.

'Who are you?' demands Ramvilas, coldly. 'Get away from MP Sahib!'

With a violent push, Ramvilas dispatches Ibrahim back into the crowd – where he is received with much derision – and addresses himself to the newspeople. 'Gopal Das will make a statement to the press tomorrow. For now he must celebrate his victory. We have to play Holi all day!'

'Mr Gopal Das!' says an insistent scribe, 'are you aware that no party has a majority?'

'Gopal Das is aware of the fact,' says Ramvilas.

'Have you offered support to Congress or IPP?'

'Gopal Dasji will consider all aspects of the matter and make a decision,' says Ramvilas.

'You are a secular candidate,' says a reporter. 'Surely you cannot support IPP?'

'Gopal Dasji is an independent,' says Ramvilas. 'He will give equal consideration to all parties, but the people of Chandni Chowk are uppermost in his mind.'

'Is your victory legitimate, considering you have won by a mere three hundred votes?'

'Gopal Dasji is certain that a recount will increase that margin,' says Ramvilas.

'Mr Gopal Das! Do you know that Charulata has refused to pledge her five votes to IPP?'

'Gopal Dasji is aware of the situation,' says Ramvilas.

'Mr Gopal Das! IPP has claimed it can get the support of two hundred and seventy-two MPs. Are you one of them?'

'Gopal Dasji will take a decision that is best for the people of Chandni Chowk,' says Ramvilas.

'Will you join with Charulata's Dalit Samaj Party before you negotiate with IPP?'

Ramvilas thinks very hard before he answers. 'Gopal Dasji welcomes all like-minded parties. He has received a great portion of the Dalit vote in Chandni Chowk. He represents the Dalits too, as much as Charulata . . .' Ramvilas continues to talk, glancing now and then at Gopal standing mutely on the box, Ibrahim nursing his resentment in the crowd, and the news reporters scribbling his answers like busy squirrels.

I am safe now, thinks Gopal. I should not have come away with Ibrahim Mian in that crowd. I am safe, as long as Ramvilasji is with me.

'Now you look like a leader,' says Ramvilas.

Gopal stands before a mirror hung from the Bournvita shelf and beams with pride at his reflection. He looks so much more vigorous in a silk kurta, and this one has diamond buttons on the front. The silk sleeves have puffed wrinkles, created by the hot iron of an industrious launderer. When Gopal pushes one back, he is delighted to see a wristwatch with a shining new steel band. There is a gold chain round his neck, sliding sinfully into the folds on his chest. What luxury, to wear a gold chain and show only part of it to the world! And then there is the oil that has slicked down the tufts of grey behind his ears, the richness of his combed moustache, the suppleness of his creamed skin, the perfection of his pleated silk dhoti and the soft cushions of his new kolhapuri slippers . . . Ah, this MP business is a good thing. It has already begun to bring him happiness, and it is guaranteed to last five years!

'Where is your shawl?' asks Ramvilas.

Gopal points to where it is lying on the counter. 'I am going to wear it after putting away these toasters.'

Ramvilas laughs. 'You do not need to put away toasters! That is Kartar Singh's job. It is his store, not yours.'

He wraps the shawl round Gopal.

'But this will hide the kurta!' Gopal protests.

'It is chilly outside. You cannot shiver in front of the prime minister.'

In spite of the shawl Gopal shivers. 'Is it necessary that I meet him?'

'Of course! He will ask for your support.'

'We can telephone him to say we will support him.'

'You will do no such thing!' says Ramvilas, sharply. 'You will meet him in his home. Do you realise what a great honour it is to meet the prime minister in Race Course Road?'

'But I will meet him anyway when I go to Parliament.'

Ramvilas laughs. 'He has called you, Gopal Bhai! When the prime minister calls you to his house, you go.'

The shawl is now wrapped tightly round Gopal, all but preventing him moving his arms.

'You don't know if he will ever call again,' says Ramvilas, quietly.

Gopal turns back to the Bournvita shelf, and the mirror presents a pleasing sight. The grey shawl gives him dignity. If he were taller, not so fat, had fairer skin, no spectacles and sufficient hair to cover the top of his head, he might even look like . . .

'Do you think I look like Rajiv Gandhi?' he asks Ramvilas, dreamily.

Ramvilas regards him with amusement, then nods.

'Then I am ready to go! Let us meet Prime Ministerji.'

'Sit down,' commands Ramvilas. 'Listen to me carefully. You are going to meet many bara sahibs. Do you know what a bara sahib is?'

'The prime minister?'

'The prime minister and other ministers, and all other sahibs around him. Anyone who sits in the same room as the prime minister is a bara sahib. Do not remove your shawl in front of them, or they will think you fidget too much with your hands. It is all right if they do not see the puffs on your sleeves. When you enter the room, do not sit down unless they ask you to. When they do, sit down slowly, and do not start talking right away. Do not say anything. Let them talk. Nod now and then, but never eagerly. Never say yes or no to anything. If they ask you a direct question, look at the floor, remain silent for a while and tell them you will think it over.'

'Can we go now?'

'He has called us at ten,' says Ramvilas. 'We need to be late.'

'What if they keep asking questions?' worries Gopal. 'Will they not expect me to answer?'

'When you cannot remain silent, turn toward me. I will always be on your left.'

'Should I say namaste to the prime minister?' asks Gopal.

'Say namaste to everyone inside the room, and to no one outside it. Do not be too eager when saying it. Bring your palms together, raise them slightly and nod. You need not utter the word 'namaste' itself. If anyone wants to shake your hand, respond with a namaste. There may be ladies in the room – the prime minister's adopted daughter, a female MP or another family member. Do not comment on her looks or dress, and do not ask how many children she has. It is all right to comment on the prime minister's poetry.'

'Will you recite his poems for me before we go?'

'Why?' asks Ramvilas. 'You have been reading his poems for years. They have often moved you to tears.'

'All right,' says Gopal, warming to the idea. 'I will also tell him his kurta always appears neatly pressed on television.'

'You must not say too much!' warns Ramvilas. 'Do not talk about your tea stall, or electrical wires in the junction box, or the drain under it, or anything related to tea. Do not talk about Dudhiya Gali or Kucha Bansilal. Do not mention Mukesh, Gauhar, the Mandal Commission or Babri Masjid. Do not talk about your wife, whoever she was. Do not ask the prime minister how many rooms there are in his house, or how much it cost to build it.'

'But I am going to have tea with the prime minister,' protests Gopal. 'Will he not want to tell me how expensive his house is?'

'The prime minister is a bara sahib. He does not discuss such matters with you. Do not ask him what his salary is, or what your salary will be as a minister. Do not ask him for a letter of recommendation, as you asked Sohan Lalji.'

'Will I become a minister, Ramvilas Babu?'

Ramvilas shakes his head impatiently. 'No, no! You must not say anything like that during the meeting. I have already told you – look down at the floor, remain silent for a while, and tell them you will think it over. If you must, turn to me on your left.'

'But, babu . . .'

'Yes?'

'This time, I would like to keep the silk kurta.'

Ramvilas looks carefully at the Member of Parliament for Chandni Chowk. 'Yes, you can keep the silk kurta.'

Gopal sits down on a stool, gratified. He will go to the meeting in his own clothes, not the borrowed ones they gave him for that function outside Gurudwara Sisganj. He is suddenly impatient. 'What are we waiting for?'

'You must get new spectacles,' says Ramvilas.

Gopal peers incredulously through the scratched panes before him. 'But these are almost new!'

With a flick of his hand, Ramvilas snatches the glasses off Gopal's nose.

'I cannot see!' pleads Gopal.

'You cannot see anyway,' laughs Ramvilas. 'You have not seen for years, Gopal Bhai.'

'Give them back to me!'

'Do you agree to change your spectacles?' demands Ramvilas.

'All right, I will go to Gupta Doctor. But that will take two hours. And who will pay his bill?'

Ramvilas slaps Gopal playfully on the back, almost tipping over the stool on which the chaivala is precariously perched, then puts an arm round him. 'Now you are an MP,' he says, 'you do not go to the doctor. The doctor comes to you!'

As if on cue, a dark blob wrapped in a white shirt appears across the counter. Gopal's flailing hands grab the spectacles from Ramvilas's grasp and return them to his nose. The blob springs into partial focus. Skinny face, large forehead, thick glasses, woeful moustache.

'Go into the back room with Dr Banerjee,' says Ramvilas. 'He will examine your eyes.'

The Bournvita shelf is swung open and Dr Banerjee strides in, lugging a wooden box that contains his tools, flashing large teeth at Gopal in a generous grin. Gopal follows him inside. 'Nothing is wrong with my eyes,' he says.

Dr Banerjee's grin widens, and his teeth seem to illuminate the dark room. He places his toolbox on the mattress, then ducks through the opening at the front, comes back with a stool, places it against a wall and seats Gopal on it. Then he measures the length of the room with careful strides and shakes his head. Too short. He needs at least twenty feet. He remains standing for a while, deep in thought, until inspiration strikes. He goes out into the store, slams the Bournvita shelf shut and plucks off the mirror that hangs from it. He returns triumphantly, but stops short on realising that there is no hook in Kartar Singh's back room from which he can hang the mirror. Unfazed, he produces a hammer and nails from his box. His first attempt to drive one into the wall causes a rectangular area to collapse and fall on to the linoleum. He has uncovered a wooden cabinet wedged into a shallow alcove, hidden behind a layer of cardboard that was flush with the wall, painted over to look like it. The alcove is stacked from top to bottom with bundles of banknotes.

Dr Banerjee stares at the money, concentrating on it with medical precision as if it were a Snellen chart, until he becomes aware of Ramvilas, who has swung open the Bournvita shelf and stands in the opening.

'You can hang the mirror there,' says Ramvilas.

He walks into the room and hammers two nails above the alcove, then hangs the mirror to cover the money, making no mention of it, as if the alcove had revealed nothing more incriminating than a dozen electric toasters. Dr Banerjee hammers another nail just above Gopal's head with trembling hands, expecting another alcove to be revealed. He produces a laminated Snellen chart from his box and hangs it from the nail above Gopal's head. Seated on the stool, Gopal can look straight into the mirror – ten feet from his eyes – and see the reflection of the chart, two room-lengths away.

Dr Banerjee's box now releases a cane pointer. He holds it theatrically, like an opera conductor, and speaks with professional composure: 'Read the letters, Gopal Babu!'

Ramvilas walks out into the store, places his palms flat on the counter and considers the two men standing on the other side. They lean on the counter like eager customers, hands crossed, elbows secured. They are both in their thirties, short, squat and dark, wearing white kurta-pyjamas and chewing incessantly on the remains of their last paans. Their tongues are stained a permanent red with betel juice, and their jaws have long adjusted to the bolas of crushed leaf that is always wedged between teeth and lower lip. They have acquired a studied manner of speech that allows them to speak while chewing, without spilling the precious concoction in the mouth. Their consonants are skewed, their vowels muted. Charulata has sent them to negotiate with Ramvilas.

'I cannot offer you anything to sit on,' says Ramvilas. 'We have no customers, these days. There is only one stool and it is inside . . .'

The men produce a vague sound that means they have taken no offence. It also indicates, somehow, that they have not come here for pleasantries.

'Charulata Behanji has heard of your man,' says the one on the left.

'Gopal Babu has great respect for Charulata Behanji,' responds Ramvilas.

'Charulata Behanji said to us, "Find out more about this man"!'

'Gopal Babu would like to meet Charulata Behanji too.'

'Charulata Behanji has met the PM Sahib – the new one.'

'He is not prime minister yet,' says Ramvilas.

'The president will appoint him tomorrow,' says the man on the left.

'If he can claim a majority,' counters Ramvilas.

'He needs one more vote for his majority,' says the man on the right.

Ramvilas nods with a smile. It is a happy coincidence, which augurs well for Charulata – with her four other MPs – and Gopal. The contemplation of this opportunity should unite them . . . But Charulata's men do not smile.

'There are five hundred and forty-four seats,' continues the man on the right. 'Five hundred and forty had elections. PM Sahib – the new one – needs two hundred and seventy-one.'

'Yes, yes, I know!' says Ramvilas impatiently. 'If Charulata Behanji supports him he will have two hundred and seventy-five.'

The men fall silent. Ramvilas studies them carefully. He wants to know if Charulata has already committed her five votes to the PM. If she has, there is no value in Gopal's vote. If she has not, Gopal's one vote can render her five useless, making her redundant in the balance of power . . . So why has she sent her men here?

The man on the left runs his tongue vigorously over his teeth, trying to remove the last pieces of paan lodged in the pockets of his mouth. He looks straight at Ramvilas. 'Charulata Behanji has talked to many small parties to form an alliance. Together, we can negotiate with the PM.'

Ah, thinks Ramvilas. She wants to negotiate for Gopal, or negotiate for herself with Gopal on her side. He must say nothing.

'The Secular Socialist Party is with us,' says the man on the left. 'So is the National Socialist Party, the Secular Democratic Alliance and the Socialist Front.'

'And the United Progressive Front,' adds the one on the right quickly, to rectify an omission.

Ramvilas sighs. He has lost track of these one-person parties. There are so many.

'Charulata Behanji is thinking of forming a front with all these parties and fronts. Ten MPs in all.'

'United Secular Socialist Dalit Front!' says the one on the left, impressively. 'USSDF.'

'Charulata Behanji will allow your man to join USSDF,' says the one on the right. 'That will make it eleven MPs.'

Ramvilas is startled. He had not expected this. They have come to discuss terms with him, and all they offer is a command to join a new front! She has sent her toughest men, of course. They have risen from the cauldrons of Uttar Pradesh, from foundries and farms and filigree workshops. They have pulled themselves out of obscurity to strut round Delhi with the arrogance of power-brokers, which is the only occupation they know. They do not understand the meaning of compromise, and that suits Charulata's style perfectly. But he will not be intimidated by these bumpkins, in spite of their bravado and elaborate paan-chewing pantomime.

'Gopal Das is an independent,' he says casually.

'What is an independent?' The man on the left shrugs.

'He cannot join USSDF,' Ramvilas declares. 'That is not his constituency.'

'No one can win a seat in Chandni Chowk without Dalit support,' says the man on the right, coldly.

Ramvilas feels uncomfortable with their manner. Perhaps he should try to end the meeting. If only they would reveal Charulata's stance . . . 'Will Charulata Behanji support this new PM Sahib?' he asks again.

'She will do what is good for Dalits.'

Ramvilas smiles. It is clear now what they want. Charulata wants to negotiate with the new PM – as soon as he is appointed tomorrow – but cannot do so if Gopal Das throws his support behind him, giving him the slimmest possible majority and leaving Charulata out in the cold with her five votes. She wants Gopal to withhold support until she has extracted her share from the PM. Very well, he will be direct with the men. They will appreciate straight talk. He stands erect at the counter and looks levelly at them. 'Gopal Das wants a ministership.'

The men chuckle at this effrontery, embarrassing Ramvilas. Has he overstepped the mark? But no, this is their way of talking him down. Why is Gopal Das any less deserving of a ministership than Charulata herself?

'Gopal Babu wants Railways,' he says quickly.

The two men look at each and burst out laughing. 'Even Charulata Behanji cannot get Railways! Who are you to talk like this?'

Ramvilas is intimidated but collects himself, with heroic effort, and points to the Ambassador that has pulled up outside the shop. 'Do you see that car? Gopal Babu is going to the PM Sahib right now to declare his support. You can go and tell Charulata Behanji that the PM already has two hundred and seventy-one!'

An opaque film falls across the eyes of the two men. 'Your man has won by three hundred and twenty-nine votes,' says the one on the left. 'That may change in a recount.'

'It may increase!' says Ramvilas, defiantly.

'Not if some boxes are lost in the recount. Or the returning officer gets a telephone call.'

The man on the right leans far forward, and Ramvilas knows fear for the first time in his life. 'Why do you want to play with Behanji?' he appeals, in a sweet voice that makes Ramvilas shiver. 'What has she done to you? She has worked all her life for Dalits, and she is asking for your man's support in her mission. Think about it! Eleven MPs can bargain better than ten. What can one independent MP get from the PM? Instead, when the PM has accepted the support of the USSDF – eleven MPs! – many things can be done for your man. He can become chairman of some board, president of the Hockey Federation . . .'

'Cricket Board chairman,' says Ramvilas. 'This is my final offer.'

'No offer is final, babu. Cricket Board is a little difficult . . . Why not hockey?'

'Then Gopal Babu is going to the PM's house!' says Ramvilas, with finality.

The two men reach a silent understanding. 'We will not stop you,' says the one on the left. 'Go to the PM.'

'Namaste!' says Ramvilas, with dignity.

'Namaste,' say the men, as they turn to go.

The man on the left holds his palms together longer than necessary. 'Think about Behanji,' he says. 'We will come back tomorrow.'

Ramvilas shudders. He watches their receding backs, afraid they will return. A sound startles him. He ducks under the counter, almost expecting a hail of bullets from a mob led by Charulata, but it is only Dr Banerjee, who has pushed aside the Bournvita shelf and come into the store. 'Ramvilas Babu, I am afraid Mr Gopal Das is legally blind.'

Ramvilas snorts impatiently. He has his hands full with Charulata's men, who are sure to come tomorrow, and he is nervous about the upcoming meeting in Race Course Road. Why must he be burdened with irrelevant matters? Why does a man need two full eyes to be an MP? And how can he be blind when he runs a chai stall, rides a bicycle and walks through the streets?

'He can see!' insists Ramvilas, irritably. 'His eyes are weak but he can see. That room is too dark.'

Dr Banerjee shakes his head. He does not know what to make of the patient. Ramvilas Babu asked him to make a quick diagnosis, so he began at the twenty over forty row – D H J B S – in the Snellen chart, skipping the first four rows. The patient was unable to read a single letter. Shocked, he had moved to the twenty over fifty row, then to twenty over seventy, and then, with his mouth open, to twenty over a hundred – L T. The patient was unable to read a single letter in any row. With trembling hands, Dr Banerjee placed his pointer on the giant E at the top, the highest and largest letter, which would mark his patient as more or less blind, and held his breath for a full ten seconds. Gopal Das stared at the mirror, contemplating the offensive E with calm neutrality, and said nothing. Dr Banerjee thought he had witnessed a miracle, or a new ophthalmologic phenomenon, until a more prosaic explanation presented itself. He was showing the poor man English letters when he should have begun with Hindi! Ashamed of his own incompetence, he hastily replaced the Snellen chart with a corresponding one in Hindi, but Gopal Das was unmoved. That was when the doctor decided to present his findings to Ramvilas.

'He has just won a Lok Sabha election!' thunders Ramvilas. 'He runs a tea stall! And you tell me he is blind?'

'How much does a cup of tea cost in his stall?' asks Dr Banerjee.

'Two rupees,' shrugs Ramvilas. 'Why does that matter?'

Dr Banerjee runs back into the room, where Gopal is dutifully seated on the stool, and holds up two fingers five feet from Gopal's face. Gopal brightens and counts them correctly. Dr Banerjee adds digits to his display and the patient responds positively to each stimulus. The doctor comes back into the store, his diagnosis complete. 'He is not blind,' he tells Ramvilas. 'He is illiterate. He cannot read a word of English or Hindi.'

Ramvilas steps away from the doctor, horrified. 'Be careful what you claim, Doctor!'

'He can count at least up to ten,' admits the doctor. 'But he is illiterate.'

'I brought you here to give him spectacles,' says Ramvilas, coldly. 'Gopal Das does not need a lecture on education.'

'I have another chart for those who cannot read or write—'

'Forget the charts!' exclaims Ramvilas. 'Give him something, anything! Any frame, any lens! Anything that allows him to distinguish between a man and a tree, a door and a window, a car and a bus . . . Anything that brings the world into partial focus.'

'All right,' says the doctor, reluctantly.

'But it must be better than what he already has,' warns Ramvilas.

'About his illiteracy, I thought I should let you know.'

'You have told me nothing,' says Ramvilas, imperiously. 'This is not a small matter, Doctor Sahib! This is a matter of national security! A very sensitive issue! Never say that again. Do you hear me? *Never* repeat it outside this store!'

The doctor nods nervously and goes back into the room.

'We must leave soon,' adds Ramvilas. 'The car is waiting.' He puts both elbows on the counter and considers this revelation. How could he not have noticed? Well, he will work with what he has. The potter must shape the lump before him, no matter how friable the clay. At the very least he has contained the damage. The doctor is a small man, easy to intimidate. That is a relief after the mien of Charulata's factotums.

With trembling hands, Dr Banerjee places a hollow frame on Gopal's nose. Into this frame he drops test lenses, holds up his hand in front of Gopal's face, and asks him if he can see the hand clearly as he moves it to and fro. He does not bother with fingers. It takes Gopal Das too long to count them anyway. With Ramvilas's impatience bearing down on him, the doctor estimates the right lenses and produces – from the cornucopia of his wooden box – three pre-fabricated pairs of spectacles with lenses that correspond to Gopal's approximate prescription. He holds up all three. 'Which one?' he asks Gopal.

'This,' says Ramvilas, coming into the room and grabbing the pair closest to him. He takes off the frame that sits on Gopal's nose and presses the new spectacles in place.

'Ganga *Maiya*!' gasps Gopal. Who is this shrivelled-up, dark man hovering over my face? Look how many wrinkles he has, look at his bloodshot eyes . . . And the plaster is peeling off the walls, which are full of spiders, lizards, cobwebs . . . How has so much detail sprung up in a moment from the haze around me?

'I will send a man with your fee to your clinic,' says Ramvilas, to the doctor. 'Collect your charts and go. Come with me, Gopal Babu!'

He takes Gopal's arm and leads him out. As he turns, Gopal's eyes fall directly on Ramvilas's face and he starts. Something has changed in Ramvilas Babu's appearance. What are those unkind lines on his cheeks? And that leer in his eyes, that smirk on his face? Why is his hair so cruelly flattened against his skull? Suddenly Ramvilas Babu looks less likeable – a man who cannot be trusted. What has wrought this sudden change? 'Stop looking at me as if I was a villain in a film,' says Ramvilas. 'We must go.'

Gopal is pushed out through the door into the store, where dozens of cameras and reporters immediately rush toward him. There are so many people, thinks Gopal, and he can see them with such clarity!

'Gopal Babu will speak to the press *after* his meeting with the PM,' declares Ramvilas. He pushes Gopal through the crowd and steers him toward an Ambassador with a flashing beacon. A chauffeur holds open the door, but there are still dozens of people between them and the car.

'Gopal Das *zindabad*!' someone shouts.

'Do not let them fool you, Gopal Das! Charge ahead, Gopal Das, we are with you! Stand up for Chandni Chowk, Gopal Das!'

'Chandni Chowk *kaa rakhvala*! Chandni Chowk *kaa chaivala*!'

Gopal makes slow progress through the crowd, pulled along by Ramvilas, marvelling at the clear outline of every human form before him. There is the man who has driven this Ambassador, holding open the rear door! Will he let him sit in it, or will he admit Ramvilas Babu and ask Gopal to follow in a bus? He must get a good salary to be driving a car with a flashing light on it. Before Gopal can speak to the man, however, he has already been ushered inside. Such a soft seat! It is covered with a white fabric that contrasts with dark wooden panels on the side walls. Ramvilas Babu has slipped into the car beside him and now the chauffeur has shut the door, cutting off the noise of the crowd. That is a relief. Why do those people shout so loudly? And what are they saying?

Now the car is trying to weave through the crowd, which is stubborn at first, then yields until the car emerges into Chandni Chowk and glides toward Red Fort.

It is wonderful being in a car in Chandni Chowk! thinks Gopal. You can see Gurudwara Sisganj, the Jain temple, the bird hospital, but you do not have to slip through stalls or avoid rickshas, cycles and scooters, or hear their horns. You can sink comfortably into soft seats and watch rickshas glide by you, and never realise how long Chandni Chowk is. Every scooter has sprung into focus, every man and woman, turban and saree is visible in all its detail.

Now the car has turned toward Daryaganj and picked up speed. Red Fort is to Gopal's left. He sees, for the first time, that it has moss climbing up its walls. He looks through the windscreen and notices there is a police jeep at the front, with constables sitting inside, looking back at the car with bored expressions. They are taking him to a police station! He looks hurriedly at Ramvilas, who sits still, expressionless. Then he turns to see another jeep following them close behind.

'Why are they going with us?' he whispers to Ramvilas.

Ramvilas chuckles. 'To protect you, Gopal Bhai.'

The answer does not satisfy Gopal but he lets it go. He will sit quietly and not give them reason to harm him. He must collect himself, concentrate on the task ahead, and prepare answers for all possible questions they may ask. An old question wells in his mind. He turns urgently to Ramvilas. 'What is the national mainstream?'

Ramvilas frowns and looks away. Gopal sighs. It is, hopefully, not something the prime minister is interested in. But what is this? The car is passing a large domed building that sprawls endlessly behind a garden.

'This is New Delhi!' he says.

'That is the Supreme Court,' replies Ramvilas, patiently.

'I have been to New Delhi with Mukesh,' says Gopal. 'I do not remember that building.'

'Your last visit was in a bus, Gopal Bhai. Buildings look different when seen through the windows of a car.'

'Is this where the prime minister lives?'

'Did you expect him to live in the cluttered dung-heap of Chandni Chowk?'

'I can see everything!' exclaims Gopal. 'I can see every blade of grass, every leaf on every tree! I can see flowers, whole gardens!'

Ramvilas chuckles. 'This is March, Gopal Bhai. Even spring knows the importance of New Delhi in the empire!'

The car sails through wide asphalt avenues lined with ashupal, jarul, mango, neem, ber and guava trees, jamun trees secretly preparing to be laden with fruit during the monsoon, and sedate gulmohars bracing to erupt into fiery red and yellow in two months' time. Red-brick walls enclose vast estates on either side and, where the gulmohars allow a glimpse, Gopal spots bungalows with colonnaded verandas set far back from the road. At every intersection, the road spins the car round in a great circle ablaze with colour – bauhinias in white, purple and mauve, silk cotton trees bursting with yellow, vines with pale green leaves, coral, flame and jacaranda. The car glides from one great circle to the next, trailed by cuckoos, sparrows and golden orioles.

They circle India Gate. Gopal watches it rotate under the shining sun. He has seen it before, when his father brought him to the Boat Club lawns many years ago, and when he came here with Mukesh. He does not remember it being so clear, so well defined. He notices, for the first time, an empty pedestal covered with a concrete umbrella. 'What is that for?' he asks.

'It once had a statue of the English king,' laughs Ramvilas. 'Maybe you can ask the PM to put your statue there.'

The car turns into Rajpath and races up the wide expanse of Raisina Hill toward Rashtrapati Bhavan, red sandstone and grey asphalt shimmering in a warm winter sun with perfect clarity, as if Nature had used a finer brush to give greater detail to her paintings. They pass the secretariat buildings and turn toward Race Course Road. Gopal, who had watched the proud dome of Rashtrapati Bhavan for a few minutes, thinking they were headed to the palace beneath it, is disappointed when it vanishes. 'Where is the PM's house?' he asks.

'He is not the PM yet,' says Ramvilas, curtly. 'But you may address him as Prime Minister. He will like that. In any case, he will become prime minister by tomorrow, because the next government will be formed by IPP.'

'Who is the PM now?'

'He has resigned,' says Ramvilas. 'He lost the election.'

'Was he not from IPP?'

'No.' Ramvilas is now impatient with the tutorial. 'IPP has won.'

'Was the old PM from Congress?'

'No.'

'Which party, then?'

'It does not matter. That party is dead. What matters is that IPP will form the next government. And the man we are going to see will be PM by tomorrow. Remember to call him PM Sahib.'

'Does he live in Race Course Road too?'

'Number eight Race Course Road,' says Ramvilas. 'With your support, he will move into number five Race Course Road, three houses down.'

'Just three houses after all this?'

'It is a great distance.'

'But why does PM Sahib need to speak to me?'

Ramvilas turns to Gopal, beaming. 'A miracle has come to pass, Gopal Bhai. PM Sahib needs one vote to become PM, and you are that one vote.'

The car is whisked through police checkpoints, enters a tree-lined avenue, turns into steel gates guarded by commandos, and stops inside a foyer created by overhanging gulmohar branches. The chauffeur springs out of the car and holds open Gopal's door. Gopal steps out of the car, straightens his dhoti, and folds his hands to say namaste to the security guards.

'Do not acknowledge them!' snaps Ramvilas. 'Save your namaste for those inside the house.'

Gopal hastily unsticks his palms and begins to climb the staircase that leads to the front entrance.

'Wait!' says Ramvilas.

He produces a Gandhi cap from his kurta pocket and presses it firmly on Gopal's bald head. 'Let me look at you.' He rotates the cap so its bow sits somewhat to the left of the forehead, then tilts it to the side and regards Gopal carefully.

'Now you are ready to sit on the Peacock Throne,' he says.

And they enter the prime minister's house.

The meeting lasts thirty minutes. The prime minister sits silently in a low chair, buried among pillows, head lowered, eyes shut in deep concentration. A young minister sits next to him, smiles benignly at Gopal but addresses himself to Ramvilas from time to time. The minister looks very comfortable in the prime minister's house. He has a thick black moustache and blubbery lips. His mouth remains open for long periods of time when he smiles, because he forgets to shut it when the smile has finished. Two aides sit behind him, taking copious notes even when nothing is being said.

The prime minister sits no more than six feet from Gopal. If he opens his eyes, frets Gopal, they will fall directly on him, and then he will have to say something. He does not like the man who ushered them into the room – a guard swaddled in khaki with a red sash round his waist, and a plume on his turban that stood erect, adding six inches to his frame, which was already so high it almost touched the ceiling. The tall guard still stands at the door, perhaps ready to forestall any attempt to escape. And now the prime minister has stirred! The young minister has been speaking for some time to Ramvilas Babu. Railway ministry, finance ministry, home ministry, labour ministry, education ministry . . . they are talking about important matters. Then they say something about Charulata. Ramvilas Babu speaks hurriedly. He looks offended. The young minister mollifies him, then shuts his eyes and smiles indulgently.

'The labour ministry is very important to PM Sahib,' he says.

'But labour is where Gopal Babu can be one with the people,' says Ramvilas. 'Or the education ministry, where Gopal Babu can declare war on illiteracy.'

'We have to take everything into account,' says the young minister. 'The low margin makes things very difficult. Three hundred and twenty-nine votes! The Secular Socialist Party wants a recount. We have asked the election commissioner to look into the matter.'

'What purpose will that serve?' asks Ramvilas. 'It will vitiate the atmosphere, incite communal violence and destroy the social fabric of Chandni Chowk. And who knows what effect it will have on the Sikh psyche?'

Gopal freezes, because the prime minister has opened his eyes, and they are looking straight at him.

'Namaste,' says Gopal.

The eyelids close gently. The prime minister massages his right knee.

'We are very sad about PM Sahib's knee,' says Ramvilas.

Gopal nods eagerly in agreement. Then the young minister and Ramvilas talk again. Gopal leans back in his chair and closes his eyes, feeling like a monument to himself. He is beginning to like being a Member of Parliament. Ganga Maiya! Here I sit opposite the prime minister, my eyes shut like his, while people discuss important matters all around me. And if our eyes should open at the same time, I will tell him I am moved by his poems. I am Arjun, I am Krishna . . .

'Gopal Babu?'

He opens his eyes in fear, because the voice does not belong to Ramvilas. It is the young minister. His mouth is frozen in a smile – or the smile has died but the lip still hangs loose – and his gaze is no longer benign. Gopal has seen such smiles: they are poisonous.

'Which ministry do you think will suit you?'

Slowly, very slowly, Gopal turns to his left to look at Ramvilas, but Ramvilas sits in deep concentration, apparently unaware of him. Gopal looks down at the floor, remains silent for a while, then gives his answer to the young minister: 'I will take all matters into consideration and make a decision that benefits the people of Chandni Chowk.'

21

Gopal Pandey wakes up with a twitch in his left eye and a curse on his tongue, and knows it is a bad day. Ganga Maiya! It is past eight, says the luminous face of his old wristwatch. He sits up slowly and uses the turmeric sacks to prop himself up on his feet. It is still dark behind the sacks, but he knows the sun has risen high in the sky. It is late March, the onset of heat. Winter is preparing a hasty retreat, its back broken by Holi. This week, people shiver in the mornings. Next week, fans in every room will churn hot air in vain, and there will be talk of heatwaves and watermelons.

Gopal collects his dhoti round his knees, caresses his teeth with his tongue – wincing when it passes over a loose one – clears his throat with a cough and crawls across the kholi to the ladder, finding his way in a dull glow cast by the ventilator curtains and avoiding the newly arrived sacks of chillies. It is not a good idea to brush against those sacks with your hands. Hours later, when you casually pick your nose or remove a speck from your eye with the tip of your finger, the chillies will find their way into your nose and eyes . . . He descends the ladder carefully, slips into his chappals, puts on his spectacles and walks down the stairs. As he emerges from the dark stairwell on the ground floor, Hameed brushes past him, carrying a sack that leaves a coat of green-grey powder on Gopal's cotton shirt.

'Dhania,' says Hameed, by way of explanation.

'You will blind me!' protests Gopal.

'Watch where you go, Gopal Bhai! How many thieves did you catch tonight?'

Gopal brushes off the powder and the insult, and stalks out of Katra Badami. He unlocks his bicycle from the pole outside the police booth and rides it through the grain market in Khari Baoli, nearly colliding with the SDM's jeep, which comes to a screeching halt amid a wail of sirens. 'Watch where you go!' scream three constables, who hop out of the jeep. The SDM himself steps out carefully, ignoring Gopal, surveying the market with proprietary poise, and saunters off toward the oilseed shops, which have rapidly downed their shutters on seeing the jeep. Gopal stands the bicycle against a pole and finds his way to a grassy patch behind the old post office, where he squats and shits.

It is almost nine when, after bathing under the hand-pump in Katra Badami, he cycles back into Khari Baoli and sees the SDM's jeep surrounded by angry traders. They have poured canisters of oil into drains in protest at his raid. They shout slogans around the empty jeep. The SDM is probably rummaging through one of their shops at this moment. 'We cannot be held responsible for the purity of our oil,' they say. 'We merely buy and sell it! Go to the factories in Haryana and Uttar Pradesh, go to the people who manufacture this oil if you must raid someone. The Khari Baoli Oil Traders Association is on an indefinite strike until all police harassment ends.'

Two constables sit inside the jeep, expressionless, unmoved by the commotion. Gopal steps off his bicycle and crosses the battlefield, hopping over freshly dug drains flowing with palm oil, soybean oil and sesame oil. He passes unmolested through the crowd, ringing the bicycle bell gently, afraid the SDM's constables will think he is an oil trader. When he is past the crowd, he mounts his bicycle again and turns into Chandni Chowk near Fatehpuri Masjid, from where he takes a detour into Dudhiya Gali to buy milk. Large vats block his way in Dudhiya Gali, so he gets off the bicycle and wends his way through them, watching the curd quiver like rolls of fat on a woman. At Banwari's shop he leans his bicycle against the counter and unhooks a basket tied above the rear wheel. Banwari opens his refrigerator and tosses six polythene packets of milk into the basket. Gopal sits down on Ram Bibek's chair. Ram Bibek prepares to shave him.

'Do you want me to dye your moustache, Gopal Bhai?'

Gopal knows dyeing will cost him ten rupees – five cups of tea. 'I will think about it,' he says.

'A man can look young at your age if he grooms himself properly,' Ram Bibek advises.

Gopal does not reply. He watches three children – two girls and a boy – take a raucous bath at the hand-pump. The hand-pump is pale green, newly installed because Banwari knows the councillor, who also helped him rebuild the glass façade to his stall after the demolition of 'ninety-six. The children are naked – too poor to wear clothes but too young to be afflicted with modesty. The girls take turns under the spout while the boy pumps vigorously, using his weight to push down on the handle. Then the girls work the handle together while the boy sits under the spout. He has long hair like the girls. It is matted down his back in dirty brown strands. His arms and legs are very thin and his belly forms a distended balloon that hangs out of his skeletal frame. They laugh at each other and hurl sharp abuse in a language Gopal does not understand. Bangladeshi children, he thinks. Poor and dark, so dark!

Ram Bibek nicks Gopal's jaw. He screams in pain.

'Behave like a man, Gopal Bhai,' says Ram Bibek, without apology. 'It happens now and then with old skin. Yours is beginning to sag. Look at the folds under your chin!'

'Ganga *Maiya*,' grumbles Gopal.

Ram Bibek staunches the blood with a lump of alum, which stings even more than the gash. When he has finished, Gopal rises from the chair and ties his basket – now loaded with polythene milk packs – to a frame above the rear wheel of his bicycle. 'The milk was watery yesterday,' he grumbles.

'It does not come out of my udders,' shrugs Banwari. 'How do I know what they feed their cows?'

Ram Bibek snorts impatiently, expressing disbelief, taking Gopal's side in lieu of having nicked his jaw. 'You need your own cows if you want pure milk, these days,' he says.

With the heavy basket strapped to his rear wheel and his face freshly shaven, Gopal cycles back into Chandni Chowk and turns left, away from Fatehpuri Masjid. It is now past nine. He swerves to avoid scooters and rickshas and turns into Kucha Bansilal. Ramesh Babu's white mannequins welcome him with upturned lips. He brings out a ladder, hoists his bicycle on to the junction box, and secures it to the louvres with hooks. Then he unlocks his stall, lifts the lid, ties it to the junction box and spreads out his cups, cans and stove. He stretches an awning of blue tarpaulin over his head, slips off his chappals and sits down in his stall, with one knee raised. The two mannequins now stare straight at him, their smiles marred by a frown that he has noticed over the last week. Can clay mannequins change their expressions? They are perhaps unhappy that his stall, when it is open, hides much of the advertisement on the wall, after Ramesh Babu paid so much money to have it painted green less than three months ago. The junction box protrudes inconveniently and dissects the name, separating 'Sushma' from 'Fancy Dresses', though that is not his fault. When he sits, the woman and the man in the advertisement are on either side of his head, and the girl's frock is hidden by his shoulder.

From behind the mannequins, one of Ramesh Babu's clerks asks for three cups of chai. Gopal pumps the stove, lights it with a matchstick and places a pan of water on it. Before the water has begun to boil, Ibrahim shuffles into the kucha, leaning on a stick. 'It is all finished, Gopal Bhai.'

Gopal looks up at Ibrahim's open mouth, and is astonished. 'Your tooth, Ibrahim Mian! Your last tooth has disappeared!'

Ibrahim grins to reveal the recesses of a dark cavern. 'It came loose last night when I ran my tongue over it. I swallowed it.'

Gopal clucks in sympathy.

'It is good that way,' says Ibrahim, squatting beside Gopal and bringing out his glass tumbler from the junction box. 'Now I do not have to worry about brushing every morning. Why waste toothpaste?'

'You are growing old,' jokes Gopal. 'One day you will have to drink tea with a pipe going down your throat!'

'Fifty-four years,' says Ibrahim, philosophically, looking like a man in his late seventies. 'When you are my age, you will view life as I do.'

Gopal, two years younger, nods in agreement.

'It is not easy to live that long,' warns Ibrahim. 'At my age a man needs comfort. He needs grandchildren, a regular pension . . .'

'If I was your MP I would get you a pension,' says Gopal, ruefully.

'Ah! That is all finished. Those Election Commission people! They say you exceeded your spending limit. They say the rickshavalas gave you too much money, and no one knows where you spent it.'

Gopal shrugs. Ibrahim eyes him curiously. 'Where *did* you spend it?' he whispers. 'Have you got it stashed away somewhere?'

Gopal shakes his head. Ibrahim's eyes twinkle with delight.

'And that garland of hundred-rupee notes, the one you gave to that whore, Gita Didi. That was campaign money! Who could have guessed you were so smart?'

Gopal nods gravely, unsure which garland Ibrahim is talking about but impressed by his own deviousness. Ibrahim nudges him in the ribs and shakes his head in admiration and disbelief. 'Twenty thousand whores voted for you, Gopal Bhai!'

'The ladies offered me full support,' says Gopal, with some embarrassment.

'Twenty thousand!' says Ibrahim, in wonder. 'But there are only three thousand whores in GB Road!' He guffaws at the thought of seventeen thousand phantom whores. 'You are a smart one, Gopal Bhai! Better than any pimp or pahalvan! Where did you get so many whores? Do you have a machine that squirts whores at the press of a button? I thought you were a chaivala!'

Gopal pours Ibrahim his tea. Ibrahim takes a generous sip. The tea calms him and his thoughts turn to more serious matters.

'That English madam has written another story about you. She says your son was with upper-caste terrorists. There was a letter in the Urdu newspaper, saying he killed many sardars in 'eighty-four. Yesterday sardar Kartar Singh said on television that you tried to suffocate him inside your stall three hours after Indira died.'

Gopal shakes his head.

'And that one-handed crook!' continues Ibrahim. 'He was a regular thief, a pickpocket. Did you know he had a gang? You reared a snake, Gopal Bhai. A snake!' Ibrahim pauses to sip some more tea.

'He was a good boy,' says Gopal. 'His baba died when he was young . . .'

Ibrahim holds up a hand to silence Gopal. 'Musalmans are angry with you. How could you play Holi like that, after saying you were a secular candidate?'

Gopal shrugs helplessly, acknowledging his lack of judgement. 'It was very kind of you to talk to the Election Commission for me,' he says.

Ibrahim puts his arm round Gopal. 'I told them everything. I said I would not leave their office until they had given me their word.'

'But you managed to convince them,' says Gopal, with admiration.

'I gave them all the papers,' says Ibrahim, humbly, reluctant to take full credit. 'I handed them your sworn affidavit. I told them they had only one course of action. It was they who decided, because only they can declare an election invalid.'

'But now it is done . . .'

'You are my brother, Gopal Bhai. If I cannot help you when you need me, what kind of brother am I?'

Gopal nods, looking at Ibrahim through foggy glasses. They took away the new spectacles, as they took away the silk kurta, the dhoti, the gold chain, the wristwatch and the kolhapuri chappals. 'The Election Commission confiscated them,' said Ramvilas Babu, 'because that was campaign money.'

'Who do you think will win the by-election for your seat?' asks Ibrahim.

Gopal shrugs.

'One of those thieves!' answers Ibrahim. 'Suleman or Harilal Gupta. But it does not matter.'

He drains the dregs of tea from his tumbler. 'When you reach my age, Gopal Bhai, you will realise that it does not matter.'

Gita Didi looks up from her desk and rests her eyes on Ramvilas's polished face. He is still thin, she thinks, but with the epicene slenderness of an energetic, fussy nature, not the fitness of an athlete. A mind that is always at work is perhaps too busy to accumulate fat round the body it controls. Yes, he has stayed thin, but he is losing hair, although he tries to hide it by combing what remains over the bald patch. And no hair is so naturally black in a man of forty-four.

He was never handsome. His appearance has always been more proper than arresting, his manner more ingratiating than attractive, and he has always looked like someone who grooms himself assiduously. But what is this? A new diamond stud at his kurta collar!

'You have been rewarding yourself,' she says.

Ramvilas fingers the stone. 'Two carats,' he says casually. 'Exactly one lakh.'

'One lakh?'

He appears pleased to note the covetous look in her eyes. 'A commission on the collection of an old debt,' he says. 'The creditor was much obliged, because it was a fourteen-year-old account.'

Her puzzlement delights him. He has no plans to elaborate. 'What have you done with that garland, my Gulmohar?'

'Do not call me that!' she says sharply.

He regards her with a mixture of amusement and derision. 'All right, what did you do with it?'

'It is safe,' she says.

'I hope so, because it was worth more than ten thousand. You could buy sarees with it. Very expensive silk sarees! Go to Sushma Fancy Dresses in Kucha Bansilal and tell Ramesh Babu I sent you. He will show you his stock of Kanjeevaram silk.'

Gita shakes her head and runs a hand over her white cotton saree. 'I will wear nothing but this from now on,' she says.

'I forgot you have an image to protect,' he says. 'Perhaps that is why you strutted about Chandni Chowk wearing that garland.'

'It was a victory rally for Gopal Das!' she protests.

She was not prepared for the newspeople, and had no ready answer when they asked her about the garland. What could she have done? It was a lapse of judgement, a stunning display of imprudence after years of being in the public eye. She told the reporters the garland was from a customer, calling herself a whore instead of compromising Ramvilas. And now he was taunting her about it! How dare he suggest that he still has a claim on that garland?

'It is safe with me,' she repeats.

She must ride out the difficult times. STREE has had some bad publicity over the election fraud. She knows that AURAT, PATITA and NAARI were behind it. They have never forgiven her for monopolising the raid on Kotha 842, and they now feel she has appropriated their other causes too. But they must know they have lost the battle, because every whore in GB Road is now *her* case, her cause, hers to keep, protect, uplift and liberate. Who are these NGOs to grudge her this constituency? If they see no incongruity in speaking glibly about whores from their expensive homes in Hauz Khas and Asiad Village, why should she hesitate to make common cause with her sisters, sitting right here among them in Kotha 842? In a year or two, these NGOs will wither away and die for want of cases, and there shall be only one NGO in GB Road, with Gita Didi at its forefront . . .

'You should not worry about STREE,' says Ramvilas, deciphering her thoughts. 'There will be setbacks but none will be lethal. What is a little election fraud? Every NGO does it, or should.'

'Will Harilalji still sanction money for STREE?' she asks anxiously. 'We made our vote for Gopal Das public, on your recommendation.' There is accusation in her voice, but he shows no remorse.

'Who knows if Harilal will even have money to sanction? The winner of the by-election could be anyone, even Suleman.'

She shudders.

'You should have the office enlarged,' he suggests. 'It is big enough for councillors and MLAs, but no MP will step into this room unless there is space for a few television cameras. You must think of the future. Look at Charulata! One day, even you could be the railway minister.'

Gita laughs, embarrassed by such fulsome praise.

He scrutinises her face. If she shows herself to be an able vehicle, he expects to be in command. She will be better than the chaivala, anyway, more capable of navigating the tortuous bends that will lie in her way. There was no point in trying to push the chaivala any further. A paper boat will float only so far. When it is crisp it will ride the waves, but once the hull has softened it will wobble, list and founder . . . He first realised that the hull had softened when Charulata threw in her lot with the PM. She had played him skilfully. She held out until the last moment, forcing the PM to turn to independents like the chaivala. When the PM went back to her, the original price she had demanded no longer seemed high, so she got Railways. That was when Ramvilas knew the boat would go no further. When officers from the Election Commission made their second visit, he knew the boat was about to list. At that point, he who does not jump off the boat is doomed to sink with it. He jumped off dutifully.

He was fortunate to have uncovered those four lakhs, or neither

Kartar Singh nor Sohan Lal would have forgiven him for this election.
He remembers the glee on Kartar Singh's face when he told him about
the cloth belts exhumed in Khari Baoli. The sardar is a clever man to
have hidden stacks of money in those alcoves before leaving his store.
No wonder the CBI found nothing! He has probably counted the
alcove money greedily. Hopefully, he noticed that two bundles were
missing. A petty theft is always more effective than a grand one. The
two missing bundles will give him pause. They might have been
misplaced, they might have been stolen, or he might have counted
incorrectly before he left the store. A seed of doubt will have been
sown about the security of his secret, and all Ramvilas has to do is
hint, obliquely, that he knows. It is useful to make a man aware that
his secrets are not safe – even when that man is as clever as Kartar
Singh, who showed such emotion at the recovery of such minor loot.
The chaivala's stash is nothing compared with the mountains inside
Kartar Singh's alcoves, or the other treasures a wealthy ex-bookie
would surely have hidden away, but who does not like an old debt
repaid? Kartar Singh ran his hands gratefully over the cloth belts,
puckered his face at the smell, pulled bundles of currency out of the
tubes and ran trembling hands over them. What a charade! There was
even a tear in the corner of one eye when he turned to Ramvilas and
said, 'All is forgiven between you and me . . .'

Ramvilas fingers the diamond stud again, aware that Gita is
watching him. A diamond stud befits the secretary of the Chandni
Chowk IPP committee. He was appointed to that post yesterday, as
soon as he rejoined the committee at a function organised for him.
Sohan Lalji recommended him, both for membership and the post of
secretary. He does not know what caused the man's change of heart,
but he can guess.

'Why should Harilalji still support me?' asks Gita. 'And why should
he listen to you?'

He is annoyed at this constant harping on money matters. Has he
not given her enough? 'Where are the thirty-six thousand that STREE
gave to the chaivala?' he demands. 'Did you buy a necklace with it? Or
earrings?'

Gita sighs and shakes her head. 'It will not look proper if I wear
diamond necklaces while appealing for STREE funds.'

'So?'

'I cannot wear jewellery,' Gita says softly. 'But *she* can.'

He leans forward eagerly. She realises she has revealed a secret, and presses her lips together. Last week he decided he had waited long enough for Kiran and descended on the kotha where she was hidden, only to find she had vanished again. The bai would give nothing away, no matter what he offered, because whoever had shut her mouth had paid even more. He had little doubt who the kidnapper was. Now he is certain.

'So it was you,' he says softly.

Gita looks frankly into Ramvilas's eyes. 'And I will never tell you where she is.'

'Ah!' he says. 'She could not be in Kathmandu, because you would never send money there. Perhaps in her own village in Nepal? No, even you cannot reach that far. Lodged inside Naari Niketan, learning to knit, sew and do filigree work?'

'You think a woman can make a living from that?' demands Gita, nostrils flaring.

'I did not for a moment think that,' says Ramvilas coolly. 'I am merely running through all the possibilities, knowing you have no place to keep her except another kotha.'

Gita does not reply.

'I will make her the happiest whore in GB Road,' he pleads.

'Do not call her a whore!'

'A sex-worker, then,' he says, with mock deference. 'Tell me which kotha!'

She looks silently at him, lips sealed.

'You had no right to give her those thirty-six thousand,' he says sullenly.

'STREE donated that money to the campaign of Gopal Das,' says Gita with a straight face. 'You signed the receipt yourself.'

He studies her carefully: she has learned to hold her own, even against him. 'I can find out from Inderlal Jha,' he lies.

'Go to him! He has moved his chauki here. It is under my window now, right outside Kotha eight hundred and forty-two.'

He knows, and she knows, that Inderlal will never betray her to him. Ramvilas is a vague threat to the SHO, but she represents to him an infinite source of income. Ramvilas leans back in resignation. He must work on her slowly.

'I have told you before,' says Gita. 'She is your daughter.'

Ramvilas sits up straight, not at this renewed assertion – he no longer believes it, considering how obviously Nepali Kiran's face is – but at the sudden reminder that he must think about marrying off his elder daughter, now eighteen. He had put it off until after the election, so he must not delay it any longer. Perhaps Sohan Lal can help him find someone from a business family. He does not want a clerk for a son-in-law.

Inderlal Jha raps his desk lightly with a baton and hums to himself.

> *'Should I lay flower petals in your path?*
> *Should I stand outside your house all night?*
> *Should I serenade you every morning?*
> *What should I do that will not devalue my love?'*

Ah! Pushpa Rani's voice is like soothing salve for the aching soul . . . But he feels no ache in his soul today. This summer he will have them install an air-cooler in the police chauki, or at least inside his office. Perhaps by next week, just in time for the fiery month of April.

He has seen many elections, but this was the best of all. The police medal for gallantry is no trinket. He has not been officially notified yet, but he has received word. The medal will be awarded by the president at the next Republic Day parade. He has looked up the requirements, and he certainly meets them – everyone is eligible, regardless of rank or service. And if *he* did not show exceptional gallantry at the explosion on 4 March, who did? The newspapers left no room for doubt: one dead and three injured, none seriously, because of the presence of mind shown by the GB Road SHO in herding people out of the area . . . That one death rankles with his pride, if not his soul. He would have liked a zero casualty figure, perhaps leading to a higher honour. Why must they count every body as one full death, considering it was only a Bangladeshi thief – a one-handed one at that! No matter, the medal will guarantee him an allowance of a hundred rupees every month, continuing even after his retirement and devolving to his wife after his death. Of course, he has no plans to die soon. He wants to savour the free air-conditioned second-class travel that comes with the medal. He has heard that a train slithers soundlessly like a snake when you are seated behind the sealed windows of an air-conditioned compartment. Or he could exchange that seat for a first-class compartment – not air-conditioned – in which case he will get an attendant of his own. Which should he choose? Air-conditioned second class, or regular first class with an attendant?

He sighs self-indulgently, sagging under the weight of good fortune. What will they give him next? An out-of-turn promotion? Might he become an assistant commissioner of police some day, even though he is not an Indian Police Service officer? If bombs keep exploding at every election, and elections are held as often as this, nothing will stand in his way.

This Gita Didi is one to watch, he tells himself. Some day she will fight elections of her own. She can be generous to those who support her, and that is important in someone who will one day enter politics. She has rewarded him handsomely for the election office she set up in Kotha 842. He will never mention it to anyone, and he does not even remember the countless burqa-wrapped whores who emerged from it that day.

He has moved the police chauki in GB Road so it now sits opposite Kotha 842. All GB Road money will flow through it, and foreign newspeople will come to write stories. There is much business to be had here, in addition to his regular allowances from pahalvans, bais and pimps. He is almost a regular contractor in GB Road, a pimp for pimps, a pahalvan for pahalvans, and a babu to all bais. These allowances must be shared with his constables, but the money he makes from foreign newspeople he will keep for himself because they pay well. 'How many women have you rescued in the last three years?' they ask. He counts them off on his fingers and notes the concern on their faces, adding or subtracting numbers in accordance with the degree of their sympathy. 'Where are these women now?' they ask.

His standard reply is, 'In Naari Niketan, learning how to knit, sew and do filigree work.' He knows that Naari Niketan has been full for a long time, and suspects that many of the girls are back in GB Road, but surely he cannot be charged with the welfare of every whore in Dilli. Besides, if they are back in kothas they can be rescued again, giving him more business. There are only so many under-age whores, and they grow up too quickly, so he must make the most of those who are in circulation.

Footsteps outside the room break his reverie. He looks up sharply. He has told his constables not to let anyone inside the chauki without asking him, but the intruder is already at his door. His scowl metamorphoses into a wide smile on seeing her, because it is the English madam who wrote that story about the chaivala. He remembers her well. He saw her in the police station years ago, arguing for the chaivala. He rises, snaps to attention next to his chair and salutes her instinctively. 'Good morning, madam!' Then he realises he has been too servile, recovers quickly and advances toward her, his hand held out in the manner of foreigners who visit his chauki.

'Namaste,' she says, folding her hands in firm rebuff.

He is befuddled. He was only trying to make her comfortable.

She walks past him and sits down in the chair that faces his desk. She does not know why the SHO displays such familiarity. She may have seen him before – she has seen them all during her career – but they look much like each other with their thick moustaches.

She has taken over my office, thinks Inderlal, bitterly. And she said namaste to me as if I were a bumpkin!

He no longer likes her. She is too tall and too wide in the shoulders, and she wears her saree like a modern city woman, not as respectable women do in his town. She is certainly unmarried. Her husband would never allow her to walk into a police chauki. But such women never marry. They go from man to man until they grow old. Yet, looking at her, he wonders who would find such a woman attractive. She is almost like a man, and she is too old to be desirable.

He comes back to his chair and stands stubbornly, facing her but looking at the table top. He knows why she is here. She is not one of the four kinds of people who come to GB Road – traders, politicians, wash-basin customers and those who seek the arms of women with sad faces – so she must be a journalist.

Chitra stares at the pot-bellied SHO. An ogre, product of an uncouth society, a human monkey who has nullified three thousand years of civilisation . . . yet she must talk to him. The chronicle of an age is a tiresome undertaking, but she must persevere through these unpleasant moments. She had hoped it would have the chaivala as its protagonist, but she is disappointed in him. It is a pity that he was unequal to the task thrust on him. She has washed her hands of him, burying the triumph of democracy under the weight of his obvious unsuitability. Perhaps these people need more than one generation to raise themselves from the dust. Until then, history will repeat end-lessly, tragedy and farce indistinguishable from each other, and she will concentrate on the task at hand. Right now, that task is her documentary for CNN, and she is prepared for the dungeons into which it will lead her. She will hold her nose, crawl through them and emerge into fresh air before they suffocate her. As soon as this fieldwork is over she will retire to the security of her office to write the script for her documentary.

'Mr Inderlal Jha?'

'Madam!' He snaps to attention again.

'Are you aware that today is Aids Day?'

'Yes, madam,' he says, unaware that today is Aids Day.

'Do you keep statistics on condom distribution in GB Road?'

The word 'condom' on the lips of a woman embarrasses him. 'We do not do such work, madam. But we help—'

'Where can I meet Gita Didi, convener of STREE?'

'Ah, Gita Didi . . .' says Inderlal, philosophically.

'I was told her office is in GB Road.'

'GB Road . . .' he repeats.

Chitra recognises the roadblock she has hit. She produces a hundred-rupee note from her purse and places it flat on the desk.

He points across the street. 'Kotha eight hundred and forty-two, madam.'

Chitra begins to rise. He hastens to retain her interest. 'Chai, madam?'

She shakes her head. At the door, she pauses. 'There was a raid on this kotha two years ago. Were you the SHO involved?'

'Yes, madam!' says Inderlal, happily.

Chitra comes back and sits on the chair facing him, pulls out her tape-recorder and places it on the desk. 'All right. Tell me about it.'

She leans back with a professional expression on her face, nodding politely as Inderlal, eyes shining and mouth flooding with saliva, begins to speak.

Kartar Singh switches on the air-conditioner and sets it to medium-cool. This is only the last week of March, not yet summer. He will soon need to keep it on all day if he wants customers to walk into his new showroom. With the back room demolished, Jasjit General Store has expanded into a large hall. He has had the walls repainted, laid a shining stone floor and constructed a glass façade toward the street, through which customers can gaze at rows of gleaming air-conditioners, televisions, refrigerators and washing-machines. At the grand opening tomorrow, in time for the summer rush, he expects hundreds of customers. He is grateful to American companies for the great new white-goods market they have created, lowering prices and improving quality to the extent that every housewife can now have her own washing-machine. And he will let them have a free twelve-inch television if they buy a washer *and* a dryer.

The air-conditioner blows a pleasant breeze into his back. It is the same brand he is planning to sell, so quiet that he cannot tell it is turned on. When customers ask him if his air-conditioners are noisy, he will challenge them to point out where his own is located.

At the front, facing the lane, he has constructed a small wooden cabin where he will keep his accounts, cash register and pamphlets. It is all legal, he reassures himself, all in plain view. What could be more innocent than an air-conditioner store? They found nothing, not a shred of evidence, not a piece of paper and not a single rupee to account for all the cricket transactions he is supposed to have conducted. It was wise of him not to keep any money in the safe. That is the problem with Godrej safes – everyone trusts them not to break, so everyone knows there is money inside them. The three alcoves he had dug into the walls had been a good idea. The CBI, preoccupied with breaking open the safe, never discovered them. He found the money intact. Two bundles were missing from one alcove, and there was a faint rectangular line at its edge, as if the cardboard cover had been removed and replaced, but it was vanishingly thin. It could have developed simply because the cardboard had been pushed out of the alcove under its own weight, causing some paint to flake off. If the chaivala had discovered it, he would certainly have taken all of the money. How, then, can he explain those two missing bundles? Maybe he packed away two fewer than he remembers. Yes, that is most likely.

The last six weeks have been terrible, living in Ootacamund, never staying in one hotel for more than two nights, constantly looking for men in safari suits who might have come from Delhi to arrest him. A dog and a sardar can be found anywhere in the world, goes the joke. It is a cruel joke, because a sardar in Tamil Nadu is no better than a dog. He understands neither the language nor the people. Delhi is where he belongs.

He was glad to be back, and set to work immediately in the back room. The linoleum was ripped out and given to rag-pickers, the mattress was claimed by beggars, and the battered steel safe is now flowing through a blast furnace in some foundry, its memories lost. He was prudent to have disconnected his telephone lines before he left. The chaivala's campaign may have saved him from the CBI. All leads to him have been cold for at least four months. They questioned the chaivala but he knew nothing, and he was a Lok Sabha candidate.

He knows the CBI will come again. So far, no one has accused him of anything, but many of the dons are in police custody so his name must have come up in interrogations. He does not know which of the dibbas, bookies and punters have been swept up in the dragnet, and who is still at large. He has heard of horrible torture chambers hidden inside Red Fort. Will they take him there too, chained in a police jeep that will pass right through Lahore Gate, never to emerge? Ah, he must not fear them. Those torture chambers are just stories. Also, they have ransacked his store and found nothing. They rifled through everything in the Vasant Vihar house and found not a speck of evidence to implicate him. Their only claim on his time is the testimony by other dons, bookies and witnesses. No one can be charged on hearsay, and he has logical explanations for his 'known sources of income', as the CBI calls it. It is not impossible for a general-store owner in Chandni Chowk to have a house, an industrial shed in Mangolpuri and a Honda City car. Everyone knows Chandni Chowk is the greatest market in Delhi, where even a paanvala earns fifty thousand rupees every month. He will hide away all the diamonds and amethysts on his fingers when they come.

He likes the new arrangement in his store. He will do everything correctly, giving no one a chance to point a finger. He will even give proper receipts for every refrigerator and air-conditioner that he sells. He does not want them arresting him on minor matters like sales-tax payments. Should the CBI come again, he will point to the showroom and say, 'What room are you talking about, Inspector Sahib? The storeroom? I used to have a storeroom, where I kept old refrigerators and washing-machines, but it is gone now because I have built a new showroom. Would you like a colour television for your bedroom?'

He is relieved that Ramvilas had found the money when Bobby hadn't. Sohan Lal had been pleased to see the cloth belts. It was not much money for a wealthy man like him, but a Marwari seth likes to balance his books. He brought out his old register from 'eighty-four, unwrapped its red cloth cover and undid the binding. He opened it to the page where an entry showed that a sum of five lakhs was owed by Sardar Kartar Singh, and entered a receipt against it. Now our accounts are clear, sardarji, he had said.

That receipt cleared more than Sohan Lal's accounts: it cleansed his heart of suspicion against Kartar Singh. It is wise to keep the trust of your friends, thinks Kartar Singh, and to regain it when it is lost. He wishes the entire four lakhs had been found, instead of the three that Ramvilas had discovered under the asafoetida tins. To think that the chaivala had had it all along, while playing innocent! But where could a chaivala have spent a lakh? Ramvilas says he quizzed him closely, but received no answers that would lead him to it. No matter, three lakhs are better than nothing. Kartar Singh is back in the IPP Chandni Chowk committee. Yesterday's function was very touching, even though he had to share it with Ramvilas. He does not much mind that Ramvilas has become secretary. His chief concern now is to try to get a ticket for the assembly elections later this year. It is not a bad idea to become MLA for Ballimaran, now that Suleman has abandoned it in his quest to become an MP . . . Sohan Lal has extended the hand of friendship again, and he is the chairman of the committee. The time could not be more fortuitous. There is an IPP government at the centre. The prime minister had no trouble in proving his majority in Parliament after Charulata threw her support behind him. He received 275 votes in favour of his confidence motion, against 264 cast chiefly by Congress, the Communists, socialists and independents. The chaivala could not be sworn in as the Chandni Chowk Member of Parliament, and was not allowed to vote, pending an inquiry into the nature of his election. The Election Commission is investigating allegations of massive voter fraud, rigging and impersonation, and there are many other irregularities about his candidacy. There are rumours that his name is not even Gopal Das! There will be a by-election for the Chandni Chowk seat. It is not clear if Harilalji will get a ticket again. His mishandling of the Chandni Chowk campaign, at a time when Naresh Agrawal's death had given the IPP its best chance of gaining the seat in eighteen years, has not been received well by the IPP high command. It is possible, *just possible*, that Sohan Lalji may push his own name forward in all this confusion . . . So it is fortunate that he has regained the trust of Sohan Lal.

Kartar Singh walks down the gleaming rows of refrigerators, holds up his hand and extends his little finger to study the amethyst straddling it. He wishes Sukhbir was still sitting in his house, waiting for him to come back from the store. And how he yearns to undo the moment when they took Jasjit from him! If his mother had sent him out to buy something that afternoon, the attackers might have missed him, and he would be walking at his father's side at this very moment, studying the refrigerators for scratches . . . But that is all in the past.

These refrigerators will keep him company this summer, when he hopes to work toward getting Sohan Lalji elected. He is going to sell the Vasant Vihar house and live in a flat in Chandni Chowk. Why does a man build a three-storey house and line the foyer with Italian marble? Why does a man spend his life consorting with havala dealers, dibbas, bookies and punters? So he can live with his wife and have his son bring a daughter-in-law into his home, and watch his grandchildren chatter over the dining-table. Jasjit never saw the house, and Sukhbir has left him to mope alone in it. He has lost all interest in it.

He thinks of Canada again. Some day, he tells himself, brushing off the thought. What would he do there now? Where is the son to love him and take care of him there? And he would have to improve his English. Take classes and lessons at his age?

He re-enters the cabin at the front, sits down at his desk and idly watches Bijoo, the boy he has hired for the store, dust refrigerators. A line of television sets sits on them, visible from the cabin. Bijoo flicks a switch and they come to life together, tuned to the same channel. It is a live telecast of the cricket match between Australia and India, being played in Bangalore. This is the last day of the last match in the series. Everyone knows India will lose. Having won the first two matches, and therefore the series, there is no incentive for India to win. No one will make any money betting against Australia in this match . . . Suddenly Kartar Singh leans forward in his chair, horrified at this train of thought. He is drifting into it again! He must not allow himself to be hypnotised by the game.

'Why must you always watch cricket?' he scolds Bijoo.

The boy stops dusting and stares at him.

'Turn off the televisions!' he commands.

Bijoo moves to flick the master switch. Well, it cannot harm anyone if the boy merely watches the match, thinks Kartar Singh. Why torture him? He is a good boy, well mannered like Jasjit. 'Let the televisions show cricket,' he says. 'But don't watch too carefully.'

Sohan Lal leans back in his leather chair and is gratified to note that there is no danger of tipping over. The chair sits on a clover-leaf base of wrought iron – heavy, stable and secure. Once you get used to these chairs they are not so bad, he thinks. The leather is especially soft. The chair swivels with you, tilts back to take your weight, and forward when you need to bend over the counter. You can sit cross-legged inside it, as if you were on a gaddi. You can collect your dhoti round your knees and arrange its pleats carefully so it is not crumpled when you stand up again. Ramesh has installed three of these chairs behind the counter. The largest – on which Sohan Lal now sits – is so wide and deep that a man might sink and get lost in its generous, smooth folds. Why, he could fall sleep in this chair! A wicked thought crosses his mind, that the folds are as soft as a woman's body. He banishes it hastily. To be dwelling on such matters at his age! Then he wonders if the leather is cow-hide and is revolted. He has spent a lifetime campaigning against cow slaughter, and if he now begins to preen himself on leather chairs, what will distinguish him from the pseudo-secularists of the Congress Party? He dwells on the matter, turning over the word 'synthetic' in his mind. He remembers that Ramesh said something about synthetic leather, made entirely from lifeless che-micals . . . Yes, he is now certain Ramesh said something of the sort. He will clear it up with him right away . . . He turns to Ramesh, sitting to his left in another leather chair, and is pleased to note that the chair has swivelled with him. Ramesh appears to be busy with accounts. He will ask him later about the leather, though it is obviously synthetic, no matter what Ramesh says. They no longer make genuine leather nowadays. It is too expensive, and did he not hear Ramesh say that this chair was reasonably priced?

The next object to arrest Sohan Lal's attention is the new fan, installed behind him, whirring gently on medium speed in the warmth of late afternoon. It will be handy next week when summer arrives. Its breeze, which now skims his pate playfully, will be doubly refreshing. There was a time when he had had a full head of black hair, in the days when he was expanding Jamna Lal Kishori Mal and Ramesh was a little boy playing on Rukmini's lap. That is pure vanity, of course. A mottled scalp speaks of wisdom and experience. It commands respect from young men. It speaks of an age when a man may turn over his business to his son and devote himself fully to public service.

He turns to his left again and watches Ramesh concentrating on a sheaf of papers spat out by the computer. A good boy, a reliable boy, neither flashy like Jugal Kishor's two sons nor weak-willed like Surajmal's four – a boy who can keep a good house and manage a good business, and is already mature at thirty-six, which is considered young, these days. He has heard of boys who continue to study until they turn forty! What kind of men do they make? There is some merit, perhaps, in knowing that the earth is spherical and heat makes the concrete in Chandni Chowk expand and crack, but should not a man close his books when he has turned eighteen – all right, he can study until twenty-two as Ramesh did – and prepare for the real lessons of life? They are not to be learned from heavy tomes but in the steady discharge of duty, in sitting on the gaddi – all right, a leather chair behind a Sunmica counter – and serving customers every day. Look at Ramesh! And look at the well-worn air he has! That is how a man must be at thirty-six as he lapses into respectable middle age – the suggestion of a paunch, a chin that sags and rounds out the face, a half-sleeved shirt and long sideburns. Everything about him speaks of contentment and prosperity – not the limitless wealth of a Birla or a Tata, but the stable resources of a man of good family – and a life led in proportion, of moderation and constancy combined with balance and stability, a life that provides no opportunity for straying too far in a world that changes slowly or not at all. He looks like a father of three children. Three boys.

Sushma sits on the third chair, beyond Ramesh, with Vicky on her lap. Well, some allowances must be made for the times, thinks Sohan Lal. Has not a woman been prime minister? It is good to have a woman in the shop. Sushma is solicitous about his health. She is always at his side, offering water or turning the fan toward him when he complains of backache or groans too loudly in trying to stand up. It is, of course, much easier to stand up from these chairs than it was to heave himself up from the gaddi. The cross-legged position was designed for the young, not old horses like him with painful knees. Even so, his knees rebel when he stands up, and he is grateful for Sushma's presence at such times. He still feels embarrassed when traders walk into the shop, look at her and assume she is an employee. But he has seen how skilfully she disarms them, and how smoothly she cajoles women into buying sarees. Ah, he must not be too fastidious. She has, after all, given him three grandsons. And look how blissfully Vicky sleeps on her lap!

The afternoon is slow. Ramesh asks if Sohan Lal would like another cup of tea. Sohan Lal gazes at the white mannequins standing behind the glass façade – bony rumps with sarees stretched tightly across them. Beyond them, he can see the chaivala seated in his stall. The old Musalman squats beside him, speaking in whispers. 'Not now,' he says to Ramesh, pleased to be asked.

I will ask for tea after that Musalman has gone, thinks Sohan Lal. The last cup is still warm in his stomach. He lowers his head to his chest to take a nap, and his eyes fall on two cloth belts lying in his lap. He chuckles. What an odd idea, to take money to the bank in these belts! Everything is done with cheques and drafts these days. He remembers the silly notion – put into his head by his father – that cash was the only safe form of money because cheques, drafts and bank accounts were traceable. The government wanted a slice of every-thing, sometimes more than three-quarters, and a hundred inspectors were swarming like mosquitoes round every shop, ready to suck it dry. The only way you could keep your hard-earned money, and run a shop worth the trouble, was to keep it in cash. Ramesh has assured him that cheques and drafts can hide money as well as cash, with none of the trouble of cloth belts. Much of Ramesh's money still comes in the form of cash because his customers prefer that, but he sends it to the bank five times a day to reduce risk. The foreign banks are much more friendly and co-operative. They will accept all kinds of notes any number of times in a day. They do not carp over torn bills or old bills, or bills arranged haphazardly. They have sweet-smelling young women in sarees, who smile brightly as they throw bills into counting machines that whir through an entire bundle in a few seconds. No more dealing with sullen babus who finger every rupee and quarrel about scratches on the note.

There is no incentive to send money outside the country. The rupee is stable against the dollar. The money he placed with his nephew Ranjan in New York, before Kartar Singh lost the last batch of five lakhs, has not appreciated significantly, certainly not enough to justify the trouble he went to in placing it, and the commission he paid to Kartar Singh. That money would have been better spent on his own business. He should never have gone to Kartar Singh in the first place. But here are the cloth belts now, lying in his lap, smelling strongly of turmeric and asafoetida, drowning the far more delicate fragrance of attar champa. But the smell of money is always pleasant. Two lakhs is not much. The mere Sunmica furnishings in the shop, with the polished wood cabinets and these leather chairs, have probably cost two lakhs. He did not even bother to count the money when Kartar Singh gave him the bags. He had written it off a long time ago, even if he had not forgotten about it. 'It is not a matter of money, of course,' he had told Kartar Singh. 'It is a matter of trust, a matter of closing old accounts.' Which was why he closed the entry with a receipt of two lakhs when the outflow was five. What matters is that Kartar Singh spoke the truth when he said people had barged into his store and stolen the money. Sohan Lal had never believed that story, always thinking the money was locked away in the Godrej safe or spirited to another hideout, that Kartar Singh was betraying his trust for a piddling sum. He was relieved to learn that he was wrong. It is gratifying to have your faith restored in men you meet every day.

What shocks him, however, is that the money was with the chaivala! Who would have thought the chaivala was a thief? But, of course, it was not really the chaivala. Even Kartar Singh does not claim that it was the chaivala who attacked him in his store. Look at the man, sitting across the lane in his stall, talking to that old Musalman with decayed gums! Could he ever have attacked anyone, at any age, under any circumstances? No, it was the chaivala's son. Was he not a hired hoodlum? A shady character, a young man without the steadying hand of a father, a wayward youth with no career prospects. Kartar Singh vaguely remembers seeing him in the attacking crowd. Once the money was stolen, it was a simple matter for the boy to sneak into Katra Badami and hide the money while his father slept. There is no doubt it has been in Sushil Jain's godown all these years. Its smell gives away its home. But Ramvilas found no more than two malodorous belts in the kholi, according to Kartar Singh. Where could the chaivala have spent three lakhs? That was a large sum in those days. Perhaps that was how his stall had expanded to include stools, benches and counters. But three lakhs? Ah, you cannot tell where vile men will spend money. It runs through their fingers like a flowing river and no one ever finds out where it went. Then again, there is the chaivala, sitting in his stall, pouring harmless tea into glass tumblers. It was the son, no doubt, who ran through three lakhs before he hid the rest. A young man can waste a fortune on frivolity – clothes, jewellery and the vile lanes of GB Road.

Sohan Lal thinks approvingly of the initiative Ramvilas has shown in ferreting out the money, not to speak of his integrity in handing it to Kartar Singh, who has been no less forthright. The sardar could have kept the money and no one would have known better. Perhaps a havala trader – even one who got out of the business years ago – is always a man of his word. Trust is his only business asset and he guards it with his life.

He will let the matter rest there because a receipt has been entered in his accounts. He is a man who likes to balance his books. He will also repay them both for their steadfastness, because that is another debt that must be cleared before all books are balanced. For now, he owes

Kartar Singh nothing after recommending him for the committee, and Ramvilas has been more than compensated. Who would have imagined that he, a mere clerk, would become secretary of the committee, so soon after breaching his understanding with the party? It is just as well that Ramvilas is the secretary while Kartar Singh is only a member. The sardar is too ambitious. No one has forgotten how he played the Sikh card to become a councillor after the riots of 'eighty-four. Ramvilas is ambitious too, but he is still a clerk in spite of his pretensions. Everyone knows he has no capital of his own, whatever he may say about his arrangement with Vimal. The two will keep each other in check, one guarding his position as secretary, the other coveting it.

There is little doubt that the chaivala's election will be overturned. Harilal Gupta has already lost once. Why should he get a second chance? Sohan Lal telephoned people in the IPP high command yesterday, saying Harilal had squandered an opportunity.

'Keep an eye open for a good candidate because there will be a by-election,' they told him.

'I will look far and wide,' he promised them, over the telephone. He has looked far and wide, he thinks smugly, and found the candidate in his own shop, ensconced on this very leather chair! He has also spoken to Harilal Gupta, who wants to stand again in the by-election. The committee will not be agreeable to the idea. He fully expects the two newest members, Ramvilas and Kartar Singh, to express disapproval of Harilal's candidacy. Ramesh, as a member of the committee, will certainly support his father. There is a general sense in the committee, thinks Sohan Lal, that it is now his turn to get a ticket. Ramesh has sensed this too, and that may be the reason for his increased deference in the last few days. Ramesh may be the master of Sushma Fancy Dresses, but his father is almost a Member of Parliament! What is a mere shopkeeper beside an MP?

Sushma stands up to greet three women who have walked through the glass door. They sit down – on the stools across the counter from Sushma – and place their beefy forearms on the Sunmica. They are swaddled in silk sarees – the synthetic kind, notes Sohan Lal, not genuine Banarasi silk. It is middle-class silk, not the silk that wraps generations of wealth. He does not need to look inside their purses to know they are empty. Of course, they will buy something. Middle-class customers always buy something to preserve their dignity, to make a point, to reassure themselves as much as to please the shopkeeper. But they do not buy expensive silks. Sohan Lal leans back in the leather chair and shuts his eyes. He knows this will be a long session – fat women in groups of three are impossible bargainers.

Sushma walks over to Sohan Lal and places Vicky in his lap. She needs her hands free to deal with the women. Sohan Lal takes the boy gratefully and lays him on his lap. Vicky wakes with a start and begins to wail, but is silenced with a lollipop that Sushma resourcefully produces. Some day, Sohan Lal thinks as he shuts his eyes, I will bless Vicky's bride, if I live to be that old. He opens his eyes again and looks at Vicky, sucking the lollipop. Ah, time moves slowly, thinks Sohan Lal, as he drifts off into a comfortable nap.

Fifteen minutes later he wakes up. Out of habit, he turns left to fold his hands toward the Lakshmi alcove before realising his mistake. The sheet of plywood that covers the alcove still rankles with him. 'Images of gods make the shop look old-fashioned,' Ramesh said, when covering the alcove.

'All right,' Sohan Lal had said. He will make his peace with a shop that has no gaddi, no cash-box and no gods, but a fancy safe hidden behind glass panels lined with Sunmica, varnished plywood and black mouldings. Every wall is a cupboard whose door slides smoothly at the touch of a finger. Fancy lamps hang from the ceiling. Mirrors in the wall are arranged in such a way that a woman may study herself from every direction with an organdie saree pressed to her shoulder.

The stench from Kucha Bansilal irritates his nostrils. He must get the Corporation to clean the drains more often. He pulls out the cotton ball of attar champa from behind his ear and puts it to his nose. The fragrance is faint. Ordinarily he replenishes it every three hours, but it is impractical to go home so many times during the day. There is no space for an attar cabinet behind the glass panels in the shop. Besides, Ramesh says it looks inappropriate in a garments shop. Sohan Lal still samples his fragrances every morning – the attar cabinet is installed in his bedroom – but it is difficult to savour them with the sounds of children in the house, and the smells of cardamom, ginger and cloves permeating the air when the servants make tea.

The three women are still there, seated like three Buddhas, immovable, inscrutable, unshakeable in their resolve to get a good bargain. He regards them contemptuously. Sushma is at a loss. She has laid before them a mountain of sarees, and they have remained unimpressed. Such customers deserve a nudge of well-meant banter, but they do not command excessive respect. In a voice matched to the occasion, Sohan Lal asks them if they would like some tea. They say yes, as he was certain they would. He sighs and calls out across the lane.

'Nanak Chand, chai!'

Gopal, squatting, turns to Ibrahim and grins.

GLOSSARY

aarti religious ceremony (Hindu)

achkan tight-fitting dress (male)

Akaal Takht Eternal Throne (seat of Sikh religious authority)

almirah cupboard

aloo puri meal of potato and fried bread

Arjun warrior in the epic *Mahabharat*

Aurangzeb 17th-century Mughal emperor, son of Shah Jahan

azan call to prayer (Muslim)

babu 1) clerk 2) accountant 3) term of respect or scorn, depending on who uses it

Babur first Mughal emperor (1526–30)

Bahadur Shah Zafar last Mughal emperor (exiled in 1857)

bai brothel madam

Bania trader by profession or caste

barfi type of sweet dish

behanji term of respect for sister or older woman

bhai term of respect for brother or another man

bhajan devotional song (Hindu)

Bhangi 'untouchable' (Hindu), scavenger

bholanath marijuana (slang)

bhujia type of snack

Bluestar (Operation Bluestar) Indian army raid on the Golden Temple in June 1984

chaat type of snack

chandan sandalwood

chauki police station or outpost

chor thief

Chou En-lai alcohol (slang)

churidaar tight pyjamas

crore ten million

Dalit 'untouchable' Hindu

Dara Shikoh 17th-century Mughal prince, son of Shah Jahan

datura poisonous plant

desi native, Indian

dhania coriander

dharam duty, religion, 'the right thing'

dharna political protest

didi term of respect for older sister or woman

Dukhiya Naari Uddhaar Sabha Committee for the Uplifting of Unfortunate Women

dupatta piece of cloth thrown over a woman's shoulders

Eid   religious festival (Muslim)

gaddi   1) mattress 2) centre of power 3) throne

gangaajal   water from the river Ganga

Ganga Maiya   Mother Ganga

Ghalib   19th-century Urdu poet

ghazal   form of poetry (usually in Urdu)

ghoda   horse

gilli-danda   street game played with wooden dowels

ginni   gold coin

Godrej   brand of safes and steel cabinets

gulaab   rose

gutka   prayer fragment from Guru Granth Sahib, the Sikh scripture

haathi   elephant

haay rabbaa!   Oh God!

haay haay!   down with!

halvai   man who prepares sweet dishes

Harijans   Children of God: term for 'untouchable' Hindus

havala   system of illegal money transfer, usually international

Hindutva   political doctrine championed by Hindu nationalist parties

Indira Gandhi amar rahe!   Long live Indira Gandhi!

Indira Gandhi randii hai!   Indira Gandhi is a whore!

Jahanara   daughter of the Mughal emperor Shah Jahan

Jai Shri Raam!   Victory to Lord Raam!

jalebi   type of sweet dish

Jana Gana Mana Adhinaayaka . . .   Indian national anthem

Jat   Hindu caste

jhola   bag

Jumma   Friday, day of prayer (Muslim)

kabaddi   game that involves running and wrestling

kalash   pot

kathak   form of classical dance

katua   circumcised man (derogatory term for Muslims)

keertan   1) religious gathering 2) chanting of devotional songs (Hindu, Sikh)

khadi   homespun fabric

Khalsa   the militant order of Sikhism

Khoon kaa badlaa khoon!   Blood for blood!

kufr   sin (Muslim)

kurta-pyjama   loosely fitting shirt and trousers

Laila and Majnu   legendary lovers

Lakshman   younger brother of Raam, hero of the epic *Ramayan*

lathi   long wooden stick

lingam   phallus (stone slab representing Lord Shiv in a temple)

Lok Sabha   Assembly of the People (lower house of Indian Parliament)

lota   pot

Mahabharat   1) Indian epic 2) the battle in that epic

Mandal ko maaro sandal!   Slap Mandal with a sandal!

Manuvadis followers of Manu
the lawgiver (derogatory term
for upper-caste Hindus)

mela fair, festival

Meraa Bharat Mahaan My India
is great

mian honorific for a Muslim
man

moksh the state of 'non-birth'
and final liberation (Hindu)

Morarji Desai former Indian
prime minister, ridiculed for
drinking his urine

Mumtaz Mahal wife of the
Mughal emperor Shah Jahan

murdabad! death to!

namaaz prayer (Muslim)

Nathuram Godse Mahatma
Gandhi's assassin in 1948

neem medicinal plant

paan betel leaf (mouth-freshener)

pagari advance payment made to
landlord, usually illegal

pahalvan 1) wrestler 2) bouncer
in a brothel or bar

Pakaro! Grab him!

Pandavs five brothers who form
one of the warring parties in
the epic *Mahabharat*

pandit 1) Hindu priest 2) learned
man

panditji 1) honorific for a pandit
2) marijuana (slang)

pir teacher and master (usually
Muslim)

prasaad food blessed by a deity
and eaten by devotees after a
religious ceremony (Hindu)

puja religious ceremony (Hindu)

pujari Hindu priest

qawwali style of communal,
mystical music (Muslim
origin)

qazi judge (in traditional Muslim
courts)

qibla the direction of Mecca

Raam Hindu god, hero of the
epic *Ramayan*

Raamleela passion play that
depicts scenes from the epic
Ramayan

Radha Krishna's lover

Rajya Sabha Assembly of States
(upper house of Indian
Parliament)

Ramayan Indian epic

Ramzan holy month of
Ramadan (Muslim)

Ravan ten-headed demon slain
by Raam in the *Ramayan*

Roshanara daughter of the
Mughal emperor Shah Jahan

ruh spirit of

saalaa 1) mild expletive 2)
brother-in-law

salvaar pyjamas (usually female)

sanyaas state of renunciation
(Hindu)

sardar Sikh

sardarni wife of a sardar

sarkaar master (literally meaning
government)

Sat sri akaal Truth is eternal
(Sikh)

savaa one and a quarter

seth 1) trader 2) wealthy man

shaabaash bravo

Shah Jahan 17th-century Mughal
emperor who built Taj Mahal
and Red Fort

shahaadat martyrdom

Shahjahanabad Delhi in the 17th century

shervani long coat-like garment worn by men

Shiv Hindu deity

shri Hindu honorific (similar to Mr)

Siachen Himalayan glacier claimed by both India and Pakistan

Sita wife of Raam, hero of the epic *Ramayan*

Swargalok heaven (Hindu)

Tegh Bahadur Sikh guru, beheaded in Chandni Chowk by Emperor Aurangzeb in 1675

Thakur upper-caste Hindu, feudal lord

thela cart

thulla derogatory term for a policeman

tilak religious/ceremonial mark on forehead, e.g. of sandalwood paste (Hindu)

Tulsidas 16th-century religious poet

ustad 1) expert 2) teacher 3) mentor

Vaitarani river that must be crossed after death, before the soul can meet its fate (Hindu)

vajoo ritual washing required before prayer (Muslim)

Vedantist expert on Vedant (Hindu philosophy)

vishkanya snake woman (mythical, Hindu)

Yamaraj god of death

zakat charitable contribution (Muslim)

zenana inner rooms for women's use

zindabad! long live!